THE RECTOR'S NEW DAWN

A Narrative Love Story

Ron Reaves

Avid Readers Publishing Group
Lakewood, California

Avid Readers Publishing Group

http://www.avidreaderspg.com

ISBN-13: 978-1-61286-344-3

Printed in the United States

FOREWORD

In our culture, religion and romance are seemingly strange bedfellows and it is intriguing to imagine them co-existing -especially if the protagonist is in love with someone who is a polar opposite of himself. *The Rector's New Dawn* is a love story that began upon my retirement after 40 years of full-time service as a  pastor in the Church. I wanted to write about some of my biblical and theological musings across 40 years. I also wanted to imagine a complicated love story as I reflected back on many tortured and some incredibly positive relationships I observed across the years in my professional life.

I offer a disclaimer that this love story is not autobiographical. The theological and biblical meanderings have some similarities to my professional life in retrospect, but the love story is imagined, at best, by the hopeless romantic I've always been for many years

ACKNOWLEDGEMENTS

I want to thank a number of people who have read and reviewed this love story in its evolving:

Micki Smith, good friend, mentor and author of a new historical novel *Fanny's Destiny* (ARPG). Micki who read the initial manuscript painstakingly and provided very valuable insights, critiques and helpful suggestions.
Pastor Julie Brigham, who gave a first read and provided me great initial insights.

Julie Gaver, professional speaker, storyteller and author of the witty *'Must Love Shoes' 'More Must Love Shoes'* and *'Random Musings.'* She motivated me to keep writing for the six years this book was written.

JoEllen Gluscevich, author of *My Sentimental Journey,* for her tireless support and care.

Pastor Mark Crispell, whose friendship and support for my writing this story was extremely encouraging.

Barbara Stokes, friend and former classmate, who was very supportive during times of doubt.

Mark Huffman, for his care in reading this story tirelessly and offered helpful input.

Audrey Asbury, Nancy Zeim and Nancy Pritchard, who read the story in its early stages and have been incredibly open.

Lucretia, my wife, who tolerated untold hours of my writing this.

Former parishioners, friends, and family members, who encouraged me to write this - even with its 'steamy segments' and its liberal theology and biblical interpretations.

Eric Patterson, Owner, Avid Readers Publishers Group (ARPG), Lakewood, CA, for his quality leadership and congenial guidance in this publishing process. teachereric18@hotmail.com

Ron Reaves

PROLOGUE

This narrative is a love story between a 'functionally atheistic,' thirty-something woman and a divorced Episcopalian forty-something rector – *me*. I'm narrating it from my recollections back to our first meeting. If she were writing this, it might read differently. But, honestly, I don't think so.

Admittedly, my life is filled with theological rambling. Not belligerent, mind you, just asking questions about organized religion, biblical stuff, about 'theology' and things spiritual. I like to chat about where the Holy One might be today. Is there a resurrection for everyone? Is there a hell? Are we going to a real heaven or are we all merely space dust floating around in the cosmos? Simple questions like that! I ponder them. For sure, answers are hard to come by. As a rector I am a pray-*er* of prayers, a purveyor of ponderings and a proclaimer of promises -the divine type. Holy Writ is full of promises and threats. Sometimes I ponder whether I'm on the right track with what I do every day as a rector. Perhaps against all odds -in spite of organized religion- my work as a rector might make a difference in the lives of others. I hope so. It's a big part of my journey.

Maybe it will connect with you. If not, this is also a love story. It's the other journey in my life – an unexpected one with a younger, unchurched woman. It's a stretch to say this within my Anglican tradition, but I believe she and I met somewhere in the cosmos. I don't believe we are strangers. I've intuited this the more we have been together. I don't know if it's our past lives, but somewhere along the caravan 's journey through the cosmos, we hitched a ride and met each other.

In these pages we travel along the seasons of the church year. We travel a lot on this good earth, too, And we enjoy its beauty. We are seekers for common ground on matters of religion and faith. We make love, too. I invite you to come along in search of one rector's *New Dawn*.

Aldie Seaver

Chapter One

LOVE AND 'ONE-ANOTHER-NESS'
Place me as a seal over your heart, like a seal on your arm;
For love is as strong as death, its jealousy unyielding as
the grave. It burns like a blazing fire,
like a mighty flame. Many waters cannot quench love;
Rivers cannot wash it away. If one were to give all the wealth of
his house for love, it would be utterly scorned.
Song of Solomon 8:6-7

What if you could stumble onto a relationship that is so fulfilling that your search is over finding the love you been seeking? Would you be willing to give away your money and possessions - even possibly your house -to enjoy this one pearl- this one uncommon love of your life? Seriously! Would you give it all up to experience love that is like heaven on earth? Most people, I'm certain, would say it doesn't exist. Some would say such love is ideal, delusional or just fantasy. Maybe so, but if it were within reach, would you put everything on the line for it? Consider what the Good Book says- roughly paraphrased: *Dude, you can't buy love like that! (Song of Solomon 8:7)* Perhaps we're all searching for it in one way or another while navigating in our kaki coils. Even so, love like this seems impossible. And if it were encountered, it would likely have a lot of strings attached to it. You'd feel like you had to be worthy of it.

Of course, looking back through literary history, there were numerous love stories of souls looking for that 'one impossible love' and, to be sure, some of them were quite torturous: Romeo and Juliet, Cleopatra and Marc Antony, Lancelot and Guinevere, Tristan and Isolde, Paris and Helena, Napoleon and Josephine, Jane Eyre and Rochester, Scarlett O'Hara and Rhett Butler, Pocahontas and John Smith, or Queen Victoria and Prince Albert. What makes them so great that they should be immortalized through literature and/or cinema? Perhaps because when we read them, they were opposites, hopelessly in love and yet separated torturously as royalty and commoners, poverty and wealth, or race and creed.

One love story I stumbled onto was that of Peter Abelard and Heloise - a monk and a nun. It was around 1100 C. E. when Peter Abelard, from LA Palais, France, went to Paris to study at the school of Notre Dame. There he gained a reputation as an outstanding philosopher. Notre Dame's Canon Fulbert, hired him to tutor his niece Heloise. You know what's coming. They fell deeply in love, had sex and conceived a child, a son, and decided to secretly marry. The furious uncle, Canon Fulbert, sent Heloise to a convent in Argenteuil. Then the Abbey had his servants castrate Abelard while he slept. *Ouch!* Abelard went on to become a monk, while his heartbroken Heloise became a nun. Despite their tribulations and obvious separation, they remained in love and their poignant love letters were later published. What a torturous and requited love they harbored! He recounts it all in his book *'Story of My Calamities.'* It may be one of the most passionate love stories in literary history and was made into a musical, *'Heloise and Abelard.'*

I'm writing a love story about two unlikely people with a few calamities of their own, nowhere near the drama of any of these notables I mentioned. I'm Aldie Seaver – an Episcopal rector with a funny name - who found myself in a somewhat unexpected relationship with someone seven years younger. How we ever hooked up is a minor miracle. Intrigue may have been part of it – the fact that we were on opposite sides of belief in a deity when we got acquainted. The universe does work in strange ways.

As a rector, I make a little over fifty grand a year with decent benefits. I wear a simple herringbone jacket and a collar most every day. My clothes look frumpy. I drive a Honda Civic with over 200,000 miles on it. I visit sick parishioners and sometimes perform extreme unction on dying ones. I've watched a few people tootle off to paradise in the middle of my prayer. Some parishioners brood and others are rude. I drop in on some seniors older than my grandparents, including some spinster types with ruby red lipstick and lavender rouge who insist on kissing me on the lips, grunt when they do it and call me 'honey.' One parishioner's grandmother yells at me and on several occasions has spit in my face in a fit of rage. Another dear lady has been stuck on butchering day on her family farm for a few years. I can almost predict the narrative as it flows out of her reality. It's been four years hearing about butchering day in Ruth's world. It's somewhat like the movie *Ground Hog Day* when I sit with her. There are very few variations in story details. Some folks from the 1800's show up to help butcher, including President Lincoln who came to help. I'm not making this up! I didn't laugh at her but expressed 'surprise.' 'President Lincoln, *really* Ruth?'

I preach and teach about the wonders and mysteries of Holy Writ, trying to make it all relevant across the great cultural and historical divide. During my preaching, I'm guessing a few worshippers pay attention and others wonder what to have for lunch. (I've thought about lunch, too, in the middle of a sermon!) Through the week I pray with all kinds of folks, visit smelly hospital rooms where dear souls have been lying in their own excrement for a while. Most Sundays I serve the 'Host' decked in robes that make me look like an ancient icon hanging on our church library wall. Kids think I look like their Granddad in funny clothes and sometimes they joyfully hang onto my leg on Sunday mornings after worship and won't let go until I gently pry them off.

For the most part my life is unremarkable, boring and my sermons beg the question: *So, what?* I suppose I am religious as my denominational affiliation goes, but I'd prefer to call myself a 'spiritual humanist hooked on Jesus,' because I am high on him more than anyone else in history. He's the 'Dalai Lama' and 'Mister Rogers' of men and, yet, a revolutionary spiritualist in his time. Even if I only know him through words written about him by people educated enough to write them down way back when, I believe in his mission. I love Jesus of Nazareth. I love Jesus the Christ (Anointed). I love him for giving up his life for the sake of God's loving this whole world. It was insane by worldly standards and divine by God's standards. And God didn't arm wrestle him to do it – he did it on his own! Jesus was so fully human that God's light shone through him and divine power worked in him. He was a 'heaven' of a guy!

I'm not a pietistic prude, far from orthodox, and doctrinally more doubtful than ever. Do I believe in the Virgin Birth? *Define 'virgin' in the Ancient Near East!* Do I believe Jonah lived in a whale's belly for three days? *No!* Do I believe Balaam's donkey talked to him after Balaam beat him three times? *(Numbers 22:28-30) No!* Granted, the Bible is filled with metaphors and imaginativeness. I believe God speaks through all of them. So, I believe the Bible is the Word of God – the Big Word within all the little ones.

Even with biblical doubts, I 'pay the rent' as an Episcopal rector. And because I have my own doubts, I have empathy for all skeptical seekers who read the Good Book with all its layers and layers of copying and editing many years ago. There were countless ancient ones who scripted this incredible library of testimony. We have no original texts to fall back on when we open up that King James or New Revised Standard Version or New International Version or whatever translation is collecting dust on our coffee tables. And even the ancient manuscripts we do have were copied many times over. Nothing is 'original' (i.e. earliest manuscripts on file) in this sixty-six-volume anthology called 'Bible.' That being said, I believe in the witness that was handed down through all those countless copied manuscripts, to be a migration and gathering of 'The Word of the Holy One.' They are, even if they aren't the original texts, 'meaningful' for me in my search for and relationship with the Holy One.

Preaching on these greatly tampered-with texts, I attempt to carefully and imaginatively extract something of the *holy* from them. In my 'preach-speak style,' I try to relate them to this post-modern, post-Christian, pluralistic 'scramble' we call religion. It's tough to do! One space scientist attending my church calls me his favorite 'astrologer.' I suppose because he thinks I get my wisdom from the stars! He's one of those 'cultural Christians' from a growing legion of modern 'non-believers' (sometimes called 'nones') who still get a kick out of the familiar trappings of the Church. He once told me: 'I love the church, Aldie, I just don't believe nine-tenths of what it teaches.' I wonder what his *one-tenth belief* is?

Dawn

So, in my 'Father Aldie' world, I met a Certified Nursing Assistant named Dawn, thirty-three years of age. She's not a church goer and defiantly calls herself a 'functional atheist'. (curious description!). Her fleeting association with any church was with the Roman Catholic Church, which she hasn't attended for more than twenty years. Even though she isn't 'religious', when I have listened to her reasons for not being, I wonder whether I am *religious* too! She said she's had it out with God on many occasions. Nothing unusual about that. Even as a rector, I've had a few rounds with the deity myself! On one occasion, she said, 'Aldie, I just dislike organized religion -period! Why would anyone waste their time with it?' she said impatiently. She must have seen the little shock on my face, because then she apologized. 'No offense, Aldie. I'm sorry."

'Not an offense at all,' I chuckled, "but I do wonder whether you might be angry at 'religion' rather than God? There is a difference."

"Mm, I guess I didn't know there was a difference, Aldie. I guess I could be angry at both"

"Well religion can be something you do by rote. Still, countless believe it brings meaning to their lives.

Dawn looked a little puzzled. We decided to change the subject.

So, after twenty years being a rector with a theological education in my bag, I looked up the word 'religion.' [1]

'Religion' (Latin 're-ligare' or to 'rebind' or 'reconnect') was once used by the orator Cicero to mean 'to rebind' something. It's an over and over again binding (like wrapping something around one's arm.) The word seems to have evolved to mean a repetitive practice as in 'holy orders' or following laws.

'Religion,' then, didn't originally have a connection to a deity. It was about practicing something so that we become proficient at it... like learning a romance language or playing the trumpet. It's about practice *(praxis)*, repetition, refining, discipline, etc. I mean, we sometimes say 'I take my gardening *religiously* or my cycling *religiously* or my baking *religiously*.' We could become pretty good at it with practice. It doesn't necessarily mean we *believe in* the trumpet or *worship* gardening.

Curiously, not much has changed since Cicero coined the word *religare*. The nature of religion as we've come to view it still carries with it plenty of should's and ought's and practicing faith, which sometimes creates guilt, anger, frustration and disillusion. I wonder who could possibly find a benevolent deity in all of that? Nevertheless, from New York to New Delhi folks *are* 'practicing' their religion in some form - whether heart-filled or obligingly, deeply or casually. Religion happens, for good or ill. Some people are addicted to it -especially those arguing about it, intimidating others with their views or, worse, killing others whose beliefs are different!

In our give and take conversations about 'religion,' I grew more curious about Dawn. Her full name is *Dawn Briana O'Shea*. She's so fascinating – especially in her disillusion with religion and her honesty. The attraction would expand beyond that, trust me! She likely has never opened a Bible; couldn't name the four gospels if her life depended on it. And as for Jesus, she would say: 'Of course, I *know* 'Jesus Christ' Aldie, his name was used all around our house most of my young life!' She found it repulsive to say it the way her father said it: *'Jesus Christ, Dawn!'* this and that. She told me: 'Although I didn't believe in a deity, I imagined that if Jesus were real, he deserved a bit more reverence beyond the blatant swearing I heard most every day of my life!'

She is very attractive with untypically 'stylish simplicity' – no make-up, plain clothes, no nylons, and yet a goddess-like physique. Actually, 'stunning simplicity' might be a better description for her. By her own admission, she seldom bought clothes, but what she wears adorns her with remarkable elegance. Even in her scrubs as a CNA she is beautiful.

Our love narrative originated in and around Havertown, PA, which is not a fictional town, but a real burb near Philadelphia – nestled among old and new mixtures of blue collar and white-collar communities like Haverford, Bryn Mawr, Upper Darby, West Chester, Ardmore, Broomall, Drexel Hill, etc., Havertown is a genuinely American town next to the big city of 'Brotherly Love.' The names of places in this story, businesses, restaurants, etc., are for the most part real. However, personal names in this story are fictional. The names of my two parishes - All Saints Episcopal Parish in Havertown and, further back, Holyoke Episcopal Parish near Gloucester, VA, are fictional. I don't want to name any religious community wondering: 'Hey, he's talking about us!'. Some of my friends who read this tell me that Holyoke or All Saints resemble churches they've belonged to. You can smell religious hubris anywhere and it smells familiar.

Our narrative is hardly *Fifty Shades of Gray* by E.L. James, which I did read in recent years. With all due respect to her erotic trilogy, I'd call our love story *Fifty Shades of 'Pray.'* We're human, vulnerable and, oh yes, sensuous! Our love story is a blend of sex and religion lived out on a 'the local parish' landscape – of all places! Well, clergy do have sexual feelings and fantasies. I know many people can be naïve about that. I think some people think we have our children by immaculate conception!

I've read that this is one of the loneliest professions in the world. I learned that first-hand knowing my friend Father 'Jacques,' who had been brought up on child molestation charges and spent a number of years at Delaware County Prison. The Roman Catholic Church may be unrelenting in requiring the vow of celibacy from their priests, but they will never know how such restraint has led to many ruined lives between priest and parishioner. Father Jacques is a 'heaven' of a nice guy, but experiencing his loneliness tore my heart out. I am reminded that, even with a myriad of human physical diseases, loneliness is still the number one 'killer' in the world. Fr Jacques lived to be sixty-nine and two years after his incarceration, he committed suicide. I often wondered if he had had a love in his life, things might have turned out differently. The 'heart *is* a lonely hunter.'

Our love story is also somewhat like a travel journal – we go away a lot. I've had the travel bug since I was a teen. Dawn and I have savored getting away perhaps too often for our own good. However, I don't have any regrets. All of them have had interesting side adventures.

I have to say that I couldn't have imagined such an attractive woman giving me a nod. I'm rather tall, a bit lanky, looking much like a priest in my Roman collar, my boring black shirt and, as I indicated, my familiar herringbone jacket. There's nothing great about my looks, although I do have a nice smile, and some have found that attractive.

But I'm not sure how I had become attractive to Dawn, who could have any man she chose. I later learned she had many, but not the way she would have wanted.

I'm not a hunk, no disrespect to all the guys who love looking at their muscles in workout mirrors. I'm a *chunk.* I gave new character to the word by referring to those among us who are *not* Adonis-like, muscle-bulging, swoon-worthy, bronze and wavy-haired guys. We are *chunks.* Many of us are a bit pudgy, maybe bald-spotted. We might have nice smiles. We'd walk on water for you if we could. We're willing to fix things, carry heavy things, reach for things high up, capture bugs and take them outside - *not killing them,* of course. We take your car to the garage for service or repairs, do the laundry, clean the house, even the bathrooms, hold your pocketbook while you try on clothing. We'll always tell you you're beautiful even if you wonder whether something you're wearing makes you look…you know! *Please don't ask us that!* You'll always hear us say: *Darling, you are beautiful no matter what you wear!* You'll be certain we're bullshitting, but you will still love hearing us say it. Right?

I'd say I'm kind of a chunk – maybe even an above-average chunk.

Chunks are average good guys. When we make love, we'll be gentle and ask what feels good. Most of the time we're fine being *snuggily-wuggily* bears –holding you close and making sure you have enough blanket. Our chunky bodies are guaranteed electric heaters in the dead of winter. And of course, we try to be hygienic, dress up nice for you and let you fuss over our clothing selection (yes, we can be clueless with color choices!) We are 'chunks' if you'll have us - imperfect, but head-over-heels in love with the most beautiful women on earth. That's me, far from a *hunk*…more like a *chunk!*

My Theological Zig-Zagging

A casualty of my profession is that I do enjoy grinding a few of my theological and biblical axes. After all, it is my world and it's what I talk about and struggle with most every day. I've been a rector for 20+ years and I've been on some crazy wild-goose head-trips in 'theology' (i.e. the 'study of God' or, as I prefer to say, *'the study of what God might be up to when God wakes up in the morning.'*

To continue my litany, I listen to hurting people, angry people and get dumped on by strangers who dislike organized religion and want to tell as many clergy as they can. I hear it on planes and trains and in public places wherever people catch a glimpse of the collar. I've heard all the excuses for hating the church – like the guy on my United Airlines flight to Chicago explaining that he hadn't been back to church since his mother died: 'Why should I believe in a God who took my dear Mom unexpectedly? '

I thought: *God 'took' her away? Geez, God is not into zapping little old ladies or anyone else, for that matter! The physical world is biology and sometimes aging, mutations and carcinogens making people tootle off.'* I told the guy on the plane: 'Sorry about your Mom, but I think God weeps a bit when our loved ones die.' He stared at me bit and didn't know quite what to say. It's okay. I expected that, and he didn't say much to me the rest of the flight. But when we landed and began leaving our seats, he turned and said, "Thanks, Father, uh… you've given me a few things to think about."

I know there will be many disagreements with my theological and biblical meanderings. Especially some of my sermon thoughts. I expect it. I'll get branded a 'flaming liberal' and others might say I'm too conservative. I sometimes hear radio preaching condemn liberal preachers like me to the fires of hell. I suppose I'm heading for the Great Crispy with all the other 'liberals' who have moved outside the borders of religious orthodoxy. We get that vitriol despite our liberal theology and notion that God does not need to confine people to Sulphur City for eternity. God has better things to do – loving, forgiving, renewing and restoring, recreating…all within God's compassion work here! Whatever 'hell' people think exists, I believe, is trumped by the Deity's unconditional grace. So, I'll sum it up this way: *I do not believe in an eternal hellfire of punishment. I believe in an unconditionally loving Holy One,* who works harder getting us into heaven than keeping us out. Whatever hell might exist is here on earth evidenced in poverty, war, crime, abuse, genocide, mass shootings, human neglect and oppression – to name a few. Hell is already around in the actions of mindless people, including not the least psychopaths, sociopaths, hate mongers, fear mongers and anyone who kills people at whim or for pure enjoyment. That's hell.

To be sure, both liberals and conservatives- and let's include extremists- have mucked up organized religion. With Christianity, fundamentalists want to hold onto their inflexible 'infallibility' theory- i.e. if one word of Scripture is not true, it's all useless. Liberals want to debunk the whole thing as myth. Extreme religionists want to kill people for not believing what they believe. Many have turned a spiritual movement based on the charisma of Jesus or Buddha or Confucius, etc., into terribly flawed institutions that essentially do the opposite of what their charismatic leaders sought. From my own denominational corner, I sometimes imagine in some cosmic way Jesus' Spirit knows how this ancient mission has turned out. Perhaps he'd prefer to spend time serving at a local soup kitchen than sit in our worship centers —save for a few great hymns and, of course, the Holy Eucharist, where he has been reported 'present.' I don't believe for a moment Jesus will 'return' as the same Jesus he was in ancient Judaism, I often wonder if he ever really left? I imagine his spiritual 'self 'creeping around our churches amazed at what we've done with his dream of revitalizing people of faith. For that perception alone, I could get me kicked out of the Episcopal Church!

I believe in a Holy Other (God) in whatever form corporally or spiritually manifested. This deity seems to be a 'nameless' one. In fact, 'God' is actually not a name, but an Old English word 'good.' The Holy One is known by metaphors -Shepherd, Rock, Redeemer, Creator, Love, etc., etc. The Holy Other -another metaphor- is mostly known by stuff that gets done… like rescuing Hebrews from slavery in Egypt. I prefer 'Holy Other' or 'Holy One' over God – but the moniker has been around for so long (Old English *goode*) it's hard to put it any other way. We could say 'Eternal Other,' 'Spiritual Energy,' Cosmic Lover,' Eternal Mindfulness, '*et cetera*. You could make up your own. For me, this deity works primarily on the ground and isn't sequestered in some heavenly throne room watching us all flounder and fall on our faces. As incarnate as the Holy One chooses to be, it seems he/she is the Highest Mind of the universe seeking to bring order out of chaos. One of the deity's highest manifestations is found in human compassion – which makes people like nurses, caregivers, first responders, countless family helpers, etc., etc. 'divine.' I trust through the sacred writings of real people attempting to work life out that there is a divine energy at work toward higher good within the finite. Still, I care about this flawed institution called 'church' or 'assembly' and my flawed work in it.

Even if we may have forgotten the reason *the Story* has continued on for so long, I've had an affair with the church for many years, its warts, bruises and all. Really! I fuss over the church because of what it could be if it sought to be a tenth of what Jesus intended. Religious communities may be perhaps the greatest hope for discovering that very 'Beloved Community' that Dr. Martin Luther King, Jr., dreamed of many years ago. The church still holds ground as a place of compassion and conversation shaped by a Holy Other seeking to hold the universe together like a parent trying to keep the family together. Religious communities are often under-rated, and their rich traditions have ended up being unearthed treasure for many. When it happens by deeds more than pontifications, I think Jesus jumps for joy. *Uncork the communion wine! Pass the pita!*

I'm decidedly tolerant of many faiths - except the pushy ones, proselytizing types who always seem to be on a 'it's my way or the highway' trip. True, they have as much of a right to exist as my funky faith family. But sometimes when fundamentalist types get pushy and punchy with their belief systems, I state my position: *You have the right to state your beliefs, but I have the right to state mine too. It would be great if we could meet somewhere in the middle and move toward appreciation for our differences rather than disagreement and animosity.*

And, of course, there are hundreds of denominations, which makes it all so much fun. We all go around pretending we believe in the same God and yet fight over our differences.

Denominations

I've had this imaginative, fun picture of denominations in heaven:

Announcer with clipboard welcomes a crowded gathering on the Other Side:

Quiet please! Quiet. Thank you. Welcome to our plenary sessions. Now here are the assigned rooms for discussion on an endless list of unresolved earthly issues. Roman Catholics, you go to the big conference *room upstairs. Lutherans, Episcopalians, you are off to the left of them, Baptists, take the next large room on the right, Pentecostals to the right of them -far right! and 'Methodists... oh my goodness, so many of you!... Consider the large third floor fellowship room. We have to add many more rooms. (Jesus did say: 'In my Father's house are <u>many</u> rooms.' - John 14:2) 'Presbyterians, you follow the signs. Please read them carefully! Non- denominational types, follow the music. Jehovah's Witnesses, if you're among the 144,000, see if your name is on the list down the hallway... and if you don't see it, pick a denomination! There's always room for a few more.'*

Ridiculous, I know. Just a little fun with denominationalism.

I don't expect *denominations* to be as important on The Other Side as we make them here. I may understand some sense of being 'Episcopalian' here in Earth Realm, so that some gathering of a heavenly plenary session for those of us who traveled the dusty roads the Anglican communion might be welcome. Why not? It would seem that memory alone might make for collective concern for the Earth Realm we left behind. I don't know —perhaps prayers from The Other Side can be powerful as they navigate to earthbound. I don't know. It would be helpful though.

How essential are denominations? Maybe such gatherings are a necessity in Earth Realm. The word 'denomination' (*denominatio* in Latin) means *'to' (de) 'name' (nominatio)* – such as *'Episcopalian'* or, those folks down the road *'Baptists' or* those folks closer to Anglican or Roman Catholic *'Lutheran,' etc.)* To be 'denominational' seems to move us away from that enormous 'beloved community' Jesus sought to forge. It divides us up, separates us out. If we're all part of God's Creation, even with all our varying creeds and constitutions, we are *most* God's people when there is unity and when we're reaching out to a broken world *together*... as one people with great diversity, regardless of our stripes. We are 'branches' of an enormous tree, which cannot function without a healthy systemic root system.

Episcopalian or otherwise, I believe all faith expressions have been under-valued, but it's sad that 'organized religion' types seldom want to find common ground. So many 'evangelists' *('evangelion'* means a 'good message') are trained to make it a one-way court press. At the end of the day I wonder if our religious pedigree really matters when it comes to experiencing God in this world? Wouldn't it be great if it were more than a one-way *good message,*' but rather a message to be shared? Wouldn't it be great if Mormons and Presbyterians, Jehovah's Witnesses and Lutherans, Jews and Roman Catholics, etc., could find a 'holy' ground on which to stand together? We might walk away celebrating a greater unity and do greater work in the world. How 'holy' that would that be! Yet all over the world 'unity' is a bad word when it comes to religious tribalism. Christians can't get along with each other; Muslims are divided to death. Neither do Jews between Orthodox, Conservative and Reformed. Further afield are Sunni's and Shi'as and Kurds, etc.

My work as an Episcopal rector is essentially a work of 'inviting- as in '*Stop by sometime if you're in the neighborhood. You're invited to listen, hear, see, taste, welcome one another, stand, sit, learn, say no, say yes, disbelieve, believe, join, challenge…*' Nothing about my work is coercing, judging, punishing, shaming, or rejecting, or especially proselytizing. I basically *invite community – especially a beloved community.* I believe that's what the Holy One is seeking to create among us – divided as we all are.

I've always had great respect for the Jewish faith, whose adherents you will never see knocking on your door to win you over to Judaism. They would welcome all to their Temple worship. Some of my most exciting conversations on faith have been with rabbi friends. But they won't be showing up at my home with a pre-fabricated program about Moses and Abraham and the message of Torah on a flannel graph.

My friend Rabbi Marv Samuelson and I talk about this. He's rabbi over at Beth Shalom (House of Peace). I remember saying to him: "You already know, Marv, that our guy is really *your* guy!

He readily agreed from his Conservative Judaism place.

He smiled. "We Jews honor Jesus – except with the title *Miashiach* or Messiah." [1]

[1] *For some Jews, the name alone is nearly synonymous with pogroms and Crusades, charges of deicide and centuries of Christian anti-Semitism. Other Jews, recently, have come to regard (Jesus) as a Jewish teacher. This does not mean, however, that they believe, as Christians do, that he was raised from the dead or was messiah.*

"I respect that, Marv. Honestly, sometimes I don't know what we've done with Jesus." I've suggested that Jesus ('Yeshua' or 'Joshua') probably didn't have in mind starting up a new religion in Israel, but most likely he wanted to reform the one he knew. (All great institutions need reforming now and then.) Jesus passionately believed in a new messianic time of God approaching. Whether he really thought of himself as a *Miashiach/Messiah* is questionable. In the Gospel of Mark, he hushes the disciples when they use the word. It seems he rather wanted to draw his beloved people back to their roots. I'd venture to say that Jesus saw himself more as a 'reformer' than a 'redeemer.' That reflection alone would likely get me kicked out of the Episcopal Church! I mean that substituting the title 'redeemer' for 'savior' would be verboten within most churches today. You will likely never see a best seller titled 'Jesus the Reformer.' Although it's been written about: *(see 'Jesus the Reformer, Rev. Roger Karban, Wednesday, March 28, 2001, 'The Evangelist')* Many would see Jesus the Reformer as a kind of reductionism within Christian orthodoxy. It would diminish basic beliefs about how God and people are viewed in the great big picture, including one of God being vindictive enough to punish some humans eternally. 'Eternity' is a long time for the deity to be punishing. The God of Jesus, I believe, has a much broader plan for restoring creation – and not just a little bit of it.

I believe starting a new religion called 'Christianity' was certainly nowhere in Jesus' mind when his ministry was unfolding 20-30 B. C. E. If some futurist/soothsayer would have cozied up to him and said, *Yeshua ben Miriam, you're going to start a new religion, which will become a dominant force in the world,* Jesus might recoil: *What you are saying, spit it out on the ground! I am committed only to my Abba-Father and his children!*

In fact, Jesus may have grown gradually tolerant of strangers or gentiles, but I can't imagine him being chummy with them.' Gentiles (*'Gentilis' in Latin, 'Goyim' in Hebrew, 'Ethnos' in Greek*) meant 'people of other faiths.' Jesus explained to the Canaanite woman who begged him to save her demon-tormented daughter that he was called to save 'the lost sheep of the house of Israel.' *(Matthew 15:24)*. Even though her persistent faith was exemplary, and she prevailed to get him to heal her daughter, Jesus still wasn't convinced the *goyim* were among his pastoral responsibility. Canaanites particularly ranked very low in Jewish tolerance in the Ancient world. Many were frankly treated harshly to the point of genocide. (Read the 'Book of Joshua!' Ugh!) It was really Paul (formerly Saul) of Tarsus, who expanded the faith teachings of Christ in the Gentile-dominated world of Asia Minor and Greece and Rome. In truth, without Paul's monumental conversion on the way to Damascus, Syria, one wonders whether Christianity would have taken off at all.

For Marv and me, our faith similarities make for good conversation. We'd like to think that Jews and Christians have a lot more in common than either are willing to embrace. If the folks at All Saints and Beth Shalom ever sat down with each other beyond just occasional Seder meals and bowling tournaments and started chatting about their two faiths, they might discover wonderful possibilities for being 'people of God.' We have more than *Yeshua* (Jesus) in common - Jews and Christians. Even our four gospels and Paul's letters have a link to Moses and Abraham. Christianity *isn't* Christianity without Judaism's historical and theological imprint. I've always appreciated the insights of Professor Amy-Jill Levine, Professor of New Testament and Jewish studies at Vanderbilt University. A primer on this is her *The Misunderstood Jew: The Church and the Scandal of the Jewish Jesus (Harper One)*. Her book has helped me understand how extracting Jesus from his Judaism can create a kind of anti-Semitist attitude among many church folks.

Look What the Cosmos Brings

Well, gee whiz, as you can tell I'm deep into this stuff! Maybe too much for my own good. But its a 'peek' into my Aldie world and my pursuit of a deeper understanding of the biblical picture. It's *faith chatter* in a real world seeking a closer connection with the Holy One. It's where I am as rector at All Saints Episcopal in Havertown. It also happens to be a love story with a myriad of twists and turns, bumps and stumbling blocks, but, at a deeper level, a potential for living more nearly a 'beloved community.'

Well, OK, let's get on with my growing enchantment with a future R.N.

I know it's a stretch for an Episcopalian priest to admit this, but I can't help but believe that Dawn and I met each other traveling across the cosmos, perhaps through many past lives - two kindred spirits discovering how wondrously they are drawn to each other even with their religious experiences eons apart. I imagine this to be a traverse of caravans hop-skipping across the galaxy, making a stop at an occasional 'oasis' (what I call a life changing and deeply meaningful connection'). And here we reach across from our modes of traverse and take each other's hand, renewing a timeless and deep kinship of spirit that has traveled far through the cosmos. As Rumi might say, *we have been in each other's hearts all along.* Do we all yearn for belonging, for that reassuring sense of community? I always have.

Our sister and brother Afrikaners have an expression: *'Ubuntu'* - which is roughly translated *'one-another-ness.'* I learned this in a speech I heard from Archbishop Desmond Tutu:

One of the sayings in our country is 'ubuntu' – the essence of being human. Ubuntu speaks particularly about the fact that you can't exist as a human being in isolation. It speaks about our interconnectedness. You can't be human all by yourself, and when you have this quality – Ubuntu – you are known for your generosity. We think of ourselves far too frequently as just individuals, separated from one another, whereas you are connected and what you do affects the whole world. When you do well, it spreads out; it is for the whole of humanity.

• Archbishop Desmond Tutu explains *Ubuntu*

---

[1] *Ubuntu is a beautiful — and old — concept. At its most basic, Ubuntu can be translated as "human kindness," but its meaning is much bigger in scope than that — it embodies the ideas of connection, community, and mutual caring for all.*

In this love story Dawn and I likely live out a form of *'Ubuntu'* - *'one-another-ness.'* (It's not an English word, by the way.) It's ironic –the very Afrikaner word that seems to express a divine purpose in this world cannot be found in the dictionary – *one-another-ness* – *Ubuntu!* Maybe someday.

Nevertheless, wherever the road of our relationship leads, the cosmos has had a hand in creating our *'Ubuntu'* and we believe it is a journey worth risking. All relationships are a risk, whether in committed relationship or not. *One-another-ness* is always risky. It implies that we all have a claim on each other's welfare. As Bishop Tutu describes it: *I am because we are.*

Before Dawn, I was in a marriage that had lost or perhaps never really had the very things I had hoped for in the institution (sadly, very common among many marriages). For me marriage is a passion to be together caring deeply, practicing daily kindness, and making genuine love with our hearts, minds and bodies. Dawn also had been in relationships that grew cumbersome. Our accidental (or maybe not so accidental) meeting seems to have been an unfolding of uncommon friendship and mutual desire for one another. Simply that.

Early on, we'd remember our first moments, those first eye-catching glimpses we had of one another. I remember the first smile, the first hug and the first kiss. Our roots begin there, but Dawn's memories of our actual beginning surpass mine. It's no surprise that I'm a guy helplessly trying to remember details of the past. What I was wearing when we first met? I have no idea, but probably a Roman collar. What was she wearing? The day, hour, etc. Women are remarkable for remembering intricate details about their lives and the lives of others and surroundings. Dawn even remembers I was wearing a green sweater when we met at my parishioners Dewey's and Eve's house that first time. (More about that first encounter later). I marvel at this, of course, as I struggle to remember what pants I wore yesterday or what I had for lunch. There's no way we could write our love story without Dawn's noticeable attention to details. She has wisdom my cranial circuitry has never known.

About Me

My full name is *Aldron Gerard Seaver.* Funny name, I know. People often pronounce my first name '*Uhl*-dron,' but the emphasis, my mother reminds me forever, is on '*Al*' as in *Al* Capone or *Al* Gore or *Al* Jolson, *Al*paca, *Al*-i, *Al*-ley etc. As far as I know there's no other person in the world named 'Aldron.' I searched and did not find *Aldron* as a first name for a guy anywhere. There's a grocery store around Philly named 'Aldi.' Interestingly, there's an unincorporated town in Loudoun County, Virginia, named 'Aldie.' It's a mile or so east of historic Middleburg, VA. Aldie was the birthplace of Julia Beckwith Neale, mother of Stonewall Jackson. Now that's a fact you really needed to know! There was a little Battle of Aldie during the Gettysburg Campaign and it's the home of the historic Aldie Mill – I've been there! So much for the town of my namesake and apologies to any other burgs named 'Aldie' in the world I may have overlooked.)

My friends call me 'Aldie,' which sounds like a car, I know. They often greet me with *'Howdy, Aldie!'* I would be happy with just 'Aldie or even Al,' but friends can be unmerciful in a teasing sort of way. I've weathered the name calling. It was tough for a while to be teased about my name. And it didn't help that I had big ears! My 'Dumbo's' could be seen for miles, I imagined. Nature just wanted my ears to grow faster than the rest of me. Fortunately, the rest of my frame caught up with me in my late teens. But *Howdy 'Aldie* 'stuck. To this day there are pastor friends, even former parishioner friends, who greet me with *'Howdy Aldie.'* At least they don't say 'Huldie, Uhldie!'

I grew up near a little community along the West Chester Pike in Pennsylvania, between West Chester and Havertown called Edgemont, across from the U.S. Army Reserve and Edgemont Country Club. My parents lived on Arbor Way, a looping street off of N. Providence Rd. It was a fashionable home, well-groomed and gave an impression that we were quite well off. My parents both worked decent jobs and scraped and saved to enjoy the amenities of our home, but I wouldn't say that we were 'well off' by the world's standards. I went to Marple-Newtown School District in the Newtown Square area. I graduated somewhat aimless about my future. An average student, I didn't play sports, but was active in Glee Club and the Marple-Newtown High School Band, in which I played the Sousaphone - that big brassy S -looking tuba that our band director said only guys should play. But one teen named Leslie was a lot stronger than I and she hoisted it around very well. Eventually I played trumpet for concert band and jazz band.

I didn't date much in high school. Girls tended to like me as a 'big brother.' I guess that was enough to feel adequate with my tall lanky frame and acned face and crew cut look. None of the girls in my class ever knew that I secretly wanted to be naked with them. But I would have died if they knew that. I carried a secret crush on Roxanne, a fair skinned, curly haired girl with dimples and pretty legs. She's the one who called me 'Aldie, my big brother.' (I had a lot of sisters in addition to my biological sister, Allison (Aldie and Ally! I always called her Ally Girl.)

Later in high school I had a continual burn for Susie Frost, long haired, sensuous eyes, a smile to melt you down to helpless nothingness. She was a majorette in the Marple-Newtown High School band. Marching behind her fueled my fantasies! (Sousaphones always stood out in front of the formation)). Later the band leader put the big horns further back! I hated that.

Back then, I had an artistic flair, so the only time I ever got close to Susie Frost was to occasionally create designs for her report paper covers. She would tell me I was 'nice.' Ugh, I hated 'nice!' When it came to any affection, zilch from Susie Frost! I was just invisible to her and found out from one of her girlfriends that she had a very determined crush on Eddie Mason, star running back for the 'Tigers'. Eddie, of course, was tall, muscular, square face of a guy, who according to a few of my occasion girl 'friends', was swoon-worthy. He was a card-carrying 'hunk' in my 'chunk' world. My social report card at Marple-Newtown was about a D- or lower! I went to the Senior Prom as part of a reserve pool for girls who couldn't get the dates *they really wanted*. Apparently, there were more of them than us. I mean, some of the girls would literally write out a list of guys that, to the best of their knowledge, hadn't been chosen. They would have died not having dates even if they didn't have the ones they wanted. So, I was part of a 'pool' of unchosen guys. We were members of the 'Leftovers' club. Chunks often ended up there. I learned about this a week before the prom and tried not to act surprised when Diane McIntyre called me and 'wondered if I was going.' I had actually saved up a bit of cash to anticipate buying a new tie and getting a corsage and White Buck shoes for dinner before the dance. Even with the extra cash, I had decided that I probably wouldn't be asked. But Diane came along. So, a few of us 'leftovers' and the girls who asked us decided to share one of the parent's Dodge van to get to the Prom and back home. It was a minimalist prom evening for 'leftover' groupies. We laughed at that. Diane didn't seem to mind it - either that or she wasn't going to say anything. The kids from family with means could drive their parents' fancy cars. Yet, with all of the minimalism, our little cadre ended up having a great time at the Marple-Newtown Senior Prom!

An Unraveled Family

Dawn Briana O'Shea had an energetically youthful spirit that could make any decent guy fall in love with her. And some did, of course. She would probably have favored our little 'Leftovers Club.'

One day at Panera's (I'm fast forwarding a little bit) she showed me a picture of herself at five years of age, I suddenly felt like 'Jell-O nailed to the wall. Her smile and energy just radiated right out of the photograph. The picture showed her standing at her kitchen sink on a chair washing her Mom's dishes. She turned and smiled for the picture from her Stepmom, Lydia. She was pure playfulness and imagination. Her older stepsister, Grace, was often her partner in crime. They both defined playfulness with simplicity. They could take wood or boxes, paper, rocks, even plain dirt outside around the house and turn it into a great adventure. Dawn and Grace in those early days were inseparable.

However, Grace Lydia O'Shea as a teen was an emotional train wreck, a lovable one. Grace was a daughter from her father's first marriage to Lydia. She was a mixture of drama queen, hyper about her looks, could cry at the drop of a hat, easily distracted, excessively girly-girl, and much too developed for her age. Yet, in the mix of it all, she was a heart of gold. She was pure enigma!

Grace's most significant challenge was falling hopelessly in love with Ahmad Ramesh, a young, Iranian stock clerk down at the Super Fresh on West Chester Pike. Ahmad was a quiet, unassuming, hardworking 17-year old, whose parents had moved to the States from Iran in the late 70's through a work assignment his father had with the State Department. After much jumping through hoops, he was able to bring his family to the States and they settled in Haverford. Ahmad's father was able to find a teaching position in Middle Eastern studies at Haverford College. Grace had been working as a cashier at Super Fresh when she met Ahmad. It was one of those romances that Grace's father, Jack, had forbidden. It turned out to be a messy situation with Grace in several 'run away' attempts with Ahmad. But, of course, they had nowhere to run away to. Her father had also attempted to dismiss her from her employment from Super Fresh, even though Grace had won top cashier award for two months in a row.

Dawn had advocated on behalf of Grace with their father on numerous occasions. And although Jack O'Shea was inclined to listen to Dawn, she realized she was getting nowhere with him regarding Grace's relationship with Ahmad. Stamping his foot, her father told Dawn: 'Damn it, he's Iranian, Dawn! It's just not going to be easy in our culture - it won't work! He's Muslim and she's Christian. What kind of world will their children grow up in?'

Dawn countered: "Daddy, she's old enough to make up her own mind. She'll be 18 in a month. It's a different world now. We're more of a global community now. Give them a chance."

Jack clenched his fist and turned red: "Don't give me that 'global community' crap, Dawn! She could find a nice Christian, white guy from the area! You can't trust these foreigners. You don't know... something suspicious might be going on in that family." Jack had obviously forgotten that his own family were 'foreigners' who left Ireland after to the Potato Famine to search for greater opportunities in the 'land of the free and the home of the brave.'

Of course, the more Jack O'Shea attempted a tighten the leash on Grace, the more certain the passion of Grace and Ahmad grew. And consequently, Grace became pregnant with Ahmad in October that year. The two had lied about an overnight school function that took them across the state line to Delaware. Ahmad didn't have a driver's license, but they hitched a ride with a truck driver friend on his way with a delivery to Baltimore. He took them to a Quality Inn on Christiana Rd. near Newark, DE. He had promised to pick them up on his return the next day. Ahmad had saved up enough money to reserve the motel and buy breakfast the next morning.

Unfortunately, their escapade proved disastrous when the truck delivery was delayed on return the next morning and through a series of miscommunications, Ahmad's friend could not reach Ahmad and the two were not able to get back to Havertown. Hitchhiking didn't prove effective either. This was before cell phones.

21

Finally, in desperation, Grace used 'reverse charges' to call her mother, Lydia, in Conshohocken to plead her situation. Her mother was a secretary at Rosemont College. She had known about Grace's relationship with Ahmad, but she was far less judgmental than her father. She listened for a while and then told Grace she would take an early lunch break and come down to meet them at the Burger King along Kirkwood Highway near Newark. That's as far as their cab fare had taken them from the motel in Newark. The two had enough money to get a soda and a burger - after which they were cashless. Her Mom got them both back to Havertown safely - but their problems were far from over. Grace's father found out there was no overnight school function and Grace was grounded 'forever' and forced to quit her job at Super Fresh. What's even worse, she came crying to Dawn on Halloween night after finding out she was pregnant. The night in Newark was blissful, but she couldn't have coordinated it better -or worse as it turned out -with her monthly cycle.

Grace and Dawn spent the entire night sorting out all the possible scenarios for this situation. Dawn had definitely advocated for her *not* having an abortion. Even Ahmad had not wanted her to have an abortion. He was willing to work extra jobs, if necessary, to help her through the pregnancy.

Grace cried and held Dawn. "Oh, Jesus, Dawn, how can I escape the wrath of our father when he finds out I'm having a baby with Ahmad?"

Dawn offered, "Well, could you live with your Mom and then have the baby and offer the child up for adoption?" "Yes, but that means Daddy wouldn't see me for 9 months? I wouldn't be able to hide it. Sooner or later he'd want to see me and then all hell would break loose. It's no use – I need to abort this child."

Dawn pleaded, "Grace, I don't want you going to some sleazy clinic in Philly. You need a healthier alternative. Daddy is always going to be judgmental about these things. Look, I'll go with you as to tell him. He's not going to beat you. I can't imagine he'd want you to end up in some unsanitary abortion clinic. Please don't back out on me, Grace," Dawn pleaded.

And she didn't.

By morning, Dawn had convinced her sister that going to her father and her mother and laying all of it on the table was a better alternative than abortion.

Fortunately, the meeting would include her mother, Lydia, and even Jack's second wife, Millie – both for good leverage, because as much as his marriage to Lydia was unsuccessful, Jack O'Shea confessed he still carried a torch for Lydia and often said he regretted the relationship had not worked out. Jack had a few decent qualities, but fidelity wasn't one of them. So, Dawn, Lydia and Millie and a few siblings came to support Grace. It was held at Millie's house in Upper Darby.

Jack wasn't aware of it, but Lydia and Millie had forged a bond after all that had gone on in these messy relationships with Jack, meeting occasionally for coffee and sorting things out on the family front. They agreed that Jack O'Shea was a piece of work. His fidelity values were destructive to say the least. He was a relationship enigma. There were affairs that they both Lydia and Miller knew about, even some they didn't know about, including one of them, ironically, that brought Dawn into the world.

The meeting with Grace was much like a Howitzer shooting it out with a BB Gun. Jack wasn't expecting all these people and protested that it felt a bit like a ganging up by everyone there. He didn't even offer eye contact with Grace. Ahmad also had shown up to be supportive of Grace.

"What the hell is all this about. I've got work to do", Jack grumbled.

There was a pause, but Lydia chose to speak up: "Jack, we're in support of Grace, who is… pregnant."

Predictably, Jack threw a fit:

"Christ Almighty!"

He looked at Grace and threw his hat on the floor.

"So, this is what I brought you into the world for?"

There was frozen silence, when Jack picked up his hat and was ready to unleash another barrage, Lydia stepped up and shook her finger at him.

"Now just a minute, Jack O'Shea…first of all, Grace is *our* daughter! So, don't be talking about *who* brought her into the world!'

Jack looked at her and then he looked at Millie, who looked as if she was ready to throw a dagger between his eyes, then looked back at Lydia and pointed to Ahmad.

"Damn it, Lydia, you know this wouldn't have happened if she had gotten involved with this *A-rab*."

Grace sat silently, her lips quivering, and tears began streaming down her face. Ahmad put his hand on her shoulder. Millie couldn't hold back. She stood up next to Lydia and pointed her finger right at Jack: "Jack O'Shea, you bigot! You know damned well you're not pure as the driven snow! You want me to mention a few of your screw-up's in life? Right here and now? There aren't enough stones for Lydia and me to pick up and throw at you if you think for one moment you're without your own faults!"

Jack, with face blood red, teeth gritting, grabbed the door handle and started walk out.

Dawn stood up. "Wait a minute, Daddy! Could we just calm down for a moment? We're here because we care about Grace and her pregnancy."

She went to her father face to face. "You can bitch all you want to about what Grace and Ahmad did, but right now Grace's health in this pregnancy is more of a concern than any indiscretion. It happened! And because she knew you would be so furious she was going to go have an abortion somewhere." Lydia and Millie gasped.

"Now is that what you want, Daddy? You want your flesh and blood to go to some sleazy abortion clinic in downtown Philly?"

Jack still had his hand tight on the door, looking to spit nails, but he paused and turned and looked down shaking his head. He may have been crusty to the core, but underneath he had some strain of values. He knew that he had impregnated as least three women and some who had also considered abortions. But he was vehemently opposed to abortion. Whatever religion lay dormant within him, he had a few beliefs and, after all, he would remind everyone he was a Republican and a conservative to the bone.

He growled at Grace. "No, Grace! I don't want you to get an abortion!"

Shaking his finger at Grace, "As far as I'm concerned, I'm washing my hands of the whole goddam matter. You made your bed, Grace, you go lie in it!" He left and slammed the door, rattling a few cupboard dishes and cups. His last words were totally useless 'wisdom,' of course, but it was the only thing that Jack could muster from within his gnarled self. And sadly, those were the last words he ever said to her.

Grace went on to have a bouncing baby boy and decided to share parenthood with Ahmad. The two had married in January at the Wayne Hotel in Wayne, PA. Grace's Mom and Stepmom pitched in for a wedding and reception afterward in the ballroom and an overnight room there. Dawn's father did not attend the wedding or reception, but did he offer to help pay for the reception. That was incredulous! He put a couple of hundred dollars in an envelope and slid into a slight opening of Dawn's car window.

Jack didn't consider himself a wealthy man, but he was known for stashing money away, readily admitting he wouldn't trust any bank 'anywhere on the continental U.S. of A.' He always paid cash for anything, did not own a credit card and still maintained a priceless 1956 Packard 'Predictor,' a coupe that his mother had handed down to him before she died. The antique would have brought a tidy sum if sold, but Jack would not hear of any offers.

'It's a damn good running car,' Jack would tell admirers. 'Mother seldom used it for more than going to Mass.' Later when he had joined All Saints, he shared with the rector that he also owned a 1950 red Chevy pick-up truck, which he once told the rector: 'I love that old truck. I want to be buried in it!" He laughed, "Hell, I ain't never seen a hole that old truck couldn't get me out of!" Supposedly the rector laughed himself silly.

Dawn had endured a rather dysfunctional family in her early years. She often said that her family put the 'fun' in dys-*fun*-ctionall. She grew up to become a kind, caring, generous, playful, practical woman. Her eyes sparkle like the sun glistening on a morning lake and her spirit can easily turn someone into Jell-O. The burning embers of a difficult childhood and youth, had refined her toward becoming an amazing young woman with determination to make the world a better place, at least the world she was coping with. I would fall in love with *all* of her - her fiery spirit and passion, her love of beauty and abiding friendship –even her disdain for organized religion.

Chapter Two

LOVE'S DAWN AT SOMEONE'S DYING

The minute I heard my first love story I started looking for you, not knowing how blind that was. Lovers don't finally meet somewhere - they're in each other all along.
-Rumi

Thinking back, our love story actually has its roots at someone's dying. Weird, isn't it? On a particularly snowy December afternoon back in 2000 while I was serving All Saints Episcopal in Havertown, I got a request to visit a dying parishioner who had suffered long and was faithfully tended to by his wife, Eve. Dewey's disease, '*Nuclearsupra Palsy*, rendered him incapable of speaking and he struggled with coughing and choking on solid foods – even with the 'host' he received from the holy sacrament. A few weeks before, Eve and I had decided to cease the way we were attempting to share this practice and just pray *as* the body of Christ. For this evening, however, I imagined trying communion with Dewey a little differently.

Arriving at about 4 p.m., I could see others were parked in the driveway. As I've learned, dying is a communal event, even if the dying one might prefer privacy. People often gather around. sometimes hovering over the dying one, perhaps wondering what it might be like for themselves when they are 'called up yonder.' Caring people and the professional types, of course, neighbors, curious types and family all come and go among the dying.

Eve, Dewey's wife met me at the door. "I'm glad you're here, Father Seaver."

We exchanged a hug. Eve is slight of stature, people often calling her 'Little Eve', in her late 70's and having a beautiful smile. The work of care and compassion for her husband had put etch marks on her face. I had known her as soft spoken and gentle. She took me to Dewey's bedroom and there I could see the visiting Certified Nursing Assistant busily caring for him, taking his vitals and making him comfortable. Noticing that I had stepped into Dewey's room, she smiled at me and came over and quietly said,

"Hi there, uh..." she looked at Dewey... "I'll be finished in just a few minutes. Do you mind?"

I smiled and nodded: "Sure. Please go ahead. Uh, and thanks for your care," I smiled.

This nurse smiled and looked into my eyes with a smidgeon of curiosity. Perhaps she wasn't used to clergy being so gentle. Some of my colleagues might march into the room as if God in heaven had arrived. *Stand back I, your Reverend, am here!* That's not my style. We are all part of a team of professional caregivers, each with his or her own gifts to share. I like it that way. I waited and watched her.

She wore scrubs and a sweater, a stethoscope dangling around her neck. I noticed her gentle hands and the loving way she went about her work with Dewey. Her salt and peppery hair laid back with a 'come hither' look. She had a natural, classic kind of beauty; she wore no make-up and I noticed modest earrings. She looked thirty-something. Eve stood with me as the young nurse finished her work.

"I don't think Dewey has much time, Fr. Aldie" she said as she squeezed my hand. As we waited at the doorway to his bedroom, the young nurse placed the covers over him and came to the doorway.

"Thanks for being patient," the nurse sighed as smiled at me and began packing her bag.

"Would you like to stay for communion?" I offered, pointing to my little kit of wafers and a small carafe of wine. "Well, sometimes he has a difficulty swallowing."

"Oh," she said as if to be surprised at the offer. She seemed hesitant, but then offered: "Well, OK, but I can't stay long. More patients before my day is over."

I nodded,

"It will only take a few minutes."

She smiled and stepped aside and let me approach Dewey. I sat my wine cup and little bread from my ciborium out on a small paten on his nightstand and poured the wine into the chalice. I placed three wafers onto the paten and offered prayer. We held hands... I was aware that I was holding the visiting nurse's hand. It felt warm.

"Lord, bless your servant Dewey this night. You know his struggles. We rejoice that your love is inseparable from life. Bless Eve and all who stand in care of Dewey. May he always be mindful of the embrace of your love and may this meal of bread and wine sustain him in body and spirit. In Christ's Name, Amen."

The sharing of the bread and wine with Dewey was never easy. With his palsy disease, swallowing was torturous with each communion. Choking and coughing were typical. I decided to use 'intinction' - a common practice of dipping the wafer into the wine- so that the wine-drenched wafer was the only thing to meet his lips and perhaps slide down his throat a little easier. I handed the wafer to the nurse, who gently let him nibble on it until it was soft enough to swallow. It worked - a slight cough, clearing his throat, but the 'Host' coasted down Dewey's throat with ease. Then I turned to Eve and the visiting nurse: "The body and blood of Christ, given for you, Eve, and you...." I smiled, a little embarrassed that I had not sked her name.

She looked up and smiled. "Dawn. My name is ...Dawn."

"The body and blood of Christ for you, Dawn," I said almost reverently as I looked into her beautiful eyes. I placed the wafer gently in her hand... she dipped it into the chalice and swallowed it.

"Thank you," she said quietly. I took a mental picture of her face. No make-up Very plain, and yet beautiful.

I bid goodbye to this gentle creature, Dawn, with whom I had shared the Meal of Christ alongside Eve and, carefully, with Dewey. I always left a little kiss on Dewey's forehead with benedictory words *'God continue to bless you and ever be with you, Dewey.'* Dawn smiled and left quietly. I spent a little more time with Eve. Then I left for home, thinking, *'Mm... Dawn!'* Her smile and beautiful eyes were imprinted on my memory. Later, when our relationship began to unfold, it seemed ironic that we should begin our journey together in this world around with the Sacrament of Holy Communion... and at someone's dying.

Those few moments with Dawn lingered on into my night as I crawled into bed. My wife Kathy was in Nashville on a CPA Account trip. Dawn's gentle care of Dewey, her kind heart, her attractive smile, her simplicity, and the way she told me her name at my giving her the Host - and not the least the way she looked into my eyes – it all left a lingering impression, a tiny lump in my throat, a tenacious curiosity. I could hardly sleep. I kept seeing her beautiful eyes, her squinted smile. She was unapologetically and simply Dawn. It would have done her natural beauty injustice to see mascara pasted on, even lipstick and rouge. Although I would have accepted the 'war paint,' if she had chosen to wear it, her natural beauty surpassed other women whom I have known who wear the war paint loudly.

Our second meeting was, sadly, at Dewey's graveside committal service. Dawn was not in the scrubs, but in a black coat with a brightly colored scarf wrapped around her neck on this bitterly cold day in Havertown. We chatted a while after the service about Dewey and how he had struggled. She told me that she was glad I had come to the house and respected me allowing her to complete her work. For a moment I took her hand and thanked her for her kindness to him. The way our eyes met was riveting as if we imagined a greater depth of one another that we couldn't possibly know then.

"Do you think the service went OK?"

She looked away momentarily and then smiled at me. "It was fine…. uh… I'll be honest with you, Fr. Aldie, I'm not practicing any religion and I'm not even a believer. I'm just not comfortable with any of it. I just don't think there is a God. Sorry" She looked away again.

"And here, I gave you communion last week…" I responded apologetically.

"It was OK, I didn't expect it and you didn't know I wasn't a believer. No harm done, please know that. In fact," she laughed a bit, "it's the first time I've had communion in, maybe, twenty years. It didn't do me harm…it's just, I'm just not practicing that stuff anymore."

"Oh," I said in with a somewhat surprising tone. "It's Okay. Thanks for telling me."

I thought: *So… she is not a believer, but she has many great qualities.*

Dawn realized my body language had changed. She looked down and then into my eyes "I love people and the world and all its possibilities for goodness and kindness and love…and whatever surges of creativity surround us with imaginativeness… but…"

I smiled. "But you just don't buy into religion and theology?"

She nodded.

"Well, to tell you the truth, Dawn, sometimes *I don't buy into it* either. There are days when I have doubts... heavy doubts. There are times when I'm preparing a sermon and I wonder, 'Is this all crap?' And frankly that's when I have to dig deeper into my own soul and ask questions...serious questions"

Dawn tilted her head and seemed surprised. "Really?"

"Really! I see the power behind what I do more in touching peoples' lives and helping them in the present, not tied to some orthodoxy or doctrine of belief.... (I took her hand)..."that's part of the reason I am attracted to you. You are so genuine." She wrapped her arms around me and we hugged. First biggy hug!

"Thank you... thank you, Aldie. That... that means a lot."

We parted as she told me she had to get back to work. I walked away still having a light-hearted feeling about this 'earth angel.' She was so authentic, no guile about her whatsoever. I hoped that I had planted a seed of acceptance and openness, that she had observed a bit of my kindness, my soul. My heart was lonely for the kind of authenticity she carried, even though we were opposites in matters of faith and religion. Beneath all of that I felt a kindred spirit between us.

This took place a few months after I had arrived as the new rector on the block in Havertown, PA. Going home to my townhouse, viewing boxes still unpacked and a general sense of disorganization -noticeably a cold pot of stew on the stove, an almost empty refrigerator, books piled here and there and old sermons in a file marked 'Holyoke,' I felt a disquieting loneliness. There was a phone message from Kathy – *Aldron, sorry I'm late from work. I may stay over to complete this corporate account we're working on. I will call you in the morning.*

I felt my spirit wedged between yesterday and some unknowable future,- especially my recent years in Virginia and a peek toward this little flickering light in my conscience, this visage of a gentle persona named 'Dawn.' Sure, I was curious about how she became disenchanted with organized religion. Was she an atheist? Could I ever be in a relationship with an atheist? Could two opposites in faith attract? Still, with some irony, that was drawing me into a twinge of fitfulness. Was it a restless longing as I had never realized -certainly with Kathy Jones Seaver, my first wife?

Chapter Three

HOLYOKE - THE PRE 'DAWN' YEARS

"You can't hold onto the past forever, but the past can hold onto you as long as you allow it."
Aldron Seaver

My years at Holyoke Episcopal Parish were ringing like faint church bells in a distant memory. They were really my '*pre*-Dawn' years. My relationship with Kathy Jones was a journey of contrasts in that place while I served Holyoke Episcopal Parish, near Gloucester. I did my priestly thing there for almost ten years, immersed daily in the highs and crazies of organized religion. Holyoke Episcopal Parish was located south on Belroi Rd. (Highway 616). Named for a city along the Connecticut River, Holyoke was founded in 1890 as a Sunday School retreat center. Then it was a simple wooden hall with a chimney and a kitchen. Later with the vision of George Mason, it became an Episcopal parish and its first building was realized in 1922.

It was part of my 'coming into my own' as a rector. Before my calling to Holyoke I had graduated from the Virginia Theological Seminary in Richmond and served tiny parishes around the County of Richmond. For three of those years at Holyoke. I struggled through my marriage to a woman who, sadly, didn't seem the least bit interested in me romantically or physically. Her name was Kathy Sue Jones, although she hated the name 'Sue.' Her work with a CPA firm and her passion for playing the cello meant she was away from home frequently. I missed her companionship deeply. Being with the guys for occasional golf games at Gloucester Country Club and Bible study breakfasts with colleagues just didn't measure up to having a soft and tender feminine companion.

I did cultivate casual friendships with women with whom I could carry on a conversation and enjoy dinner now and again.

Believe me, I resisted companionship with women in the parish. And to be sure, there were a few spinster types at Holyoke who made it their duty to watch my every move. I heard that the Eastern Shore of Virginia was a breeding ground for rumors about 'the rector at Holyoke.' I couldn't verify if this had happened in the past, but I do know that organized religion sometimes thrives on this kind of rumor-milling.

Even at that, people in the parish knew that Kathy Jones Seaver was elusive and more absent from worship than present. People seldom saw us together. And, if the truth were known, there were a few people in the parish who assumed their rector was single. Kathy Jones seldom worshipped, although she claimed she was Christian.

It amazed me that any time I ventured out to enjoy the companionship of women, there were 'eyes' to report my 'indiscretion.' *He's married, you know!* some would say. Of course, I swear on a stack of King James bibles that I did *not* sleep with any of them. As it turned out, someone at Holyoke did send a letter to the suffragan[1] Bishop about the rector's 'indiscretions.' I have a good idea who, but it didn't seem to matter after a while.

In the realm of 'ecclesiastical instabilities,' let me introduce F. U. Frank - short, pudgy, balding, a slight scowl on his face, seldom smiling and, notably a personally, downright nasty man. F. U. (Forrest Ulysses) used to yell at altar boys or girls right in front of gathered worshipers. As the suffragan Bishop for the Episcopal Diocese of Virginia, he decided to make it his business to put me through an earthly hell for my faltering marriage to Kathy Jones and for having social contact with women. He knew that my relationship to Kathy was tattered. We had talked about it. He knew it before he became suffragan Bishop. Of course , F. U. really wanted to be a bishop, not a suffragan.

---

[1]A *suffragan* bishop is an assisting bishop who does not automatically succeed a diocesan bishop. A suffragan bishop may be elected bishop or bishop coadjutor. In 1814 James Kemp was consecrated Suffragan Bishop of Maryland, even though the office was not authorized by the Episcopal Church's Constitution. From 1829 until 1910, different General Conventions discussed proposals for electing and consecrating suffragan

bishops. The 1910 General Convention enacted "Of Suffragan Bishops." A diocese may elect a suffragan bishop, but no diocese may have more than two suffragan bishops except with the special consent of a General Convention.

-*The Episcopal Church*

Having served a parish in our diocese, F. U. Frank apparently discovered that he was better at managing and manipulating others than trying to be a priest to them. I had heard that he had botched a few churches in the Tidewater area and for that, the diocese, in its inestimable wisdom, decided to 'reward' F.U. by making him a suffragan - a somewhat feathery reward I must admit. I observed how he soaked up the authority immediately, bossing priests around and inflicting his self-righteous drivel on many of them. Those of us who had fallen on difficult marriages were good fodder for his 'authority hunger' games. For the most part, the little Episcopal parish I had served near the Virginia's shore was quite willing to embrace my 'fallen' state, but not 'F.U!' (I'll spare you how we used those initials in clergy circles.) Sadly, I consider people like Forrest to be part of the reason the Episcopal Church is in decline today. Across the Episcopal union, our membership numbers are lagging, and we are apparently not attracting young people.

F. U. became my nemesis throughout my ten years of my ministry, most of which were at Holyoke. He would snip at my heels like a nasty sheepdog, especially during those last three years of my *non*-marriage to Kathy Jones Seaver.

As I tried to figure where all this crap came from, I decided F.U. probably disliked me because of my close relationship with Diocesan Bishop, Benjamin Asher Cargill, or 'Ben' as I call him; he also graduated with me from Seminary and we were close friends throughout the rigors of training to be pastors. I had been a confidant through some of his own struggles in his marriage. He was elected Bishop from resumes of some fifty applicants from within the Eastern Diocese and beyond. I'm sure F. U. was among them. Ben was personable and charismatic, a dynamic preacher and down to earth. On the other hand, F. U. Frank had been removed from a parish outside of Richmond for being a bit of an ecclesiastical asshole. The former bishop, the late Aston Derwood Young, had decided to bump him up to an administrative position and then to suffragan Bishop, which had also substantially bumped up his ego. It was no secret in the Diocese that F. U. wanted desperately to become an Episcopal Bishop, but Ben had moved far above him in the election and F. U. would remain a suffragan. The title *suffragan* is synonymous with 'subordinate' or 'assistant' and F. U. certainly couldn't stand being subordinate to anyone, let alone Ben Cargill. Further, F.U.'s awareness of my friendship with Ben put me on F.U.'s radar for any missteps at Holyoke... as well as later at All Saints (yes, bless him, F. U. Frank is a suffragan to the Bishop of the Episcopal Diocese of Pennsylvania even as I write this!) Suffice it to say, F.U. would have skewered me in any way possible given his official capacity, making me an 'example' to Ben as if to suggest: *'See what kind of a friend you have chosen!'*

So, as an act of ecclesiastical 'dissection,' with his scalpel sharpened and ready, F. U. Frank decided to send an investigative team to Holyoke to see if I should be censored or possibly removed as a priest. The investigation cost the Episcopal Diocese of Virginia about $7,000. Ben had deplored wasting the already tight budget of the diocese on this investigation, but F. U. wielded his ecclesiastical muscle to make the intimidation possible. The work of this 'lynching' team included random interviews with my parishioners.

On arrival, the team demanded from me a documented listing of everywhere I had been the last two years at Holyoke and environs, etc. Yes! Seven hundred and thirty days of documented personal navigation! I flatly refused to do this and sent a registered letter of complaint to the Bishop's Office indicating my refusal and indignation at F. U. and his 'minions' (well, I didn't use that word) accusing them of a gross violation of my privacy. I would have left the parish if it had been pressed upon me to do this 'shit.' - the only decent word I could give it. I was ready to make this a 'legal' issue if necessary, with my friend in law, Tim Grimes in Gloucester, on retainers if necessary! My reading of the constitution of the Episcopal Church saw no reasonable requirement of statement of a priest's whereabouts for even one day under its 'Discipline of Priests'.

As expected, my refusal to fulfill this requirement gave F. U. just the ammunition he needed for his final report to the diocese. There were seven 'praying mantises' for the investigation – five men (one a psychologist, himself a former Episcopal rector), one retired rector from Hampton Roads, three men and two women from the ordinary ranks of diocesan churches. F. U. had called together this Committee on Discipline after I formally refused to account for 'everywhere I had been in the last two years of my life,' but the Eastern Diocese Council and Bishop Cargill threw out F.U's request and threatened his censure should he insist on this provocation. F. U. backed off, but the inquisition would gain even more steam.

The folks at Holyoke had never had this kind of 'lynching' (their word) and, when announced to the Vestry and then to the congregation, returned with loud indignation.

Monday early, the team descended upon the parish and began to randomly go through our pictorial directory and parish address book to begin their interview process. I was pissed off at that, because that seemed like a violation of institutional privacy. Photo directories are not intended for anyone's use other than parishioners. A number of parishioners flatly refused random interviews. In the 1990's, privacy laws were not yet reaching the general community. My Secretary cried when one of the team minions indignantly asked for the parish phone directory as if she were investigating a crime. As it turned out, my Senior Warden was the first 'casualty' of this interview field skirmish. It began with the question, *'Do you have reason to believe that Fr. Aldron Seaver has been morally lax and professionally irresponsible?'*

Wilbur Forcey looked at her haltingly:

"'Morally lax and professionally irresponsible?' Jesus, woman, the man's an excellent priest if I ever I knew one – human, sure like the rest of us, but, Christ, he can give a decent sermon in eight or nine minutes!" (Wilbur was one of those blue collars from the other side of the track in Philly. He worshipped the Flyers, the Phillies and Eagles, but he was a true-blue Episcopalian. He didn't mind saying what was on his mind – even with me!)

Uptight Investigator: "Please, be reverent when using the name of our Lord and Savior!"

Wilbur: "Why don't you leave Aldie alone, for Christ's sake? I've been through three marriages myself and I can take the Jesus juice with my head held high!"

(Did Wilbur actually use the phrase 'Jesus juice?' Wilbur! He was known for dropping some irreligious language on occasion, especially when he was angry.)

Uptight Investigator: "Uh... OK, Mr. Forcey, this interview is over. I will not tolerate your language. How did you ever become a member of this parish let alone Senior Warden?" She closed her notebook and put it in her satchel and stood up and left the room quickly. He told me later he shook his head as she was slamming the door and muttered 'What a bitch!'"

Many parishioners apparently told the investigative team to proverbially 'take a Flying Nun's leap,' which got the team's dander up and, with the exception of the psychologist, were ready to actually recommend disciplinary action for the entire Holyoke Parish – *me included of course!* What! I have no idea how you do that? Could they bolt the doors? Bring in the militia?

But then, no surprise to me, a powerful voice emerged from the ranks of the parish - *Molly Malone Mason,* known as '3M' around the parish. She actually contacted F. U.'s office to request an interview on grounds that she had much to share about Holyoke's 'delinquent rector.' Molly Malone Mason was the great, great, great, great... and maybe one more 'great'...granddaughter of Holyoke's founder, Dr. George Marshall Mason, IV, the first Senior Warden at Holyoke. He was a professor at the School of Engineering at Virginia Commonwealth University in Richmond. Word had it that George single-handedly financed and carried out the leadership development of Holyoke, handpicked the first priest-developer and helped construct the first church building - now called 'The George Marshall Mason IV Memorial Chapel,' I guess sometimes it takes only one very wealthy and powerful person to *raise a church.* His legacy has continued until now in the likes of Molly Malone Mason - a bit strange in that, although she saw it her mission to keep his legacy alive, she consistently alienated many folks because of an attitude of self-importance based on her lineage. Apparently, sometimes in churches, 'who' you came from can matter. And I'm not just talking about baptism in Jesus either!

She was by her own description a 'teetotaler.' If the truth were known, she likely abstained from most everything else, too. She was also very orthodox in her religious beliefs. She never married and once muttered at someone's comment about her being an 'old maid: 'Only Jesus Christ himself would ever be worthy to carry me across the threshold.' That's so mindboggling that the thought of it actually kept me awake one night! Sometimes the *heir apparent* of George Mason IV's legacy would refer to her abstinence from, as she always put it, *'you know what'* as the crowning achievement of her life. It would be hard to imagine '3M' even having *you know what!* She was not an unattractive woman, but I had to wonder what happened to her that made her such a spinster of sorts. Somewhere at her core she was very angry at life and I had become the misguided target for her unleashed fury.

Appearance-wise, at times she seemed to have jumped right out of Laura Ingalls Wilder's *Little House on the Prairie,* but unlike Miss Beatle at Walnut Grove school, '3M' was kind of rigid and mean spinster. She wore her hair in a bun, a high neck blouse buttoned tight and long black skirt, black hose and black shoes. Although her face seemed like it ached for a smile, her occasional smiles were almost torturous. Her small-framed glasses rested on her nose and when she spoke, her words had that slow and deliberate Eastern Virginia drawl. I wondered whether there was a 'feminine' Molly yearning to crawl out of that rigid persona. Should she ever dare to let down her guard and allow some restrained *joie d 'vivre* gush out of her, she would die right on the spot! She was an enigma.

I picked up from the Holyoke grapevine that '3M' didn't like me because I once professed that I didn't believe in the Virgin Birth of Jesus. I don't think it was a public pronouncement, but it might have been overheard when I was casually chatting with parishioners and questioning some of the more archaic doctrines of the Church. There are a number of them I've never warmed up to, like the Second Coming and the Atonement.) Nevertheless, this overheard statement about the VB was an anathema for 3M. Whatever was spoken …and I almost…*almost*… regret that it leaked out… created a perfect storm for this wiry worm of a woman. She seemed to be obsessed with the Doctrine of the Virgin Birth as if it were the only important belief in her life and everyone else's–if she had her way. I learned that when she served on a Call Committee for a new rector, she insisted that the question must be included: *'Do you believe in the literal Virgin Birth of Jesus?'* Those who answered in the affirmative had half a chance of being called to Holyoke. Those who admitted they struggled with it were immediately eliminated from consideration under 3M's voracious protests. No one dared disagree. I happened to survive that, because '3M' was *not* on that Call Committee when I interviewed, and the Committee insisted that the question be dropped. Wilbur Forcey told me that Holyoke actually lost some good candidates for rector because 3M's forcing of the question. When it was revealed that most members of the Call Committee also had issues with the Virgin Birth belief, Molly Mason Malone resigned from the Committee and almost left Holyoke to join Abingdon Episcopal Church (c. 1650), down on Route 17 in White Marsh - a beautiful and quaint colonial church along the George Washington Memorial Highway. However, there were two problems with Abingdon for '3M'. First, they were an open community, welcoming both conservative and liberal views. And second, George Marshall Mason, IV, didn't found it. She knew very well she would have been a little fish in a bigger pond at Abingdon.

This Virgin Birth issue actually blew up in my face at a gathering Bible Study with the Dorcas Society, a group of well-heeled women who insisted that I join them in 'feeding on the Word' every Wednesday at 10 a.m. with tea and sweet rolls. I was *not* invited to lead the sessions, but to be the token priestly presence. I loathed these gatherings and their pious pretensions. 3M called them "Two Holy Hours with Jesus.' We usually met in her suffocating living room, sitting around on her creaking, period furniture and discussing the 'women of the Bible.' No one at the gathering was under 70 years of age except 3M and me. Molly and her neighbor, Agatha Whistlewaite, would do most of the talking. I often wondered whether the rest of the women who sat on their hands around her dimmed and uncomfortable living room as 3M and Agatha chattered away wondered why they bothered to come to these gatherings, since only Molly and Agatha ever said anything.... Until my appearance that humid late morning in May.

"As I've said, I've always been proud of my abstinence," 3M muttered and fluttered referencing our study of 'Mary, Mother of Our Lord.' I've felt honored to have something in common with her virgin status."

She looked straight at me as if to say *'Of course, our Rector doesn't believe in the Virgin Birth..."*

I believe it was Mildred Torrance, the local town librarian, 'that liberal woman' as some referred to her, who found her 'Dorcas Bible Study' voice:

"Well, I guess I've always wondered about the Virgin Birth. I mean, when you read the Gospels, Jesus had brothers and sisters. Didn't he?"

Molly interrupted, "Oh, Dear, Mildred, you don't want to imply that Joseph and Mary had... *you know what...*"

"Had intercourse?" Mildred interrupted? There was a gasp.

I offered at great risk, I knew: "You know, ladies, the word 'virgin' in the Bible simply means 'young woman.' I'm inclined to believe that God can favor human procreation to bring about someone as transforming as Jesus. We've turned sex into something ugly as if God is disgusted with it. So, what if Mary had sex with Joseph or perhaps was raped by some Roman soldiers? Not uncommon in that day. She wanted to bring this special life into the world. Life was cruel and unfair in those days. Maybe God brought something beautiful out of human cruelty."

The stone silence was shattered by a deep sigh from Molly Malone Mason as she looked around the room shaking her head. It was a tectonic shift beneath the creaking chairs and clattering teacups. It was a verbal earthquake and we were right at the epicenter and, figuratively speaking, Molly Mason Malone's Victorian edifice was crumbling on Duvall Avenue from embarrassment. And here I was the ecclesiastical seismic rumble tearing it down. Molly tried to gather her composure. Agatha Whistlewaite, with no eye contact, chided me for suggesting that the Mother of Our Lord could have been raped. "Eh...now Fr. Seaver, you don't know that. It's all speculation."

I smiled but retorted gently:

"So is the speculation of 'parthenogenesis' - the idea that a woman not having had sex with a man would become pregnant and conceive a child. Look, how does a Spirit impregnate flesh, Agatha? If God created human beings and said that they were 'good' - as the Genesis creation account suggests - why on earth would Mary not conceive a child and see divine participation in the way human beings are brought into the world? Why would we think of that as dirty?"

I knew I had stepped into a boiling caldron. It was clear by her body language that 3M wanted to drown me in it. Her buttoned up blouse was tight around her neck, her face red and her neck arteries strained.

She said tersely:

"I'm not implying that...that... well *you know what*...is dirty! I just believe God didn't use that base earthly encounter as a way of bringing about the Son of God, Jesus. It's important for me to believe that Mary was a virgin!"

Mildred Torrance, her 'Dorcus'-voice now up-pitched, jumped in. "Base human encounter? Come on, Molly, that's so.... so Catholic! People just aren't going to the wall with Virgin Birth any more. Can't sex be part of the miracle of God-becoming-human? I, too, would rather have Jesus come by natural birth and become one of us than imagining God having sex with a teenage girl."

"Mildred Torrance," Molly Malone retorted, "you've been reading too many of those liberal books down at the community library! And, for the record, I do go to the wall for Virgin Birth. Someone has to defend the Blessed Virgin!"

Now all eight of the women were starting to jump into some 'verbal fisticuffs' about the Virgin Birth. Everybody was getting their 'Virgin Birth' voice on- (pro or con) – perhaps for the first time in any of the sessions since I'd been there. Louise French, one of the bakers down at Old Dominion Cake Shop said she was going to talk to Father Jakes, her priest at St. Therese's about it. To which Mildred Torrance, who was getting up a head of steam for a woman short of stature, said:

"Louise, goodness gracious! You don't even attend mass! You told me you were angry with St. Therese's Parish because they requested large sums of money for the building of the new Fellowship Hall."

"Doesn't matter!" She sat up and folded her arms, "Father Jakes is still my priest," Agatha started reaching for her kerchief and began to cry: "God must be angry with us, I swear! It's a wonder lightning just doesn't come down from the sky and wipe us all out for thinking this way."

Damn, if it didn't happen! A sudden clap of thunder rattled the 3M's house and they all looked at each other in frozen fear. A late morning thunderstorm was making its way into the Gloucester area —certainly common at this time of the year in Tidewater Virginia. One enormous clap followed by a lightning nearby with 3M's quaint chandelier flickering and then came a second clap. The timing was perfect! Three of us laughed... my laugh being the heartiest.

3M spoke with a half a smile: "Well, ladies. I guess God *has* spoken."

Papers were shuffled, teacups picked up. Mildred Torrance snickered. Louise and Agatha nodded to each other in agreement. The rain poured down solidly for fifteen minutes, amounting to a late May deluge. The lightning flashed around the area, with 3M's lights continued flickering as if anticipating loss of power. It all seemed surreal, like divine fury being unleashed and I imagined the Almighty thundering: *I loathe your petty arguments! And you, Aldron, look what you've created!*

I realized at this thunderous moment that I really didn't belong to this group - at least not my sorry ass liberal theology sticking out like dirty underwear. My own theology had grown way past the rather retro theology of these dear 'Dorcus' ladies, God love all of them!

'Dorcas' in the Book of Acts is Greek for 'female of a gazelle' or in Hebrew 'Tabitha –the name means 'Emblem of Beauty.' Who was I to burst their bubble, these *'emblems of beauty?'* Who was I to publicly doubt their sacred beliefs? If they wanted to believe in a Virgin Birth, they should have at it, embrace it, defend it, and advocate for it – just as 3M had. Yet, I did discover in this session that a few were struggling with it and were willing to come out of their cloistered theological closets of belief. It doesn't matter that it's a doctrine I've long disbelieved. Why am I trying to change their model of their world of faith?

So, I apologized for my stirred cauldron of beliefs and told them that I needed to move on (which I *really* did mentally and emotionally). I made an excuse that I needed to make a few rounds at Riverside Walter Reed hospital. I prayed with them, asking that God might open our hearts and minds so that we could live into the wonder of God's creation and see its good amid the complexities of our beliefs and spiritual growth. Getting ready to leave, I thanked Molly Malone Mason for her hospitality. She still was throwing mental daggers at me, but managed a civil, half smile at the front door:

"Good Bye, Reverend."

The storms had passed - outside and inside. The deluge had produced puddles here and there along Molly's walk to Duvall Ave. My feet were sloshing in my shoes by the time I got to the car. The mud from the drive way found its way to my trouser hems. The day had become very humid as it surely always does in Tidewater Virginia in May. I imagined how the Dorcus ladies were relishing conversation about me... and why not? I was like a sudden lightning and a clap of thunder myself, a storm that had startled these 'emblems of beauty' seeking to find Jesus on the quaint tree-lined Duvall St of 3M's Gothic home. Although in the greater picture of the current shifts of the theological climate, it wasn't all about me at the center of this storm. Even in the 90's there were winds of change in the speculative world of theology and belief systems. People were being challenged to ponder a Deity greater than human doctrines and dogmatic beliefs, larger than Bible verses and the thinking of those who wrote down their perspectives of God. We are all micro urchins in the expanse of God's creation, scrambling around for security in the uncertainty of our days. We all have something to prove, to be sure of and much to control. We struggle with the hint of theological and spiritual chaos in this new age theology, forgetting sometimes that it was out of 'chaos' that the world itself was fashioned by a benevolent Creator. In the fragile gathering of these little 'two great hours with Jesus,' I had unleashed a thunderous bolt of doubt: *maybe God is greater than our doctrines or our arguments about human virginity!* But walking through the hospital entrance I wasn't proud of myself at all.

I thought to myself: *'Seaver, sometimes you are such an asshole. Shame on you for stirring up tempests in circles where the gathered just want their time with Jesus!'* I quietly prayed: *'Forgive me, God of Love, for being so disruptive in the fragility of human beliefs. Teach me tolerance. Amen.'*

Molly Malone Mason barely gave me eye contact after I had tossed the 'Virgin Birth' thunderbolt from my liberal perch. From that time on our relationship deteriorated rapidly. I was aware that she observed every detail of my ministry at Holyoke, especially since F. U.'s lynching attempt had proved unsuccessful. She looked for anything to complain about – how I often forgot to fold my vestments properly at the conclusion of Mass. or the Sunday I gave the wrong date for the upcoming annual Mission's Picnic to raise funds for supporting our missionary in Indonesia –even though it was plain as day in the bulletin announcements! She was going to be in my life whether I wished it or not –to remind me that I was not worthy to be in the shadow of George Marshall Mason, IV. Could anyone convince her that she was already loved and accepted by the One she was desperately trying to be good enough to be loved? I wanted so much and couldn't freely say:

'*Molly Malone Mason, you don't have to do this charade to get God's favor... you're already loved and in that enormous circle of divine acceptance.*' Yet it was painfully clear to me that she was not ready to accept that.

So, as it turned out, F.U.'s 'Gestapo'-type descent upon Holyoke, had only one complaining interview in the investigative team, not enough to merit my censor and now the Diocese was out $7,000 with nothing to show for it. Of course, F.U. wrote a scathing report about my behavior and presented it to Bishop Ben. Copies shared with the Discipline Team, merited a few chuckles and the entire team politely thanked F. U. for his work and did *absolutely* nothing but accepted the report as 'information.' It never got on the agenda. F. U. was '*FU*rious!' Word got around that Bishop Ben Cargill personally criticized F. U. for wasting of Diocesan money and the energies of Discipline team and demanded he put his energy elsewhere.

'3M' continued milking my 'indiscretions' for all it was worth. Life at Holyoke became an unwieldy challenge with her 'Rift with the Rector' Campaign. She verbally voted against every salary increase and every proposal I made as a rector on behalf of that congregation – including the effort to send Malaria nets to sub-Saharan Africa. Holyoke Parish ended up raising, interestingly enough, $7,000 toward Malaria nets, despite Molly's dissenting vote. It was a delightful sum in many ways, ironically off-setting the Diocese's waste on investigating my so-called 'indiscretions' at Holyoke. Many people came to me plainly embarrassed by 3M's behavior.

There *were* 'indiscretions' of course – my liberal theology, my non-stop fury with F.U. and, not the least, I was a terribly horny rector. I lived with a wife who feared intimacy and getting pregnant and, I wondered, might be asexual or gay.

New Calling

I spent another year in the Tidewater area of Virginia's Diocese before interviewing and being called as rector of All Saints Episcopal Parish, Havertown, Pennsylvania, in the summer of 2003. My leaving Holyoke was difficult for many, although I imagined that for '3M' it was a bit of a *tour d' triumph* for 3M's 'undo the rector' cause. She would have tried anything to get me out of Holyoke. She had become brittle beyond description, even more than I could have imagined sitting in the stifling living room of her pale green and gray Gothic a little over a year ago chatting about the Virgin Birth. I had never anticipated as much hate in an individual as I did from Molly. My paranoia had grown to the level of dreaming she murdered me one late evening in my study with a letter opener, sneaking up behind me and stabbing in the back of my neck.

Just about the time I was submitting my resignation to Holyoke, I began receiving some interesting revelations about 3M's earlier life. I learned from one of her cousins that Molly Malone Mason had been through a very disappointing love affair with a young man who had actually attended Holyoke but had never joined. She had dated him for almost seven years, but he had never sought marriage. Rumor had it that he looked like the very early pictures of George Mason IV. 3M had sought the counsel of the rector at that time about her long-suffering relationship with the young man, troubled because the relationship had not moved toward marriage. Then by some revelation from one of her best friends, Molly learned that the young man she was in love with for seven years had another relationship that he had been harboring secretly for all those years and had decided to marry that woman. According to her cousin, the revelation was so devastating that Molly Malone Mason turned into a bitter woman overnight, vowing never to seek the affections of a man nor ever to wear a wedding ring. Some in the parish thought she had gone mad. Others suggested she might be 'evil.' Molly had always been firmly imbedded in her fundamentalist beliefs, but apparently according to some older folks in the parish, there was a time in her early twenties when '3M' was gracious, smiled frequently and was enjoyable to know. And even with her conservative edge, she had been more tolerant of others' beliefs. But after this heartbreaking rejection, a very dark veil of descended over her persona. And she wrapped herself in it and intended for revenge on every male clergy she encountered.

I was one of the very few people who knew what had really happened. Her cousin had sought me out in confidence because she knew how 3M had been literally badgering 'the hell' out of me at Holyoke.

And, as if it could get any more intriguing, the most shocking revelation of all was that the young man who rejected her during those years, was a student at the Virginia Theological Seminary in Richmond - a colleague of mine in the Diocese of Eastern Virginia – Ed Cameron. We weren't close friends, but he knew where I had gone to serve and there was never a word mentioned about Molly Malone Mason. Now I could kick his ecclesiastical ass for not warning me.

Anyway, 'hell's bells!' Stuff like this can really rattle your perspective when you learn its impact on a person's emotional landscape. It gave me a different perspective of Molly and why she seemed out to destroy me.

Her hatred for Ed lived and as far as 3M was concerned, any rector at Holyoke who was not impeccable professionally would have been on her radar, targeted for vicious emotional disembowelment. And you might guess how many impeccable clergy there were in the Episcopal Church - other than possibly F. U. Frank! Still, I wondered if I had known about this jolting relationship with Ed Cameron, might I have approached Molly Malone Mason less defensively. Believe me, I pondered this for a long time.

Strangely and certainly unexpectedly, after my resignation letter, 3M wrote me a letter that included, among other niceties, her *'great appreciation for all I have done for Holyoke'*... (What?) In one sentence she even wrote: *'You have helped our search for the grace we yearn for from our Savior.'* Wow!

In fact, Molly cried the day I left the parking lot of Holyoke Episcopal Parish. Was she finally coming 'unstuck'? There was a surprising shift in her attitude toward me. Was her reign of terror over? Did my resignation vindicate her?

My wife, Kathy Jones Seaver, had moved out that week to stay in a hotel in Havertown, PA, claiming that she was anticipating several interviews with CPA firms in Philadelphia. The movers were scheduled to leave for Havertown that afternoon during my protracted 'good byes.' A reception had been held in the Community Room with generous gifts from both individuals and the parish itself. I felt embarrassed that I was leaving with a treasure trove - gift coupons, checks and cash. The treasurer had given me one additional month's salary and the congregation had culled together a generous 'purse' of $10,000. I was tearful as I opened the envelope in front of 175 people gathered for potluck and a sheet cake that read *'We love you Father Aldie.'*

Many stayed in the parking lot to wish me well. In this profession it seems you never know how much people love you until you leave! As the crowd waned, 3M finally approached me and seemed like she wanted to hug me – it was surreal. The woman, who for the last six years could not stand my persona, detesting every strain of my liberal ass theology and every program I recommended for the Parish and who had complained to F. U. Frank that I was 'the worst rector Holyoke had ever called' *was standing in front of me crying because I was about to drive out of the church parking lot forever!* You just never know about people who claim to be your enemies. The most ponderous question for me became: *'Was 3M truly my enemy?'* In the theology of Genesis, God's intent for creation was not that creatures should be enemies, rivals, injurious, assaulting... but rather benevolent, peace-seeking, nurturing, caring, and just. Regardless of '3M's' attack on 'me,' did I truly understand her? I don't think so! *Dear God, did I have a great big gob of regret deep inside!*

I put my hand on her hands and felt a sizeable lump in my throat:

"Molly, take care of yourself. I know I've disappointed you far too many times in my years here. I'm so sorry and regret any unkindness toward you. I hope you find a much-deserved happiness."

Yes, my eyes were a bit misty. 'Thank you for your... your kind letter.'

Suddenly she wrapped her arms around me and kissed my cheek and held me tight for a few seconds... and then turned and left hurriedly toward her vehicle. In the realm of the surreal, that was possibly the 'surrealist' of all. I felt my heart racing and my tears well up.

I pulled out Holyoke's parking lot at 1:23 p.m., tears streaming down my cheeks and blowing my nose and reaching for my water bottle to quench my dry mouth. I had to have music, too. Something soothing.

Driving up Interstate 64 and around Richmond on I-295 and up I-95 to D.C., I spent a lot of time reflecting, continuing with '3M,' what she had been through with Ed Cameron and how it had turned her life into a tormented journey. This spinster in her late 40's, perhaps early 50's, had lived in the wake of an ever-widening and deceitful relationship. All my disdain for her rigid persona, her fundamentalist beliefs, especially hanging desperately onto the Virgin Birth belief made sense. I began to melt away into a regrettably belated compassion for her. I suddenly felt a needed to hold her. I even imagined making love to her! But more realistically I had a slight impulse to sit down and write her a long letter. Yet I knew I couldn't look back. The future was calling me toward a new community, maybe more '3 M's,' - lonely, tormented people who were living out unresolved anxieties and regrets. So, I prayed out loud that Molly might indeed find a new meaning for her. She had taught me something, shared a gift I needed, even in her vitriol toward me – a gift, sadly, too late, *Molly, Molly, I'm so sorry... may your yesterday's disappear so that today might embrace you with peace and love. Dear Jesus, I thank you for Molly, for the gift waiting to be open in her.*

Leaving a parish is a lot like leaving a family! I had married, buried, baptized, prayed over, confirmed, taught, fought, visited people in distress, led the Mass publicly and privately in peoples' homes, comforted the afflicted and sometimes afflicted the comfortable, cried with a few, laughed heartily with some, and argued lovingly. Being a rector is a special kind of 'social and spiritual' dance. When I was called there in 1994, I had promised to share the spirit of Christ with these folks and be among them as his servant. It wasn't just a professional relationship, it was intimate, transparent and being like a parent. I carried their secrets within me. I knew of their indiscretions, I listened to and forgave their wrongs 'in the name of Christ.' I was often among them in the ups and downs of their daily lives.

I recalled sitting in the bedroom room of a parishioner, James, who was threatening to commit suicide. On his nightstand lay a loaded revolver. He seemed resolved at his great age to end his life and spare his wife of his debilitating depression. I listened to his sobbing and inconsolable wife in the next room. I was shuttling back and forth between the two until, exhausted into the wee hours of the morning, I brought Ruth back to his bedroom and sat her down and sighed:

"I cannot spare you two from your agony here. You both have got to find a way to resolve this situation and promise me you'll seek a counselor, someone with better credentials than my own, to help guide you into some positive resolution. All I can say is that you were both created by a benevolent God and nothing is so insurmountable that it cannot be brought before that very presence. Before I walk out of this room, I need you both to tell me that you hear me... otherwise, I'm going to sit here with you and wait for the sun to rise!"

I said it with such conviction and strength, that it drew a long silence. Soon they both nodded and actually took each other's hand and I took both their hands prayed my heart out to the One who needed to be called upon in this fragile and uncertain situation:

'Benevolent Creator, in these hours of the night, we feel the deep darkness of our own human frailty. We call upon you to enter into the lives of Ruth and James with your powerful love. They are both shattered by their own weakness and torment. Their tears and their fears wear on them heavily. Come be their Guide and Healer. I pray you enter mightily into this dark hour with your Love that they may know for certain that you are God, their Rock and Fortress. Even as we boldly say, 'Amen.' (I squeezed their hands and Ruth and James muttered 'Amen.')

I went home at about 3:45 a.m. worn to the depth. Kathy didn't even hear me come to bed. Tired as I was, I couldn't go to sleep wondering whether James might have followed through with his threat to scatter his brains all over the bedroom walls. At some point sleep did overtook me, and I gladly surrendered.

I learned the next day that Ruth and James had stayed together that night. They held each other and cried and promised that they would find a path toward healing for James's broken spirit. I knew it wasn't that I had not observed James' life was tormented. Draining as the profession is at times, I learned one thing: I live within a matrix of Divine Presence that seeks Love to find a way to work within uncertainty and sometimes uneasiness of the human condition - including my own. That Love –sometimes hidden, yet always there, was a Pillar of Light I followed tenaciously, a Shepherd's crook I held tightly, a benevolent Hand I grasped securely when I felt myself sinking into despair. Being a pastor, priest, rabbi, imam, and shaman –whatever the title- holds no power or authority over human behavior, only the conviction that the Holy One is always within the shadows of mortals like me with a 'care and share' spirit.

Though I walk through the valley of the shadow of death, I will fear no evil, for you are with me... that part of the shepherding role was, the sure-footed steps of the shepherding role, could never be journeyed without the Divine Shepherd up ahead. *I am able to lead only because I am able to be divinely led.*

Suddenly I was aware of weightiness hanging over me, a mountain to cross over. I was facing new names, new circumstances, unfulfilled lives, hurting spirits, anger... all of them waiting for a new member of the frock to nibble away at their helplessness and neediness.

Nevertheless, I could not have imagined as I approached this new venture, that someone who was 'already in my heart' – as Rumi had written – was waiting to meet me.

Chapter Four

HAVERTOWN HOMECOMING

The hometown skies seem bluer than skies that stretch away. The hometown friends seem truer and kinder through the day; and whether glum or cheery, light-hearted or depressed,
Or struggle-fit or weary, I like the hometown best.
Edgar A. Guest, **Hometown**

By five o'clock that afternoon my old Honda Civic -210,000 miles and still going strong- arrived at what was essentially a 'homecoming.' The' townie-turned-preacher had returned. Back at Holyoke on the Eastern Shore of Virginia I had l been a 'sojourner,' a transplanted Pennsylvanian settling in the backcountry of Tidewater Virginia, across the York River from Williamsburg and Newport News/Hampton Roads. Gloucester, the 'Daffodil Capitol' of America. I was a Virginia flatlander, 'a 'Holy-*okel (the affectation given to priests at Holyoke),* a 'Tidewater Trawler' - although I never once fished the tidewaters. Now the call to All Saints was like the prodigal son returning home and I was at its gate, welcomed as a kind of native son on the rebound. I sighed as I pulled off onto I-476, the 'Blue Route,' and exited eastward onto Route 3, West Chester Pike. I was hungry and would have enjoyed feasting on the 'fatted calf,' but a Big Mac and coke would suffice. The 'McD's' was a familiar haunt just beyond Eagle Rd across from The Shops at Manoa Center were there. The familiar golden arches building now renovated to a modern theme, the arches smaller than the old crowning arches of days gone by. Some of the familiar haunts remain after many years -places I remember shopping in my youth –Radio Shack, the irresistible 'Krispy Kreme,' Ruth's Hallmark, where I bought many a card, and, of course, the Acme Hardware store, where once as a teen I made a noble effort to help people find tools and countless other things I knew very little about. I noted Bill's Shoe Service was still around as well as Essex

Cleaners, where at 16 I first met Susie Frost, who I thought was the love of my life.

Nine miles west of Philadelphia city limits, Havertown is an unincorporated community of Delaware County, PA. Most locals will tell you that Havertown is the birthplace of 'Swell Bubble Gum,' which closed its doors recently and is now being replaced with the new state of the art Havertown YMCA.

Looking back, a segment on Philadelphia News 10 shared:

On a cloudy Wednesday morning, the Swell Bubble Gum factory, a Havertown, Pa. landmark for decades, began to come tumbling down. Workers started demolishing the 200,000-square-foot Eagle Road factory to make room for new development. Bubble gum and confections were produced at the site from 1948 until it closed this year. Since then the plant has been an eyesore for local residents as legal battles over the actual value of the property kept the site from being developed, according to the Delco Times. With the demise of the bubble gum plant comes a state-of-the-art YMCA. The 70,000-square-foot facility promises to serve 20,000 local residents and create 150 jobs, reported the Delco Times. On Wednesday, though, as bulldozers ended the bubble gum plant's run, residents were left remembering what was before the bubble popped on Swell. - Wednesday, April 13, 2003, NBC 10 Philadelphia

Perhaps a lesser-known fact about Havertown is that it has the largest Irish-American populations in Pennsylvania. Of its 51,000 residents, over 11 thousand are of Irish descent. All Saints Episcopal Church, my new calling, hugs the suburbs of Havertown on a quiet lane off the West Chester Pike.

With the city of brotherly love looming across the Schuylkill River All Saints Parish is a quiet little oasis of encroaching urban life. Like Havertown itself, All Saints is made up of a number of Irish members like the McAllister's, McCoy's, McCleary's, McLaren's, McCormick's, McGill, McNamara, McClellan, McCafferty... and the O'Connor, O'Connell, Oh my! I wish I had been Aldie McSeaver!' or 'O'Seaver. Dawn's Irish descent came through her father, Jack O'Shea, who I've already introduced. Jack looked every bit Irish and with a faint Irish brogue. *Christ-a-mighty!* you could hear him say, or 'God-dammit!*

He no longer darkened the doors of All Saints. He was very active back when he was married to Lydia (Grace's mother, Dawn's stepmother). Lydia had persuaded him to get involved at All Saints. It was short-lived, however. Jack was known for having a short fuse and had fallen out with my predecessor, Vernon Ivan Powers, over a property dispute – a long-held vision of the All Saints, to build a Great Hall for congregational fellowship. Building new structures can be a source of all-out war in many churches. The congregation weighed out over Jack O'Shea's insistence that the addition would bring financial ruin to All Saints. At the vote in favor of building the Great Hall, Jack dramatically walked out the Nave door and never was seen again. In a very rare case, V.I.P. had won a victory in a congregation that had essentially tolerated him and building a new Great Hall at All Saints was the one thing they could agree on. It was a beautiful structure with varied community uses that benefited the area.

Dawn had attended church only occasionally back then. Her best friend from school, Sissy McKinney, attended St. Faith's Episcopal Church on Brookline Blvd. Her father was fine with her attending there with Sissy and her parents. He reminded her: "Just stay away from that money sucking excuse for a church, All Saints. That's all I care about!"

Dawn's ancestors had come from County Kerry, on the south edge of Killarney, close to Muckross Lake - near where the famous Ring of Kerry Road ends and returns to the city. Her father, Jack, was the great grandson of Martin Bailey Clifford O'Shea, one of eight generations of famous Irish butchers. Having left high school, Jack had begun his career as a butcher from the tradition of James Whelan Butchers of Dublin.

I would meet Dawn for coffee at Hanne's. It was heart-felt on both side. It was a bit of a break from all the venting about religion. She shared so much information about the difficulties of growing up not knowing who her mother was. Her father had had two wives and during the second marriage had had an indiscretion with someone who apparently was Dawn's mother. She said somewhat pensively:

"Somewhere out there, my flesh and blood Mom is walking around wondering about me as much as I am wondering about her."

"So, did your father raise you?", I said as I took her hand.

"Yes. It wasn't bad, really... at least in the early years. I know that I have a very different worldview from my Dad – maybe not as provocative as Grace's. My father had a seductive way about him, which often made me realize how it was with the women in his life. I remember when I had become a teenager he made a comment: 'You're the woman in this household, Dawn!' I was somewhat flattered by that comment initially, but as I grew into my later high school years, my father was expecting me to make supper, do the laundry, keep the house clean and go grocery shopping. I was exhausted between going to school daily and working at home being this teenage 'housekeeper.' I ended up being some kind of surrogate wife. I hated that part. And he seemed to sabotage the notion of my dating - until"... until, Aldie, he got involved with his own girlfriends. Then I pretty much lived alone in our house. I came and went and, unfortunately, got over extended with boyfriends."

As the weeks went by and Kathy seemed to be evaporating from my life, I found myself cuddling with Dawn and sharing kisses, very sweet kisses and feeling ardor. I sensed she was being drawn to me, maybe in a quasi 'big brother... girlfriend' sort of way. I may have been horny and filled with fantasies, wondering what beauty lay beneath those Navy-blue scrubs she wore, but I wasn't ready for sex with Dawn and wanted to be cautious. I was still a married rector, albeit a very lonely one.

Being cautious became more difficult the more we met and with her sweet lips melting me down. Each time we found ourselves breathlessly caressing. The physical desire unfolded so naturally and with mutual yearning. We agreed that sexual intercourse was still too risky. We laughed that it felt like we were high schoolers in serious petting mode. She could feel my swollen member as we held each other. I was permitted to caress her soft legs and reach the pleasure zone and then kiss her breasts.

I'd release my pent-up urges at home during a midnight shower. It seemed like most nights Kathy was nowhere to be found. I would always be asleep when she arrived late in the night and before she left for her work the next morning. I'd make coffee and we'd talk casually.

"You worked late last night, Kathy."

"Oh, we have so many accounts that need to be completed, Aldron. It's been awful. Between the orchestra and the firm, I hardly have a moment! I'm sorry. Are you doing OK?"

I looked at her and drank my coffee. "I'm fine."

As she left for work, I realized that I had experienced more intimacy with Dawn in a few months, than any single time in my courtship and marriage with Kathy Jones Seaver. My feelings about Dawn were beginning to occupy more space in my mind and heart. I knew that I was never going to be the love of Kathy's life, nor she mine. It was unsettling though. I wasn't ready to let the talented cellist, my wife, disappear completely. I tossed and turned the night before. *Was Dawn for real? Could I really love her with so many differences between us? Was it more physical than soulful, since sex had not become part of Kathy's and my life?*

Chapter Five

'FLOWERS APPEAR ON EARTH'

My lover spoke and said to me, 'Arise, my darling, my beautiful one and come with me. See the winter is past; the rains are over and gone. Flowers appear on the earth; the season of singing has come; the cooing of doves is heard in our land...

Song of Solomon, Chapter 2, verse 10-12, New International Version (Holum Bible Publishers, Nashville, 1984)

Gosh!…how unforgettable it is the first time you make love to someone, regardless of how clumsy it might have felt! Marta was my first, of course. But Dawn was my first sex with a woman I heartily loved. I came to appreciate the difference. Dawn and I certainly seemed to be heading to this moment in our secretive connections.

One Thursday, we both had endured a monumentally difficult day. I had been at Mercy Community Hospital where the family of Marty McLeaf, a former senior warden at All Saints, had decided to 'pull the plug' on his respirator. Marty had a rare form of brain cancer and in just a few weeks from the diagnosis, his health declined rapidly. He was 89 and in reasonably good health until the headaches had gotten so bad that he required hospitalization and the MRI showed a fast-growing tumor in his parietal lobe. During his consciousness at one of my visits at Mercy, Marty told me he was ready to 'meet the man upstairs.' He managed a chuckle. He didn't really seem to be afraid to die, just that he didn't want to linger in some vegetative state. He slipped into unconsciousness this past Tuesday and the family decided, based on his 'Do Not Resuscitate' directive, to follow his wishes and not allow his life to be prolonged. Pulling life support is always intensely emotional for families, of course. His wife, Margaret, held me so tight I could hardly breathe. His daughters, Lisa and Lauren held each other and wept. At first Marty gasped for breath, but within a short time he slowly breathed a welcomed relief as his life slipped into the abyss. I gently placed oil on his forehead in the form of a cross and said: '*Martin, the Lord bless you and keep you. The Lord make his face to shine upon you and be gracious to you. The Lord lift up the light of his countenance upon you and give you peace. In the Name of the Father (+) and of the Son and the Holy Spirit. Amen.*'

I spent another half hour with the family around Marty's body. Lisa was sobbing as she hovered over him. She had been the daughter who had strayed often from her father's graces. She had born a child out of wedlock with someone for whom her parents had disapproved. Her grief was deep, because her Dad had waited patiently for her to find a way back into his life. Recently, she had met a man who was kind to her and accentuated her good qualities. They both had approached me about being married and she was looking forward to the possibility that her Dad would give her away. But that wasn't going to happen, and she knew it sorrowfully. Lauren was much more subdued in her grief. As they were able, I invited both daughters and Margaret to talk about Marty. Lauren preferred to be alone with her thoughts. She was the 'daughter who had chosen to stay home.' According to Margaret, she had had several disappointing love interests while attending Delaware County Community College, where she was preparing for a career in energy technology. She was the introvert of their two daughters.

It was three o'clock and a knock at the door indicated that Logan's Funeral Home had arrived for the body.

"Just a few more moments, please," I indicated to the funeral personnel. They nodded. I turned to Marty's family:

"Could we just pray before they take Dad?"

They each gathered around the bed touching Marty. Margaret put her hand around his faced and leaned hers next to him, planting kisses. Lisa put her head over his abdomen and held his head. I put my hand on his forehead and prayed, thanking the Lord for sharing Marlin with us these many years. Lauren held his other hand and bowed her head. After the prayer, I hugged each one and told them I would be in touch about the details of Marlin's Service of Remembrance.

I looked at my watch when we were finished, and it was 3:45. I needed to get going. I thanked the good folks at Logan Funeral Home and left. I arrived at Dawn's townhouse about ten minutes after four and was relieved to see her white Camry parked in front. Greeting me with a smile and the taste of her gorgeous lips, I could sense immediately there might be love in the air. I can't say I'm always aware of the 'air' of love, but she was wearing a low cut white blouse and a short bronze thin skirt that revealed those shapely legs. I confess she was an ocular charge. Most of the time I'd see her in hospital scrubs. She was barefooted and held a glass of wine. I knew it had been a tough day for her because she doesn't ordinarily drink wine. Her text to me earlier indicated that she wanted to take me to *'Giampino's'* for a 'romantic Italian dinner' on West Chester Pike.

"Wow, Sweetheart - you take my breath away."

With a seductive kiss, she looked me in the eyes and said: "Aldie, after dinner I want you to take off that stuffy collar!"

It's hard to describe what a beautiful woman in this attire saying those words does to a rather horny Episcopal rector like me! Of course, I had forgotten that I was in my 'work duds', my Roman collar and black shirt, my boring-but-predictable herringbone jacket and gray pants. I looked every bit like a stuffy priest. I decided to remove the collar anyway, at least not to draw attention at the restaurant. There in her foyer for a few moments, we enjoyed some sweet kisses. That got my libido kicked into high gear.

Quiet on weeknights, dark and candle lighted, this *Cucina Italiana* defines romantic dining. Dawn and I had begun routinely to share an entrée at restaurants. We saved money on good food and cared for one another in the process. Sometimes patrons would stare at us sharing plates. And, of course, most restaurant don't like that

Nevertheless, we arrived a little late at *'Giampino's.'* Eduardo, the new *maître'd*, found us a comfy table for two, He introduced Benito, who would be taking our order. He looked about 18 or 19 years of age, a schmoozer of sorts, seeking to entice us into expensive wine and entrees. We waved off the wine and decided to order the Chicken Voldastano, stuffed with smoked mozzarella cheese, broccoli rabe and prosciutto finished in a mushroom sauce. (That's how the menu described it.) We also ordered an appetizer, Cozze, sautéed mussels in a white wine sauce.

"You only want one order?" Benito lamented. Dawn recited our typical response: "Benito, we share everything we enjoy...and we enjoy everything we share."

We learned Benito was a second-year student at Delaware Community College. We guessed he wasn't used to people sharing entrées, but this evening was a learning curve.

As the order was taken and Benito finally disappeared, Dawn poured out her heart about the frustrating day she had on the floor at Frankford. Apparently, one of the nursing instructors had found a note from a vindictive nursing student. This instructor was noted for being a bitch on wheels. As the students gathered in the morning, she let out a barrage of allegations based on the note and chose to punish the whole class if the culprit didn't come forward. Needless to say, no one did. So, we were served notice we'd have to work the weekend and stay sequestered at Frankford in the student area of the facility. There were of course deep gasps of indignation.

"What!" June O'Reilly piped up. "I've got two children home. My husband works weekends!" "

Ms. Grandfield shook her head. "That's tough, O'Reilly. You'll just have to get a sitter."

There was unrequited grumbling around the room: "Listen here -all of you... you'll all do this at 0800 on Friday a week from today. No excuses!"

Dawn stood up and said, "But, Miss Grandfield, it's not fair to punish all of us for one person's complaint."

"Get off your high horse, O'Shea! Now, Ladies, if no one's going to' fess up to bitching about me... you all pay."

Then, amid more grumbling around the room, Bonnie Wratchford stood up and said, 'Ms. Grandfield, I wrote that note. I'm sorry."

"God, Aldie, we were all stunned! Bonnie Wratchford! -one of the best nursing students in the class - punctual, studious, helpful, serious - never one for 'I'm better than you,' not an arrogant bone in her body. As mean as Meg Grandfield was as a nursing instructor, she would sometimes compliment Bonnie on her work. So even Ms. Grandfield was shocked that it was Bonnie!"

Fumbling papers, she told Bonnie: "Ms. Wratchford, I want to see you in my office right now. The rest of you, get on with your duty assignments today. I'll rescind the weekend work details. And, ladies,"…shaking her finger at us… "don't belittle me with notes like these. If you have something to bitch about, bitch to me in person. Now get out of here, all of you!"

'We cleared the auditorium and watched Bonnie walk out of the classroom with Grandfield. We looked at each other in disbelief as we filed out. Later that day, we learned that Bonnie Wratchford was removed from our group and assigned to several weekend work details as punishment. It stressed all of us out on this particular Friday before the weekend. We wondered what the now famous 'note' had said. Bonnie was not one to complain and no one ever heard an unkind word from her mouth. It's not that she was self-righteous either, but sometimes we'd say with resignation: *'God, I could never be like Bonnie Wratchford!'* "

I said holding her hand, "Wow! No wonder you had a glass of wine in your hand when I arrived this evening!"

The *Cozze* appetizer wasn't as tender as we had enjoyed previously, but the Chicken Voldastano was excellent. Benito kept insisting, 'Why not share a dessert.'

'We'll skip dessert,' Beautiful Dawn said with determination.

'You could share a dessert maybe? The tiramisu is out of this world'. *Magnificato!* Benito lobbied.

"*Grazie, Benito, tráigame la cuenta, por favor.*" Dawn looked like she was on a mission. The *cuenta* paid, we parted Giampino's. On our way to her home, Dawn told me, "Aldie, I'm so ravenous this evening! I want to make love to you so desperately. I mean… it's time! I can't stand it anymore!"

My heart kicked into overdrive and my face flushed. Arriving home, we practically stumbled into her front door in a heat of passion, landing on her carpeted foyer. I kicked the door closed. We tore away at our clothing as if our bodies were aflame. Dawn was incredibly seductive, her skirt wrapped around her waist now. We kissed and caressed and shared all manner of guttural sounds. She pulled me closer until she could feel my phallus begin to penetrate.

"Aldie! Oh, dear heavens, that feels wonderful!"

She confessed later that, other than 'Vince the Vibrator', she hadn't felt a real male goad in years. As for me, I was praying I would be sustained adequately throughout the lovemaking. The more I penetrated, the more Dawn held me tight.

"Aldie, please don't stop, for God's sake. Oh, my goodness, Aldie!"

For a few moments, we were caught up in a rocking rhythm, the carpet cushioning beneath us. My thrusts made her bounce against me, until she screamed. "Oh, Good Lord, Aldie! just... just ... *Oh!* Her ecstasy soon took me to the threshold of that irreversible moment of release welling up in a male when all the forces of erotic imagination blend in with one powerful physical sensation and *Voila!* ...the eruption!

I yelled: 'Oh, Sweet Angel of God!'

As I released, I felt the sweat in the smallness of my back. I'm not the most athletic rector in town. I'm a 'chunk!' But I was holding my own. I was so breathless afterward I thought my heart would leap out of my chest. It was the first time I had experienced honest-to-goodness sex with a woman since my one and only embarrassing episode with Marta late one evening down in the stacks of Temple University's library! (More about that later.) This encounter was so genuine, so sensational. My words are inadequate!

After our pleasure softened into sighs and caresses on her living room carpet with *'I love* you!' and gentle kisses, we lay in contented rest. Our delight in each other simmered into babbling contentment. Finally, sleep took hold there on the short weaves of the carpeting by the coffee table. Somewhere near midnight, I awoke aware that my arm had fallen asleep beneath her neck and was numb.

"Darling, let's go to bed," I whispered.

She yawned and smiled and said nothing, got up from the floor, gathered her panties and shoes and blouse and skirt and walked with me up the stairs. We removed the remainder of our clothes, pulled back her puffy comforter and fell into one another's arms for the remainder of the night. Only a pale light filtered through the venetian blinds. It was the first time I had shared her bed. The night spent itself and carried us on proverbial gossamer wings. A beautiful reverie – our first real love-making. Although, almost amonth before this, we had an 'almost first' love-making time in the church after the service one Sunday. I'll share that another time.

Although it was risky, we spent more and more time at her house, squeezed in between her demanding nursing training shifts at Frankford Hospital and my busy work at All Saints. Kathy never asked where I was, because she was barely at home. By now it didn't seem to matter, because obviously being with me wasn't what she needed.

Dawn and I became quintessential conversationalists, chatting about most anything and had a great deal of synchronicity in our values. My religious beliefs and her traveled atheism remained unspoken for the moment. For the present, our passion kicked into high gear!

By mid-October All Saints knew its Rector was enjoying the company of a woman. Dawn would make a few discreet appearances at our contemporary service. She admitted she enjoyed the 'peppy music,' but she also liked to come in and listen to the magnificent organ sound that Helen McFarley mustered with Bach or Buxtehude. Sometimes the ushers would say to me, 'Fr. Aldie, there's a young lady that comes in from time to time and then leaves. Do you know her?" I gave a rather non-plus answer. "Oh, uh she's a friend who is… uh… searching, she told me. You know, a seeker type."

One thing Dawn refuses to participate in is the Eucharist, calling it 'contrived communal nonsense.' She remarked later, 'Who wants to eat and drink Jesus, Aldie?" I made a few failed attempts to defend the sacrament, but I wasn't going to convince her any time soon. How does one defend the holy eucharist to a non- believer? Explaining 'consubstantiation' and 'transubstantiation' gets my own tongue tied up. I wasn't going to explain it to Dawn. I recall when I attempt to give the 'consub' and 'transub' talks, I get blank stares -even among my own parishioners. When I'd try to explain it, kids in my 7th Grade confirmation classes I'd get a resounding 'Yuk!!!' - even when trying to imagine a 'magical mingling' of bread and wine that recalled Jesus' life-giving self. Still 'Yuk!!!' I had pondered often, even in seminary days: *Did Jesus' last meal give him the jitters when the sharing of the cup of wine (red) and breaking the unleavened bread (his broken body) gave a whole new meaning to this Passover commemoration?* Could Dawn understand that we don't 'munch' on Jesus or sip his blood? Could anyone embrace that in the 'meal of thanksgiving' itself

was what Jesus sought to commemorate? 'Do this to remember me '
… 'Do this'… gather, share a meal and remember me. *Therein lies a
thankful gathering.* The word communion means literally 'common
union' – something that draws us together and creates community.
Meals can do that. We know that from our potluck luncheons! We're
never more cordial than when we bring our dishes and chat around
our tables.

This notion – that the 'Sacrament of Holy Communion' is
the commemoration of Jesus in a communal gathering - breaks with
a long tradition within Christian orthodoxy. Teaching it could get
me defrocked. Yet I still wonder whether the meal itself, a 'memory
meal,' is the essence of the sacrament. We do something similar with
our commemoration of Dr. Martin Luther King, Jr. in January –
having a communal pot-luck and sharing his 'I have a dream' speech
with neighbors in the Havertown area. We keep his memory alive by
striving to be a 'beloved community.' Don't we do the same with Jesus?
Well, *consubstantiation* and *transubstantiation* will always have the
floor on the debate. We like the *mystery* over practicality. A memory
meal as figurative, metaphorical, and doesn't cut it for traditionalists.
We want to say that Jesus is 'present' in the meal… yet we can't accept
that the meal itself is his presence.

Chapter Six

THE ANTECEDENTS OF A DIVORCE

It ended, and the morrow brought the task. Her eyes were guilty gates that let him in by shutting all too zealous for their sin: Each sucked a secret, and each wore a mask. But, oh, the bitter taste her beauty had.

George Meredith on a failed marriage, 'Modern Love.' (1862)

I can't go further without sharing the narrative of my Pre-*Dawn* years - my previous marriage and subsequent divorce to Kathy Jones Seaver. I've been hedging on this, because it's been a thorny thicket I've passed through in recent years. I had kept our crumbling marriage under wraps at both churches to protect both of us. For a while I wasn't sure how our marriage came off the tracks. She wasn't unkind and was very supportive of my work as parish priest in the early years. But there was a tectonic shift in our emotions and her feelings toward me. I wondered what I had done to push her away — even with all her physical inhibitions and sounding the death knell on our physical intimacy. Our courtship was probably more of a pleasant memory than marriage itself. Sadly, it's often the case in marriages today. I've read a lot about 'sex-starved' marriages. People drift away from intimacy for countless reasons- most of them through the utter failure of marital communication.

While attending Virginia Theological Seminary in Richmond, I met Kathy Jones, who was attending the University of Richmond School of the Arts. I had a small job helping in the Admissions Department there. I'm a great lover of the classics, so I would occasionally slip into the auditorium to listen in on the Department of Music's orchestra rehearsing for upcoming performances. Kathy Jones had caught my eye as she played the cello with noticeable artistry. I love that instrument and got the courage to introduce myself at a rehearsal break. Our conversations proved enjoyable, so we met again. Slim and graceful, Kathy's intimacy with the bow and cello was remarkable. Although she didn't smile often, her occasional smile at the conductor quickened my heart. When she'd talk to me about a musical piece she was rehearsing, her animation had almost a sensuous quality about it.

After a few weeks, I was smitten. And she seemed – stressing *seemed* - smitten too – prompting our getting together for dinner and visits to her little flat in Westover Hills. She would often ask to be held and I detected an unspoken 'love-me-but not too much" feeling about her. Weeks of cuddling made me obviously desirous of her. Her small frame just cocooned into my arms. Everything about her coaxed in me a yearning for intimacy. I sometimes wondered whether her certain aloofness fueled that desire or not.

Eventually, our first attempt at making love was disastrous. We started with gentle caresses in our underwear. Her fair skinned legs were soft and almost silky. She watched as my hands gently caressed them. She had confessed that she was not comfortable with her body, let alone a man's body and apologized, assuring me that it wasn't me. I wondered whether she had had difficult experiences with men in her past. She was such a gentle creature. I hated to even imagine that. Her movements were swan-like, graceful, almost dance-like. But intimacy with a man seemed to be the least of her desires.

I had decided our lovemaking just needed time to unfold and that, if anything at all, my patience might be rewarded. I chose to be gentle in every possible way with her. I praised her beauty, her stylish dresses. She wore slacks most of the time and her dresses were always long. I would often listen to her practice, affirming her skills, listening carefully as she would at times be frustrated learning a particularly hard piece. She appreciated my patient listening.

When we were once again drawn to intimacy, she would only allow me to fondle her in the dark and she insisted that Rachmaninoff be played while we caressed. Really! She apologized about Rachmaninoff, but she submitted that she always needed to have some article of some music as well as one article of clothing on. I didn't mind Rachmaninoff now and again. However, Sergei all the time was getting a bit monotonous. She was also adamant that I not touch her breasts. Eventually she accepted cunnilingus from me as long as I would not kiss her lips afterward and required that I not touch other body parts while I performed it. Curiously, none of my caresses or even oral care in her softest region ever elicited pleasure. Eventually she would say, "That's enough, please Aldron."

She also confessed to me during our fondling: "I've never been enamored with a man's phallus, Aldron. I'm sorry. I know that's not how other women feel, but I just don't like handling them. They're just...well, to me, unclean. I just feel they're saturated with germs."

The inhibitions were growing longer and longer. We reached a point where I was required to take a shower before 'intimacy.' And then, following our fondling, she would immediately run to the bathroom and shower for a good long while with her friend, Sergei, helping her wash me away. I decided this was just all too much fuss. I just didn't attempt honest-to-goodness sex and lived in our controlled intimacy.

I know it's too much information, but once when I accidentally penetrated her, she confessed it hurt and would I mind not 'doing that.' Oh my! It was a fleeting but incredibly beautiful moment! I apologized for the accidental penetration and she apologized even more. Kathy may have been frigid, inhibited sexually and a bit phobic, but she was excessively kind. 'I'm sorry, Aldron.' Every inhibition was followed by three or four apologies. So finally, sweet kisses and cuddles and caresses were the extent of intimacy – which is not bad, but I just had to accept with enormous frustration what we could share, because there were so many good things about this shy, talented cellist.

Even with all of these yellow flags and, not the least, my male horniness and naiveté, Kathy and I were married at the Court House in Richmond the summer of 1997. We had known each other for almost a year and a half. I must have had some undying belief that marriage would change her inhibitions and maybe 're-write the score' of our naively-shaped romantic interlude with a marriage contract. I should have known better.

My mother came down from West Chester for the wedding and Kathy's mother drove over from Charlottesville, VA. Her father was deceased. And, no surprise to me, my father was a no-show. I've forgotten which excuse my mother gave for him this time- maybe his back or not liking the drive to Richmond.

The wedding day seemed very conversationally strained. Kathy didn't smile much and seemed to have a veiled but anxious look during our civil ceremony. She wore her hair in a bun with flowers and a beige slim dress with lacing at the top and bottom. She was amazingly beautiful! I tried to prompt a smile by cupping her face and she barely managed even one tiny smile. She hesitated before she responded, '*I do,*' to the judge. And she never looked me in the eyes as we made our vows, looking down and to the side. Even the judge wondered out loud, 'Miss Jones, are you sure you want to do this?' She nodded with a rather benign smile. Even our invited marriage kiss brought her pause. It was more like a peck on the lips with a painful expression. I had officiated a number of weddings, but I never witnessed a bride so aloof, detached and anxious as the one I was promising my life and love. I hid my sadness and feigned a celebrative face, trying to pump a modicum of joy into these constrained moments. Even in the photographs, everyone was smiling except Kathy. It all seemed quite funereal.

Our two mothers had not met before that day in Richmond. We exchanged cordialities at the luncheon following the ceremony. There was plenty of polite conversation and the delicious food at the *Café Rustica*. It was an unbearably hot July day in Richmond. We talked about Angelica's work (Kathy's Mom) at the University of Virginia's library, her specialty being Thomas Jefferson's memoirs, and my mother's work at the University of Pennsylvania library as an Information Specialist. Library talk continued to generate a modicum of conversation with their common interests. It was as if Kathy and I had little talk about.

She seemed a million miles out in the cosmos. When I'd put my hand on top of hers, she would give me a faint smile and then look away. She seemed riddled with anxiety? I wanted to take her away and just hold her. When she excused herself for the powder room, I wondered whether she was sick. Later she told me that she had thrown up because of a nervous stomach. My wife, my joy, however constrained, suffered an anxiety disorder. I thought, 'in sickness and in health…'

Angelica asked me: "Now just where is Holyoke, Aldron?"

She knew of Gloucester- but was not familiar with the parish. I probably over-answered the question as if I were some docent for the town, offering historical details about the Episcopal Church in Tidewater, Virginia. Actually, I was trying to fill in gaping holes in our rather uncomfortable time together. For a while, it seemed like Angelica and I were the only one's conversing. My mother tends to be an introvert around people she doesn't know. Neither she or Kathy had much to say to each other. 'Awkward' summed our wedding day in Richmond. I was beginning to feel it was a bit ominous. Of course, I had yearned to be in a partnership, to have a spouse to share my life, but I would not have counted our wedding day convincing of marital love and celebration.

I know I keep harping on this, but following our wedding day, there were feigned occasions of intimacy – fondling, etc., but very little else. There were mounting excuses for not having sex - physical illness, stress at work and the biggest of all, her fear of becoming pregnant. She finally confessed that she had never wanted to have children and knew that was a burden for me. I suggested birth control, but she seemed disinterested in a response. Still she would always apologize, of course.

In months that followed our wedding day, I began to suspect that I was not the *love* of Kathy's life – that Kathy might be gay. We never broached that subject, even after we moved to Havertown. I sensed that she was looking for the courage to tell me. After Holyoke, she had joined a CPA Firm in Philadelphia and the new venture finally brought her out of the closet. One Sunday after I returned from worship and with take-out, she nervously told me that she intended to move out of our townhouse in July, ironically three years to the date of our wedding Richmond.

Ratcheting up her courage, she held my hand:

"…Aldron, I think you've guessed by now… I *am* gay. I always have been gay, but it's only been in the last couple of months I've had the courage to deal with the truth. I was afraid of hurting you. *Six of the most dreaded words no one wants to hear!*

Tears were streaming down her face and my heart was pound-ing. "You are a decent man, Aldron. That's what attracted to me you.

But...I'm sorry, I've... I'm sorry, I need a decent *woman* in my life."
A stunning admission!

She sat down and sipped her espresso and began a torturous confession. I was about to find out that not only was Kathy Jones an accomplished musician and a Certified Public Account with Pierce, Monk and Satterley, PA - she was by her own admission a very talented liar. While working at PMS, Inc., she had two same gender affairs. The first was a woman client whom she had met for dinner and then, after a while, several overnights and weekends away. Kathy would tell me that the firm was sending her to work on client accounts in Atlanta or New York or Los Angeles or Phoenix, and she'd be gone for several days, usually over the weekend or in two instances, more than a week on several occasions, but she was really with her lovers in Aruba, Cozumel, Bahamas, etc. Dear God, I was so naïve and never spotted a paper trail! Never looked at her passport!

When she'd return home, we were decidedly not intimate, despite my desire for her. The usual excuses were travel fatigue, not feeling well and, the usual, fear of pregnancy. I never understood why birth control wasn't an option!

The first of these unfaithful encounters she confessed when her lover had become so insistent about their moving forward quickly and moving in together - not to mention her physical demands on Kathy. I wonder if she had made love with Sergei in the background? *My little dig – shame on me!* She told me that their separation was bitter, with harassing E-mails and angry texts.

The second affair was with an older woman who decorated herself with tattoos and owned a late model Harley. She turned out to be a dominant female, which just didn't work for gentle Kathy. That relationship only lasted a few weeks, but without a bitter exit. The tattooed lady just disappeared in the sunset (so to speak) on her Harley.

Then as if 'three's-a-charm' she met Anita, who, according to Kathy, was a 'kind and sensuous, not pushy - just right' partner. She admitted that she had met Anita a month after we were married. The relationship grew slowly with Anita's frequent travels as one of Pierce, Monk and Satterly's top account managers. No wonder all the anxiety and our awkward wedding day. She was in a different world already, wrestling with her feelings for Anita and for me! It all made sense. *But why had she even married me?...* I thought, as she was going through these affairs.

As she confessed this, I swallowed hard, my eyes moist, my hands were shaking and my face red. Even if I had grieved the total absence of intimacy with her, I valued our closeness, our good conversation -especially around our mutual interest: classical music. I made it a point to attend all her performances, including a very memorable concert featuring her playing the demanding *Concerto for Cello in E Minor, Opus 85* by Edward Elgar. *'An acclaimed performance,'* wrote the *Richmond Times-Dispatch* the following Monday. I had beamed with great pride at her accomplishment and sent flowers at her concert studio room. Eventually, we dissolved all kissing, even cuddling. We essentially co-existed under a roof.

In my years of ministry, I had been very open to same gender relationships, perhaps beyond the judgmental attitudes of many of my colleagues and parishioners. I welcomed partnerships and counseled those who were struggling to find their courage and voice amid fears and uncertainty. However, I discovered that, until I became suspicious of Kathy's sexual preference, I had not imagined what it would be like if I were facing this with my own wife. Why had I been so naïve with Kathy, why such a blind eye and deaf ear?

Marta , a guilty pleasure

Looking back, I lived somewhat of a chaste life, even up to my young adulthood, secretly idealizing women and more attracted to 'nice girls' than the slutty types, although who am I to judge 'slutty?' But notably at Temple University in my senior year, I had my first and only honest-to-goodness sexual encounter with a lab partner named Marta. There was so much sexual tension during our work in the Physical Science lab, I would often have to hide my visible ardor. Our hormones were working on supercharge. She was sensual, but very plain with long, frizzy blonde hair and freckles. Sometimes she would wear her cheerleader outfit to lab and I couldn't keep my wandering eyes off her perfect legs. On occasion she would be deliberately careless. Once during a blackout from an electrical storm, she welcomed my caresses to explore- in an *unscientific* way - her wantonness and wetness. Then she encouraged me to release her right there under the bench beneath the Bunsen burner. She squeezed her legs tight against my fingers while planting kisses on my lips. The blackout created a noisy interlude as the instructor went to find a reset switch in an electric panel down the hall, so no one could possibly have noticed our tryst. It was so sexually intense in the back of that lab that I realized that I had released in my shorts just as the lights were turned back on.

A month later, one evening, Marta and I were studying in the stacks of the library basement for an upcoming Chemistry exam. It was so quiet, save for the sound of the AC. I had drifted off to sleep, slobbering on my chemistry notes. There was no one around. Marta got up from her desk, awakened me and took my hand and silently led me over to a quiet and dark part of the stacks marked 'Ancient History.' For a fleeting moment, I thought it was a dream. Marta faced the stacks and then lifted up her skirt as if to say: '*You know what to do.*' Maybe I was dreaming, but I was startled as she carefully pulled her cotton panties down. In the dimness of the shadow of the 'Ancient History,' volumes, there was enough existing light to see her beautifully rounded butt. I looked side to side and pushed down my own shorts. And there for the first time in my life, I allowed my honest-to-goodness inexperienced shaft to find its way deep inside the tender wetness of a woman. It was remarkable! I penetrated her and breathed out the words, 'Oh God!' I got so overly excited deep inside her that I quickly lost control and jettisoned helplessly deep into her before she was ready for her own orgasm. It was so embarrassing for me – as if I had selfishly denied her the pleasure she was obviously looking for.

"I'm so sorry, Marta," I lamented breathlessly, kissing her perspiring neck.

"Oh, don't be, Aldie, it felt incredible to me. I loved hearing your rapid breath and sighs and how engorged you became! That's a total turn-on for me! Now, just...just put your hand here..." It was Physical Science lab all over again! She guided my hand and placed my two fingers where she needed them to be.

"Oh! ... yes!. Now place your middle finger there... Oh, that's it!... right there...Oh, don't stop!... yes!!! Don't stop. Oh my God!'

Her body jolted and undulated - her voice lifted into an ecstasy with indistinguishable words. Surely some student was roaming around and could hear us. I marveled – feeling like a schoolboy learning the fingering on a saxophone, amazed at the sound it was able to squeak out. 'I did it! I thought '…and twice!'

With the school semester almost over and summer beginning within a few weeks, Marta and I parted ways and I heard later that she had transferred to a school in Pittsburgh. She was sensual, of course, but not the Virgin Mary by a stretch – not that I was looking for the Virgin Mary! She was the kind of girl, sadly, the guys around Temple would often refer to as a 'conquest,' like hunters bagging game in some safari. I didn't need trophies like that. It wasn't really me. I did write a letter of apology to Marta for that night in the stacks. Even though she had invited the sex, I felt I had treated her as if she were a sex object. She was my 'guilty pleasure' memory -one I very much regret and yet can't forget. I anticipated a return letter, perhaps some acknowledgement or words of forgiveness. My letter returned with a 'No Known Address' notation.

Our Uncoupling

So, now Kathy had found her 'authentic voice' and I was hearing her. Since my affections for Dawn and our growing intimacy and mutual care for one another, I wasn't thinking of Kathy as often. I didn't see her often. However, I did marvel that she hadn't told me earlier on… back when I was falling in love with a gracious cellist who sent me soaring. What had allowed her to stay with me and lie?

"Why so long, Kathy, after a courtship and marriage?" I would have released you to your preference…"

She interrupted and confessed: "You were a tender, sweet man, Aldron – a safety net in my anxious world and my cloistered sexuality. I fell for your kindness, patience, understanding. I'm so, so sorry. I knew your ardor would suffer. Before I met Anita, I would have stayed. But.. in another way, your kindness and patience gave me….well, it gave me courage. You… you lifted me up, Aldron. I will always be appreciative of that."

In the divorce settlement, Kathy wanted nothing. She signed over the house to me, which I found remarkable. The monthly payments, the $976 mortgage payments to Wells Fargo didn't disappear, of course, but now I was the sole owner. I wasn't jumping for joy. It took me three weeks to remove all of her pictures, scrapbooks, clothing she had left behind for Planet Aid, books, and DVDs. You've probably guessed already that her cello and other personal items were going with her to her new home.

Tearfully, I told her: "I *do* love you and honor you and now I'm letting you go with my blessing. It's not easy, Kathy, because not being with someone you love is harder than I could have imagined."

She looked up at me, wiping a tear.

"Aldron, you deserve someone to share your life with. I hope something works out for you. I'm hoping there will be a very special woman in your life. I'm sorry I'm not that woman."

It was the following Thursday in August when we stood in our kitchen, hugging for the last time as she waited for her partner to arrive. Kathy's overstuffed 'American Tourister' stood silhouetted in our hallway. While I had been at work, she had moved out most of her clothing and belongings to Anita's place on Rittenhouse Square, where apartments sell for nearly one million dollars.

When the car horn sounded, it was as if Kathy had summoned a cab set to embark on a long journey. It was going to be difficult to see her go out the door one last time. I had seen her go away many times, thinking that Pierce, Monk and Satterley was sending her on another client account junket. She had been 'leaving me' more often than I knew. There were many nights when there was no text, no call with 'Hi, Aldron. Thinking about you.' I couldn't remember the last time I ever heard her say, 'I love you.' I soon just never expected it. Even when I initiated it: 'Kathy, I miss you... I love you,' she could only muster. *Me, too. Take care, Aldron... I'll be home Sunday evening.* The only 'I love you' in her heart was the for one driving her away from the townhouse once and for all.

This is Kathy's *Bastille Day!* Myriads of balloons are arising from the *Ille de la Cité*. She pulled from my embrace and took her suitcase handle and pulled it out the door and down the walkway to a silver Mercedes Benz. The day was overcast with a slight mist. Anita appeared and opened the trunk. She was wearing a gray pants suit. She was tall –about my height, slender, her hair pulled back and a ponytail bouncing around as she moved about the car. They hugged and kissed for an extended time -which was an unfamiliar sensation for me – Kathy kissing another woman. I imagined it had occurred often alongside other shared intimacies. I didn't feel jealous, just a bit weird. Soon they drove off and I could see her looking at me from the car. The picture of her blank face looking out the passenger side of that Mercedes Benz brought the first swell of tears to my eyes and I sat at the kitchen table and cried openly for the first time in a long time. That blank stare ripped me apart. Such feelings are so raw. It was like watching death! When I had exhausted every tear, I made a cup of comfort tea and was aware of an unexpected rush of relief – not 'well good riddance, Kathy' 'but 'Good for you Kathy Jones! You did it! You have courageously met the future!'

I never heard from her after that. A month later, I read that she was accepted into the Philadelphia Orchestra as second to the principal cellist. I felt a tingling of pride and a brief memory surfaced sitting in her apartment listening her 'dance' with the cello. The paper referred to her as 'Kathy Jones Kramer.' So that's Anita's last name.

Life in Transition

Of course, Dawn knew well about Kathy and our sufferable journey and impending divorce. Her empathy and comfort sustained me in the weeks ahead. I was spending most nights with Dawn. My townhouse was the empty shell of a dead marriage. I would stop by my study occasionally between visits with parishioners to pick up items I needed. But for me, it was simply a dark, empty cavern. I decided to put my townhouse on the market.

Life seems to have many 'deaths' and many 'resurrections' in the span of years. The Holy One desires to hunker down with us and help us toward new beginnings where old orders pass away and new ones become possibilities. They are often waiting on the horizon when we are ready to let them find us.

As Fall leaves were blanketing the ground around Dawn's townhouse, I was really feeling settled there. What was unsettling was imagining what my parish might think knowing their divorced rector was living with a single woman. 'Misconduct' by any account in this business is not tolerated, yet it happens often. F. U. Frank would surely find my divorce from Kathy Jones Seaver and living with another woman feeding his hungry grist mill. Dawn and I decided to keep it quiet at great risk. She was not a parishioner and neither of us were married. So, for the sake of ecclesiastical decorum, we were 'girlfriend-boyfriend.' Of course, Dawn was still resisting coming to All Saints. There were countless questions to be hashed out and I was a willing companion in all her fretting.

I knew already that she had grown weary of 'organized religion' early in her teens. Haven't most of us? Now she was into her academic career at Drexel. Many people arrive in their twenties and thirties with heavy doubt about organized religions and its claims. I've often wondered about the difference between 'organized religion' and '*dis*organized religion! My experiences have been the latter! Our 180 degrees with religion was no longer something I feared – if I had ever. Most of our sentiments about the failure of religious institutions were the mutual. She was curiously being drawn into deeper questions about my experience of 'Church.' I was curiously drawn toward her disdain and admission to a total lack of understanding of the Bible. Getting the perspectives, the good, bad and ugly, of an active rector became daily conversation. She wasn't afraid to throw darts at my biblical understanding -especially about the nature of God in the Old Testament and the violence in the name of the deity. *The rape of Dinah (Genesis 34), the genocide in Joshua (chapters 1-12); the dis-membered concubine (Judges 19); the beheading of John the Baptist (Mark 6); the killing of Ananias and Sapphira (Acts 5)* She had culled texts from various places the Bible on violence.

I had to really dig deep into my theological speculation, wondering whether God changes from one generation… or do we humans create God 'in our own image' rather than the other way around… that God is the highest good, the highest love, beyond human imagining. And it has always been that way from the beginning of time.

"You mean that *we create God*, Aldie?"

"I confess, sometimes it seems that way, Sweetheart. Humans have been fashioning images of deities since the beginning of civilization. There are evidences on cave walls all over the world of deities with both human and animal forms. It was the only perception of a 'divine being' they could imagine…one that looked like them. We've been doing that for eons upon eons."

"Wow, that blows my mind!"

"There's some measure of truth to it, Darling. Who can know the mind of God? Culture can pin a lot of human dysfunction and violence on God. We can't believe in a god we can't see. So, we try to imagine one. Monotheism grew out of a robust polytheism in early times. The earliest of religions had all kinds of gods for just about everything phenomenon they could experience and *not* control. Fire gods, rain gods, wind gods, mountain gods. The earliest of Hebrews had their own – El Shaddai, El-Roi, Elohim. Monotheism (the belief in one God) was a convenient way to reduce the overly populating 'gods' of the ancient world to one God.

It was a ponderable point with her. She seemed to acquiesce a bit. One morning over breakfast at Hanne's, she surprised me:

'Aldie, I... I've never... I've never prayed. I guess I couldn't comprehend some entity on the other side of anyone's prayerful words. I know this sounds a bit shocking, but... perhaps you could pray. I mean... would you do that?

I was shocked? Startled too! Maybe feeling a bit awkward.

"Are you sure, Sweetheart?" I probed.

"I know this sounds weird, but I need to hear you pray to a God I haven't believed in but am curious about."

I felt a little 'on display', but I muttered a prayer...*"God beyond reason, we live in awe of the bounty provided for us from your graciousness. Thank you for the many ways you stoop to love us in our real world....* something like that with no 'Amen.'

"Thank you, Aldie. I'm amazed that you can just... just spin out those words!"

Chapter Seven

A BROODING THANKSGIVING

Dead leaves are reddening in the woodland copse, And forest boughs a fading glory wear;
No breath of wind stirs in their hazy tops, Silence and peace are brooding everywhere.

'Thanksgiving' – Kate Seymour Maclean (1880)

With October over, the winds of November were now transforming the landscape into flying dead leaves and barren trees. and early morning mists. We looked out from Hanne's on a dreary Saturday, the fog so thick we could barely see across the street. There was a foreboding and yet enchanting feel about it.

Dawn used the extra coffee fills to share with me the most treasured family connection she had –a colorful and rather ornery but delightful gem: her Grandma Wilma Burgess. As I would come to learn: if there ever was a God-fearing but stalwart individualist and feminist beyond her age, Wilma Francine Burgess was it.

I delighted hearing about this feisty octogenarian, who lived almost six hours west in New Castle, PA. I was curious about the emotional impact she had on my Beautiful Dawn.

Dawn adored Wilma Burgess save for two nasty habits. The first was her 'religious zeal.' (Yes, that *could* be a nasty habit!) Wilma Burgess was a 'card-carrying-hardcore, close-to-militant-Roman Catholic.' She was sure all other denominations were on the slippery skids to hell! And Wilma adored her parish priest at Holy Family - Father José Marcantonio. As far as she was concerned, Father José was next to Jesus and the disciples in the heavenly pantheon. If Father José would've declared the moon made of green cheese, Grandma Wilma would have given a rousing *'Amen!* As feisty and fiercely independent as she was about so much of the rest of her life, she was galvanized in her religious beliefs and certain in the conviction that Roman Catholicism was the true religion...or at least the most directly connected to Jesus Christ. All others were failed attempts at Catholicism and suspiciously subversive –especially Lutherans and Episcopalians! She once told Dawn that she was almost certain Lutherans and Episcopalians would rot in hell with all other 'non-Catholics.' I chuckled at the prospects of my future plight.

Notably, Wilma Burgess was *not* Beautiful Dawn's 'biological grandmother'. Wilma was mother to Lydia, the biological mother of Grace O'Shea, who, as I've already indicated, was Dawn's stepsister. However, Grandma Wilma adored Dawn since she was the *only* one from the family who ever visited her – including her own daughter, Lydia and granddaughter, and Grace, whom no one has heard from since she and Ahmad Ramesh slipped off in oblivion to Tulsa, Oklahoma, after the baby was born. The word circulating was that Grace and Ahmad had better job prospects there and they wanted their asthmatic child, Christopher, to grow up in a healthy climate. But there has not been any communication for some time from the only biological grandchild of Wilma Burgess. That grieved Grandma Wilma, because she adored children.

So, Grandma Wilma, this devout Catholic had 'adopted' Dawn as her own granddaughter despite Dawn's Non-Catholic affiliation and the two have gotten along famously.

And on this recent visit, Wilma Burgess asked her beautiful granddaughter, cupping her face:

"Honey, you are attending Mass, aren't you? Please tell your dear old Grandma you're attending Mass! "

Dawn looked at her pleading grandmother in amazement. How could she lie? Shaking her head, she looked down. "No Grandma... I'm not..."

"Now Honey, don't let your dear old grandma die knowing that her favorite granddaughter is going to hell..."

"Grandma!" Dawn interrupted, "please, I'm not Catholic. I'm a busy girl. Frankford owns me right now. I'm so busy, I just don't have time for... church."

"But, your soul, Dawn! Who owns your soul? Why don't I ask Father José to come over..."?

"Grandma! I love you, but let's not talk about this now. Please?"

Silence filled the room as Wilma's eyes fell to her busy hands. She liked to massage her dry hands.

Dawn hugged her: "I'm sorry, Grandma. 'I just... I just love *you*. That's what's important right now."

It didn't keep dear Wilma from talking about religion. She may not have been sure about many things, but she knew for certain that hell was a real place and damnation was forever. She used to tell Dawn that she could almost smell the Sulphur of the deepest caverns of eternal damnation. It drew swells of fear deep in her own soul. She shared that she once confessed to Father José that she had lost her virginity in the back seat of the family's Desoto with her drunken prom date, Ollie. She did her penance for that and had gotten it on the good word from Father José that she was eternally forgiven for her indiscretion. In fact, moving beyond penance, if the truth were known Holy Family 'owned' Wilma Burgess. The word from the family grapevine was that her bungalow and one quarter acre on the corner of Oak and Forest Streets in New Castle had already been willed to Holy Family Church.

Apart from her obsession over her eternal salvation, Grandma Wilma was a delight. She would make sure there were plenty of foodie comforts for Beautiful Dawn when she arrived from the long trip from Philadelphia and the comfy little guest room was always made up fresh for her late Friday night arrival. Wilma Burgess was Southern bred, the daughter of a Mississippi tobacco farmer. She knew about hospitality. Her husband Vinnie Burgess used to say that Wilma Burgess could 'charm the chrome off of an Oldsmobile.' In her day, by some of the old photographs she shared with Beautiful Dawn, Wilma Burgess was a knock out -slender, leggy, and so girly in her flapper-style dress (1926-1928) and her short hair and bonnet. It wasn't until she moved to Pittsburgh in her early twenties that she discovered the 'flapper' woman's style. Dawn savored stories about that era of her early life, which was far more interesting than listening to her obsession over religion. That obsession hadn't emerged until she buried her husband Vinnie in 1976.

There was a *second* irritating indiscretion – probably far more dangerous than her militant Catholicism or even those wild 'flapper' days in the 20's - she was an incessant smoker and, as if brand were even a matter of discussion, she had smoked 'Camels' since she was about 13 years old. She'd talk on occasion about her need to 'give them up.' Even Father José had been fussy about it on occasion, especially the time she was sent to Jameson Memorial Hospital with an acute respiratory ailment.

'Wilma,' he pleaded, 'when are you going to let go of those smokes?'

Of course, Fr. José was one to talk. A few parishioners remember seeing him lighting up one cigarette after another at the Lawrence County Fair. Wearing his Hawaiian shirt and Panama hat, Fr. José certainly looked out of character, but it raised a few eyebrows to see him smoking like a chimneystack.

Holding Wilma's hand, Father admonished: "Don't you know that God may want you around for a few more years, Wilma? You may not think so, but as your priest... I'd like to have you around for a few more years." One might have thought Fr. José's words alone would have changed Wilma's obsession, but Dawn knew that Grandma Wilma was addicted to cigarettes and it was the one thing for which not even religion could make her to change her mind.

One of Wilma's hospitalizations scared Dawn half to death. She had made a special trip from Frankford Hospital in Philly one Tuesday in mid-September pleading with her instructors to let her take a day to visit Grandma. The pulmonologist had told Wilma it was time to take drastic measures - get the patch on or get into some kind of treatment program for quitting. Wilma promised, of course, but did little or nothing. She secretly told her neighbor, Mrs. Frieda Carlson, that she was hooked. So, you see, Wilma could do great penance for that indiscretion in the back of the old Desoto many years before but couldn't count her smoking as one of her 'deadly sins.' And she smoked in her house, which was always a struggle for non-smokers. Dawn would leave house smelling like a chimney and sometimes tried to lovingly convince her to smoke out on the porch, but it was for naught.

"Honey, I gotta have my smokes," she'd tell Dawn. "I'm 89 years old. If I've got a short time as your old grandmother, I'm at least going out puffing!"

This visit before Thanksgiving, Dawn saw her coughing and labored breathing growing worse. Yet at eighty-nine years of age, Wilma often admitted she was very lonely. Dawn's nursing regimen was a different kind of fussing. I call it *'love fussing'* - a kind of love that cares so deeply that fussing is just an added dimension of the love relationship. It was very clear that Grandma Wilma was loved. Beautiful Dawn had learned so much from this little bundle of energy from New Castle, PA.

Just a day shy of Thanksgiving, Wilma Burgess had turned for the worst after a terrible bout of pneumonia a week before Thanksgiving that year. The doctor had said the rattling in her chest was the worst he had ever heard. Hooked to breathing apparatus, Wilma lay in ICU bed #4 for almost three days before rallying to scribble on a tablet next to her bed: "Where in the hell am I?" Dawn had arrived just after Thanksgiving Break had begun, battling a freak November snowstorm to make it to Jameson Hospital in time to see her grandmother.

"Well, honey, I guess I'm paying for my sins," Wilma Burgess wrote illegibly.

It was the first time Dawn shed tears as she grasped her Grandma's hand. She knew enough through her nursing training that only a miracle could pull this stubborn old woman out of this. Dr. Wahlberg had told Dawn outside the ICU room that Wilma's chances were slim to none that she was essentially drowning in her own fluids.

"We can give her morphine and keep her sedated until she dies. I'm thinking it's only a day, if that. She'll be gone."

She looked down at the tiled floors. There was something in Dr. Wahlberg's manner that grated on Dawn. ('This is my grandmother,' she thought. I don't want her sedated and pumped with morphine. Dying is part of living. I want her to have what's left of her good mind - her caring heart- until death comes.') Dawn told Dr. Wahlberg to withhold the morphine unless she's in pain. And no sedation was requested. He could see she was serious.

Dr. Wahlberg acknowledged and shrugged his shoulders, marked his charts and walked away. Dawn was amazed how calculating and uncaring he seemed. Balding, with a goatee, he looked about 50 years of age. He didn't smile and there was no evidence of a compassionate bone in his body. How could he even begin to understand what this beautiful woman meant to her? Vices aside, Grandma Wilma was almost like the mother she didn't know and wondered if she ever would know. Suddenly an overwhelming feeling of anger blanketed Dawn. The more she sat there watching Grandma Wilma wheeze the angrier she became. She couldn't rest and felt tormented by Dr. Wahlberg's flippant manner. Finally, she stood up and marched to the nursing station and announced:

"I'm taking her home."

The charge nurse stood up looking bewildered. "What?"

"I'm taking Mrs. Burgess home."

That's unadvisable, Ms. O'Shea. Your grandmother's very sick," the nurse said, coming around from her station.

"I'm well aware of that. I'm signing her out and getting SouthernCare Hospice in New Castle to come in. If she's going to die, she's going to die in the comfort of her own home and as alert as she can possibly be! Please get me the paperwork for her release."

The charge nurse shrugged her shoulders nodded and began to pull out the release forms and, of course, then called Dr. Wahlberg back to the nurse's station. Dawn texted me to tell me *'I'm bringing Grandma Wilma home to her own house.'* She had just finished signing the release forms when Dr. Wahlberg appeared from around the corner.

"You're not doing this, Ms. O'Shea. Your grandmother is too weak to be moved."

"I *am* doing it, Dr. Wahlberg. She's going to die at home under hospice care," Dawn said defiantly, looking the doctor square in the face, almost nose to nose.

"She won't make it home, Ms. O'Shea. I won't have you move her," he said loudly as if he was going to pull authority over her. Dawn got even closer and shouted:

"Then hear this, Dr. Walhberg: You're fired! You can no longer have anything to do with my grandmother. Now if you'll excuse me, I need to call for transportation."

Dr. Wahlberg stepped back, shaking his head and sighed.

"Well, it appears the doctor-patient relationship is broken. As you wish, Ms. O'Shea."

He hurriedly signed something on his clipboard, gave it to the nurse, turned around and left.

Expectedly, no 'Good bye' … or 'Sorry for your loss.' Dawn knew too well that sometimes certain people in the medical profession are unfeeling, calculating and pompous asses. Dr. Wahlberg was among them. Whatever he knew about pulmonology (which was obviously a great deal, to his credit) was diminished by his heartless, unfeeling attitudes that looked at Wilma Burgess like a medical throwaway, heaped on some grim reaper's wagon for disposal. At least that was Dawn's impression.

Grandma Wilma was very weak, but she did make it home in an ambulance through a snow squall and was very appreciative when she awoke the next morning in her own bed. The November dawn was beautiful, the air crisp and bountiful leaves everywhere in Grandma Wilma's sparse, fenced-in backyard and on the little balcony outside her bedroom. She sat up in bed and took her Granddaughter's hand.

"Thank you, Dawn! Thank you! I thought I was going to spend my final days at Jameson before, hopefully (she looked up) I saw my Lord and Savior face to face." She looked around and snuggled in her quilted blanket and then proceeded into a coughing fit that brought up blood all over her blanket and gown. Dawn immediately cleaned her up and replaced her blanket. Then she proceeded with a sponge bath, which Jameson had planned to give her that morning.

"I can't think of a better place than home for you, Grandma. I've talked with SouthernCare Hospice and they'll be here in a few hours to help you," Dawn said as she stroked her Grandma's hair.

"Will they let me smoke?" She put her two fingers to her mouth. "Oh, by the way, where are my smokes?"

"Grandma, please," Dawn responded as tears welled up in her eyes.

Her grandmother drooped her head as if ashamed at what she had said. She realized she was addicted to them like an addict to cocaine.

"Please bring me coffee, dear. You know how I like it - black, no sugar."

"I've already made it. Here, Grandma."

Managing a smile, Wilma Burgess sipped it and lay back to sleep. In fact, she slept most of the rest of that morning until the Nurse and CNA at Hospice rang the doorbell and stepped inside her bedroom and began to gently go to work to make her comfortable. Dawn had gone to the grocery store to stock Wilma's fridge. She thanked the hospice CNA for taking care of her grandmother and then left with the nurse.

When she awoke, Wilma saw the Hospice CNA attending to her personal care. They exchanged 'hello's' and Rose McDermott introduced herself and what she was going to help her within the hour she had with her

"Honey," Wilma asked the Hospice CNA, "would you mind going over to that top drawer and pulling out some smokes for me?"

"Oh, Mrs. Burgess, Rose said with a smile, "as much as I'd like to, you're on oxygen, remember? We both don't want to blow up together on Oak and Forest, do we? She gestured with her hands opening and her eyes grimacing. "You know... Kaboom!

Wilma laughed with a rattle and then coughed.

"OK, I hear you. So, this is what we're going to do, honey: Disconnect this damn thing for a moment" (referring to her oxygen mask), "and go get my heavy coat and put me in that damn, creaky wheelchair and roll me out to the porch and let me have a cigarette!"

Rose McDermott was not a smoker and was an advocate for people quitting. She had seen too many cases in her young life of people panicking for a cigarette when a pack was empty. She was not a prude either and she believed that at the end of life, people should really do whatever they want. If they want to eat dessert first, they should be permitted. If they want to spend all day in their pajamas, they should. So, she bundled Wilma up, grabbed the pack of Camels on the top drawer and a cigarette lighter and rolled Wilma out on the covered front porch and, standing upwind from Grandma Wilma, let Wilma smoke away. Dawn had gone to town for groceries and reminded Rose: *'She's almost 90, Rose. Give her what she wants.'*

Rose was just one of those special CNA's. In her mid-forties, she was gentle and had a very sweet way with every terminal client she met. Her reputation followed her and families requesting hospice care would ask for Rose McDermott. Of course, SouthernCare Hospice didn't work that way with clients and their families - as do most Hospice communities. Dawn felt privileged to have Rose there. It was a real fit.

Wilma smoked two cigarettes and coughed up some blood, which Rose was prepared to clean up, after which she got Grandma Wilma back into her bedroom and back on her oxygen, provided clean, comfortable cotton sheets, a brief bathing, fluffed up pillow, helped her into her favorite pajamas and opened her favorite Yoplait. She only had two spoonsful and then lay back to sleep. Dawn had returned appreciating Rose's sustaining care. Hospice has been consistently one of the most beautiful care organizations for the dying the civilized world has ever known. SouthernCare Hospice was no exception.

As the day wore on, Wilma began to sleep more. Alloy Oxygen stopped by to replace her tank with a new supply. Even with added oxygen, Wilma Burgess wasn't going to get better. In fact, another hospice nurse, Cathy, Rose's R.N. team member, noticed that Wilma's oxygen level had even decreased dramatically within the day. Her breathing had become labored. Dawn had run errands and picked up a few groceries at the Giant Eagle. When she got home, Cathy immediately updated her on Wilma's low oxygen levels and how much she had been sleeping. She had become agitated around 4PM and Cathy had given her some Ativan to calm her down. Cathy also indicated that she would be sending Beth, another hospice nurse, later that evening to check in on Wilma. Beautiful Dawn decided she wouldn't sleep in the guest bedroom, but instead put a cozy chair next to her grandmother's bed. Curled up in the chair, she reached up for her grandmother's hand. She had been in nursing training long enough to observe that life was rapidly slipping away from this feisty and adorable woman.

She wondered why someone she loved so dearly could allow a burning object between her lips and inhaling it and taking in carcinogens enough to eventually kill them. It just seemed so senseless.

Now and again her grandmother would squeeze her hand as if she knew what Dawn was thinking. Dawn stood up and reached over and kissed her. *'I love you Grandma,'* she uttered tearfully. Then she wept with resignation for a long time, until Beth, the hospice nurse, came into the room and gave her a comforting hug.

The Dream

Sleep eventually overtook Dawn. Now a vivid dream had her walking hand in hand with her grandma through a breathlessly beautiful garden filled with every imaginable color and sweet aroma of fully blooming flowers. Smiles radiated from Grandma Wilma's face. It was an ecstatic moment that Dawn never wanted to end. Her grandma was smiling uncontrollably, lifting her hands in the air and almost dancing along as if every pain in her gnarled body had slipped away. Amazingly, smoke was leaving her mouth and nostrils as if being vacuumed out of her rejuvenating body, replaced with fresh air from all around her that was like wind blowing in every direction.

Soon Grandma Burgess looked at Dawn and smiled ecstatically and, embracing her and kissing her cheek released her hand as she was drawn toward a blinding light with an indigo backdrop. There was an energy that seemed to be pushing at her like a fierce wind at her back. Grandma Wilma's arms were outstretched as if she were waiting for a glad welcoming. Now Dawn heard voices that were speaking and laughing from within a hollow. The lights all around were dazzling, a luminous animation, a myriad of fireflies, only bigger, dancing all around her as she seemed to step into something, a kind of floating vessel. The music in the background was unlike anything that Dawn had ever heard, like thousands of voices echoing in perfect harmony the matchless joy of the moment *Allelu...Allelu!* There were people embracing her, spontaneous laughter, like a welcoming, a reunion. Her grandmother's clothes changed into a kind of multicolored pastel robe. Dawn tried to stretch her head to get a glimpse, but she just couldn't see.

Now all around the gathering were millions of colorful butterflies flapping their wings. Dawn kept wondering if she should pinch herself. Perhaps she had died and was being transported to this strange, new world. Now Dawn felt her heart racing. She felt everything was out of control, that she needed to wake up soon or she would explode. Still the dazzling light and view of her Grandmother floating away on some enchanting vessel was so breathtaking. The dream seemed more vivid than she could imagine in real life. She remembered just being filled with love for her dear Grandma and she longed to go with her on that mystical transport, but she couldn't go any further and she knew it. She was standing on the shore observing something so transcending that words would fail to describe it. Now, suddenly, Dawn was being nudged away from this mystical scene; tugged and shaken, she awoke with a start and realized that the hospice nurse was standing over her with a hand on her shoulder.

"Honey... Mrs. Burgess has passed."

"What... oh no! I... I fell asleep!"

She arose from her chair and saw her dear grandmother's ashen face, her mouth gaping. It was a picture of death she was all too familiar with. She ran her hand over her face and laid her head over her breast and became so aware of the lifelessness of this once animated woman. Dawn cried uncontrollably for the first time in many years - the way she once cried as a little girl when her beloved collie, 'Shakespeare,' was hit by a car along West Chester Pike. Nurse Beth held her for a few moments, her head resting on Dawn's back and her hand massaging her arms. After being depleted with crying, Dawn looked at the clock. It was 4:56 in the morning. And she realized it was Thursday and it was Thanksgiving Day. She could not help but feel robbed. *'There is no God!'* she grimaced. *'If God loves us, why does he take love away from us? What kind of God does that?!'* She laid her head on her grandma's belly and held her still hand. More tears flowed. Beth completed the hospice work and left with hugs. Dawn scrambled for the Yellow Pages to look for the number of DeCarbo's Funeral Services.

Shaking her head and cupping her face and looking at her lifeless grandma, she sighed and said aloud: "I dread this part!"

Back in Havertown, I had drawn the short straw among local clergy to preach at the Havertown Community Thanksgiving Service that Wednesday evening before Thanksgiving. Actually, it wasn't a 'short straw.' It was my turn in that annual rotation of local clergy preaching on Thanksgiving Eve. The worship was being held at Hope United Methodist Church over on Steel Road, and it usually gathered a hundred or more faithful souls. The tradition had been around for more than fifty years, but each year the gathered seemed to decline in numbers. This year was no exception. There were perhaps fifty souls -bless them! I preached on the theme *Gratitude, the Attitude: The Twice Blessed Leper.* The Gospel text from Luke 17:11-19 narrates one of those parables Jesus told to try to provoke deeper understanding about the larger picture of thankfulness. Ten lepers are healed by Jesus' very words, the story is told. He doesn't really touch them, just commands: 'Go show yourselves to the priests, the guys having final say on 'clean.' *I referred to it as a kind of migration emancipation'. The lepers are healed as they go on their way and rejoice as they watch their skin return smooth. One, realizing he was already clean, just needed to return and thank the Healer. The priest can wait, you know? That's an uncommon attitude that, when shared, makes the healing complete. I find that few people are offended by words of gratitude. A relationship is blessed when gratitude is offered.*

Returning home, I couldn't sleep. I kept thinking about Dawn in New Castle and that things were grave for her grandmother. Her texts to me relayed how death was certain in a short while. I called her late and asked her to keep me informed, shared an abundance of *'I love you"* and then settled in for the night at the townhouse.

On Thanksgiving Day at my parents' house after Thanksgiving dinner I was watching with only casual interest the game between the Redskins and the Cowboys. The familiar buzz on my phone caught my attention and it was Dawn. I walked into the hallway to listen.

Grandma Wilma died at 4:56 a.m. The funeral will tomorrow at the church. She wanted a late afternoon mass and a graveside committal immediately afterward, no visitation. She had it all worked out with DeCarbo's Funeral Home.

I immediately texted her back: '*I'm so sorry, Darling. I've been so worried about you. I love you. I'll be leaving in about a half hour.'*

She replied: '*Be safe, Aldie. I miss you so much.'*

Dawn had expected to call me sooner, but she knew that Hospice had to finish their work and she had gone back to bed emotionally exhausted waiting for DeCarbo's Funeral home to come to remove 'the body.' She turned on the little corner TV downstairs to make the Macy's Parade a distraction away from watching her grandmother being zipped up inside a body bag and carried out of the house. The DeCarbo staff was very comforting and kind to her. Since her Grandma's funeral plans included 'a very quick burial,' the staff and Dawn talked about the Commital service following the Mass around 3:30PM.

Wilma Burgess Remembrances

Now the house was hauntingly quiet. Dawn felt so alone. When the Macy's Thanksgiving Day Parade could no longer hold her interest, Beautiful Dawn wandered through the bungalow looking for 'signs of life.' She gazed at every wall hanging, especially one that was an early oil painting she had completed for her Grandma one Christmas. It depicted a snowy scene with pine trees. Her grandma had treasured it and made sure it had a fit frame around it to display in her living room. Remembering how much of a fuss Grandma Wilma had made over it brought more tears as Dawn's fingers slid over the texture of the oils and the initials, 'DBO, 'Dawn Briana O'Shea.' She was twelve years old when she painted that winter scene. She had been inspired to paint the scene because of their walk through a snow-blanketed New Castle one Sunday afternoon. She and her grandma had put on boots and shuffled through this wintry wonderland. Beautiful Dawn had thought it was one of the most beautiful winter days she had ever known. The memory in that painting became so vivid in those lonely moments at her Grandma's house it was as if she had returned and felt her Grandma's hand leading her through the snow and into the pine grove. Then it occurred to her: *'Now I know why we took that walk! She had taken me to a place where she and her beloved Vinnie had frequently walked to get away from the crowds.'* She described how he had first kissed her there. She pointed to an old tree stump, as flat as could be, and how Vinnie sat her down one November day and got on his hands and knees and presented her with a ring asking her to marry him. (There in the middle of the pine grove, Dawn had painted that old stump just as she remembered it.)

'Did you say 'Yes,' Grandma,' Dawn had queried?

"Of course, I did, Honey. I didn't really want him to know it, but I was head-over-heels in love with him. Well, in those days, a girl wasn't supposed to let on. But when he placed that diamond on my finger, I couldn't stop kissing him. I acted like a silly schoolgirl! Oh, what a fool I made of myself!"

Dawn's Grandfather Vincent was a handsome man - tall, square-cheeked and a with a sprouting handlebar mustache that made him look so distinguished. He wore ties and suspenders wherever he went, even when he was out pushing the hand mower or chopping wood. He was manly but gentle. The first full-time Editor of the *The Daily City News (later to become 'The New Castle News.')*, Vincent's old boss, Fred L. Rentzell, had hired him on as a 'Printer's Devil' at the age of thirteen for twenty cents a day doing odd jobs around the news building. When Rentzall's son, Julian, took over the news publishing for his father, Vinnie had already proved himself as an occasional writer. With more and more calls for those skills, he was eventually asked to become Editor in Chief. Dawn remembers him as a kind man, who liked to spoil her with candy, which he carried in his pocket all the time. Grandma Wilma complained that he was going to create decayed teeth in their granddaughter with all the candy he was giving her, but Grandfather Vinnie didn't listen one bit. He'd often cup Dawn's cheeks and call her his 'Little Dawn.' Sadly, Grandfather Vinnie died in summer of 1980. Dawn was 14 years old and was devastated to see her Grandfather Vinnie stretched out in a casket. She and her Grandma Wilma cried holding each other as they gazed at the lifeless shell of Vincent Matthias Burgess, his handlebar mustache neatly groomed and his receding hairline prominent and those prominent square cheeks. Dawn remembered how real he looked, wondering if he'd wink at her or whether his pocket might have candy tucked in it.

Dawn walked from room to room reminiscing, mindful of how Grandma Wilma had been a widow for so many years and had never taken an interest in another man. People around New Castle who knew Wilma - even Fr. José - would try to 'fix her up' with eligible bachelors. Even Dawn would ask her if she ever wanted to meet someone.

"Why would I want another man, Honey?" she responded, "I'd never find any one as charming and caring and kind as your grandfather. Even when he was rascally, I worshiped the ground the man walked on." Her grandfather was not without his faults. He liked cigars and would smoke them while watching Friday night wrestling on the Philco. Grandma Wilma could never plan anything on Friday night for fear he might miss his favorite Rocky Marciano knock someone out of the ring. Her grandfather also had a nasty gambling habit, frequenting 'The Club', a back room at the old Odd Fellows Lodge. Grandma Wilma said he would always wager too much. And in matters of church, he was a 'C & E' Christian (Christmas and Easter). As much as she tried, she could never get him out of bed on Sunday's to take her to Mass. She would threaten him with 'withholding sex', but it didn't matter. He'd tease her:

'You're going to use sex as a leverage for me are you, Wilma Burgess?' He'd tease and taunt her: 'Well by gum, I'll just go out and find two 20-year-old's... that's what I'll do!'

Looking in Grandma Wilma's cedar-lined closet, Dawn discovered a box with a note taped on in: 'For Dawn - Christmas.' She pulled the box out and gently opened it. There was a beautiful yellow Irish wool sweater that was obviously an unfinished gift - the skein of wool still connected to her last needlework on it. Crouching down beside the closet door, Beautiful Dawn cried openly and held onto it and pledged that she would finish this beautiful sweater as a tribute to her grandmother. She had always wanted an Irish Sweater and yellow was one of her favorite colors. What a treasure she had discovered deep in that old cedar closet in the hallway! Hanging there were many of her grandmother's dresses and sweaters, many of which she had never given away. Some still had the price tags on them! Fingering among familiar outfits, most of which she would wear to church or to weddings and funerals, Dawn discovered the black suit her Grandmother Wilma had worn to the funeral of her beloved Vinnie. Wilma never wore slacks. She believed that a woman wasn't a woman unless she wore a dress.

Memories of her grandmother loomed large after her death. Her ambling through the house produced tearfulness in every room. It was like a leisurely walk through the halls of a museum with captions of a life shared and loved. How could she be gone when she was larger than life? Dawn wondered. It was as if her Grandma Wilma was there as a docent, pointing out each glimpse of herself: Bric-a-brac from her many trips out west, old calendars with vintage automobiles, photographs of herself and Granddad Vinnie and much older photos of herself in her flapper days. She was a stunning beauty in her stylish dresses and make up and fiery eyes. There were ashtray collections from Spain and the Hawaiian Islands and Jamaica and San Juan.

Back in Havertown, I was ready to leave for New Castle. My Aunt June lives just outside Kennett Square, PA, near Route 1. It was our tradition to go there for Thanksgiving Dinner with my sister Allison and her family and my nieces and nephews. And of course, my father and mother would join us, although my Dad didn't much like Aunt June and Aunt Wisteria. He would shake his head:

"They're too damn gossipy, the both of them! Hell, you can't get a word in edgewise at the table...."

Not that Dad was an avid conversationalist at Thanksgiving Dinner. It was usually "Pass the potatoes... gravy... filling will ya?" The women would talk to each other and the men just asked for food. Now and then my Dad might look at my Uncle Howard and say, "How 'bout them Flyers, Howie? What ya think? " Or..."Hell, Harry, what's wrong with the Eagles this year." After dinner, the men folk would 'repair' to the den to watch the game while the women folk would clean up the kitchen and sit down for some serious girl talk. It is true that my Aunt Wisteria was the poster child of 'girl talk.' She knew just about anything that was happening in the family and around Kennett Square (where she has lived as a divorcee for almost 24 years). The joke in the family was that Aunt Wisteria was too busy gossiping to cultivate a relationship with an interested suitor. She was not unattractive: a slender and shapely build. She dressed well with lots of bling and 'girly' qualities - but her gossiping was a bit over the top. The kinfolk would always wonder how much was truth and how much was fiction when Wisteria would gab.

Now that Dawn's phone call had arrived, I told my parents I was going to New Castle. (The family always forgot I meant New Castle, Pennsylvania, on the other side of the state, not New Castle, Delaware, down the road). They knew about 'Dawn' - the love interest of my life.

"Be careful, Aldie!" Mom stopped me as I was preparing to head to my car. "The Weather Channel is predicting light snow later this evening. "

She poured me a cup of coffee in a thermos and stuck a piece of her delicious pumpkin pie in a bag and sent me on my way.

My Dad was too engrossed with the other guys in the game. He didn't even hear me say, "Heading to New Castle, Dad", although I repeated it. I was soon on the turnpike for the five-plus hours' drive across Pennsylvania. I missed my Beautiful Dawn and couldn't wait to hold her in comfort.

Turning onto I-476 and heading toward the turnpike, I recalled how she had been so comforting to me when my grandfather died. I needed to be with her and comfort her in her loss. After a long siege with lung cancer, my Grandfather had finally succumbed into a coma one stormy July evening. The passing storm had shut the power down and an emergency generator had been switched on to help with his oxygen flow but soon after the lights came on, I felt my Grandfather's amazing grip on my hand as he gasped one final gasp, his mouth wide open and his eyes looking straight to the heavens. Then he settled into the mystery sleep of death, that sense of nothingness and yet peacefulness and whatever world lay beyond shell of his breathless body.

Dawn had arrived only minutes after my Grandfather succumbed. The storm had delayed her arrival since the traffic lights and street lights had been shut down by a lightning strike on the main Penn Power stations in Havertown. When she arrived and saw Grandfather had expired, she cried and held me tightly, which allowed my tears to flow and my mother's too. I remember Dawn's words:

"Oh, Aldie, Sweetheart, I know your grandfather loved you."

And I loved him, even during the stormy years when he defied my going into the Episcopalian Church as a priest. The menfolk in my family sure had a problem with my becoming an Episcopal priest! I wondered whether my grandfather might thunder and lightning from beyond because I was still an Episcopal priest.

Interestingly, the night of his death, electrical power went out when he took his last breath. PP&L would be summoned to the area. John Holden Seaver "Jack" as he had been known then, had worked for Penn Power (Pennsylvania Power and Light Co. or PP&L - back before it was called that. PP&L actually grew out of a number of electric utilities from the 1880's like the Edison Electric Illuminating Co. of Sunbury, PA, which Thomas Edison actually used to perfect central-station incandescent light in small cities and towns across Pennsylvania. By 1900 there were 64 of these companies throughout the state. And then, like most small companies, by the early 1800's they merged to become PP&L, which through the 1900's acquired additional companies. Jack kind of grew up with the evolving companies that became this mega electrical utility in Pennsylvania.

He was a trouble-shooter for times just like that night he died when electrical power went out and he'd have to go out into the community with 'the team' and try to restore power. Following his stint with PP&L, he got a job with the Pennsylvania Utility Commission for 38 years before his heart attack in 1993. After his recovery, the Commission had asked him to be an inspector for local transformers. He called it his 'stinking desk job.'

Knowing I was heading to the seminary, he told me one evening after dinner: "The church is a losing cause, Aldie. Why do you want to waste your time with it? It's all politics and raising money and shit like that! Come work at Penn Power. Your old grandfather can get you a job working with your hands."

It was hopeless trying to explain to him what a 'calling to ministry' was. I had graduated from Temple with a degree in philosophy and a minor in literature, both of which my Grandfather and my Dad thought was a pure waste of my time.

"Why not business or accounting or…. crap Aldie, you could become a lawyer or engineer! What the hell does a pantywaist degree in philosophy get you?"

It was tough to hear that at twenty-one years of age. Fortunately, neither of my parents or my grandparents had paid for my studies at Temple. I had managed a scholarship designed for Pennsylvania residents and had worked about 20 hours a week at Temple's Samuel L. Paley Library. Temple has several libraries. I was in charge of microfilming documents (this was in the days before data processing!) I managed the historic documents donated by alumni. In addition, Temple needed someone to help with Undergraduate

Admissions and hired me on for 10 additional hours filing student applications and setting up interview schedules. Between the two jobs and a scholarship, I earned enough to pay for tuition and books (used ones), while commuting from my parents' house in Newtown Square and maintaining my 1980 Honda Civic with over 100,000 miles on it. I was also trying to pay off my education loan from the Pennsylvania Higher Education Assistance Agency, to whom I nearly owed my soul. But with a loan at 2% interest and no hurry to pay it back, I couldn't complain.

So, now I was going to New Castle to comfort my Beautiful Dawn in her time of grief. It felt so right. A time of grief draws upon the fire of mutual love and passion. We would feel deeply for one another in the helplessness of death.

The snow began falling outside Everett, PA, where I stopped to fill up the Honda and relieve myself from Mom's strong coffee. It was a menacing wet snow. I opened the bag on the passenger side seat and savored Mom's slice of pumpkin pie before pulling back onto the turnpike.

The snow stayed mostly wet through the balance of turnpike travel. The temperature back at the Food Mart indicated 35 degrees. It was about 10:11 p.m. when I turned into the driveway of Wilma Burgess's brownstone bungalow at Oak and Forest for the first time. The porch light was on and Dawn was sitting on the first step. I could see her smile and wave from my headlights, but I could also see her swollen eyes. We embraced within 30 seconds - my engine still running and my lights on

"Aldie, I love you..."

"Darling, I'm so sorry. I love you so much."

We held each other tightly for the longest time. The windshield wipers were still on and the lights cast a shadow of us against her Grandmother Wilma's front porch. I kissed her forehead and put her head close to my neck as I massaged her back. She wasn't wearing a coat. I turned off the Honda and walked her inside.

"I'm OK," she assured me,

"I've had some good cries and I feel a strange peace... like she's walking through a beautiful garden."

That's when she told me in vivid detail the dream she had had by Wilma's bedside. I stroked her hair:

"What a beautiful dream, Darling. There's enough mystery about life to wonder at times where heaven and earth, time and eternity, cross through each other's paths." I suggested that we go inside and warm up. I had stopped at the McDonald's near State Street after I got off I-676 outside of New Castle and picked up two Hot Chocolates and some chocolate cookies (comfort food). I turned off the Honda and brought my overnight bag inside. Dawn helped bring in the refreshments. I held her close as we sat on her Grandmother's overstuffed couch. She shared so many 'Grandma' stories, including remembrances of her Grandfather Vinnie. She lamented how the cigarettes had taken over her life and health.

Tearfully, she continued, looking around the kitchen. "But, as angry as I was about the cigarettes, I could never have stopped loving that dear woman. She will always be a treasure in my memory."

She recalled how her stepmother, Lydia, and Grandma Wilma (like my Grandfather and Dad) were never close. Part of it was the way Lydia had fallen out with her father, Vinnie, who had had a love interest at thirty-three years of age. Beautiful Dawn had forgotten this story until Grandma Wilma had brought it up years after his death. A certain secretary at NEW CASTLE NEWS had carried a crush for Vinnie for a number of years and, especially during Wilma's pregnancy. Lydia's sister, Veronica (now deceased) discovered her father's indiscretion on some notes she found in his pocket while washing his clothing. By the time she had found them, however, the tryst was over. Unfortunately, the damage was done, Veronica never talked to him again. Even stranger, her mother knew about the indiscretion and had forgiven him when she found out.

The conversation Beautiful Dawn remembers her grandmother having with Lydia went like this:

Wilma: "I wasn't available to your father for sex, Lydia. I was so miserable with my pregnancy with Veronica, I wouldn't let him touch me. "

Lydia: "That's no excuse, Mother!"

Wilma: "But we worked through it... you have to understand. I forgave him, and we moved on."

Lydia: "How could you forgive him, mother? There are other ways for men to deal with their urges than having trysts. It's just unacceptable!"

Of course, the same thing happened to Lydia and Dawn's father, Jack. It was one of the reasons Lydia said she would never marry again. Their relationship had been cordial, but the trust was gone. Sadly, Lydia turned against her mother for tolerating something she herself could not tolerate – her own husband's infidelity. Dawn had marveled how Grandma Wilma could forgive and forget her husband's indiscretion and yet her own daughters could not.

It was almost two o'clock in the morning when we finally fell asleep on the guest bed. We had not shared intimacy in almost a week, but neither of us felt compelled to make love. We just held each other until the alarm awakened us next morning.

The service was held Friday afternoon at 2 p.m. at Mary, Mother of Hope Church Catholic Church, downtown, New Castle. Father José's Mass for the Dead was, to be honest, 'deadly.' As an Episcopalian priest I knew 'deadly' services. I probably officiated a few! I had often wondered why I didn't attempt to write a new kind of remembrance service that animated life rather than focused just on death. Father's sermon was good enough. He didn't over-preach death and resurrection. He mentioned Wilma as a tender human being who loved the Lord and cared for her family, especially her granddaughter, Dawn. Looking directly at Dawn, Father José Marciano smiled and commented.

"I heard more Dawn stories each time I visited. She was proud of you, Dawn, in your pursuit of a nursing career and loved the way you fussed over her."

This brought a tearful smile to Dawn.

Lydia had come to the service wearing dark glasses (perhaps to disguise the remorse she felt at not having a relationship with her mother.) In fact, Lydia left as soon as the service was over, only taking a moment to speak to Dawn. It was the first time I had met Lydia. I observed a ton of issues navigating within her persona.

"She was quite a woman," Lydia managed, "but I guess so many years passed between us, a lot of turbulent waters under the bridge."

Dawn hugged her, but Lydia's response was somewhat lifeless. Pulling away, she smiled briefly:

"Thanks for your kindness to my Mom, Honey." Then somewhat apologetically, she muttered: "I need to go before my mascara gets messed up."

She was a bit of an enigma. She mentioned nothing about driving all the way from the West Chester area to New Castle. Was she by herself? She mentioned faintly something about getting ahead of traffic.

The drive up to Castle View Memorial Cemetery took more time than we anticipated. The afternoon was blurring into dusk by the time we reached cemetery. Dawn held onto my arm. I reached over and kissed her forehead and placed my A-lettered handkerchief in her soft hand. She leaned her head on my shoulder at the graveside Committal Service. Fr. Marcantonio read the familiar words, *Rest eternal grant her, oh Lord, and let light perpetual shine upon her.* Then, leading the *'Our Father,'* he ended the Committal with the benediction. Grandma Wilma was laid to rest and Beautiful Dawn plucked a flower from her grandmother's floral bouquet on the casket. We walked leisurely through the cemetery, her hand in my arm. There was a raw chill in the late November air. All around us were sobering signs of life's great finality. There wasn't anything bad about that. Graves are essentially places of memory and Beautiful Dawn and I would return here again, especially around Thanksgiving. Still, we both acknowledged that being alive - being aware of our own feelings, life's animation and spirit... those were the things we needed to return to. Stopping at a large stone statue of a grieving angel, we noted the engraving of Luke's Gospel, Chapter 24, verse 5b:

'Why do you seek the living among the dead? He is not here but has risen.'

"That's it, Sweetheart!" I remarked pointing to the marker. "All of this is about remembering, but it is not the place for the living. Let's remember your dear Grandma Wilma in her vitality! Sweetheart.... Are you OK?"

She nodded vigorously. "I'm going to be OK," she promised.

We stopped downtown for an evening meal and lots of chatter about Wilma. She was as big as life even if she was buried. Dawn's questions, her 'why's' lingered. There was anger at Wilma's wasted life with cigarettes as well as adorations of her loving personality.

"She died without assurance that I was a Jesus follower, Aldie. Did I fail her?" Her question drew tears once again.

I responded as I cupped her face and wiped tears gently with the thumbs. "No, Sweetheart, you didn't fail her. She was speaking from her own faith tradition. She was from that generation that can speak zealously of the need for others to become religiously the way they practice. Just let me say, the God I experience, doesn't coerce people into faith. Your Grandma Wilma wasn't being unkind."

We chatted for almost an hour and a half there at Chuck Tanner's Restaurant. Dawn was looking emotionally exhausted from these several days. We shared a light dessert and headed back to her Grandma's bungalow. It was after 8:30pm. There were a few dishes to wash and put away, some items Dawn wanted to show me from her grandmother's closets. By 9:30pm, we were depleted.

We quickly undressed and crawled under the heavy covers of her grandma's guest bed – a comfy place for Dawn since her youth. I snuggled behind her. The streetlight at Oak and Forest brought subdued lighting into the small window behind the old creaking guest bed. The old furnace in Grandma Wilma's house had rattled on for the first time that evening. It had grown cold and our warm bodies were entwined for the night securely beneath an old quilted blanket Grandma Wilma had made. It was surreal, as if she had mysteriously nestled down with us beneath the beautiful fabric made with her own hands. The blanket had a 'Grandma Wilma's House' presence and scent – an aroma of her Victorian living room, a lingering hint of her kitchen herbs, a faint scent of her bathroom soap, all mingled from years of Grandma Wilma's presence. Even the faintly lingering smoke odor from far too many cigarettes left a distinctive scent. She was gone, but she was very much alive within that old brownstone bungalow. Comforters are just that, beautifully designed fabrics of 'comfort' in a cold and dark world. Life needs more of them.

Thanks to that feisty and loving presence of Wilma Burgess, now nestled in her own secure 'somewhere' beyond the abyss of this cold November night, rattling furnaces and her wonderfully lingering scent, Beautiful Dawn and I slept peacefully and deeply into the early morning.

Chapter Eight

A DECEMBER TO REMEMBER

Isaiah 9:6-7
Of the greatness of his government and peace there will be no
end. He will reign on David's throne and over his kingdom, establishing
and upholding it with justice and righteousness from that time on and
forever. The zeal of the Lord Almighty will accomplish this.
New International Version (NIV) Holum Bible Publishers
(1984)

We awakened that Saturday morning to the spirit of Eros - a yearning that could no longer be withheld. Our intimacy was wanton. The wind was howling as an early morning rainstorm pelted the windows. I was engorged within my beautiful Dawn. Her moisture intensified as did her moans. Our rhythm became rapid and with it the bed was creaking wildly, almost willing itself to plummet to the kitchen floor below. Dawn held onto me, kissing my neck with repetitive Oh, Aldie incantations. Our rhythmic movements became so intense as if we were racing toward a finish line. She was begging me. "Please Aldie, just fuck me!" (This was a word I had never heard her utter!) It kicked my libido into high gear! Suddenly her orgasm jolted her into undulations against me so powerful, I thought I would fall out of the bed. Her tremors were reverberating like a wild animal. And that is when I gave off a Tarzanesque sound that I had never never heard myself peal. If the neighbors had heard this, they might have wondered whether a murder had been committed at the old brownstone bungalow of Wilma Burgess. Dawn and I lay there in breathless amazement at our erotic catharsis at this conclusion of very emotionally intense days. She apologized for the 'f-bomb'. I laughed and kissed her cheek.

"To be honest, Sweetheart, it kind of kicked my libido into high gear."

"Gosh, Aldie, I've just never felt that intense before! I felt like I was outside myself."

Sex is sometimes more momentous because of life's stresses. The whole week had been so tense for her.

After a leisurely breakfast and more reflections on Grandma Wilma's life, I would make my way back to Havertown. Our 'good byes' seemed to linger for an hour or so. I really didn't want to leave Dawn, but I had to. The approaching First Sunday in Advent back at All Saints was already breathing down my neck. I gave an extended kiss and got into the Honda and left Oak and Forest and that memorable brownstone bungalow.

As I travelled the Pennsylvania Turnpike eastward from New Castle, All Saints parish was unavoidably on my mind. I hoped that the McFarland's completed their annual faithful 'hanging of the greens' and preparations for Advent. They and a few other folks were the Advent team at All Saints. Some members would gather to share hot chocolate and cookies and spend Saturday before Advent transforming the Nave of All Saints into splendid blue and green and lavender decorum. The long artistic banners for the four Sundays in Advent would transform the Nave into wonderful images of expectation – waiting and watching, the often-forgotten themes before the Christmas rush. The Advent Wreath at All Saints was especially beautiful, a tall wooden stand with four enormous candles – three blue and one pink and a generous draping of greens around them. Carved into the wooden stand were images of a fiery John the Baptist and additionally a young woman overshadowed by an angel Gabriel with outstretched hands and finally a couple in traverse – the Holy Family. And finally carved were four words that, for me, capture the essence of Advent: *Wait, Watch, Wander and Wonder.* I had commissioned Ian McAllister, an art instructor and sculptor at the Philadelphia Institute of Art, for this piece of artwork. I had officiated his wedding to one of our parishioners at All Saints recently. Ian and I had become fast friends when he had expressed interest in my doodles as a liturgical artist from my early days as an Episcopal priest. I had refused a fee for officiating his wedding, so he promised me a piece of sculpture at some future date. The idea for the Advent Wreath had come up and I commissioned him with a few designs and the beautiful woodcarving that holds the Advent wreath that had been complete a year ago. Ian considered it to be one of his best works. We dedicated it on the First Sunday in Advent with most of Ian's students present to fuss over it. I treasured the memory of it as well as our friendship. I teased him that I would owe him a thousand times more than my regular wedding fee for this beautiful work of art.

So I was on my return on the turnpike. The late November rainstorm was followed by a temperature moderation. The snow that followed Thanksgiving weekend in New Castle had melted. The Turnpike was crowded with people either returning home or on their way to Christmas shopping. It was the day after 'Black Friday.'

The Somerset Plaza was crowded, too, with holiday weekend cars refueling. Once I was able to fill up, I found some coffee and a donut for the next stretch through tunnels and some scenic parts of the Pennsylvania landscape. I resumed the mental 'tweaking' of my sermon with some fresh stories, including some shared by Dawn about her Grandmother Wilma. The remaining four and a half hours went by speedily until arriving at Havertown late afternoon. The sun was brilliant, the temperatures now turning crisp. The Philadelphia area had been spared the snow that had fallen in western Pennsylvania, but the traffic was outrageous along the Blue Route (I-476). I arrived home to numerous calls, Emails and one frantic mother, whose teenage son had run away from home and was busted on drugs found in his vehicle. I was glad I had prepared my sermon on the way home because I was no sooner home and then once again out the door to Delaware County Prison in Glen Mills.

Sunday Services at All Saints were festive even with the subdued theme of Advent. The colors within the Nave, those Chrismons handcrafted ornaments with Advent and Christmas symbols for the nave tree, the brilliant banners and Ian McAllister's beautifully carved Advent wreath holder - all lifting up the theme of these coming four weeks.

I was restless most of the day following the liturgies, anxious about my Beautiful Dawn's return. The townhouse needed some cleaning, so I took broom and dust pan to the kitchen, vacuumed the carpeting and cleaned the bathrooms. It was a necessary distraction. There was soup in the fridge I warmed up with some French bread. I found an NFL game on TV and eventually dozed off on the couch. I was awakened relieved to hear a car drive up. It was 8:56 p.m. I rushed out to help Dawn carry in a quantity of bags and her suitcase. She showed me two speeding tickets from her drive home – which made her grumpy. I tempered my initial enthusiasm for her arrival. I had prepared some muffins and tea, but she wasn't hungry and preferred to relax on the sofa just to quiet her brooding spirit. It was truly a brooding Thanksgiving. Not-the-least, she would need to go to bed soon because training at Frankford would resume in earnest early the next morning. I held her close until she fell asleep. At 11 p.m., I led her upstairs and we crawled under the covers for the night.

"Sorry I feel just emotionally crappy, Aldie. The trip home was a dark cloud hanging over me."

I massaged her back, "It's okay, Darling. You've had a draining week – hardly a Thanksgiving celebration."

"That feels so good though, Aldie…"

She savored gentle cuddles, a back rub and quickly fell asleep.

Death drains the human spirit, of course, and robs our physical energy, too. It intrudes upon our emotional landscape and tears away at the few securities we hold onto in this world. Dawn had every right to feel the aftermath of sorrow. There was an empty space in her life because Grandma Wilma was more than just that feisty lady out in New Castle who was adored. Wilma had filled that empty space in Dawn's family life… *that mother she didn't know - that mother she longed for.* Sleep is a wonderful salve for the body and spirit, for broken hearts and life's draining moments.

The Following Saturday

According to the Haverford-Havertown's newspaper *The Patch,* there's nothing like the Christmas trees at 'Tree Guys' at the Manoa Shopping Center, where each year they offer 300-400 Christmas trees of all shapes, sizes and price ranges. Owner Doug Rosado can usually be found there near the True Value hardware and can offer a quality tree from $20 -$50 for Fraser Fir, Douglas Fir or Balsam Fir. It was a Saturday late morning on December 6th that Dawn and I went in search of one of 'Tree Guys' offerings. We had earlier enjoyed a savory breakfast at Hanne's Breakfast Nook and Luncheon on West Darby Road. There are no menus at Hanne's. You just tell them what you want, and their chefs will meet your breakfast needs.

Following breakfast, we went to 'Tree Guys,' where Doug was busy showing a Balsam Fir at their location near the True Value Hardware store. It was busy, and it was clear to us that many trees had been picked through since Tree Guys' opened for business around Thanksgiving. There was already snow on the ground this December 6th. Each year it seemed that some kind of snowy weather or Nor'easter came through the Philadelphia area on or around December 5-7. And this year was no exception. About two or three inches had fallen the night before in the Havertown area and snow plows had been out in earnest for the growing Christmas shoppers who would be using places like Manoa Shopping Center.

"Hey folks!", Doug greeted us with a Norwegian Spruce upright in his hands. Sweeping his hand, he told us, "they're moving fast - especially the Douglas Firs."

"Any Douglas Firs left?" I asked, looking around.

He looked at the assortment quickly. "Believe it or not, less than ten remaining. Let me see here... follow me."

We went deep among the stacks of trees and found the few Douglas's left. Dawn saw one that was a bit larger than she had wanted for her living room. Eleven feet! Doug pulled it out. It seemed pretty full. "We can size it down for you, Ma'am. No extra charge. This one goes for $50.00, but I'll sell it to you for $35.00."

"Thank for you kindness, Mr. Rosado," Dawn said in that sweet voice that won my heart a long time ago. She could make reading the telephone directory sensuous and sweet. When she drives through McDonald's to purchase a sandwich, she'd say: 'You have a pretty smile.' I always want to reach over and kiss her hand or lips.

"No problem," Doug smiled. "And you can call me Doug. About how tall does this tree need to be?"

Dawn's ceilings were about 9 feet tall, slightly taller than the average townhouse ceiling. So, she suggested an 8' tree. Doug barked an order at Susheel, a student from Haverford College – a guy with a chainsaw in his hand looking eager to buzz away. He had the look of 'Oh boy, more noise!' Susheel did some measuring of the Douglas Fir and then cranked up the Craftsman. I paid Doug and waited for Susheel to trim it down. But there was a problem. Like an over-zealous barber, he trimmed the tree much less than half its size'.

"Uh, Susheel, I think you might have trimmed it too..."

He raised his eyes," Didn't Mr. Doug say you wanted a small tree?"

"No, actually he said..."

I looked at Beautiful Dawn, who was smiling and nodding... "you know what Susheel, why don't we just stop where you are. It's perfect."

"So sorry, Mister Seaver."

"Not a problem. We will make it work, Thanks, Susheel!" I gave our happy tree cutter a generous tip and off we went with our 'whatever' length Christmas tree. We were looking forward to our first Christmas decorating at Dawn's house.

"It's beautiful, Aldie. Really. I'm glad you didn't..."

"I know, Sweetheart. I couldn't criticize his chainsaw massacre. Well, it wasn't a massacre. I guess we were both wanting something that reached the ceiling. We'll just have something to remember about our first Christmas – a tiny tree!"

Susheel's creative version of a formerly 8-foot Douglas Fir actually turned out just fitting in Beautiful Dawn's living room, in the corner next to her favorite rocking chair. We found the perfect table for it and Dawn draped it with a beautiful Christmassy skirt. While we were decorating it, I realized that I had never decorated a Christmas tree. That was always my mother's job, because she was so meticulous about decorating the tree that neither my Dad nor I could ever measure up to her expectations. So, we both just wandered off when it was time for Mom to 'do the tree.'

Maybe I was maturing a bit, but I found just taking Dawn's direction about how our little tree should be decorated was fun enough. She too was meticulous... but in a fun way. I liked that.

Adventing

My favorite season of the church calendar is probably the least known and often the least favored season- *Advent*. The Advent tradition began most likely in France during the fourth century C.E. (Common Era) as a penitential and devotional time to get ready for the 'Christ Mass' or Christmas. It's somewhat as Lent became in church history - a crash course on austerity and penitence in preparation for baptismal candidates for Easter. Historically the Church believed that sacred celebrations like Jesus' nativity, death and resurrection were so necessary that people got reined in by 'cleaning up' their personal lives and practice spiritual discipline in advance. I don't know that people do that much anymore. I may be wrong.

This curious season of four weeks and traditions like Advent wreaths, caroling, candles, finding Christmas trees, buying gifts, drinking eggnog, eating mince meat pies, drinking hot cocoa… gives me pause: *What would it mean if the Creator God really wanted to live in our lives? What would it mean if the Holy One wanted a relationship with us?* There is so much wonder about a deity who incarnates – who would rather meet us by taking on our form than staying in heaven. In Greek mythology, the gods are capricious with humans, poking fun at them and their earthly limitations. It seems scandalous that God would desire to incarnate (become human flesh) so that we might know 'God*ness*' over against our often '*un*Godly' existence. The Creator is not 'playing with us' so much as reaching adoringly toward us the way a sculptor adores the sculpted image she or he shapes it or the way a new Mom embraces her infant. God's reach is so ponderous, of course, and Advent can barely scratch the surface of its breadth and depth. I mentioned in my sermon:

I wonder… why would the Holy One seek to become less than divinity, less than the Holy One?' That's a head-scratcher for me. Maybe that's why the birth motif in the Christmas message is so strong: it seems that in 'weakness' -i.e. by human measure - God is actually stronger than we could imagine. God becomes less God, so that we can become more God-like. Or, maybe the strength already within us needs to be awakened by a neighboring God so we can be more alive with divine presence. Or, maybe one step further: God in Jesus form gives us a greater glimpse of

God in divine form. It's the mystery. God's reach for us in the nativity makes for a holy connection.

Some of the folks at All Saints get really angry with me because I don't rush into singing Christmas carols during Advent. It's one of my pet peeves, because culture is already piping in Christmas carols abundantly, especially where we are invited to spend our money I would appeal: 'Help me discover with you the rich texts of these four weeks before the baby is born." But, of course, for the sake of unity, I sneak a few Christmas carols each Sunday.

Dawn was still not signing on the dotted line with Church. We spent quite a while wandering through the mystery of incarnation. Still, she was very curious about my work and this peculiarly inward journey I was on.

"Aldie, honestly, your parishioners are nice folks, but I just can't buy what you call the 'liturgy' and people paying lip service to something someone else has written. So, no offense, Darling, but I'm just going to sleep in on Sunday's. Don't get me wrong, I honor what you are doing... I'm still not sure I believe in God, although maybe in the back of my mind I want to."

"Well, Sweetheart, why don't you just give it a try without making a commitment? People enjoy meeting you."

I knew immediately I shouldn't have ventured that!

"Aldie, please... I'm not ready, I'm just not sure about the whole church thing and I'd rather be left alone!" She walked out of the room wiping her hands on her dress from dishwashing. I heard her close the bathroom door. I hated myself for bringing any expectations.

Of course, we had a 'kiss and make up' return and an apology time. I held her close and assured her that I would honor her need for distance. Our love superseded any differences we had about religion or belief or faith. And that was that. I knew even with all our differences on the subject of religion, church, theology, Bible...I was so in love with Dawn. And more and more, it seemed mutual. We spent untold hours inviting her doubts and questions. Often our conversations would end up with our clothes coming off and unbridled intimacy. Perhaps our honest talk about religion needed that kind of exhaust. I gave her all the room she needed for doubts and even anger about her 'untraveled faith.'

As we faced the holiday, we made the first mutual decision in our togetherness journey, our *ubuntu*, and that was not to give each other gifts, but to give to some great need in the area – and the decision was to donate to the 'PEC' -'Peoples Emergency Shelter' of West Philly.

The Unexpected Gift

I can be impulsive, I know. But there would be one special surprise 'gift' for my Beautiful Dawn this year. I drove over to Faden Jewelers on Eagle Road to find an elegant diamond for her. I had saved up money from weddings and baptisms and funerals to put some serious money toward a 'rock' – *a girl's best friend* I am told. She had all but finished her training at Frankford Hospital's School of Nursing. We had talked frequently about being married, but we never settled on a date or even mentioned a ring. I'm kind of a hopeless romantic, so I 'did the deed' going to Faden's one Thursday afternoon on her last day of nursing raining before Christmas. I chose an emerald cut ring with rectangular stone and rounded corners. I believed it would look absolutely beautiful on her hand. The next plan would be to plot a time to present her with this exquisite ring the likes of which I had never laid eyes on. One place that came to mind was the historic Dilworthtown Inn in West Chester, PA. Built in 1754, the Inn was nearly destroyed in the Battle of Brandywine twenty-two years after it was opened. Located on Old Wilmington Pike, the Inn probably exceeds most restaurants in all of Philadelphia for its romantic ambience, candlelit dining, warm hospitality and consistent quality of food. I imagined springing for two glasses of its rare wines like the 1994 Chappelet Cabernet. The menu seemed so promising with candlelight too - like sharing a cup of Dilworthtown Mushroom soup and smoked Trout salad, a serving of Pistachio Crusted Sea Scallops and a starch and vegetable to be determined For dessert I would plan a savory chocolate parfait served with a small white box in which the delicate diamond would be waiting, and with its opening my proposal to be somewhat like this: taking the box in my hand and taking her hand, I would first kiss it and then say: *My darling, Beautiful Dawn, you have so won my heart's adoration and devotion. I would be honored and most overjoyed beyond words if you were to accept my proposal to be your partner in life.* (Of course, I would have memorized this.) Then I would open the box and show her the Emerald stone and place it upon her left hand.

A wet snow had passed through - a squall blowing down the Schuylkill Valley during the rush hour. We were delayed a bit on the Media Bypass and finally turned onto Conchester Pike (322) before turning onto Route 202, Wilmington Pike. Old Wilmington Pike is off Brintons Bridge Rd. The snow had changed to a sleet-rain mix as we arrived.

"Feels good to get away for the evening," Dawn sighed. "I still feel like my nursing exams are spinning around in my head. Dr. Conise's Physiology Exam was a bear. God, it was terrible, Aldie! I was glad to get a B- on it!"

I returned:

"Tonight, we'll forget about Physiology Exams and Dr. Cronise and School of Nursing and Frankford Hospital, Love."

I reached over and kissed her.

"Pre-Merry Christmas, Sweetheart! Love you."

"Love you, too, darling." Getting into the Dilworthtown Inn was simple. I decided on using the valet parking. We were seated next to a window with a candle on the sill and real holly surrounding it and a little Nativity Scene. We both chuckled, since it seemed to be the only Nativity within eye reach.

Once Dawn was seated, I excused myself to use the Men's Room. Actually, I was taking the boxed engagement ring to the kitchen and asking for our server, Eduardo, to serve it with a parfait dessert. He knew what it was and smiled.

"Very good, Mr...."

"Seaver. Uh, 'S-e-a-v-e-r.'" He looked down at his reservation list.

I shook Eduardo's hand,

"Very good, Mr. Seaver. We'll take care of this for you... with the parfait. OK."

The meal, to say the least, was flawless! We toasted our wine glasses:

"To release from the clutches of Ms. Conise's painful physiology classes," I tipped my glass to Dawn's.

The first sip 1994 Chappelet Cabernet was incredible, and the crusted scallops proved savory beyond measure. We savored and chatted and laughed and sipped. Then it was time for dessert. Eduardo, whose service had been flawless until this point, seemed delayed in bringing the parfait.

"Mr. Seaver," Eduardo approached reluctantly, "might I possibly have a word with you, Sir? Excuse us, Madam."

I arose a little frightened at what news Eduardo might have: a dying parishioner - a family issue, emergency in the parish, death? In the foyer of adjoining dining room, Eduardo confessed,

"We seem to have misplaced the box."

"What? Jesus!... I mean, what do you mean?" "

"We assure you, we are looking for it and will not be content until we find it."

"Oh, my God! "

It felt like blood was sinking from my brain to my stomach. I turned Eduardo around with my hands on his shoulders firmly.

"Go! Please find that ring! It's an engagement ring!"

I regained my composure to make a return to the Table. Beautiful Dawn looked curiously at me... almost suspiciously.

"It was nothing, Darling." I tried composure, but my heart was burning inside. "He wanted to make sure the scallops were to our liking."

"He took you to the next room to ask about the scallops? Darling, is there something I need to know... did you get a call?"

"No, Sweetheart....actually I misplaced something and they're looking for it."

"What, darling?"

I can't lie to the woman I want to marry and adore with all my heart. What am I going to tell her?

"It's... It's a small gift I intended to share with you during dessert."

My eyes looked down. A broad smile fell over her face:

"Aldron, did you buy that Seiko watch I've been talking about? I thought we weren't going to do gift exchanges. We were going to put our resources together for the homeless shelter!

"No, it's not a Seiko watch, Sweetheart."

I took her hand.

Suddenly, Eduardo appeared with the manager holding a generous dish of chocolate parfait with a sparkling candle on it.

"Happy evening, Mr. Seaver. Happy evening... a parfait to share with the lady and, oh... what is this... a little box too!"

I felt my life return to me, although my heart was still beating wildly. I smiled at Eduardo, who placed both the parfait and the little white box on the table in front of Dawn and then quickly disappeared. My smile fell upon my Beautiful Dawn who had that look of 'I-know-what-this-is-OMG' all over her face.

Could I now remember the proposal speech? I was so rattled by the mini disaster! I got down on one knee, held the box before her and mustered up courage to give my little speech.

My darling, my Beautiful Dawn, you have so won my heart's adoration and... uh... my devotion. I would be thrilled beyond my pale words...uh... to you this night... if you were to accept my proposal to be your partner, uh...well, your husband for the rest of your life.

She was speechless, her mouth open and covered and looking for something to say. I opened the box and the emerald diamond was brilliant in the candlelight. By now a few couples nearby were straining their necks in quiet anticipation. All conversation had suddenly hushed. It was deafeningly silent except beyond tables who couldn't see.

"Aldron... O my God, Aldron! What?"

Her eyes were fixed on the ring and widening with her gaping mouth.

"O my God!"

She began laughing hysterically. Yet, tears were streaming down her face. The elderly woman next to our table pleaded "Come on, say yes!" Looking back at her husband, she sighed: "Charles, I never saw anything so romantic" Dawn looked radiant in her surprise. I swear her smile makes me fall all the more in love with her. She cupped her hands over her mouth and then looked me in the eye.

"Yes! Yes! Yes!"

Everyone broke into clapping wildly. The word must have gotten around. Taking the ring from the box, she asked me if I would put it on her finger. I kissed her hand gently and began sliding the ring on her left finger:

"I'm yours forever."

We kissed a long kiss, our lips locked and our embrace inseparable until one older gentleman across the room yelled,

"Hey, get a room, you two!" He laughed heartily.

And that brought down the house. We barely finished the parfait. There were pictures I took on my iPhone and other folks offered to take photos of us. The lady with Charles gloated all over Dawn as she came to our table.

"Never had anything nearly this romantic from Charles. He just handed the ring to me and said, 'Hope this fits...whatta you think?' What kind of a proposal is that, right Charles?"

Charles just shrugged his shoulders and smiled.

Needless to say, finishing our dinner with dessert was hardly a memory. Beautiful Dawn just kept looking at the ring and admiring it and laughing and holding my hand.

Leaving Dilworthtown Inn, I noticed sleet and snow had finally passed through Chester County when we had the valet return the vehicle. The night sky was crisp and clear. Dawn clung to me as the car door was opened for her.

"I'm really going to be Mrs. Aldron Seaver... how about that!"

"Thank you for saying 'Yes!'" I said with relief.

December 24th

It wasn't the worst Christmas Eve ever at All Saints Parish, but by some accounts, nearly the worst in recent memory. I learned that back in 1834 Rev. Dr. Barrick Farber Gasden, rector of All Saints, was hit by a horse and buggy as he attempted to run across the street for the services one snowy Christmas Eve. He slipped on the slippery road. His parishioners pulled him to the steps of the Nave, where he died in the arms of his warden. I read this in the history of All Saints of Havertown. According to records, the horse and buggy never stopped after trampling Gasden. Some who saw it gave chase, but the night darkness was too much. Needless to say, I am careful at parking my

Honda and crossing the street on Christmas eve or anytime. Needless to say, that was the worst Christmas in All Saints' History.

It had become unusually warm the morning after the mixed precipitation of the day before Christmas Eve. The weather was quite balmy, which meant that last minute shopping at Springfield Mall and the Manoa Shopping Center in Havertown was wild. I had spent Friday morning working on my Christmas Eve message based on Luke's Christmas text from Chapter 2. The temptation to find a sermon on line was a little overwhelming, because I had preached on Christmas for so long, I had run 'out of gas.' All the warn-out motifs, such as how Luke puts Jesus' nativity in the context of socio- economic contrasts of the day, how Mary and Joseph, soon to be parents, were homeless and somewhat helpless in providing an adequate setting for birth; how angels came singing of Jesus' unsanitary birth to nameless shepherds in their nocturnal work of protecting sheep. The truth is that I had ceased to believe in this broad literary crap about Jesus' nativity.

The writers of what became the gospels weren't particularly interested in Jesus' nativity - only that the word of his teaching, proclaiming God's unfolding reign in his life and mission, might give hope and strength to the communities who followed him. It was Jesus' passion and purpose that fueled the writers to put together stories that became manuscripts and then distributed among the churches. The nativities of famous people seem to become important only as their fame grew. We want to know more about a sitting president's place of birth or where a monarch got his start, or famous folks' hometowns, education, interests, etc. much more so after they have passed from this world.

The problem with Jesus' life is that we know little about any of it except the few sources we have that came many years after he lived. Nothing was written down until some forty years after his death and those sources were based on stories from communities who sought to remember who Jesus was: For example, one proclaimer might declare: *This is what I was told by Hezekiah's people over in Capernaum.* Of course, the remembered conversation might eventually be written down. The first Gospel, probably Mark (which doesn't have a nativity within it), wasn't likely written until around 70 C.E. (Common Era) or maybe a little later, which, if true that Jesus was crucified around 30-33 C.E., was much like writing about someone 40 years after he or she died. Imagine how we might write about Martin Luther King, Jr's assassination in April 1968 if we were the first to write about his life and nothing had been written down until 2008. That's forty years after the event. In the case of Jesus, we would, of course, not have photographs or TV clips or newspaper articles to go on – only stories passed down from parents or grandparents about Jesus' So the gospels are remembered history written down much later by men who were wealthy enough to write.

Regarding the gospels, the floating stories shared from one community to another seemed adequate to stir the imaginations and hopes of the Church, so that whatever Jesus was doing was advancing the work of God in their lifetime. This was big, *really* big! And carving out a nativity without any kind of written birth record was, to say the least, wildly speculative. That doesn't take anything away from the idyllic Christmases we keep culturally. Those are iconic, of course, and nothing should disturb the meaning we give to them. It's just necessary to say that if we are trying to look for accurate accounts of Jesus' birth, even the two gospels with birth narratives – Matthew and Luke- but they're all very speculative.

I had decided that I wanted my preaching to focus on 'presence' vs. 'presents' and how some of my best Christmas memories were fueled by our families being together; how necessary it seemed to seek the 'presence' of the Holy One *here in our world.* Sometimes that's not so easy. Our families exchanged presents and that was fun, of course, but it couldn't compare to the excitement of togetherness. The Creator God's 'joy to the world' seems to be found in how God became a 'presence' to us, so present that our own sense of community presence, our empathy and our motivation, our altruism, might best be expressed on being, like the Deity, 'present' with others. I realized such a preaching point might be stinging for some who wanted the idyllic crèche scene – shepherds, angels, magi –the whole package of Luke 20:1-20, Matthew 2:1-6, etc. We would have all of that, of course.

Aunt Bernice

Dawn had travelled down to Claymont, DE, Christmas Eve morning, to visit her Aunt Bernice, a younger sister to her Grandma Wilma. It was a tradition for Dawn and Bernice to go out for lunch somewhere in the area on Christmas Eve day, just the two of them. Unlike her sister Wilma, Bernice was a non-smoking, tea totaling Southern Baptist and passionate reader and, in her own right, an excellent writer. She had worked for the *Philadelphia Inquirer* for many years as a copy editor, known for her eagle eye in catching not only grammatical errors, but also out-and-out misinformation on the *Inquirer*. Staff members knew that Bernice was known for going to the sources to check the accuracy of something that seemed a little suspicious to her. As such she often drove editors straight up the wall on some articles they had spent inordinate time on as they attempted to beat a deadline. Some editors tried to get her fired; one even concocted a lie suspecting she might be involved in a subversive organization trying to infiltrate the *Inquirer*. That remembrance became a joke around the *Inquirer* because Aunt Bernice may have been feisty about her job, but she was hardly espionage material. Her favorite past time was knitting patriotic scenes, many of which were hanging in her living room. She was known for her unwavering patriotism and was a senior member of the *Inquirer* copy staff. Even after her retirement at 72 her boss had begged her to stay on as a consultant.

Other editors found it necessary to stay on Bernice's good side. They would frequently send her notes and gifts of appreciation for her hard work. They had a saying in the Editorial Department that *'nothing gets by Bernice's evil eye'* - including the tryst back in 1994 between one of the Administrative Assistants and the Chief Editor.

Dawn knocked on her door at 11:15 a.m. Bernice was overjoyed at seeing her favorite niece (I think 'favorite niece' because Dawn was the only one among the other nieces and nephews who ever stopped by or paid any attention to Bernice.)

Looking over her head to foot, Bernice said: "Ah, my sweet little Dawn... look at you! You are just gorgeous!"

"Aunt Bernice!"

They hugged and rocked side to side in the doorway.

"Well, come on in. Here we are standing out in the cold. Oh, honey, it's so good to see you!" She stopped and looked at Dawn's finger. Beautiful Dawn was holding it out almost deliberately waiting for her to notice.

'O my goodness! O my goodness! Honey... my little Dawn Briana O'Shea is engaged? Will you look at that? It's beautiful. Who's this lucky man?"

"Aldron ... or Aldie Seaver. He's an Episcopal rector at All Saints."

Bernice looked in amazement. "You're marrying a priest?"

"No, an Episcopal priest. You know, the marrying kind." Aunt Bernice looked away and then took Dawn's arm to lead her in. They walked to the large kitchen table right under the window with a view view of her backyard. Dawn and her aunt had two very passionate things in common: flowers and gardening. December memories of Bernice's spring and summer flower gardens were welcome conversation, especially on this unusually mild Christmas Eve day. Bernice had tea ready for pouring and her famous biscuits right out of the oven with exotic jams. She prided herself on finding creative jams.

They talked of engagement and wedding plans, nursing school graduation coming up in January and Aldie's work at All Saints. Bernice looked at her for a moment and was silent.

"Honey, are you sure you're ready for the life of being a minister's wife?"

Dawn didn't know what to say. She hadn't been asked that question before until Aunt Bernice brought it up. That's when her aunt dropped a bomb.

"I never told you this, Honey, but I was once engaged to a Baptist minister."

"Aunt Bernice! Why didn't you..." She put her hand on her lap.

Her aunt interrupted her.

"I just couldn't bring myself around to tell you, Honey. I was young and foolish, you might say. He was single and vulnerable. He lived in a big manse outside of Haverford. Mm! the kindest man

116

I've ever met. He treated me so good. And I was a promising young editorial intern at the 'Inquirer.' He was writing the history of Temple Baptist Parish and wanted to submit an article for 'The Patch.' He was tall with blond wavy hair and square chin. His smile made my heart sink. We dated and before too long, I was head over hills in love with this man of the cloth. Oh my!" She sighed.

"I followed him to visits with parishioners, attended services faithfully and even helped in the secretary's office. It was just about this time of the year that we ...." (she turned and looked out the window)... well, he asked me to marry him. And, of course, I said 'Yes!'"

Aunt Beatrice went on to tell how her pastor-lover was so over-extended in his work there at Temple Baptist, working to exhaustion. One day as she waited in the church parlor to join him for lunch, she found herself perplexed at his tardiness. Usually he emerged from his office in plenty of time. His secretary had already gone to lunch. Beatrice waited 15 minutes and then five more before she decided to go to his office door and knock. There was no response. Could he have gone to the hospital? Finally, she pushed the door open and there was her fiancé -pastor slumped over in his chair. Medical examination at the morgue showed that he had died of a massive heart attack. So now Dawn seemed determined to go to a Christmas Eve Service, not for any strong beliefs in religion, but just to support me

"Oh my gosh, Aunt Beatrice, I never knew!" said Beautiful Dawn

"I'm sorry. For a long time, I couldn't tell anyone. And then it... it just faded into the background. That's why I'm saying; Are you sure you want to marry this Pastor Aldron? I know love is love. But as far as I'm concerned, the life of a minister is a killer life."

Beatrice and Dawn talked about many things that morning - including their passion for flower gardening - but the one thing that lingered more than anything in Beautiful Dawn's mind was the revelation of Aunt Beatrice's story. So now Dawn seemed determined to go to a Christmas Eve Service, not for any strong beliefs in religion, but just to support me.

Christmas Evening

I had finished my Christmas Eve sermon about 4 o'clock in the afternoon before deciding to take a stroll over to Testa's bakery for some coffee cake and a latte. Before I was even out onto the sidewalk, Dawn came rushing into the church parking lot in that familiar silver Camry.

"Anything wrong, Sweetheart!" I hugged her.

"Aldie, darling, we have to talk right now!"

"What's wrong, my Darling? I'm about ready to..."

"Now... we have to talk now!"

We returned to my office and closed the door as Dolores, my secretary smiled and greeted Beautiful Dawn. She didn't even sit down. She kicked off her shoes and turned to me: "You know I love you very much..."

"Uh oh, I sense something is about to happen." I put my hands behind my head and stretched back in my chair.

"Seriously, Aldie, I need you to listen. I'm not.... not sure I'm ready." She put her hands firmly on my shoulder.

"For Christmas?" I chuckled.

"Be serious! Aldie, I'm not sure I'm ready to be married to you."

I sat up in my chair. This is the woman who just a few days before said *Yes, Yes, Yes!* Now she was about to say *No, No, No!* My smile turned to an eye-widening look at her.

"What? What do you mean? What's going on, Sweetheart?"

I put my arms around her and kissed her forehead. She held me tight and began crying. She told me Aunt Bernice's story and how terribly shaken she had become thinking about me, about and the work at All Saints.

"I... I don't want to go through what Aunt Bernice went through. Don't you know how precious you are to me, Aldie? How do I know someday I'm not going to walk through this..."?

"Stop, Sweetheart!"

I pulled back and put my hands on her shoulders, looking into those tearful eyes, I said:

"You're being irrational about this."

"I'm not being irrational, Aldie. I love you!" She pulled a white tissue from my desk box and blew her nose.

"I love you, too, darling. But... but I'm me."

I helped her find the trash to throw the tissue away.

"My health is good. I work out at Planet Fitness over at Ardmore. I walk at least two miles a day. I try to eat right, save for my obsession with chocolate cookies! And I get regular physical check-up's. Darling... I take care of myself. The truth of the matter is that at 43, I'm healthier than when I was 34. Or at the least I'm more conscious of my health and what to avoid."

I walked around to my desk and put my fingers on my desk pad and then crossed my arms around my chest as if to say: 'Case settled!'

"But your job is stressful, Aldie...."

I returned briskly: "And your work at nursing training isn't stressful, Sweetheart? Remember when you had to visit Dr. Hanchek over at Havertown Primary Care, because you weren't sleeping? Remember what your blood pressure was?"

There was a pause as she wrapped her arms around herself and looked down to the carpeting, perhaps feeling a bit vulnerable. I gave her space to think and respond. It was a very pregnant pause before she looked up and came around to wrap those arms around me.

"Aldie, darling, I just don't want to lose you."

Kissing my cheeks several times, she whispered, "Promise me you'll work on easing the stress around here. Call an Associate Priest. Take more time off." Then with a slight devilish smile, she said: 'Make more love!'

"That's a deal darling! I promise."

Leaning her head on my chest she admitted, "I guess I was overreacting. I'm sorry about wanting to delay the wedding. I *do so* want to be Mrs. Aldron Seaver." We embraced for quite a while and shared some loving kisses. Time had gotten away, and I *gladly* gave up the piece of coffee cake at Testa's and the latte. I looked at my watch and realized that the first of the Christmas Eve services was only an hour and a half away. I invited Beautiful Dawn to help me in the Vestry and begin preparation for the evening. The vestments were to be laid out. My Beautiful Dawn now was resolute to be my helper and make sure I went into the 5PM liturgy, the 7PM liturgy and the 11AM Midnight Mass stress free. We made some coffee and spent the next hour in the Vestry. She told me that she planned to attend all the services, that, even if she still had problems believing in the Deity, she secretly loved Christmas Eve services – the candles, the music, all the Christmas decorations.

"Hey you two! Hi Dawn." Senior Warden, Bob McGyver greeted as he dropped in.

She nodded, fixing up her hair nervously and not knowing where to put her hands except to sweep them along her pants.

"Forty-five minutes to show time, Fr. Aldie. Anything you need from me?"

"Thanks, Bob. Are the candles ready for five o'clock?" I gestured with a single wave of my hand.

"All out in baskets ready to be handed out," he replied. As I indicated earlier, this Christmas Eve at All Saints was not a total disaster, but I would have given anything *not* to have experienced what was about to happen at the five o'clock service.

The crowd filing into the Nave was substantial. Bob McGyver had enlisted some of the men to add folding chairs in the Gathering Area and alongside the pews. By estimate, there were approximately 250 attendees, three quarters of which were children. This was our 'Family Friendly' Christmas Eve service begun about eight years ago when some parents approached Fr. Vince, the acting rector at that time, to add an earlier service that allowed for families to enjoy an earlier service for all the activities that would unfold at home before the late evening. From what I could gather, Fr. Vince was reluctant to do this and went into it kicking and screaming when the Vestry prevailed and allowed for the extra service. So, the tradition of the Early Christ Mass began and so did the annual cacophony of little drama kings and queens who wished they were anywhere else but stuck in a room filled with adults trying to keep them quiet. The Nursery Coordinator had refused to be available for nursery duty at the service. The first year we attempted to provide a nursery attendant, she almost had a nervous breakdown with seventy-five little people in a free-for-all and demanding every ounce of her energy for one and a half hours. We paid her double for that evening, but she still refused this year.

They were all there crowded into our Nave as the Praise Team began the Rock and Roll version of *'O Come All Ye Faithful.'* It was a snappy version of the old hymn. It took me a while to get used to this version with its strummed, almost march-like accompaniment. Bob, Dawn and I looked out at the sea of chaos. I kissed Dawn and she said as she rolled her eyes,

"God luck, darling!"

I walked to the pew to be seated with the acolyte and settled in with my bulletin and for a moment, scanned a few notes from the sermon. The Praise Team started the second song, a combination of *'God Rest Ye Merry Gentlemen'* and *'We Wish You a Merry Christmas',* which always amazed me, but it was Christmas Eve and there were no holds barred here.

Things went rather well, although Holly Graebel's little Riley managed to scream through most of my message about 'Presence and Presents' and, poor Holly, bless her, had no way to get out of the crowded pew until a few teens sitting near the side finally stood up and allowed her to take Riley (now into full tantrum mode) to get him back to the Narthex. We were blessed with Riley's version of 'Joy to the World' until he was eventually taken outside.

It wasn't until we were ready with the *'Silent Night'* (contemporary version) that my acolytes with their candles and the Nave lights were dimmed so that only the Christmas tree filled the Nave began to make their rounds of giving light to the whole congregation. (I had instructed them on Sunday after the eleven o'clock service: *Don't tilt your lights – worshippers will tilt them toward yours to receive their light.*)

They looked at me in a daze. I smiled and said: "Consider that you're a human candle and people are getting their light from you."

What we weren't prepared for was what happened to little Stone Graebel, Holly's other angel, who was sitting on his Grandma Ivy's lap and proudly holding his candle. Since Holly was still outside listening to Riley's version of 'Joy to the World,' Grandma Ivy had grandson duty for both Billy and Stone. Faster than Grandma Ivy could even imagine, Billy held out his candle, took his light (which was scary enough), but then Stone grabbed it from him, since he wasn't handed a candle, and proceeded to set himself on fire. I turned around in my pew and saw Stone Graebel fully aflame.

"Jesus, Joseph and Mary!', somebody yelled, and panic struck the entire front left quadrant of the Nave. No sooner had I heard *Jesus, Joseph and Mary*, there were a hundred gasps as Bob McGyver was standing there with a fire extinguisher the size of a Mack truck and suddenly Stone Graebel was receiving a powerful spray of dry chemicals on his little suit and tie, which made him scream bloody murder, but the fire was out instantly. Grandma Ivy, who looked like death warmed over stood and moved Billy aside and screamed 'Oh God!" Oh God!! 'The Praise Team had stopped its version of 'Silent Night' (far from 'silent') and the house lights were turned on. Holly Graebel was summoned and came running in screaming with Riley still in a verse of his own version 'Joy to the World', "Bob McGyver (a seasoned rescue volunteer Station 56, Havertown Fire Company) picked up Stone Graebel and realized that, as quickly as it all happened and apart from black smudges all over his little suit and some on his face, the burn had not penetrated his skin, but he smelled like an overly cooked baked potato. In reaction to all of this, Stone's screams were no match for Riley's *Joy to the World!'* Holly was crying uncontrollably, and I was holding her as Dawn came over to comfort her and Holly gave screaming Riley to pale Grandma and held screaming Stone as tight as she could, and it was a 'Barnum and Bailey' circus at All Saints!

Things gradually calmed down on that scary quadrant of the Nave. The whole crowd was either sitting or standing, chattering loudly. Holly took the kids and Grandma Ivy out with Bob McGyver and escort. A few parishioners who knew Holly and her boys attended to her. The Praise Team waiting for things to calm down started their version of *'Little Drummer Boy.'* I looked over and saw Beautiful Dawn rolling her eyes. Remembering her own meltdown earlier in the day about the stress of a pastor's life, I can only imagine what was going through her mind. I thought to myself, *'Great timing, huh Lord?'*

Before dimming the lights and resuming candle lighting and singing of *'Silent Night'*, I decided to venture two announcements:

"In light of what just happened here…and I use 'light' sparingly… I ask two things. First, I ask you to pray for Holly and Stone, of course … he's OK… and Riley and Billy and Holly's Mom. Holly is a single Mom who works very hard to keep her boys well fed, dressed and out of harm's way."

"Second, I ask you, please, do not give your small children candles to be lighted or I will excommunicate each one of you!" (That brought laughter). "I need parents to really help me with this. Our children are curious and at the same time very vulnerable. Please? Okay, let's dim the lights again and continue our service."

I knew what the future would be based on this incident. Jerry Castleman, the local Fire Marshall, was sitting on the third row, pulpit side, with his wife. I knew he would be calling me first thing Monday morning to forbid anymore candle-lighting at future Christmas Eve services. The 7PM, 9PM and 11PM Services went without a hitch. I was enjoying some FairTrade coffee with Beautiful Dawn, when I got a call from Holly Graebel on my cell phone. She was calm and thanked me for having Bob McGyver ready with the fire extinguisher.

"I apologize for making such a scene, Fr. Aldie. I should have taken Stone out with me, too."

"No need to apologize, Holly," I said with assurance. "You work very hard as a single Mom and I can only appreciate that it's not easy at all. I just want to make sure that Stone is OK. I've been thinking about him all evening."

"He's completely fine. We stopped at the hospital just to make sure there weren't any burns. It could have been worse. But he's OK. He told me he wants to keep his burnt clothing as a 'souvenir'! Can you believe him?" Holly Graebel has a funny little laugh. I laughed.

"I'd say 'Merry Christmas', Holly. But I know it hasn't been very merry. I want to stop by after Christmas and share something with you," I invited. The congregation's Social Concerns Team had already been thinking about Holly Graebel and chose her for a generous gift of food gift cards and money to bring some help for the holidays.

"Oh, that would be nice, Father Aldie. Thank you."

After the Midnight Christ Mass concluded and the church was locked up, I looked at my watch and it was 1:23 a.m. Beautiful Dawn and I got in the Honda and started home. She was yawning, and I was completely depleted. She held my hand and kissed it. We didn't say much, except to reference Stone Graebel's little 'light show' at the 5 p.m. Service

"I'm just glad he's OK, Aldie."

"Oh, God, I'm so grateful, Dawn."

It was one of those nights when any lovemaking was the least on our minds. It didn't take us long to crawl into the comfort of our bed and pull the covers around us in a cocooning fashion. I kissed her on her forehead and wished her a Merry Christmas. She blinked a few times with 'Merry Christmas' whispers and we were fast asleep. She slept between my left arm and chest all night. For a few moments, I just planted little kisses on her forehead and hair. In the 'treasured gifts' category, she was my most valued and I thanked God for her countenance, her presence.

Christmas *is* about 'presence' I thought, and I truly felt that Presence in this quirky night of screaming children, panicked Moms and good ol' Bob McGyver and our ready-on-spot, super fire extinguisher. The Cosmic Creator seeks a place within us to 'hang out' so that we might know who God really is even as we are known. This is the nearest meaning we have of 'Emmanuel.'

It's still a mystery to this preacher - four sermons to midnight - how a Creator who fashioned the world, is 'with us.' Can the sculptor fall in love with her work – like Shaw's iconic 'Pygmalion?' Can the little girl make the doll part of the human family? Can the beautiful painting of a summer day become *that* very day? In our imaginations, perhaps. Nevertheless, the *divinum mysterium* -divine mystery-lives on, God looking upon the created world and saw that it was 'good.' Despite of human rebellion, our ever-restless human will, the Creator loves and cherishes us. Humans, when left to their devices, don't function very well as God's creation. The mystery of this relationship between Creator and the creature is that God continued to be animated with divine presence even with our fleshly personas. The Nativity is just the beginning. The neighboring presence of God is a wonderful expansion of the greater story. As thin as Christmas is in its historical context, its greatest truth is that we are embraced by God's 'cosmic cuddle.' As I cuddle my sleeping Dawn, I am appreciatively aware how we rest in that wonderful reality: God is here. That may sound like pious drivel in a world so complex as ours, but it's where I see The Grander Picture. Even as my eyelids droop and my brain quieted itself down, I pray that Love may overtake this world...and...

Christmas Day

In the early hours of Christmas Day snow had laid heavily in the Delaware Valley. I hadn't checked the weather forecast. But it didn't matter. Dawn and I had nowhere to be particularly, except to stop and be with family later in the day —our Christmas 'presence.'

The Weather Channel said our area could expect four to six inches before noon. It was a perfect morning to cuddle and make love and anticipate making breakfast together and playing some Christmas songs. We stayed in bed until 10 a.m. Dawn pouted teasingly:

"Aldie, I'm ravenous for you... but I'm also ravenously hungry!"

I got out of bed and reached for her white Terry Cloth robe from the closet and my own. We stretched and kissed and made our way to the kitchen, which was soon alive with pots and pans, juice glasses, the smell of coffee, eggs and sausage, wheat toast and some gift jams from members of All Saints. We sat down to the sound of 'Vivaldi's 'Four Seasons' – appropriately the 'Winter' section. It was amazing to be snowed in and unhurried on Christmas Day. Let it snow! We just enjoyed an abundance of 'presence' with one another.

Chapter Nine

A WONDROUS, WOEFUL WINTER

O Morning Star, how fair and bright! You shine with God's own truth and light, aglow with grace and mercy.
-Philip Nicolai, 1556-1608, Hymn for the Time After Epiphany

January in Havertown! The sidewalks roll up after 6 p.m. and there's less traffic on the Pike. There's little to do except catch up on movies still sitting in a pile or get to that novel that's been waiting to be read. Or you could head over to 'Jack Quinn's Lamplighter Tavern' or over to 'Murphy's Pub' or maybe 'Peabody's' or the 'Ivy Inn' – or you could hoist a Guinness at 'Paddy Rooney's Pub.' They're all open each night to help you endure the cold, dark month of January. The chatter is always about how cold the weather has become. Some folks are munching on peanuts and downing a pint or two. Some seem lonely and needing somewhere to belong. It's similar to the TV series 'Cheers.' With the strong Irish population, it isn't any wonder that there are Irish-sounding names associated with 'pub crawling' around Havertown. I'm not a 'pub crawler,' although I enjoy a Guinness now and then. I know there are a number of male parishioners who frequent these nocturnal naves of Havertown. I go out now and again and have a Guinness with them. They used to be reluctant to see me arrive in a collar and my green parka. But now they're used to seeing me as a regular guy 'chewing the fat' with them and laughing at their terrible jokes. They call me 'Rev' and sometimes actually start talking about religion and church until one of them chimes in and says: 'Uh oh, this is getting too damned serious!" And we all laugh and go back to being regular people...which, of course, churchy folk are!

Now and then I'll stop at *'Paddy Rooney's'* just to talk with Phil O'Rourke, bar tender *par excellence*, all around great guy and purveyor of sound advice and uncommon wisdom. He could've been an Irish Priest but wouldn't be caught dead with a Roman collar! Frequent flyers there at 'Paddy's' tell me that Phil has good insights in almost everything - from what to do about an obsessive-compulsive spouse to what's the best way to fix an ailing furnace. And he doesn't flaunt his wisdom. I find myself running ideas past him about life and programs at All Saints – like the Stewardship campaign or some solutions to the ailing 11 a.m. Liturgy. Phil's a great guy to chat with when the January days are short, and the nights are long. His wisdom is not unlike a fountain - it kind of wells up within him with good advice in colorful tones (he still has a devilish Irish brogue.) Everyone enjoys a splash of Phil. He just has that certain way of bringing it together, a logic that makes my own reasoning seem useless.

"Phil, tonight I'm stuck on Stewardship," I'm telling him as swallow some peanuts with a Guinness. "Looking for a theme for my Stewardship program. It happens every year."

He wipes the bar top with his chamois.

"Stewardship eh? I hate the word 'stewardship, but I tell ye, when me *figurs* how generous the good Lord has been here on *'urth*, there's no other way of bein' when it comes to figuring out church except 'generosity' Me thinks the word 'stewardship' doesn't cut it, Aldie! How 'boat' *'Taking Care of God's Dream?'* He looks up and writes it in the air. "Ye think now… aren't we all wee custodians of that great big cosmic dream?"

I'm amazed as Phil spun out his wisdom…I downed an entire Guinness and wrote it all. *"Taking care of God's dream!"*

Brilliant! I kissed his balding head and gave him a five-dollar tip and went home and finished it up before 10 p.m. My Stewardship Team thought it was brilliant too; I was a bit embarrassed to tell them that I learned it from Phil the bartender over at 'Paddy Rooney's!' But they weren't surprised, because half of them know Phil and frequent the place. They liked it. We made posters and stationery with Phil's *'Taking Care of God's Dream'* splashed on it. I eventually took pictures and shared them with Phil. He grinned from ear to ear and insisted I have a pint of Guinness on him. I'd elect Phil O'Rourke bishop of the Episcopal Church! Well, you know….

All too soon the Christmas decorations that made our church nave glow were taken down and put in storage. Now, preparations for Epiphany had our Worship Design Team moving about quickly. Apart from January 23rd , our Annual Youth Sunday, when the kids get a chance to lead liturgy and read lessons, pass out bulletins and help with the Mass, the seven Sundays in Epiphany are as strange to many as the four Sunday's in Advent. The Gospel of Matthew, beginning with the story of the Magi - another one of those *'Did this really happen?'* stories. *I mean, can a star in our galaxy stop and start up again guiding Persian kings across a desert and stand still over a manger somewhere in Israel?'* The lectionary continues with other narratives about how the manger baby Jesus grew up and started showing light and life at large. If Christmas concludes that *'God is with us!'* (Emmanuel) then Epiphany, among other things, asks: *How did the kid become the king?* Or maybe, *'How is God really with us in this Jesus fella?'*

Light is one of the central themes during Epiphany. We have a nifty star we hang from the center ceiling at All Saints. The people on Property Team who know how to do this fashioned a wireless device that allows for the star to shine during the worship. The way this large star hangs from the center gives quite an effect to the theme of Epiphany. Joe McLeaf, our property guy, fixed it so that each week the star gets brighter and by Transfiguration Sunday (the Last Sunday of the Epiphany) it would be dazzling- just as Jesus glowed on the Mount of Transfiguration. Some Sundays when we're having one of those gray January days, our Epiphany star is magnificent to behold. I complimented Joe at pulling this project with such excellent special FX. Some traditions suggest that at the time of Jesus' birth there had been a super nova, a collision of stars that allowed for a magnificent light show in the heavens. Like many symbols in Scripture, I think of Light and the Transfiguration that concludes Epiphany as imaginative ways of describing how Jesus counters the darkness of the world with his presence, his teaching, his miracles and, not the least, his compassion. Some of my conservative friends think I've bailed out on the literal translation of the Bible. I tell them:

"Are you kidding? The light of Jesus is what the story means! Parables, riddles, sayings, metaphors, allegories, miracles... they don't have to be *true* for me to find *'truth'* in them. My faith has taken a quantum leap since I gave up Biblical literalism for those poetic metaphors I draw from the Bible."

Sylvia O'Connor heads up our Worship Design Team. She was once a diaconal minister having received additional training and then became an Episcopal priest. However, the pressures were too much, so she left the priesthood, got her doctorate in 'Sacred Theology' and became a professor of liturgy eventually and now teaches courses at the Lutheran Seminary in Philadelphia. Lutherans and Episcopalians like each other these days since they now share communion across their denominational borders. That so-called 'communion' didn't happen without some kicking and screaming as the two judicatories struggled with what they did *not* have in common. Sylvia is very comfortable with organizing and designing liturgy. The star was really her idea. So, the setting for Epiphany Sundays would necessarily include 'Kid Size Bites' (our version of Children's Sermons) that focused on light. Sylvia got Jeff Stearns, one of our youth mentors, to teach children the song *'This Little Light of Mine'* with little flashlights in their hands. He told them: "Remember, kids, Jesus is like the flashlight we need to find our way around the dark world."

My own sermons during January were preceded with people acting out the Gospel story in a minimalist way rather than my reading them. I'd write the script, for example based on Mark 1:4-11 (the Baptism of Jesus) by having a John the Baptist characterization, a Jesus persona and a narrator. As soon as the drama was concluded, I would emerge for the kids' sermon on Baptism of Our Lord Sunday, I'd give the sermon from the baptismal fountain, positioned in the center of our Nave. At the conclusion, I'd invite those who wish to gather around it, place their hand in the font, and make the sign of the cross as a reminder of their baptism. I announced at the font:

"Even if you've not been baptized, know that you are welcome to make the sign of the cross on your forehead. Our hope is that it will be a sign of something that is perhaps beginning to unfold in your life. We can all grow in the Spirit of a Living God."

Usually I'd place bergamot oil in the font - a citrusy fragrant oil (usually lemony) to add intrigue to the ritual. Sometimes the children would just lean over to smell the fragrance. Once I recall a little girl cupping the water with both hands and washing her face.

"This is how I wash my face in the morning, Pastor!" She beamed from ear to ear." I loved it, although her mother was mortified.

"It's fine," I whispered, "she's enjoying it. It's great that she can have the meaning she's seeking. Who knows, maybe it's her spiritual connection."

I liked our Epiphany worship for the lift people needed after the Advent-Christmas cycle. With weather unpredictable and diminished light, worship at All Saints was a luminous worship experience and a rather exciting place to be. Our banner makers always provide colorful images that highlight Epiphany. I like the one that Barbara McCaskey made that reads in bold silver and gold against a deep indigo that includes stars... *The Wise Still Seek Jesus... His Light Still Leads.* Christmas and Advent need an afterglow and these seven weeks before the time of Lent are perfect for allowing the message 'God with Us' – *Emmanuel* - to catch hold of our shivering, darkened spirits.

I must admit I suffer from a bit of Seasonal Affective Disorder (SAD) during January. I'm a light and color person. Not that I don't appreciate the special beauty of darkness, but I've always appreciated the longer daylight. For a period of time when January rolled around during my days at Holyoke Parish in Virginia, I'd sometimes disappear in the middle of the afternoon to my bed or favorite chair and sleep for hours.

One year while at Holyoke late in January I attended a Preaching Conference for Clergy held in a large hotel opposite Walt Disney World - the Marriott World Center. I continued making that late January early February pilgrimage while at All Saints. Some of my friends in the parish called it 'the rector's annual escape to golf.' I do participate in clergy golf tournaments, where we raise money for special outreach concerns (like Malaria Nets for third world countries for which we raised almost $8,000 in the previous year). But more than golf, I enjoy the ambiance of warmer temps and great conversation with speakers and colleagues.

I'd tell close friends the Orlando conference gathers 'depressed and burned out clergy' who often deny they are 'depressed and burned out' to get them somewhat revitalized only to get more depressed and burned out later when Lent and Easter approach. I'm teasing, of course. But no mountaintop experience lasts. Speaking for myself, the Conference was just what the doctor ordered when I'd get these winter blues after the big Christmas 'blowout. 'Since All Saints pitches in on the expenses for this two-week hiatus, I welcome not only hearing the well-known speakers at the conference, but also getting out for two or three rounds of golf and exploring EPCOT and Magic Kingdom and Animal Kingdom. Since I usually traveled this alone, I didn't hesitate to let the kid in me come out to play at the 'happiest place on earth.' That wasn't going to happen this year.

Dawn will be tagging along to experience 'the World' with me this year and I couldn't be more delighted. I didn't announce it to the congregation that Dawn was going with me. 'We planned it with just enough wiggle room built in that it didn't seem so structured. Three or four days to get there would be enough to stop and smell the roses along the way with stops in Charleston and Savannah and Saint Simon's Island and then a straight shot to 'The World.'

We had planned to leave just after the youth service on January 23rd

It was refreshing to let the kids flex their leadership muscles. Apart from my needing to officiate the masses that day, I applauded them taking over much of the services. Kids put their hearts and souls into doing what adults normally do -even taking offering plates and collect offering (or, as one kid said, collecting the loot!) One of our senior youth gave a five-minute sermon that had people applauding afterward.

I teased the congregation before the offering was collected and announced that 'Jeff Billingsley' would be our new Assistant Pastor. That brought even more laughter and clapping. All with good fun.

Florida

I wasn't running out the front door that 23rd Sunday in January, but I was sure determined to get away with my Beautiful Dawn as soon as possible to recalibrate my priestly spirit down in Orlando. She had spent the morning packing and tidying up the townhouse. I met her at the door and the suitcases were packed. The Honda was gassed up and roaring to go.

The sky seemed ominous and the weather channel was pre-dicting a late afternoon snow to descend upon Havertown -three to four inches. It was time to get onto I-95 and leave the cares of All Saints to those priests whom I had asked to shepherd the flock while I vacated. Beautiful Dawn had prepared a sandwich, some fruit and, of course, chocolate chip cookies as well as some green tea to take with us on the initial leg of our trip that would take us over the Delaware River into Maryland and around Baltimore and around D.C. By eleven o'clock that evening, these 'snow birds' hoped to be in Fayetteville, NC, about halfway to the Florida border. There's a big rush about preparing to get out of town -especially when you're heading to warmer climes!

We talked about a myriad of things down I-95. She was remembering her graduation from Frankford. It was a snowy Saturday in Philadelphia when the auditorium was filled with some 80 graduates, all decked out in their hospital nursing whites. There were three males in the class. She already had received her Associate Degree at Delaware Valley Community College and was ready for the last step toward her goal, passing her NCLEX examination. (National Council for Licensure Examination). In fact, she had brought along a number of preparatory texts for that exam and imagined sitting on the beach in Florida with her head buried in the book.

We stopped for dinner in Fredericksburg, VA. It had begun to snow pretty intensely, although it was a wet snow and the roads were passable. I recalled a neat little French Restaurant I visited during my Seminary days in downtown Fredericksburg - *'La Petite Auberge.'* If it was still on the menu, I invited Beautiful Dawn to share an entree I savored their once, a Jumbo *Lump Crabmeat Auberge.* Turning off Exit 130A of I-95, we followed Route 3, Plank Road, which becomes Williams Street and lead us to *'La Petite Auberge.' (it means 'a little hotel')* We weren't disappointed. The Jumbo Crabmeat entree was shared with delight. We finished our dinner sharing a chocolate Ganache cake for desert and left Fredericksburg about 6:30 PM to continue our journey southward. The wet snow had turned to all rain as we turned onto I-95 south once again. It was going to be a good stretch of 270 miles or four and a half hours of driving yet before our stop for the evening, with an estimated arrival about 11-11:30PM. The speed limit for the most part on I-95 through North Carolina is 70 mph, so perhaps our arrival could be sooner. Our reservation would be the Hampton Inn on Cedar Creek Rd., along I-95. We turned on some New Age music and Beautiful Dawn settled into some serious knitting, working on a beautiful sweater she was creating for her friend, who was making her first trip to Ireland in the Spring.

Between the Kitaro music and smooth ride, Dawn was soon sleeping soundly. I would gaze at her from time to time as we rounded Richmond on I-295. In sleep, she was as beautiful as ever.

We were nearing Rocky Mount, NC, when I noticed that the rain had turned to snow again and there was sleet mixed with it. The area was slightly elevated and nighttime temperatures were hovering around freezing. By the time we reached Wilson, it was apparent the roads were getting a bit treacherous. The usual 70 mph speed limit was now slowed down to a crawl. Beautiful Dawn was still asleep at 9 pm when a passing 18-wheeler lowered its gears and woke her.

"My goodness, Aldie. It looks bad!"

"Yeah, I'm being very cautious. It's hard to trust others, though, like this guy (pointing to the 18- wheeler carrying Toyotas and who seems in a hurry)."

We still had about 80 miles before Fayetteville and I could see that, considering the road conditions, it could be much later than 11:30 PM until we arrived at the Hampton Inn. We navigated the treacherous stretch of I-95 as a team. Beautiful Dawn was keeping an eye on who was approaching and my trying to keep a distance from cars in front. There were a number of vehicles that had slid off the highway. Fender-benders were everywhere. Many of us realizing conditions were OK driving slower and didn't mind hovering in the slow lane. It was the worrisome risky passersby that seemed more treacherous than the road conditions themselves.

A few miles north of Benson, an eighteen-wheeler (ironically the guy trying to get around me some miles back hauling new Toyota's) had overturned and blocked the entire southbound lane of I- 95. There were new Toyotas scattered on each side of the highway, smashed with strewn glass and car parts. Police were diverting us to exit at Benson and take the old Route 301 south toward Dunn. The cars were moving by inches to get off I-95. By now, we were aware of needing a potty-break. I had regretted not stopping in Rocky Mount to take care of this, but now it was looming large for both of us. Full bladders and tense driving don't mix very well.

"I know what we can do, Sweetheart!" I slapped my knee. "Underneath my back seat, I have one of those hospital pee bottles that I use for emergencies."

We looked at each other curiously and then laughed.

"Do you think we can do it?" Dawn asked. There are lights all around us."

"Well," I resolved, "it's either that or this new Honda Accord is going to need some major cleaning tomorrow."

"OK," Dawn joined in.

She reached behind me and produced the hospital urine bottle. "You start, Aldie. I can wait until you're finished."

We were moving along now at a snail's pace and the exit was still about a mile away. So, I unzipped my fly and with my right hand produced my spigot. With my left hand, I secured the steering wheel. Mind you, I am laughing myself silly, which didn't help the bladder situation! Dawn held it up to me tight and my bladder and said, 'Do it, Big Guy!" I peed and sighed in welcome relief. It didn't matter who was looking. It felt good. Beautiful Dawn had a tissue ready for my happy hose. I zipped up my trousers, which caused me to turn the steering wheel slightly... which made me think I was going to be off the highway, but I caught it before slipping and sliding.

I asked Dawn curiously. "How are you going to do this, Sweetheart?"

"Hey Aldie, I'm a nurse," she chuckled, "adaptability and nursing are inseparable." I held the urine bottle while she hiked her skirt(no zipper to her advantage) quickly slid her panties down to mid-thigh. She deftly took the bottle from me and lowered it so that the bottle's opening could be tight against her. And then felt her relief. Love shares everything!

"Oh my goodness, Aldie, that feels so good!"She leaned her head back.

We both chuckled at this anecdotal moment in our journey. By the time she had finished, the said urine bottle was full. Carefully she raised it so that none leaked out, put the cap on and returned it to me to hold while she pulled her panties back up and lowered her skirt - an act that required her to raise herself a bit off the seat. Mission accomplished! We were almost to the Benson exit.

The filled urine bottle would require a bit of time before we would empty it. Turning onto Route 301 south was not going to guarantee a faster ride south of Benson. But relieved bladders made the slow trip much more tolerable. It took us 45 minutes before Route 301 provided a return access to I-95 below Dunn. The snow and ice had now returned to sleet and rain and traffic on I-95 finally picked up moderately.

Since my gas tank was nearing empty, we stopped at the Exxon station in Wade, NC, to fill up. Dawn discreetly took the bottle filled with our relief and emptied it in the Women's restroom there. Coincidentally, another woman passenger was emptying her own bottle. They exchanged laughs and memories of getting around Benson, NC, with bladder relief.

We were about 12 miles to our exit for the Hampton Inn in Fayetteville, NC, and, believe it or not, we arrived only fifteen minutes later than I had planned for. The snow had become scattered flakes as we arrived about 11:45 PM and our room was waiting for us. Dawn had enjoyed an extended nap after Fredericksburg and, although I was tired, I must admit the image of her peeing into the hospital urinal back around Benson, NC, and raising her skirt was an inviting image even in mixed light and darkness. We spent about an hour in very passionate lovemaking, the lights very dim. The tensions of driving and the almost seven hours on I-95 melted away in sweaty intimacy and noises of ecstasy, the *'Ah's'* and *'Ooh's!* And as we had grown accustomed, after our unrequited lovemaking we fell asleep in one another's arms. I barely remember turning out the lights and turning off the Samsung TV. It was dark, and our souls and bodies wrapped in each other. We were spent for peaceful dreams.

"Omigosh, Aldie's it's almost 9:00!"

Dawn had awakened with brilliant sunlight peeking through the partially opened curtains. It was Monday morning and we had planned to leave much earlier for our stop-over in Charleston.

It was actually 10:30AM when we checked out of the Hampton Inn and found the Cracker Barrel near-by for breakfast. The temperature was rather moderate that morning in Fayetteville - just a smattering of snow here and there. The thermometer read 50 degrees. Dawn and I shared a stack of multi-grain pancakes and some poached eggs, one large fresh squeezed Orange Juice and two cups of coffee. I paused to say a few words of thanks.

For a new day and safe travel, for mindfulness of gifts that we might share this day and gifts so freely shared with us, we come hand in hand with grateful hearts, Creator God. Keep safe all who travel with us. Let this day bring us awareness of your caring presence. Amen.

"I'm getting used to this praying thing, Aldie. It's something that has been long missing in my life. I mean, I'm still not particularly religious and still struggling with the whole organized religion thing, but I'm kind of living vicariously through your own traveled spiritual journey, Darling. I think I'm beginning to understand why religion is communal"

I smiled at her and said: "Love you too. You are really my *beautiful* Dawn, this morning, Darling!" She was adorned in a sleeve-less wool sweater with images of sheep grazing, a beige button-down shirt and wearing her corduroy pants. I could not be more fortunate to have someone so beautiful in my life.

Our bill was $15 with our shared breakfast. Jenny, our server had four stars on her apron. It meant that she had graduated in degrees toward being a seasoned server there. She bubbled with personality added with that sweet Carolina accent. She got closer and looked both ways and said:

"I saw you two praying before breakfast. I love it when couples pray. I hope I find a boyfriend who would be willing to do that. None of my boy friends are interested in religion."

Dawn quickly caught my eye, then turned to Jenny.

"I hope you do find someone, Jenny," Dawn said, "Thanks for your service this morning. And for that beautiful smile."

We left her a generous tip, almost the total cost of the meal. Why not! We browsed a bit around the store. 'Cracker Barrel ' always has neat stuff! Dawn found a CD of relaxing music that she thought would add to our travels. We were on our way back onto I-95 south.

It's three and a half hours to Charleston, SC, from Fayetteville, NC. There are very few highlights along that stretch of highway that eventually takes us onto Interstate 26 East to the city of Charleston. One of them I mentioned was the several-mile stretch of bridge across Lake Marion, the largest lake in South Carolina, fed by the Santee

River and other tributaries. It was built in the 1940's as part of the Santee Cooper Hydroelectric and Navigation Project. I remember an uncle of my Mom's had worked on this project and spent several years in Sumter, NC. He said that it was the hardest he had ever worked on anything in his life. Another highlight along I-95 is the iconic *'South of the Border'* South between Rowland, NC and Dillon, SC. The previous day while it was snowing in parts of North Carolina, we noticed signs for 'America's Favorite Highway Oasis' - like *'Chili Today, Hot Tamale!'* and all the 'Pedro' sayings. 'South of the Border' was founded as a beer stand in 1950, since it was just over the South Carolina border from Robeson County, NC, which was a dry county. Eventually through its development, 'South of the Border' became a favorite gas and restaurant stop along a somewhat boring stretch of highway where Route 301 and I-95 crisscross. We made a 'curiosity' stop there, just to browse at the shops and enjoy some hot chocolate and fuel up at the Shell Station.

We arrived in Charleston about Noon. It was overcast with patches of blue here and there. Condé Nest Traveler Readers' Choice Award voted Charleston the 'Top City in the U.S.', which is one heck of an honor! It's apparent from the time you step out of your car at The Battery' or at your preferred lodging, Charleston feels like one friendly place. However, we chose to have lunch at the Charleston Crab House on the waterfront over on James Island across the Ashley River from Charleston. It had been quite a few years since I had their She Crab Soup and a Low Country Crab Cake. Beautiful Dawn was eager to try both. So, we made an order to share with a large glass of lemonade. We enjoyed the waterfront and plotted our afternoon in and around Charleston, which included a carriage ride around The Battery as well as a visit to Ft. Sumter, where the American Civil War began officially on April 12, 1861, when Confederate artillery opened fire on this fort. Fort Sumter surrendered 34 hours later. The island the fort rests on was made of more than 70,000 tons of granite and other rock. For over a decade, contractors from as far away as New York and the Boston area delivered this material by ship and dumped it on a shoal in Charleston Harbor. 'Fort Sumter Tours' boat gets you over to Ft. Sumter, about a 30-minute cruise through Charleston's scenic and historic harbor. We enjoyed the historian who narrated the firing on Ft. Sumter.

The boat trip back was very choppy from a Nor'easter that was moving up from Georgia. Charleston Harbor had some steep swells. We both became nauseous until we moored at the landing back in Charleston. Needless to say, we weren't in the mood for an evening meal - coke and bag of chips sufficed until we felt our stomachs settle.

As evening drew near we decided to forego the carriage ride and walk this beautiful city as the sun was setting. We loved admiring the old homes from Washington Square Park up to Meeting Street to Cannon and down along East Bay Street all the way to The Battery. We met a few folks on the Ghost Walk and they were having a great time looking for spirits. Everywhere you turn in Charleston, there's history staring at you. I enjoyed taking a look at St. Michael's Episcopal Church at the corner of Broad and Meeting. We walked hand in hand, enjoyed some ice cream at Kilwin's Chocolate and Ice Cream Shop on Market Street, where we had a delightful conversation with Bruno, its owner and enjoyed sharing a waffle cone with French Vanilla Ice Cream and some of the best chocolate sauce my palette has ever engaged.

"You haven't told me where we're staying tonight, Aldie?"

"Well, my sweet one, I found this wonderful vintage mansion, 'Wentworth's,' located not too far from here. It's rated as one of the best hotels in Charleston - a place guaranteed to have a friendly staff and many amenities to enjoy."

It was about 7:30 pm and we were both ready to check-in and take off our shoes and prop ourselves up on a king-size bed in a room fit for a king and his queen. A description of the Wentworth's suggests that it tries to capture the ambiance of a bygone era. Everything is about elegance and comfort. We valet parked our car and took our overnight bags and entered the lobby. It's as if the Staff was waiting for us to arrive. The check-in was quick, and we were able to make our way to one of the Garden Rooms at the Wentworth, a very spacious room with an oversized whirlpool and an original gas fireplace. It didn't take us long to take off our clothes and get into the whirlpool and let all day' driving tensions melt away. The lighting around the whirlpool and the light classical music in the backdrop began to create a romantic feel that would eventually lead to climbing over the tub and drying out and putting on our white terrycloth robes. We climbed into the king-size bed with its beautiful golden draping at the head and the gas fireplace off to the side and dimmed the lights until just the shadows of our naked bodies were all we could see. Our kisses followed our foreplay and the feverish pitch of our lovemaking began to find intensity so great that I could no longer contain myself. It wasn't just sex. It was delightfully mutual love-making – the kind that I never thought existed back in my testosterone-saturated teens and college years. I thought about sex back in those day…a big 'lot' of imagining. Most of those thoughts were more about pursuit than mutual love-making.

It was a bright sunny Tuesday morning that awakened Dawn. I was lying behind her with my arm around her and my lips right next to her hair. She turned and put her hand on my lips.

"Good morning, Darling Aldie."

"Sweetheart," I kissed her, "I had this most amazing dream that we had been in this beautiful hot tub and then found our way to this gigantic bed and... wow!"

"It wasn't a dream, silly goose!", she gave me a swat on my arm.

We enjoyed our morning shower and stretching. The shower at this Wentworth Mansion room was bigger than most bedrooms in our homes. There was a large walk-in, glass-enclosed shower big enough for a whole family. We lathered each other with the most fragrant soap, something that smelled like a summer's day on a tropical island. We made early coffee in the Keurig and spent an hour looking forward to our day on Saint Simon's Island. The breakfast prepared by the staff at Wentworth was one of the finest breakfast buffets I've ever tasted. The eggs were all moist, the bacon just the way you might want it - lumpy or crisp. It was 8:00 AM when we sat down and prayed. Beautiful Dawn offered the most beautiful prayer of thanksgiving.

In the middle of our breakfast at the Wentworth, I received a call from my mother. Dawn saw my face suddenly crestfallen. She heard me say "Oh, Mom!" as I covered my face.

"Aldie? What's wrong?"

I put the phone to my chest:

"My Dad died of a coronary embolism early this morning."

Dawn began to cry and took my hand.

"We'll be home as soon as we can, Mom... yes, yes, I'm glad that Allison is there with you... yes, we will... I love you, too." Putting my iPhone on the table I stood and held Dawn.

"Aldie, Darling, it's so awful! Just awful!"

My eyes were moist. I was stunned.

Dad had suffered a coronary embolism at 2:35 AM and was rushed to Chester County Hospital, but he died in route. Our trek to warmer climes ended haltingly. We checked out of the Wentworth quickly and began the 10 ½ -hour drive back to Pennsylvania. Beautiful Dawn held my hand and put her head on my shoulder. Dad was 78 years of age and, until his recent diagnosis of COPD and coronary bypass surgery, had been in reasonably good health. As I grew in years I had worried about his smoking (not unlike Dawn's worrying over her Grandmother Wilma's smoking). After his by-pass I had hoped he would stop the damn weeds, but he was stubborn about it and once told me, *'I'd rather die than give up these babies!'* Well, he had his wish. If the truth were spoken, my Dad's smoking got even more intense after his bypass surgery.

A disappointment settled into our journey homeward knowing the remainder of our Florida trip was not happening. I had so looked forward to this time. I suggested to Dawn that we might wish to continue our trip after the funeral, but I knew it would take several days to plan all the details of communication visitation times and allowing for relatives coming from out of town. My clergy conference wouldn't begin until a week from the day we returned home, so perhaps we could fly down and carve out some remaining time.

In her comforting manner, Dawn said:

"We'll figure this out, Aldie. Don't worry. For now, let's just concentrate on what lies ahead. I love you, darling." I held her hand and let my tears flow. She leaned on my shoulder with such a warm feeling of comfort.

My remembrances of Dad flowed quickly during the long trip to I-95 from Charleston and onto I-95. We were just on this route the day before. Already the 'South of the Border' signs were visible.

Dad grew up north of Louisville, Kentucky, the son of the groundskeeper for Churchill Downs. It didn't take long for Dad as a young man to be smitten by the horse racing industry. My uncle was able to get him a job working with the jockeys' horses. After a time, my Dad served in the U. S. Army in Korea as an airplane mechanic. He was wounded when a tank exploded near his barracks during the Battle of Inchon in 1950. He suffered the partial loss of his left thumb and forefinger but had full use of his right arm. He was shipped home and continued to serve at Ft. Bragg until his medical discharge in 1951. He had been able to get partial prosthesis for his hand at Walter Reed Army Hospital in 1989. Still he battled other struggles after the effects of his combat tour of duty, including the worst one – depression - for which he had never gotten help. He once ranted, "The therapists are all screwy...a bunch of damn money grabbers!"

There was some alcohol abuse for a while and the smoking had become constant. My mother would call me each Saturday morning when Dad was having coffee with some of his buddies at McDonald's, Mom openly vented, because she had plenty to complain about, especially my father's depression and lack of self-care.

"He never listens to me, Aldie. Maybe you could talk with him," Mom lamented.

Of course, I never did talk to him. I learned very early that the last person who would ever receive advice from me was my Dad.

After what seemed an eternity with stops and gas and eats, the sunset and darkness, we approached the Philadelphia area. Some late January weather had moved into the West Chester area when we arrived at my parents' house. Sleet and rain had made the trip through Maryland and Delaware a little dicey. We pulled into the driveway at 11PM. The kitchen light was on. After college, my parents moved from Edgemont to a modest, but well- manicured property on Mulberry Ln. in the Newtown Square area (off of West Chester Pike) west of I-476 and Havertown.

We greeted Mom with hugs and tears. She had made cookies and tea suggesting that we that we were into the night for a long haul. She narrated the events of the day in dreadful detail. Dawn and I both held her hand as she poured out her exasperation over my father's failure to watch his health these past few years. My sister Allison arrived about 11:30PM and joined us in anticipating all the necessary arrangements for the days ahead. It had been a family agreement that we would use Donohue Funeral Home on West Chester Pike. They had served my Dad's sister Aunt Jean's funeral a few years back as well as both my grandparents. The folks there are good and delicate folks to deal with on these matters. We sat around the kitchen table with Mom's goodies spread out now to include cheese and crackers and coffee and left-over Christmas cookies.

"Aldie, what do you think of having the service at All Saints?" Dawn asked me. I agreed that it was a great idea, but I also wondered whether it might be better to consider their home congregation.

My parents were token members of Church of the Holy Trinity, an Episcopal Church in the heart of West Chester on South High Street. The Rev. Rick Riverton often spoke of my parents (especially their absence!) while we were on the greens pretending we knew how to putt. He was a young rector, still a little green behind the gills. I remember being like that.

"They're really good people," I remember saying to Rick, "but my Dad's always been a curmudgeon and not much of a churchgoer. My Mom refused to go without him. So, church was a continuing nothing.

Of course, when death comes, all seems to be forgiven or forgotten when it comes to someone being a 'no show' at church. Fr. Rick was expected at my parents' house on Tuesday. My mother was nervous about the visit, still embarrassed that my father had refused to participate in the Capital Campaign to add an addition on to the Educational Wing at Holy Trinity two years ago. Now at this most vulnerable time, would the community be supportive? Rick seemed like a nice enough fellow, looking and feeling all priestly-like. I remember those days when, fresh from the halls of seminary education, you felt like the world was your oyster. Now somewhat seasoned by his approximate year at Holy Trinity, Rick arrived looking priestly, but much less 'I'm in charge here!' In fact, he was very compassionate, hugging my mother, Dawn and my sister, Allison, and sharing words of sorrow with us. He allowed for some moments of silence looking at us and then I invited him to be seated in the overstuffed Lazy Boy that my Dad use to sit in while watching his favorite shows like 'Swamp People.' Dad and TV were inseparable, my Mom would remind us. I learned to never call or stop by during 'Jeopardy' and 'Wheel of Fortune.' I did that once and found myself in a non-conversation with him. He'd occasionally look over at me as if to say:

"Oh, were you saying something?" Then he'd turn back to the TV and answer "Who is Genghis Khan?' you idiots!" Dad loved to shout at the TV. He had a sharp mind, but a bit of a dull spirit. Mom would tell you he could get so many of the 'Jeopardy' answers correct, but when it came to things happening in the family, names, birthdays, places, etc., he didn't have a clue. Sometimes he'd forget the names of some of his own grandchildren - Allison's kids. Still beneath that curmudgeon-geezer persona, my Dad had had a tender side for my mother. He knew that she was the softer version of their marriage and that if anything was to be done, cared for, planned for, bought, thought through, etc., he could rely on her. Allison and I never received cards or gifts for any occasion where Dad's signature was visible.

"I rely on your mother to do those things", he would say unapologetically. "I can't remember birthdays or anniversaries. Hell's bells! I can't remember my own!"

He'd say that from his Lazy Boy when some TV show wasn't occupying his diminishing brain cells. It was a real blow to me when he refused to attend my ordination. Mom made all kinds of apologies. "Your father hasn't been feeling well, Aldie. I told him to take something for his back. He told me that sitting in the hard pews might be unbearable."

I chuckled when she told me that, because the Old Man would sit for hours in front of the TV and never move a muscle. Besides, the seats at the Seminary Chapel were cushioned. I expected as much, but I was still disappointed. Ordinations come around only once in a while. I can say with certainty that Dad was never really enamored with my going into the priesthood and, as I've already mentioned, advocated vigorously for some alternative in my younger days. The only quote Dad knew from Karl Marx was 'Religion is the opiate of the masses.' (Actually, he said: *"Die Religion ... ist das Opium des Volkes". (Religion is the opiate of the people).* People tend to take the statement out of context. Here is what he really said about religion:

[1] Religious distress is at the same time the expression of real distress and the protest against real distress. Religion is the sigh of the oppressed creature, the heart of a heartless world, just as it is the spirit of a spiritless situation. It is the opium of the people. The abolition of religion as the illusory happiness of the people is required for their real happiness. The demand to give up the illusion about its condition is the demand to give up a condition which needs illusions.

[1]About Religion. Is Religion the Opiate of the Masses?

———

Dad was suspicious of communists, Russians, Jews, Catholics, Asians, Arabs and women in government. Of course, I didn't mention that about Dad when Father Rick stopped by to plan the Service of Remembrance.

"So, this was your father's chair, huh?" Rick nodded.

"Yup, he spent a lot of time in it," I nodded with a wry smile.

Rick is a very nice guy, but he is very systematic. With the 'Book of Common Prayer- Priest's Edition' he scripted out a Funeral Liturgy that crossed every 't' and dotted every 'i.' Listening to him narrate the flow of Dad's funeral service reminded me how I had grown to depart from 'rote' funeral liturgies to something freer, sometimes written in my own creative expression. In fact, I had given up calling this end of-life-events 'funerals' and preferred 'Service of Remembrance.'

Allison had requested the hymn *'On Eagle's Wings,'* based on Psalm 91. She loved the words:

'You who dwell in the shelter of the Lord, who abide in this shadow for life, say to the Lord, my refuge, my rock in whom I trust. And he will raise you up on eagle's wings, bear you on the breath on dawn, make you to shine like the sun, and hold you in the palm of his hand.'

I agreed. Perhaps Dad never realized it, but he did live in 'the shelter of the Lord' and the same Lord who, Dad perhaps never really knew, was often there to 'raise him up on eagle's wings.' Fr. Rick, amazingly, was not familiar with the hymn but said he'd look it up. My mother wanted the hymn 'Peace Like a River. ('It is Well with My Soul') Perhaps that's what she would have wished for my Dad's restless spirit - or perhaps for herself in her constant attempts to soften his rough edges.

"And you, Aldie, what would you want to include?"

I hadn't thought of what I'd like. I'm so used to being on the inquiring side of that question. "Perhaps a bit of remembrance time, Rick. I'd like to have 'the last word' for my Dad."

I chuckled a little. I recall that the word *eulogy* literally meant 'good word.' "I'd like to have the last 'good word' about my Dad,' which would, of course, remember a man, who, despite his view of the world, tried to cope with this life and maybe never realized he was a child of the Creator Father. My relationship with Dad worked its way toward grace. Despite his reserved judgment for my having become a priest in the Episcopal Church, he loved me in his own way. That was the peace I sought for myself. I'd want to share that we all are seeking the love we want from our parents, but sometimes we have to discern the love we can realistically have. My father and I never said 'I love you' - it just wasn't on our father-son landscape. But there were times when 'love' surfaced without condition. When he got me the job at Churchill Downs, he had told one of the trainers *'I'm proud of the boy. He's got a good head on his shoulders.'* The trainer had told me that and I reveled in it for years. Later after my ordination into the priesthood, which my Dad refused to attend, he told my Aunt Jean, *'I'm not a church-goer, but any church he serves will be fortunate to have him.'*

I reveled in hearing that from her, although I would have loved hearing it from him. I knew that wouldn't happen. The sadness for me was that I never told my old man that I proudly watched him doing his job at Churchill. He was faithful to the racing industry at one of the most prestigious tracks in the country. I would enjoy hearing him talk about a particular horse in the starting gate and whether he thought it had a crack at the Triple Crown.

Love between a father and a son is one of those iconic images of American life right out of a Norman Rockwell painting. But when both father and son meet each other beyond the stereotypical male model of competitiveness, sports and small talk, is very uncommon. Should Beautiful Dawn and I ever have a son, I had already envisioned a relationship of open hugging and verbal expressions of meaningfulness and where saying 'I love you, Son' was like breathing in and out.

The visitation at Donohue's was sparse throughout the day that Thursday. The weather had again turned dicey and by afternoon, it was snowing pretty heavily in Newtown Square. Family came by, aunts and uncles, our neighbors, including the Williston's two doors down from Mom and Dad. Some of Mom's 'Red Hat Society' ladies came by (yes, they wore their hats, having come from their luncheon meeting.). One of the ladies attempted to bring into the funeral home their mascot 'Little Punkin', a miniature Dachshund with a red ribbon bow around her neck and pink booties. But Donohue's gently but firmly said 'no' to animals in the funeral home.

"Molly Seaver loves our 'Little Punkin'" she insisted.

"Little Punkin!" my mother cried out as she saw the yipping little critter through the open doorway. She ran past Ken, one of the assistants and grabbed 'Little Punkin' and proceeded to shower kisses all over it, it's little tongue enjoying my Mom's rouge.

"Mrs. Seaver, no offense, but we're not permitted to bring animals in here," Ken said with a firm but kind notation. Mom frowned at him and then surrendered:

"Oh, all right Ken.... oh, cute baby!" she said with affection to the little dog. "OK, Mildred, let's go outside. Mean ol' funeral home!"

Grief is a difficult thing!

Dawn remained close throughout the visitation day. She held my hand often as I stood with folks by Dad's open casket. The folks at Donohue had done an amazing job of crafting my father's dead body into 'lifelike' likeness. It's not classic art, but it is an experienced artistry to transform a dead body into life-likeness. Good morticians are creative with their embalming skills. I don't fault them, because it is therapeutic for loved ones' last images of their family member to see an image of peace and rest. On the other hand, I've seen some botched mortuary that made some family members cringe.

I'd remind folks, "From my faith perspective, of course, Dad's not in there," I'd remind those who asked me, "not in *that* body wearing *that* suit as if he was going to jump out and start whistling Dixie. He's left that body and it will decompose. But I can only trust that in whatever way God makes it happen - and I don't have a clue- Kenneth Edward Seaver, Jr., will transition into a new body suitable for whatever lies ahead." Dawn was particularly interested in that suggestion.

I certainly don't have the last word on this. Many have written about it. St. Paul did in his epistle to the people of Corinth in their wild religious practices and thoughts about life and death. Paul declares these kaki coils of ours are 'corruptible,' which I take to mean 'aren't worth a damn' when life can't sustain them any longer. My Dad's lungs from years of smoking must have looked like burnt charcoaled meat; 'corrupted' because the body *is* corruptible. Smoking certainly corrupted his.

Whatever resurrection is or isn't, it will be beyond the abyss of time and space. I am just imagining from my perspective that God must hand us a new set of duds to put on for the big heavenly party. Scholarship and biblical narrative aside, everything is up for grabs on this. I'd like to think I'll be forever 30 years of age and built like a virile athlete fit for the Olympics. I'd like to think we're more than space dust floating around in the outer reaches of the cosmos - that God's clever gifts of love and life will be worked out in us beyond the limits of this earthly experiment. I'd like to think we live beyond death in whatever form it turns out to be. It's probably the most popular topic we *never* talk about.

One of my Confirmation students came by for the visitation time, Mindy McGyver (Bob's granddaughter), and asked me point blank:

"Fr. Seaver, where is heaven?"

"Uh, good question, Mindy. And I've asked myself that too —actually many times. 'Where' is hard to pinpoint, but I believe it's wherever 'Love' (capital 'L') is complete and unconditional and embraces others. Sometimes when you really care about someone and time seems to stand still, that's at least a kind of heaven on earth. But most of all, I believe it's where God's love is as real as life itself."

"Oh, "she responded with a curious look on her face. "So, you think it's possible there might be a heaven here on earth?"

"Yes, it's possible. The truth is, Mindy, life is still a mystery... life, death, forever - you know, as we've been chatting in Catechetical Class. And it's a good mystery to continue to trust. I think we have glimpses in this world of heaven that are worth noticing."

Hank Byrd, Dad's longtime bowling buddy, stopped by. Dad bowled until the time of his first heart attack, about a year after his retirement and before he and Mom moved to West Chester. Each Saturday morning, he and Hank and two other buddies would meet at McDonald's for what they called 'their bullshit session'- griping about government, economy, etc. And then go over to Ardmore to Wynnewood Lanes and bowl until 11 a.m. Wynnewood was a special place. Back in 2006, it won the 'Best of Philly' Main Line award for bowling alleys.

"Ken Seaver, you ol' son-of-gun!" Hank gestured patting my father's arm.

He turned and looked at me. "Your Dad was a helluva guy, Aldie. I will sure miss him!"

Hank had been faithful in visiting my father in the hospital and at home following his second heart attack. My Mom would say that Dad would light up when Hank would come through the door. They'd talk politics (both die-hard Republicans) and sports (both die hard Eagles/Flyers/Phillies fans). Then Hank did something unexpected. He leaned over the casket and kissed my Dad on the forehead and began to weep. "Aw, Kenny. Damn it. Say a prayer for the Eagles next season. "I put my hand on his back and rubbed it a little. He had a flannel shirt with a tie on - not exactly a fashion plate that Hank! He stood back up and took out his handkerchief and wiped his eyes. Then he wrapped his arms around me real tight and without looking at me or saying a word, turned and left Donohue's. I realized at that moment that Hank shared something with me that my Dad and I had *never* shared - *a hug*. It was tempting to think maybe vicariously, whatever mystery lies beyond the fringes of life and death, that maybe... just maybe Dad and I were sharing our first father and son embrace.

The Service would be Saturday morning at 11 o'clock at Holy Trinity Episcopal with Fr. Rick in charge. Helen McFarley, organist at All Saints agreed to play. She was quite gracious about it and even offered to bring along her granddaughter, Penelope, a voice major at Westminster Choir College, New Jersey, to sing my Mom's only request, *'Ave Maria'*. Usually reserved for weddings, and things Catholic, I was a little amused by the request, but who was I to argue with my mother at this hour of her grief.

"Well," Dawn mused, "she did endure a lot with your father, Aldie. Maybe this is her 'last word.'" I laughed and agreed.

The day of the funeral saw additional snow accumulation of 1-2 inches. This was one wintry January! Traffic was light on the West Chester Pike. A limo from Donohue's picked us up at Mom and Dad's house at 10:11 and dropped us off in front the church doors at 10:30. I've never liked limos or the statement they try to portray, but Mom insisted. A few kind souls had gathered already and some women from both All Saints and Holy Trinity had already arrived to set up the luncheon.

The crowd at five minutes before the service was decent. Holy Trinity is a rather contemporary A-frame, stoned-faced building with a beautiful circular-shaped Narthex entrance. The walks were cleared and easily accessible. Some folks from All Saints greeted us as we were escorted to the fellowship room reserved for families. Fr. Rick looked seasonally ornate with his Epiphany stole and images of three kings and a star beautifully woven into the fabric. Helen was playing stirring organ prelude music (as I had requested). I detest the schmaltzy stuff. My sister Allison loves schmaltzy -the schmaltzier the better. I figured since I had requested very little for the service, I could request music such as 'A Mighty Fortress'....'Joyful, Joyful We Adore Thee.' from Beethoven's Ninth Symphony and 'Jesu, Joy of Man's Desiring'... I wanted Bach and Handel. In death, let there be life - let there be stirring confidence that God is the creator and we are the creatures. I believe our lives are ultimately in a divine embrace. Ken Seaver would not have been turned away at Heaven's gate. He'd often wonder whether that would be possible because he had a grim view of religion's 'pie in the sky promises.' He never asked my opinion. I would've suggested: 'Dad, The Guy Upstairs has a mercy that we could hardly fathom.'

Dawn and I sat together hand in hand. During Fr. Rick's homily, she put her head on my shoulder. I knew that some measure of her own grief over the loss of her dear Grandmother Wilma had been welling up inside her ever since my Dad died. Grief is cumulative. One loss reminds us of another. We go through this life holding on to one another, because it's all we can do in the face of loss or when tragedy occurs. I looked over at my mother. There were no tears, just a blank stare. Forty-five years of marriage - sometimes it was an embattled union. They fought often and at times I wondered how they could possibly have survived those years. And yet, for all my father's idiosyncrasies, she would have done anything for him. When the chips were down and one of them was ailing, they were two people really in love. When my mother had her hysterectomy (back in the days when they were five days in the hospital), I was at Temple deep into my studies. But on visits to her room, I watched my father sit by her bed and hold her hand. They were inseparable.

"Geez, Hon, get better. I'm tired of Campbell's in the can," he'd tell her. I knew what that meant. As condescending as it may have sounded to some, it really meant, *'I miss you Hon... come home soon.'* My Dad was a little like Archie Bunker, but a little skinnier.

My sister Allison was very tearful through the service. She was never one to hold back her emotions. Her husband Will had his hand around her shoulder and at times she leaned against him. Allison was the daughter who was always second-guessing whether her father really loved her. I observed along the path of our youth (I'm six years older), that Allison spent an inordinate amount of time trying to please my Dad. And sometimes she was just flat out disappointed that 'Daddy' didn't pay attention to her. It isn't any wonder that Will, the love of her life, married previously, is ten years older and somewhat like a father figure. Will was a much softer version of Ken Seaver. Allison had always been the 'pleaser'... the 'earner' (she had to earn her father's graces). In school, her grades were always higher than mine, her achievements stellar. She was always the 'top' of anything she did -cheerleading, writing, playing the clarinet in the school orchestra and, not the least, swimming competition. She did everything well, except getting the affection and affirmation she needed from 'Daddy.' Also, not surprising, Allison sometimes sparred with my Mother as if competing for my father's attention. What family dynamics! In these later years, she was doing better with it, having sought out some individual counseling with an excellent woman therapist in Philadelphia. So, much to her credit, Allison's grief was pretty open.

Fr. Rick finished the homily and then invited me to come and share a eulogy. I came forward and spent just a few seconds scanning the attendees.

"Never one for lack of words, I do come here without anything written or prepared. I suppose that I am speaking for myself, but for my dear sister, Allison, I say that we loved our father. To be sure, he was a curmudgeon at times and not one to express a lot of affection. But neither Allison nor I had a worry for want as we grew up. Living in Louisville, Kentucky early on, we watched Dad work hard to provide for all of us, alongside my dear Mom, Molly, whom we thank for her long-suffering care for Dad and for all of us." I looked at her and said

.... We love you, Mom!

My Dad and I had contentious moments along the way –probably as many sons and fathers do. I'm sure he would have preferred that I not become an Episcopalian priest. I know that, because he tried to talk me out of it a number of times. But our journey can be summed up as 'moving toward grace.' I believe God's grace is as mysterious as life and death. Somehow as messy as life can be here, we do come out on the receiving end of limitless grace. I'm not sure if Dad was always convinced about that, but somewhere within the deep roots of my own faith... and a kind of hunch about the old curmudgeon, I think he believed it. Nevertheless, a homecoming has happened. A prodigal has been welcomed at the gate. The robe has been placed around his shoulders, and the ring upon his finger and sandals upon his feet. And one amazing feast is going on. On behalf of my sister, Allison, my dear Mom, Molly Seaver, and the rest of our family, we say 'Thank you' for being mindful of us and for continued prayers.

The Committal Service and burial were held at Arlington Cemetery - not the one in Virginia of course, but in Drexel Hill on State Road. I asked Fr. Rick to remind folks they were invited back to Holy Trinity for lunch and fellowship. He didn't, so I gave the announcement before the benediction.

As Fr. Rick finished the benedictory words at the chilly January graveside, my sister Allison suddenly rushed to the casket and draped over it and cried, "Oh Daddy, I loved you so much!" Will tried to hold her, but she seemed inconsolable. It was almost like she was going to go down into that pit before the dirt was laid over him until he said: *'I love you, Ally girl!'*

Then I began to cry. My Mom burst into tears. And we were off to the races. Dawn embraced me, and she started crying. Then

Allison turned and put her arms around my mother and they held each other. (That was long overdue!) Allison's children started crying and her poor husband Will had his arms around his whole family. It was a chain reaction. Will was the only one - bless his heart -who felt he had to be stoic and not cry.

Chapter Ten

FLORIDA RETURN AND UNEXPECTED VISIT

Pull back, Grey Shroud, that of late imposed your pall upon my spirit! Death made its claim and now days have passed since Earth yielded one spent life. Is there no light so bold, so bright or morning so brilliant as to raise these spirits?

I waited... weighted down... waited and sleepless until morning light came bursting through the pall of grey covering my salty tears. The journey will call me from the night of death to earth's new light;

And there I sprang from grim shadow to light and life and hastened my journey once more.

- Aldron G. Seaver - During a sleepless night after his father's funeral

We decided to resume our trip southward Saturday morning with an early nonstop flight to Jacksonville, FL, on USAirways. Everything was planned and completed on-line, including picking up a rental car at JAX and driving to the coast for a couple of days at Fernandina Beach on Amelia's Island. The plane was late getting into Philadelphia International with weather in Boston causing travel delays, so our departure was about an hour and a half later than it should have been. Once airborne, though, we were about two hours from our destination. The coastline approach to Jacksonville was stunning with blue skies and miles of beach. In our final approach to JAX, I pointed out to Dawn Amelia Island and even Fernandina Beach, our first destination in Florida after landing. When we stepped out of the airport to pick up or rental, the air was warm and the sunshine intoxicating and so inviting. From the airport, we were only about 45 minutes to the coast. We had made reservations two nights at 'The Fairbanks House,' considered by Fodor's and Frommer's as well as 'Southern Living' as 'one of the best romantic escapes in Florida.'

We were greeted at the steps of 'The Fairbanks House' by the resident cat of Theresa, our hostess, who went out of her way to make us feel as if we were the only guests staying there. (It turns out we *were* the only guests!) She showed us around the house and then invited us to our upstairs front room, 'The Tapestry Room' with its huge four-poster bed. Beautiful Dawn just fell in love with the place's charm and amenities and chatted with Theresa about what to see around Fernandina Beach and the rest of Amelia Island - referred to as 'Florida's First Coast.' In the 'It's a Small World' category, Beautiful Dawn discovered that Theresa knew some of her family in Maryland and could talk about certain acquaintances.' We decided to enjoy some tea and crumb cake on the porch before walking downtown Fernandina Beach - about a ten-minute walk from The Fairbanks House. The warmth of the late afternoon sun was such a pleasant contrast to what we left in our Philly area winter. The stroll led us eventually to the pier to watch the sun set on the Amelia River. A later- afternoon Ferry from the Cumberland Sound with passengers from St. Mary's, GA, arrived. Many were bicyclists who had ventured out that day from Fernandina Beach to enjoy some cycling on the more primitive Cumberland Island to the north. We enjoyed the ambiance of Brett's Waterway Café and watched the sun disappear and enjoy some native Florida seafood, especially the taste of mullet.

There were thunderstorms making the rounds the first night at 'The Fairbanks'. Florida storms have nothing to bounce off such as our hills provide in the north. So, the thunder was louder and the lightning brighter and the rain more torrential. You get the feeling of a weather Armageddon just settling down on top of you. Of course, it made for cozy cuddling, snuggling and lovemaking in our four-poster bed, dim lights around us and the smell of scented candles burning. As we held each other and enjoyed our always gentle and sensuous kisses, we listened to the storm slip away into the distant. It was easy to segue into the most beautiful rest that I had experienced since my father's death. I was aware that my sleep had been unsettled in the past week, frequently awaking and thinking about my father. But this rest was very welcoming and sustaining.

Father Redux

However, a vivid dream came somewhere in the night. My father entered our Tapestry Room and was sitting at the edge of our poster bed, smoking a cigar, which isn't allowed anywhere in the Fairbanks! I suppose it was tolerated in my dream. Dad seemed to be giving me a fit about misleading him about this 'heaven thing.' I don't recall having a conversation with him about 'this heaven thing!' I lay there mystified that I was speaking to my recently deceased father. He had on his familiar grey cardigan sweater and plaid red shirt. Suddenly we were transported to the edge of an enormous cliff overlooking the most brilliant lights in an indigo sky that I could ever imagine.

"What's not to like about this, Dad? It's crazy beautiful!"

I looked around and felt my own heart racing at this panorama. It seemed like it was night and yet there was beauty and tranquility at every movement of my eye.

He took a deep puff from his cigar and looked at me and looked out:

'It's OK, but they don't have TV and the Phillies. Geez, Aldie, I miss the Phillies!'

I looked at the cigar: 'How did you get that cigar, Dad? I can't even fathom smoking on this... this wherever we are!'

Dad went on: Yeah, it's great! Oh, the cigar isn't real. They tell me that because I smoked so much on The Heartshadow Side, the habit sort of follows me around.'

Heartshadow side? I wondered.

But no one can smell it. See? He breathed into my face, but I felt nothing, nor did I smell anything.

'Christ, Aldie, the place is so sanitary. I get to craving a mess now and then. But it's the same temperature every day, the same brilliant sun with billowy clouds, same beautiful flowers. It rains in the afternoon and out comes rainbows... I mean – it's not that everything isn't beautiful. It is – unlike anything I ever laid my eyes on! But... I don't know..." My Dad is looking away as if he were lost.

'What are you doing with yourself here?' I asked him.

Dad is animated: 'Watching people move about. One guy told me he transported himself to Nepal. I thought, 'Jesus, why would you want to go to Nepal?' He paused. "I miss my chair, Aldie. I miss your mother. I can't seem to penetrate her Heartshadow. You... you were easy! You must have some spirit layer or whatever the hell they call it. I don't know. It's fascinating – the whole thing. I just miss the world as I knew it.'

I laughed. "But you complained about 'the world as you knew it' all the time, Dad. Even the Phillies and Eagles. You'd yell and curse at the TV. You hated Democrats and liberals... you even hated that I became a priest." Wow, it takes a weird dream for me to tell the Old Man how I felt about this!

He looked down, tipping his cigar of excess ash: "Yeah, okay... okay, I know... Geez, Aldie, I'm sorry already." He put his cigar down and placed his hand on my shoulder (Another first!) "You did the right thing" He looked at me and then scanned the panorama again."

"Thanks, Dad!" I was amazed that I was receiving a fatherly blessing from beyond!

"The creepy thing about being here is that the feelings I had on that so-called Heartshadow side just kind of hang on me like morning dew. Hell, it sticks like glue, Aldie!"

I looked back at him: "It sounds like you're still stuck on this... whatever Heartshadow side, Dad. Why don't you get yourself an Astral Spirit Guide?"

Still puffing away, he shook his head:

"I don't know, they keep asking me about having one. I'm kind of curious, but I just want my comfy chair and TV. Christ, I miss your mother, Aldie!" He put his cigar out (where?!) and looks down pensively.

"There are things I wish I had said to your mother – many things – I guess I'm still... "

Suddenly my late Dad seemed to turn his head and fade out, like a TV reception being lost. I swear I thought I smelled his cigar when he faded! I felt a chill up and down my spine, a tugging between wanting to stay in this dream sequence and wanting to get back to my bed. I awoke and realized I was still *in* my bed! Dawn was resting on my shoulder and deep in sleep. But where had I been? Had I stepped across the abyss to the mysterious 'Other Side?' I thought that happened only when someone was dying. I had heard about NDE's

—Near Death Experiences, but I wasn't dying. Was I an interloper in my father's new existence? Why did he say that my *Heartshadow side* was easy to penetrate? What is a 'heartshadow.' I've been trying to figure that one out ever since!

Our conversation had been so vivid, like Dad was really at the foot of our four-poster bed. I lay there wondering about such dreams —what happens in REM mode and deep sleep, whether we take journeys into what some call the 'Astral Plane.' I have no idea, but dear old Dad seemed a bit lost out there —wherever 'there' was. I thought: Is it possible consciousness and memory can connect us across the abyss of two realities? Or was this just a crazy dream? I looked at the clock. It was 1:23 a.m. It took me an inordinate amount of time to get back to sleep.

When I awoke at 8 a.m., Dawn was already in the shower. I gazed out through the large window of our Tapestry Room. It was overcast with some evidence of blue skies. I had slept straight through since that vivid dream about Dad. I still wondered whether we do at times in sleep mode visit that Other Side, or whatever it might be, and whether we get visits at times from those who are, like my father was most of his life, still restless. He wasn't especially a 'people person,' except when he was around his bowling buddies. My mother used to complain that it was difficult to carry on a conversation with 'your father' that didn't include bitching about those 'damned Democrats' or 'the world is going to hell in a hand basket', 'goddam liberals' and Pennsylvania politics. You'd never want to get Dad started on Democrats in Pennsylvania. He believed the worst thing that ever happened in Pennsylvania politics was the election of James Buchanan, a Pennsylvanian, as President of the United States. Dad knew where I stood and it's a wonder he didn't disown me!

When Dawn appeared from the bathroom, she was in a white terry-cloth robe and a white towel wrapped around her head.

"Good morning, my Beautiful Dawn. You're an image of dazzling white!"

She smiled and crawled in bed with me. She smelled of such fragrant bath oils and her hair, too, with a citrus-like shampoo scent. We enjoyed an extended 'Good morning!' kiss.

"This place is so amazingly beautiful, Aldie! Magnificent inside and out. The bathroom is so elegant. The shower was so soft and the bath oils. Mm. Let's buy it!'

I chuckled.

Then I began sharing my dream about my Dad. "It was so vivid, Sweetheart. I think the old man is restless beyond the perimeters of this earthly side. I wonder if crossovers between this world and the next are possible?"

"That's amazing, Aldie! Now we both have had dreams beyond the perimeters. If I were a woman of faith, I'd think your Holy One had been communicating."

I showered and as I was toweling off, I wondered whether the phrase 'heartshadow side' might indicate that, from 'The Other Side,' our former selves leave a trace of our essence (heart, soul etc.) for all those astral folks to penetrate us, as if they were shadows. Is it like catching Wi-Fi on someone's computer? A 'shadow' is usually something that follows us around as light shines on us. It seems attached to us. Our hearts and souls beyond our bodies must have some spiritual marker for those on the other side - a heart shadow someone can see or experience. Then I wondered, why some and not all. It is all speculative. Do we carry with us a trail of existence that lingers for a while in life after life? Why was mine easy to penetrate and my mother's not? Or... maybe it was all just a dream and that's that!

The sun had begun to cross the wooden floor. The lacey curtains produced beautiful shadow patterns over our bed. I had chosen denim pants and a mock white turtleneck top. The day had promised to be in the seventies in northern and central Florida. This warm front was even making temperatures mild in the Philadelphia area. Dawn had chosen beige shorts and a shaggy, floral print top. It is not for nothing that I sometimes call her 'Beautiful' Dawn.

And, wow! Our hostess, Theresa, had put together a veritable Florida breakfast with coffee to die for, fresh squeezed OJ - so welcoming! The scrambled eggs and French toast combination with delicious Florida citrus on the side brought a hearty *bravissimo!*

After breakfast, we rented bikes and rode down to the wharf and enjoyed Fernandina's morning ambiance, watching fishing vessels trolling in and out, looking at the old rusted rig down at the end of the long wharf. We then rode through the residential area, enjoying the stately old homes along the way. When the shops opened, we secured our bikes and ambled along Atlantic Avenue. There was an Irish Shop 'Celtic Charm' on Atlantic Avenue we both thoroughly enjoyed. It spawned a conversation about one of our 'bucket list' items: a trip to the Emerald Isle. Beautiful Dawn has a cousin there and she's always wanted to see it. Exhausting the shopping details for a Saturday morning, we decided to ride our bikes out to Ft. Clinch.

Ft. Clinch is part of the Florida State Park system. Although no battles were actually fought at Ft. Cinch, it was garrisoned during both the Civil and Spanish-American wars. During the 1930s, the Civilian Conservation Corps began preserving and rebuilding many of the structures of the abandoned fort. We learned that daily tours with period re-enactors bringing garrison life at the fort up close and personal.

On the return road from Ft. Clinch, we enjoyed viewing the Amelia Island Lighthouse, and then took the beach road to enjoy the ambiance of the Atlantic Ocean. Our legs were tired when we finally returned to 'The Fairbanks.'

At refreshment break, I called my mother to let her know we were safely in Florida and to just check in on her. Although she seemed eager to let the funeral and reception go, I knew that her feelings were fragile and that she missed my father. The conversation seemed subdued. I wasn't going to share my dream with her. That would have been a bit overwhelming.

"Your father had a good heart, Aldie! Not the physical one… but underneath that crust was a softer person than he let on."

"I know, Mother. I know. It took me a while to recall that. I was just such an impressionable teen."

I realized as our conversation went on that my mother was weeping. I was glad that her grief was being felt. Their married life so often was torturous. Mother carried the scars of a repressed wife. There were times I knew she longed for the love that he was not able to give her. I recall once she told me that they had long since abandoned sex. Dad would always forget her birthday and their anniversary. They never exchanged gifts at Christmas and put all the focus on 'the kids' and the grandkids. They never went on vacations, although once Mother had taken a trip to Nashville, TN, with the Red Hat Society to attend a Grand Ol' Opry performance. Dad fussed about it the whole time she was gone, even though she had prepared meals and had frozen them for him the five days she was gone. He complained about having to thaw them out and heat them up. My sister Allison had to remind him of her instructions how to turn the oven on for heat-up's. Dad was totally helpless on his own! No doubt he programmed himself that way. Many married men act as if they are married to their mothers.

"It's OK, Mom. I know you miss Dad.... What's that?" She had wondered through her tears whether I thought my father was in heaven... or not. "Mom... I just trust that God's grace is much bigger than we can imagine... you know? Dad was a product of his generation. There are things I'm certain he chose not to learn or just wasn't capable of learning. I'm sure I have much that I need to learn or maybe have resisted learning myself. The world seems like one big distraction, Mom. Dad had a few bad habits…"

"I thought we were going to have to bury him in that LazyBoy! And honestly, Mom, so often I wanted him to go somewhere with you... take you on a vacation or something."

She chuckled again and recalled: "Oh, I know. We had arguments about that. The Red Hat Society had a bus trip to Niagara Falls for ladies and their spouses or friends. He just killed it with his 'what if's'... what if my colon acts up, what if the weather gets bad... what if the driver is some wacko communist..." She sighed. "I just gave up on it."

I sighed with her. "Well, anyway, you're so right... he had a good heart, so to speak. But life just hedged him in with a lot of settled in ways. It can happen to all of us. Maybe now you can do some of things you've wanted to do all your life, Mom."

"Maybe… maybe."

I knew this call was important. She needed her son to just grieve with her a little. It was a lonely existence and she was seeking to express some of those raw feelings – the regrets, the anger, the brokenness. She wasn't saying 'I know you're in Florida, however....', but I knew that's what the conversation was leading to. The years of marriage were like an old, familiar blanket wrapped around her. It the familiarity of it all, she missed him.

The conversation wound down with Mom's: '*Well I hope you're having a good time, Aldie*', I offered:

"We're enjoying it. I love you, Mom, and we'll talk more."

"Yes, let's do that, please." she sighed.

"Bye, Mom."

I told Dawn, I had a twinge of guilt leaving the day after my Dad's funeral. I realized I needed to get away and she needed to get away and that loomed larger than concern for my Mom. Although my sister Allison is like a 'hoverer-protector' and assured me she would check in on Mom.

"She's got a good support system, Aldie", Dawn reminded me. "The Red Hat Society had all kinds of plans to bring food and chatter."

She patted me on the cheek, "She's going to be OK, Love."

We continued on our biking trail from Ft. Clinch and past the Amelia Lighthouse and back to town.

That evening we enjoyed cocktails and snacks back at the Fairbanks House compliment of Theresa and Bill, both owners. A new couple from Tennessee had registered that day. Cocktails were followed by our reservations at '*29 South*', located at 29 South Third St. It seemed very unpretentious. It was kind of a chic neighborhood bistro with classic world cuisine served with a bit of modern twist. Sharing our entree, we chose a Dekalb Family Farm Pork Chop on Macaroni Gratin with warm Blackberry Preserves and a Grilled Heart of Romaine Salad with Maytag Blue Vinaigrette. We gave '29 South' four and a half stars!

The temperatures had remained mild in northern Florida for this time of the year. There were gentle breezes around us as we sat on the porch and enjoyed the sunset and some green tea.

"I'm still thinking about your dream, Aldie. Do you really think your father visited you?"

"I don't know, Sweetheart. I have to admit I've been thinking about it all day. Part of it is spooky. Another part makes me wonder whether there are cosmic 'crossovers' -you know? Do you believe in Near Death Experiences, Love?"

"A couple of nursing friends and I have read about it and talked about it. There seem to be enough of recorded information about it to get even physicians' attention. Jenny McFadden told me she encountered it with a supposed DOA after a traffic accident outside of West Chester. The woman was in her seventies and was revived in the ER. When she was recouping in the ICU, she asked Jennifer stop in and began describing in vivid detail the so-called 'tunnel light' and seeing the Christ-like figure with indigo eyes standing in front of her and how she felt the most overwhelming peace she had ever felt. The woman described things to Jennifer that she had never even imagined... like how the Christ figure navigated around effortlessly with this caring person. But his face was so filled with love and warmth unlike any she had experienced on earth. Jennifer remembered how incomparably beautiful the woman was. She saw butterfly-like animations all about her of so many rich colors. And there were people in some kind of transport, but they weren't like automobiles. The woman told Jennifer that she felt such an amazing peace, that she wanted to continue.... Uh, like visiting some beautiful place on earth and never wanting to leave there. When the comforting voice said, 'It is not your time,' in such beautiful words... not so verbal, but almost like someone reassuring you... the woman protested something like 'No, please let me stay here!', but she found herself being drawn back to the light over the gurney and people hovering over her. She heard someone say, 'We've got a pulse!' And she was back. It freaked Jennifer out and every time we get together, we talk about it.

"I believe there's something to it. I don't think this earthly scramble is all there is," I speculated.

The next day, Dawn and I left Amelia Island for the trip down to Orlando to register for my preaching conference at Marriott World Center. It was another brilliantly blue sky over Florida's First Coast. We took the southern 1A route across Nassau Sound through Ft. George Island and the Timucuan Ecological Historical Preserve and then past Mayport Naval Station (Route 105) Heckscher Rd., finally connecting to I-295 around Jacksonville and I-95 on our way southward. It would take about two hours to reach Orlando.

The annual conference is usually held at the Marriott World Center, an enormous monolith of a hotel across I-4 from Disney

World. The Center was capable of holding a number of conventions at the same time. By the numbers of folks checking in, there must have been quite a few. We already missed the intimacy of The Fairbanks House at Amelia Island. Our World Center room was on the 12th floor overlooking Downtown Disney and with some view of EPCOT in the background. Beautiful Dawn had never been to Florida and already her view of the sprawling area was piquing her interest in Walt Disney World - 'The Happiest Place on Earth.'

I shared with Dawn: "Tomorrow, after the morning classes, we will have the remainder of the day free, Darling. I'm going to introduce you to the 'World,' whose mission statement is four words: *'to make people happy"*

"I can't wait, Aldie. I feel like a kid already."

The evening buffet was a mingling of clergy and some of their spouses. Most people assumed that Beautiful Dawn and I were married, although neither of us were wearing wedding bands. Instead we wore 'friendship rings' we shared with one another the Christmas after Beautiful Dawn's Grandma Wilma had died. We had realized we needed something to express the love we had found and yet agreed it was a little awkward being an unmarried clergy and attending a clergy conference with a girlfriend. I wondered whether some of my Episcopal clergy colleagues might report back to F. U. Frank. Do I sound paranoid? F. U. had been happily absent for most of my two years at All Saints – apart from a few administrative calls and 'hello's' at Diocesan meetings. Rumor had it that he was being evaluated by the Philadelphia Diocese for possible transfer based on some typical *f.u.'s.'* - a term a few of us in the diocese use when he grates on us. You can figure out what it means.

The speakers the next day included Dr. Tom Long, our preaching track professor from Atlanta, GA. I've admired Tom for some time and count him as one of the top preachers in the country. I've also appreciated his articles in my favorite 'trade' magazine *The Christian Century.* The other morning speaker, Dr. John Dominic Crossan, 'Dom' as we know him affectionately, wowed us with his work on the antecedents of The Lord's Prayer. The morning sped quickly by in 'The Palms' banquet room. There were 240 gathered from all across the country made up of varied denominations - most of us, a frozen bunch (down from the tundra of the Northeast and Midwest), reeling and recharging from the demands of Christmas and already anticipating Easter. Ministry can easily wear clergy types down physically and emotionally. Now with my father's death and burial just few days past, I felt exhausted. Florida was a good diversion from the rigors of organized religion. Or as I like to say, '*disorganized* religion.'

The next day, I rushed out of the session and found Beautiful Dawn sitting in the atrium reading a book. She didn't see me at first, but I saw her. She was wearing a red skirt with yellow bees on it and a beautiful flower-printed yellow blouse. Where did this angel descend from?

"Good morning, Beautiful. Do you come here often?"

"Why, are you flirting with me, Reverend?" She looked at me with a teasing smile, quickly bookmarking her page. She put her book down and stood up and gave me a slow kiss.

"I've missed you this morning, Aldie. Did you get breakfast?"

"Yes, Love, hope you did, too."

"I ate too much. Their breakfast buffet over there is gargantuan!" She pointed to the other side of the lobby.

Dawn had enjoyed indulging in a little shopping at some of the World's Center huge gift shops. She proudly pulled out a beautiful and smart looking lavender cashmere sweater."

"Can't wait to see you in that, Darling. I imagine you in an off-white or beige skirt. Mm."

We put our personal items - her shopping trove, my book, iPad and Bible in the security boxes assigned to us near the Concierge station and left with cameras in tow for 'The World' and Dawn's first step into Magic Kingdom. There had been an early morning rain, but the sun was making its way through the clouds. It's how you can imagine 'The World.'

The funny thing about Disney 'World.' is, of course, it's really not 'the world,' that is, the one we know every day. It's another 'world' we long for, imagine. When you pay the park entrance fee and step into that world wondering how spending so much money on a park entrance fee could 'make you happy.' The parking fee at the Magic

Kingdom is $20.00. The entrance fee for a one-day pass for two people is $290. Dawn flipped out over that.

"Aldie, I had no idea it costs so much! That seem so excessive."

"I know, Darling. But, it's the 'world' within the 'World.' You could easily spend that much or more on a rock concert ticket or a Mayweather fight or an expensive dinner or on a new coat. And let's say they have twenty thousand go through the turnstile today, they will have made over 2 million dollars today – not to mention the foodies and souvenirs, etc. So (we now were going through the turnstile ourselves) it's the 'world' of economics within the 'World' of Disney's magic.

Walking into the Main Street of the Magic Kingdom, Dawn stopped in amazement. "Oh my God, Aldie!" For the next half hour as we roamed around, there were all kind of superlatives coming from my Beautiful Dawn. Her little point-n-shoot was clicking away.

I reminded her that in this 'World', you do find yourself in a kind of childlike euphoria, which is normal. Adults might be embarrassed to admit that. You do smile more, laugh a lot and marvel at all the colors and kindness from the staff and it's all the great fun. You get high on good feelings walking down Main Street in the Magic Kingdom, gazing up at that Magic Kingdom castle patterned after Mad King Ludwig's Bavarian castle in southern Germany. It's crazy wonderful! You want to get close to the Disney characters as if they really are who they are and not some pint- sized teen sweating profusely behind the persona and wishing you'd drop dead. Of course, I'm being facetious. They're getting paid to make you happy regardless of what they may feel.

Dawn, whose kindness to others is so evident everywhere she goes, was so touched by the Disney mystique. "Aldie, everyone's incredibly friendly, like they can't wait to help you. Gosh, I heard the guy pulling trash whistling and he even said to me, 'Howdy Ma'am!'

"It's their job, Love. Remember their mission statement is four words. *to make people happy.*

On Thursday, however, I skipped out and joined my Beautiful Dawn on an all-day excursion to EPCOT (Experimental Prototype Community of Tomorrow). Disney wanted to create a utopian city of the future. He wanted to build a model community as a home for twenty thousand residents to embody the ideals and values of a self-sustaining community. Disney had hoped this vision would catch on for the rest of the country. An 800 million-dollar project, EPCOT opened in October 1982. On its opening day, one of the photographers looked around and suggested to one of the park attendants. *'Too bad Walt Disney didn't live to see this.'* The park attendant returned:

'Oh, he did see it. That's why it's here!'

If the Magic Kingdom was 'magical' with its childlike spontaneity, EPCOT quivers with its futuristic rides and World Showcase. After paying (I should have looked into the 'park hopper' passes!) we went through the turnstile, we queued up to the almost ageless 'Spaceship Earth' ride taking us from the dawn of civilization to the future with all its animatronic vignettes, followed by Ellen DeGeneres's delightful journey at the 'Universe of Energy' pavilion that took us back to animatronic dinosaurs and first awareness of earth sources of energy - a ride with whole units of perhaps 50 people per ride moving us through imagined pre-civilization all the way to modern modes of energy use and conservation. Following these initial rides, I suggested to Dawn that we make our dinner reservations. We enjoyed the selection possibilities and decided on *'Les Chefs de France'* for a 5:30PM visit. It was warm that Thursday (for the latter part of January), but it was incredibly beautiful in Orlando - low humidity, light breezes, blue skies and white puffy clouds. Walking hand in hand through the World Showcase proved glorious. It required an entire late morning and afternoon to make our way around to each showcase, enjoying especially *'Visions de France'* with its stirring classical French music and breathtaking images of France. We also savored the 'American Adventure Pavilion' with the vocal entourage of American music that precedes a stirring animatronic program of American history. You always leave that pavilion 'proud to be an American.' Other showcases we enjoyed were the ride through Mexico, and the pavilions of Morocco, China, Germany, Italy and Norway. The drumming and dancing energy at the Japanese pavilion always intrigues me. The circle vision tour for Canada was also enjoyable, although I always get a little queasy with circle vision presentations. Some of the funniest theatrics are to be found at the Britain pavilion where taunts at Henry VIII are acted out complete with audience participation.

By the time we arrived at 'Chefs de France' we had walked our legs off. My flat feet and tendonitis were rebelling against any plans to walk further. By now you can guess how Beautiful Dawn and I ordered from the menu of 'Chefs' and you would be correct if you said, 'shared an entree.' Unlike other restaurants we've been to, Madeleine at 'Chefs' didn't even bat an eye.

Merci, I will bring a second plate.

We chose the entree that I can only read in print if I slow down and pronounce it - the *Demi Poulet fermier roti, pommes risolees et tomate grillee.* (half of a roasted chicken, risssole potatoes and grilled tomato.) We chose also to share a glass of *Cabernet Sauvignon.* The elegant setting of 'Chefs de France' created a romantic feel. Dinner music was Debussy's 'Afternoon of a Faun,' *L'apres-midi d'un faune.* We exchanged some smiles and blown kisses and I felt Beautiful Dawn's foot reaching for my pants leg. It was always a sure sign of 'later, stud.' Even after a long day walking around EPCOT, our feet tired and the enjoyment of the day a fleeting memory, Beautiful Dawn could be sensual. Not the least, the wine was a fast-acting elixir for her. She admitted not being given to strong drink, because it affects are quickly. And the shared *Crepe a la pomme et cannelle, glace vanille, caramel jus de pommes* (Crepes filled cinnamon, apple, vanilla ice cream and apple caramel sauce - both paved the way for Beautiful Dawn's psyche to be fixed on making love.

After the fireworks, we were back at the Marriott World Center, she pushed me onto the bed and said she was interested in slow lovemaking with dimmed lights and a few scented candles she had picked up in one of the gift shops. She put on a sheer beige, hip-high nightie that didn't take me long to respond to. With dimmed lights and flickering candles scented with vanilla, I held her with soft kisses and rubbed her back. Her hand reached for me. She had dipped her hand in coconut oil and began to massage me slowly. Our lips were locked as she took my finger to her soft and moist orifice.

"Let's have a baby, Darling!"

Startled, I looked at her for a moment, deep into her eyes.

"Sweetheart, are you... are you sure?" She nodded, smiling:

"By my calculation, it's the perfect time *right now.*"

I continued: "But, you've barely begun your nursing career. And you have to pass your boards for certification."

She smiled: "I can do all of that, Darling, I'm young ... and I'm woman... and having a baby with you at this time of our lives seems... seems so right, ...so beautiful...so us After all Fr. Aldie, you are not getting any younger."

I stopped suddenly. I looked her in the eyes and looked off to the side.

"Aldie?'

I sighed and rolled off of her and sat on the edge of the bed.

"Aldie, I'm sorry, I didn't mean to imply..."

"No it's OK... it's OK Darling. You're right. I sometimes forget that I'm almost 43...and you're 36. I can't deny you wanting a child. I... I..."

She wrapped her arms around me. "Please, Aldie, I shouldn't have reminded you..."

"It's OK, Dawn! You're absolutely right. I *am* getting older. I haven't thought much about our age difference. I do worry sometimes that my libido will run out of steam well before you are ready. And I..."

"Please, Aldie, I wasn't implying that. You know I wouldn't... I never meant to ... Oh, I'm so sorry!!!"

Dawn began to cry and rushed off to the bathroom.

"Dawn, I didn't want to upset you. I just have to think about this baby thing... and...

She shut the bathroom door abruptly and I heard her crying.

Damn! Why did I have to be so sensitive! I went over and knocked on the door. She had locked it.

"Sweetheart, please open so we can talk."

"Aldie, just leave me alone. I need space right now."

I walked back to the bed and crawled under the covers. The WDW fireworks were going on in the distance and I could see the light from our Marriott window. Dawn and I had only one or two tiffs since we had met. I felt empty, embarrassed, guilty. I had momentarily drifted off to sleep, when the bathroom door opened. Dawn turned out all the lights and quietly crawled into bed and reached over to wrap her arms around me. I started apologizing. Quickly she put her finger to my lips.

"Let's just hold each other tonight, Aldie."

She drifted off, snoring in my arms. I lay awake for a long time, imagining myself as a father – a roll I hadn't honestly entertained for quite a while. I knew it would never have happened with Kathy Jones Seaver. We could not even muster an intimate moment, let alone making a pregnancy possible. With Dawn, there was youthful energy, amazing sensuality, which this evening I had successfully sabotaged! Had I allowed her to become a woman of my fantasy, stuck in the pages of pin-up magazines. I'm an Episcopal rector, why would any woman 7 years younger be head over heels in love with a rector anyway?

I soaked my thoughts in self-doubt for a moment. Maybe I was a welcome alternative to her crusty father? Was I a safe and secure fatherly figure who could provide her kindness and care and family love? I realized I had to trust her love for me and not allow self-doubt to invade what we had cultivated. I was capable of fatherhood as much as she was so fit for motherhood. Love like this can bring about life. That's what biology and Eros make possible.

I nodded off. At 4 a.m., I was aware of lying behind my sweet love with an erection that ached, nestled behind her. Eros summoned both of us. I effortlessly eased into her – almost as if she were anticipating my readied phallus. She seemed half awake with moans I heard in quiet tones.

'Oh, Aldie…'

'I love you, Darling.' We moved at first slowly in our dance of intimacy. Her moisture made my movements intense and beckoned me as if I were moving toward an irreversible release. Soon that moment arrived when I let go of any inhibition of my age or ability and jettisoned deep in her. Her moans continued until she quieted and sleepily reached over and kissed me.

I whispered as I withdrew:

"I want us to have a baby, my Beautiful Dawn. I would be so happy to share a life with you."

She kissed me and thanked me several times and then rolled over and fell sleep. It was 4:56 a.m.

Morning

Dawn had awakened and walked into our little living room area there at the Marriott.

'Did I dream what happened last night, Aldie?'

I kissed her and assured her that my whole self was completely connected to her.'

After the last morning session of the Pastors Conference concluded, we checked out of the Marriott and left for a trip eastward along the 'Beeline' Expressway (Route 528) to Cape Canaveral's Kennedy Space Center, where we immersed ourselves into the history of the space program and toured some of the launch pads as well as the enormous VAB (Vehicular Assembly Building), one of the largest buildings per square foot in the world. In the afternoon, we followed I-95 northward for an overnight stay in Daytona Beach at the 'Bahama House' on the ocean.

Among other conversations (and we had many), one my beautiful Dawn just blurted out:

"You know, Aldie, if we are pregnant, I guess we really need to start finishing up our wedding plans, don't you think? You know, first the marriage and then the carriage."

We both had a good laugh.

We approached Daytona Beach's southern end with a drive to one of my favorite lighthouses - Ponce Inlet Light. The skies had brightened over the Atlantic while the high cirrus clouds dotted the inlet. Crossing the Dunlawton Bridge on Route 1A, we would turn right onto South Atlantic Avenue and travel a couple of miles southward to Ponce Inlet Light, located next to a Marine Laboratory, where rescued wild life is restored. after injuries from boat and fishing nets. The lighthouse is one of the most beautiful and one of the tallest along the Atlantic coast (among its rivals: St. Augustine Lighthouse, FL, Tybee Lighthouse near Savannah, GA, St. Simon's Lighthouse, GA and Cape Hatteras Lighthouse, Outer Banks, NC.) There are 175 steps to the top of the lighthouse with breathtaking views of the Atlantic shore. Beautiful Dawn thought she would be OK making her first lighthouse climb. As the passageway narrowed, our legs felt the strain of the climb, but the reward for all of it was stepping out into the top landing (where the Fresnel light rested) and walking around the windy balcony access, amazed at the blue sky and span of the beach northward as well as looking over to Smyrna just south of us. Lighthouses are one of the iconic treasures of America's shores. I loved studying their histories as well as climbing them for their vistas. The wind was so wickedly strong, so we shortened our stay and made the long descent so that we could enjoy some of the history of Ponce Inlet Lighthouse in a wonderful self-guided tour of the museum inside its white picket fence.

It was mid-afternoon as we left the lighthouse and enjoyed an iced tea and shared some crab legs at the Lighthouse Landing across the road from our visit. They have a spacious deck there with great inlet views toward Smyrna. Then we proceeded northward to Daytona Beach to find our lodging. Since this was going to be our only ocean stay in Florida, I had chosen Bahama House, because I had stayed there on previous visits to Florida. They have a wonderful staff and the place is impeccably clean. Every room at the Bahama House has an ocean view. We took our overnight bags to our assigned room on the 12th floor. We sat on the balcony and relaxed for an hour with the breezes and spectacular ocean views and sound of seagulls - all of which invited naps from both of us.

Toward evening, we took the all-important beach walk. Somehow you haven't been to Daytona Beach unless you've done that. The long shadows of beach hotel high rises were evident as we walked the beach. We walked hand in hand with random conversation about our families and life together.

Recollection of Our 'Almost First Lovemaking' Time

We recalled the 'almost' first time we made love. It was after one of my worship services one Sunday back in the early days when Dawn was hesitant to even attend All Saints. One Sunday she decided to attend our 'Relaxed Service'- an abbreviated 11:15 a.m. service of worship based on hymn tunes. Our worship team of guitarist, keyboardist and two vocalists lead the service and most everything about the gathering was informal. I get to go *sans* vestments and roll up my sleeves there. After everyone had left (I'm usually the last one out of the building), Dawn stayed around to help put a few worship items away and turn off lights. As we were leaving, she took my hand.

"I've been thinking about us, Aldie. I'm really...mmm, I'm really so smitten by you."

I returned with: "Trust me, the feeling is mutual. I have to confess that I think about you most all the time."

Stopping and looking me in the eye and putting her hand on my chest, she reached up and kissed me.

"Do you find me attractive?"

"Do I find you attractive? Sweetheart – Holy Moses, I am *so*...attracted to you!" She looked deep into my eyes:

"Are you... are we ready to...mmm..."

She placed her lips on mine with a more sustained kiss. "...to make love?"

"Here, Darling?"

I'm not sure whether we were at the entrance to my office or closer to the Fellowship Room, but all I remember is that suddenly we were fondling each other with abandon. She felt my instant erection and my hand had reached beneath her skirt to feel her soft legs. Our movement now, almost consuming, took us into my office, where I closed the office door and locked it. I moved us toward my desk, which, thankfully wasn't too cluttered and I hoisted her on top of it and she leaned back. She was wearing a white skirt with black polka dots and a soft while blouse. She voluntarily raised her skirt and I began kissing her soft legs ...when suddenly there was a forceful knock on the door.

"Father Aldie?"

Immediately Dawn sat up, straightened out her skirt and pointed to the chair – the one I usually reserve for folks I counsel.

When I unlocked the door and opened the door partially, I could see it was Rick, one of the homeless shelter guys who is a 'frequent flyer' at All Saints seeking handouts and gift coupons to McDonald's. I reminded myself: 'Damn, I forgot to lock the front Nave entrance!'

"Rick, can I see you another time?"

That's when I saw he was pointing a gun at me. I felt blood rush from my head to my stomach.

I had never seen Rick with a gun.

"Uh, Rick, why the gun? You know I've always helped you..."

Beautiful Dawn gasped. Rick was breathing hard.

"I'm in real bad trouble, Fr. Aldie.... *real* bad trouble."

I locked the door and stepped outside and closed the door, so he might not see Beautiful Dawn, when I closed it. But he may have caught a glimpse of her. I mustered up some courage and assertiveness.

"Well, I'm sorry to hear that, Rick, but this isn't the way to tell me about that. Now would you please put that gun away? Let's go over to the lounge and talk about this. You know I've always helped you...why would you bring a gun in here?"

"I shot a man this morning, Fr. Aldie," Rick shuttered fearfully, "and they're looking for me. I heard the sirens. I didn't know where else to go. I'm just feeling jumpy about this. I don't want to harm you, really! But I don't know what to do. I'm coming apart, Fr. Aldie!"

He kept pointing the gun in my direction. I felt like my life was very much on a short string for the moment. Rick was delusional, scared and who knows what he was capable of. Not much at Seminary prepares you for what to do when a .38 handgun is staring at you in your House of Worship. All the counseling courses, including the Clinical Pastoral Education, don't equip you for what exactly to say to a homeless man entering your space and announcing that he shot someone and makes you wonder whether you might just be next. All I knew was that I had to keep talking and get him to put the gun down. That much I recall from my counseling courses.

"OK, Rick, I'm asking you to put the gun aside and tell me what happened. I'm your helper - you don't need to be pointing that at me, okay? You know I've helped you along the way."

"I know, Fr. Aldie...I know.... I know... But I'm awfully scared and confused right now," he said with an intense grimace on his face. "I'm.... I'm." His hand was shaking, and his finger locked on the trigger!

Meanwhile, I was hoping that Dawn was calling 911 from my office phone. I knew that if I was going to survive this irrational moment in Rick's life, it would depend on her quick call for help and whether the front door of the Church Nave was still unlocked. I trust that fact, since Rick did not have a key and found his way in.

Rick now managed to at least point his .38 in another direction. He went on:

"My life's been a mess, Fr. Aldie. My Dad hated me and use to beat me and throw me across the kitchen floor for nothing. That's because the son-of-a-bitch would come home drunk, beat up my mother and then go after me. Christ, I hated the bastard!"

He clenched is gun and raised it toward the ceiling.

"I'd a shot his goddam head off if...." He then pointed the gun toward the Lounge Door.

I interrupted: "Rick, guns don't help. I've told you, you have to find a way out of your anger at him and channel it in a better direction."

"I know you've said that...but what do I have goin' for me.... preacher?"

I didn't like the angry tone of 'preacher,' so I took a different approach and asked him to tell me what happened this morning. He looked away. Perspiration was streaming down his face:

"Billy G, he was givin' me some lip about my girlfriend and all. I told him to go easy, you know, and he kept going. Then he told me if I didn't get her out of the shelter, he was going to fuck her. That got to me, y'know? If that son-of-a-bitch' so much as laid a hand on her..."

He shook his gun like he could aim at any one.

"... And the next thing I know, he told me he had fucked her twice, right outside the shelter on the ground on a summer night."

Rick was silent momentarily, shook his head and there were tears of rage.

"Son of a bitch!"

Then he acted out his moment of rage with Billy, snorting at me.

"I took this .38 and shot that mother fucker between the eyes. I blew his goddam brains out, Fr. Aldie!"

It was then I spotted remnants of brain tissue on his white tee shirt. I had a sudden sick feeling in my gut. He turned and looked toward the lounge, waving the gun away

"I ran out of the shelter and down to the 'The Palms' Lounge and told the bar tender to set up 10 whiskeys. I'm sure you know by now I'm drunk, Fr. Aldie. And I need your help, because, Christ, I don't know what to fuckin' do!"

He broke out in fitful crying.

By now perspiration was pouring own my neck. I took a deep breath and gently told him the first thing he had to do was hand over the gun to me. I gently told him we weren't going to find help for him as long as he had that in his hand. It took him thirty seconds, looking at it, pondering and shaking his head and was ready to hand it over... when I heard footsteps coming through the hallway. Dawn must have called them. A flash of relief came over me.

"Oh shit! Who's that? What's ...?" Rick suddenly panicked. "Goddam...they're here!"

Rick jumped up and grabbed my arm as if he was ready to take me hostage. He stared at me for a moment that seemed like an eternity. His strained neck and panicked eyes pierced me. I could smell the alcohol and the brain tissue.

"You had someone call the cops, that woman you had in there... I saw her. She called the fuckin' cops!"

I knew this was a defining moment in my life. I was either going to take a bullet to my head and die on the spot, or the cops were approaching, they were going to apprehend him. I knew this was possibly the last moment of my life. My heart was already pounding wildly. I thought about Dawn, petrified behind my office door. I thought about never seeing her again or the possibility that she may see my head blown to bits. Suddenly everything blurred as I felt Rick grip my arm and saw his gritting teeth. Perspiration was dripping down his stubble. A terrifying frown came over his crimson face as if he was morphing into a monster.

What happened next will be forever imprinted in my memory. Rick pushed me back and stuck the barrel of his .38 into the roof of *his* mouth and began to pull the trigger. Within seconds I would be showered with brain tissue and blood from an exploded head.

Instead, all I heard was a 'click.'

The Havertown Police squad entered the Lounge with their guns pointed at Rick. I moved back and shouted:

"Don't hurt him, officers. His gun is ...empty!"

They immediately restrained Rick and pulled the gun from his hand. Then I fell over on the couch just to catch my breath. I felt as near to fainting as I had ever felt in my life. My stomach churned, I did everything in my power to keep from throwing up. My eyes were blurred, and my mouth was so dry it felt as if I had swallowed sand.

"You OK, Reverend?" one officer squatted down next to me to ask.

"Catching my breath..." Hyper breathing, I continued, "He was going to pull it on himself when he heard you coming. But it ... it just.... clicked"

Gathering some semblance of composure, I told them I had been working with Rick for a year or two and knew he was homeless. As I did, I could see Rick was totally silent and amazed, probably that his brains weren't decorating the white walls of our ornate lounge.

By this time Dawn darted out of the office and toward me and I jumped up and she caught me before I fell over in the hallway. I remember gagging while I was on all fours and attempted to throw up, but finally I settled down.

"Oh my God, Aldie! Are you OK?" We held each other for the longest time. Dawn was shaking and crying uncontrollably. Finally, she pulled me up. I was hearing the officer read Rick the Miranda rights. Rick had already been handcuffed and was cursing. The officer approached us:

"Are you the little lady who called us, Ma'am?"

She nodded to the officer, tears streaming down her face.

"You should be mighty proud of her, Reverend. She even told us where you were." He managed with a smile

"I am. Oh, God, thank you, I am proud of her!"

Then with a business-like voice, the officer said: "Uh, we'll need you to come down to the Police Department tomorrow and fill out some papers."

I nodded as I removed sweat from my brow with my handkerchief. "Of course. I'll be there." I looked Rick in the eye with a modicum of compassion.

"I wish this hadn't happened, Rick. God only knows, I want that lost child in you to be found." Looking at the officer, I pleaded:

"He needs lots of help, guys." The officer in charge looked at me: "He'll get the help, Reverend... right now he's a suspect for Murder One and he's facing additional charges of holding you hostage with a dangerous weapon. That's all we need to deal with for now."

As hard as this horrific experience was, I watched Rick being led away thinking: his life is over. I recall the number of times I handed Rick McDonald's coupons and cash from my pocket so he could get something to eat. Some of my parishioners saw him turning the coupons back for cash and heading up to 'Wine & Spirits Shoppe' to buy some bottles. My Social Concern task force warned me I was wasting my charity with Rick. But I always thought, 'I'd rather err on the side of compassion than no compassion'. It would be hard to live this one down at the next Vestry meeting or listen to my Senior Warden on Monday. Sadly, people around the church usually grimaced at seeing Rick approach at worship. Bob once threw him out because he was inebriated and peed on the steps leading into the Nave.

Dawn and I held each other for the longest times as tight as we ever have. Wiping her eyes, she said, what is that horrible smell, Aldie."

I told her what Rick had done back at the shelter. "It's.... it's brain tissue, Sweetheart. Sorry." We were tearful at 'what could have been' and grateful for what was. Then I washed up in the Men's Room and Dawn helped me. I secured the front door and we made our way home.

Granted, our first intimacy opportunity had been thwarted. We were both so shaken by the 'what if's' that lovemaking was the farthest things from our minds. We knew we would get there some time and that the passion we felt before the knock on the door would be revisited. But for now, life was feel fragile and raw. We were grateful for our friendship, for being alive and able to look in each other's eyes and just know that a cosmic kind of Love navigates us through the thorns and thickets of daily life. If only that Love could find its way into Rick's life.

I believe all genuinely caring love has essential divine properties within it. I'm not sure God matches people up, but I do believe that God presents opportunities for kindred spirits to find each other. There's much we need to learn while we're on the planet and one learning may be that our hearts are looking for others to help round out our yearning for 'love' – an overly simplified word. There are many layers of love. The highest and seemingly inaccessible Love while we here on earth is worth every waking breath of our lives. It is God-driven love. Rick had lost his will to seek that Love.

Once I visited him while he was living in a refrigerator box beneath the Schuylkill River along I-76 and, on a cold January night with subfreezing temperatures, offered him lodging at the local Economy Lodge. I took him for a hot meal and helped pay his lodging. Once he told me I was the 'only friend' he had – now he will likely hate me for the rest of his life.

Kindness and helpfulness can be skewered when life's circumstances hedge a person in. Rick *had* forgotten who he really was. The son of a well-known Philadelphia anesthesiologist and an alcoholic mother, Rick's tortured life of alcohol and having very few friends became a perfect storm for falling into despair. His father had supplied his mother with an abundance of painkillers following back surgery, fueling her addiction. Her alcoholism became more intense alongside her addiction to those painkillers. She was a terrible model for Rick's own disillusionment. He followed her trail. Sadly, Rick was lost before he was 17, shuffled around the System for theft and selling drugs on the streets of center city Philly.

Dawn and I stopped in the sand and held each other for a moment and sighed. "We'll never forget that time," I said as I kissed her on the forehead. The night-lights of hotels along Daytona Beach were providing whatever light we had to make our beach walk, so we decided to go back to the street and drive somewhere to eat. We had packing to do for the journey home on Sunday. Our flight from Jacksonville back to Philadelphia was scheduled for 2 p.m. We drove to the 'Stonewood Grill' to share an entrée in our usual Dawn and Aldie

'Care and Share' fashion. We realized that our visit on Daytona Beach had been consumed by conversation - talk about baby possibilities and the marriage and remembering the first time we *almost* made love on my office desk at All Saints. We arrived back at the Bahama House tired and ready to sleep in one another's arms with gentle kisses and quiet 'I love you's.'

Sunday was overcast. From our hotel window we could see the faint line of sunrise way off into the horizon. There was a front moving in, according to forecasts. It was a much-needed rain according to locals, since Florida had experienced one of its driest winters on records. After breakfast, we made our way back to Jacksonville, the torrent rain whipping us around.

We arrived in Jacksonville about 11 AM and decided to turn in our rental car early. Since I had already printed out our flight boarding passes at the hotel, we only needed to check our suitcase through. JAX is a rather modern airport not far from downtown Jacksonville. Bustling, but not crowded, the airport shops and dining attracted our attention. Beautiful Dawn was intrigued by 'Brighton's' and they're expensive but beautiful handmade purses. We settled into 'Chilli's Too' to share a little lunch. Afterward, we made our way through security to find our gate and anticipate the flight home. Flight 3282 a Boeing 737-200 had taxied in just as we had passed through security. Boarding would begin in about a half hour. The attendant indicated that it would be a full flight. We noticed that the sun was beginning to come out and some welcome Florida blue sky. The weather in Philadelphia was clear and chilly - about 24 degrees. Take off was on time from JAX, but it was a bumpy ride along the coast. That front that was moving into Florida was producing some upper atmospheric winds that were playing havoc with our plane. The Captain mercifully offered to move us up a thousand or so feet and that seemed to calm the air down. But the continued turbulence and stirred up Beautiful Dawn's stomach a bit. The queasiness caused her to hold my hand and close her eyes. I gave her some Dramamine, but I wasn't sure it would be helpful thirty minutes into the flight. But it must have helped, because she fell asleep with her bridal magazine open on her lap. She slept most of the two-and-a-half-hour flight to Philly. I decided to catch up on some reading.

The skies were blue as we began our descent over Washington, D.C., about 40 minutes out before landing at PHL. I could hear the engines slow up a bit. The cabin servers were beginning to gather the trash items.

"How are you feeling, Sweetheart?"

"Fine, Love"... she smiled as she stretched a bit.

Approaching Philadelphia, I could see that there had been some additional snow in the area. Soon we were descending with a steep bank to the left over the center of Philadelphia. I could look down at the top of the Comcast Center until the plane evened out for its final approach to the runway. Its flaps pulled up and the landing gear engaged to provide the typical drag for approach to Runway 27L. We landed at 2:34 p.m.- on schedule. Stepping through the chilly jet-way to the gate, we already missed the warm winter that Florida was enjoying. But it was also good to get home, to that sense of 'normalcy' (if there ever really is). Life needs some predictability. Dawn was ready to hunker down on some last-minute study.

Chapter Eleven

THE SHADOW OF GRACE

Today is far from Childhood -- But up and down the hills I held her hand the tighter -- Which shortened all the miles –
Emily Dickinson, 'One sister I Have in our House'

On our return to Havertown on January 27th, one among many of the phone calls was a call from Dawn's stepsister Grace, 'MIA' since she and Ahmad had slipped off to Tulsa, OK, after their baby arrived. We had talked about her a number of times, wondering how she was doing. The communication lines had essentially been cut. We weren't sure why they were cut off. If Grace had any family member with whom she would have stayed in touch other than her mother, Lydia, it would have been Dawn. But Grace had no cell phone number, no E-mail and no LAN line number. Dawn had made a number of calls to Tulsa just to see if they had a listing for 'Grace Ramesh,' but nothing was available. She wondered why her stepsister would be angry or uncommunicative. And her father was no help, shrugging his shoulders when asked if he knew where Grace was or how she was doing. Lydia, Grace's Mom, also was puzzled and couldn't share any information.

But here, after a number of years, Dawn was listening to her sister's voice

Hi Dawn. I know it's been a long time. Gosh, so many things have happened since I last talked with you. First, tragically, Ahmad was killed in an automobile accident here in Tulsa a year ago. I was crushed and ended up picking up some drug habits I had to work through. I had to take Christopher and move to Oklahoma City, where a friend took me in. Ahmad had no life insurance and I was left with some debts. I had to make some money, so I worked for an escort service in Oklahoma City. I know – a glorified prostitution service! I got busted by the Oklahoma City Police and I spent a little time in jail. Long story short, I'm back in

181

Tulsa and I met this wonderful guy, LaMont, and remarried a few weeks ago. He is a Target manager and makes pretty good money. Life has been topsy-turvy to say the least. But I've just been longing to talk with you. I fell out with my mother because she wouldn't lend me some money when I so needed help. Another long story! You're my only family connection, baby. I just needed to hear your voice. Call some time. I love you. Bye.

Dawn called Grace immediately and talked with her for almost an hour. It was a long-awaited reunion. Grace wanted to come and visit Beautiful Dawn in the Spring and crisp up their family connection. The two plotted when that might be – a few days perhaps.

She realized that Grace was her only sister among other stepsiblings. She pondered all that had happened to her since they last met, how she didn't know that Ahmad had been killed, how she had to succumb to prostitution on the street.

'*It was terrible, Dawn! I can't begin to tell you how humiliating it is – men groveling and slobbering all over you, smelling like booze and sometimes their BO... ugh, it makes me nauseated just thinking about it. But, it paid a few bills and helped Day Care for Christopher while I went job-hunting elsewhere.*'

Then she mentioned her father, Jack O'Shea:

I haven't seen or talked to Daddy since the day he left and slammed the door. I know you remember it well. You saved my life Dawn. I've picked up the phone a couple of times attempting to reconnect, but I just imagined his disgust and anger with me lingering. Please tell me he's still alive, Dawn.

She assured him that he was still 'Daddy' but hoped he might soften should she want to call. The conversation ended with the promise of a sister reunion.

They may not have shared a common mother, but Grace and Beautiful Dawn shared a common bond. Why hadn't Grace let her know about Ahmad and her subsequent hard times? It was an answer Grace just seemed incapable of giving.

I offered:

"Sometimes, Darling, it's just too difficult to let even those who are close to you know the truth of your life. She may have felt ashamed to tell you, Sweetheart. Prostitution is a difficult admission for any woman."

"But I'm her sister, Aldie, I've seen her through tough times with my father and... but, you're right. I guess her life was so troubled, she couldn't tell me. It still hurts."

Sadly, a month and a half later on Maundy Thursday, she received a letter from a woman named Juanita from Norman, Oklahoma, who wrote:

'*Dear Ms. O'Shea: I trust this will reach you. I'm so sorry to inform you that your sister Grace died in an apartment fire here in Norman February 9th.*

Dawn gasped and grasped my arm..."Oh, Aldie, no, no...." She sat on the couch and cried and tried to continue reading:

'*....They discovered she had been smoking in bed and had fallen asleep. Sadly, her child Christopher also perished in the fire. I'm so sorry to share this news with you. She worked with me at the local shelter helping battered women and children. Her new husband, LaMont, had abandoned her for another woman and she had moved into an apartment here in Norman. It turned out that LaMont had become abusive and had made life miserable with drug addiction. That's another long story....*

I just felt I needed to reach you so that you would know what has tragically unfolded. I am so sorry to share this with you. I wish you well. You were the one person your sister often spoke about and missed dearly.

Sincerely, Juanita Gomez

Dawn sobbed in my arms most of the afternoon. It was such a tragic loss. It seemed as if Grace couldn't find that one break she needed to make her life work. Her struggle with her father, whose last words to her were '*You make your bed, you lie in it*' haunted her all days. Ahmad was likely the highpoint of her troubled life. Unlike her father, he had accepted her and loved her unconditionally.

Once Dawn was able to get through the crying, she knew that her next tasks were very difficult: to call her father and Lydia. I had offered to help her by calling them, but she needed to make that connection.

At the news, Jack O'Shea, was silent. Dawn could hear the slight whimper, the sniffles, which caused Beautiful Dawn to openly cry:

"Daddy, I'm sorry. I know she was your flesh and blood, like me. I loved her too. She's the only sister I feel I have ever had... I will truly miss her."

Gathering composure, he said, "It just seemed like once she left home, nothing ever worked out... Christ!" The conversation was muted and finally Dawn said, "Well, I just wanted to let you know. I love you Daddy." Jack O'Shea just couldn't say the words 'I love you' back. He never could. He could only muster: 'Thanks for letting me know, Dawn' And he hung up.

It didn't help my Love's grief that her father could never say the words she longed to hear from him, *'I love you.'* Even if he was a father and a husband to a few, it seemed that nothing could coax those words out of his heart or his mouth. It seemed like he was spiritually dead.

Expectedly, Lydia O'Shea, hearing the news, was drowning in shock and tears about the news. She cried for a long time on the phone.

"Oh Dawn! I can't believe it – my baby! Oh, Dawn...! Oh, Dawn... Oh, God!... Oh God! I missed her so much and that beautiful Christopher. And I should have...I should have sent her the money. She needed $1,500 and I just couldn't afford..."

"Lydia, don't beat yourself down. We all loved her, but Grace could never find a break. It's not your fault."

"What about your father, Dawn? Have you called him?"

Dawn sniffed and wiped her tears.

"I did. He seemed to cry silently about it. Our conversation was awkward." She sighed.

"Well, you know Daddy."

It took Lydia a while to gain her composure. Their phone conversation finally ended with 'Thank you' and 'I love you.'

Beautiful Dawn knew for a long while that the money issue would bring guilt to Lydia It's hard to imagine that money could separate a mother and daughter. It's certainly not an unfamiliar story. The anguish about money – the need for it, the obsession over it, the dreams that are fueled by its very existence has always plagued humans. The Good Book suggests '*The love of money is the root of all evil.'* *(1 Timothy 6:10).* It surely seems a timeless truth. Grace may not have 'loved' money, but it plagued her life at critical times.

In one of my sermons on money I recall suggesting: *Loving money is tough, because it really can't love you back.*

Dawn agonized for days how best to deal with her sister Grace's tragic death. Coincidentally, an unexpected package arrived from Norman, OK one morning soon after the tragic note. It was the same Ms. Gomez. In the box were Grace's ashes.

It rattled Dawn, because Juanita had not hinted that she would be sending them. For a long time, Beautiful Dawn just gazed at the box on the counter top in her kitchen. Finally, she took my hand and said:

"What can we do, my Love?"

She just seemed frozen in her thoughts and shook her head. I suggested one course: to have a remembrance service. And that's what we did on May 25th at All Saints Church. Helen McFarley provided suitable music and Jack did come to the service, but he remained very subdued and barely talked with anyone. Lydia came. Some of Grace's high school friends were there. Grace's other stepsiblings came late. The day was a 'miracle gathering' of sorts. I marvel how much healing can come from gathering in a sacred space and with a liturgy sustained by the scriptural words and the fellowship. Sometimes the family dysfunction and agonies over unfulfilled love just blur a bit. Ruth McGill (our beneficent angel of hospitality) provided a nice spread of food for our gathering after the service. Grace Ramesh O'Shea had her proper closure and sending from this world.

Thanks to the folks at Logan Funeral Home, we were able to find three bronze containers and put Grace's name on them.

My meditation at Grace's Service of Remembrance focused on some feeble thoughts in light of Grace and Christopher's living hell. I had no idea of the measure of Grace's spiritual journey. I just knew that she seemed to be yearning for 'Love' – this elusive and yet transcending, unconditional Love of the Creator. I shared that life and death seem to be mystery yoked together. Certainly, death is a mystery – the 'why' of it, both youth and great age fall into it. Death is most often a painful, agonizing, a lonely surrender. No one can do our dying for us. And neither can anyone do our living for her. We seem as St. Paul wrote, accounted for sheep to be sent to the slaughter daily.

I continued:

'All I know, family and friends, is that Love in the godly sense seems to hold this fragile human planet together. Just as some scientists have observed that the earth is a 'privileged planet' by degrees (that is, this planet couldn't survive if it were tilted by a small measure of degrees in one direction or another), so I think Love is really what makes this world go around. My unqualified belief is that Grace, in whatever lies beyond this earthly realm, has finally found the Love she yearned for. And I could only hope that she is immeasurably happy as I hope the same for Christopher. I say that with a great deal of trust in a Greater Other, a Holy One, that my mind tries to comprehend at this juncture of my life.

And finally, I believe that the Jesus of our faith, the one who was as close to his Father-God is as anyone could possibly be in this world... that he believed and ultimately surrendered his own life to show that same Love."

Ashes

All life begins, the biblical story reminds us, 'from the soil' *(adamah)* and to the soil we return. Within that process, life unfolds and not easily. The anguish of birthing continues through 'soil life.' We are bound to it through the length of our days in this world. Within those limited days, we struggle with human will, control, desire, uncertainty, and improbability. It seems even in death, these ashes, these chards, these remnants of physical life – whether in urns or fancy caskets –are sent back to the soil.

Still *Love (the godly kind)* endures faithfully to give form and purpose in us for all the opportunities that this world may provide. I wondered what Grace's contract in this world was? It seems we are born into this world with some purpose other than existing... She may have learned –or maybe she didn't – that *Love* is greater than the human limits from which our yearnings are expressed. We all struggle with that truth regardless of what part of the globe we inhabit. It may take us a lifetime (or perhaps beyond) to learn that we were created from the soil for soulful love, so that as we draw life from it, we have opportunity in this earthly walk to open ourselves to *Spirit –the inner essence.* Yet life is raw. How does the Spirit find a Somalian child in sheer poverty, where disease and hunger will end life before love and benevolence find her? Where does an aborted fetus know Love? How does a crack cocaine newborn convulsing in pain know Love? Christopher, Grace's child, burned in his mother's dwelling with his whole life cut off. Where is the benevolent deity?

Dawn and I spent an inordinate amount of time reflecting on Grace in the weeks ahead. The ashes in the urn remained on the fireplace mantel. Their presence became an unlikely source of comfort to her. They were chards of Grace's life, but for Dawn they became part of a sacred remembrance. And beside the ornate bronze urn was a picture of both Grace and my Dawn taken during those turbulent high school years when Grace's 'little sister' was her best friend, her confidant. They pose with arms around each other, with happy smiles – a glimpse of sibling love, a captioned moment of what Grace had yearned for all of her remaining days.

Chapter Twelve

INTO THE HEART OF THE HOLY

The cosmos dreams in me while I wait in stillness, ready to lean a little further into the heart of the Holy.
I, a little blip of life, a wisp of unassuming love, a quickly passing breeze, come once more into Lent.

-first two verses from Lent 2001, Joyce Rupp

So much had happened in two weeks, including the tragedy of Grace and Christopher. Early February was proving to be as wildly cold in Havertown as January was mildly warm in Florida. Since February 6th we had been pounded by two blizzards, including a Nor'easter that had piled almost 20 inches of snow on us, making even Route 1 barely passable one Saturday morning. I never cancel church services as long as I can get my butt up the steps of All Saints and turn on the lights (hoping the electricity and the heat are functioning.) That was the case February 14th (Valentine's Day) when we awoke to an intense overnight snowfall that dumped an additional six inches on the Philadelphia area.

My Senior Warden wasn't too happy that I did *not* cancel worship since he drives down from Wayne. The roads on Route 30 were passable but had numerous slick spots.

"Geez, Aldie, its winter out there! Even the Lutherans have cancelled services."

"Stay put, Buzz", I said on the phone at 5 AM.

"I don't expect you to plow through this stuff. I'll take care of things. Really! They'll be a few stragglers coming in from nearby... you know, my usual walkers - Blanche McCusker, Janet Mellon, of course, and... what? Yea, I know. It's OK. Sleep in this morning. Margaret will enjoy having you home for a Sunday. .... Okay, maybe not..." I chuckled. "Sure, OK, Bye."

Buzz Sawyer (we call him 'Buzz Saw' around the church because of his high energy) is my late father's age, easily excitable and a church worrywart. Snow is one of his big worries. He'll be worrying about getting the walks shoveled out in time for church, spreading the salt on the walks to melt the ice, and making sure that Mick's Snow Removal will be around in time to move snow from the two lots All Saints provides. He'll worry about the kids slipping on the walk as well as the elderly who will be sloshing along and who may fall, especially where the ice drips at the entrance doors. Buzz Saw knows for sure that dripping water will turn into ice, which means someone will have an icicle fall on them or another will slip and break a bone and sue the congregation.

Apart from being a worrywart, (who am I to judge?) Buzz is still one of the best Senior Wardens I've had in my career so far. He's an exceptionally reliable and thorough Senior Ward. (Bob McGyver was certainly neck-to-neck with him.) At our vestry meetings, he's fair and balanced and he's a great fit for our people. He seems to be able to talk reasonably with our more fiscally conservative parishioners as well as those who think we ought to be spending money rather than saving it. He's a great negotiator at our Annual 'Family Fights' (otherwise known as our 'Annual Meetings'). On balance, All Saints does well with muddling through the annual meetings, save for the Gruber's and the McFadden's, who fight over what the fiscally conservative Gruber's call the 'battle of the budget bulge.' Although I don't care to know what people give or don't give, I'm told that the Gruber's are generous folks with All Saints, but their views of church budgets are woefully shortsighted. So, the annual budget proposal becomes a military war zone because the McFadden's think the church should be about outreach and spending for things like the local Soup Kitchen and the Wesley House over in Chester (one of the ministries near and dear to the Ellen McFadden). 'Buzz Saw' just mediates his way through their chatter over the budget in a way that surprise both sides, suggesting replacing this item for that item and shifting money every which way. The budget team winces at this as they try to keep their calculators working overtime.

It was about an hour and a half before the first church bells would ring. My Honda seemed to drive effortlessly through the new fallen snow and hard-packed ice beneath. I had thrown in my shovel from home and some salt bags. I noticed as I turned into the first parking lot that Mick's truck was busily pushing snow to the side. I shoveled the walk up to the Great Hall entrance and walked to my office. I'm always aware of countless Post-It notes on my desk. When I switched on my iMac, I realized there were plenty of email messages.

A copy of the *Christian Century* was there, with half the cover page ripped off. There were the usual advertisements for copiers and church renovation services and things clergy can't live without. I also noticed a formal letter addressed to me from the Suffragan Bishop F. U. Frank. It's usually bad news when F.U. writes to you, something he needs to slap your wrist for or worse. I stuffed that in my pocket for later.

My desk phone lighted up. The caller ID said 'R SAWYER' so I knew Buzz (whose real name is Robert) was calling to see if I made it in OK.

"Hello. Yes, Buzz I made it in OK. No, not a single problem... Su... Sure, Mick's is digging out the lot even as we speak. No Buzz, you don't have to... no, it's... I'm...OK. Well, I shoveled the walk into the Great Hall and...Buzz! ...OK, suit yourself, but navigate at your own risk, my friend... You take care, too, Buzz."

There were approximately 40 attendees at our 9AM Liturgy that Sunday. By 8AM, Moser's had cleared both parking lots and Buzz had cleaned all the walks with the snow blower (Buzz loves to operate the snow-blower!) and enough salt to cover three or four winter storms. The sun came out about 8:30AM and the sky was a cloudless, brilliant blue. The temps climbed to about 38 degrees and it was evident that Route 1 was now passable, albeit slushy. We used an abbreviated liturgy and only about four of the usual 20 choir members were in attendance.

Sunday School was spotty in attendance, understandably. Fran O'Shea, our choir director, not related to Dawn, came with her husband, who loves to get his 4-wheel jeep out and 'play' in the snow. Fran was a bit *fran*-tic when she arrived for the 11 o'clock liturgy! The attendance at 11 turned out to be a decent 70, although the baptism that was scheduled for that hour had to be rescheduled. God will wait, of course. Baptism, I figure, is a communal celebration of a spiritual connection the Creator has already made. There's no hurry.

This was Transfiguration Sunday on the liturgical calendar. I had prepared my sermon on the Gospel from Mark - Jesus taking his inner circle of learners, Peter, James and John, up on a mountain to pray about his mission and purpose- an ascent that turned out to be one super-sized God-revealing moment (or 'theophony). Of course, as dramatic as it appeared (and the gospel writers really do it up well!) this God-revealing-moment had a limited audience – three 'students' (disciples) of Jesus about to experience their teacher on something like spiritual steroids. While up there in some meditative state, Jesus suddenly appears in a blazing aura and connecting with two ancients, Moses and Elijah. Okay!

Those two must have transmuted from some alternative reality! Or at least Mark wanted to divinize a fleeting moment. In my heart of hearts, I can't be sure what really happened, but I reckon the gospel-writer tucked it in there as a foreshadowing of Jesus' Resurrection. Something happened – but maybe not this dramatically. No one could know for sure.

It was one of those events that only the inner circle could talk about, because trying to explain it to the rest of the crew down at 'Base Camp' would likely have ticked them off. *Why did you guys get to go up there, anyway? Are we chopped liver down here?* But I wonder how any of us would have managed moments as these select three disciples experienced up there, watching Jesus transfigure into something totally other-worldly for a moment. It puts chills up and down my spine imagining it. Ordinary life just isn't ordered this way. One moment Jesus is sweating from the climb and then, as if time just froze, he's lighted up like a super nova. Chalk it up to one of those rare moments when the cosmic curtain is pulled back a wee bit for less earthbound types to experience.

I remember once being on the top of Rockefeller Center at sunset. The elevator led us to the 67th Floor where we got to see spectacular views of Manhattan all around us. But on this particular evening, the sun was setting and for a single moment there was a brilliant light between velvety lavender clouds and blue skies spreading an incredible splash of gold on the buildings of Manhattan's north side from the East River to the Hudson. Those who were my view-mates gasped. And my camera just clicked away. It's as if the Creator just made one sweeping brushstroke all over town. Some light on the enormity of glass windowpanes on the tallest of buildings made us squint and turn out faces. It was almost unbearable. Words were difficult to describe it. Instead of three dispel types drawn to it, there were fifty or sixty people from the 'top of the Rock' gasping in sheer delight. And in one fleeting moment the west side of the Empire State Building looked like a pillar of fire. . What a holy moment to celebrate our connection with a Holy Otherness. Trying to explain it to others- even sharing pictures – did it no justice. It was a transcendent moment. That's what 'Transfiguration' Sunday tries to capture – God's fleeting, spectacular, self-revealing presence (known as a 'theophany') captured in a Galilean peasant Jewish teacher's day on a mountain.

Throughout the Sundays of January, these 'God-revealing-moments' had recounted how Jesus moved from helpless baby to influential traveling teacher pushed by the winds of divine approval and Spirit. It's sort of like your father saying to you, *'Son, you're doing a heck of a job and I'm very proud to have you in the family!'* (Something perhaps many of us may never have heard our fathers say). The gospels recall divine-like revealings ('epiphanies') in which Jesus turns out to be more than a wandering Jewish rabbi/mystic/healer. The church would echo John the Baptist pointing to Jesus: *This is the Lamb of God who comes to clean up God's world.'* Jesus had many titles circulated and some stuck. 'Lamb of God' was one of those titles the Gospel of John uses. Yet how did he get that title? Was it added later as writers remembered the Jewish sacrificial system of a pure lamb offered for atonement for human wrongs? Or was Jesus viewed as an adoring recruit for John's wild wilderness ministry? Was Jesus short of stature and kind spirited- innocent like a lamb? That's all speculation of course. But it makes us wonder. My mother at times in my late high school years would call me 'my little preacher.' (I loathed hearing that. After all, I was tall!)

So, these past weeks of Epiphany (time after Christmas) offered gathered stories of Jesus emerging in his favored status of 'Son of God' into a country peasant rabbi seeking to draw people back to

God's determination to clean up the world. The way the early church understood it, John's 'Lamb of God' is 'earning his sacrificial lamb-hood for messianic work.

Transfiguration Sunday, then, is this last biggie 'Epiphany. Our, Joe McCleaf, who works with "Buzz Saw' had mounted a large star from the Nave ceiling with a mechanism that allows it to grow brighter each Sunday. It was a gray overcast day with snow on this last Sunday of Epiphany. John cranked up the star and it seemed the 'Son' was truly shining brilliantly there – Jesus our *Morgenstern*- 'morning star'- in a fleeting glimpse of eternity.

I saw Dawn come into the Nave while I was making announcements. She waved from the back of the Nave and I so wanted to yell, *Hey there, Beautiful One!* I realized when I saw her sit down that tomorrow, Monday, February 14th was Valentine's Day. She had told me the evening before to make it home early for a Valentine meal. I would scramble to get a mushy Valentine's card and take some roses along with some of her favorite chocolates in a heart- shaped box.

I had the joy at worship of having 7 children for our 'Little Bite Sizes' time. I asked them if they knew anything about Valentine's Day. Wilson, our very active second grader, went into a pretty long description about how on Valentine's Day you make up cards and give them to people you like, but if you didn't like them you wouldn't give them a card (!) That drew a chuckle. I suggested that perhaps Jesus was God's 'Valentine' to us. A child might understand that, but it was a theological stretch, I realized.

"This word 'love' is a pretty difficult word, isn't it? Do you think it's possible to love everybody in the world?"

Wilson McKenzie, of course, had his hand way up in the air. But little Bonita Sanchez with the beautiful curly black hair and a smile that can turn you into Jell-O put her hands on her hips and declared, "If God had wanted us to love everybody in the world, we wouldn't have time to do anything else."

That also drew a chuckle.

Wilson blurted out, "Yea, our arms would get tired of hugging so many people." He stood up, going in circles with his arms rounded so that he was pretending he was hugging everyone.

I came back with:

"So, do you think God needs us to help by loving the world right where we are."

Wilson again blurted out: "Well, I love most everybody -- except my sister!" That brought laughter. I noticed Wilson's Mom and Dad shaking their heads. His little sister Rebecca looked at him without smiling and stuck out her tongue.

"Well," I concluded, "I guess God has a great big job loving the whole world. And during this time called Epiphany, God wants us to know that Jesus is like the biggest Valentine card God could possibly give us. And just to remind you, I've brought some heart-shaped cards with 'Jesus loves you' printed on them. Would you do me a favor? Each of you is getting 10 cards. Would you be willing to share some of these cards with someone who might enjoy being reminded they are loved?"

The kids scooped up the cards and spread them out through the congregation sharing their 'Jesus Loves You' cards. There was about three minutes of purely wonderful chaos with lots of smiling big people - even a few teens! I noticed some of the kids –especially Bonita Sanchez - hugging every person who received a card.

Dawn and I chatted for a while following the services and decided to head for Hanne's for some lunch. She talked mostly about her certification exam coming up at the School of Nursing at Frankford. She was scheduled for February 22nd at 9AM. She admitted that for the first time she was getting butterflies.

"The academics were easy, Aldie. These exams are going to be tough!"

I offered:

"May I help you with some question and answer time, Sweetheart? I'd be willing to do that. A lot of the questions are multiple choice." We chatted about wedding plans on our full-court press to put things together. Then I happened to remember that I had a letter from F. U. Frank. I pulled it out of my pocket. I forgot I had this in my pocket. "What is it, Darling?" she asked curiously.

"A personal letter from F. U. Frank!" I said with rolling eyes. I opened the letter and began reading it:

'Dear Father, Seaver: Blessings in this Epiphany tide. It has come to my attention that you are currently in a relationship with a woman who worships in the parish. Considering the close proximity of your recent

194

divorce, this may be compromising your relationship with the good folks of All Saints.

'Oh, crap!' I thought.

...Although I write with a heavy heart knowing that recently you have experienced the death of your father, Yes, I feel your compassion – not!)... *I felt it was necessary to let you know that the Diocese does not look favorably upon relationships so close to an Anglican priest's divorce. It is important for the good order of Anglican Diocese that you discontinue this relationship immediately....'*

Dawn and I looked at each other.

"That mindless ass is at it again!" I said in a rage. "prying into my personal life." I folded it and put it into my pocket. I intended to follow through with this piece of crap from 'Fr. Asshole!'

"My goodness, Aldie! What does this mean?"

I took a deep breath and fold the letter and put it in my coat pocket.

"It means nothing, Darling. It means that F. U. Frank is flexing his authority muscle again. He's out to get me!"

"But what can he do to you, Aldie? And who told him about us? And what's so wrong with it? Your divorce is court record!"

"I know, Sweetheart. Truthfully, he can do little except slap my wrist - ecclesiastically speaking. He's a jerk! I have no idea who told him. I probably have a few enemies in the parish; I only have a suspicion of who they are. Anyway, I have a lot of secrets about F. U. I carry around in my back pocket... Sorry, Sweetheart...I guess I'm just pissed. Forgive me. I'm even angrier that 'organized religion' seems to have a fixation with rules. It's part of the downfall of the church today! Don't worry about this, Sweetheart. I feel the Creator has drawn us together. The institutional church cannot separate us. I love you."

"And I you, my darling! Let's talk about it over dinner tomorrow evening. It's Valentine's Day and I've cooked up something special for you."

I crawled into bed around 11 p.m. with a book. I realized I had read only a few paragraphs and didn't remember one thing I had read, because 'the letter' was invading my reality. My beautiful Dawn was drifting off to sleep.

The next morning, I was on the phone early with F. U. *'Got your letter, Forrest. I must say I was surprised in light of the number of divorces and rebounding relationships that are going on even on my backdoor here in the Philadelphia area.'*

There was a slight pause.

'It's standard procedure, Aldie.'

'Bullshit, Forrest! Everyone knows the Bishop himself had a girlfriend not long after his wife revealed she was gay ...'

'Yes, but he's the bishop....'

'So, there's a double standard --is what you're saying? The bishop is the chief pastor of the church, so he can do whatever the hell he wants to...'

'Calm down, Aldie...'

'I'm not calming down! You think for one moment, you stupid son-of-a-bitch, that you can tell me to discontinue a relationship that is the one thing in this world that I cherish and especially now with my father's recent death! Stop this stupid sh-t, Forrest, or I'll spill the beans about your little tryst with your secretary after you left Spring Grove. You're such a stupid piece of sh-t....'

'Aldie, calm down.'

'I'm not calming down, you bastard! This is why the frickin' institutional church is going down the toilet: stupid rules fostered by people like you who can't manage a parish worth sh-t, but want to run others' lives...'

I knew immediately I had gone way over the top. There was silence on the other end of the line.. *And then* ...I heard the 5 a.m. alarm come on! It was morning and I had dreamt my vitriolic call to F. U. Frank. My heart was galloping, and my palms were sweaty. I had dreamt what my runaway rage was trying to express. I settled and thought it all through... and prayed: *'Calm my restless heart, O God.'* Dawn was in the shower and had no idea what I had dreamt.

I did call Forrest around 11 a.m. from my office. It took a while for F. U. to answer, but eventually he said.

"Hello, Aldie?"

"Forrest, I'm not sure how to respond to your letter. It really hurts considering what I've been through losing my Dad. Dawn O'Shea is a good person and well-liked in our parish. I feel like the

Diocese is judging me, like trying to control my search for a loving mate.... Can you imagine what that must feel like?"

"Aldie..."

"I'm deeply hurt by your letter, Forrest. Do you remember who officiated the wedding of Bishop and Sabrina after his divorce?"

He sighed. "I know... you did. But..."

"And you know he found Sabrina within a few months after his wife left him for another woman. We can't be having double standards, Forrest, can we? So, I just appreciate your hearing me out. I want you to know I *will* continue my relationship with Dawn O'Shea. And if there is a problem, I'll be visiting Ben myself and in consultation with you and the diocesan representative, work this out. (Ben Cargill is now the Bishop of the Episcopal Dioceses of Philadelphia.) "(Sighing) "Okay, Aldie. "

"Thanks for hearing me out. And Forrest..."

"What is it, Aldie?" Another sigh was evident.

"Please don't send letters like this. You know the ministry has much more to do than this. There are so many other effective ways to be the suffragan Bishop then picking on someone's lifestyle. There are congregations in Camden that need support. You know that. There are priests who are burning out and need to be cared for. I know there are circumstances that are intolerable, of course. Sexual abuse, child molestations. Etc. But this is far from abuse.

And Forrest, you know that All Saints contributes more to Foreign Missions than any single Episcopal Church in the Diocese. (I really needed to pour this on a bit). "The diocese needs to lift up the good work that's going on... the things that our parishes are doing well. Think about it, Forrest. Thanks for listening. Take care."

More signing. "Thanks, Aldie."

"And will you pray for me?" I invited.

"I ...I will."

"Thanks. And I will pray for you, Forrest. Good bye for now."

I hung up. I had to milk it mightily to spare me from slipping into the terrible viciousness of my dream! Okay, this was less vitriolic – still, I'll admit, it was a bit menacing. My dream of dumping a full-metal jacket of negative energy on the suffragan Bishop had scared the crap out of me. I don't like the side of me that becomes like that nightmare before the 5 a.m. alarm. Dawn would be relieved that I just stated my intent... no cursing and vitriol. It's just not who I really am… except in a dream maybe.

That evening my beautiful Dawn welcomed me home with candlelight and the smell of lasagna (one of my favorites). She had outdone herself. I had arrived with a dozen short-stem roses, a heart-shaped box of her favorite dark chocolates and a mushy Hallmark card attempting to share my sincere love for her. "Mushy" was acceptable to her. The words beneath the image of a discreetly naked man and woman embracing next to a large campfire *'the spark that ignited a flame in our hearts continues as a raging fire of passion.'*

I did a little 'shop talk' with Dawn and mentioned some of the Lenten preparations I was involved in and her curiosity about 'Ash Wednesday,' a service she was planning to attend. We enjoyed feeding one another with lasagna and sharing the French garlic baguettes she had bought.

For dessert, Dawn had baked a lemon meringue pie. "I have these special napkins just for the occasion, Aldie. I'll be right back." When she returned, she placed the plates of lemon meringue pie on our tables with forks and a folded napkin. When I opened the napkin, a little knit bootie fell out and landed on my lap.

"What's this, Darling?"

"Mm...What does it look like, Aldie?"

"It's... it's a baby's bootie..."

"That's right, Sweetheart. I wanted to share with you on this Valentine's Day, my love, that... we're going to have a baby!"

My reaction must have been quite monumental as I sat there examining the bootie. My eyes were wide open as was my mouth. I stood up and went around the table and wrapped my arms around her and kissed her, accidentally knocking her dish on the floor along with her napkin and fork. We laughed.

"We're really going to have a baby, Sweetheart? We're really going to have a baby!!! "

"Yes, yes, yes.... I'm pregnant. I found out yesterday with the test I bought from Walgreen's Oh, Sweetheart, I love you so much."

We held each other on the couch for a long time, just mesmerized by this new reality. We recalled that romantic.... well, eventually romantic night at the hotel in Orlando. It had been over a month since that sensuous moment when Beautiful Dawn looked up at me and said, *'Aldie, let's have a baby!'*

Our kisses were sweet there on the living room couch. Nature worked its wonders in the weeks that followed, and life was now unfolding within her womb. Our love, as the Song of Solomon suggests, was *'like a raging fire'* at times. I shared with her in whispers in the quiet of our cuddles that I believed our love had so much mind-body- spirit energy about it - all of it positive energy, nothing negative at all. Dawn and I are so blended with synchronicity. We intuit so much of our feelings and awareness of each other. When we make love, the body draws upon spirit and spirit draws upon mind and mind draws upon memory and memory celebrates all three. I don't pretend to know the mind of God, of course, but I am certainly aware of an Eternal Mindfulness that finds its way into our finite life and love. In such it may be possible to experience oneness with God. beyond lust or libidos. Our intimacy is co-equal, co-respondent and co- existing. The self is free to be who it truly is meant to be. It is, in some measure, the highest form of being within an imperfect world where love is too often exploited.

Geez, lofty thoughts, I admit! And they can't replace the Nature that is embedded in the pursuer and pursued - an earthly anima that brings about conception. Regardless of my idealization of the body-soul-mind- tri-unity, lovemaking is essentially a physical endgame, a mingling of bodily juices with Nature's impulse augmented by desire - the male and female dance. *It is a circle of desire that enters into the circle of life, drawn from a circle of Love.*

The next day, we awoke with tenderness and kisses and 'I love you's.' Dawn jolted out of bed and realized she needed to get to the library for a last full-court press on certification for nursing licensure. And I knew that I had to get bulletin information and details for that night's Ash Wednesday worship at 7:30 p.m. We parted after quick coffee and cereal and a brief scan of the '*Inquirer.'*

Ash Wednesday, February 16th

Ash Wednesday -the day of the imposition of ashes on worshipers' foreheads- is for many one of the most meaningful worship
experiences they could ever recall. There's something about the
imposition of the ash mark that just 'settles it' for their place in the
cosmos. Kathryn, a former Roman Catholic-turned-Episcopalian,
described Ash Wednesday to me as 'the great reckoning with God.'
The ash mark spoke boldly: *'OK, God you're the creator and I'm the
creature.'* Or as Father Jim over at Immaculate Heart used to say to me
before Ash Wednesday: "We're more than space dust, Aldie - *but not
much more!"* From a biological standpoint we are both a miracle and
yet, given the linear years we face, seventy and more if we're lucky –
we're basically dust... *to dust...ashes to ashes.*

The ash mark is symbolic at best and poses as a kind of spiritual
high ground for many folks annually. *Why is this so appealing?* Maybe
at their root... their soul level, it creates a longing for the Creator
relationship. Like the lost pet longing for its owner. Or the grieving
father longing for his 'Father' in heaven.

On another level Ash Wednesday awakens us to our sense of
finality.

Of course, Thursday morning people are back to reality and
have already washed off the ash mark. Others like to show them off. All
Saints invites a noontime Ash Wednesday service as well as an evening
7 p.m. service. I recall last year that Heidi McWilliams, who works as
a Secretary at Aramark Corporation, Center City Philadelphia, wore
her ash mark to work, because, unknown to me, I had imposed on
her forehead an almost perfect, cold, black ash mark in the shape of
a cross. She had purposely not washed her forehead that morning,
so she could flaunt this accidental 'genius' of art. Someone knew an
Editor over at the *Inquirer*, which sent out a photographer to capture
it for an article on Ash Wednesday –which made the paper the day
afterward. Needless to say, I was surprised to see Heidi's 'perfect ash
mark' on the front page of the *Inquirer*. Believe me, it was purely
accidental! But I enjoyed a little fifteen seconds of notoriety.

All Saints offers two Ash Wednesday liturgies. One at 12
Noon (for workers and those who might not wish to go out at night.)

After the Noon time service, I have a 'drive by ash opportunity from 12:45- 1:30 pm. I rushed outside after the service to the curb side and cars were already lined up. My thumb looked like burnt toast, but I schlepped ash marks for a solid hour with those haunting words: *Remember that you are dust and to dust you shall return.* The other liturgy was a full one at 7:30PM. Over a hundred people came for the 12 Noon liturgy and 225 at the evening service. I was so appreciative of our organist for offering the traditional organ piece I had come to know and love, Tomas Albinoni's *Adagio in G Minor.* She always captures a kind of *this is how it is, O Lord God* spirit. Albinoni's piece has a strong grip on me to just lay our human condition right out there. It's felt in the music's quietude and deep crescendos. I almost feel as if my arms are outstretched before Christ, pleading for mercy for my self- consumed life.

Combine the *Adagio* with Psalm 51's *'Create in me a right spirit...'* motif, and you can sum up the spirit of Lent. It's a great start to an inward journey for the soul (perhaps one of the most challenging for the noisy, busy world we're use to).

My sermon entertained a 'Happy Lent' for everyone - only because the news of war and our mounting national debt to foreign countries, the greater disparity between rich and poor and because of all the bad things that were happening to people, giving a chokehold on these past weeks. Lent (loose translation 'Spring in progress') always seemed to me to be about being open to life's possibilities rather than self-negating for what is broken in us – not that we aren't 'broken' and need fixing. The ancients looked to Spring as a time of renewal even as the earth awaited its own new birth. Our ancient cousins celebrated birth and longer days of light. I found only hints in the appointed lessons and Gospel for Ash Wednesday. The theme of such openness might make Lent a happy one. Although, I suggested, 'Walt Disney World' Lent is not! The texts are filled with constraint, minimalism, and reductionism and other 'isms' I can't think of.

Joel's solemn assembly (Joel 2:1ff) calls for exercising earthly constraint, piety and self-denial. Matthew's Gospel (6:1-6, 16-21) in the heart of the Sermon on the Mount reminds readers that focusing on 'things of the spirit' shouldn't be showy, since our relationship with God is so deeply personal. For Matthew, piety isn't for being seen as much as about awareness that the Creator God is seeking a space within us. Honest piety invites a closet kind of humility, a self-examination that yearns for God's mercy without showiness.

If we need showy humility, we're admitting we need congratulations. There's a Gospel story of the Law Teacher and the sinner (different as night and day) going to the Temple to pray. Fair enough. The Law Teacher wants to be heard and seen by God and others. It's : a fleeting reward, accessible and short lived. It's a self-congratulations and hoping someone will notice. But the other guy, bent over with his behavior lapses and moral missteps, sees nothing in himself to congratulate, but instead finds necessary to stand a far off from the other guy and lay it out to God: *'I can't live without your mercy, O God! I can't even look at you! Just as I am I come to you – Have mercy!'* The religious teacher is so full of himself that he must utter to God how he stands apart from this lowly one bowed over. He gives a litany of his good deeds as if to expect God might be congratulatory. Truthfully, he doesn't know how else to be –except his life seems devoid of mercy, compassion. Of course, God seems more drawn to the lamenting one down on his knees and pleading. God seems to be a sucker for people like that.

I've mentioned, of course, that sin is one of those inescapably difficult words in the scriptures with many meanings: *missing the target, rebellion against God, being perverse, going astray, deceiving, causing one another to go astray, etc.* 'Sin' for us seems like a stone we keep tripping over along the road. But I advocate for a fresh interpretation of it. It always seemed to me that my greatest self-disappointment is *forgetting who I really am,* falling way short of what God might be calling me to be. That's as close to sin as I can imagine. One Hebrew symbolism was 'missing the target,' the notion that we are arrows being drawn toward a target, inclined to miss it completely as if the arrow has a mind of its own. I'm capable of thinking that God is not a particularly convenient target, until I realize that God is only the target, the bow, the arrow and the archer all in one. So being at-one with God is about being in alignment with my mind, body and spirit, so that I see God clearly. I mentioned in my sermon:

'I know it's a weird analogy, but I'm a little like my car when I neglect to keep it aligned...it can go wobbling along the West Chester Pike. And I'll say, 'Hey, this Honda needs an alignment.' So, I take it

for service. It seems Lent is time to focus on our 'spiritual alignment.' It's the creature aware of its wobbly creature-nature. Something in that connection with the Creator needs adjusting. Lent seems to invite us in that direction.

Winter returned with a kind of vengeance the next few weeks in Lent. The snowstorms that dropped on us were all weekday snows, starting on a Monday morning and ended midweek. The one that dropped by this past week left a blanket of 14 inches in Havertown. Several midweek worship services had to be cancelled and my Bible Study on 'Job' met only once, the Tuesday after the First Sunday in Lent. I had been looking forward to that study, not only because Job is an intriguing story within the wisdom literature of the Bible, but because of the image of God it portrays - one seemingly willing to cause suffering in Job's life for the sake of a bet with the Satan. The writer may not have intended that, but it sure comes across that way. Even at that, I tried to imagine the world view of the writer of Job at that time. Job seems to have a resiliency about his life in spite of God letting the Satan have a few knockout punches. At times, he does curse the day he was born, yet he will not let go wondering how a good and just God would allow this tormented 'testing' and suffering to happen. His so-called friends spend an inordinate amount of time arguing that somewhere in his life he must have slipped up badly to get this divine treatment.

Coming toward Holy Week, I was once again up against the 'atonement' thinking in the Christian tradition. I wondered sometimes whether the concept of atonement in the gospels was far different from what early Christianity believed it be. To *'atone'* means to be 'at one' or be reconciled, to find agreement. As in the past, it seemed that religion had put God in the same category that the writer of Job had: as a kind of passive-aggressive deity, sitting by while his 'Son' is nailed to a Roman cross on a flimsy verdict of sedition (i.e. undermining government authority.) The God of Good Friday seemed scandalous to me - on one hand calling Jesus' *'Son, Beloved, one who pleases me'* and yet willing to cave into the human scenario of judging Jesus as seditious and setting him as an example through crucifixion for those who would pass by his cross. I said:

Looking at it from a very human perspective, the God of Good Friday seems impotent, passive and uninterested in the fate of his 'beloved'

Son. I struggle that God could be indifferent to the worst of the human condition, even in Jesus's Roman execution. Did God walk out when the Holocaust took millions of Jews to the gas chambers of Dachau? Was God disinterested when those planes rammed into the World Trade Center or Pentagon or the field in western Pennsylvania? Is God turning the other way when girls are sexually mutilated in the Sudan? I can't imagine. Sometimes I wonder if God isn't a silent sufferer when humans make destructive choices. Even human will in doing evil doesn't make God impotent or disinterested. Yet God is not a 'Superman, 'nor is Jesus a 'Super Hero.' Neither are 'in the nick of time' types. Human will – for good or ill –is always part of the great risk of divine nature. From God's perspective, there is power in the surrender of Jesus – the spirit of God in the human suffering, dying so that the human might be raised beyond this finite life.

We're reminded, too, that God is not 'up there,'- a casual observer of all human life - but rather dwelling here 'on the ground' and within positive energy, compassionate communities and our yearning hearts? How do we become empathetic and reaching for the underdogs in an unfair world? Is it found in our 'spiritual DNA?' Altruism has a source somewhere in human creation.

Jesus was an exceptional person with a deep God-presence and compassion within. Might we agree that the cross was the result of Jesus' own down-on-the-ground ministry, his willfulness to go beyond the perimeters of the religion and 'Messiah dreams?' There were many 'messiah pretenders' in those days. Do we have to pin the crucifixion on God and not allow that Jesus took up his cross willfully and challenged the lie of human power over against the power of self-giving love and compassion? In doing that, Jesus was revealing the essential nature of God. In the passion of Jesus, we still hear the 'Immanuel' we heard a few months ago at Christmas: 'God with us.' It's mind bending! This is a sufferable marriage between the divine and the human, two entities searching for each other in the world. Jesus helps us see the greater picture of this Love within our struggles for hope and Godly love and justice in this world. On the brutal cross of Roman punishment, Jesus took his mission to heart - showing the extent to which God loves the world.

This time of the year can send us deep into the holy... a divine mystery. And, yes, I've been rambling.

Chapter Thirteen

'OUR LIVES JOINED MORE COMPLETELY'

We entered into each other's lives and experienced love and happiness. Today I am confirming my promise for all of my life to love and respect you, to be faithful and honest with you, to give you encouragement, strength and trust, to stand together in our times of joy and of sorrow. I pray that our home will be one of love and understanding and patience ... not to remain the same, but to grow better and stronger with the passing of time, and through the love we have for one another. Our lives have become joined with the times we have shared, and will be more complete by the memories ahead, ready to be made.

I am promising from this day forward that I will be your husband and walk with you throughout all your tomorrows.
I love you, my Beautiful Dawn
Our wedding vows, March 14

I remember one of my colleagues telling me he never officiates weddings during Lent. I found that curious considering that in much of the imagery of *divine restoration,* God's intent to clean up the world, seems like a divine yearning, the Creator's courting, - perhaps divine flirtation, if you will. God wants a relationship with us even within the great limits of our human condition. The first miracle of Jesus in John's Gospel happened as he was enjoying a wedding in Cana, a hill country town on the slopes from Nazareth. There, Jesus is somewhat coerced into showing the abundance that is possible with an embarrassingly diminished wine supply at a wedding. (Weddings could go on for a week back then!) He proceeded to turn a quantum of water saved for rites of purification into some of the best *vino* ever to touch the lips of these inebriated guests at the wedding reception. God seems to favor the world with of abundance of Divine Love – a love so rich that the bouquet of its sweet nectar never fades. Although in the early Church Lent was an intense time of preparation for Easter, it is no less about the Christ energy of God growing ever larger (in Jesus the Nazorene)–as in the Sundays of Epiphany.

Second, the marriage imagery is often used to describe our waiting on God, somewhat like the bride waiting to go to the bridegroom's chambers on her wedding night. Throughout Israel's history, God is often Israel's 'husband' and she - nationally-speaking- his 'wife.'

Thirdly, God's relationship with Israel is much like a lifelong marriage– sometimes fraught with human infidelity vs. God's fidelity - symbolic of Israel's unfaithfulness to her contract with God. Marriage and relationships (rocky or otherwise) seem potent forces in biblical literature and the narrative of God's desire to be with us. Well, so much for my rationalization about getting married during Lent!

All of this to say that Dawn and I decided it was important to celebrate our marriage soon. We settled on a date in mid-March, actually March 14th, a Saturday evening, in the Great Hall, our parish fellowship room, inviting members of the parish to join us in celebrating our new beginning. We decided to invite a friend of mine, Stan, from 'across the aisle,' a Lutheran pastor from St. Paul's Church, Ardmore, PA, to officiate. My friend, Mark Crenshaw, another Lutheran, was unavailable to come up from Maryland. I had once met Stan and his wife for dinner and officiated their wedding a few years back. He didn't mind at all officiating during Lent, which was our first big hurdle cleared. Stan, like me, was a liberal when it came to theology and liturgy. We were a lot alike save for one thing: he was a significantly better golfer than I with a 10 handicap. My handicap nearer to my age.

Beautiful Dawn and I met Stan and Bonnie for lunch to talk over wedding details. The girls hit it off well, focusing on details that ran circles around Stan's and my depth of interest, although we listened and said often 'Whatever you say." Bonnie decided she would be our Wedding Coordinator and teased Stan and me that we needed to 'remove our collars' and let the girls take over. We gladly did that, and Stan and I talked (what else?) about golf.

The wedding would be simple, inviting the women of All Saints Parish to provide a buffet for the reception, for which Beautiful

Dawn and I would make a generous donation. Our wedding invitations would go to the parish, our families and our intimate friends. We would ask for *no* gifts but invite guests perhaps to make a donation to their favorite charity in honor of our wedding. Few people, however, knew of Dawn's pregnancy – Stan and Bonnie included.

The Dress

One thing you must know about my sweet Dawn - she hates to shop, to buy clothing and spend time at Malls. I know, for some women this might seem incredulous. She will happily tell you that many of her clothes come from thrift shops - many with famous brand names, including Liz Claiborne, Alfred Dunner and stores like Coldwater Creek and Talbot's. This startles many of our women 'retail enthusiasts,' who would rather die than shop for clothes at Thrift Shops.

Of course, I honestly cannot understand the allure of shopping –part of my 'clueless male wiring'. Most women find shopping infinitely better than chocolate and sex (in that order). Not Dawn. The order of her desires would be the three 'C's: 1) Cuddling; 2) Coitus *(Come on – you know what it means!)* and 3) Chocolate. I find it amazing she put coitus ahead of chocolate!

Nevertheless, in her attempt to find a wedding gown (with Bonnie's support), my beautiful Dawn had one requirement only: to buy a gently used gown at a thrift shop one.

"What?" Bonnie responded in amazement, "you're going to a thrift shop for the dress you're going to wear on the most important day of your life? Honestly, Dawn!"

She admitted this was a bit shocking initially, but once she heard Dawn's rationale, she thought otherwise. So, it was no surprise that the two of them had planned coffee one morning and a visit to 'Sylvia Berkow's Resale Shop' on Haverford Avenue and City Ave., Philadelphia. Just a strip shopping center store, but it's packed with great bargains. Sylvia was so welcoming and introduced Dawn and Bonnie to a special room with just 'gently used' wedding gowns. Sylvia explained how many of the gowns were sold soon after the wedding from brides who had no interest in keeping them.

She went on:

"Many brides today aren't sentimental types – especially the young brides with wealthy parents! No offense, of course, but it's just a different day. So, look around and let me know if you find one of interest."

For Dawn and Bonnie, it was much like entering a candy shop with enormous succulent variations to choose from. The room was packed with gowns of all makes and sizes. Dawn probably looked at every one of them. And, within an hour, my soon-to-be bride found a perfect fit from a favorite selection: a Vera Wang Taffeta Ball Gown with 3- dimensional floral embroidery on the bodice. I'm not making this up in my head. Only a detailed description by my beautiful wife *after* the wedding could possibly have made this perfectly understandable to the women who are reading this now!

According to her description, the gown had 'feather-light layers, which made for a magnificent tossed tulle skirt design, complimented by a corded lace bodice.' Originally retailed at $1398, this perfect fit, used-once Vera Wang was amazingly priced at $350 at Sylvia's. Dawn was ecstatic and paid cash. Bonnie couldn't believe her eyes. The dress was like new –not a blemish, not a tear, looking like it had never been pulled from its original rack. When she tried it on, Dawn looked into the mirror and began to cry. Bonnie became tearful too.

Dawn laughed through her tears:

"Gosh, Bonnie, I didn't want to make *you* cry."

"No, Dawn… I'm crying because I paid over a $1100 for my wedding gown!"

Ruth McGill, chair of the Fellowship Bunch at All Saints was the logical choice to ask to coordinate the food. A pastry chef by profession, Ruth had tons of energy for dinner gatherings. When she was asked at a meeting with Beautiful Dawn and Bonnie to lead this, she literally jumped up and down.

I'd love to!! I'd love to… I'm on it!

And immediately she took her clipboard and pad and started writing details as Dawn and Bonnie started imagining the day. We agreed that, depending on the number of folks who would pass through the reception following the ceremony, the extra food would be given to the Wesley House down in Chester, PA. Stan and I hammered out the ceremony details, with Dawn and Bonnie present. We didn't mind some traditional elements of a wedding ceremony and favored a Unity symbol called a 'Unity Bouquet,' where flowers would to be placed in an empty vase by designated family and friends and, finally, by Dawn and myself. The flowers were to be among Dawn's favorites.

The news of our wedding became 'viral' throughout the parish. Through a parish letter of invitation, we would ask that folks join us and that they RSVP no later than March 10th. By March 6th, we had received 200 responses in the affirmative. Dawn was overwhelmed with the number, but we agreed that it was an important event for the parish to experience our wedding. It was the first time a rector had been married while serving All Saints. The saying around the church was *this is the rector's new dawn!* And, for sure, it was!

Joy and Life Interrupted

Sadly, the night after Bonnie and Dawn had wrapped up all the details for our wedding my soon-to-be bride miscarried our child. She had felt very tired and prepared for bed. While peeing she felt a sharp cramping in her abdomen and then she passed several large blood clots. She called me to the toilet and cried. I helped her to clean up and held her until the cramping subsided. We both knew what had happened and the helpless feelings it would bring. I prepared a warm bath for her and gently stroked her neck and back. After I toweled her dry, I helped her dress and we went to Mercy Hospital to make sure that she was cared for. The doctor on call and nursing staff were wonderful and comforting. We returned home at 2AM and spent the rest if the night holding each other in our sadness. We chatted about 'what may have been' and I sang to her an old campfire song *Kumbaya, my Lord, (an old Spiritual, 'Come by here, my Lord.'*

Only God in heaven knows how much I loved her at this challenging time - how much I wanted to reassure her that she was still the most beautiful partner I could ever imagine embracing.

She slept in my arms, a blanket around us -a beautiful afghan made by her Grandma Wilma. It was a blanket Grandma Wilma 's own Aunt Nina had made for her in the early 1930's when Wilma was pregnant. It had, of course, the fragrances of yesteryear, soft, warm, strong and the memory of comfort. We also slept under another blanket - a warm and comforting blanket of Eternal Love that knows human tears and disappointments and stands harbor with us. It was four a.m. now and I switched off the light and held her close on her couch until the dawn's sun reached through the living room blinds. It was Thursday, the 12ᵗʰ of March.

The Rector's New Dawn

As difficult as the miscarriage had been several days before our wedding, it became certain that Saturday, March 14ᵗʰ was one of the most beautiful gatherings and celebrations I had ever experienced. The skies were partly cloudy and the temperatures moderate.

I had orchestrated all manner of worship in my now twenty some years as a pastor. I could never have put together such a beautiful liturgy of worship as our wedding. Although she was very nervous, my dearest Dawn was radiantly beautiful in her Vera Wang gown. I was teary-eyed at the very sight of her coming down the aisle - caught on camera, I should tell you! Since her father was a no-show for the wedding (he never responded to the invitation, Beautiful Dawn had decided to come down the aisle alone. Her flower girl was little Dreama McFarland, a beautiful child of Downs, the six-year old daughter of Danica McFarland. Her ring bearer was Paul and Bonnie's youngest son, Kirk, a handsome nine-year old, who took his job very seriously.

It's hard to describe the magic of facing my ravishingly beautiful bride and holding our hands as we repeated our vows to one another, prompted by Stan. I barely got through my words, my tears were freely flowing, and I wondered what half my parish was thinking as they watched their rector being a bowl of jelly through his marriage vows. Beautiful Dawn on the other hand was as cool as a cucumber. This Beautiful Flower, who was worried her nervousness might make her stumble down the long aisle of All Saints, looked me straight in the eye and repeated her vows, placing her hand over my cheek, and drying it with her thumb. (I recall whispering 'Thank you. I love you.') How sweetly she repeated after Stan as she looked into my eyes:

We entered into each other's lives • and experienced love and happiness. Today I am confirming my promise • for all of my life • to love and respect you •to be faithful and honest with you • to give you encouragement, strength and trust • to stand together in our times of joy and of sorrow.

I pray that our home • will be one of love and understanding and patience •... not to remain the same • but to grow better and stronger with the passing of time • and through the love we have for one another. Our lives have become joined • with the times we have shared • and will be more complete by the memories ahead • ready to be made. I am promising from this day forward •that I will be your wife • and walk with you throughout all your tomorrows.

What a beautiful moment to hear Stan call us 'husband and wife.' Our kiss was unapologetically passionate and the whistles and thrills from the gathered approved.

There were a few anecdotal moments, including the ring bearer, Kirk, getting a bad case of the hiccups that started early on in the ceremony. Stan was officiating our ceremony and Bonnie was standing there as Matron of Honor, her flowers in one hand and Beautiful Dawn's in the other —both parents were helpless as Kirk hiccupped away and loudly. We both laugh as we review the audio-visual of the ceremony provided by Bob McGyver, my Senior Warden. Oh, and one more anecdotal memory of the ceremony. During the recessional, Kirk took Dreama, the flower girl's hand, but she refused to hold onto it and, in trying to pull away, they both fell flat on their faces in the middle of the aisle. Whatever rose petals were left in Dreama's basket was now strewn over the aisle and over both of them. Kirk, being the little gentleman and somewhat embarrassed, gently helped Dreama up. She looked at him and started smiling and reached up and kissed him on the cheek. The unexpected kiss now turned Kirk's complexion to almost the color of the rose petals scattered on the floor. He shook his head, took her hand and walked out to the applause of all the guests. Brit, our volunteer for video recording, got it all! Since we were walking together in front of them, we greeted them with hugs and kisses of our own. I told Dawn, "That'll look wonderful in the movie!"

The congregation was so congratulatory and welcomed Dawn as if she were a daughter . Many of them enjoyed ribbing me, saying to Beautiful Dawn, *"We hope you get a chance to see him now and then!"* Or *"Thank heavens, now his shirts will get ironed!"* I had a tendency not to be effective with keeping my shirts from getting wrinkled.' The truth of the matter is that I was pretty lazy about laundry and dry cleaning. And Beautiful Dawn had made it clear from the beginning that she didn't own an iron. Does anyone own an iron anymore?

The hospitality and food organized by Ruth McGill was stupendous. She had mustered twenty large batches of lasagna and quantities of mini sandwiches (including P&J sandwiches for kids). She had arranged for an enormous wedding cake that looked like the edifice of All Saints! Ruth's favors, flowers and extras were spectacular. We couldn't have been luckier than to have known Ruth McGill. Our church's worship choir had even joined together to offer an arrangement of one of Johannes Brahms' love songs *Neue Leibesleider, Opus 85*. We both were teary-eyed over the song. What a gift! All Saints' worship choir was exceptional, although short on tenors, and capable of delivering a wonderful variety of worship music. They loved occasionally singing 'outside the box' –such as the Brahms. Four of the men even formed a barbershop quartet that had won some awards in the Philly-area Society for the Preservation of Barbershop Quartet Singing in America – SPBQSA.

Despite our plea for *no* gifts, a number of people left cards with gift certificates and cash. Some folks just never listen! We later decided to donate the cash to a local battered women's shelter. By 9:30 p.m., I could see that my beautiful bride was very tired. Having experienced her miscarriage and having prepared so many details, she was not sleeping well. Additionally, she was only a few days until her board exams. Bonnie very graciously made an announcement that we would be finished no later than 10 p.m. and invited the Bride and Groom to be dismissed before that. Yes, the congregational attendants and friends had some fun teasing about that! The party would continue with our well wishes and rich memories of care and friendship. We both fell into sleep until 7 a.m

Chapter Fourteen

EASTER - LIFE IS NEW AGAIN

Death's flood has lost its chill since Jesus crossed the river
Lover of souls from ill, my passing soul deliver. Had Christ, who
once was slain, not burst his three-day prison, our faith had been in vain.
But now has Christ arisen, arisen, arisen!

-Verse 3, 'The Joyful Eastertide', Text George Woodward; Music:
Dutch Folk Tune, Vreuchten

So, it had been an up and down Lent for us in Havertown. The 'down' was, of course, the miscarriage my sweet Dawn endured, which sadly had to be kept a secret from the parish. My ecclesiastical ass would have been kicked all the way to Valley Forge with the public knowledge that we were expecting a child before we were married. It would have F.U. Frank percolating in high ecclesiastical style. It was our intention to have the wedding before physical evidence of the pregnancy, which even a mathematical dullard would have figured to be 'conception' before 'reception' (i.e. wedding reception).

However, the 'up' part of Lent was certainly our wedding on March 14th , two days after the miscarriage. Nothing could have been more therapeutic than celebrating our nuptial beginning as husband and wife shared with the parish, family and friends. The folks at All Saints Parish are a blended group of traditional Episcopalians from the Philadelphia area and not a few 'burned out' seekers looking for some 'divine mystery' they might trust. Mingled with them are transplanted folks from other Episcopalian communities living in the area because of jobs or education for research. We were a motley crew of old and new Episcopalians'- a number of gays, lesbians and transgendered folks, not a few singles' ethnically mixed folks and many internationals working in research and technology among our academic communities and our technical and scientific communities.

Our faith community is a beautiful tapestry with colorful patterns and weaves.

Easter was approaching after the Three Days that had us in church for Maundy Thursday, Good Friday and the unique Easter Vigil of late Saturday.

'Death's flood has lost its chill' the Woodward's Easter Hymn suggests.

Back in the day when the Vernal Equinox rolled around, my hometown went all out for Easter. Mother would always make sure we had new outfits for Easter Day and our community actually had an Easter Day parade, which began a little after 12:30 p.m. at the conclusion of most worship services. We'd gather at St. Clem's School and walk to Havertown Senior High School, where photographers waited in droves to capture our new outfits. One year my photo in my new suit and bow tie ended up in the Delaware County News. My mother clipped it and had it on the fridge for years. I looked so dorky in black rim glasses, a multi colored black bow tie and a suit jacket that looked a might small and pants that seemed a might too short, green colored socks to match my green jacket. My 'jumbos were sticking out of course, since my head still hadn't caught up with my ears. 'Dorky' is the only word I can find to remark about that picture.

As far as I know, Easter parades are mostly a thing of the past. Few parades exist today save for the hoopla on the Fourth of July Spectacular Feast of Bands. In New York City they have an Annual Easter Parade and Easter Bonnet Festival, held on Fifth Avenue between 49th and 57th Streets. It's hardly a 'parade' in the normal sense. Mostly it's a mingling of people wearing colorful costumes and funny bonnets. Some countries around the world still have Easter Parades - including Spain, Asia and The Netherlands .

I recall my early high school years, marching with my Sousaphone on hot days in April melting in my uniform and hating my band director for not allowing beverages until we had marched the distance to St. Clem's! My lips were so parched I could hardly 'oompah' any more. But I was not the worse for wear carrying that enormous oversize brass plumbing over my head. I always had to be careful about turning and bending over – which I learned fast after

I whacked Tommy Bintzer in the head at a practice one afternoon on the football field. Tommy whacked me over the head with his trombone and we were off to the races. Two stitches later we were laughing and saying we were just 'two pains in the brass.'

I caught up with Dawn one afternoon at Starbucks. We shared and sipped our favorite Caramel Macchiato Grande on a rainy late March afternoon.

She admitted: "While I look forward to attending Easter services, Aldie, I must confess I'm still not sure where I am in the whole resurrection thing. I have so many questions running around my head about the existence of God or that there is such a thing as the Resurrection."

Of course, I'd been there myself. Not many people realize that clergy can tiptoe through a *'mind'-field* of doubts like most of their parishioners. They seldom admit it though. I was plagued with my own doubts - including the Virgin Birth doctrine, which set up a firestorm with Molly Mason back at Holyoke parish in Virginia. I also wondered about the Resurrection. It wasn't going to affect my Easter sermon, but I have to admit that when it comes to Resurrection, I embrace the witness that Jesus, although dead as a doornail, certainly didn't 'go away' especially after the gospels were written and two thousand years of 'Church.' He was a new version of the same Jesus or as I liked to say: 'a resurrected earthy Jesus with new duds.'

"My Grandma Wilma would roll over in her grave if she knew I had such doubts," Dawn admitted as she shook her head.

I suggested:

"Well, darling, we certainly can't see the whole picture of God in a short time. It's like... something has to awaken within us - an ever-expanding vision, a way of seeing beyond worldly views of life and death. Doubt is like a shaky footbridge across a deep ravine called 'faith.' We want to cross but pause there and take a look around us and wonder if we can make it across. Jesus never gave a picture of heaven. Frankly, I don't think he knew. Although, I suspect he was more interested in trying to make a better world here on earth.

"Do you believe in resurrection, Aldie? Do you think Jesus walked out of his own grave with a body that had been broken and put to death?"

215

I pondered a moment.

'Well, as I've matured, I've found I have more questions than answers – like: *What kind of resurrection are we talking about?* For example, consider Mark's gospel where Jesus is missing bodily from the resurrection story and some of the women are running away in fear of heavenly messengers inside the empty tomb. Mark's story is a 'go and tell' story that has frightened women running from the tomb. Or Matthew's resurrection story where the resurrected Jesus is visible to the women and then the disciples meet Jesus coming and going. In Luke's Gospel, the women are coming to do the burial duties and are terrified by an angel who announces Jesus had been raised just as he said he would and they go back and tell the disciples, who regard it as 'gossip.' Finally, there's John's resurrection where Mary mistakes Jesus for the gardener (she's been crying her eyes out) and, once aware that it was the resurrected Jesus standing there talking with her, she wants to hold onto him for dear life. The four gospels are a 'Resurrection Hodge-Podge'- which one do we believe –if any?

I looked at my sweet Dawn pausing. I put my hand on her cheek and kissed her. "I haven't answered your question, have I? She kissed me back with 'No.'

"Truthfully, darling, I've had to question it and read and question more until chalking it up with two words: *mystery and faith.*"

"Goodness, Aldie, so even *you* have doubts about it," my surprised wife remarked.

"Not so much doubt as wonder, Sweetheart. When things can't be proved beyond a doubt, I guess I just live in awe of how God goes about being God within this finite world. Sometimes it seems that 'wonder' is the only foundation on which to build something like 'faith' –another mysterious word.

I paused for a moment searching for words. "I figure that creation is a great big 'God-work' within infinite time and space. I can't imagine God would just leave us in the galaxy as space dust ... or like some unfinished piece of furniture that God just got bored with and left along the cosmic road. Life seems to have enough love and meaning attached to it that makes us curious about where it's all going. Life has a kind of holy 'mindfulness' about it even if I can't be sure what the 'divine thinking' is about, except with hints in the Bible. Even God's 'mindfulness' of us behind some cosmic curtain is a mystery. Through it all, the mystery seems suggest that God *is* with us. Sometimes I just have to surrender, *whether we live or die, we are connected to this Holy One.*

"Geez, Aldie, that's so deep!" she scratched her forehead.

"Sorry, Sweetheart." I am 'deep,' of course. Theology is creative and reflective guesswork, pondering what God is or does when God is out and about being God. Theologians and churchy folks across the years turned 'imagining it' into 'doctrine,' and doctrine into 'rules,' which we attempt to turn into a 'religious system.' I've had a love-hate relationship with that system ever since being at Holyoke and dancing my sorry, theologically liberal ass around the likes of fearful people who need to protect the Bible and God.

Too bad there aren't more church reformations. As church writer Phyllis Tickle suggests: 'Every five hundred years or so the church needs to hold a rummage sale to get rid of some useless stuff... not the least of which might include some of its own beliefs.

"Wow, Aldie Seaver! It's interesting to hear you talk about these things. Here I am now married to you and I love the folks of All Saints – but I just haven't made that 'church' connection in my heart yet. Things are so 'cloudy' in my spirit."

"It's OK darling. Hey, you can sit in the back and duck out if it gets to be too much. Just know I'll chase you down for a kiss and a cup of coffee!"

Easter Sunday was warmer than most days had been. By April 8th , we expect Spring-like climate. But this Easter Sunday was almost summer-like. The first liturgy at All Saints was packed with my regulars, the faithful throng who would never considering going anywhere but their own parish, but who delighted in dragging their visiting families into the Nave to show them off. It was interesting to observe how totally clueless these poor folks were coming in and wondering what on earth it was all about.

Beautiful Dawn came to the Contemporary Mass at 11 a.m. When she walked in, I caught a glimpse and she took my breath away. She was wearing a flowery-print yellow dress and white belt. The dress complimented her shapely countenance. She was wearing small white pearls and carrying a small white purse. I almost tripped on my robes to rush back to hug her.

"You're gorgeous, darling!" I said in a whisper.

"Thank you, Aldie. It's shorter than I thought. I hope it's not too provocative."

"I like it!" I smiled broadly," but just stay away from the men folk here!"

The 11 o'clock Mass was packed with 'EC's or 'Easter-Christians 'as we like to call them. A large part of the worship was contemporary in nature - two vocalists, a keyboardist, and two acoustical guitars. Mitch Willingham, a transplant from the Church of England and himself a Londoner, led the Praise Team. They are a unique cadre of people who meet on Tuesday evenings for their 'jam sessions,' and sort through contemporary praise music suitable for the liturgical calendar. They start rehearsal by reading the lessons (in this case the Easter texts) Then they pray together hands in hands and 'give it all to God' for the rest of the week.

With the mass over, I fumbled around with books and notes I had written that morning essential to my weekly schedule. I wondered where Beautiful Dawn was. Most everyone had left the Nave. The financial team for the day had packed morning offerings and prepared to take them to Night Deposit. *Where was she?* I wandered toward the Gathering Area near our entrance - a large foyer that lead to the main entrance and exit of All Saints. Perhaps she was outside chatting. Peering out, I saw only the money counters parting ways and getting into their vehicles. Something seemed wrong. I turned off the light in the men's room and then I heard what I thought was someone whimpering.... It seemed to be coming from the Women's bathroom.

"Sweetheart?" I heard her broken voice in the Women's room. Daring to stand outside and opened the door, I said:

"Darling, are you OK?"

Seconds passed, and she stood up from inside the stall, emerged wiping her hands on her dress and smiled at me, her mascara running down her face.

"What's wrong, Sweetheart? Are you thinking about your grandmother?"

We embraced.

"Aldie, we need to talk." Every time I hear that I get a lump in my throat. I tend to think the worst. I took her hand and we sat down on the couch in the Fellowship Room, a place I often used to counsel people. I held her close. Tears once again streamed down her face. She attempted to compose herself and took her time to search for the right words.

"Aldie, darling, I know you adore me and love me as I am, but my past has been far from impeccable. I mean..."

"Sweetheart? We all make lapses in judgment."

"Please listen, darling. There are things I've never told you... and I must."

She began to unravel a narrative of the darker moments of her young life twenty years before, how she had been born outside her father's marriage to a mother she still doesn't know and how she had had one sexual encounter after another in her early teens into her 20's. She recounted growing up frequently shuttled between her step-mother and father and grandmother Wilma in New Castle, PA. Her older sister Grace had once told her:

"You're not my real sister, Dawn. I heard Mom and Daddy arguing about it one night at the supper table. They said you came from one of his girlfriends. But I love you. As far as I'm concerned, you *are* my real sister!"

Dawn remembered crying about that so hard in the closet under the steps to upstairs that she fell asleep and no one knew where she was for hours. When her stepmother, scared out of her wits, found her, Dawn just held her tightly and cried all the more.

She recounted how in her teens she had been raped after a school dance outside the school gymnasium by an older boyfriend who offered to 'take her home.' When she had shared this with her High School friend, Maggie, she took her off to Immaculate Conception Church one afternoon following school to confess it to the resident priest. Dawn had never been to a Confession before. She felt a little claustrophobic inside the confessional booth and was startled when the green light came on and the priest opened the curtain quickly and the grill between them became visible.

Prompted by Maggie's instruction, Dawn broke the silence by saying, "Uh, OK....Bless me, Father, for I have ...uh...sinned. It has been..."

There was a large pause.

"Yes, my child?"

Dawn was squeamish and whispered,

"I forgot what to say next..."

The priest replied, "Tell me how long it's been since your last confession."

Another silence fell upon the exchange. Dawn finally mustered up the courage to say: "Uh, to tell you the truth, I don't think I've ever confessed anything, Father.... except, well, that my earthly Father, not you or the really big "Father,' of course, had me by one of his girlfriends and here I am confused about who I really belong to. I was happiest at my Grandma Wilma's house in New Castle, Pennsylvania. It was the one place where I really felt loved. She had a comfortable bed and often baked me lemon meringue pies and..."

"Child!"

The old priest coughed and said: "Please, just tell me what you need to confess."

Dawn told me it was such a pivotal moment for her. What *was* she going to 'confess' to some priest she didn't know? Everything in her life seems to have been 'done' to her. No priest or adult or parent or pushy boyfriend was going to control her life any more. Suddenly she picked up her pocketbook, stood up and walked out of the confessional booth, grabbed Maggie's hand and ran out of Immaculate Conception onto the pebbly parking lot. Maggie pulled her hand away and was indignant:

"Holy Jesus, Dawn, you don't just walk out on a priest in confession! How are you going to know what to do to get your sins forgiven?"

Dawn stopped in her tracks and turned and looked Maggie in the face angrily:

"I'm not the one who needs to confess, Maggie! There are other people who should be in that confessional booth right now telling that priest about their sins *against me!* I'm not perfect and there are sins I do need to confess, but I've had so much abuse done to me that I can't think straight! I've met so many guys who only had one thing on their minds...to get my panties off and fuck me!"

She yelled it so loud that people on the other side of the street stopped and looked.

Maggie gasped in response. She was a naïve Catholic teen and hated the 'f-word.' Dawn was unfazed,

"Damn it, Maggie, I'm going to work this out on my own! To hell with any priest who believes he's going to work out my life for me by making me say 50 Hail Mary's and 100 Our Fathers!' Don't you see... *I've* got to work on me!"

Dawn turned with her books in hand and walked away to a stunned Maggie. That was the last time Dawn saw Maggie McNeal. Perhaps Maggie realized that Dawn was out of her league. For Dawn, it was the last time she had entered a church... until she met me.

It would take Dawn a long time to realize that her inner beauty was more important than her outer beauty. And it mattered greatly that she refused to be subject to people's perception of her. She recognized her own submissive ways and her frailty, but a lot of stuff had been dumped on her that she did not solicit. Boys told her how 'gorgeous' she was, but none of them cared about how she felt, what she thought or what she wanted in a relationship. They just wanted fondling and sex. She was starving for genuine love. Every submission to having sex only made her realize how needy for acceptance she was, wanting to please others to win their favor.' She realized that the problem wasn't the mindless attitudes of boys and their immature sexuality... but it was her problem and she needed to claim a 'new dawn.' in her life... and she was going to make that 'new dawn' happen without a priest or the church.

We sat in the lounge chair of the fellowship room and held each other. She kissed me tenderly and said: "When I came in here today, I realized that all of that 'stuff 'of my life that made me a frightened teen was only pushing me away from valuing my own soul. In fact, when I was being forced to have sex, I decided I didn't believe in God, because I couldn't imagine any good God allowing my life to go on this way. But I realized today I had pushed God away- not the other way around. Aldie, today when we got on our knees for the confession and I heard the words *Your sins are forgiven*... it wasn't you or the Church or some priest in my past I needed to hear say that - I heard in my heart some divine reality beyond my tormented life *accept… affirm* the whole ill-begotten mess of 'me' - and here I am warts, bruises and all, darling! Can you still love me?"

Tears were already streaming down my face. She wiped with her thumbs. I held her.

"My heart breaks for all you've been through, Love. If God can embrace you in your brokenness, how much more will I embrace you and love you. Besides which…I promised my commitment to you in a kind of 'for 'better or for worse' way."

I kissed her gently on the lips and cupped her face. We held each other for the longest time. We could have rocked together in our loving embrace all afternoon, both of us with not a few tears.

As we left the Fellowship Room to get some lunch, I thought to myself that Beautiful Dawn's connection in worship today was itself a 'resurrection.' She didn't use that word, but that's what it seemed like. I wondered about all the 'resurrections' I have ever known. Along the path of my priesthood, many people fought hard to love themselves or allowed themselves to be rescued from seemingly impossible places life had pushed them. I'm convinced the difference is Love – the patient, sustaining love of one human being for another that emerges from the very heart of a Creator God, coaxing each to be awakened. Beautiful Dawn loved me enough to bare her past agonies, to be transparent about a broken part of her life and open herself to the God of her being to be healed in her brokenness and to even trust that my love would sustain her. It wasn't the sermon that spoke to her this Easter Sunday, but it was the Confession and Forgiveness. That was her 'resurrection.'

Chapter Fifteen

DAWN BRIANA SEAVER, R.N.

It takes courage to grow up and become who you really are
- e.e. cummings

It was Tuesday, April 30th that Beautiful Dawn got the letter she had been waiting for regarding her certification as a Registered Nurse. She refused to open it right away. I was away on pastor's retreat for a day and wouldn't return until 4 p.m. She looked at the letter on our kitchen table all morning. What if she had not passed? What would she do next? It was probably around 2 PM after returning from grocery shopping that my Beautiful Dawn put the groceries on the dining room table and just took the letter in her hand and opened it hastily. *What is all this hesitation,* she thought to herself? *It's an either-or. Life goes on either one way or another. If I have to....* Her eyes casting a glance, she immediately knew by the tone of the letter that she, Dawn Briana O'Shea (Seaver) was now a Registered Nurse. Relief broke out all over her like a rash. She walked from room to room reading the letter over and over just to make sure the formal institutional tone REALLY said she was certified. The laminated card that came with the letter indicated 'R.N.'- it had to be true!

She decided to text me, *'Dawn Briana O'Shea Seaver R.N!* I wanted to jump up from my conference seat and pull down my fist in the air with a resounding *'Yes!'* but I just sat there and texted back, *'Congratulations, my Beautiful Dawn.... I'm so proud of you, Darling! Dinner out tonight for celebration!'* She texted me back with three smiley faces.

She had interviewed at Frankford Hospital first, but there were no pediatric nursing positions open. However, Children's Hospital of Center City was interested and had granted an interview for a position in the Pediatric ICU. It was an area of nursing that was one of the most demanding and yet could be the most meaningful.

The commute would not be bad from Havertown. It would take a few days for the interview to be processed. She had two interviews on Wednesday and Thursday. When she returned home exhausted late Thursday afternoon, she revealed the interview process had been a 'bear.' She was certain she did not get the position.

"They grilled me on stuff fresh off my nursing exams." Aldie. Remember how I studied and studied. They asked me about detailed procedures and instrumentation I hadn't fully learned."

On Friday, she called me at my office: "Guess what, Aldie, I'm heading to Children's Hospital on May 15th! I have to go in this afternoon to fill out all the paperwork." The celebrations continued with a meal at *Shogun's*. Why not?

Chapter Sixteen

ROMANTIC INTERLUDE AT BROOKSIDE COTTAGE

O, to have a little house!

To own the hearth and stool and all! The heaped up sods upon the fire, The pile of turf against the wall!

To have a clock with weights and chains and pendulum swinging up and down! A dresser filled with shining delph, Speckled and white and blue and brown!

I could be busy all day Clearing and sweeping the hearth and floor, and fixing on their shelf again My white and blue and speckled store!

I could be quiet there at night Beside the fire and by myself, sure of a bed and loath to leave The ticking clock and the shining delph!

Och! but I'm weary of mist and dark and roads where there's never a house nor bush, And tired I am of bog and road, And the crying wind and the lonesome hush!

And I am praying to God on high, And I am praying Him night and day, For a little house, a house of my own, Out of the wind's and the rain's way

- An Old Woman of the Roads by Padraic Colum (1881-1972)

Before her work began at Children's May 15th, we planned a weekend getaway in Western Pennsylvania. Again, I know what you're thinking: *Here you go again!* We pursued a Western Pennsylvania destination at 'The Brookside Cottage,' an idyllic off-road Bed and Breakfast nestled in the Laurel Highlands of Pennsylvania south of Somerset. Traveling west on the Pennsylvania, and taking Route 281 (Kingwood Rd) south of Somerset, we found the 'Brookside' to be on a long gravelly road about a mile and half off the Kingwood Road. Dave and Wendy Bischoff, owners, spread enormous 'Highlands hospitality' before their guests. The cottage looks like a large old Irish estate nestled on a hillside with beautiful vistas of the Laurel

Mountains. A beautiful walking bridge across a gently drifting stream is viewed from the breakfast room and lovers often stand on the bridge and embrace and kiss. This little European-style crafted bridge we call 'Kissing Bridge #3'. We initiated it with a sustained lip-lock. A large wooded grassy area spreads out deep in the back yard almost to the woods. Many large Adirondack chairs painted in European settings await occupants for chatting or snoozing. I often spot deer grazing their way through the wooded area. Sometimes the carefully maintained flower gardens circumnavigate the large trees out back but most of them surround the cottages themselves. I should say that Brookside has a few special small cottages that guests can choose apart from the large center cottage.

Beautiful Dawn loves flowers. I get a little giddy when she gives the name of flowers as we walk by. Around flower gardens, I sometimes say: "Darling, did you notice how that yellow rose sort of blushed when you walked by with your stunning beauty?" To walk with Beautiful Dawn as she names these flowers and takes pictures and delights in them is unparalleled joy. "Aldie, look how they've planted the Mountain laurel shrubs and laced them with all the wild flowers. Don't you love the yellows and whites and pinks and reds? Here, please take my picture next to this group here."

I gladly obliged. Standing there in her sleeveless white dress and corral lacey skirt billowing with the Highlands breezes, she kicked my heart into a high gallop. Her smile melted me down to helplessness. I'm sorry... I'm a guy. Her gorgeous thighs are to die for!

"Make sure you get as much of the mountain laurel as possible," she maintained her pose.

Noticing my ardor, she said teasingly, "Now, Aldie, are you enjoying looking at the flowers or me? Oh my," she sighed, "you're such a naughty boy!"

We stayed out on the grounds and reclined in the Adirondacks chairs until sunset and chatted just about everything from the insanity of politics to why organized religion is struggling so much. Ever since Easter Sunday at All Saints, she has asked more about faith matters than any other subject I could have anticipated. She was now affirming that she seemed 'in the circle' of God's enormous love, opening enormous spiritual vistas for her. Lately, Dawn had taken to reading the Scriptures and bought a big Bible Commentary to help her weed through the larger 'God story' spun by the people's stories of faith. Sometimes I'm a Bible mentor in these conversations. We talk about trying to understand the context of those stories.

"Commentaries are kind of like looking under rocks. What was going on beneath the words that eventually became 'the Bible?'" I said. "It's asking 'What lies beneath the biblical story?' And for sure, there's always life teeming beneath those rocks."

We talked about 'metaphor'- how to avoid the trap of 'literalism' (everything happening as written) rather than allowing the meaning writers gave to their God experiences to surface and become appreciated from our own world view.

"I believe God peeks through those old stories," I suggested.

The Baldowski's

We arrived early for dinner at the 'Black Forest Room,' an elegant European style room finished in pine and displaying some of the most beautiful artwork of the Laurel Highlands. We ordered an entree of portabella mushrooms stuffed with crab imperial and wine sauce, redskin potatoes and green beans. As always, we shared it liberally. Irish music played subtly in the background.

We were finishing up the entree when we heard a scream from the next room. Everyone turned a looked and an elderly man appeared from around the corner holding his throat.

"Oh my God, Aldie, he's choking!"

She quickly put down her napkin, pushed the chair back and ran toward him. Within seconds she had her arms around him and was performing the Heimlich maneuver. I was startled, since her strength was far greater than I imagined it to be. There was absolute silence as we sat around.

She whispered, "Come on, sir. Let's get this out."

She gave him several tight squeezes around his midrib, pulling upward, until the old man just coughed up a pretty sizable piece of chicken bone. He fell to his knees and Beautiful Dawn with him. Dawn wrapped her arms around him as he coughed and tried to catch his breath. His wife stood there stoically as he looked up at her and then turning to Beautiful Dawn, gasping, he cried:

"My God, woman...you saved my life!"

Dawn smiled and said: "You made me work hard for that one. I'm Dawn... I'm a new Registered Nurse - thankfully. But I've only practiced it on manikins before. Are you OK? Let's get you up on the chair. "Everyone gave a polite applause as the staff surrounded the man. An ambulance had already been summoned. His name was Richard Baldowski, *Lt. Col* Richard Baldowski, and his wife, *Major* Helen Baldowski - both retired from military service and living in Fairport, New York. Throughout the weekend, we would bump into the Baldowski's at breakfast and walking around the grounds. He would reach over and kiss my Beautiful Dawn and thank her profusely. Then came the delivery of a dozen yellow roses. I think Helen was beginning to see more than just gratitude. Lt. Col. Baldowski was enjoying kissing this beautiful woman from Havertown, PA, and who could blame him?

I was recalling that the night she gave the Lieutenant Colonel the Heimlich, we later became ravenous in our lovemaking. Our spacious bed inside the upstairs cottage room called 'The Snugglery Room' was romantic enough with its dim candlelight and sweet aromas, but we were barely through the door and our small talk about the beautiful quilted comforter over the bed, when she pushed me on to it with as much strength as she used to squeeze the chicken bone out of Richard Baldowski's throat. Some part of her energy was, perhaps, a feeling of triumph at saving a life, After all, she was now a Registered Nurse!' (Proudly stated!) It seemed to me Beautiful Dawn was realizing life was good. There are days, admittedly all too fleeting, when everything around us and within us seems to be perfect. That Wednesday at 'Brookside Inn' was one such day. The puffy clouds and brilliant blue skies, the shadows and shades of green reminded me of a Matisse painting. Brookside Cottage was just what was needed in our busy lives.

Thursday at The Brookside was glorious, beginning with a special breakfast served up by owner Wendy Bischoff. We greeted the Baldowski's at breakfast as usual and Richard had reduced his greeting to Beautiful Dawn with a kissed hand. (Perhaps Major Helen had given him a serious chat about his going overboard with gratitude.) We decided to enjoy the day driving around the 'Laurel Highlands.'

Friday

Heavy morning thunderstorms and a torrential downpour couldn't dampen our Friday beginning. We lay in each other's arms and the sound of a clap of thunder jolted us to open our eyes at the same time. The storm prompted spontaneous morning lovemaking. For many, storms are one of the biggest turn-ons for romance. Our bodies were inseparable and Beautiful Dawn's eyes just invited me to continue our fondling fest from the night past. This morning, though, with the crashing thunder and pounding rain sounding like Armageddon, we both knew it was time for slow, sensual lovemaking.

Our deliberately slow cadence could only intensify and make us have to wait until we couldn't stand it beckoned a mutual release of intense joy. We fell breathlessly into one another's arms. And in our restful contentment, we both fell back to sleep and were awakened by the sound of a truck rumbling along the stony service road not too far from the parking lot.

Richard and Helen were the only two at breakfast that morning when we arrived, drenched from the short walk down the outside stairs and around the walkway to the entrance to 'The Black Forest Room.' The smell of roasted coffee and bacon was intoxicating. Richard and Helen gave a subdued but polite 'Good morning.' Richard only made brief eye contact with Beautiful Dawn. It was a bit awkward. We were used to his falling all over her with gratitude, his kisses on her hand and sustained hugs. It was as if we were suddenly strangers passing one another with just casual greetings. I almost asked Richard how he was feeling and, Helen, what plans they had for a rainy day. But she made no eye contact and just held her coffee to her lips and stared at Richard almost as if warning him: 'Don't you say a word!'

We sat in an adjoining room as Simone, our super server welcomed us and talked about the weather (obviously the topic of the day). She recited the breakfast menu: Eggs Florentine, Applewood bacon, Almond crusted French Toast and savory fruit and cream sprinkled with cinnamon.

"What do you make of it, Sweetheart?" I whispered to Dawn.

"Curious, isn't it?" she whispered, sipping on her coffee. "I wonder if 'Major Helen' is having a major jealousy attack?'

Looking out the bay window at the torrents of rain, I mentioned: "It's so different out there this morning, but it's beautiful, isn't it? We both nodded.

Dawn looked down at her plate. "Mmm, this almond-crusted French Toast is to die for!"

We never saw the Baldowski's after that. They apparently checked out soon after we began breakfast. We asked Simone whether they were OK.

Simone thought for a moment.

"Oh, I don't know, but now that I think about it, I heard this morning that Mr. Baldowski got a call last night... something about bad news in the family. I don't know."

Beautiful Dawn and I nodded to each other. We chatted about how we 'missed that one' and how perceptions can be so deceiving. After breakfast, we walked through the library thinking about some catch-up reading for part of the morning. Beautiful Dawn had spoken of perhaps catching up on her embroidery. It was that kind of day. We could walk through the rain, but somehow lounging a bit seemed inviting. Luis, the young man at the reception desk spotted us and came over quickly and handed us a written message. It was from the Baldowski's. Beautiful Dawn and I read it together:

Dear Aldron and Dawn: We meant not to ignore you this morning. We received bad news last evening. Richard's son was killed in a motorcycle accident on his way to work in Reading, PA. He was 39 years of age. And his wife is expecting our first grandchild. So tragic! We will always be grateful for your kindness and especially, Dawn, your heroic act of sparing Richard's life. We wish you both well. Yours, Helen Baldowski.

It was such a ponderous moment as we sat on the huge Queen Anne couch chatting about such an unforeseen tragedy.

The storms ended about Noon and the sun eventually broke through the clouds. We walked through the slushy grass around 'Brookside.' The torrential rains had beaten down a lot of the blooms in the garden.

"I wonder why they didn't tell us, Aldie?" Dawn pondered.

"I don't know, Sweetheart. The shock of it all... no doubt a sleepless night. People are unprepared for tragedies like this. It completely turns any decorum of life inside out. They were both officers in the military. Maybe it's hard to get rid of the 'Teflon coating' in public."

Dawn, stopped and looked at me.

"So maybe the choking really stripped away his decorum! It was humiliating and yet he realized I had saved his life. The hugs and kisses and roses... they were Richard Baldowski's attempt at removing the Teflon.

"You may be right on, Darling!"

We checked out of the Brookside around 11 a.m. to a long trip back to Havertown. It would be a soaking drive, but we were drenched with lively memories of our few days there.

Beautiful Dawn's work would begin on a drenching, windy Monday morning. Overnight rains, the off shoots of 'Hurricane Dorothy', had dumped floodwaters in low-lying areas of the Delaware Valley. The winds had knocked out power in areas toward King of Prussia and nearby Kennett Square. My proud new nurse made it to work in her Honda just fine –even through downed traffic lights and some high standing water. Even in a storm, a career in pediatric nursing must be launched.

Chapter Seventeen

THE KILLING HEAT OF SUMMER

Tis the Last Rose of Summer

Tis the last rose of summer left blooming alone; All her lovely companions are faded and gone:

No flower of her kindred, no rose-bud is nigh, to reflect back her blushes, or give sigh for sigh.

by Thomas Moore

It was 'Bummer Summer' in Havertown. It didn't start out well for All Saints and it wasn't because the attendance had dipped, Temperatures had become stifling, the humidity indexes were off the chart. A Bermuda high had settled in the whole Eastern Pennsylvania region. It lingered for days in June, as if promising a month of killing heat. Already there were a few brown outs in the Northeast. Even Boston, usually still moderate from cooler ocean temps in early June, was stuck in the 90-degree indices. The grass had turned brown and water restrictions were on all over the area. The kids had been released from school by the first week in June. Everybody wondered what kind of summer we were heading for.

I was attending the annual national conference of the Episcopal Church in Cincinnati. Why I went, I have no idea! Well, probably just to see old classmates. Beautiful Dawn was working a couple of extra hours to cover senior nurse vacations at Children's Hospital. Rookies get to do that, of course.

It was about 10 PM on a Wednesday night and I was in the final minutes of a boring meeting about budget cuts and the presiding Bishop pressuring us to help meet national deficits. Always one of my favorite topics! I got a cell phone call from Bob McGyver, our Senior Warden and stepped outside the Conference room to answer it.

"Hello Bob, what's up?"

"Aldie, we've got trouble here. Several kids broke into the church this evening and one of the kids shot and killed another boy right next to your pulpit."

"What?! ... Oh, Jesus, Bob! Were any of our people in there?" I sat down on the windowsill looking out over the Cincinnati skyline.

"No one was in the building, although the Wee Folks School staff had just left from a meeting about an hour before it happened. According to the police, the boys were 16-18 years of age and part of a gang around Havertown. Did you know we had any gangs, Aldie?"

"Not surprising! Are you there now, Bob? Are the police with you and may I talk with one of them?"

I was pacing now.

"I'm here, yes. Crime Scene detectives are here. They've got the church roped off. The uniforms are helping out. Det. Quincy is leading the investigation."

I paused for a moment, my thoughts caught somewhere between catching the earliest flight home to managing this from my end.

"I'm trying to decide, Bob if I should get on the first plane home?"

There was a pause from Bob: "Mm. I'm not sure, Aldie. To tell you the truth, my worry is the media blitz. KYW News just arrived the parking lot to set up their broadcast van. They tried to interview me, but I told them I couldn't interview anyone until I spoke with you."

"Good job, Bob! I'm going to call Dawn and see if I can catch a plane back to Philly tonight. Tell the Detective I'll talk with him as soon as I get in."

"Her..." Bob corrected me.

"Oh... her...tell her I'll be there as soon as I can."

As soon as I hung up, I called Delta Airlines to see how soon I could get out. They got me on a midnight flight direct to PHL. I checked out of the hotel and told no one at the conference, got to the airport and was checking in about 11:12 PM. The Delta DC9 took off exactly 12 midnight and I was picking up my car at PHL parking garage at 2:20 AM. I had called Dawn to let her know I was heading back to Havertown.

"Aldie, All Saints is all over the news tonight. It turns out the teenager who was shot where you stand in your pulpit is the son of a City Council member, Jake Glyndon."

"Aww…No! … Jake Glyndon's son? Jake and I are serving on the rezoning project for our district. I've met him in my office several times. Oh, my God!"

When I arrived at All Saints, Detective Quincy was waiting for me and I shook her hand. She was a young African American woman, short of stature, but with a commanding personality and very business-like. I told her that we've never had a murder at All Saints.

"Actually, you have, Fr. Seaver. Our records show that 1972 a young Hispanic man was stabbed to death in your Narthex."

That must have been hushed information. I hadn't heard it. The detective showed me where the breaking and entering had occurred. They had a suspect in custody that fit the description of the shooter. CSI showed that there apparently had been a struggle and that drugs were likely involved. I could see blood on the pulpit and some scratches on the altar railing. The pulpit light had been knocked over and the light bulb crushed to pieces where I sometimes stand. Detective Quincy indicated that the large door on the side (out of public view) had been jammed open with a big crowbar. It's not sure why these guys needed to get into the church except to steal and get drug money from their take. It wasn't clear yet. Nevertheless, Bryce Glyndon was shot while in the pulpit.

Dawn dropped by with coffee and pastries for the whole team and it was appreciated. I kissed her quickly and whispered, 'I love you, Sweetheart.'

I had to answer some questions. I dreaded it that my familiarity with Jake Glyndon was going to come into question. Any time local politics are mingled with a crime situation, things get messy. Jake and I had been at odds over some of the zoning appeals from the congregation and myself. Jake advocated for aggressive redevelopment in the zone that includes All Saints. It was a friendly debate, nothing personal. But, one on one, Jake had confessed that his son, Bryce, had been struggling with some drug problems. Although the Glyndon's were not regular attenders, Bryce had come to a few youth events and when he had been caught was some marijuana a few years back, he had done some community service at All Saints, which I supervised on behalf of the court order. To make it all a bit complicated, it was well known that Jake Glyndon was running for State Senator.

About 3:45 a.m., KYW, Philly's CBS Affiliate, parked their satellite van outside the front entrance, and the team was preparing to come inside. I downed the rest of my coffee and met the reporter at the door. I was going to have to weigh every word carefully, because I knew it was likely I would be on TV later in the day. The news reporter was KYW's Elizabeth Hur. She's always seemed a fair reporter on air. She greeted me with a pre-dawn smile. She had obviously been up early, make-up on and ready for business. I introduced her to Detective Quincy and we were off to the media races.

Once Elizabeth was able to clear access for KYW News, the cameras were rolling - first an interview with Detective Quincy. I could see the camera panning the pulpit area and then zooming in on the interview with the detective. It was strange seeing the pulpit area yellow taped as a 'crime scene.' There was something so unsettling in my psyche about that. Then for a moment, the camera panned to me. I didn't look at it directly – just looked meditative. Detective Quincy had shown me where the shot had been fired, there was still a lot of blood around the pulpit – a chilling scene given my use of it. Although I often give my homilies from the aisle, closer to the folks seated.)

Then Elizabeth sought me out. I had been catching up with Bob McGyver and his twist on things. I was waiting in the pew in front of the pulpit. Elizabeth was setting up the interview, giving me an advance on some of the questions she intended to ask. The camera guy was given the go ahead to begin filming. I took a big breath as the interview began.

KYW –"Father Seaver, you are the rector here at All Saints. What's been on your mind as you've sat here close to the crime scene?"

ME –"It's been surreal that a place I generally use for things of the spirit, for encouraging love and peace as the way of our faith tradition –now realizing that a young man was shot to death up there. It's just been rattling me, of course."

KYW – "I'm sure. I understand that you knew this young man. How did you know him?"

ME- "Well, he's participated in some of the older youth activities here at All Saints. Although, he wasn't a member, his family has attended with him."

KYW - "And you are aware that the young man is the son of Council Member Jake Glyndon, a candidate for State Senator?"

ME - "Yes, I am aware of that. Jake and I have served on the Rezoning Commission. I obviously respect Jake's position, but now I'm tremendously concerned about Jake and June and their family at this senseless tragedy. My heart goes out to them as they will soon know."

KYW - "Are you aware of any of the circumstances that led to this shooting and their son's death?"

ME- "I am not. I was attending our Annual Episcopal Church Meeting in Cincinnati yesterday when I got the word. I know nothing except that there was an apparent break-in and the young man was a victim here."

KYW - "Were you aware of any problems or troubles in his life that led this tragedy."

ME- "None that I could imagine". (Lie!)

KYW- "Father Seaver, why do you think a young man who was attending your church would end up this way?"

ME - "These are tough times for our kids. Many can't get jobs. Many have deep identity issues... they don't know where they fit. Our kids need hope - they need help. I'm glad we have community agencies and religious institutions as part of the outreach to them. But, of course, as you may be aware, County budget cuts and city budget cuts have eliminated some key after-school programs and key activity centers have been closed."

KYW - "Thank you, Father Seaver." Turning toward camera: "For KYW TV News, this is Elizabeth Hur from All Saints Episcopal in Havertown. Back to you Stephanie..." Camera off.

I breathed a sigh of relief. Elizabeth saw that I was nervous and smiled: "You did fine, Fr. Seaver. Is there anything else you would like to add for the article I'll be writing?

"I don't know. I would imagine that we might be having a Service of Remembrance here for his family. I'm not sure. That needs to be worked with Jake and June. I will be calling them today.

Bryce was an only son. He had been adopted from a foster care family at the age of one year. He was the answer to Jake and June's prayer on the long road of infertility. When Invitro Fertilization had failed to produce any results, they turned to adoption from Lutheran Social Services and Bryce came as a result of a long search. Until his 12th birthday, he was a happy and gifted child. His parents spared no expense to provide for him (perhaps therein may be part of the issue). It's only natural for a coddled child to begin to see himself/ herself at the center of the universe. Jake admitted to me after a City Council meeting only a few years before that things were getting out of control with Bryce and that he suspected his son was into some kind of drug recreation.

Bryce's first bump with the Law came at fifteen, when he was caught at the party of a friend's house smoking marijuana. The parents were so naive to realize it was going on beneath their feet (i.e. the downstairs family room). The Haverford police received a tip from a neighbor and were on the spot within one half hour. Bryce was busted along with twelve other teenagers. *'The Havertown Patch'*, of course, wrote about it in the next day's edition and Jake and June were significantly embarrassed. This had happened soon after Jake made public announcement of his bid for the State Senate race. Bryce was booked and charged, along with the 12 other teens. The parents of the host kid for the party were fined. It was a bad scene all around.

What a night! My eyes were puffy. And making the things worse, I felt a major head cold coming on. I realized that I hadn't picked up the misery of a cold in almost three years, but between the lack of sleep, the stress of this crime in our own church, maybe the rarified airplane cabin airflow in that DC-9, and not the least, that half the Bishop's staff had head colds, it was, indeed, a 'rare day in June.' I immediately popped two Coldeeze's and downed an OJ with a bagel. I had texted Dawn indicating I was feeling a head cold coming on from the airport, so she put two Asani water bottles in that bag she brought me.

By now, the sun was beginning to rise and I was heading to meet Jake and June Glyndon at their home. I had called them before taking a quick nap. The Glyndon's live on Paddock Street, opposite the Merion Golf Club West. I greeted June with a big hug, her eyes puffy and red, a handkerchief rolled up in her hand.

"June, it's so awful! Just awful!"

She cried in my arms. I could see Jake sitting in the big overstuffed chair in the living room.

"Jake! I'm so sorry." I put my hand on his shoulder and squatted facing him.

"I can't believe it, Aldie. I just can't believe it. I'm crazy wondering whether I did enough to prevent this from happening."

I responded: "You gave him love and time. Jake. You gave him a starting chance."

Jack pounded the arm of his chair: "Pardon me for saying it, Aldie, but it's a goddam evil world out there. The police were over and told us that the kids broke into the church with a crowbar! Jesus, Aldie, I tell you I can't believe it!"

The Glyndon's were nearly inconsolable, but I just invited all that anguish to flow out. What else could a priest offer at this point? What else could I do or say? It was my presence they needed. There are no magic words, religious sayings.

Once Jake and June had expressed incomparable grief, I asked them if I could share anything that might in some measure offer hope in this seemingly hopeless time.

June offered: "I know we're not regular churchgoers, Fr. Aldie, but could you offer prayer."

Jake nodded: "God must be on vacation, Aldie, but I'll appreciate some appeal to the Almighty."

"Let's try,"

"God of this great mystery called Life. We come empty of spirit and drained of energy at the loss of Bryce. It's hard to find even prayerful words we might say in the wake of this terrible tragedy. I had to interrupt my prayer with a sneeze! *...Please be here in your own comforting way for June and Jake, especially in these difficult days ahead. Help them to find in this terrible absence some borrowed strength to be sustained. They feel such a tremendous void at the sudden loss of their only son. Help them*

to find steps, however small, to go forward in certain strength and good memories of Bryce. I give them to you for your caring embrace. In Christ, 'Amen.'"

We talked about the possibility of remembering Jake in some special way, possibly through worship.

"We'll think about it Fr. Aldie, June reflected, we've just been in such a state of shock we're barely able to talk with John down at Stretch's Funeral Home. I'll call you tomorrow."

Jake offered,

"But I think we'd certainly want to consider having something to remember him. Don't you think, June? Looking down, he cried, "But.... I can't bear to think about having the service in the place where he was killed. I don't know, Aldie. Christ, I can't even think straight! I hope you understand."

I nodded in agreement.

June looked at Jake.

"Well, we certainly want you to be involved wherever this happens, Fr. Aldie."

"Oh, yeah, Aldie. That we do want,"

I hugged them both- trying not to transfer my cold to them. The Cold-Eeze was helping somewhat, but I was glad for my handkerchief. I gave them my card and told them to feel welcome to stay in touch.

I knew that Sunday worship would be tough -even with folks being away for summer travel and vacations. It was quite evident by the KYW TV News and 'The Havertown Patch' and not the least The *Inquirer* that All Saints was the top news item. The 9AM Liturgy was well attended. During the initial Joys and Concern Gathering time, I shared:

"It was the kind of week in our congregation when we found out just how vulnerable we are, even in Havertown. It's not Philly... and yet, in some ways, only a few miles away... it *is* Philly. The pulpit has always been sacred ground for me, but now it's surreal that blood has been shed in the very place where God's Word of love and forgiveness is preached." I just couldn't get that out of my head!

I assured worshippers that all efforts have been made to bring justice to bear in the death of Bryce Glyndon, but I asked for prayers for the perpetrator, for the others who were involved and their families, but I especially asked prayers for June and Jake Glyndon. Unbeknownst to me, June and Jake were sitting in the back row. People would extend to them their heart-felt expressions of sympathy, their hands and hugs. I knew it took courage for them to show up.

I also mentioned that I had a rare summer cold and that I would respectfully forgo my handshakes and hugs today. I was thankful we kept the bacterial soap near the altar and behind the pulpit. I was asking my Assisting Minister, Ginnie Grayson, to share the bread after I consecrated it with white gloves. I keep these on hand just for occasions like colds.

It was June 16th and it felt like most of the summer had already happened. I spent my 45th birthday with my pesky cold and a little dysthymia hovering over me like a gray cloud. Dawn was giving me wifely nursing care. Sometimes she was direct and firm:

"Aldie, you need to get to bed soon and rest. You don't need to rob yourself of sleep during a summer head cold. So, Darling, leave the sermon soon and crawl into bed, or I'll spank you with a wet noodle!" I needed that chuckle.

The 11 o'clock Liturgy that Sunday was larger in attendance than usual, also. There's nothing like 'murder in the cathedral' to bring the curious out. Doris McDaniel and her daughter, Fay (both widows) had not been to church in three years. When the church musicians moved the piano they had donated in memory of Doris's mother, it set off an emotional earthquake and they had become invisible for a few years. The move was six feet from its original placement and was to accommodate a new stand for altar flowers. Memorial Gifts are 'sacred cows.' But here Doris and Fay were, curious like many after the media blitzed this story of 'murder in the cathedral'. I found that even CNN carried a short segment.

John at Stretch's Funeral Home called me on Monday morning to let me know that the Glyndon's had been there and asked him to request if All Saints might be available for the service on Wednesday morning. I told John I was surprised, since that seemed to be the farthest from their minds when I visited.

"I sensed they just wanted to return the space to, uh, you know, reclaim its sacredness."

My second visit with June and Jake was not nearly has emotionally draining for them. Thankfully my cold had subsided enough to help me feel more alive. Also, June and Jake had a little more of an emotional shift. They still had moments of crying about Bryce, but they were more resolute to have a Service of Remembrance and to have it where a gathering of family and friends could heal in the very space where evil intent had hurt life and taken it away. Sometimes the best way to overcome evil is to transform its context. Give it a sacredness, more life.

I thought of the biblical Joseph and his brothers story. (Genesis 42-50) recalling how Joseph's brothers, in a jealous rage, had sold him into slavery in Egypt. There in Egypt Joseph rose mercurially to become a governor of Pharaoh. And when his brothers went to Egypt to seek grain during a time of great famine back home, they didn't recognize him to be Joseph, their brother. When he finally reveals that he is their brother, whom they had sold into slavery, his brothers had to come to terms with what they had done to him. Finally, Joseph tells them:

Don't be afraid. Am I in the place of God? You intended to harm me, but God intended it for good, to accomplish what is now being done, the saving of many lives. (Genesis 50:19-20)

I wondered at Bryce Glyndon's Remembrance Service:

Sometimes it seems that the worst things that happen have evil designs attached to them -whether it's war or famine or the brutality of one human being toward another. God created us not for ill, of course, but for good. God intended for Bryce to grow into his full humanity. Even so, God chooses not to be that proverbial 'Superman' and be everywhere in nick of time. We could fault God for not being that 'Super Deity,' but unconditionally loving us requires granting us the freedom to make choices —good ones, bad ones or none at all (which is a choice). It was God's riskiest venture, as any parent understands, to let God's own love grant us free willfulness. God knew would make bad choices. Can we wrap our minds around that? It happens. It happened here. Even with that, Bryce Glyndon should be alive.

God intends for good - even in the worst of scenarios, God seeks to bring life where there isn't any. God's heart must be broken. After all, God knows what it's like to lose a son.

Many of Bryce's classmates from Havertown High were there, many of them sobbing. At their tender ages, what happened to Bryce Glyndon at the pulpit where I stood seemed incomprehensible. Ordinarily, these youths were filled with invincible determination, unstoppable independence.

I offered the kids some reflections.

To the kids of Bryce's class at Havertown, I offer this: in the fullness of your energetic lives, make room for things of the Spirit, where you might discover your inner essence, your soul, the highest possibility of 'you.' You already have the capacity to care for one another and console one another. I see that right here today. You know that you have emotions, doubts, fears, anxieties mingled with your many skills and confidences. They're all OK but know that your Creator has given you opportunity to pay attention to your soul, which provides ways of dealing with these unintended, unanticipated sorrows of life. And there are, as you know today, many sorrows.

Then I walked down in front of the pulpit where, appropriately, an 18 x 24 portrait of Bryce stood on a stand, with flowers around it. I looked at the class of 2004, Bryce's class.

There are things, I know, you would want to say to Bryce that perhaps you wish you had when he was among us. I want to give you an opportunity to do that after this service. Near the entrance to our Church Nave I have placed a large piece of newsprint with multiple color markers. If you wish, write on it things you would want to say to him... or maybe things that his death makes you aware of. I will send it with your class president, Jaden, and invite you to post it, with permission I trust, somewhere in your class memory location.

The reverberation of the 'murder in the cathedral' (as some around Havertown were referring to it) was enormous. Many of our folks reached out openly to Jake and June, providing meals and housecleaning. Donations came pouring in from many a charity in memory of Bryce: a scholarship fund for Haverford College, where Bryce had intended to go after high school to major in Communications. More than $5,000 had been received already since the obituary had been placed in 'The Patch.'

The montage I had invited to be made during the Service, turned out to be quite a memory piece. In addition to many sentiments, some of the class artists drew pictures. Others later added real photographs of themselves taken with Bryce. The class encased the newsprint in a large frame and placed it in their class location location at the high school community board. Sometimes even in the most tragic choices, a 'phoenix' does seem to rise from the smoldering residue of human tragedy. Needless to say, one person's action that killed another was now transforming us into an outpouring of human love and care in Havertown. The Holy One was truly at work.

Chapter Eighteen

SUMMER ESCAPE:

Painted Ladies splash the town;
Waves and sandpipers dance ashore;
The sea and Old Cape May, we found
Were respite from these days we bore.
The ocean swelled, our griefs were drowned
With music from a different score;

Painted Ladies splash the town
While waves and sandpipers dance ashore.
The sea and Old Cape May, we found
Will make our dampened spirits soar.
                                        - Aldron Seaver

It must happen yet again! Getting away! Dawn and I had a long weekend to look forward to over July 4th. She had worked over-time for three weeks in a row and had earned Thursday and Friday off before July 4th returning on Monday. The work at Children's Hospital of Philadelphia was very demanding, but she was finding great satisfaction helping children in the PICU Unit in special rehabilitation, especially post-cranial surgery where tumors both malignant and benign had been removed. She enjoyed the challenge of setting up a plan of motor skill redevelopment with the rehab staff. Even at that, she often came home exhausted physically and emotionally. My work often permitted me to be on 'Dawn Care' when she arrived. Neck massages, hugs, something sweet and savory with tea.

We left Thursday night, July 1st (July 4th was on Sunday) for a welcome stretch from Friday to Monday at Cape May, New Jersey, to spend a few nights. The weather was surprisingly cool for the end of June and we arrived for some cool ocean breezes. Cape May is about two hours from Havertown. We took the Atlantic City Expressway down to the Garden State Parkway South and directly into Cape May. Although another hurricane, Ernestine, was making landfall in Florida and Georgia, the East Coast was expected to enjoy clear weather through the following week.

The decision to go to Cape May was prompted by an embarrassingly generous gift from Jake and June Glyndon for a package of four nights at the Queen Victoria Bed and Breakfast, one of the most elegant B & B's on the historic inn registries. We were given 'The Crown Jewel 'room, perhaps the most elegant of rooms at the Inn. Beautiful Dawn and I were guilty because of the elegance of 'The Crown Jewel,' arranged in two stories, with the staircase taking you to the Juliet balcony and the posh sleeping loft with a two-person marble-surrounded whirlpool tub, gas Franklin stove -would've been great for December – and a king- sized pillow-topped bed. We felt like royalty! Beautiful Dawn and I have enjoyed overnight amenities like 'The Fairbanks' in Florida, but this was definitely over-the-top.

We couldn't begin to imagine a value on the package deal for our four nights at the Queen Victoria, but a quick search on the internet determined that the per night rate for the summer was $515. *Good Lord!* The Glyndon's generosity was overwhelming. Standing on the spiral staircase of the 'Crown Jewel,' we looked around and pledged that we would make a contribution in kind to the 'One-Day-At-a-Time' Homeless Shelter in Havertown. Maybe it would assuage our guilty pleasures at the Queen Victoria. The room was like stepping back into the Victorian era and so comfortable. We felt like royalty.

Cape May is a little treasure at the southern tip of the Jersey shore. A two-hour ferry ride runs between Lewes, Delaware and Cape May. The Cape May lighthouse is open to the public. The 'painted ladies' –those beautiful old houses so colorfully decorated- are in abundance. And the Cape May Lobster House is to die for at least once during your visit. You can always take in one of the shows that are part of the Cape May Theater Companies - the Cape May Stage (The Robert Shackleton Playhouse) or the East Lynne Theater Company at the First Presbyterian church. There's also Elaine's Dinner Theater.

We shared an entree at the Island Grill on Mansion St., with its Caribbean specialty of grilled fresh fish with tropical fruit salsa.

After a leisurely walk around the shops, we went to see a hilarious production of *'Nunsense'* at the Robert Shackleton Playhouse. On the way, we caught a glimpse of the most beautiful summer sunset. I chose to take a photograph of us with the sunset in the backdrop. A couple going past us offered to take a photo. We held each other as the wife framed us against the backdrop and took the photo. We offered to do the same, since they too were in awe of the sunset, which seemed to grow intense in the moments that followed. We became conversational and realized they, too, were going to the theater production. Their names were Edgar and Wynetta James, from Brooklyn, New York. They had been spending some time in Rehoboth, Delaware, and took the two- hour ferry shortcut to Cape May, where they intended on staying for several days before returning home to Brooklyn. They were enjoying staying at the 'Angel-of-the-Sea' Bed and Breakfast. Before entering the theater, we exchanged cards and hoped that we would see each other again.

"What a beautiful couple, Aldie! There was just a wonderful connection I felt with them. They are so attractive together and kind. Did you sense it too?"

"I did, Sweetheart. I don't know, it felt like an instant friendship, as though we've known each other before."

We all crowded into the theater. And the *'Nunsense'* production was hilarious. When we left the theater, Edgar and Wynetta were waiting outside for us. We greeted them and shared how much we enjoyed the production.

"Would you join us for drinks and dessert at the Ebbits Bar and Lounge?" Wynetta offered.

Beautiful Dawn responded:

"Sure, why not - Okay with you Aldie?"

"Oh, sure – it's right next to where we're staying, the Queen Victoria B & B. We'll meet you there."

We departed and returned to our B & B to park our car and meet the James'.

"I'm sure you've noticed that Edgar hasn't really said anything, but he has a great smile?"

"Yes, I was just wondering whether he was shy."

"Wynetta's doing all the talking", I said, "but he seems

fine." When we greeted them again, Wynetta said the Ebbitt's Bar and Lounge had one table for four left. It was a few minutes before 10 p.m. As we settled into our chairs, Wynetta put her hand on Beautiful Dawn's.

"Before we begin, I must tell you that Edgar is not able to speak. He is mute. He had a rare tumor in his brain that left him incapable of speaking. He can hear us" (Edgar smiled and touched our hands), "he just can't express it in words, which is why we are often tactile."

He took Wynetta's hand and kissed it.

"It's been socially difficult for us - for me. I guess most folks just have a difficult time communicating."

"Do you use ASL, Edgar?" Dawn both spoke and signed.

He gestured back, smiling broadly and signing that he did indeed know the language. Then he took her hand and kissed it.

"Oh, thank God! I'm never sure until I have to ask," Wynetta said with relief. She looked at me and said,

It was an awesome late evening of conversation and friendship-building with Edgar and Wynetta. With only Saturday, Sunday and part of Monday remaining, we both decided we'd enjoy as much time with each other as possible.

Before departing from a beautiful evening of conversation and dessert, we agreed to meet the next morning on one of the favorite brunch places in Cape May, 'The Mad Batter' - next to the Queen Victoria B & B.

It was about midnight when we walked back over to the Queen Victoria. Dawn and I commented on Edgar's condition and how neat it was to communicate with him. Beautiful Dawn was glad for her ASL skills.

Neither of us were particularly sleepy, so we decided to enjoy the whirlpool. Without a stitch of clothing, we embraced each other and kissed as the water came jetting into the tub. Eventually we stepped into the tub and, holding each other tightly, sank into the heart of a summer night. There must have been magic in the tepid water. Before too long, Beautiful Dawn was sitting on my lap. The feeling of the jettisoning tepid water was like an aphrodisiac. We found ourselves suddenly groping at each other with playful abandon.

The next morning at 'The Mad Batter', Edgar shared that before losing his speech, he had played for the (then) California Angels as an outfielder. As I looked it up later, Edgar had a .680 batting average and in 1986 had the fewest errors in the majors. I have to confess that I'm not an avid baseball fan, although I do enjoy getting out to a Phillies game from time to time just to root for the home team. But I wasn't into following the MLB statistics. Edgar signed at breakfast that he had accomplished this, and I confessed that I had not known its. He laughed silently as he signed 'Don't worry.'

Edgar was a statuesque male. He was muscular and yet had a great smile and a very handsome face. Wynetta was also a beautiful woman with a radiant, kind and gentle smile. She adored Edgar and would lean on him, holding his arm. We could tell they were very much in love.

Wynetta reminisced:

"We were married while Edgar was in the minors waiting for a chance to go to 'The Bigs.' I was a flight attendant for American Airlines. I had met him on one of his road games flying across country. Without even knowing he was in baseball, I found his smile infectious."

Edgar interrupted with a signing that said, "She was a total homerun out of the park!"

When our conversation shifted to my profession, Wynetta remarked, "I told Edgar I thought you were either a minister or a social worker. We are both Episcopalian, although Edgar is still a member of the Abyssinian Baptist Church in Manhattan. That was the church of his family, many of whom still go there, but we're closer to St. Luke and St. Matthew on Clinton Avenue in Brooklyn."

Wynetta shared that she grew up in Brooklyn and was the daughter of a congressman from the State of New York - Winston Coles - formerly a cop for the N.Y.P.D. Now she teaches Social Studies at Bishop Loughlin Memorial High School and doubles as a School Counselor in career studies.

Edgar signed that she was modest about her work.

"She's been considered one of the top high school educators for the five boroughs of New York City."

After her time with American Airlines, she completed her undergraduate degree at Brooklyn College with a major in Sociology and a double major in School Counseling. She graduated with top honors and went on for a Graduate degree at Manhattan College in Education and Health. I shared with them that my Beautiful Dawn has a tough job as a PICU RN at the Children's Hospital of Philadelphia. I shared that she was my hero with the kind of challenges she meets every day to help brain surgery kids in their recovery process.

"Honey, you would be my hero, too. I so appreciate the hands-on work you have to do with these precious children," she said holding Beautiful Dawn's hand.

"Oh, Thank you!"

Beautiful Dawn grasped her hand with a big smile. Edgar also signed with appreciation for her work. He shared that, having gone through therapy following his larynx issue from the brain tumor, he wouldn't have made it without the kind and patient nursing staff at the Brooklyn Hospital Center.

We so enjoyed the James's. They announced that they would be heading back to Brooklyn that afternoon. Wynetta was due for some meetings prior to school opening in August.

Wynetta went on to say: "And Edgar always has some project going on at home. Since he retired from 'The Bigs,' he's become a master woodworker. You should see the projects he has going in his shed. I call it his man cave. He works away while listening to his other passion."

"Oh," I said, "another sport or something - maybe soccer or football."

"No," Edgar smiled and signed, "Italian opera." He wowed us chatting about his love for Italian opera, especially Verdi. He signed enthusiastically: "I love *Aida,* of course, but also *Falstaff, I Lombardia all prima, Il Trovatore, Oberto, Othello, Rigoletto...* you know, Verdi composed 28 operas."

Dawn wasn't sure she picked up the Italian names with his signing, but he repeated them, to be sure, all too soon our breakfast time ended. The James were going to meet the ferry back to Lewes and then on to Baltimore to meet some family.

The James's were a special gift during our visit to Cape May. Beautiful Dawn and I realized that the cosmos often seems like a God-befriending place. People come along, connections are made when kindred spirits find each other and open themselves to the possibility of friendship. We exchanged address and Emails and phone numbers to make sure that we would stay in touch.

Our Cape May get-a-way was a welcome salve. The grueling incident at the All Saints pulpit had taken its toll on my energy. On Sunday afternoon, we advocated for a leisurely time beyond breakfast to lounge for most of the day. The big porch at Queen Victoria B & B invited such lounging. Dawn crocheted, and I caught up on reading. We both contracted to have some talk time and refreshment time together along the course of the day. The sea breezes felt good and there were big puffy white clouds and blue skies everywhere. We lucked out. It was still very hot, but ocean breezes cooled the air nicely.

"Wow, Aldie, this really feels like a vacation, doesn't it?"

I agreed.

"Mm-mm. I've only dozed off twice while reading. The breeze is intoxicating."

"I noticed." She smiled.

We went for some coffee and a pastry to share before our seaside walk. The glistening of the sun on the ocean beneath a beautiful sky was also intoxicating. We walked hand in hand and talked about many things - a renewed conversation about the magic of our friendship with Edgar and Wynetta.

"How would you *really* feel if I discovered I was pregnant, Aldie?"

"Great! I'd feel great, Sweetheart. How about you?"

"Oh... it would be wonderful, but it would mean a dramatic shift in our lives. The focus on the baby would be 24/7 and getaways like these would be on hold for a little while. We'd have to prepare a nursery. There's an enormous responsibility on the road ahead for us. I'd want you 100% part of that, Darling." Beautiful Dawn wrapped both hands around my armed and peered into my eyes.

"Of course, "I said patting her hand, "and I do know it's 24/7. I would ask All Saints vestry for paternity leave for a few weeks. I'd want to experience all the feelings of welcoming Amy Dawn into our..."

"Or... maybe Adam Aldron!" "Or Adam Aldron... into our lives."

We stopped and embraced with a kiss and then continued our walk. Farther down the beach, we saw a crowd of people at the edge of the ocean. As we got closer, we wondered whether there had been a drowning. A police officer was standing there, but there were no emergency vehicles. When we arrived, we looked into the circle and saw a porpoise had beached. We noticed it was injured – perhaps by a boating propeller or a large predator. Beautiful Dawn was heartbroken to see the defenseless animal hurt. I asked the officer if the Marine Laboratory or something like that were contacted.

"Not sure. We have a call into Wildlife and Natural Resources."

"Can it be airlifted somewhere? There's a National Aquarium in Baltimore."

The Cape May officer checked with one of the attendants about the National Aquarium as a place for the porpoise. I quickly asked 'Siri' (on my iPhone) for a number and produced a direct line for Marine Laboratory personnel in Baltimore. In less than a minute I had a technician on the phone that immediately called her boss to the phone.

I told the officer:

"Thanks for letting us know. Is there someone I can contact to check on the porpoise?" The officer standing by pointed to a City Councilman, who had just happened to be out on the beach when the beaching occurred. Before long there was a plan being formulated to fly in a chopper that could airlift this porpoise to National Aquarium in Baltimore.

Beautiful Dawn and I stood around with the crowd and got to know a few folks who were there on vacation also. It took about 40 minutes until we heard the approaching helicopter. The Cape May Police Officer got the crowd to move way back from the chopper approach. I decided to film the scenario, since I noticed there weren't any local media around. It took about 4 minutes for the Bell 206 chopper to land on the sand. Occupants jumped from the vehicle and immediately gathered around the porpoise. I noticed the familiar National Aquarium logo. Now the tricky task of mounting the injured mammal onto the lift would begin. Beautiful Dawn decided to name the gentle sea creature 'Penny Porpoise.'

"Gosh, I hope they can save her. She's such a beautiful creature. Aldie, say a prayer quick."

I looked at her. "I...you mean..."

"Say a prayer, Darling." She smiled and pinched me on the cheek..."It's your job!"

I complied: "Well, OK...Father of all Creation, for all your creatures great and small, we give you thanks. Bless....Penny Porpoise..." I started chuckling. I couldn't help it.

"Aldie, don't laugh in the middle of a prayer!"

I couldn't stop laughing.

"Father Aldie, shame on you!"

"I'm sorry, Sweetheart, if you hadn't named her ..."forgive me. Let me try again."

I cleared my throat:

"For all your creatures great and small, we give you thanks! Bless this dear porpoise..." I started laughing again.

Beautiful Dawn shook her head and took my hand and continued with: "Bless your dear one... Penny Por..."

Then Dawn started giggling!

"...Penny Porpoise."

"Aldie," shaking uncontrollably with laughter, "I feel terrible laughing and there's a defenseless poor purpose... I mean...porpoise!"

Now she's falling onto the sand in gales of laughter.

"Stop it... Stop!" She pinched my leg. I pulled her up from the sand .

"Pity poor Penny Porpoise!" I wasn't helping the situation!

Dawn tried to gather her composure:

"Silly goose!" She dusted herself off and began to swat my behind with a teasing swat. We decided the name was downright funny.

It took almost twenty minutes for the Aquarium crew to load 'Penny Porpoise' on a lift gurney. Some of the staff poured water on her inside a rescue tank. Although she was small, she was not light. Soon the Bell 206 started its engine and within two minutes started its lift as the helpers held onto Penny's gurney. Giving the high sign that she was off the ground, the chopper made a slow lift to about 30 feet, made a turn westward. It would take about a half hour to get her to Baltimore.

We resumed our walk on the beach back toward the Queen Victoria. By now it was mid- afternoon and we were thirsty. I apologized once again for interrupting my prayer with laughter.

I think you're right, Aldie. 'Penny Porpoise is a little funny. I just felt so bad for her. And she may not even be a 'she.' It could be Peter Porpoise or Paul Porpoise or... or ..."

"Or 'What's your Porpoise?," I clamored. She gave me another good swat on my arm and kissed me.

"What am I going to do with you, Reverend Aldie!"

Our last evening meal in Cape May, we chose to enjoy 'The Lobster House,' at Fisherman's Wharf, a landmark for seafood eating in Cape May, nestled on Cape May Harbor. Added to sharing an enjoyable entree at The 'Lobster House,' we enjoyed viewing the 130-foot-long authentic Grand Banks sailing vessel, the 'Schooner American,' moored at dockside. Although we're not big cocktail drinkers, we did enjoy the atmosphere and sharing a drink on the schooner and taking a leisurely tour.

Later we enjoyed watching the sunset from our Cape Harbor seating, the pale orange sky on top of deep orange and red with seagull silhouetting the background. It was a fitting way to conclude our visit to Cape May. We reminisced about the lovely 'Painted Ladies' we toured, those beautiful Victorian houses of an era gone by. As we sat and sipped the rest of our fruit drink, Beautiful Dawn told me they were the highlight of Cape May -not that she didn't enjoy the Lighthouse and ambiance of the Queen Victoria, one of the most beautiful 'ladies' of all or the memorable beach rescue of 'Penny Porpoise' (we hope she's getting along OK at the National Aquarium) or the great food and meeting Edgar and Wynetta... and certainly not the least our intimacy.

It seemed almost fitting that on Monday morning as we were leaving the Queen Victoria Bed & Breakfast that it should begin raining. Some of the offshoots of another hurricane, 'Ernestine' had finally reached the coast. It gave a kind of justification for going home. Sun and fun were put away for the time being. We had been blessed with an abundance of good weather and good times these four days, but now it was back to reality. We 'vacated' and finally the storm of our stress that eroded our emotional shores had subsided and it was time to occupy the places of our reality - my parish still reeling over a young man shot to death where the Word of God is preached; Beautiful Dawn's delicate rehab nursing work among children recovering from brain surgery at the PICU unit of Children's Hospital, a place of daily dramas and daily rewards as children try to learn to walk again or speak again or perhaps smile again. We listened to New Age 'Kitaro' music as we entered the garden State Expressway. We didn't say much.

She fell asleep and I thought about Jake and June Glyndon and this most generous gift they had given us. In the wide spectrum of things, I had done little more than bring a presence, a comforting. I was someone who could stand with them in the unthinkable - their only son, Bryce, murdered in a 'house of God.' Bryce's guidance counselor, James Fellowes, had given one of the eulogies at the Service of Remembrance. He mentioned that Bryce had lived a 'full life in his short years.' Time can be deceptive, of course. Often time takes us well into late years until we can say, 'I've lived a full life.' Others like Bryce cram many years into a just few. Still I can't help but believe this loss was so unnecessary. What could have prevented this senseless tragedy in our Church Nave? What word from Bryce's parents or myself or his school counselor might have guided him toward better choices, toward a fuller life, a longer life?

Of course, there are no answers to that. We only know that everyday life is subject to random choices and our unshackled wills. In my years as a priest/rector thus far, I find myself still caught up in the mystery of life and death together and of the One whose hands have already and continue to shape this world. We are here, I believe for a singular purpose manifested in many ways, *to care for the world God has created, including one another.* It sounds so simplistic and unreachable, yet a necessary pilgrimage.

It was just about Noon when we pulled into our driveway. There was a city patrol car sitting there - a bit jolting for a homecoming.

"What now?" Beautiful Dawn stared at the car. "Aldie, did you steal the sheets from the Queen Victoria?!"

"It's Detective Quincy. Maybe she wants to help us carry things into the house," I chuckled.

Detective Quincy greeted me and wanted to give me a follow-up sheet to the events leading up to and including the murder of Bryce Glyndon. As rector, I needed to sign papers to confirm that a full investigation of the crime in our facility had been completed. It was like stepping back into the reality of that murderous event after having dreamed a beautiful and fleeting dream.

There was enough adventure in June to fill an entire year. Now in early July summer was proving to be as hot as June. It had become quite dry and already Havertown was issuing some ever-greater water restrictions. Other than the rainy offshoots of Ernestine, it hadn't rained since May.

A Promotion

We were back to work with mid-July approaching. I had a backlog of pastoral calling and worship planning. Several ministry team folks were waiting for me to look over some Fall proposals There are always a few intra-congregational 'fires' to put out. Beautiful Dawn had been working some weekends at Children's Hospital to cover vacations. In fact, for two weeks counting she worked six days a week. While continuing to love her work there, she would be the first to admit that it is a challenge for her physically. Her hours were long and exhausting, but one late afternoon she came through the front door with a radiant face.

"Sweetheart? Did you get a promotion?"

She laughed.

"Somewhat. Aldie... Darling.... I'm pregnant again!"

My gaping mouth and hug gave me away. "Oh, Darling... that's wonderful!"

We held each other for the longest time in silence. We knew what the silence meant, both of us wondering if this pregnancy would be for real.

I prepared lasagna, Caesar salad and picked up Italian bread and tiramisu for dessert. Since it was nearly ready, we talked as we prepared the table and Beautiful Dawn finished heating up the Italian bread.

"I'm praying this will be our opportunity to bring a child into our world, Aldie." She touched my shoulder and kissed my neck.

"It's our time... it's our time, darling."

"It is Sweetheart." I smiled and clapped my hands "Wow, I've got to get back to work on that nursery we started!" Beautiful Dawn nodded: "I know...we've been using it as a catch all room for clothes and boxes." Visits in the next week to Dr. Maria Greenburg, was one of the doctors at Children's as well as a GYN doc with an office in Havertown, showed a normal pregnancy unfolding. The morning sickness was initially minimal and Beautiful Dawn continued working and was very robust in the pregnancy.

Chapter Nineteen

A WEE WEDDING NEAR ENNIS

If ever I'm a money'd man, I mean, please God, to cast
My golden anchor in the place
Where youthful years were pass'd
Though heads that bow are black and brown must meanwhile
gather grey
New faces rise by every hearth, and old ones drop away-
Yet dearer still that Irish hill than all the world beside;
It's home, sweet home, where'er I roam, through lands and waters
wide.
And if the Lord allows me, I surely will return
To my native Ballyshannon,
And the winding banks of Erne.

- William Allingham, Irish poet (1824-1889)

Okay, I admit it...we *are* certifiable travel junkies! Take my Visa card away from me, please ! But this is one of those *carpe diem* travel stories. It's travel with a *porpoise*...purpose! A very happy one. On a very humid Saturday morning we arose early and decided on breakfast at 'Hanne's Breakfast Nook.' As the coffee was being poured out, I noticed Beautiful Dawn seemed pensive.

"Sweetheart, I know something is on your mind." I took her hand. "Are you alright?"

"I am, Darling. I've been thinking about...." She twisted her napkin... "about Ireland."

"Ireland?" I grinned in a 'you're kidding' sort of way.

"Why Ireland?"

"Well, I got an Email from my cousin, my father's nephew, Ryan O'Shea. We've kept in touch across the years. He wrote me the other day and said he is planning to marry Mary Margaret Boyle

257

in late August. Ryan lives in County Clare where his uncle owns a little sheep farm. I think it's near the Cliffs of Moher. I'm not sure. Anyway, I was just thinking that, before our baby arrives, it would be so beautiful to go to Ireland and enjoy Ryan's and Margaret's wedding as well as travel around Ireland for a few days. My vacation options at Children's are open. I don't have to work there for a stretch of time to earn vacation time. It was one of the incentives."

As is the case with any priest, my thoughts immediately turned to my schedule. I recall that I had a wedding in mid-September 22nd and a two-day conference in New York City during the mid- week.

"Mm. Let me look at my schedule, Sweetheart. I'd enjoy going back to Ireland myself. Do you know the specific date of the wedding?"

She put her hand on mine. "Believe it or not, it's a Wednesday, August 24th. Apparently, in Europe they hold weddings any time!"

I did some juggling of my schedule in the next few days and by Friday had paved the way for Beautiful Dawn and me to fly to Shannon on Sunday, August 21st for ten days in Ireland. I had to arrange for a supply for my Service on August 28th and Mark Crenshaw down in Maryland agreed to come up and supply for me on my one Sunday away. We already had updated U. S. Passports, so within a week's time we were set for Ireland.

Beautiful Dawn kept in touch with her cousin Ryan and his fiancée, Margaret. Both were elated that a few family members from across the pond were going to be part of their wedding. The Irish do love it when family from 'The States' come to see them. The plan was that they would hold the wedding on Ryan's uncle's farm behind the cottage they owned. Father O'Murray, a 'priest for hire,' would perform the marriage. I had nothing to do except to be a 'go-for' guy. Ryan also knew of Beautiful Dawn's love of flowers, so he convinced her to be part of the flower arranging for the wedding. The reception would be held in a tent in an open field very near the barn and the cottage.

Following the services at All Saints, I rushed home to complete packing for our late afternoon departure for Boston. Beautiful Dawn played hooky from worship for all the necessary preparations.

It was a mixture of clouds and sun as we sat on the tarmac at PHL for a short hop to Boston's Logan Airport. There were two other planes ahead of us. We lifted off about 4:56 p.m. In Boston we would connect with our Aer Lingus flight to Shannon, about six hours and forty minutes.

The flight to Boston was about fifty minutes. The plane touched down about 5:51 p.m. We knew that we would have about four hours of layover time. So, we decided to enjoy dinner at 'Legal Seafood.' There is no other Clam Chowder better than Boston Clam Chowder! Naturally, we shared a bowl and enjoyed some sourdough bread with it. Strolling around the international terminal, we realized that we still had about an hour and a half before the Aer Lingus departure. Time seems 'interminable' in terminals during long layovers. But with reading and nodding and watching CNN on the monitor -there was an oil spill at Prince William Sound in Alaska – again. Time went by quickly. Soon we were being called for boarding the Airbus 330 to Shannon Airport in County Clare. Beautiful Dawn had never been on the bigger Airbus. The A330-300 has lots of room and you can enjoy the TV offerings on the back seat in front of you. She became so fascinated by this that we hardly spoke.

"I'm sorry Aldie. I was so caught up in these computer games. They're so addictive. "

The evening meals were distributed about nine p.m. DST. I reminded Beautiful Dawn it's important to eat to catch up with the change of time – a six-hour difference in Ireland, meaning it was only three a.m. in Ireland. We decided to both order meals and share them (since they are very small). Afterward, I shared some of my memories of Ireland and its beautiful people and how once I had kissed the Blarney stone. She asked me my favorite places. I'd been to Killarney, Cork, Connemara National Park, Cliffs of Moher and a little town named Cong, where the 1950 movie 'The Quiet Man' starring John Wayne was filmed. In fact, one of our stops was at a B and B in Cong. I certainly also enjoyed the small towns around Shannon and many treasures of Dublin.

We were due into Shannon at 6:30 a.m. (Ireland time.) The plan was to stay at a little B and B outside Ennis while we were enjoying the wedding. Beautiful Dawn was paging through the DK book on Ireland, while I settled into a movie with a bit of an Irish connection, *'P.S., I Love You!'* starring Irish actor, Gerard Butler and

American actress, Hillary Swank. As the lights dimmed following coffee and tea service, it wasn't long until my Beautiful Dawn was asleep against my shoulder. I put a blanket around her and kissed her forehead. As for my sleeping, it never happens on planes. I may occasionally doze. It's just my nature. However, when the credits for the movie were swiftly moving by, I found myself curling up a bit with my Sweetheart and a space of time drifted by until we were awakened by bumpy air. The seatbelt signs were turned on. as the captain announced that he would be climbing to about 39,000 feet. After a while, it worked as the air smoothed out. It was about five a.m. Irish time and 11 p.m., Daylight Savings Time (Philadelphia) when the sunrise was becoming apparent on the horizon. It was the first time Beautiful Dawn had seen the ribbon-like orange and purple light up the sky.

We landed in Shannon at 6:30 a.m. Irish time, 12:30 a.m. Philadelphia time.

Ryan and Margaret happily greeted us outside baggage claim after we cleared passport control. Ryan O'Shea, Beautiful Dawn's cousin, and his wife-to-be Margaret Boyle, live in a little cottage outside of Ennis near the farm site of the wedding. Ryan and Margaret's cottage is a wee too small for us. They hesitantly offered accommodations in their tiny space, but we insisted a B and B would be ideal. The 'Abbey Lodge Guesthouse' was a mile from their cottage. Beautiful Dawn had not seen Ryan since his visit to the states for her Grandfather Vincent's funeral, quite a number of years ago. Neither of them remembered what year it was. Nevertheless, Ryan had taken Vincent's name as his own middle name – Ryan Vincent O'Shea.

Margaret was a sassy red-haired lass, a year older than Ryan and slightly taller. They had met through Ryan's work as a veterinarian tech in Limerick. His specialty was sheep. There wasn't anything Ryan O'Shea didn't know about sheep. And since there were countless sheep farms in Ireland, his work was in demand. Margaret O'Boyle was a bit of a Renaissance woman. She taught Celtic to elementary age children, danced in a local clogging group, played a mean Irish harp and wrote for a children's magazine. Margaret had raised a few sheep of her own and wanted advice on some of the health concerns she should be aware of her for her black heads. Ryan was more than helpful, he ended up asking her out and the rest is history.

We stopped to visit the Abbey Lodge Guesthouse and to check-in. It was so clean and comfortable. Meg and Fred O'Reilly, the hosts, knew Ryan and Margaret, who had used the Abbey Lodge once when her family visited from County Wexford. Meg and Fred proved to be a very relaxed older couple. They allowed us to drop our bags in the comfy room reserved for us, while we visited Ryan and Margaret in their home and worked on a few wedding preparations. Beautiful Dawn was very excited about helping Margaret with the floral arrangements. And me? I would be on 'gopher' duty, which was exceptionally light duty for me in my usual wedding officiant duties. It was one o'clock in the afternoon and we decided to visit a pub in Ennis – a favorite among locals, Michael Kerin's Bar. Ryan is one of those unique menfolk in Ireland, for whom many of his male friends have great sorrow. He is allergic to beer. To live in Ireland and be allergic to beer seems like cruel and unusual punishment from the Almighty Himself. Ryan loves wine, so he happily indulges some of his favorite wines – including, on this day and the occasion of their nuptials coming up and the visit of his favorite niece, Dawn O'Shea Seaver and her husband, Aldie, chose a glass of *Protocolo Tinto,'* a Spanish wine. Margaret, on the other hand, loves beer and is not shy at ordering herself a pint of Guinness.

"Oh, I don't give a wee rat's ass whether it seems like a man's beer, you know, I love the way it goes down me gullet."

I ordered a Smithwick Ale for *me*-self and Beautiful Dawn, preferred the Irish coffee. We toasted our safe arrival to the Emerald Isle and the upcoming wedding of Ryan and Margaret. We ordered some sandwiches and soup. Of course, Soups in Ireland are some of the yummiest to be found! Beautiful Dawn and I decided to share a bowl of Irish stew with bread.

"So how did the two of ya meet up?" Margaret asked us.

Beautiful Dawn shared the narrative of our finding each other and how the relationship has been knitted into a beautiful weave of 'us' –friends, lovers, and marriage partners. I shared how much I valued the foundation of friendship that got us started. I added as I looked at Beautiful Dawn:

"Of course, I thought she was beautiful and it ratcheted up my pulse rate a bit. She still does!

Ryan added. "And 'yor' going to have a baby... congratulations!"

"We just found out two months ago." We're thinking the baby will arrive sometime in April – maybe Easter!"

After our leisurely lunch at 'Michael Kerin's Pub,' Ryan drove us up to the Cliffs of Moher. When you're in County Clare, it's almost required by the Board of Tourism to visit the 'Cliffs of Moher'. It had become breezy, but the sun was shining. When we arrived, I could see a great many changes had been made since I visited in the late 90's. Now there was a Visitor's Center built into the crest of the Eastern hillside before ascending above the Cliffs. Lahinch is the largest town near the Cliffs of Moher. Beautiful Dawn became overwhelmed with the beauty of the Cliffs. We walked up the side of the cliffs to the tower for a magnificent view. The day was so clear, we could see Inisheer, one of the first of the Aran Islands, where Aran wool comes from those iconic Irish sweaters we love - so warm and cozy.

Margaret and Ryan admitted that each time they came to Doolin to visit the cliffs, they saw something new. They had never seen Inisheer look so amazingly clear in the afternoon sun. In fact, Margaret confessed that she had not been atop the tower before, so this day was a first.

"It's quite a view from here, don't you think Ry?"

"'Tis, Margaret dear, especially today. It feels as if I could reach out and touch Inisheer Island." Ryan reached over and kissed his soon-to-be-bride.

From a distance we could see fog moving in over the Cliffs. We were told that this happens often because of the winds and the energy of the sea at the western edge of Ireland. Showers pop almost every afternoon. The fog descended on the outer edges of the Cliff and you could barely see its expanse, just a silhouette of sorts. The winds began whipping around and Margaret's and Beautiful Dawn's billowing skirts were flying helplessly against its ferocity.

"Ah, Dawn 'tis bad day for the ladies' flying dresses and knickers views. Of course, the gentlemen don't mind it all, do they?" she lamented teasingly

"Oh my!" Beautiful Dawn agreed as she struggled to keep her own skirt from flying. The effort seemed impossible. So, both of them just surrendered to the wind's fury.

"Oh, what the heck. Let'em have a peek if they must. We both have gams to show, don't you think, Dawn?"

"Well, that's what Aldie tells me!" She rolled her eyes and looked at me and shook my arm.

"And I'll say it again, my dear!" I smiled broadly and kissed her cheek.

The storm was approaching fast and the rains eventually beat down on the Cliffs. We managed to get to the Visitor Center a bit drenched. But the showers only lasted ten to fifteen minutes. Unless there's a strong storm brewing, the rains in Ireland only last a short time. Soon the winds diminished, and the sun returned. We made a pass on the other side of the Cliffs for a different view of these rocky ledges.

Eventually we left the beautiful cliffs and drove around Doolin and enjoying seaside looking toward the Aran Islands. We ended the excursion back at Ryan and Margaret's cottage to relax a bit and talk about the wedding. Their cottage was part of a farm near Drumcarron More, off Lahinch Road (N85) just west of Ennis. Ryan's Uncle, Rory McKeldin, a gentleman farmer and software engineer from Ennis, owns the farm behind Ryan and Margaret's cottage. A rather large dirt lane with large rocks on either side leads back off the road to the farm site. We walked back the lane to view the wedding site. Already a large white tent was erected and anchored to accommodate the reception site. The wedding site was beneath a large willow tree not far from the silo and farm pond. Chairs were stacked there. Ryan had mowed the area and it looked very attractive as a wedding location. Margaret showed Beautiful Dawn inside the barn, where the flowers for the wedding had been delivered that morning. Margaret's Irish Setter, 'Pike,' followed us back to the barn and nestled on the floor as if to watch over the flower arranging.

"Oh, my goodness, Margaret, my work is cut out for me!" Beautiful Dawn sighed. "Might we get these Dahlia's in some water? I want them to look as fresh as possible for tomorrow."

"We'll bring all the materials ye need to put the bouquets together, Dawn. And over there are the flower stands." She was pointing to two white stands that were shaped like Corinthian columns. And, of course, the trellis is over there. We have some special flowers and Baby Breath for that. You won't need to make my bridal bouquet or the nosegays for the bridesmaids. Those have been special ordered and....as a matter of fact, they should be here... oh, here's the box over here." Beautiful Dawn looked in the box. "Margaret, they're beautiful! Oh my."

Ryan and I walked around the perimeter of the farm while the girls talked wedding details. He rubbed his goatee; "My uncle Rory is a typical gentleman's farmer, Aldie. He can afford all the best of equipment...look at the magnificent Hattat four-wheeler over there....and the hauler and mower. But, the truth is the man rarely gets a chance to come out here and ride them, since he's so busy with his software business. I actually handle most of the mowing and tending the sheep and the few cattle he has. He gave us a good price on the cottage in exchange for my watching out for the farm. You'll meet him this evening for the rehearsal."

I raised my eyebrows scanning the property and thought: *Everybody needs an 'Uncle Rory.'*

"He'll be fluthered a wee bit soon after his toast and the reception began and by the end of the day he'll be asleep on a haystack, mind ye."

"Fluthered" I scratched my head? Ryan laughed. "It's Irish for 'drunk!' He can down'em, Aldie. And he knows how to make good craic!"

Again, my puzzled look.

"Oh, yes, *'craic'* is slang for having a good time. Good craic... pronounced 'c-r-a-c-k.' His wife, Mary, gets on with him about it. I suppose when you're working on software all week long, making good craic is a balance for the stress. I tell ye, the man makes enough money, but he works too damned hard for all he does."

Beautiful Dawn got very busy the balance of the afternoon, organizing and making the floral bouquets and dressing the trellis. You could tell she was in her 'element.' If Beautiful Dawn had not become an R. N., she would have been a floral designer.

Ryan and I went into Ennis to pick up a few groceries for Margaret. She was planning on making us an Irish dinner. If Beautiful Dawn's gift is arranging flowers, Margaret's gift was culinary arts. So as soon as she had Beautiful Dawn situated for the floral arranging, she would be back to the cottage to begin dinner. Ry and I went to

Meere's Butcher's in Lower Market in Ennis to buy the meat and other items around the store and then stopped by a 'Ma and Pa' market nearby for the remaining items. While driving about, another swath of rained passed through. I was glad that Beautiful Dawn had the shelter of the barn for her work. When we got back, Margaret was waiting impatiently to get started on her gourmet meal.

"Ye were buying the whole store, we're ye, O'Shea? If I didn't know ye never drank, Ry, I'd think ye stopped for a pint!"

"Y'know I don't drink the stuff, woman!"

She kissed him on the lips and grabbed his crotch, Margaret laughed and winked at him. "Just checkin' to see if yor still alive down there, ya know." She laughed and put on her apron and got started with meal preparation.

Margaret is a lusty woman with fiery red hair, and she's no wallflower. She will let you know how she feels about most anything - no guessing, both good and bad – and I could imagine she might show a flash of temper when she needs to. Robust, certainly not petite, her smile is radiant and devilish the way her eyes look at you. She's not Irish, but Scottish, and unapologetic about marrying an Irishman! Margaret was born in Oban. However, Ryan, was born near Ennis and had lived here since he was a toddler. He's very laid back, a gentle kind of guy with a dry wit. He doesn't smile a lot, but he can tease in a fun sort of way. Margaret seems passionate about life, a loose cannon of sorts. Ryan is a steady rudder in the sea. It's always interesting to observe couple dynamics – the balances that make up the relationship. I imagine that Margaret wears her emotions on her sleeve, will laugh heartily. Ryan keeps a lid on his emotions and, at times, is the Rock of Gibraltar when Margaret needs him to be. He grounds her. She unbuttons him when he's too grounded. Nice combo!

I walked back to the barn to see how Dawn was faring in the flora. Ryan had a few chores to catch up on with the sheep. Dawn was busy arranging flowers on a table that Ryan had placed in the barn. There were ribbons and scissors and papers with drawings, buckets with flowers and ties and strings and many things.

"Hi Sweetheart, you're really working hard."

"Oh, Aldie, I'm so nervous. I want this to be just right for the wedding. I'm glad you're here.... would you hold these while I put ties around them?" She pointed to mixtures of floral bouquets.

"Of course!" I winked, "I'm honored to be your floral helper."

"Thanks. Just hold them like this... a little higher so I can see underneath. That's good."

It was neat to see her in her element. I gazed around and saw the fruits of her work unfolding beautifully. She was truly in a floral design crush. "Sweetheart, you're doing some neat work here. It's beautiful."

"Oh, thank you, Darling. I just hope I can get all of this ready in time."

She took the flowers from my hand and asked me if I would bring over the brass vase behind the chair. "Thanks, Darling. Could you just wipe it off a bit with the white towel? There are some things I can't do until tomorrow. But at least this will have the bouquets ready for the columns. Aren't they beautiful, Aldie? They look so genuine."

I sat and watched her and shared some of the good feelings about Ryan's and Margaret's relationship and how enjoyable it was being here. It was the kind of relaxed travel I had not had opportunity to enjoy. My earlier travels to Ireland involved hosting groups. While at Holyoke my ex-wife Kathy and I had hosted a trip to Ireland with about 40 people, not all from the parish. I was so exhausted when I returned, looking after older ladies and some teens traveling with us. Kathy had developed pneumonia during the trip and required a brief hospitalization in Galway. And one of the women fell and broke her leg in Connemara National Park, which required an overnight at the hospital in Killarney. The next day she received crutches and I had to make arrangements for her flight home, since she would have had a difficult time navigating the balance of the trip.

Most, there was one unforgettable incident, in which I lost one of our teens, Jordyn Childress, in Dublin during the city tour. She had boarded one of the coaches that looked similar to ours after our tour of St. Patrick's cathedral. When she had realized it was the wrong bus, she got off and started looking for our coach. She didn't realize that we were parked near the front end of the long line of parked buses. She started walking away from the buses thinking that she would find us. When I finished my count and realized that she wasn't there, I told our Guide-Driver, Joe, I would look for her.

He told me that he couldn't remain in the spot, because other buses would be pulling in for other tours. He told me that he would be in the Georgian section of Dublin, where all the fancy doors are. I knew this area, just beyond the Museum of Art. So, I told him that I would catch up with him there or possibly at the entrance to the Book of Kells, Trinity College. And if I missed him, I knew where the Gresham Hotel was on O'Connell Street. So, I'd get a cab and bring her back there, since our afternoon would be free. Jordyn Childress was a perky, adventurous (I underscore 'adventurous') teen at Holyoke. She was actually a niece of Molly Malone Mason, although Jordyn would deny that. She was about 180 degrees from her Aunt Molly's lifestyle. This was her first trip to Europe and her parents thought it would be good for her and Brie McKendry, her best friend, to experience Europe before graduation. Jordyn and Brie roomed together, but I sometimes got the impression that Brie thought Jordyn was going to spring loose. Well, perhaps not by design, Jordyn did 'spring loose' at St. Patty's Cathedral, sending panic through my sinews. Dublin was a city of about one million people, give or take. And, while I love the Irish people, a city of one million! I tried to think logically where a teen who got lost at a cathedral like St. Patty's and in a formidable city might go to next?

These were the days just before GPS. (How did we ever survive?). I did remember that Jordyn had on a bright blue jacket with her high school mascot, a cougar, on it. And I remembered the number '1' being on the back of the jacket. Jordyn had blonde hair and her earrings were rather large circles. I tried to imagine Jordyn's parents at this moment, their daughter suddenly lost in a large city. (I'm glad we weren't in London or Paris or Rome!) Since it had only been about 20 minutes, I figured that she couldn't be too far. I first went back into St. Patrick's and asked the security personnel, having given a description, to keep a watch for her. If they found her, they were to call the Gresham front desk and contact Joe (the Guide/Driver, who had a phone on his bus. I had that number at least. And, yes, mobiles were at least advanced that far). Joe would bring her back to the hotel.

I scanned the crowd (there were enormous crowds at St. Patrick's) and I didn't see the bright blue jacket. I stayed just a few minutes just to see if she might re-enter the cathedral. Then I walked through the gardens by the cathedral just to see if she might be there. Finally, I exited and started heading north on 'Patrick St. Close' somewhat retracing the route of our approach to St. Patrick's. The cathedral is south of the Liffey River and it seemed logical she might follow (I prayed) the more populous streets we traversed. Now and again I would ask passersby if they had a seen a blonde teen, rather tall, with a bright blue jacket with a numeral '1' on it. Two little ladies passing with shopping bags did mention seeing someone of that description along Church Street. (Ah, a start!). I kept watching both sides of Church St. all the way to the Liffey. Just before High Street and where Dame Street begins, I spotted her standing at a light!

"Jordyn!" I yelled at the top of my lungs, startling most of the walkers in front of me. She spotted me and put her hands atop her head. I could tell she was relieved.

"Stay there, I'll come across the street." I caught the next green light and ran over and held her. She was crying.

"I thought I was on the right bus, Fr. Seaver! I didn't know what to do..."

"It's OK Jordyn... it's OK. It happens. I'm just glad I found you."

I thanked God for helping me find her and keeping her safe. Her parents had warned me that Jordyn was a free spirit and to feel free to 'keep her under wraps.' But this wasn't the free-spirited Jordyn they were speaking of. This was the Jordyn who just happened to get on the wrong bus for the right reasons in the heart of busy Dublin. I took her into a pub and asked to make a phone call. They were kind enough to let me call Joe, our Guide/Driver. He was just getting through one of the streets in the Georgian area and said he would be stopping at Trinity College, so folks could view the Book of Kells. The bus would be parked along Nassau Street (along a black iron gate). From our position, I was only about 15 minutes from Trinity College. I told him that we would catch up with the group at the entrance to the Book of Kells. I bought Jordyn a Coke and we proceeded on Dame Street toward Grafton and Trinity College. She held onto my arm the whole time. We arrived at the entrance to the Book of Kells just as the group was passing the tower clock. When they saw us, cheers went up and everyone extended a hug to Jordyn –especially Brie who was crying and holding onto her.

"God, I thought I'd never see you again!"

The excursion was an adventure. We got everyone home and I was exhausted. Kathy swore that she would never attempt group travel again. She didn't really like Ireland, with the exception of Dublin. She was a very 'urban cowgirl' type. The country gave her the 'creeps' (her word.)

On the contrary, this trip with my Beautiful Dawn seemed more relaxed so far. The touring was unhurried. There was no on and off the bus, pushing through crowds of other tourists, trying to stay together, folks complaining about their seats, their view, the limited time, the regimen, etc. I found myself *really* enjoying the Emerald Isle for the first time. My Nikon was working overtime –especially at the Cliffs of Mohr and surrounding area. Even the farm area and Ry's and Margaret's cottage were scenic.

After Margaret's delicious meal of tender Irish beef and potatoes with green beans, we chatted by the fireplace. The Cottage was idyllic. Although somewhat small, it had a good size kitchen/dining room combination, with a living room off to the side. There was a bath and a half. The master bedroom was small but comfortable. The guest room was really Margaret's 'girl shack' where she did her sewing and watches TV. The Cottage is in stone. So charming! Even though it was a farmhouse, Ryan and Margaret had fixed it up to include a porch off the kitchen, where we spent the evening before our jaunt into town, where we were already checked into the Abbey Lodge B&B.

Ryan took us there about 9PM. The note on the door said: *'Fáilte, Dear Friends! 'Breakfast is at 7- 10 tomorrow downstairs.'* We realized that it was 2 a.m. back in the States. As much as we would have enjoyed beautiful lovemaking, but the long plane ride, the touring and all the flower arranging, there was only time to give a kiss, turn out the lights and fall into the big four-poster bed.

I peered out the window at 6 a.m. The wedding day was beginning with morning showers, we were glad we didn't set up the chairs, stacked and covered by tarp). We had told Ry and Margaret that we would have breakfast at the Abbey Lodge and plan to meet them at 10 a.m. Returning to bed, Beautiful Dawn wrapped her arm around me. We savored vigorous lovemaking in that large poster bed, with the sound of the battering rain and wind. As we lay entwined, feeling energized, we realized we had to get our showers and get ready for a busy day.

Breakfast with Meg's cooking was delightful. There were two other couples already seated. Delightful Irish music was playing in the background. We enjoyed eggs and bangers, quantities of cut fruit, cheese and ham, Orange Juice, tea -- 'Barry's' of course- and pastry delicacies. We finished breakfast and enjoyed a brief walk around the Abbey Lodge, waiting for Ryan to pick us up. The day had become brilliantly aglow as the last of morning clouds disappeared. The grassy area was a bit soaked, but, sparkling with the sun.

The wedding was scheduled for 2 p.m. We had four hours to zero. Margaret was already at her hair appointment in Ennis and Ry had a 'honey-do' list a mile long. Beautiful Dawn headed back to the barn to finish the flowers and began setting up the Corinthian columns pedestals. My job was clear: set up the white folding chairs and create an outdoor chapel and, essentially, stay out of the way and play with Pike, who had been neglected.

Ry and I would eventually move the trellis to the wedding site after Beautiful Dawn transformed it into a floral presence. Carrying it out of the barn, it almost fell over, which caused Dawn to scream, which then set Pike to barking. Ryan and I were able to right it, but it was a close call considering the flowers intricately delicately placed on it! We were able to set it securely with some spikes dug into the ground and cable connected on both ends.

YUM Catering, Ltd., arrived from Ennis about 11:30 a.m. They were allotted a separate tent for food preparation. At 12 Noon, Ry picked up Margaret from the beauty salon and she disappeared into her bedroom for the rest of her 'beauty hand-to-face combat', appearing occasionally for food and a pint. When Beautiful Dawn had finally finished her flower work, Margaret summoned her for beauty duty and bridal assistance wrapped into one. The master bedroom became "Wedding Central' and Ry was to get lost and get dressed in the only logical place available: the tiny built-in bathroom the farm next to an old milking house. Rory had put it there when his wife and two girls had taken over The Cottage and created a nylon jungle and a lipstick lagoon. The window in that tiny bathroom looks out over a field with rolled up haystacks and views of Ennis. No matter where you look in Ireland, there is beauty to behold.

Around 1 p.m., the Irish harpist arrived. and asked for a chair and location of his space during the wedding. Ry was on hand to show him. At 1:15 p.m., Father O'Murray arrived in his black Mercedes. Ry's Best Man, Patrick, had joined him at the barn and Margaret's Matron of Honor had arrived at The Cottage – now there were three girls squeezing in the Master Bedroom- half bath space. I ended up being a gopher between Ryan and Margaret. I had already savored the dress Beautiful Dawn was going to wear at the wedding. She had bought back home at Talbot's. It was a beautiful floor-length gown of summer green, a sleeveless, silky pattern with a white webbing design from the shoulder to the waist. The gown allowed for some cleavage showing and the belt was a white webbing matching the design around her bosom. Her Matron of Honor was wearing a green gown with summer flower patterns throughout. The women decided on white low heel shoes for the walk across the rough grass to the altar. The girls all had a circle of flowers in their hair.

Ry and Patrick wore the basic black tuxedo with green cummerbunds and green kerchiefs in their jacket pockets. Their vests were a green pattern. Just to make it even more Irish, they wore green wing-tipped shoes. Where they found wingtips, I have no idea! Guests started arriving around 1:30 and Patrick's job was to welcome them and hand out programs. He had been an altar boy in Father O'Murray's church in Limerick back in the 1980's.

Father O'Murray was a 'retired' priest. Of course, priests technically never retire, they are just put out to pasture. Father O'Murray was literally 'out to pasture' today there in Drumcarron! He had the capacity to officiate secular marriages (as the Roman Catholic Church called them in Ireland) – which are simply weddings not performed in a Catholic church building. Since the Father didn't have an official church, he was enticed to officiate the Boyle-O'Connor ceremony. Ry described him as a 'corker.' O'Murray once told a friend he'd do weddings just for the whiskey. Rounded and short of stature, Fr. O'Murray had very red cheeks and few hairs upon his head, but he could laugh long and hard –especially at Catholic jokes. He knew them all. And, well known, he enjoyed his

271

Michael Collins Single Malt whiskey, one of the top Irish whiskies in the country. An unsubstantiated rumor had it that the good reverend had stock in Michael Collins or maybe he was just 'stocked well' with it at his refectory in Limerick.

Puffy clouds were emerging on the horizon. This usually signals an afternoon shower, but the wind was calm, and the weather forecast did not indicate rain. We were now ready to seat the guests and within 20 minutes of the ceremony. Fr. O'Murray was cracking jokes with Ry and Patrick.

Knowing I was from America and had hosted tours to Ireland. Fr. O'Murray couldn't resist telling me this joke: "A group of Americans was touring Ireland. One of the women in the group was a real curmudgeon, constantly complaining. The bus seats are uncomfortable. The food is terrible. It's too hot. It's too cold. The accommodations are awful. The group arrived at the site of the famous Blarney Stone. "Good luck will be followin' ye all your days if you kiss the Blarney Stone," the guide said. "Unfortunately, it's being cleaned today and so no one will be able to kiss it. Perhaps we can come back tomorrow." "We can't be here tomorrow," the nasty woman shouted, "we have some other boring tour to go on. So, I guess we can't kiss the stupid stone." "Well now," the guide said, "it is said that if you kiss someone who has kissed the stone, you'll have the same good fortune." "And I suppose you've kissed the stone," the woman scoffed. "No, ma'am," the frustrated guide said, "but I've sat on it."

I laughed heartily, of course, the groomsmen with me. Ry shook his head. I had settled in my seat when I noticed Beautiful Dawn motioning for me to come to the Cottage. The harpist had begun his beautiful strumming. I excused my conversation with another wedding guest and walked toward the house.

"Aldie, Margaret wants to speak with you."

"Of course," I said curiously. Her Matron of Honor came out of the bedroom and smiled at me and then Beautiful Dawn closed the bedroom door. There was Margaret Boyle, looking radiant. Her beautiful countenance in the long dress made me realize that all brides are beautiful. Margaret smiled and then lowered her eyes. "Aldie Boy, I'm sorry for drawin' ye in here right before the weddin'. I'm.... I'm not a church attender, you know. Christ, I'm not much of a believer at all. Ry calls me a 'token atheist.' Before God, whoever God is, I'm not much. But I do believe in the goodness of human creation... in fact, all of creation. Fr. O'Murray is basically a 'hire.' He's not my priest. God knows I love the man dearly...in fact, I could down a Michael Collins wit'im right now! But he's a friend, not my priest. I have no priest. But you... you're a decent man and you are an Anglican and, God willin' after I confess to ye, still a friend! And yor married to Ry's first cousin, so yor family. I'm needin' to tell ye somethin', Aldie. I'm feisty and sometimes lusty and I've got a Scottish temper. The Good Lord knows, it comes with the territory! I'm a 'Boyle.' And sometimes on someone's arse - forgive me, Aldie! In a wee bit of time I'll be standin' before the likes of a good man, Ryan Jameson O'Shea and promise me life-long love to him. I'm needin' to get this off me chest – pardon the expression."

She confessed that several years before she met Ry, she had dated a man from County Galway and had gotten pregnant one evening after a drunken stupor in one of the pubs in town. Discovering that she was pregnant had rattled her to her senses. It was a 'fork in the road' experience. She told no one, not even her parents and certainly she didn't tell Ryan about it after she met him, but she had planned the next day to get an abortion in Galway. However, during the night, she had a horrific dream in which the fetus she was about to abort had taken form and had come to the foot of her bed trying to reach for her the way a frightened child reaches for its mother. The fetus was crying and pleading. It was an awful image she couldn't shake.

"Aldie, I stayed awake and I cried and cried me-self to derision the night long!. The next day I called the clinic in Galway and cancelled the appointment. I moved to Limerick and for the next nine months, went full term with the wee one in me belly. With the help of friends like me Maid of Honor, I was able to make it through and deliver a beautiful baby girl named Anna Margaret. Today, Anna Margaret is four years old and livin' with her adopted parents in County Donegal. I visit her on occasion with their permission. I swear to you, Aldie on a stack of King James bibles, someday I'm going to tell Ryan every detail."

She looked at her watch and sighed.

273

Blessed Jesus, I'm late for me own wedding! I just needed to tell someone who was a Man' o 'God like yer self that although me life had lapsed in the pregnancy with Anna Margaret, I intend to do what was right and share it with me dear Ryan."

I gave her a hug and a kiss on the cheek and nodded.

"Your confession is safe with me... and the God I have come to know will love you through it. Thanks for not aborting Anna, but even if you had, there would have been forgiveness. I believe that."

She smiled and kissed me on the cheek.

"Oh, thanks to you, Aldie Boy, and that Dawn of yours is one lucky lass! Now I need to get me big arse down the aisle before Fr. Murray starts on his first Michael Collins!"

I left the room and winked at Beautiful Dawn. It was exactly 2 p.m. The harpist was waiting. The guests had all been seated and the procession was about to begin. I hurried to my seat. My Beautiful Dawn first appeared and dropped white flower petals on the grassy pathway to the altar. My heart was racing as she moved gracefully down the aisle. How I loved her, this intoxicatingly beatific vision of a flower maiden! This enchanting nymph, made all of these beautiful flower arrangements happen. I recalled that it was more than five months ago that we stood together to promise our life-long commitment to one another. I wanted to run up to her and just tell her all over again how much I adored her.

Though the day had brought a mixture of sun and puffy clouds, there was no rain. The wedding of Ryan Jameson O'Shea and Mary Margaret Boyle went off without a 'hitch'... except of course, they hitched up and become Mr. and Mrs. Ryan Jameson O'Shea! Margaret, stunning in her emerald gown, wore the traditional Irish lace around her shoulders. Ry placed the Claddagh ring upon her finger, his first gift to her. The ring was her mother's and her grandmother's. The Claddagh ring was named after a fishing village in Galway. It featured two hands clasping a heart. And mounted on the heart was a crown. The symbolism of 'love' (heart), 'friendship (the hands) and 'loyalty; (the heart)- are all necessary qualities of a marriage. As they placed the Claddagh rings on, Fr. O'Murray asked them to recite their vows, which were very traditional and a bit weird, I must admit.

I vow you the first cut of my meat, the first sip of my wine, from this day it shall only be your name I cry out in the night and into your eyes that I smile each mornin'; I shall be a shield for your back as you are for mine, not shall a grievous word be spoken about us, for our marriage is sacred between us and no stranger shall hear my grievance. Above and beyond this, I will cherish and honor you through this life and into the next.

My only role in this wedding was to stand and deliver the Irish Wedding Prayer. So, when it was time, I took my reading forward to the podium and with a little Irish rogue of sorts I read:

May God go with you and bless you. May you see your children's children. May you be poor in misfortune and rich in blessings. May you know nothing but happiness from this day forward. May joy and peace surround you both, Contentment latch your door; And happiness be with you now and God Bless you ever more. May you live your life with trust and nurture lifelong affection, May your lifelong dreams come true for you,

May the road rise to meet you, May the wind be always at your back, May the sun shine warm upon your face, the rains fall soft upon your fields.

May the light of friendship guide your paths together, May the laughter of children grace the halls of your home. May the joy of living for each other trip a smile from your lips, a twinkle from your eye. And when eternity beckons, at the end of the life heaped high with love, May the good Lord embrace you with the arms that have nurtured you the whole length of your joy-filled days. May the gracious God hold you both in the palm of His hands. And, today, may the Spirit of Love find a dwelling place in your hearts.

Father O'Murray, smiling broadly pronounced that Ryan and Margaret were husband and wife, and invited a little peck on the cheek. Everyone laughed heartedly as Ryan planted an extended lip-lock on his sassy bride, to which she responded with bending him with an aggressive lip lock of her own. Fr. O'Murray notched up his glasses, looked at his watch a few times and smiled broadly.

"Did ye not hear me? I said a' peck on yer cheeks!"

That brought gales of laughter. The harp strummed recessional music and Margaret danced down the aisle with her groom, shaking her hips and waving her flowers. When she got to the back, she bent over and raised her skirt and showed everyone her knickers – including Fr. O'Murray, who adjusted his glasses once more and was heard to say: "Oh, dear Jesus!"

Beautiful Dawn and I kissed each other soon afterward. "Mrs. Aldron Gerard Seaver, you are stunning! I love you."

"Thank you, Mr. Seaver! You're a handsome lad yourself."

A little post-script on the Wedding Reception: Guests, of course, participated in the traditional Irish Wedding Toast with Beautiful Dawn, the Matron of Honor, Patrick, the Best Man, gathered around Ryan and Meg and Patrick, reciting as the mead glasses were raised:

Friends and relatives, so fond and dear, 'tis our greatest pleasure to have you here. When many years this day have passed, fondest memories always last. So, we drink a cup of Irish mead and ask God's blessing in your hour of need.

Then the guests raised their glasses of mead and said: *On this special day our wish to you, the goodness of the old, the best of the new. God bless you both who drink this mead, may it always fill your every need.*

The caterers spread a tasty feast of Irish soda bread and corned beef and cabbage. But they also served Irish stew and an assortment of baked hams and sliced roast beef with, of course, boiled potatoes.

'The Mad Hatters,' from Newmarket on Fergus, south of Ennis, provided the Irish music. Margaret was a friend and they were happy to have work on a Wednesday evening. Guests raved about their music and energy. The dance floor was smoking with their Irish songs.

Fr. O'Murray enjoyed four or five glasses of 'Michael Collins Malt Whiskey' and passed out around 6:30 p.m. At 8 p.m., he awoke and threw up on his plate and chair and most everything immediately around him. He was embarrassed, but we survived it. The caterer cleaned the mess up in little time. The guests, agreeably, all moved outside for a little while! Oh, and Margaret's Irish Setter, 'Pike,' got loose during the ceremony and climbed on the table and assaulted the wedding cake with his powerful jaws before the caterer was able to drag him away and place him in the barn. Cake remains were fine and still served most of the guests, although some politely passed up the offer.

Ry succumbed to a dare or two that he would down a pint of Guinness. There was a 150 Euro bet on the dare and he proceeded to drink it all in one fell swoop. Margaret was dared to show her knickers once again —which she accepted without hesitation.' There was a bet of 300 Euro in wedding money. Never one to turn down a dare or money, Margaret proceeded to bend over and hoist her wedding gown around her waist to show the crowd her well-rounded derriere. The red print on Margaret's knickers read *'Kiss this lass!'* This is the only wedding I've attended where the bride twice gave a full view of her underwear! Margaret's mother almost fainted, but her grandmother Lillian Boyle, from whom Margaret inherited her Scotch mojo, clapped and shouted, "Now who's gone to wear the pants in this family, ye know!" Another crowd knee slapper!

By 9 p.m. Beautiful Dawn and I were reaching a threshold of spent energy. We had both learned a little of the Highland Fling and other dances. But the time difference from back home and the excitement of the wedding made it necessary for us to call it a day. We called for a 'hire' —McMahon's Taxi Service. Ryan wanted to take us home, but we insisted not. We told Margaret we would come the next day at 12 Noon to bid good bye. McMahon's dropped us off back at the Abbey Lodge and soon we were fast asleep.

My last thoughts before sleep were: *'New beginnings are a lot of energy... but thank God for them!'*

We both awoke at 6 a.m. to another hard-pounding rain and howling wind. The summer weather pattern had changed over-night. The moon had been full and the skies clear the night before. The sounds awakened the spirit of *Eros* in both of us and suddenly we were entangled in each other with rapid breathing and moans of unrequited desire.

There's always something about howling winds and beating rain that triggers the impulses of the libido. We stretched our passion over almost an hour. By 7:30 a.m. the sun was blanketing the area and we were off to the shower to cleanse ourselves from all the previous day's sweat and toil. We both agreed, as we washed each other with sponges, that it was an incredibly beautiful Irish wedding. Once spruced up and packed, we enjoyed another fabulous Meg O'Reilly breakfast. We were the only couple at the Lodge overnight. When I handed Fred my Visa card, he waved his hand.

"It's been paid for ya, Mr. Seaver."

I was stunned. I tried to insist that we pay for our own lodging.

"No, your friends 'wor' adamant. "

Beautiful Dawn looked at me in disbelief. "We'll work this out. Thanks, Fred. You and Meg have a wonderful facility here. It's been a joy to stay here."

I presented a 50 Euros tip.

Fred insisted on taking us to the cottage.

"It's only 5 minutes, don't ya know. Let me help you get those in my car." Fred dropped us off at the cottage at 10:15. Margaret was outside doing chores. We prattled back and forth about the generous two nights' they paid for at the Abbey Lodge, but Ryan and Margaret would have nothing to do with our offer to reimburse them.

"Would ye consider for one moment the amount of work ye put into the flowers, Dawn?" Margaret was serious. "And Aldie, in addition to all your help, your listening to me before the whole show came off was priceless. You helped me get me head and me heart straight, for sure."

Ryan piped in. "It was the least we could do. Thank you both so much."

We shared some hugs and some tea and then Ryan and Margaret carted us off, backpacks and all, to the train station in Ennis – our first Irish Rail ride awaited us, and we would head southward bound for Killarney. Everyone has to visit 'Old Killarney' at least once! The route would take us to Limerick and then southward to Tralee, where we would board a bus to Killarney – about three hours total travel time. The trip by rail was a visual smorgasbord. We appreciated the various shades of green within the rock boundaries for sheep and cattle farming.

I was amazed at the number of golf courses we passed along the way. In the course of the three hours, we had sunshine, a pounding rain, a mixture of clouds and sun and then brilliant sunshine as we pulled into Tralee station and changed to a Killarney-bound bus – about 45 minutes.

It was about 4:30 p.m. when our cab dropped us off at Chelmsford House, a beautiful Bed and Breakfast on Muckross Road just five minutes from downtown Killarney. (Beautiful Dawn marveled that she was in a community where her father's family had once lived.) It was a joy to check in there and meet our hosts and their staff. Erin, daughter of the innkeepers had grown up in Killarney and knew everything there is to know about the town – what to see, pubs that are outstanding for their music and ambiance, the beautiful Muckross estate and Kerry guides for those interested in the Ring of Kerry.

We were both a bit hungry, so we favored walking downtown and enjoying the ambiance of Irish music in a recommended pub, '*The Danny Mann*' located on New Street. It was about 5:30 p.m. when we arrived, and the Irish music had already begun, and we enjoyed good food as the music entertained us. Even though we could hardly hear each other, the flavor – the violinist, the harpist and the accordion player- as well as the food (a bowl of Irish Stew and some fish and chips) were well worth our time there.

We were even treated by a special visit of Step Dancers from the Connemara area. I learned from one of the locals sitting next to us that the reason the upper bodies and arms are still, is that in the 19th Century, dancers had limited space to perform their dances, sometimes even on the tops of barrels. The emphasis was on the percussive sound of the toes. Dancers were instructed to dance a step twice –first with the right foot, then with the left. Their cadence, of course, matched the particular Irish tune being played. We were mesmerized by the performance of these girls and their step-dancing skills.

We stayed at '*The Danny Mann*' until after 8 p.m. The sun had set in Old Killarney and we spent the rest of the evening walking around town and enjoy the Irish music from one pub to another.

We walked back to the Chelmsford and enjoyed the ambiance of our room, facing the Muckross House and one of the several Killarney Lakes, which we would visit some time the next day. Everything electronic we were carrying needed re-charging that night. We unpacked our bags and, like the previous night, fell into our bed fast asleep.

The morning sun awakened us and cast a spell on our holding each other. We had become morning lovers since our trip to Ireland began, since most evenings, influenced by the changing time back home, had become unbearably exhausting. Making love in the sunshine in an elegant bedroom awash in yellow walls and white lacey curtains in a four-poster king size bed was very alluring. It was seven o'clock and we were looking forward to a jaunting ride to Muckross National Park, the elegant house (a Tudor like mansion) and the Muckross gardens. The breakfast by Chelmsford Staff was very elegant, like the Inn itself.

We took our cameras and some snacks and hailed a jaunting driver for the first ride out to Muckross around 9 a.m. It is a beautiful estate designed not by an Irishman, but a Scottish architect named William Burns and built in 1843 for Henry and Mary Balfour Herbert (she was a well-known watercolorist). The house has 56 rooms. Queen Victoria stayed in it in 1861 after it had undergone extensive renovations. The latter mentioned renovations financially ruined the Herbert family and it was sold in 1899 to Arthur Guinness and then in 1932 sold to a wealthy Californian, who bought it for his daughter and his son-in-law as a wedding gift.

We enjoyed the tour throughout the house for a small fee. We were able to return to town to hire a guide to take us around the Ring of Kerry (correct name: the 'Iveragh Peninsula) for the afternoon – certainly one of the highlights of any visit to Ireland. A guide-hire for the Ring is one of the best ways to see the peninsula and we had Peter Kilpatrick to do just that. It took us from 12 Noon to 6 p.m. to take the most leisurely van ride around the 111 miles of the Ring, savoring little towns like Kollorglin, Leane, Ladies View, with its panoramic viewpoint, the Gap of Dunloe, the Bog Village, Rossbeigh beach. We continued through Moll's Gap, Waterville (the summer residence of the late Charlie Chaplin) and the quaint little town of Sneem. Peter was superb with his humor and great knowledge of the area. Those of us who were photographers had all the time we desired for pictures. We returned to the Chelmsford to enjoy light fare at their pub before retiring.

The next morning, we were up early with an Irish hot breakfast and then took a bus back to Tralee to board the Irish Rail to Cork, where we arrived at approximately noon. We purchased a round-trip bus ticket to Blarney Castle outside of Cork and spent the afternoon partly at the Blarney Woolen Mills, where Beautiful Dawn found and purchased a stunning canary yellow Irish sweater for the Fall and winter months.

A greater part of the afternoon was spent following the footpath across from the mills that winds its way by a gentle stream and ends up to the entrance of the Blarney Castle grounds. I know that most everyone who makes a stop at Blarney are interested in kissing the stone atop the castle and thereby assure themselves of the promise of eloquent speech. But I succumbed to that journey once and found it rather claustrophobic, not to mention a bit of the fear of heights and falling through that narrow section where you bend backwards to kiss the iconic stone. "It's something to do," one of the guides mentioned. "Thousands of people do it every month just to say they did."

Beautiful Dawn had no interest climbing to the top of the tower. She was somewhat fearful of heights and felt that she could vicariously live it through me.

"You kiss me, Aldie, and then I'll have the eloquence of speech!"

We wandered through the serene grounds beneath the Blarney Castle. There were idyllic gardens and walkways and bridges across the stream. It's the kind of setting where you almost feel your blood pressure lowering by a few notches. There are places around the Castle where you sense that at any moment a leprechaun may just jump out and greet you. The afternoon sun, which had grown brilliant, provided for beautiful photos of the area. Police officers on horses came down to the stream to offer their horses cool drink. That provided a good photo setting with the castle draped in the background.

On our way back to the footpath leading to the castle, I suddenly heard my name called out. "Father Seaver?"

I looked up. I couldn't believe my eyes. It was Jordyn Childress, the teen whom I had lost in Dublin a number of years ago – now a beautiful young woman with two daughters!

"Remember, I was Jordyn Childress –You took me to Ireland... and I got lost in Dublin! I'm now Jordyn Childress McKendry.

"Yes, Jordyn! I can't believe we're here again!"

I wrapped my arms around her and introduced her to my Beautiful Dawn. They hugged too. Jordyn continued: "This is Shrushsti. She's six. And this Phan, who is now ten." I gave them both hugs

"You roomed with Brie McKendry... you must have married her brother."

"Well, actually... I married Brie, Fr. Seaver."

I didn't see that coming, but I accepted it easily.

"Wow, congratulations Jordyn!"

"Thanks. She's actually in the bathroom right now. Please wait... she'd love seeing you."

"This is so wonderful, Jordyn!"

Jordyn continued "We grew close after that trip. It wasn't too long after we returned that you moved to Pennsylvania. It took us a long time to realize that we were drawn to each other. Well, we both went to the University of Virginia and got our degrees. I'm an architect now for an industrial engineer company..."

"Father Seaver!!!! Oh my God! "I heard Brie screaming as she ran toward me. and wrapped her arms around me.

"I can't believe you're here in Ireland!" Brie introduced herself to Beautiful Dawn and then put her arm around Jordyn.

We all were amazed at the improbability of meeting one another at Blarney Castle on that particular day at that particular place. We took pictures and enjoyed chatting. I offered congratulations on their partnership and their two adopted children. After they partnered, following graduation from University of Virginia, they both got engineering jobs, Jordyn as a structural design engineer for Bechtel Corporation, and Brie, a software engineer for Northrup Grumman. They now live in Vienna, Virginia. Since they both travel worldwide, they felt it was important to live near Dulles Airport. The girls have an excellent daycare provider and, if both Brie and Jordyn are on work travel, Brie's Mom lives in Purcellville, VA, not far away.

We chatted for quite a while, catching up on life for both our families.

Finally, Brie offered: "Well, we need to let you enjoy the castle and the grounds. It's beautiful here. I think we stopped here on the trip we made, didn't we Jordyn?"

"Yes, that's why we're back here... partly. Brie's working on an assignment in Dublin for a few days, so we decided to make it a family trip and retrace some of the steps. I'm happy to say I haven't gotten lost yet!"

I hugged them and the girls; Beautiful Dawn hugged them all too, and we parted. It still amazes me the probability of meeting someone you know in that setting, especially someone whom you remember as a teen, who scared the wits out of me, lost in Dublin!

"Life is different in the twenty-first century, isn't it Sweetheart," I mentioned to Beautiful Dawn. "There was a day when the idea of two grown women sharing adoptive children and having two professional careers would have been unheard of."

"We've come a long way, Aldie. I'm happy for that," she remarked as she held my arm.

"Me too, Love!"

We went back to the restaurant at the Blarney Woolen Mills and enjoyed some Barry's tea and dessert and then walked to our overnight, the 'Blarney Vale Bed & Breakfast,' five minutes from the Woolen Mills. This four-star B&B was one of the most delightful we stayed at in Ireland. Ann and Ray Hennessy are charming Innkeepers. As we settled in, we asked them where we might enjoy dinner. Among the choices they offered, we chose the *'Blair's Inn'* in downtown Blarney. And we weren't disappointed. Beautiful Dawn and I enjoyed an Irish Seafood entrée in this very romantic setting. (Irish music, of course, was included.)

It was Sunday morning and the weather had changed. There was a system moving across Ireland that made for clouds and rain. Somehow that's not all disappointing. Part of the reason Ireland is so green is that it is never without rain somewhere in Ireland. It is an island with windward and leeward coasts. 'Windward' at one time was synonymous with the 'weather' coast. And western Ireland was the weather side of the country and we were experiencing that.

Today we would be taking the train back to Limerick and then connect to Shannon Airport for our trip back home. We both knew that there was a lot more of Ireland we would love to have seen. But like other islands, Ireland calls you back. We imagined that one day, we might, like Jordyn and Brie, bring our child to this beautiful place and explore other sites like Galway and Connemara National

Park, Sligo and Donegal and, of course, Dublin and the Wicklow region. Our Limerick-bound train departed at 9:10 a.m. The Irish countryside never disappoints. There's so much to take in. And the green is green even in the cloudy rain. I went to take a picture of one of the mountains with clouds hanging over it and suddenly realized, I didn't have my camera. I looked in my backpack, my jacket pocket, nowhere!

"Darling," Beautiful Dawn put her hand on my hand. "I have it. Remember, you wanted me to take a picture of Jordyn, Brie and the girls yesterday."

I sighed. "Thanks, Sweetheart!"

She handed me the camera and I captured the mountain range as we approached Limerick. We transferred to a bus for Shannon Airport, about a 40-minute ride west.

"I've enjoyed this so much, Aldie. Thanks for making this all possible. You did all the arranging. Thanks, I know there is so much more to see, Darling. But we both have to get back to work."

Our flight out of Shannon was somewhat delayed by storms, but by 1:30 p.m. we were bound for Boston and then for our connection to Philadelphia.

When we arrived, the weather in Boston was much like Ireland– cloudy, rainy. It was August 29th and 6 p.m. Boston time. We cleared customs and passport control and walked across to the domestic terminal to check in our US Airways flight to Philadelphia. Touching down at Philly at 8:02, we made our way to Havertown. The humidity was stifling. The skies were still unsettled and there appeared to be storms on the horizon as walked into the townhouse exhausted. It was 9:10 p.m. It was a bit surreal being back there after a long time. Beautiful Dawn knew that she had to be up by 6 a.m., in her uniform and working at Children's Hospital. I would be inundated with calls and E-mails. It's sobering to be back home with the magic of Ireland somewhat like a blur. It's like a pleasant dream and you wake up with: *'Oh, yes, I remember now – a wee wedding in Ireland!'*

Chapter Twenty

BE IT EVER SO HUMBLE...

To thee I'll return, overburdened with care; The heart's dearest solace will smile on me there; No more from that cottage again will I roam; Be it ever so humble, there's no place like home. Home, home, sweet, sweet, home! There's no place like home, oh, there's no place like home!

- John Howard Payne

After traveling to Ireland, we took a few days to get back into the 'zone' because of the six –hour time difference between the East Coast and Europe. Mornings seem to be high energy and by 8 p.m. we could hardly keep our heads up. We realized one evening at dinner that with a few exceptions our lovemaking had been put somewhat on the backburner. Travel and time differences can crimp that impulse. Over dinner, we looked at each other and Dawn put her hand on mine.

"That's it... we're going to catch up on our... *'luv!'*"

We hastily removed our clothing and made the dining room carpeting our bed. Our libidos were jumpstarted as our bodies were clinging in abandon. It was as if we hadn't tasted its Eros' nectar for months.

A *real* thunderstorm now descended on the Delaware valley. We both looked out our sliding glass door as the thunder rattled with frequent lightning strikes. It was quite a summer storm as heavy darkness settled in. The lights began to flicker and then we lost our electricity. It didn't matter. Our undulating bodies were visible by flashing lightning. This was 'stormy sex', torrid, unrequited, as if we were on a chaise lounge on a screened-in porch on some tropical island in the Caribbean in the middle of rain and wind and lightning. Sweat rolled off our bodies as I thrust her deeply and then came that irreversible height of Our consummation was mutual and with it, we fell breathless near the dining room table. I watched Dawn's little tremors following our passionate release and I planted gentle kisses on her lips and thighs. We fell into a deep sleep right there on the floor next to the dining room table.

About 2 a.m., the electricity came alive and jolted us awake as the house lights brightened the blackness and the whirring sound of the AC vibrated the floor. We realized that we had been in a deep sleep almost six hours - almost as if we had been anesthetized. We helped each other up and walked up to our bed and continued our nocturnal journey. It was sleep that both of us needed, a delayed rest - the re-energizing kind. Ireland was a wonderful memory of a far-off place we could now enjoy in conversation with others and one another, with our photographs and the CD's we brought back. But as always, enchanting travel is alluring, of course, but we both knew we had to step back into the real world - balancing budgets and managing houses and jobs with their necessary time and energy requirements.

Life at All Saints was in full 'September Rally' mode. Our Director of Christian Formation is Rose McKenna - Brown. hardly anyone at All Saints who doesn't have an Irish name. I would probably have been better off being Aldron McSeaver!) I came to my office early Tuesday morning for an update. Rose is so unlike me, a workaholic. She already had the sample brochure for the coming year in Education and Youth ready for my review. Rally Day would be September 8th. The kiddos go back to school on September 9th. We would be having the 'Blessing of the Backpacks' and Rose and I would distribute mini 'Back to School Kits' for those who attend. One of the Dad's came up with his wee one and brought his briefcase for blessing. I told Dan I admired him for that.

Bob McGyver, my Senior Warden, stopped by to give me a building analysis. There are things needing major attention, especially the HVAC system and the roof over the church Nave - the older portion of the building - not the least of which it has a beautiful but leaking steeple! I dreaded that we were heading for major capital funding for the near future. Raising money has always been my Achilles heel! The rector, which interestingly enough means 'ruler'- has a lot of involvement in building issues and capital funding and money transfers, all of which my Beautiful Dawn calls 'funny money.'

My Worship and Music Coordinator was standing in line also to see me. There is the matter of liturgy settings for Fall as well as the rift between the Choir Director and the Organist. I knew this was coming before I left for Ireland. Our Choir Director, Helen, is new. And our Parish Organist has been there since 'Hector was a pup.' Helen is filled with new ideas and suggestions for contemporary choral offerings. And our Parish Organist, who is also 'Helen' –Helen McFarley, 78 years old and perhaps in her own mind 'irreplaceable', but she'd rather play Bach and Buxtehude than the 'new stuff' as she calls it that Helen Goodman selects (You can tell our Choir Director is not from Havertown, she doesn't have an Irish name!)

The rift had finally come to blows the Sunday I was gone when three women from the choir planned to sing 'I'll Fly Away' and used a guitarist to accompany them, instead of Helen's 'mighty Möller' as we like to describe the church organ. Helen McFarley decided to abandon her Möller and walk out just as the presentation was about to begin. They had to scramble for a pianist for the balance of the service. When it comes to church musicians, it's not a perfect world

The congregation is blessed with one of the last and best organs to come out of manufacture at the Möller plant in Hagerstown, MD, before it was bought out by a Yamaha parts manufacture. Without someone's donation, the congregation would never have considered purchasing this powerful Opus 11738 (next to the largest one, Opus 11739 at Calvary Church, Charlotte, NC, built there in 1990.)

M.P. Möller, a native of the Danish island of Bomhold, put Hagerstown, MD, on the map with moving his business there. Until his closing the plant in 1992, he had built over 11,000 'Mo's. 'The tracker action links the organ console to a pipe chest by solid-state electronic means. A little bit of trivia I learned is that the last Möller organ built was in 1992 and was delivered to Chapel-by-the-Sea in Fort Myers, Florida. My Aunt Wisteria, when her husband was living, was a member of that church. Feisty Helen McFarley was a master at our Opus 11738, but it wouldn't even be standing at All Saints had it not been for a generous donation by F. Pitman McPherson, a Philadelphia financier, who loved organ music and he happen to love All Saints as much. I have never seen the final cost of All Saint's Opus #11738, but I know it was nearly or, perhaps, exceeded $1,500,000.

Bob McGyver remembers Pitman as kind and generous. The rumor is that he single-handedly found Helen McFarley to be the organist and, even more, she had been one of his love affairs back in those days. (Wonder if that's hearsay? But for sure, I would never ask Helen!) Nevertheless, Helen could make the Möller stand up and salute M. P. Möller himself- especially when she took to the keys and played Bach's powerful *Toccata and Fugue in D Minor* or *Charles Widor's Toccata from Symphony #5, Opus 99.* There was no second-guessing that our 'Opus with the Mostest' was *her* instrument.

Rumor also had it that the previous rector was so angry at her Nazi-*esque* nature with the organ, because he loved playing it himself. Even when the rector would play the organ while she was out of town, she knew the instrument's setting so well that she could tell he had played it. Word from the parish is that the rector tried to get her fired – and he himself ended being fired! (Another possible hearsay.)

So now here I was caught up in the 'Battle of the Helen's' in one of those 'duties as unassigned' situations. It didn't take long for both to make appointments with me to make their cases.

Helen: "Fr. Seaver, you're going to have to set Helen Goodman straight. All music played at our traditional service must require organ accompaniment."

Me: "But is that a written rule, Helen, or one of those unspoken rules?"

Helen: "I have no idea. My position as organist requires me to offer accompaniment. That's why I get paid."

Me: Okay, but how about the piece itself. 'I'll Fly Away' is a Negro Spiritual. Wouldn't it seem a bit odd accompanied by a Möller organ?"

Helen: "That's not the point, Father Seaver. No one mentioned to me that this guitar was going disgrace our Nave. It would make my skin crawl to hear a guitar at our Book of Common Prayer service."

I thought for a moment.

"Me: Okay, Helen. I think we need to get other folks involved in this. Perhaps we need our Worship and Music Team to look into the matter and form some policy. Helen Goodman is coming by this afternoon and I'm sure she'll have her view of the situation."

She looked at me with one of those 'There is no other view' looks and then looked down.

I waited a few seconds.

Helen: "Well, I just think we need to get this resolved."

I ventured a little further before the conversation ended. "Helen, I need to know whether you feel you can work with Helen Goodman."

Helen paused and looked down. And then - totally unexpected - began to weep. Honestly, I had never seen her weep!

Me: "Helen, I didn't intend on making you cry. Are you okay?"

She went on to tell me that she had recently been diagnosed with Parkinson's disease. The tests did confirm it, but hers was a mild case at this juncture. The picture of her unyielding resistance was becoming clearer.

Helen: "I just know that this is going to end my career – I just know it," she lamented.

Her weeping continued. It had never crossed my mind to give Helen a hug. She's never seemed like a hugging type. But I did take her hand to offer compassion.

Me: "Helen, I'm sorry. I didn't know this was going on. I can see how that brings out all kinds of feelings."

She put her hand on mine.

Helen: "It's OK, I just didn't have the courage… you know… until now. Thank you, Father Seaver."

I also knew that Helen was, by her definition, a non-believer. She had confessed that to me some time back. She was one of those 'I-like-Jesus-but-I-hate-organized-religion' people. She once wrote down all the doctrines and beliefs she didn't believe – she called it her 'religion dirty laundry list.' I had to admit there were many on her list I didn't believe either! But I didn't share that. Once when her son lost his job and was evicted from his home, she asked me to pray for him.

I prayed anyway -especially that Godly calm would come over Helen in the wake of her news about the Parkinson's diagnosis that she might know of a love beyond her limits and fears to sustain her in these days of uncertainty.

"As long as you are able, Helen, you will be our church organist."

She thanked me and allowed me to hug her. Of course, I knew I wasn't going to tell Helen Goodman about this diagnosis. Helen McFarley was a very private person. I watched her leave with a renewed sense of understanding. I was still imagining how this might all work out. A message came from my Secretary:

"Fr. Seaver, Helen Goodman is on the phone for you."

"Yes, Helen... sure I'm here. Come on over."

Helen Goodman works at the library part-time and is a private piano tutor in her home. Helen is also a professional harpist, having played in the Delaware Symphony Orchestra and the Chester County Pops Orchestra in West Chester. We heard about her through the Westminster Choir College in New Jersey. One of her gifts is understanding liturgy and being willing to explore new ideas within the choirs. We have a chapel choir, which sings on alternative Sundays and the regular choir, which is faithful each Sunday. Helen grew the choir adding more than 20 voices to the existing membership.

She's a very pleasant person, but she started right into business.

"Please, I have the highest regard for Helen McFarley. I'm not here for the purpose of complaining about her, but to share some concerns about our working relationship. I know Helen is a traditionalist and, to some extent, I am too. I just think that a variety of music – traditional, contemporary, even country, can add a blended spirit to worship."

"Of course, I agree with that, Helen. Just to let you know, Helen called me up shortly after you did. She was in here about a half hour earlier... anyway, I agree with the idea of variety. Could we meet together on the issue? Is that OK with you?" I asked.

"I'm certainly willing, Aldie. I'm not a fighting kind of person. I just didn't agree that a guitar in our Nave with a song like 'I'll Fly Away' was a problem."

"I agree, but I want us to all talk about it."

Helen started reaching for her calendar. "Okay, do you have a date in mind?"

"I'll talk to Helen and get back to you."

"Good. By the way, we have brass quartet lined up for Christmas Eve. I found some students in their undergraduate program at West Chester University that are eager to earn a little extra Christmas money. I'm hoping I can use remaining budget monies for their being among us for the 9PM and 11PM services."

"Great! I love brass – as an old Sousaphone and trumpet player." I said appreciatively. Helen was out the door.

The two Helen's and I met on a Saturday morning in my office. Both were cordial and professional. Organist Helen seemed calmer about the situation. Both seemed to be in a mood for 'working things out' rather than being at odds. We resolved to come up with a more expanded policy in our Worship and Music Team to provide for more effective and advanced communications about music selections. Organist Helen seemed more open to the possibility of alternative musical instruments used for musical offerings. Both women embraced each other at the conclusion of our meeting. Needless to say, I was relieved. Was Organist Helen in a different space in the wake of her news about the Parkinson diagnosis? I'm not sure, but I knew I would hear more about that.

Chapter Twenty-One

DEATH IN AUTUMN

Yes, thou art gone! and never more
Thy sunny smile shall gladden me;
But I may pass the old church door,
And pace the floor that covers thee.
May stand upon the cold, damp stone,
And think that, frozen, lies below
The lightest heart that I have known,
The kindest I shall ever know.
Yet, though I cannot see thee more,
'Tis still a comfort to have seen;
And though thy transient life is o'er,
 'Tis sweet to think that thou hast been;
To think a soul so near divine,
Within a form so angel fair,
 United to a heart like thine,
Has gladdened once our humble sphere.

-Reminiscence by Anne Brontë

The leaves were turning yellow and orange and red when Beautiful Dawn and I learned of the deaths of our favorite aunts, coincidentally on the same day- her Aunt Bernice in Claymont, DE - the one she had visited at Christmas who was less than enthusiastic about her marrying a pastor, and my 'Aunt Char,' Charlotte Frances Weldon Fraser in Lebanon, PA.

Unbeknown to Beautiful Dawn, shortly after Christmas, her Aunt Bernice was showing signs of dementia. Her cousin, Bernice's daughter, Veronica, had not contacted Beautiful Dawn about this, but apparently it was progressing quickly. By March she was admitted to Arden Courts of Wilmington, DE, just a few miles from Claymont.

Knowing that almost nine months had transpired since she had visited her aunt made her sorrowful and a bit angry. Why hadn't Veronica or someone in the family told her? 'Ronnie' (as Veronica is called) knew that Beautiful Dawn was in touch with her aunt.

Ronnie: "Didn't you know?" Ronnie lamented. "I told my husband to call you and he didn't! I don't know what I'm going to do with George. Here I thought perhaps you had a falling out with my Mom or something."

Beautiful Dawn: "Oh no, not at all. I'm so sorry, Ronnie. I just didn't know. I should have contacted her sooner. The year has just gotten away from us. I married Aldie Seaver, an Episcopal priest back in March. It's been a whirlwind year."

Ronnie: "Congratulations, Dawn. I think my mother had told me you were involved with a member of the clergy. But when her mind got bad, I just wasn't sure what was reality and... you know."

Beautiful Dawn: "It's OK. I guess there are a lot of things in life we just don't have any control over."

Aunt Beatrice's Service of Remembrance would be held on the same day as my Aunt Charlotte's, almost the same time. My cousin had asked me to lead my aunt's Service of Remembrance, since Charlotte had not been a churchgoer. Actually, I never remember my Aunt ever going to church, but she was one of the finest and most caring women I had ever met in our family. I never heard gossip or a negative word about anyone from her. She had been a Professor of Philosophy at Lebanon Valley College in Annville and was probably the most influential person in my life in the development of my openly liberal side. Even her children, Bud in particular, used to tell me: "Mom's a little out in left field with her ideas."

Of course, I never felt that way. The truth is, I could talk to my Aunt Char about ideas on the universe and God that I couldn't even discuss with my colleagues. I can't say that she was an atheist - perhaps more agnostic- but she was one of the most progressive people in the Weldon side of the family. My mother, her sister, would often say that Charlotte was a kind of 'black sheep' in the family. Bud and Cecilia were her children by marriage. She had married late in life and was only married a few years before divorcing because of her husband's indiscretions with a number of women. Manfred was from

Wales, a charmer of sorts, and as he went about selling a particular brand of women's hosiery, Aunt Char was certain he was selling more than women's stockings! She told me: 'He was probably putting them on them too!"

So, I had the duty of saying 'the last words' over my dear Aunt Char. When you are clergy, you get roped into 'family chaplaincy' situations from time to time.

"Wait a minute!" I told my cousin Bud Fraser up in Palmyra, PA. "She was my favorite aunt, Bud. What am I going to say?"

"Well, just say that, Aldie. I don't care. We just need someone to say some words over Mom".

I accepted the invitation hesitantly. Bud was relieved and gave me the number of the Buse Funeral Home in Palmyra.

Beautiful Dawn and I regretted that we were going to have to go in different directions on that upcoming Tuesday. Gebhart Funeral Home (part of the Greico Funeral Homes) was handling the arrangements for her Aunt Beatrice in Claymont. And I'd be driving northwestward to Palmyra to Buse's to do the honors for dear Aunt Char. She was almost 90 when she died. Bud told me she really hadn't been sick long. She had developed an allergy and coughing and subsequent tests revealed that she had a sepsis developing in her blood. She died in the hospital.

It was a beautifully crisp morning in mid-October when I kissed Beautiful Dawn and started my way westward on the Pennsylvania Turnpike toward Exit 266 (Route 72, Lebanon Rd.) and then to Route 322 (Horseshoe Pike) and finally to Route 117 into Palmyra. It was going to take me about an hour and a half to get there for the 11 a.m. service. I noted how beautiful the fall colors were near Denver, PA, and along the State Game Lands. I hadn't prepared any meditation, so I allowed myself to remember my Aunt Charlotte and try to organize my thoughts. What do you say at a Service of Remembrance as a Christian pastor about a woman who actually despised organized religion?

The first person I saw outside Buse's was my cousin Bud.

"Man, am I glad to see you, Aldie. We've got a mess on our hands."

He was wringing his hands.

"What kind of mess, Bud?"

"Oh, my sisters and brothers. They're all up in arms because Mom, according to them, is 'going straight to hell!' And they can't believe an Episcopal priest would have a Christian service for a woman who didn't believe in God."

"Bud, how do they know she's going to hell or, for that matter, didn't believe in God?"

He hesitated and scratched his head.

"Well, that's your department, Aldie, whether she believed in God or not, but I'm sure as hell glad you can run this thing."

I shook my head and looked off to the small crowd gathered. I continued:

"Well, Bud, I'm not sure we can conclude that she didn't believe in God. I mean, yes, she had a disdain for organized religion. But who hasn't? When was the last time you went to Church?"

He gave a little nervous chuckle.

"Well, I guess Christmas. But that's not the point, Aldie. My sisters and brothers are over there wondering how you could lead a Christian service. I didn't know what to tell them.

I managed a sarcastic smile and said: "Well, who in God's earth is going to do it if I don't?" I put my hand on his shoulder. He was a good guy and I knew he was in a squeeze.

"I'll handle this, Bud."

"Please!" He had the look of exasperation.

I went over to the 'gathering' bunch of cousins, some with the kids around them.

"Hey, everyone."

"Aldie." They all mumbled. They all looked uncomfortable.

"Sorry for your loss... uh, we have a bit of dilemma. Bud tells me you don't want me to do Aunt Char's Service of Remembrance."

Sue Ann was the only person to look me in the eye and seemed to have some civility about her.

"Aldie, no disrespect, but we're... we're just not sure how you can officiate Mom's funeral when... well, you know, she didn't believe in Christ."

The rest nodded in agreement. I thought for a moment and took a deep breath, looked away and then turned.

"Look, I just want to say that, in my visits with Aunt Char, she *did* believe in God - she just had a struggle with organized religion. We had talks about this and I have to agree that, as an Episcopal priest, now and then, I have problems with how the church is run – I can't imagine you don't have problems with it from time to time. I'm passionate about Jesus and the message the Church carries, but sometimes I'm fighting with the organization, too. I think you're underselling your Mom."

Joe Fraser, Bud's younger brother, spoke up.

"Aldie, she was a member of a cult, for Christ's sake!" (Mm, great 'Christian' talk!)

"A cult? My Aunt Char was a member of a cult? She never mentioned a cult."

Sue Ann interrupted.

"Aldie, what Joe's trying to say is that she was a member of that Unitarian Universalist Church."

I shook my head and chuckled in disbelief.

"Sue Ann, you think that's a cult?"

Joe defended Sue Ann. "They don't believe in God or Jesus, Aldie!"

"You don't know that, Joe. Come on. Have you read about their faith? They use the wisdom of many world religions, including Judaism and Christianity. They just broaden their faith a bit to support the 'free and responsible search for truth and meaning.' It says that right in their manual. Christians have their heritage in Judaism and the Old Testament. It's *not* a cult. And by the way, the word 'cult' is when people break away from a larger religious tradition. Isn't that what happened when early followers of Jesus broke from Judaism? But we're still Judeo-Christian. Jesus was Jewish!" Cults today are more like Jonestown or Waco."

I knew I wasn't going to convince them and was wasting my breath. They all looked at me as if I were a smart ass – which, I agree, I probably am. I already think I went too far with this. They were stone silent and fidgety. Their kids were even more fidgety. I continued. "Look, I'm sorry… Sue and Joe and all of you… I just want to say some good words over Aunt Char."

Joe shook his head.

"Mother was just a flaming liberal, Aldie. As far as we're concerned, she's not saved,"

Nancy, Joe's wife, said defiantly: "And, sorry, we're not going to attend. No disrespect to you, but Joe and I and our children are going to wait in the Fire Hall until the service is over and join everyone for the reception.

I looked over my shoulder and saw Bud prancing around. I looked back at them and decided that this wasn't the time to argue over these matters.

"OK, I'll do the best I can to say some good words, Take care."

They nodded and seemed a little more relaxed, the kids were getting restless and trying to pull them away. Sue Ann rounded them up and they left. I went over and told Bud they didn't want to be part of the service. We both shrugged our shoulders. He responded:

"Suits, me Aldie. It's their loss. She's our mother – I owe it to her apart from this religion thing."

Bud Fraser was different from his siblings. He wasn't a churchgoer, but he had strong values when it came to family and the treatment of others. I recall he was always trying to keep the peace among the siblings' regarding their Mom, and yet he felt he was letting his Mom down in not trying to build a bridge to her for them.

I headed for Buse's clergy entrance and sat down in the clergy room and began to write some notes for what I might say. After the service had begun... with only a smattering of friends and locals sitting there, I stood up and began the service with a few prayers and several readings from the Scriptures, the standard Psalm 23, Romans 8:31ff and John 14:1-6 I paused for a moment and looked around. There were a few cousins and nieces and nephews. I had no idea who the others were, perhaps colleagues and friends. I decided to forge ahead. I stood at the podium:

Martin Luther once said something to the effect that we're all beggars before God. We don't go out with stuff that will guarantee our safe arrival on the other side of this learning curve called life. My Aunt Char was a 'beggar' of sorts. Her hands and heart were always open to receive what the Creator was happy to share. For her, being open was found in the gifts of reason and discernment. We may not all have that, but they were certainly Aunt Char's gifts.

297

Aunt Char attended the UU Church (Unitarian-Universalist) - that was about as close to organized religion she was willing to invest herself. It doesn't matter. I'm going to suggest to you that there are many 'ladders' we may climb to meet this Holy One we call 'God'. By the same token, my tradition offers that God has intentionally made a reach for us and is revealed in places we may not even look. I know for me, Jesus was one of those ladders. I learned to love Jesus at an early age, but the Jesus I know now in my 40's is a much different from the Jesus I knew in Third Grade or in college. I would say that Episcopalian or Baptists or Lutherans or Roman Catholics or Unitarian Universalists are not the only ladders to climb toward the Holy One. As a matter of fact, I'm not sure it's so much that we climb to the Holy One or the Holy One comes down the ladder to meet us. Ladder is a metaphor for a relationship that is seeking. We meet somewhere in our search. Nevertheless, I consider Aunt Charlotte a pilgrim with us in the search to understand truth and meaning and godly love. She might say to you, if she were standing here today, 'I may not share the same creed as you, but I share the same search to know the God of our being as you do.' She wasn't an enemy of faith, she just struggled with how our faith communities function in this world organizationally. I even remember her fretting a bit about how the UU Church was organized. I'm sure that if we all examined our thoughts, we might admit the same struggle from time to time – to believe in God versus believing in the church we connect to within that search.

So, good for Aunt Char for having the courage to say: 'My path is not the only path, it's just another path.' I will miss her. She helped my spiritual formation as a person, a seeker, someone in search of different paths. Now she is at peace, I believe in the comfort of the Holy One who gave her life and opened her eyes and mind to a myriad of new insights into how this amazing mystery of life and death and new life really are. To that I say, 'Amen.'

The reception at Citizen's Fire Co. #1 over on North College Street was like a frigid January morning. The family did their best to distance themselves from me even if I had given my blessing for their not attending the service Truthfully, I'm not sure I gave them a blessing, but it seemed to them I must have had an infectious disease and they wouldn't dare want to be close to me. Aunt Char would not have liked her reception. Bud did manage to put a collage of photographs together for the viewing and carried it from Buse's to the reception site. A few people would stop by and view them. I sat with people I did not previously know, enjoying conversation about Aunt Char. Some were former philosophy students who had migrated to other parts of PA and had remembered how insightful she was. A student, now herself a Philosophy professor at Lebanon Valley College, told me that my Aunt Char was the one who opened the path to her own faith journey.

Other than that, it was a strange reception. The guests and distant cousins were more open than the family. Some of the family parted before the event was finished. Bud did stop by and thanked me.

"Uh, Aldie... I do appreciate you're coming by. And I'm sorry for the family not speaking with you. It's probably about the money." He handed me an envelope with a check for my mileage.

"Bud, you didn't have to do this," I said trying to hand the envelope back to him.

"No, you go ahead and take it. You deserve it."

With that he put his hand on my shoulder and left. He started gathering the collage of pictures and folded up the tripods. In truth, this whole service and gathering wouldn't have been possible without Bud Fraser's hard work. Some of the grandkids helped. And before you knew it, Aunt Charlotte's family had vacated Citizen's #1. I decided I had enough time to text Beautiful Dawn

'*Sweetheart, strangest Service of Remembrance reception I've ever attended. Will tell you later. Hope it went well for the Service of your Aunt Bernice. I love you, Darling.'*

She texted me back:

"*Love you too. OK, here, Sweetheart. Some anomalies with Ronnie. We'll have things to talk about.'*

Heading back to the highway, I kept thinking 'It's probably about the money?' What did Bud mean by that? Was it the funeral honorarium I received - $100 – gas money and effort? Strange family!

Beautiful Dawn was already home when I pulled in our driveway. The weather had grown colder and the skies were overcast with the expectation that another Nor'easter was soon to arrive from the Carolina coast. We sat with coffee and chatted about our aunts' funerals. Beautiful Dawn was appalled that Aunt Charlotte's family had boycotted the service of remembrance and had frozen me out at the reception. Then I told her about my cousin Bud Fraser's comment about 'It's probably about the money.'

Sifting through the mail, Beautiful Dawn handed me an envelope.

"Could this be what it's about? I had to sign for this when the mail carrier came by just before you got home."

I picked it up curiously. It was from 'Caldwell & Kearns, Professional Corporations', Harrisburg, PA.' Opening it, I found a formal letter indicating that I had been the recipient of the Estate of Charlotte Frances Fraser in the amount of $300,000.

"I can't believe this!" I looked at a check made out to 'Aldron Gerard Seaver' from PNC Bank for.... *what?*

We looked at each other with incredulity. My heart was pounding. For the rest of the day walking around the house seemed surreal. A hand-written note from Aunt Charlotte had been folded and included with the check:

Dear Aldie. First of all, I want you to know that my dysfunctional family is in my will —especially my son, Bud, the only one who visited me. The others despised my views and beliefs (or lack thereof), but I wasn't going to leave this earth with a grudge. Secondly, please know that I've wanted you to be a recipient of part of my Estate, because I found you to be the most open and genuine member of my family. Your visits and conversations were the most meaningful of my late years. The balance of my estate will be divided between Lebanon Valley College's Philosophy Department (Annville, PA) and UU Church of Palmyra, PA. Rev. Julie VanMeter, pastor at Unity Church, who like you was truly one of the most open people in my life. Thank you for caring about me. I don't know what lies beyond these limited moments of my life. I'm not sure whether there's a 'heaven' or not (we've had this conversation, remember?) I just know that if there is heaven on earth, you were part of that for me. Love, Aunt Char.

The letter brought tears to my eyes. Sometimes we never know just what impact we're going to have on other people. We were shocked at such an enormous amount of money. The only thing we knew for certain was that the some of the money would be directed toward a cause near and dear to our hearts: *the homeless of the Philadelphia area.*

The money represented another ticklish situation in our family. My mother and Aunt Char, her sister, had not spoken to each other in over forty years. When I'd announced I was going to visit her, my mother would get silent. Even more, when I shared with her that I was officiating her sister's funeral, she shook her head at my invitation to go along.

"Good Lord, Mom, she's your own flesh and blood!"

"I'm sorry, Aldie. Your Aunt Char and I fell out many years ago. May she...rest in peace."

She'd never tell me what happened. Yet I never invaded her comfort zone on it... that is, until I shared the news about Aunt Char's death with her.

"Well, thanks for telling me, Aldie."

She hesitated at my invitation and then looked out the window and then turned and said, "No. The wounds are too deep."

"Too deep? Mom, you need to move on with this. She's no longer with us. What benefit has 40 years of isolation provided for..."

"You don't understand this, Aldie!" she interrupted angrily... "you don't have a clue!"

"You're right, Mom... I don't 'have a clue,' so why won't you tell me the story. And now with her death, are you going to carry this to your own grave?"

She began to cry resting her head on her folded arms on the kitchen table. I had stepped too far into her discomfort zone. Damn, why did I do that? So, I held her while she cried. She put her head on my shoulder and I just let her cry it out. Perhaps it was a cathartic release of years of pent-up energy over dislike for her only sister.

Finally, Mom removed her apron and thanked me. We sat down at the kitchen table and she started telling me the torturous story of jealousy, anger, and competitiveness. Charlotte was fifteen years older than my Mom. She was a free thinker. Added to that, because she was beautiful and sensuous, she seemed to always attract men, some of them well-to-do types. After graduate school at Brown

University with her degree in Philosophy, she jet-set her way around the world with a man from Philadelphia, a well-known corporate attorney. They were married on a yacht in Greece while my mother was struggling through college working odd jobs to make ends meet.

"I became so jealous of Charlotte; I couldn't sleep. I'd send her letters and she'd never return them. One day, when my mother (my grandmother Leona Weldon) was hospitalized, we thought we were going to lose her. Your Aunt Charlotte waltzed into the hospital and announced she would take Mom home and have round-the-clock nursing care. She didn't consult with us, she practically ignored us and when the move was made, she was very controlling and even limited our conversations with mother."

Mom clenched her fist and shouted skyward:

"My mother was so miserable in Charlotte's house. She felt imprisoned and controlled! I blew up at Charlotte on one of the visits and threatened to take legal action to return Mom to a nursing home or something Charlotte threw us out of the house and I've never talked to her again. Your father complained to the Department of Social Services, but nothing was ever done. Your grandmother died at Charlotte's house and... and I never had a chance to say, 'Good bye!'"

She fell into tears once again, her eyes swollen from crying and her face blood red. I was silent for a long time and just held my mother's hand across the kitchen table.

I realized that I had carved out a piece of my life with Charlotte that was totally removed from this mysterious distance my mother and she had with each other. I had met Aunt Charlotte on a different landscape, sharing that part of her life where she had blossomed and become a free thinker.

It was clear to me from my mother's catharsis that my Aunt Char had a few demons within that lofty persona she carried around. I had never asked Aunt Char why she and her sister, Molly (Weldon) Seaver, were not talking. Aunt Char did ask me after my father's death,

"How is your Mother doing since your father passed?"

It was small talk, of course. So, now in the days since Aunt Char's death, a revelation comes out about a darker side of Aunt Char with family. It's amazing the deep wounds that can divide people and fester throughout their lives. Here is my mother living a tortured life not having been with her own mother when she died – having been essentially kept from visiting her. Here was Aunt Char, in a twisted journey of jet-setting, likely sexual escapades and writing and teaching philosophy and alienated from her own children - children she had had with her first husband, a blue-collar worker in the Steel Industry. They had lived in Millersville, PA, during the hay day of the steel industry. Aunt Charlotte was teaching courses at Millersville State Teachers College (now Millersville University). Willie Fraser had done well financially, but, according to Charlotte, he was conversationally 'a boob' and a kind of social dud. It was when she had talked Willie into her taking graduate courses at Brown University, that her jet-setting life ignited and when she met J. Barclay Bielfeldt, Jr., one of the most aspiring corporate attorneys of the law firm of Bielfeldt, Baker and Brown, PA. The story has a storybook path - an affair, a divorce and Charlotte off into her self-indulgent life with a famous attorney.

The illusion of that self-indulgent life was itself fleeting when it was discovered that Biefeldt had been living a double life with a French woman from Paris, Madeleine. A nasty divorce ensued and, let's just say that Aunt Charlotte walked away with millions of dollars in that settlement.

She returned to the Lebanon area and later, with a degree in Philosophy at Brown University and a book in print, she settled down and met a local banker at PNC. Benjamin Franklin Tipton was a good cross between Willie Fraser and J. Barclay Bielfeldt, Jr. He was solid, intellectual and yet he could tame the tiger in her. Charlotte decided to keep the name 'Fraser' for the sake of her kids. Ben helped her to properly invest her money and they lived happily together until he died in 2004. Of course, Ben Tipton left her even wealthier with stocks from PNC and a generous life insurance policy. The $300,000 she left me was likely a 'small' stock she had sold that was due for some kind of investment option - a tawdry sum compared to her net worth. I really don't understand these investment strategies. She had left a modest sum to each of her children. But the estimate of her gifts to Lebanon Valley College and the UU Church was in excess of 5 million dollars.

Three days later my Mom signed for registered letter from the same attorneys I had received a letter - Caldwell & Kerns, PA, Harrisburg.

When she opened it and began reading it, she broke into tears. There was a small handwritten note from her sister that read:

'Dear Sis, I'm sorry we never found a path to reconciliation. I was wrong in many things I did and I regret that we weren't closer as sisters. I know I can't undo this lapse in our relationship, but I hope the enclosed check will help. I love you, Sis. Charlotte.'

Attached with it was a PNC Check made out to Molly Jane Seaver for $200,000 dollars. That was the day my mother came knocking at my door desperately needing to be held by her son.

Money can't heal, of course, but it can help. The note from Aunt Char held intrinsic worth in ways the large sum could not.

Pregnancy

A week later -- I awoke hearing Beautiful Dawn throwing up in our bathroom. I dreaded that she would experience the morning sickness, but this was not the first time. She had complained about some nausea during and after our trip to Ireland. This was the first bad episode. The OB/GYN Doctor, Maria Greenburg, watched her pregnancy like a hawk. She obviously knew Beautiful Dawn had miscarried last year. She was going to do everything in her power to let this pregnancy be a good one. When Beautiful Dawn returned from the bathroom, she smiled sheepishly.

"Darling. I'm so sorry." I said as I held her.

"Oh, no, don't be sorry. I expect the morning sickness. I've had times of nausea, but this just was just worse. It does remind me that this is a process. She half smiled and rubbed her abdomen. I'm going to fetch some saltine crackers. I'm craving salt, Aldie."

Chapter Twenty-Two

A HOLIDAYS... A HOLY DAZE!
Holidays

TThe holiest of all holidays are those kept by ourselves in silence and apart; the secret anniversaries of the heart, when the full river of feeling overflows; the happy days unclouded to their close; the sudden joy that out of darkness starts as flames from ashes; swift desires that dart the swallows singing down each wind that blows!

White as the gleam of a receding sail, white as a cloud that floats and fades in air, white as the whitest lily on a stream these tender memories are fairy tale of some enchanted land we know not where, but lovely as landscape in a dream.
-Henry Wadsworth Longfellow

Dawn and I presented a check to 'Project H.O.M.E.,' Philadelphia, for $100, 000 to help chronically homeless men and women. H.O.M.E. (Housing Opportunities Medical Education). Dear God in heaven, I've never written a check so large! Additionally, we presented 20 boxes of toiletries, cleaning supplies and clothing - new underwear, new socks, towels, washcloths and bottled water as well as school supplies - for the children. As part of our gift, we would volunteer hours organizing street outreach programs and deliver some of the items needed urgently for these folks. This is the kind of holiday I love – sharing from abundance. The Holy One provides abundance and we are more fortunate ourselves when it is shared.

The Thanksgiving Day chow down at my Aunt June's in Kennett Square was especially energetic with all the talk about the baby – I should add among the women folk. Our mothers were ecstatic. So, when the turkey feast was over, the men scattered to the NFL games and the women enjoyed 'baby chatter' with Beautiful Dawn. No surprise. Aunt Wisteria was all ears and suggested a couple of names if the baby were a girl:

"I like Claire... or Amanda... and, just saying, Wisteria's not bad either!"

Aunt Wisteria's subtle humor.

My mother offered a couple of boys' names: *Chad... Stone.... Jared.... or what about Aldron, Jr.*

"Where did you that name 'Aldron' anyway?" I had asked her once. She told me it's not found anywhere and it's a rearranging of the name 'Ronald', which would have been her second choice. I reminded her that it could also be arranged to spell *'Arnold'*... I could've been 'Arnie' rather than 'Aldie.'

I recall once imagining baby names with Dawn. "I don't have any male name preferences, but if this love child of ours is a girl, I like the name *'Amy Dawn.'*"We agreed on that name.

"She will be almost as beautiful as her mother, with long, curly hair, fiercely independent, yet a 'girly-girl' in many ways. She will grow up with every opportunity to learn, discover and be open to the world God created and we will teach her to care for it and love others. What greater gifts!"

By mid-afternoon on 'Chow Down Day' the men were slouched down in their chairs, except for Bill Schneider, the "Texan," who was rooting for the Cowboys and couldn't sit down, jumping around like an old geezer cheerleader. The women had gone for a walk through Anson B. Nixon Park. My Aunt June lives near the park.

I thought to myself: Women know how to be social creatures, - to be a community and look after one another. They're great at "care and share" ways. They're heathier emotionally psychologically and physically than men. Women hug each other freely! I watched them file out down the steps to the sidewalk, on a journey of togetherness.

I sat there wondering why NFL was so darn fascinating. Part of me wished I could just get up and follow the women on their path. I'm a coward, because that would be some gender code violation on my part. I stood up and walked into the Aunt June's large kitchen. The dishes were put away and pots and pans were being washed by the sound of the monotonous sloshing of the dishwasher; the refrigerator neatly packed with uneaten turkey and trimmings and the dining room table as clean as I have ever seen it. They all did that together.

We didn't offer help! I did ask if I could help put stuff away, but they shooed me off to the NFL cave. It's a two-way problem often. How might it have been different if we had? Well, we would have surprised our dear ones and rolled up our sleeves and helped them. Of course, they might have said, 'No, you guys go enjoy your football!" Women know men aren't the best conversationalists.

I took a soda from the fridge door and walked out onto Aunt June's large canopied balcony. The fresh air felt good. The women were walking together hand in hand! Mothers on both side of Beautiful Dawn, I knew their conversation was mostly about the baby. Most men want nothing to do with conversations... especially about pregnancies and babies. What if I had ventured to say to these NFL jockeys during commercial breaks, something about imagining fatherhood and how Beautiful Dawn wanted nothing to do with birthing at the hospital, how we want to birth our child where we love and play and care and stay. I'd tell them that, between my presence and encouragement and the midwife's work, it would go off well. I'd tell them I'm looking forward to being a dad – a hands-on Dad.

But I knew such conversation on NFL Turkey Game Day would be crossing some forbidden boundary: 'Don't talk while the game is on!' Violation of some stupid 'man code.' If I ventured to talk about our plans, there would probably just be some stares or grunts or... 'Hey, I need another Bud Light. Somebody going to the fridge?' Or, knowing our family when the women aren't around, someone would fart and then everyone would laugh. Sometimes I just find it's disgusting! I am a guy... a chunk...I fart too – but privately! As far as I know, women don't sit around and fart and then laugh - at least not the women in this family. They genuinely like each other as women. They work as a team to serve and clean up. I didn't do a damn thing to help with this feast... except to pray. And Uncle Bill would chortle, 'Don't make it too long, Aldie! I'm hungry.'

I watched Beautiful Dawn ambling along. Wow, to listen in... to hear what they're saying about life and things they fear or what makes them happy or what makes them sad. Maybe they were chatting about ordinary, practical wisdom or the 'what if's' or maybe spinning out old wives' tales or stories of people they know. Look at us - lazy-assed, 'farting, football fanatics! That's all we are! The women are out walking. These wise and gentle creatures aren't interested in viewing men crashing senselessly into one another over an odd shaped ball. They're interested in life and ordinary days and feelings and coping with family dramas. I'm sure, not the least, they talk about us – what they wish we might be.' Maybe.

What a strange union – men and women! How is it possible we co-exist? Men get up, fart, eat, go to work, come home, grab a bear, read the paper in their comfy chair, ask when supper will be on the table, fart some more, growl and grump about the food, fart some more and then fall asleep watching the evening news. They barely recognize what joy to behold God has created in the wisdom and beauty of women! They don't have to be a beauty queens, but in their softness, their smiles, their kind and caring way, they are infinitely more heavenly than the lug that sits on the Lazy Boy and farts and snores until it's time to go to bed.

OK, enough on 'farting!' Got that out of my system!

With trepidation, I ventured an interjection mid-flatulence: "Hey guys, can I tell you a little about getting ready for this baby thing? Dawn and I..."

They just looked at me with a kind of, 'What-frickin'–planet-did-you –get-off-of?' look. Chortling a bit. Predictable! They turned back to the TV. Then I heard Ted say:

"Christ, look at Aikman throw that frozen rope... Aw shit! And Emmitt dropped the frickin' ball.... Damn it, Emmitt!"

My 'future Dad' interjection was dead in the water...or on the fifty-yard line. I grew silent and waited for the women to return. I asked Beautiful Dawn later: "I'm curious what you and the women chatted about on your walk, Sweetheart. "

She smiled and touched my arm:

"It was so enjoyable, Aldie. I learned about the wonders of birth from the aunts' and mothers' memories, even my birth, Aldie, which I had never discussed with my mother. I learned that I was a breach baby and that my parents thought I might not make it!

Beautiful Dawn's pregnancy was coming along fine as Christmas approached. She grew more beautiful each day with her baby bump. And on evenings after dinner, we'd spend time talking to our little cloistered gift, singing songs (even favorite hymns!) We especially enjoyed singing *'Jesus Loves 'You' this we know, for the Bible tells us so...rewording the song a bit* to make it a little more personal. We hoped that Anna Bartlett Warner (who died in 1915) wouldn't mind our revision of her famous words. Few people realize that the words really appeared as a poem in a novel called *'Say and Seal'* written by Susan Warner, published 1860. She was the older sister of Anna Bartlett Warner, the poetic writer of *'Jesus Loves Me.'*

We were within a few days of Christmas Eve and I decided that it would be great to return to Dillworthtown Inn, the place where I proposed to Beautiful Dawn one year ago. To make the evening special, I purchased an 'Eternity Band' that would remind her how much she had captured my heart forever The Eternity Band was wrapped in a little gold box.

"Aldie! I thought we said no gifts! You're my gift... our little bun in the oven is our gift. "Why did..."

"Please forgive me, Darling."

I pushed the ring box over toward her. "I just thought this was a great occasion to share something with you that tells you how much you mean to me – especially since this is the anniversary of our engagement."

She opened the box and was overwhelmed with the Eternity Ring. It was a 'Princess Eternity Ring' from Timepieces International, London, England, with sparkling gems in a solid cradle setting. The way the gems are mounted shows off glittering Princess cut gems, flawless D colored and with gem weight of 4.6 carats. It fit her perfectly and she kissed me in delight and then looked at it several times.

"You paid a fortune for this, Aldron Gerard Seaver, didn't you?"

"Actually not, Sweetheart." I got a little defensive.

"Come on, Aldie!" She smiled devilishly as if I were not telling the truth. "Be honest with me: $700? $1000?" I kissed the hand that wore this new Eternity Ring.

"Less than $125. Regularly $239. It was on sale...honest."

She was amazed... also relieved. She kissed me again in gratitude for not being excessive.

"Thank you, Darling! It *is* beautiful!" She looked at it admiringly often. One thing you know already about my Beautiful Dawn is that she isn't into expensive things. She still talks about the Queen Victoria opulence we experienced at Cape May! I had to remind her that it *was* a gift. Sometimes gifts come.

Christmas Eve

Here we are again, a year later after a memorable Christmas Eve 'light show' with little guy, Stone Graebel, who scared the wits out of us when he became inflamed from a lighted candle. He made the Christmas Eve service exciting' to say the least. So, one essential difference with Christmas Eve at All Saints this year: *no* candles - thanks to Jerry Castleman, the Havertown Fire Marshall. I knew that I would get a lecture after Christmas last year from Jerry after our incident.

I had accepted Jerry's final word on this graciously. To tell you the truth, I was greatly relieved. The burden of not having candles wasn't going to fall on me. So, it was that All Saints would have its very first *sans*-candlelight Christmas Eve as far back as anyone could remember. And thanks to the generosity of Jerry Castleman and his wife, Virginia, All Saints is now the proud owner of 300 battery-operated candles - of course, we were responsible replacing the batteries! The Christmas Eve masses went well, except that I noticed that attendance was not nearly the same as the previous year. I couldn't attribute that to battery-powered candles or my preaching. I'm a decent preacher, usually sermons between 8-10 minutes. So, the answer may have been that holiday traditions do shift: more people go away than stay home; more people have Christmas Eve activities and go out to dinner; and, the well-worn excuse: organized religion just isn't the priority for many people as in days gone by. Everyone was feeling the pinch - even our friends at Enon Tabernacle Baptist Church in Germantown, having grown to over 14,000 members the last five years, felt the shift. Rev. Alyn Waller, the lightning rod develop of that megachurch, observed that the number of people tithing had dipped. All Saints folks numbered almost 600 attendees for our three services Christmas Eve, down from about 750 in the previous year.

Yet we were free of dramas such as happened with Holly Graebel' son immolating from live candlelight last year. I considered myself fortunate getting through this night without a hitch. Well, there was one child who threw up in the Narthex before the 5 p.m. service. But that's benign compared to human immolation!

My sermon on Christmas Eve included these reflections:

Here I come asking again: Why would a mysterious God share the gift of 'Self' (Capital S) wrapped in Jesus of Nazareth? What's so appealing about us on this planet —where, unfortunately, the worst of the human condition can and does take center stage? The good and beautiful are rarely lifted up. Why would God care? I would never pretend to know the mind of God, but I do imagine a God 'hopelessly in love' with people shaped from a divine ideal —to love us, even if we are mindless at times about who we really are. Yet we carry within in, because of this incarnating God, a spiritual DNA -'Divine Nature Attribute.' Is God blind to our foibles, our selfish preoccupations and our aimless wandering through this world?

God sees us, <u>really</u> sees us, beyond the world's lenses, fixated with restoring us in our human frailty, our finiteness. That's the mystery we hold onto at this Mass of Christ. Such a revelation is a gift, wrapped in an enigma, Jesus of Nazareth, and delivered with Love written all over it. It is the gift, as the commercial suggests, that 'keeps on giving!'

Chapter Twenty-Three

WINTER WONDERLAND, FLORIDA REDUX

The Road Not Taken

Two roads diverged in a yellow wood, and sorry I could not travel both and be one traveler, long I stood And looked down one as far as I could to where it bent in the undergrowth;

Then took the other, as just as fair; and having perhaps the better claim, because it was grassy and wanted wear, though as for that the passing there had worn them really about the same,

And both that morning equally lay in leaves no step had trodden black.

Oh, I marked the first for another day! Yet knowing how way leads on to way, I doubted if I should ever come back.

I shall be telling this with a sigh somewhere ages and ages hence: Two roads diverged in a wood, and I, I took the one less traveled by, And that has made all the difference.

- Robert Frost

The forces of nature and the erratic national jet stream that had kept the Northeast frigid since the first week of January now left an abundance of snow over the Martin Luther King, Jr. Holiday. Schools were already closed for that day, but they wouldn't re-open for several days. Parents were grumpy because many had to work and arrange for childcare. Grocery stores were under-stocked because delivery trucks were stranded out on I-476 and I-76, which had been closed since before midnight until snowplows could get to them. For the first time since I had pastored All Saints, I had cancelled Sunday Services, because I couldn't get out of my driveway. Beneath the blanketing of the snow that started Saturday lay a sheet of ice that made motor vehicle driving almost nonexistent –- save for the 4WD jeeps and SUV's that some were privileged to own.

312

One such 4WD jeep arrived early Sunday morning to take Beautiful Dawn to Children's Hospital. Physicians and Nurses were a priority for emergency transportation. She texted me and said it was 'the ride of a life time' since the roads were barely passable - even West Chester Pike. I had used several means to communicate the weather cancellation: our Facebook page, which reached probably about two thirds of the congregation. I left a voice message on our phone system. And I called WXPN's Snow Cancellation access number with a voice mail. And I called Gertrude Patterson, our LAN Line contact, who had accumulated all the people who did not have the Internet. Gertrude had created a network among the fifty or so people, mostly senior types, who would never imagine having Email or a computer. Gertrude's pyramid of contacts had everyone contacted within fifteen minutes. Gertrude's daughter, Mindy, is also our congregational treasurer, so you can imagine what she was thinking about at church's cancellation announcement.

Oh my, Fr. Aldie, it will take a while to make this up. We're behind already in January. We might have to borrow from our Reserved Fund, our 'Rainy Day' fund.

Weather like this January's is no friend to fragile, fresh church budgets.

With Beautiful Dawn's 'wild ride' completed and arriving safely at Children's, I settled down hardly knowing what to do. *The 'Inquirer'* stuffed with advertisements was sitting on the kitchen table. I could surf the religious channels and see who was on (or pre-recorded before the snowfall). I could watch old Fred Astaire and Ginger Rogers musicals. I could tweak some photos on Photoshop. I had a ton of photos that were begging for attention from months, years! I could just go back to bed and sleep another hour. I chose the latter. Beautiful Dawn texted me during my extra sleep to let me know she arrived and felt she was in it for the long haul at Children's.

I called my Mom to make sure she was OK.

It's strange to have a Sunday open like this. I looked out the sliding glass door at the snow piled perhaps twelve or fourteen inches. Birds were fetching whatever food in the birdhouse they possibly could. The snow was a soft, fluffy snow, but as I slid the glass door open, I swear I could almost hear it coming down -as if the millions of flakes reaching ground made a gentle sound. Or was it the tinnitus in my ears? I am plagued with ringing in my right ear. I thought about Beautiful Dawn, working with those special children and thanked God for getting her there safely. I had worried that with her pregnancy, jolting around in a Jeep would have an impact on our child she was carrying. I went into my study - a little bump out from the dining room - and gazed at my sermon notes - the sermon that might have been! - Jesus turning water into wine:

'Wow! What a morning for this miracle! I wrote. *I picture some hillside town and a rather large room where people were coming and going and Jesus whooping it up with some locals dancing. Maybe a particular girl he had his eyes on might chat with him later about his latest exploits, hob-knobbing around with his fishing friends and talking about a 'new time of God.' 'Why is that so important?' she might ask.* He might respond, *'Because all the signs are there... the time is ripe, like the harvest, the Holy One's gathering from what has been sown.'*

'You talk silly! (She laughs.)

'This is not silly. Our people have yearned for God's new reign for a long time. Don't you want to see Jeremiah's prophecy come true - that God will know each of us in a new way, not by the statutes we keep, but by the agape (godly love) we share?' It has been written... so it will be.'

She looks at Yeshua ben Yossef (Jesus, son of Joseph) and wonders about his strange talk. How could she know about Jeremiah and God's new reign? She only knew that someday she wanted to marry a tradesman who would keep her safe and secure and bring her family the blessing of a son in her womb.

Just then, his mother, Miriam (Mary), stepped up and interrupted him: "A word with you, Yeshua?' Jesus moved away from the dance circle and listened. 'You should know, they've depleted the wine and the wedding feast is far from over!'

Impatiently he looks away and folds his arms.

'And what am I to do about it, Mother?' Then looking at her suspiciously and opening his arms and hands. 'So, you think this should be the time of my coming out?'

Miriam, her arms crossed, silently ponders her son's curt response and turns and goes back to the Wine Steward. 'Talk to him. Maybe he has a plan.; (She rolled her eyes with that 'exasperated mother' look.)

Yeshua left the party and stood looking out over the valley. He heard a rooster crow and bleating sheep and bawling cows. The valley was alive with sounds and smells and familiar images - his senses took it all in. Alive! It's all there, including God's plan to bring the spiritual harvest and a new time of divine rule. Maybe this was his 'coming out'... his strategic move to proclaim God's New Time! Was the depleted wine a signal, a sign?' Look at the grape vines!' he thought. 'There's abundance everywhere. God's reign is like that, not scarcity! The wedding wine may be depleted, but the grapes are abundantly ripe.

When he returned to the gathering, he could see that most people were already three sheets to the wind. He told the steward, 'Give them what's left, even those purification water jars if necessary. Who knows what God can do with what is already around us?'

The Wine Steward was almost indignant – purification water as wine? What a drunkard! Still, in his desperation to do something, he proceeded with the young man's crazy suggestion. He wondered: 'I say, who knows what God can do with this drunken crowd?' And you know what happens next.

I never get further than seeing this story from John's Gospel as a metaphor for God's abundance - particularly when the world is drunk with its own version of 'wine.' After all, wine is a metaphor for joy and contentment and laughter and togetherness. If drunkenness is the only goal of indulging in such sweet nectar, then it will only mean that sleep and numbness follow. That's not being alive and using our senses to experience God. I have to go deeper with this wine metaphor... beyond a local wedding and a limited supply of vino. What God is doing is bringing a new kind of wine and feasting into the world - the kind that never runs out, where all are fed and drink from the joy of God's liberating presence. That's what Jesus was trying to tell the flashy girl who caught his eye. It's God's presence we need most. And the need has never diminished! It's even greater now than ever.

Isn't it true of the world –it 'runs out' of a lot of things (milk and toilet paper supplies on snowy days in Havertown?) But what's really plentiful is what God provides and replenishes abundantly – God's own presence captured in gifts of the Spirit, kindness, unconditional love, peace, joy, healing, etc. Jesus' world was so lopsided. He was a peasant Galilean Jew in an impoverished culture. Yet when Jesus looked at the world God

315

had created, there was abundance everywhere to be shared. Why must there be hunger and nakedness and peril and sword and famine? Surely his Abba-Creator would seek to clean up the world and restore what he had created abundantly for all to enjoy. That was the essence of his approaching reign: a cleanup and restoration operation. And to be sure, this idealistic, passionate Galilean peasant Jew would be at the forefront of what John Dominic Crossan calls 'God's great cleanup operation.)

Sermons live inside you in this work. Wish I could have preached it. (Well, I did, didn't I?)

The snow wasn't going to let up any time soon. The Weather Channel was expecting six more inches for the Delaware Valley. I wondered whether my Beautiful Dawn would have to stay at Children's tonight. In a week, should winter give up its death grip on the Northeast, we were planning for a second trip to Orlando to attend the Pastor's Preaching Conference.

The Delaware Valley was, indeed, blanketed with not quite twelve inches of new fallen snow and, yes, my Beautiful Dawn did have to stay Sunday night at Children's Hospital. We texted all afternoon and evening, sending *'I love you's'* and smiles ;-) and even photos of each other 'longing' for one another. It was a pathetic case of *'Miss you's.'* The nursing staff and physicians were provided empty patient rooms for sleeping shifts and food prepared from the cafeteria. Cell phones were rapidly clicking away messages to loved ones. I was awake before dawn, but received my first text around 7 a.m. There had been an emergency surgery on a little girl from center city Philadelphia who had been rushed there with a suspicious skull injury. Beautiful Dawn had been called into the OR to assist. KYW-TV was reporting that I-76 was beginning to be opened, but secondary roads were still impassable. I found a few eggs, made coffee, drank the balance of the OJ and settled down to finish the Sunday papers I had not yet read. Martin Luther King, Jr., always the third Monday of January, began with unexpected brilliant sky and lot of noise of heavy equipment removing snow

By late morning MLK, Jr. Day, the temperatures had moderated enough that West Chester Pike was completely open and most business parking was cleared out. Grocery stores were descended upon en masse. I decided that, until Beautiful Dawn got home, I really needed to get some groceries and decided to get the Honda cleared out and the drive way so I could venture out to 'grocery-land' and the expected long lines. Giant Eagle was the most accessible and the greatest challenge - first, finding a parking space and, second, finding anything on the shelves. It took me two hours and tons of patience, but I eventually bagged enough groceries to last through the week ahead. I knew that Beautiful Dawn would be ravenous with hunger when she got home. Her hormones were in a full-scale ambush on her body and not having any food in the fridge would be just short of marital mutiny. When I got home, I was shocked to see vehicle tracks had been my space. Carrying groceries to the steps, my Beautiful Dawn met me at the door. I was elated. I hoisted the groceries inside and dropped them and embraced her.

"God, I missed you, Darling!"

"Aldie, Sweetheart, I love you and I missed you... please tell me you have food in those bags!"

"I do. Let's feed you."

Rummaging through the bags, she said, with wantonness, "Good, Aldie I'll eat those chips and every chocolate chip cookie you have and that fresh bagel ...right now."

I didn't hesitate. It was time to feed two, not just one. I made her several sandwiches, poured her milk, and opened the chips and a bag of chocolate chip cookies. She inhaled them all! Then my role was to sit down, shut up and rub her back.

With her eyes closed, she whispered:

"Mm, that feels so good. I need a bath badly, Aldie,. As soon as I gorge myself, I'm going to get naked and sink myself into a hot bath until next Tuesday! And then I'm going to sleep until Saturday! Oh God, I am so exhausted!"

I cupped her face and kissed her gently. Her breath smelled like the Russian army had tracked across it!

"I'm so sorry, Darling. I'll prepare your bath and massage you while you're sitting in the tub."

I was determined to be in full 'care-for-my-pregnant wife' mode. For the balance of this day, everything else would take a back seat. I helped her take off her clothes and into the bathtub. Scented candles were lighted and lots of bath gel and shampoos to soothe her were available. I put relaxation music on. I washed her back, her legs, her feet and planted little kisses of 'I-missed-you-Darling' all over her. I brushed her teeth and she rinsed in the bath cup. Then I fed her Bon-Bons. As she munched them, she narrated the more expanded version of her text attempts to explain how exhausting and painful it was during her two days at Children's Hospital. My Beautiful Dawn remained at her bath for over an hour and, after toweling her off and putting a comfy robe on her, I escorted her to bed and she fell fast asleep and continued sleeping well into the evening.

It was past nine o'clock when she awakened, and we had a conversation about the day and held each other. She had been the equivalent of a triage nurse in a M.A.S.H. Unit at Children's Hospital of Philadelphia and, until the roads had opened at 7AM on MLK, Jr. Day and replacements were able to get there, she had worked with 19 doctors and nurses as a virtual ER for west Philly for twenty-five hours non-stop.

"I know it was a big snowstorm, Aldie, but it was more like a war zone. I've never worked so hard in all my life without a minute to sleep and no food, except crackers which made me want to throw up. I kept thinking, 'I've got to feed this little bun inside me!'"

I gave her some hot chocolate and a pastry and soon she fell back to sleep. I turned out the lights and slept by her side through the night. Before she drifted off, she told me that Children's had granted her Tuesday and Wednesday off.

Although the MLK, Jr. weekend snow had left a heavy blanket, it didn't take long for the temperatures to moderate and melt the piles and trillions of it so that by Friday, the temps were in the 50's (a heat wave!) which left standing water most everywhere. We were due to leave the following Monday on USAirways Flight #2960 from Philly at 6:10PM, arriving in Jacksonville at 8:38PM. The temperature moderation continued favorably until by Sunday morning, the indexes were in the balmy forties! Beautiful Dawn hardly knew how to pack. Indications were that Florida was experiencing a warm winter spell. We packed lightly and with layers, light jackets and sweaters for the rental car. and keeping them available in our rental car. Beautiful Dawn's wardrobe included baby bump changes, of course. Although she was incredibly beautiful as a pregnant woman, she appreciated being comfortable.

My Senior Warden, Bob, at All Saints, brought a retired Episcopal Rector from Philadelphia, Rev. Fr. Scott Keeney. He had filled in leading worship and preaching a time or two before and liked his preaching style. He was a humorist, known for telling a few jokes, and a bit of a cynic - a great combination. The Bishop once reprimanded him for his open criticism of some of the Episcopal Church's existing polity. He was my hero in that matter! He was known for bringing out in song while preaching. Once he did an Advent 'John the Baptist' impersonation that brought down the house as well as getting some really poignant teaching across. He used a few Muppets for his 'Little Size Bites' sermons for children. Pastor Bob was not only a supply preacher he was Sunday 'mass' entertainment.

Barring bad weather, I knew the worship services would be well attended the next few Sundays I'm OK with it. I'm not a 'cowboy' like Scott Keeney. He told me once he essentially preaches the same sermon as he makes the supply circuit. He just adapts them to whatever the lessons are on a particular Sunday. He admitted, *I essentially plan the sermon in the car on the way!*

His joke 'well' is fairly deep. I've only heard a few that he probably gets a lot of mileage out of telling. Some of them can be a little risqué, although he always seems to get his point across.

We enjoyed an unusually smooth two-hour flight along the coast toward Jacksonville, FL. We touched down at 8:37PM, one minute earlier than scheduled. Our goal was to pick up our rental and travel southward to Daytona for a return visit to the Bahama House before heading to Orlando and a return visit to the Marriott World Center. We thought it strange that there wasn't too much of a difference in the temperature in northern Florida than the moderation in Philadelphia. Since plane food is nonexistent, we stopped at a 'Chik-fil-A' a mile from the terminal on Airport Road just beyond I-95.

It was about an hour and fifteen minutes to Daytona Beach from Jacksonville. We arrived at The Bahama House at 10:20PM and checked in on the 12th floor. We unpacked and snuggled in bed, tired from our trip and the drive, and were contented to go to sleep with the sound of the ocean. The temps were warm enough to leave the sliding glass doors open.

The next morning the winds were strong and the ocean choppy. The morning light filtered through distant clouds at miles out on the horizon and formed a beautiful circle of light that was keeping my Nikon busy. Soon the sun was brilliant above the clouds and morning was a breathless wonder of blue and red and orange and lavender.. My camera was clicking crazily.

Unexpected Storm

Beautiful Dawn's pregnancy was robust. Now beginning her third trimester, she was filled with energy and enthusiasm for every task. A trip to Florida with moderate weather - as it turned out, very mild weather - was going to be great opportunity for some walking and exploration. That is why after late morning brunch we decided to travel to Ponce Inlet at the southern tip of Daytona Beach and spend the rest of the morning and afternoon walking the beach perimeter. The Ponce Inlet lighthouse was visible from everywhere. The surfers were out *en masse* since the Nor'easter that was approaching was bringing enormous swells to the ocean and the waters between Ponce Inlet and New Smyrna Beach to the south became wild. The wind was exhilarating in the brilliant sunlight. Seagulls were tossed around as they battled against prevailing breezes. It was evident that the temperatures were cooling from when we had started out our walk. Standing on the pier that extended out from the inlet coast and watching the 'locals' fish, we both realized it was time to walk back to the car and fetch our jackets.

There were moments as we walked toward the beach parking lot that the wind literally pushed us along. As scary as this moment was, it reminded me of the tremendous power of 'Spirit.' The Hebrew word *ruach* has the same sense of wind - not a gentle breeze, but almost like a fierce rush of wind, an invisible force that can bend trees, uproot them even. Florida is not unacquainted with hurricane strength winds. The intensity of the wind was growing there along the Inlet. Spirit energy in God's realm is unsettling, almost menacing, as it blows where it wills to remind the world *'I am here and everywhere!'* Never one to sit on thrones and pontificate, God is more about an Energy unleashing its fierce yearning to love the world. It's the same kind of energy the gospel writer Luke is describing in Acts on that first Pentecost after Easter when the Spirit whirled about in a somewhat menacing way of telling the gathered worshipers from many different regions, *'I am God and you are my people. Listen!'* It was (historically speaking) the 'second wind' the Church needed, still reeling without a bodily Jesus to lead it and hunkered down wondering whether following Jesus was a dead-end street. The Spirit's 'wind energy' (which is ultimately God's love energy) doesn't prefer region or race or creed. It's there to push followers of Jesus to go and be living, walking, breathing, serving 'gospelers.' (good newsers). I'm thinking about this as I am holding onto Beautiful Dawn and pushing with great resistance against the *ruach* of Ponce Inlet!

Clouds soon mushroomed under the brilliant blue sky and reduced it to tiny patches. Now Beautiful Dawn and I were finding it hard even walking forward. I held on to her with all my strength. Beach umbrellas and hats were flying past us and now the surfers were beginning to edge closer to the shore. It would seem that only the most experienced surfer would dare ride the white caps and tremendous sea spray that played havoc with the shore. There was no one high up in the viewing deck of Ponce Inlet light. The wind was getting downright frightening as we stepped onto the sand near the parking lot. The sand itself was stirring in the wake of this mighty wind, creating little spouts. Sand would hit our face and sting us. I put my jacket around her face, turned her back to the wind and walked her backward, trusting my embracing and walking her toward the car. We were caught within a large wind spout, the sand swirling around us so that I could barely see.

"I don't know if we can make it, Aldie!"

"Just hold onto me, Sweetheart... I'll guide you. I see our car." "Okay," she said breathlessly, "I've never experienced anything like this.

"We made it to our rental car, which had a sand covered windshield, almost like snow blanketing it. I managed to get the front passenger door open, until Beautiful Dawn crawled in holding onto my arm. She was exhausted from battling the winds. I held her hand for a while.

"Are you okay, Darling?"

"I will be in a minute, Aldie, as soon as I catch my breath. Oh my, that was scary!"

The sand accumulating on my windshield now blew away and I could hear the screaming of the wind as it violently shook our rental car. As I mentioned, there isn't anything particularly malevolent about the wind. It is a force of nature, simply that. It is true that property and life can be wrenched away by it, but it doesn't have a conscience that 'wills' that life should be squelched by it. The planet is a living organism whose physical properties are very much alive- from dust storms in the Arabian Desert, to shifting tectonic plates creating earthquakes that spawn tsunamis in the Pacific Rim, to raging forest fires in Colorado or volcanic eruptions in Iceland. The rage of weather on the circle of the planet is nature being itself.

Now the rains began to pummel the Inlet along with the wind. Forces of nature are forces of unrelenting energy, sometimes lethal at worst and renewing at best. For humans in the helpless grips of these forces, for good or naught, Nature is a mystery. So too is God's force of Love energy. Where Nature can seem malevolent, God's continuing creative energy is wholly benevolent. It's not so much that God chooses to resist rescuing us from the flood or fire or fault-line, but that God brings a love so powerful as testimony of Jesus' resurrection bears that not even the darker forces of nature or the darker wills of human beings can separate us from that love. (Romans 8:31ff). I shared some of my thoughts on this as we sat there mesmerized by the shaking of our rental Buick.

Beautiful Dawn had that look of, 'My God, he waxes theological even in a scary Nor'easter!' But she didn't say anything. Instead, she asked:

"This is so ponderable. Aldie. Does it mean the Creator has two sides - a malevolent side and a benevolent side? Does God get pissed off at us, Aldie?"

I shared as I looked out my window:

"Sometimes it seems that way. This 'privileged planet' seems to have so many fragile settings by just miniscule degrees... like a giant circuitry board that holds the whole operation all together... things like climate, oxygen and carbon dioxide and human will may influence our very existence on earth. But I still believe that the Creator's intent is not malevolence, but benevolence."

"Thank you, Sweetheart, but the 'benevolence' side seems to have gone on vacation today," she chuckled somewhat nervously.

The tempest continued to shake our rental car. The troughs of wind and water danced all about while seagulls seemed to make little progress trying to fly in any direction. Surfers were barely managing through the winds with their surfboards as shields from the sand. I tuned on the radio to Beach 92.7, which indicated that hurricane type winds of up 90 miles an hour were hitting the coast and that the Daytona area is on high wind alert. Electrical outages were reported in parts of Volusia County. Beaches from Flagler to Cocoa Beach have were closed and school on lockdown until the Nor'easter passed, anticipated to end by 2 p.m. Some of the roads in the area, because of the high wind and water, were reporting floods and now impassable. Beautiful Dawn and I had a decision to make: to either wait out the storm (which now had tons of rain added to its windy fury) or we could drive northward to our hotel and at least remain in the lobby until the storm passes.

I suggested:

"If the roads flood, I wouldn't want to get stranded on 1A going back. It might be better if we just wait it out here. If they have electricity, there are places nearby to eat."

"I think that's best, Aldie."

I suggested: "Would you like to try the little restaurant across from the lighthouse? The sudden cool weather would make for a hot bowl of soup."

"Mm! I'm a bit hungry."

I started the engine and began to back up. It took a lot of hand control on the wheel to keep moving, but we managed to leave the parking area and headed for the road around the lighthouse. The Inlet Harbor located opposite the Ponce Inlet Lighthouse facing New Smyrna. and New Smyrna Inlet. The lighthouse certainly is imposing above it. Although the wind continued hurling its fury, the Inlet Harbor Restaurant seems to be shielded from some of the crosswinds. There are lights on and cars parked around the restaurant. The rain now seemed to be falling horizontally. I decide to pull rain gear from the trunk (I have no idea why I put it there, but I'm glad I did.) I grabbed the gear and was immediately soaked as if a bucket had been emptied in my face. Quickly entering the vehicle, I placed one of the jackets around Beautiful Dawn, who began to put it on in the limited space she had. I quickly slid my own gear on and suggested I quickly get around to the passenger side and help Beautiful Dawn out. We found the maneuvering to be a challenge considering the horizontal wash we were getting, but we managed to move quickly to the entrance. It certainly felt like the morning shower all over, except with clothing on.

Once we entered the restaurant, we found others, like us, seeking shelter from the storm. We traded stories of being caught up in the first Nor'easter of the year. It was January in Florida and, until now, seemed very moderate and very spring-like.

"If you were giving Nor'easters a name, such as we do with hurricanes, what would you call this one?" I gestured to one of the guests and pointed upward.One suggested 'The Whale' -as in 'Jonah and the...' because this damn thing seems to have swallowed us whole! And it may take us three days to get out of it!' As the rain now beat against windows and the wind continued to howl the rage of the Nor'easter, Beautiful Dawn and I settled down to share a warm bowl of Cream of Crab soup with crackers and a soda. Within minutes of our service, the lights of the Inlet Harbor Restaurant went out. It didn't take long for little candles to appear in the darkened early afternoon. There was a touch of romance that blanketed those of us gathered around.

"When are you due?" the voice from the next table asked. A casually dressed man smiled at us. His name was Javier and he was from Porto, Portugal. He shared that he was an obstetrician there.

"Mid or late April," Beautiful Dawn smiled and responded.

His companion, who introduced herself as Catarina, smiled along with Javier.

"Ah, but you must have a very good obstetrician. Will you have your baby in a big hospital in the states?"

"Actually, we are going to have our baby at home with a midwife and with my husband helping," Dawn smiled smartly.

"Oh, but this is so good that you do this," Javier clapped his hands. "I have been an advocate for home delivery. Our ancestors did this before there were big hospitals. Good for you!"

"Thank you," Beautiful Dawn obliged.

Beautiful Dawn seemed surprised that an OB/GYN would be so accepting of this traditional method of childbirth. But Javier seemed like an extraordinary person, open and nonjudgmental. His wife, Catarina, was shy and smiled generously. We surmised that she was learning English and listening carefully. The Portuguese are beautiful people, often tanned and dark haired and kind and generous people. Javier shared that Catarina works with his practice as a Registered Nurse and helps him deliver babies.

"She's much better at it than I am. She comforts the women and speaks to them with encouragement. She told me that when we have our second child, she, too, would enjoy a midwife." Looking at Catarina with his hands cupped outward, "Parteira?"

She smiled broadly agreeing, clapping her hands as she looked at my Beautiful Dawn. "Obrigada! Obrigada! (Thank you! Thank you!)" I offered on Dawn's behalf. We spent time with Javier and Catarina for almost an hour until the lights returned. We noticed the wind had diminished considerably and soon the sun was evident and patches of blue. *The Whale* had released its grip on us and decided not to swallow us. So, we said *adieus* to our friends from Porto, Portugal, and wishing them an enjoyable remainder of a stay in the 'sunshine' state, which for a few hours here, was far from sunny. Javier and Catarina watched us as we pulled away.

"Gosh, they seemed so friendly, Aldie," Beautiful Dawn commented as she watched them waving from her passenger side mirror. "Mmm... that's odd. Javier is writing something down, Aldie."

"Huh..."

Route 1A (Atlantic Avenue) back to Daytona had some standing water, but it was passable and now the day had become sunny with cotton puffy clouds. It was still breezy from the Nor'easter's grip of the Daytona area and it remained substantially cooler from our earlier visit to the Inlet. By the time we returned to the Bahama House, it was glorious and sunny. We decided that we had had enough outdoor venture for one day. We bought some picnic items - a whole pineapple, some teriyaki chicken, potato chips, coleslaw and delicious raspberry-strawberry sangria punch to take to our room. Afterward, we enjoyed lounging on a breezy balcony. It was 3:30 in the afternoon and we both fell asleep amid sounds of screeching and hungry seagulls and the energy of the waves. When we awoke at 4:30pm, we were aware that we both felt amorous and moved to the bed, quickly removing our clothing. We enjoyed 'spoon' lovemaking, because it's gentle for the baby's sake and makes for easy gliding in. The rest that followed was so welcome. We slept naked under the covers for an hour and we would likely have slept well into the evening if my cell phone had not buzzed.

I scrambled to answer it. "This is Seaver."

"Mr. Seaver, this is Quinn at the front desk. There are several police officers here and they would like to speak with you." I swallowed hard with curiosity

"For me? Uh, I'll just need a few minutes and then I'll be down."

"What is it, Darling?"

"There are police officers in the lobby and they want to speak with me.

"They finally found you! Oh my goodness! Did you take the silverware from the restaurant again, Aldie?"

Then she gave me a serious look. "There really are police officers down there?"

I nodded and chuckled nervously, but the anxiety level was heightened significantly as I descended the elevator to the lobby. Reaching the front desk, I saw the two officers, who greeted me with handshakes. They invited me into one of the conference rooms and asked me if I had seen the man in the picture they presented me. It was Javier!

"Why, yes. Javier. We spent a few hours with him and his wife, eh, Catarina at the Lighthouse Landing Restaurant during this Nor'easter that passed through late this morning."

Did you notice anything unusual or disturbing about him," they asked?

""Disturbing? Not at all," I said defensively. "Both he and his wife are from Portugal, where he is a physician. Although, my wife did notice that Javier was writing something when we departed. I thought that was a bit curious."

The officers looked at each other and nodded and then looked at me.

"Mr. Seaver, they both were picked up this afternoon for an armed robbery of the local SunTrust Bank." I sat down in the chair with my hand over my forehead.

"Armed robbery? Oh my God! They seemed like such a nice couple. But... how am I implicated in a robbery?"

The officer looked at his notes: "As you observed leaving the restaurant, he must have written down your license number and your name. He looked up your information. When he robbed the SunTrust Bank, he wrote your name on a piece of paper and demanded money.

"They produced the folded paper and showed your name 'Aldron Seever' misspelled"-: *'I am Aldron Seever. I demand $20,000 in unmarked bills. My wife has a weapon at the door and will shoot anyone who attempts to sound an alarm.'*

I felt a little limp. Looking up at them startled, I asked: "My God, what's keeping you from arresting me?"

"That's simple, Mr. Seaver. SunTrust's sophisticated cameras caught the guy in living color. Our computers identified him almost immediately. You were his decoy - your name and tag numbers. We traced your rental back to JAX and verified that it was your rental, not his. Turns out he's been wanted for a string of robberies along I-95 in the last six months. By the way, his name is not Javier and his wife's name is not Catarina ... and they're not from Portugal. He lives in Ft. Pierce and his name is Mendez - Albertus Mendez. Her name is Cecilia and she's not his wife, some girlfriend from San Juan, who turns out to be an illegal immigrant. Anyway, Mendez is wanted for murder in the Miami area. Our stats show that he's actually been on the run for almost two years. When the Nor'easter came through, he was apparently batting down the hatch before a robbery attempt until the storm passed and decided to place you in the middle of his scheme while he waited. He's played so cool with people, well-groomed, off white suit and jacket. He befriends people and then tries to lead them into a robbery attempt with a false ID."

The other officer piped up. "Yes, and we were able to trace his information back to his home in Juniper, FL, where he runs a sophisticated operation. We found a number of Oozies, AK-47's, explosives and lots of bank blueprints."

"He had a list of some twenty banks in Florida he was apparently planning to rob. This was number 6 - and thankfully his last. We just wanted to verify who you were and let you know...well, you can't judg'em by the cover, Mr. Seaver. I need you to sign some papers regarding our conversation and as a witness to having met Mendez."

I read it over and signed it. I also read that I could be summoned to court at government expense if necessary.

"I just would never have imagined it, officers. I can't thank you enough for letting me know."

"Our pleasure. Thank the sophisticated bank cameras, Mr. Seaver. They now have a link to our computer system - a very sophisticated software that takes face recognition and matches from a central mainframe across the country. Within a few second, we knew practically every detail about Mr. Mendez. He won't be robbing any more banks. But, as you probably know, there will be others like him."

I looked away.

"God, my wife's going to be so upset. She's five months pregnant and her..." The officer interrupted. "I know. Her hormones must be working over-time.

I nodded

"My wife has one in the oven, too. She cries at the drop of a hat. Good luck with that one." Shifting and putting his notes away, the officer stood, "Well, we'll be on our way. Be careful out there, sir."

I thanked them and shook their hands. As I expected, telling Beautiful Dawn about this sent her emotions into a tailspin. I told her his name was 'Albertus Mendez,' not 'Javier' and that he wasn't Portuguese.

"Darling," she cried (and she really did cry!), "we could have been hurt, maybe killed!"

The balance of the evening filled our time with reflection. We nibbled on some fruit and some nuts and were just amazed how kind and trusting the couple seemed to be - how duped we were into thinking they were the people they imagined themselves to be.

"There is such a thing as evil!" my tearful angel blurted out.

"I've certainly asked that question many times."

I stroked Dawn's hair. I wondered with her. "What triggers someone to become an 'Albertus Mendez' if they were created in God's image? Do they reflect the image of God when they steal and murder? Obviously not! So, there must be a spirit of evil, some malevolent force, that finds its way into the human psyche and worldview. It would be fascinating to speak with Albertus right now in some lock-up unit, to ask him, should he care to speak, 'What happened in your life that you should make these perilous choices, that you should rob and kill? What's the satisfaction?' Considering how his worldview turned out, I'm not sure I'd get a civil answer. I'm not sure he'd even want to see me! Unless....darling, do you mind if I go down to the Volusia County jail for an hour?"

"Are you permitted to do that, Aldie? Do you think they'd even allow you to visit?"

"I never leave home without a clergy black shirt and Roman collar. I have one with me. I just need the satisfaction..."

Beautiful Dawn shook her head. "Please be safe, Aldie. We've had enough excitement for one day."

I kissed her gently and told her I'd be safe and bring back some Moose Tracks ice cream. She clapped her hands joyfully and then put her hand over my lips. "Just come home safely, Darling – and with the Moose Tracks!"

I put on my well-worn, a bit wrinkly black clergy shirt and Roman collar and grabbed a light jacket and headed over to Volusia County Corrections, only a mile or so from the Hotel on Red John Dr., right off of West International Speedway, Route 92, shortly beyond I-95. I was driving there to request priestly duties to a known felon and murderer who had duped me in the middle of a Nor'easter at Ponce Inlet. I was curious. A bit angry. Slightly insane perhaps!

The warden was reluctant, but after checking with his superior, he permitted me to share a room with Albertus Mendez.

When he entered the room, he grew pale, "Shit! You're a goddam priest?"

I swallowed hard and then looked at him: "Albertus Mendez, also known as 'Javier' correct?" I looked him in the eye.

Albertus: "Look man…"

Me: "Why did you do it, Albertus… you and 'Catarina?'"

He just looked at the floor. The prison guard waited at the door and kept looking in.

Albertus: "I don't want to talk, Man. Why do you wanna come down here? I'm busted - I hope that makes you and your little lady happy! You can take your righteous dribble and your silly God and get the fuck out of here." He turned toward the guard and waved him in and then looked at me and spat in my face. I wiped it away and felt the heat of his hatred toward me. The guard didn't see him spit on me.

Albertus: "The visit's over, asshole!" The guard took his arm.

Me: "I'm not here to talk religion, Albertus. I just want to ask one question." He stared at me as if he didn't care on one hand and was curious on the other. "What hurts so much in you that you have to rob and kill in order to feel good about yourself?"

He didn't know what to say, even though I knew he was smart enough to ponder it. He looked at me and shouted:

Albertus: "Because love was stripped away from me, you bastard. The only love in my life was stripped away! Son of a bitch!" He walked away crying.

The guard looked at me gesturing as if to say: 'This is what you wanted to visit?'

I sat there at the table momentarily and then cried for the first time since my father died. The human condition is so messy, so incredibly tattered. Albertus Mendez had completely forgotten who he really was, lost in deep bitterness from some anger that I could never have known. The prison system may not be helpful. In fact, it most likely will never even begin rehabilitating Albertus Mendez. He will be warehoused somewhere and possibly, because of the murder he committed, be put on death row. The script written for his life has been by his own hand. Society will advocate for a 'lock him up and throw away the key.' He may completely reject any modicum of divine grace. He's angry at a 'god' that doesn't even exist. Or maybe he's just angry at himself and cannot embrace it. Apparently, I was the part of his last attempt to rob and harm and it was foiled. The storm that had descended upon the peninsula had ended with a second 'storm' - the deceit that bore down on Albertus Mendez many years ago –playing out a final affront on him. Its torrent unleashed a rage within, a beast that, like the winds that almost knocked us off our feet, moved mightily at will at the inlet.

I felt more sadness than anger. I didn't care that he spit in my face, that his feigned kindness to us at the restaurant was a scheme. When the 'what if's' fears dissolved from my emotional landscape, my sadness was that a creation of God had been terribly lost. Had anyone reached out to him? What was the story of the love 'stripped away from?' Was some divine-human 'link' overlooked when one person might have represented 'Godly love' to him? Who allowed the negative energy of hate and resentment and will to hurt flood his emotional arena? I learned from the records that Albertus Mendez was my age - 44. What was the true difference between us? Am I lucky and Albertus not? Is there some kind of favor extended to me that Albertus did not or could not receive? I realized I could analyze this all to death! The world is unfair and such unfairness can reach deep into us, so deep that there is no resolve. *Where is the Holy One in such helplessness?* The divine seemed so completely absent in that prison room.

I returned to the Bahama House about 9 o'clock with a half-gallon of Moose Tracks Ice Cream for my pregnant love. She was reading a favorite book of poetry and finishing a box of chocolates. Before she could even ask me about my visit with Albertus Mendez, she held up a spoon.

"I borrowed this from the kitchen. Aldie, I went down in my sweat suit and asked for a spoon. I'm so pathetic - I've had Moose Tracks on my brain ever since you left. Just bring the carton here."

It seemed in a flash the ice cream was out of the bag, opened and her spoon deep into it.

"Sorry, Darling. Were you able to see this Albertus *aka* Javier? I'm listening," she said between her savoring spoonsful.

I shared the scenario in painful detail. Seeing him and his recognizing that I was clergy, his totally different demeanor –his cursing, the spitting, and the terrible absence of kindness that we had known earlier that day. He was far from the 'Javier' at the Lighthouse Landing and had now created an unforgettable new image - Albertus Mendez, felon.

"Did you pray with him?"

"No, he wasn't happy to see me, obviously. I shocked him when he saw the collar. He shouted obscenities at me and then… spit on me.

"Oh, Aldie, that's awful!"

"It's OK. He asked the guard to come in. I asked Albertus what hurt so bad in him that he had to hurt other people to feel good about himself. He shouted, 'Because the only love of his life was stripped away from him.'

She stopped and looked at me, realizing the tragedy in those words and shook her head.

"That's so deeply sad, Darling, so deeply sad." Her sadness turned to tears. I held her for a few moments and kissed her cold Moose Tracks lips.

I curled up behind her and scraped what little Moose Tracks was left.

"I'm so fortunate to call you my wife, to share my love with you."

The Hershey's Moose Track ice cream was gone and Beautiful Dawn soon pulled the covers up around us and the lights were turned off and the sound of the ocean, and remembrances of a day that had been so terrifying with howling winds and biting sand, horizontal torrents and unexpected people we might call 'friends' falling far down in the crevices beneath grace and truth - a day that we now give over to a greater Power, an energy we can only trust is finally a sustaining, healing Love for the world.

If there ever was a reason I call my love 'Beautiful Dawn,' Tuesday at dawn on Daytona Beach just as the sun was eclipsing the darkness was it.

I kissed her gently on her lips. 'Sweetheart, you asked me to awaken you when there is a beautiful sunrise.... Look!'

Just as she rubbed her eyes and inched herself up to an upright position, mindful of a great urge to pee, there was a light burst, that first splash from the long-distant orb, skipping across the sea and piercing the sliding glass doors of every room that faced it. "Aldie, it's breathtaking! ...Uh-oh, I've got to pee badly!" She hurried to the bathroom. I took photographs of the sunrise, trying to capture the burst of light dancing across the now calm waters of the Atlantic. What a contrast this was from the 'roaring of the sea' the previous day. The long shadows of early walkers made for photographic artistry.

I thought about Albertus Mendez, what kind of morning he was having in the Volusia Correction Center; what he was having for breakfast; whether anyone might tell him today 'I care about you, Albertus.' (I seriously doubted that would happen in a prison cell.) Perhaps a letter from a loved one might use the word 'love.'

"Good morning, Darling," my Beautiful Dawn draped her arms around me and pinched my behind, rubbed my belly. I could feel her baby bump up against the small of my back.

"Oh, my goodness, the little pooper is kicking its heels this morning. I felt a tap dance on my bladder. Sorry I couldn't enjoy more of the sunrise".

She gazed out through the sliding glass door and pulled it open a bit to feel the breeze and hear the ocean.

"Oh, it's invigorating, Aldie!"

She walked out completely nude and stretched her arms to welcome the dawn. Her breasts were full and taut. A couple passing beneath must have thought she was waving at them, '

"Good morning up there!"

Beautiful Dawn waved: "Good morning! It is chilly!" She wrapped her arms around her breasts. The wife below shouted, "What is your due date?" "April sometime," she shouted. As she was turning around, she was startled as she looked to the left to see an older man sitting with a cup of coffee, gazing at her.

"Oh my goodness, I'm sorry, sir. I didn't know you were sitting there."

He stroked his mustache. "Honey, I'm 84 years old. You don't have to apologize. You just made my day! Maybe my decade!" Beautiful Dawn laughed. She turned quickly and stepped back inside.

"Well, that was a little risqué, Aldie!"

We both chuckled at this and then hurriedly prepared for our day in Orlando. There was, of course, a bountiful breakfast for Dawn and frequent pee stops down I-95 and I-4. We still kept a hospital pee bottle from last year, just in case. We arrived at The Word Marriott Hotel to familiar surroundings. Our room was no on a higher floor than last year, but it was more spacious. For Beautiful Dawn's comfort, I ordered a suite this year, complete with a hot tub, snack bar -which I'm sure will be used and replenished! Our little pooper has been really active since we came to Florida. I think he/she is beginning to like our environs.

The opening banquet that evening featured keynoter Garrison Keillor of Prairie Home Companion fame. His 'It's-been-a-quiet-week in-my-hometown-Lake-Wobegon...' monologues are always priceless. How the conference speakers were able to arrange for Keillor to be there is a mystery (although later indications were that he was taping part of a musical revue at Disney. Garrison Keillor has always been intrigued with pastors and gatherings such as this.) He announced that he was sure Pastor Iynqfist of Lake Wobegon Lutheran was planning to attend, but was having a hard time getting out of Lake Wobegon because of winter snows and ice in Minneapolis-St. Paul. Keillor's keynote talk made for an enjoyable evening for the gathered clergy and their spouses. Beautiful Dawn even had an opportunity to have her picture taken with him later. He commented on our 'little bun in the oven' and hoped the little one would grow up being like the children of Lake Wobegon - 'above average' and 'strong like her mother.'

Our suite on the fourth floor wasn't cheap, but it was worth the comfort to Beautiful Dawn for the four days at the Pastor's conference. She teased me that she'd be spending most of her days reading in the Jacuzzi and eating chocolate éclairs and reading romantic novels.

During the first session of the Conference the next morning, she texted me that she was actually planning to slip into the Jacuzzi and watch 'The Today Show' with a bowl of Rice Krispies.

"Sorry, Aldie, I'm having an affair with 'Snap', 'Crackel' and 'Pop!'

Wednesday afternoon the rains settled into north Florida once again. Until January the weather had become extremely dry and the water levels were dreadfully low. But not on this Wednesday! Our afternoon plans would necessarily become indoor plans. When I returned to the room to ponder with her what 'Plan B' might look like, Dawn was in her terrycloth robe on the bed. She smiled at me, but I could tell she had been crying. Her eyes were swollen and red from tears.

"Darling, are you OK?" I immediately got onto the bed.

"Aldie, I don't know who my mother is!" She grabbed my

hand and pulled me toward her. Her tears began to well up again. "We're going to have a baby and I don't know who my mother is! I just can't stand it!"

I held her for a long while and, thinking about it, wondering when my she might finally reflect on this. This rainy day was an opportunity. She shared how her father had strayed far too many times from my stepmother, Lydia. And while Beautiful Dawn does have a relationship with Lydia, she knows that she's not her biological Mom.

"Aldie, I'm sorry... it just hit me hard this morning. The torrential rain and I'm lying here being terribly pregnant... and"

"Don't apologize, Darling. When it hurts, it hurts." I turned and looked out onto the balcony. Let's just stay in the room for a while and talk, I could order up some lunch and we could just enjoy the afternoon here. Florida weather changes quickly. Maybe later on this afternoon it will clear up and we can venture out."

"That sounds great, Dear. They made up this room just a while ago, so we can just stay here."

I ordered lunch It appeared the rain was going to linger for a while. Beautiful Dawn went on to tell me the torturous tale of what she remembers of her father's escapades when she was only five years of age. He had already divorced Lydia, with whom he had had Grace (their only child). But shortly after Grace's birth, her father had an affair with Millie, who had several children of her own. Beautiful Dawn does know that Millie is not her mother. Millie does talk openly about the shifting morality of her father, but she's honest that, as much as might wish she were, she is not Beautiful Dawn's mother. And sadly, Millie does not know who Dawn's mother is either. She only knows that it wasn't more than a year into their marriage that she discovered Jack was 'fooling around' again. She had been forewarned by Lydia, but foolishly married him anyway. To this day Lydia and Millie are friends because of their common misery over Jack O'Shea's infidelity.

"Darn, Aldie, only my father knows who my real mother is, and he refuses to discuss it!"

"Well, Sweetheart, it may be time to have a face to face with your Dad. I mean... Darling, you have a right to know. By May you will be a Mom and it's an important identity. Lydia and Millie are OK, but they're not connected with you biologically."

Beautiful Dawn dismissed herself to pee. Our little critter was doing tap dances on her bladder! Crawling back into bed, she continued the monologue about her parentage.

"I remember as a little girl, Daddy would come and sweep me up for a truck ride, but it was after dark and I knew I had kindergarten the next day. We went to a house and, Aldie, I remember vaguely there was a woman. Oh... crap! I wish I could remember what she looked like! All I remember was that she smoked and that she was thin. Daddy would set me on the couch to color and read some books while he went to another room to 'talk' with her a while. I always thought it was important business. Of course, now I know better."

"But, it doesn't add up, Sweetheart, I thought for a moment and looked out at the rain. You were five years old. She would have had some interaction with you if you had been her child? Did she kiss you or hold you?"

"Mmm. I just don't get a feel for her I just remember the smoke and the..."

Beautiful Dawn stopped suddenly and looked out at the rain as if something was about to happen. Then she cupped her mouth. "Oh my God, Aldie! *Lorraine McCardle!...* it just jumped out of my memory bank! Oh, Dear Jesus, Aldie!" *Lorraine McCardle!*

I was curious. "Who is Lorraine McCardle, Sweetheart?"

"Lorraine McCardle! Look at my features, Aldie... I know I'm not thin, but how would you characterize my face, my hair."

"Beautiful, Darling!"

"No, not that. How would you describe my features?"

Carefully, I described my Beautiful Dawn as having a slightly rounded face with naturally flowing, somewhat curly hair. She had a pointy nose and a pleasant squinty smile. Her lips were full and she had a somewhat pointy chin.

"It's Lorraine McCardle, Aldie! Oh my God!" She got out of bed and pulled my hand to look into the mirror with her. "That's just incredible! I've had a flash back to her. It's like the curtain was pulled back and the lights came on... suddenly there she is! Oh...my...God!

I can't believe it!"

Her memory was now working feverishly as she paced back and forth in our room: "My Dad worked in maintenance at Temple University for about six years. He hated the job, because he swore he'd never work for anyone. But apparently the money was tight in the sixties and he found this position. Lorraine McCardle worked in the accounting office there and would process all his work orders and payroll – as I recall. Yes! Yes! Six years... that makes sense. I was five when we'd go to her house several nights a week. Somewhere within those years... Oh my God, Aldie! ...*Lorraine McCardle* is my mother!"

She went on to say that her father had mentioned her by name several times when she was growing into her teen years. But then she ... she just disappeared off his radar. And mine. It's coming back to me. He mentioned how she had gotten another job or something and I...we... never saw her again. And Daddy just never mentioned her after that." Dawn just stood there looking out at the rain.

"I remember her smile. She may have been kind. I didn't like the cigarettes. It seemed hard to breathe in that living room. Even the overstuffed couch was filled with smoke... everything. My goodness, Lorraine McArdle may..."

"Emphasize '*may*' Sweetheart," I interrupted.

".... No, Aldie,' '*is*' my mother! Aldie, I've got to find out."

Lunch arrived from and I took care of receiving it, signing and tipping.

We ate sandwiches and chips and coleslaw. Green tea came with it and a couple of cookies.

"How best to do that, Sweetheart?" I asked curiously.

She thought for a moment. "I'll find a way, Aldie. I will find a way!"

The remaining days at the Preaching Conference were different. Our afternoon and evenings were not spent outside much, save for finding dinner and one afternoon at Disney's Animal Kingdom. So much of the time Beautiful Dawn seemed preoccupied with her laptop. I think she was trying to find every possible 'Lorraine McCardle' she possibly could. She could have re- married, changed her name. It seemed like the search of a life time– and I fully appreciated how much it meant to her.

"I came up with twenty-five Lorraine McCardle's, Aldie! There is a 'Lorraine McCardle' in Drexel, PA, according to the White Pages. But the number is unlisted."

She paused: "Sorry this seems to be taking up so much of my energy, Aldie. Suddenly it's become so important in this pregnancy to know who my mother is and possibly meet her."

The weather had improved remarkably mild from Wednesday's torrential rain. It was windy with a cool front moving in, but very welcome sunshine favored our day. We decided that a brisk walk would shake the stress loose. Beautiful Dawn was so fixated on Lorraine McCardle, she struggled to enjoy the beauty of the day. She told me several times: "I'm so determined that our baby knows his or her grandmother, but I swear it's like rummaging through an attic looking for old pictures."

Chapter Twenty-Four

HOMECOMING AND REFLECTION

"...real childhood scars heal, but not when Band-Aids replace self-reflection." - Cameron Conaway, Caged: Memoirs of a Cage-Fighting Poet

It was February 2nd when our plane touched down at PHL. We heard Punxatawney Phil had NOT seen his shadow, so that was a promise of an early Spring. It was a bit drizzly in the Delaware Valley. Re-entry is always difficult after a time away. We both had cushioned our time to return to work by two days. A new blanket of snow covered the Delaware Valley on top of several inches received while we were away. Our neighbor, Doug, had graciously removed snow from our sidewalk and placed our mail and the 'Inquirer' inside our door for us. He is an Airline captain for US Airways.

After the 'go-through-the-mail-throw-out-the-advertisements' ritual, we paged through voicemail on the LAN line. There was one curious message from Dr. Greenburg's OB/GYN office. *'Ms. Seaver, Dr. Greenburg would like to speak with you when it's convenient. Please call to set up a consultation.'*

"Aldie. I'm wondering what this is about?" "Mmm, had Dr. Greenburg been concerned about any part of your pregnancy, Sweetheart?"

"No, but she did take blood during my last visit."

We put this on the shelf for a bit and resumed our scan through messages. I noted at my computer that Emails had piled up. I decided in earnest not to keep checking them when I was in Florida. *Bad idea!* I had so many it would take me a few hours to go through them.

With a fridge lacking in food essentials, I offered to go to Giant Eagle and help restock. Beautiful Dawn was very tired from the travel, so I was soon out the door with a list and my ravenous pregnant one's hope for some lunch to return home with me. I don't mind grocery shopping as long as I am not hungry. The aisles at Giant

Eagle were hoping that I would be hungry. While there, I bumped into Marge Freeser, a regular at All Saints, who expressed disappointment that she had been in the hospital and no one visited.

"Oh, gosh, Marge, I'm sorry. Did you let anyone know you were there?"

She paused for a moment. "Oh, I guess I didn't. That's silly of me, Fr. Aldie. I guess I just assumed people knew I was there."

"It's OK, it happens a lot. I sometimes chuckle and remind people 'If I don't know, I won't show.' Anyway, I trust you are fine now. How did they help you?"

She explained it was gallbladder removal, which they had performed laparoscopically. She unfortunately, had some complications, because the gallbladder had imploded and sent some infection spiraling out of control. They had to keep her several days to make sure the antibiotics were ridding the infection. She was good-natured about not having visits. I gently reminded her to always have someone call the office, so the word can get out. There are at least five other parishioners who regularly go to the hospital in addition to myself. We chatted for a few minutes and then I resumed my list. As often happens, it was 'All Saints Congregation Day' at Giant Eagle. Fred and Ruth Johannsen, octogenarians, were out picking up groceries after their morning workout at the YMCA in Ardmore. They were telling me a new YCMA is being built in Haverford, near where they live. They could walk to it. Fred and Ruth are one of few Scandinavians at All Saints. They chuckle that the whole church is buried with folks of Irish descent.

"Someone has to represent the Norskies!", they would tell me.

"I know," chuckling in response, "when you two came to All Saints, I thought there was a mistake in the print. I told my Secretary, are you sure it isn't '*Mc*Johannsen?'" Fred likes to remind folks that his name is spelled 'Frederik – without the 'c.' Ruth now and again reminds folks that her maiden name was McCarren and that she proudly grew up in Havertown, even if she did live in Bergen, Oslo, for almost eighteen years. That's where she met Fred, who worked on an oil rig on the North Sea.

"So, I do have Irish blood in me!"

When I returned home, Beautiful Dawn looked alarmed. "Sweetheart?"

"I called Dr. Greenburg's office, Aldie. The blood test shows the possibility of a child with Down's syndrome. I had requested it as a precaution, but Dr. Greenburg wants to check it again." She shook her head. "It could be a false positive, but I remember this from nursing training, Aldie. When there's an extra #21 chromosome, it will likely indicate a child with Downs. Dr. Greenburg wants me to do a diagnostic test, which will require a needle to draw out fluid from my placenta."

We sat in silence for a long while. I held her hand. I offered: "There's everything in me to accept 'It's OK.' Our child will be loved and accepted no matter what. Yet, I think we just assume our child is going to be one particular way."

Beautiful Dawn was puzzled: "I didn't see this coming, Darling. Dr. Greenburg said that 1 in 700 women have indications of Down's. I don't know why it should bother me. I work with children with Downs at Children's Hospital. They are some of the most beautiful kids in the world. I even remember saying to myself. 'I could accept being parent to a child with Downs.'"

We had a little bit of a cry over the possibility of child with Downs. I whispered prayerfully: *'Please help us, Creator God, to embrace what we must face with grace and determination. Let your love flow through us and through others. Bless the child in this womb. We trust your will is already present in this little life. Amen.'*

Beautiful Dawn asked me if I'd mind if she went out by herself for a while. "I'm OK, Aldie... the possibility is sobering, but I'm OK. I just need some 'Dawn Time.' I nodded, affirming her. I knew what 'Dawn Time' was. Occasionally, Beautiful Dawn just needed to explore some of the breadth and depth of her own feelings on her own. I cleaned off the Honda for her and warmed it up. She put on her winter coat, scarf and gloves and headed out for a drive.

"I know you'll be safe, Sweetheart. Here's a sandwich to take along and an apple and a chocolate chip cookie." I handed her a brown paper bag. "And here's a Snapple of Pomegranate Juice." She kissed me long and slow.

"I love you... I love us. We will get through this," she assured me.

"Remember, Sweetheart," I reminded her, "we still don't know for sure."

"I know, Aldie. I'll be back. I have my cell phone." I later learned that Beautiful Dawn had driven over to Cobbs Creek Park, a beautiful spot near Havertown, where Cobbs Creek flows into Darby River and winds its way into the John Heinz National Wildlife Refuge and then eventually out to the Delaware River near the airport. The day was cool, but the sun warmed the air enough for sitting in one of the park benches. She ate her sandwich and spent some pensive time meditating on child rearing and Downs syndrome and whether Lorraine McCardle was her biological mother.

She noticed a man walking a dog coming toward her, but she didn't think anything of it. Finishing her sandwich, she placed the wrapping back in the bag and then was startled when the man stopped.

"Dawn O'Shea?"

She looked at him startled.

"My goodness, Lenny! Lenny McCracken! Oh my God!" She stood up and gave him a hug and kissed him. Lenny was her high school sweetheart at Havertown High.

"You look... you look amazing, Dawn...and... you're... you're pregnant."

"I am, Lenny. Into my seventh month."

"Aw, that's terrific, Dawn," He continued to hold her.

Lenny McCracken was one of the nicest guys she had ever met at Havertown. He had a gifted voice and was an artist and writer. The truth of the matter is that Beautiful Dawn fell in love with Lenny and would easily have married him. For a while, they were 'an item' in the Senior Class. They dated and enjoyed so much together. When Lenny would sing solos in the Choral Group, Beautiful Dawn would swoon. His voice brought chills up and down her back. His kisses were incredible. He treated her like a princess. But there was something curiously missing. Lenny seemed to be uninterested in petting or admiring her physically. Sometimes she would dress in a slightly provocative way, just to get his eye. She had a short, red and yellow flower print skirt that she would often describe to me, could get the 'eyes of the guys.' She would flaunt her legs in subtle ways.

And guys would notice. But not Lenny McCracken. In the car on a Friday date the two of them were discussing this.

"Dawn, it's not that I don't think you are beautiful... you are."

Then Lenny did something unexpected. He began to weep and put his arms around her. "I have a problem, Dawn, and I'm afraid to tell you... I'm afraid to tell anyone."

Dawn looked at him ponderously and finally, putting her hand on is shoulder, asked: "Lenny, are you... gay?"

He nodded 'Yes' with tears streaming down his face. "But I care deeply for you. You're my best friend", he returned emphatically.

It was such an emotional shift for a 17-year-old girl. She had always wanted a nice guy to make love to her one day. She thought maybe Lenny, one of the nicest guys she had ever met and with who she was madly in love, might be that guy.

Torturous Prom Memory

The truth of the matter is that Dawn never wanted to go back to sixteen when she was date raped by the captain of the football team. Richie Cullison was good looking, muscular and had a devilish way about him that had girls longing for him. Imagine her surprise when he invited her to the senior prom her junior year. Dawn was in heaven! Their dances were so sensuous. His strength just danced her around the floor as if she were a rag doll. She drank him dizzily into her imagination.

Then came the latter part of the evening. Their 'after prom' drive and petting late into the night in Richie's car. At first, it was intoxicating. She felt limp in his strong arms. His strong hands were soon feeling her thighs and edging into her sheer panties. Quickly her lavender dress was around her hips and Richie was advancing in his intent to aggressively manhandle her. Everything was happening so quickly. At a particular point in that advance she began to shift from intoxication at his physical presence to unwelcome insecure and fear. She had not thought this was going to happen on her first prom date. She may have idealized sex with him. But not yet. This seemed all too familiar.

"Let me get these off of you quickly," he said, breathlessly, pulling at her panties.

"Wait, no, no I'm not ready for that, Richie," she pleaded.

He ignored her plea and his strength became overbearing. With his hands he pulled her panties away from her body.

"Please, no! Richie, I'm not...ready... Richie!"Stop... No!"

"Shut up," he growled, "you know you want it, Dawn! Every girl in the school wants me to screw her."

He pulled her up with one arm holding her and unbuckled his pants with the other. She tried to push his shoulders to pull herself out of his grip, but his strength held her tightly. With no underwear on, his large, engorged penis was ready and moving around her vaginal area and he began pushing himself into her forcefully.

"No! No, Stop.... Richie!"

He kept forcing his penetration until her natural wetness allowed his phallus to find its way deep inside her, but not with her welcome at all. *'This is rape,'* she thought and began sobbing as she continued effortlessly to pull away from him. But he held her even tighter. His penetrations became rapid.

"God, you feel good... Oh, baby... Damn ... Oh, baby... I'm going to come!"

Suddenly she could feel him grow so large that sharp pains shot down her vaginal wall. She felt his ejaculate jettison up against the back of her vagina, his undulation so intense that she was feeling nauseous. He jerked inside her for what seemed an eternity. Although she was aware that she had climaxed and was undulating on his engorged penis, whatever pleasure she might have felt was dulled by her humiliation. Tears were streaming down her face. It was forced pleasure, but in no way was this emotionally satisfying, because as much as she had fantasized about his strength, his manliness, she didn't want forced pleasure, forced sex. This was rape! She had endured too many situations where sex was forced upon her, she yearned for cultivating mutual love - first. Richie was scary the way he manhandled her. Other boys had their way with her, but it was adoration and lust and petting. Richie's aggression was criminal. Her idealizations and fantasies about romantic love with him were ripped to shreds by forcible rape. Now he was forcing kisses on her lips.

She pushed away and fell over on the passenger seat and cried as he removed his dripping member from her.

"Why are you crying, Dawn? Shit, are you some kind of virgin?"

She grabbed her shawl and pocketbook and her shoes and crawled out of the car and slammed the door.

"You raped me!" she screamed at the top of her lungs. "You raped me!!"

He quickly jumped out of the car and yelled at her as he pulled up the zipper on his tuxedo pants.

"Christ, Dawn! Shut up! I thought you wanted me. You were coming on to me, you know! You pressed against me during our dancing. You know you did. Dawn, come on, talk to me...."

She screamed back at him. "You son-of-a-bitch!"

He begged her to stop screaming. He looked around, seeing if there were any cars or people nearby. Then he got back into his car and sped off quickly.

Dawn disappeared into the darkness in the wee hours of the night, one shoe on and carrying the other with a broken heel, clutching her purse, her shawl wrapped around her neck. She had no idea how she was going to get home or even what part of town she was in. Nothing looked familiar. She was aware as she moved, that she felt Richie's ejaculate dripping from her. It was such a repulsive feeling! She realized that her torn panties were still in his car, but nothing mattered. It loomed all too heavy, her surrender to immature boys' fantasies a few years back. Stumbling along dark sidewalks, edging toward street lights, she started to feel dizzy all of a sudden. She fell on her knees in the wet grass and threw up her supper. When she was finally able, she got back up and walked toward some lighted street.

In the middle of the street, she waved down an off-duty cab and convinced the cabbie to take her to the hospital. She confessed she only had eleven dollars in her purse. He got out and helped her into the cab The cabbie knew that something horrible had happened, gazing in his mirror, noticing her disheveled look, her mascara and dripping down her neck. He heard sniffles.

"I don't know what happened, lady. But we'll get you to the hospital quickly."

He called the E.R. ahead to let them know that Cab 6445 was bringing someone who needed help right away. The cabbie refused her eleven dollars for fare and helped her inside. The E.R. nurse checked her and confirmed the rape. She spent some time talking with her and recommended a Rape Support Counselor in town. Beautiful Dawn used the eleven dollars to get a cab home. She looked at her watch. It was 4:56 a.m. With her key, she quietly entered into the dark house and to her room and pulled the covers around her and tried to sleep. She didn't even know whether her father was home. It didn't matter, because conversation with her father would have been difficult. Peeking through his bedroom door, she realized he was not home. She was alone and frightened. She cried as she imagined how an understanding mother to confide in would have been so comforting at that moment, but her father wouldn't know about this rape. Jack O'Shea would have pulled a shotgun from his cabinet and gone after Richie Cullison, hunting him down and shooting him in the groin with his 30.6 high-powered rifle. She didn't want that. She was tired of anger and revenge. As much as she felt violated and humiliated and foolish, she just wanted … peacefulness, kindness. Suicide had crossed her mind, but not now – she just wanted to sleep. She fell into a deep sleep until 12 Noon.

After the episode, she never spoke to Richie again. Even when he wrote to her apologizing, she refused contact with him. It took almost six months of psychotherapy for Dawn to even consider another date, let alone consider pursuing a new relationship. Although encouraged to press charges against her date by her therapist, Beautiful Dawn chose not to. As angry and humiliated as she had felt that May night, vengeance was not going to be her path again. Never.

She concluded with the therapist:

"You know, it's on his conscience – if he has one. For all I know he may be a sociopath! I want to move on, to be cleansed of that memory and be open to kindness and people who don't want to possess me and control me... but love all of me. Frankly, I hope he still has those panties he ripped off of me.... at least the memory of that humiliation would live on inside him. Maybe not. My only regret is that I had allowed myself to swoon over him... to be mesmerized by his strength and good looks. Looking back, I don't think he had a soul... there was nothing three inches beneath that narcissistic ego and heartless emptiness inside him. I'm... I'm just a... just a 'fuck memory!'"

She was almost eighteen when she met Lenny McCracken. In so many ways he had been the man of her dreams (if it was possible for any man to be that). Even after he had revealed that he was gay, she remained a friend. He always treated her with kindness and had an attentive ear. He was her most loyal friend – more than even some of her closest girlfriends.

Now fifteen years had gone by since Lenny had gone to undergraduate school in South Carolina. And now here he was, walking his little Schnauzer through the park on this day of her pensiveness – this time wondering about her mother... wondering whether the child that was growing within her womb was a child with Down's syndrome and how different the future will be because of that.

Lenny sat down with her, much to his dog's yelping frustration. She learned that Lenny had gone to grad school at Boston College in International Business and was now working with the World Bank in New York on global investment strategies. His partner of ten years, Jason, managed a Wells Fargo office in Philadelphia. They talked for an hour until I texted Beautiful Dawn to make sure she was OK. She said 'Yes' and that she would be home shortly. Lenny and Beautiful Dawn parted with a warm hug and kiss.

"I'll be thinking about you in anticipation of your baby's arrival, Dawn. I'm glad you found Aldie."

Beautiful Dawn smiled:

"I am, too. Thanks for being a friend. And all the best to you and Jason. You're a good guy, Lenny McCracken!"

The afternoon sun was now descending closer to setting; the air had become a biting chill. Beautiful Dawn hurried back to her car. Returning home, she just asked to be held all night. She wanted scented candles - something peach-scented. She wanted me to know that I was her emotional anchor in the many storms she had faced. I couldn't fix the past, but I could sure heal it with my presence. And I gave her everything she wanted all night long until we could welcome the beautiful dawn back.

The next morning, she told me all about Lenny McCracken and Richie Cullison– two polar opposites– and how much she appreciated the goodness of our relationship – how I was like Lenny in spirit. She kissed me and thanked me for an understanding heart and my gentle care.

Although I was horrified by the details of her date rape, I so appreciated how she had chosen to move on from the horrendous experience. I was learning that she was strong of mind, spirit and body. Not every woman who experiences such atrocities can claim to have 'moved on.' There are countless women who carry deep scars and bruises physically, mentally and spiritually from rape. The world of rape comes most often from men who are unfulfilled and who sometimes carry misdirected desire. It can carry the heavy freight of resentment, anger and rage. Who knows what led a high school football star to exploit an innocent teenager who happened to be one of many girls who idealized him. Power over women is an aphrodisiac. It's been around since our civilization began. It will continue to be around.

Chapter Twenty-Five

HAVE YOU SEEN MY MOTHER?

Have You Seen My Mother?
Have you seen my mother?
My natural Mom, in an alley they might call 'Despair?'
She's looking for me and I'm certain you see, that my mother must still be aware
That her daughter is lost, disconnected by years, and abandoned by family division;
So, I'm making this search that I've started for now, and it is my very own decision.

Have you seen my mother?
It's far too dark… could she be alone in our city park?
She wears a soulful kind of sadness beneath her cloak of untold madness.
She might have waited, her spirit deflated, beneath some lamppost light?
I'd put on my coat and walk out to see, but I'm afraid to go out in the night!

Have you seen my mother?
She just might be (I'm waiting to see) that lady who lives down the street,
Who always wears those fancy shoes upon her dainty feet?
She laughs and sings and seems so kind, so she might be this mother of mine!
If I could just get up my nerve, I'd walk right in and query
But my nerves are not so strong these days and I'm scared and kind of weary.

Have you seen my mother?
She's seeking a child, who looks a lot like me,
A child who's wondered about her mother since the age of three!
My dress is a mess, I must confess -there's a smudge on my face as well;
But I'd hunt my Mom clear up to heaven and all the way down to hell!

Have you seen my mother?
I know she's hunted what we both have wanted: a time we've longed to share;
She'll see me in plain dresses and a face I confess is quite dirty – but I don't care!
I'll have certain graces despite smudgy faces and charms I know how to use
To help me pursue her and be led right to her with arms she'd dare not refuse!

Have you seen my mother?
One day, I'm hoping after years of coping, that I'll finally ask no more:
'Have you seen my mother?'
I'll look no further when she walks right through the door.
What tremendous relief! What stupendous belief - that we might hold each other
I, her long lost daughter am found, and she my long-lost mother!
Aldie Seaver, reflecting on Dawn's search for her mother

According to Beautiful Dawn's unrelenting research, Lorraine McCardle, resides, or did reside, in the Drexelbrook Apartments in nearby Drexel, PA. Her phone number was unlisted. Dawn said she had driven by the apartments six or seven times after work and, on one particular afternoon after returning from work, she stopped and inquired whether they had a 'Lorraine McArdle' residing there.

"I'm sorry, Ma'am. We're not allowed to say who lives here unless you are the Police or there's an Emergency," the office manager told her.

"Well, it's kind of an emergency," Beautiful Dawn sighed, "I think she may be my mother. I've never met her, and I've been searching for her all my life."

"Oh...."

The apartment manager stood up and gazed at her. He looked off to the side and said.

"OK, I'm going to share this with you, but you must promise you didn't hear it from me."

She gave him her confidence.

"There is a Lorraine McArdle here. But she's seldom home lately. In fact, she's one month behind on her rent. I've asked a few people and the lady across the hall from her said that she has a boyfriend or someone in her life. She's a nice lady. But she's seldom here and, as I said, I'm concerned about her rent being behind."

Dawn moved a little closer to the manager. Her heart began racing. "Uh, do you mind if I ask – what does she look like?"

He thought for a moment and then he looked at Dawn with wide eyes:

"Well, she has hair somewhat... like yours... but she's thin and... "To tell you the truth, now that I look at you, you're a spitting image of her. I don't know if that's any consolation, but there's a strong resemblance"

Beautiful Dawn was more certain than ever that she was going to meet her biological mother. "Thank you! You've been so helpful. Do you mind if I pay her rent? How much does she owe?"

The manager perked up.

"Well, not at all. We don't mind where it comes from... just so we get it. We have utilities to pay, you know. She owes $650 for the month of January."

Beautiful Dawn got out her checkbook and wrote a check for $650 to 'Drexelbrook Apartments' and handed it to him. Just at that moment, the manager heard the door open and looked up surprised.

"There you are! There's someone..."

Then he paused. Beautiful Dawn turned around and her heart really started pounding. Standing there was the woman who had given her birth, the mother she had been looking for all her life. She was thin with pepper and grey hair, holding a pack of cigarettes, chewing gum, her hair drawn back, and underneath her parka was wearing a pretty white polka dot and black dress and high heels. Their eyes met. And her mother was just as startled as Beautiful Dawn was.

"I'll let you two alone," the manager said as he backed away and went into his office.

"Mom?"

"Dawn?"

Beautiful Dawn began to cry. Lorraine wrapped her arms around her, "Oh, baby! O my God, Dawn Briana, my precious..."

"Mom! I can't believe I'm holding you."

They held each other, rocking back and forth – mother and daughter, reunited after almost 30 years, crying their eyes out! It was incredulous! For most of those years, they were only a couple of miles apart and now they were desperately holding onto each other as if that nothing could ever separate them again. They found a common area and sat down together and continued crying in their embrace. Lorraine told Beautiful Dawn that she was not permitted to see her because of Dawn's father, Jack O'Shea.

Through her tears, Lorraine told her daughter:

"I had always hoped that you would find me. I sat down so many times and started writing you a letter, but I worried that it wouldn't get to you. Oh, baby, you look so beautiful and"....looking down at her daughter's belly, she became wide-eyed: "Oh my God, Baby, you're pregnant!" Lorraine kissed her on her forehead and felt her baby bump and marveled.

Beautiful Dawn couldn't stop crying. She held onto her mother and leaned against her bosom. The conversation lasted for two hours. Beautiful Dawn knew that I was at a Diocese Meeting over in Bryn Mawr and wouldn't be home until late. She excused herself to pee and quickly texted me: '*I found my mother!!! I'll tell you more later!*'

They talked about everything, remembering how her father had brought her to the apartment - it was an apartment closer to Haverford -and how they both would sing to her and play games. Beautiful Dawn admitted that all she remembers was being on the sofa, coloring then then falling asleep and then waking up the next morning in her own bed at home.

"May I see your apartment... Mom?"

"Oh, honey. I'm afraid.... I'm in trouble with my apartment. I'm a month behind on my rent and..."

"Oh, I already paid it, Mom."

Lorraine looked startled. "Baby, you didn't have to go and do that."

"It's OK, the manager told me, and I was so eager to see you, I just paid it."

Lorraine hung her head and cupped her face.

"Oh my God, I need a cigarette. Baby, I've been..."

She shook her head. "I lost my job last September and I haven't been able to get on my feet. And, yes, I know I'm addicted to these darn cigarettes. But I go on one job interview after another... which is where I was when I came in... and there's just nothing out there for Administrative Assistants."

Beautiful Dawn looked into her mother's face. There were so many character lines revealed, etched deeply, made likely by one relationship story of love and hurt after another. She wreaked of smoke, most likely self-medicating perhaps farther back than my father's tryst with her. For a flashing instance, Beautiful Dawn saw her Grandma Wilma in her mother.

Lorraine shared volumes of information about her life. She was once simply Jack O'Shea's girlfriend, a lover - a 'fling' - an affair. Beautiful Dawn was the product of one of those nights when her father would drive the truck to wherever she lived and make love to her without protection. For four years, after Dawn was born, Jack O'Shea financially supported her mother but cared for Beautiful Dawn at his house. But he never wanted to marry Lorraine. He would tell people asking about Beautiful Dawn that he had decided to help in the foster care program and that Dawn was his latest foster care child. Lorraine hated admitting that her father never trusted her caring for Beautiful Dawn. He was sure that Lorraine would run off with a man and take Beautiful Dawn with him. Jack O'Shea, it turns out, was a very jealous man.

"So much water has gone over the dam, Honey. Your father did help me, but he just never wanted to marry me."

"So, how do you survive now... Mom?" Beautiful Dawn asked. The word 'Mom' just felt so good to say.

"I have a friend, Honey!" She smiled broadly, "...he helps me over the hurdles, with groceries and my bills. He's a good and decent man. His name is Clint. He doesn't want me to live here. He wants so badly for me to move in with him and... well, honestly, that's where I've been this past month."

She opened her purse and pulled out seven hundred dollars and handed it to Beautiful Dawn.

"Here, baby, I was going to pay the Apartment Manager for my rent and tell the manager I was moving. Thank you for thinking about me, Honey." She kissed her on the forehead.

"No, Mom..."

"Please, Baby, Clint gave this to me. He's so kind to me. He owns a number of ZIPS Laundry stores in the Philadelphia area.

She smiled. "He's crazy about me. Sometimes I have to pinch myself. I've never had a man just adore me so much. The only thing, he doesn't like is my...well you can probably guess... my smoking."

Beautiful Dawn looked at her mother. She was a beautiful woman. She wore very little make-up. She was thin and shapely. Her simple dress and large earrings made her seem sensuous.

"If you're sure you don't need this..." Beautiful Dawn held the money out to her.

"Oh, Honey, no... it's not mine. Thank you." "Well, here's $50... Mom... it was only $650."

"Well, okay, Honey."

"So, Clint really is looking after you?" Beautiful Dawn asked.

Lorraine nodded and shared how Clint had met her at one of his ZIPS laundries He owns eight in the Philly area. She didn't have enough change for the pick-up. He overheard her and went to the counter. He told her it was OK, that he was the owner. He looked at her and seemed smitten by her natural beauty. They were in conversation for a few minutes and he asked if they might have coffee later in the afternoon. She felt a bit shy. He was dressed in a grey suit and, although he was a bit stocky, he had handsome features, silvery hair and beautiful eyes and a kindness that radiated from his face.

She explained to Dawn that the relationship unfolded quickly. Soon she was having dinner at expensive restaurants and going to movies and even theater. The sex was gratifying, too. Clint was apparently as generous in bed as he was in person.

"Again, I have to pinch myself, Dawn! Here I was on welfare and navigating from one job interview to another. And then Clint came along." She added that she would likely be moving into his home, a fashionable house in Newtown Square.

Before I left my diocese meeting, I had received this text from Beautiful Dawn.

'I've met my mother, Aldie. It's incredible! I will be home later this evening.' I wasn't sure whether Beautiful Dawn was happy or sad from the tenor of the text. 'Incredible!' could mean different things. I was hoping that she was happy. I was just relieved that the persona of 'Lorraine McArdle' was no longer an endless search. The energy (not the least fueled by hormones) she had given to in this pursuit since Florida was at times overwhelming.

When Beautiful Dawn arrived home at 10:45 p.m., I let her exhaust every ounce of her energy from the afternoon and evening with her Mom. There was no way she could go to bed, even if she had to be at Children's by 7AM. I knew that regardless of the outcome, Lorraine McCardle was going to become an important part of our lives. She chatted energetically into the night about her Mom – picturing a woman broken by relationships and still more beautiful than she could have imagined, even with the effects of smoking. For the next several months her talk energy was like a machine gun!

"My Mom and I look alike, Aldie. She's thinner than I am... well, anyone is thinner than I am right now! I'm beginning to feel like a Beluga whale! But I mean that our builds are different. And I'm glad that Clint is in her life. He seems to have the means to support her and is wealthy from owning eight ZIPS Laundry Centers around

Philly. When I first heard her talk about welfare, I had a flash of worry that maybe she would want to come live with us. I don't know what the future holds. Her track record with men is pretty bad... my father included. I feel hurt by my father right now, Aldie. I don't hate him, but he's kept me from my biological mother all these years! She told me Daddy warned her to stay away from me. He was just embarrassed for his 'little mistake.' I hate that! I mean, I know he raised me and all of that, but this is about life and relationships. It's about a woman who's going to be a Mom wondering about who her own Mom is. Well, at least, now I know that my Mom and I have a future... I hope. She wants to meet you, Aldie. I told her all about you. She's going to talk with Clint and see if we can get together for dinner somewhere. Is that OK, Darling?"

"Of course, Sweetheart. I want to meet them both," I said adamantly.

For the next several weeks, Beautiful Dawn was on a euphoric rollercoaster ride. She and her Mom would get together for coffee after work and spend an inordinate amount of time catching up. She learned that Lorraine had finished her Associate of Arts degree at Delaware Valley Community College after almost 10 years. She learned that her father had made arrangements to pay for her birth and child care but refused to allow Lorraine to see Beautiful Dawn after it was discovered that Lorraine was having an affair with one of the professors at Temple University, where she was an Administrative Assistant. Even at that, a double standard existed, because at the same time, her father was also having an affair with a Delaware Valley School bus driver named Daisy. Infidelities reigned in Delaware County. There must have been something the water!

The Mom-Daughter visits eased up a bit after several weeks. Lorraine had closed out her apartment at Drexelbrook Apartments and moved into Clint's very fashionable house in Newtown Square. Lorraine also put her job hunting for an Administrative Assistant position on hold when Clint gave her a position helping with some of the ZIPS bookwork. The next time Beautiful Dawn saw her was at the new house, I was invited along and the four of us met there before going to dinner. I was immediately struck by how similar Lorraine did look like Beautiful Dawn, although my dear wife was infinitely more beautiful and healthier. Clint was as Lorraine had described him. I enjoyed meeting both of them initially. Clint was friendly, but his wealth wore a bit arrogantly on him. He and Lorraine were a study in contrast. She gave the perception that she was nothing compared to him... and he treated her as if she was a bit mindless, although it was subtle. Although, Clint did seem to adore her. They were visibly affectionate. Still, something seemed unsettling about the two of them. Clint seemed pretty self-absorbed; he never asked about my work, even though he knew I was an Episcopal priest. Like many men with power, he had little to do with religion. Lorraine would often stare at me. I was curious what she was thinking. Lorraine was in a beautiful blue dress and large circular earrings hung from her ears. Her hair certainly seemed to have been styled. At some point we gathered our things and left together to have dinner at *'Teikouku's'* an Asian restaurant in Newtown Square on the West Chester Pike. I had seen it often but never had occasion to eat there.

Conversation around our table was a bit awkward with our different personalities sitting across from each other. Although he was friendly, Clint seemed uncomfortable to say anything beyond teasing Lorraine and referencing her smoking.

"They're going to kill you, Baby, I've told you."

"Oh, I know, Clint. I've got to stop." She looked and Dawn and me as if exasperated with herself. It was a huge awkward moment, because it was awfully true and creating a gaping silence. Lorraine just stared at her noodles and shook her head.

Meanwhile, it seemed Clint wasn't sure what to say to me - perhaps because of my profession. Beautiful Dawn would try to make conversation with her Mom, but she seemed a little uncomfortable about it – often turning toward Clint as she preferred to focus on him.

"What do you think, Clint, honey?" She would say as con-versational bait.

As you may guess, I'm an extrovert. I'm in a profession where my job is to make people comfortable, not uncomfortable – although my sermons may sometimes make people uncomfortable. Anyway, I thought to myself: "How might I help this situation from becoming a social disaster in an Asian restaurant?" So, I launched into deliberate conversation:

"So, Clint, Dawn tells me you own some ZIPS Dry Cleaning Centers. How did all of that come about? I know there are ZIPS around the area, and I've used them."

Well, Clint was off to the races! As we ate our Shirataki noodles, Clint began a narrative that extended almost through dessert, sharing the story of how he had worked in a Laundry in center city Philadelphia and when the owner had a heart attack, Clint managed the store through his recovery. Of course, he didn't have two dimes to rub together, but he was able to convince 'ZIPS' management to help him to buy and restore two other stores. When all was said and done, he owned eight stores and was now considering buying two more. On and on he went like a charging bull talking about 'ZIPS number four', where he had to fire the manager who tried to overcharge customers and pocket the change. Unrelenting he prevailed speaking about the fire at a Zips Dry Cleaning in Bensalem. It was just what was needed in the awkwardness. Not to blow my horn, but I was able to ask enough of the right questions, to create that comfort zone that we all need when different personalities are thrown together in a social context.

By 9PM, the evening had shifted and now Clint was saying, "Well...uh, can I call you Aldie...how is the religion business?"

"Sure, Aldie's fine. I actually prefer Aldie to Father Aldron or Reverend, etc. Anyway...the religion business? I hate it, Clint. I'd rather work in the dry-cleaning business. Man, I have to deal with so much 'dirty laundry' that I think I'd do more good at ZIPS than at the Church."

Clint laughed hard. He loved the comparison. "Hey, maybe you could come manage one of my stores!"

"Where do I sign up, Clint? "

I paused a moment and then said: "No, fortunately or unfortunately I got into the 'soul' business twenty some years ago and, despite the imperfections and as much as I hate the politics of religion, at the end of the day, I kind of feel I am where I need to be. However, I might feel differently if you ask me tomorrow."

Cliff chuckled a bit and then looked down at his *Saki* with a serious look on his face. His whole demeanor changed. And then looked me in the eye:

"Actually, we need you guys."

Looking into dead space, he confessed:

"I got disillusioned with the Catholic Church after my divorce. My wife was heavily into it. You might say she was addicted to it. Then... humph (shakes his head) she ran away with one of the priests! He got defrocked, of course, and they got married in Ft. Lauderdale and he ended up selling automobile fleets for businesses. They had a bunch of kids and I suppose are living happily ever after. Hell, I don't know!"

I leaned up toward him. "Geez, Clint! That had to be a punch in the gut."

"Yeah, I told Lorraine, it soured me on organized religion. I know I shouldn't let one priest color the picture. But it hurt for a damn long time. No offense to your profession, Aldie."

I smiled broadly and put my hand on his shoulder.

"No offense taken. Organized religion sucks at times, but for all of the human crap, I believe the message is still worth it."

Clint returned curiously:

"How would you sum it all up, Aldie? I'm 58 years old and I haven't a clue."

I looked down for a moment and then at Clint smiling:

"I suppose I'd sum it up saying... God is around on the ground seeking to be close to us. We just don't often see it. It's not an 'in your face' closeness. We have to go hunting for it. Most people just quickly bail out on the search. And then there some, like me, who try not to give up on it."

Clint raised his eyebrows: "Wow. I have to think about that one!"

By now, Beautiful Dawn was ready to change the subject. "Did Lor... did my Mom tell you Aldie and I are going to have a baby?"

Clint smiled and leaned back on his chair: "Oh, Jesus, I'm sorry...I meant to say 'Congratulations!' When is your due date, Dawn?"

Lorraine piped, "It's April 30th , Honey. I'm going to be a grandmother! I'm in heaven. First, I get to see my daughter after all these years" She turned and took Dawn's hand ... "And then she is going to gift me with a grandchild!"

"I have three grown children," Clint offered. "Two are in banking and the other... I have no idea where she is. She got hooked up with some dope addict and the last thing I heard she was up in Brooklyn or one of the boroughs with a few grandchildren I've yet to meet."

Lorraine offered: "I told him we should try to find her. She may be in trouble! Her name is Shari and she's twenty-three."

"Good kid in principle," Clint looked down, "but when her mother left with Father Francis, her whole demeanor changed. This perky teen with her future ahead of her just did a 180."

And then something happened that I didn't see coming. Clint began to cry. It was one of those crying spells that seemed uncontrollable. He put his napkin up to his face and he was crying like a baby! Lorraine immediately went over to him and wrapped her arms around him, his face in her bosom. Beautiful Dawn and I looked at each other with one of those 'where did this come from?' looks. This wealthy, egoistic man rolled up in a ball of emotion. I reached over and put my hand on his shoulder.

"Man, I'm sure sorry, Clint".

Clint dried his eyes with his napkin.

"I get so damned emotional about Shari. We almost lost her when she was born. And I can't believe my little girl is living with some crackpot in the Big Apple!"

I continued to have my hand on his shoulder. "Clint, I can only appreciate how tough it has to be as a father."

Even with Clint's emotional meltdown, dinner turned out to be a social delight as well as a culinary delight. The conversation had picked up in a different direction. It seemed we covered the gamut from *ego* to *let-go*. The ice had been broken and we left *Teikouku's* practically arm in arm. Clint had spilled his guts, Lorraine had felt good comforting him, Beautiful Dawn had her pregnancy acknowledged and I turned out to be a very human Anglican priest. As we got into our cars, I got a bear hug from Clint. I also got a kiss on the cheek from Lorraine. Beautiful Dawn got a tender kiss from Clint.

"You do look like my Lorraine there, Dawn"

Beautiful Dawn got a rocking hug from her Mom. Life was good as we parted *Teikouku's*. It was a pleasant *sayonara*. Sometimes life is accidentally 'good!'

On our way home, Beautiful Dawn touched my arm.

"Thank you, Aldie. You saved this evening. We were all dying socially in there. Oh my God!"

"Thanks, Sweetheart. You know, all I did was to shift the focus to the neediest personality. Clint is powerful and egotistical, but he covers up his vulnerability well. Your Mom's ego is suppressed. I can tell she wants to like herself, but she hasn't found the courage yet. So, she hangs her emotional hat on Clint, who eats it up whole. I just did conversational 'window dressing.' It's the power of 'interview.'"

"Interview?"

"Yeah, if you really want to bring someone out, you start 'interviewing' them –like TV or talk radio, asking folks questions about themselves. We all love to talk about ourselves. Clint is no exception. Once I started asking him about his ZIPS laundry history, he was off to the races!"

"Ha-ha-ha! And I thought he'd never stop!" Beautiful Dawn mused.

"But notice how after he exhausted, he did stop... *'How about you, Aldie?'* Remember, he started being interested in me."

"It worked, Darling". She leaned on my arm.

"We're all hungry for affirmation. Even the rich and powerful... Many people can't buy that kind of notice."

Beautiful Dawn reflected that she wasn't sure where it would all turn out – this new relationship her Mom had with Clint. All she knew was that it felt good to meet the one who gave birth to her. It was like a circle was finally complete for her – that becoming a Mom in a few months, it was important to connect with her own mother. I was glad, too, that this circle was finally closed

I continued: "As far as your Mom and Clint, it may work out, Sweetheart. It seems to me, despite Clint's earning power and ego, he's just as needy for her compassion and care as she is for his attentiveness. I'm not sure whether God is a matchmaker in relationships, but I'm convinced God sometimes sends us the right people when we've been off looking for the wrong ones."

"You're right," she returned with sarcasm, "and my father, God love him, has never seemed to be the 'right one' for anyone!"

Chapter Twenty-Six

LETTING THE FUTURE TAKE CARE OF ITSELF

Do Not Worry

Let us not worry about the future. Let us only do the right thing today, at this moment,
Here and Now. Let the future take care of Itself.

Omar Khayyam

I do worry a lot, I know. I don't often let that be known because of some illusion that rectors are always supposed to be in control. *Not!* Yes, I'm an extrovert and conversation starter, a decent Episcopal priest, but I'm pretty vulnerable too. I'd give my 'Rev Rating' maybe a generous B-. I have people in my parish who 'adore' me, although I wonder why. I have a few who dislike me for reasons they keep secret and would never tell me face to face. Then again... standing back and looking at the big picture, I work hard for what I am called to do. The hospitalized are regularly visited, the homebound are communed, kids have some 'Rev' time at our 'Whale of a Wednesday' evening programs. My sermons are OK, not long or painstakingly personal. I have energy to do my job. What could go wrong? That's what I was soon to find out. In fact, it may or may not surprise you what happened after a demanding February at All Saints.

Beautiful Dawn and I were aware that March 14th was coming soon, so we started chatting about where we might celebrate our first anniversary. Again, I had saved up some 'wedding money' and 'funeral money' – honoraria for doing these pastoral duties, unsolicited as they were – and still had a healthy nest egg from Aunt Char's generous inheritance, so I suggested we have a get-away-weekend in Ocean City, MD - 'downy ocean, hon,' as Marylanders like to say. O.C. is about two and a half hours from Havertown. We wanted to be within reach of our hotel knowing that 'Baby' Seaver might choose to make his/her debut a little earlier than anticipated. We had already decided that we were going to have this little person at home with my full participation and with the help of a favored midwife, Nancy Gresham.

We chose the Hilton Suites Oceanfront. Located at 33rd and Philadelphia Avenues, the number one rated hotel in Ocean City and especially during off season. We arranged for a Sunday night, Monday and Tuesday stay at a very reasonable package rate. Even though she felt somewhat 'like a Beluga whale,' (Her description!) Beautiful Dawn was robust and energetic. Did I mention her appetite? We left after church on Sunday, March 12th and enjoyed the leisurely ride down through Delaware and straight into Ocean City. I arranged for two breakfasts to be at the hotel, one evening meal there and our Anniversary meal, Tuesday, March 14th to be at a special, yet to be determined place. We were like kids getting out of school following the services that Second Sunday of Lent. We grabbed a McDonald's drive-thru and were on our way. The weather had begun to moderate in the Delaware Valley, a lot the snow had melted and there was mud galore in our little mini pre-Spring thaw. Other than a necessary pee stop (there were tap dances on a pregnant lady's bladder), we drove straight through and arrived at the Hilton at 3:45 p.m. and were able to check in immediately.

Dawn was quick to say, "I have my walking shoes ready, Aldie. I want to get down to the beach and walk until my legs fall off! I want to get deliriously intoxicated by the salt air and the sound of lapping waves and seagulls screaming their heads off."

"Let's preserve those beautiful legs, Darling!"

Beautiful Dawn was changing her shoes when she got a text from her mother (These began to be frequent since her Mom got a new phone.)

"Oh, Mom texted and says that she and Clint had their first fight over furnishing the house."

I countered. "Let them work it out, Sweetheart. If you respond, she'll be texting all night."

"You're right, Aldie. It's our anniversary!" She grabbed my hand and turned and pulled my arms around her. "Thank God we're in Ocean City!"

We were down to the Lobby and out for some serious walking from 33rd , where we could pick up the Boardwalk later, but now it was down to the beach and our walk along its skirt. I held her hand and then she switched and held my arm as we walked and admired the azure sky and white puffy clouds off in the Eastern horizon.

"Aldie, do you think my Mom is starting to get too clingy?"

"Mmm. I think she's not used to this Mother-Daughter relationship and is making up for lost time. And...yes, she is clingy. Remember, she's not had an easy life, Sweetheart."

She nodded, certain that it was a new experience for both of them. What she feared most was that her Mom might be so overwhelming just about the time our baby came into the world needing our 100% focus. Beautiful Dawn knew that her mom's life was lopsided. She had expressed to her daughter her fear that Clint would see through her 'warts and bruises' and eventually reject him. Beautiful Dawn also knew that her mother lacked a great deal of self-confidence. Even though she had successfully completed her degree work at Delaware Valley Community College, her Mom was a lot smarter than she had allowed people to know about her. Once during coffee, she revealed being sexually abused by a few men. She assured Beautiful Dawn her dad had not been one of them.

"Baby, your father was one of the gentlest men I had ever had. Yes, I know he was controlling and had some weird ideas... and he proved unfaithful to me... but he was kind and supported me."

"I don't really want to hear about that, Mom. It's.... it's just a tender area for me right now." "Oh, sure, Baby." Although she was somewhat relieved that her father had not abused Lorraine, Beautiful Dawn still had major issues with her father's secrecy about her real Mom and forbidding her from contacting me. She worried about confronting him on it (although she felt the impulse to let him have a verbal tongue lashing!) She didn't want vindictive repercussions with Lorraine. She was going to have to focus on that a bit.

Our beach walk had netted a good-size bag of seashells. Ocean City is not known for an abundance of seashells, but a few earlier storms that week had left an abundance of all kinds – conks, welks and scallops. She had an idea of making a mobile for the Baby Room and hanging them with ribbons of oceanic blue and green.

Included along with her many gifts, my Beautiful Dawn is very crafty – or perhaps I should say talented with making craft items. I imagine our Baby Room being colorfully bright and fascinating for a child to behold. We will marvel as she moves playfully and her eyes open widely, fascinated by the colors. We had moved up to the boardwalk.

As I was imagining this seashell mobile, I suddenly felt woozy.

"Sweetheart, wow! Suddenly I feel like I'm going to faint."

"Aldie?"

I held my forehead and began to feel my head spinning and my legs were like jelly. We sat down on one of the benches along the boardwalk and I put my head between my knees as Beautiful Dawn checked my vitals.

"You feel clammy, Sweetheart. Just sit here a while." She stroked me and let me rest on her shoulder. I began to feel a little better. My pulse had been about 180 and now slowed down. Dawn decided the episode merited a visit to O.C.'s Urgent Care Unit. My protests met a nurse's roadblock.

"Aldie, I'm not letting you ignore this. Your body is telling you something. We're going to Urgent Care!" She was right, of course. My male wiring was at it again. I was in Urgent Care in thirty minutes with blood drawn and vitals taken. This is not how I expected to celebrate our anniversary.

After what seemed like an eternity and Dawn's love fussing about how hard I was working at All Saints, my eyes focused on a rather under-tall woman in a white coast and a stethoscope around her neck. "Fr. Seaver, we've begun some tests – the whole gamut. Sir, thus far you're looking clean – BP was a little high, but within the normal range. Your heart seems fine, your cholesterol seemed normal... sugar normal. You're the picture of health, Sir. We just don't know why you passed out. I have ordered an MRI and some additional tests. How do you feel right now?"

"I feel fine. We're celebrating our first anniversary... I'd kind of like to get back to that."

Beautiful Dawn insisted "Aldie, we should check things out ... that's most important."

This little interlude, or rather interruption, proved to be nothing. I was declared a 'picture of health.' We just don't know why I felt the syncope as I did. Obviously, I wasn't going anywhere until Dr. Patel, the resident neurologist, would look me over. He was a tall man with bold glass frames and short, spikey hair. He looked to be about as old as my nephew James (my godchild) who was now 26.

"Rev. Seaver. I'm Dr. Patel. How are you feeling?"

"Fine now, Dr. Not sure why I checked out on the beach a while ago."

"Well, all of your neurological tests are normal. With all the other tests, there seems to be nothing wrong with you, Rev. Seaver —my only question to you: Have you been under stress?"

Beautiful Dawn and I looked at each other with raised eyebrows.

"Not really, Dr. Patel." I stroked my chin.

He went on: "When someone like you has some syncope episode and goes through a battery of tests as you have this afternoon and they all come back normal, I begin wondering about an anxiety disorder. Simple as that."

"Anxiety disorder? You mean like panic attacks," I responded with surprise?

Dr. Patel nodded.

"I can't imagine what makes me anxious."

"Well, Darling, we *are* expecting a baby," Beautiful Dawn chuckled.

Dr. Patel smiled and looked out the window and drew a serious look.

"I'm not going to second guess this, Rev. Seaver. Would you be open to a consultation with a psychotherapist back home? I understand you live up in Havertown. I know the area – I did my residency at Jefferson Hospital in Philadelphia."

"Well...I guess so. It's what I would recommend if I were hearing someone describing these symptoms."

"Good. I know Dr. Williams, a great Psychotherapist in Philadelphia. I'll make you a referral."

The rest of the evening was moving in a direction neither Beautiful Dawn nor I had anticipated. Sitting in the restaurant at the Hilton Suites, we talked about me.

"Aldie, you're always looking after me, worrying about me... why shouldn't I have a turn?"

"But, Sweetheart, I can't imagine what's wrong that I should have almost fainted on the beach."

"Well, my darling, maybe you *are* having some anxiety."

It was hard to find another dinner topic. We did talk about 'Baby', especially because we were anticipating Beautiful Dawn's test to determine if we might have a child with Downs syndrome.

In the middle of the night I awoke sweating and trembling. I thought my heart was going to jump out of my chest. Yet, I was shaking to my bones. Beautiful Dawn sat straight up in bed.

"Aldie? Darling? Do you want me to call an ambulance?"

"No, Sweetheart. Let me catch my breath and sit up. It's.... it's not pain, I'm just...trembling and scared to death. Could you just hold me?"

Beautiful Dawn turned on the light and leaned toward me and began to hold me and rock me.

It was frighteningly clear to me that something was wrong. I cannot ever remember being so anxious in all my life except for those few occasions when something was just frightening – like once when I was stuck in an elevator at an old nursing home. Waking up trembling and sweating profusely, that was like a blind-sided attack. Beautiful Dawn checked my pulse and it was racing at 190. I had no chest pains, but I was feeling every racing beat of my heart. And my palms and feet were sweaty, my face flushed. I described my feelings as 'impending doom.' For the first time in my life, I actually shed tears of fear.

"Do you think we should go back to Urgent Care, Aldie? I know they are open 24/7."

I thought as I sat there shaking. "No, Sweetheart. We just did all the vitals check today. You heard Dr. Patel. Everything came out normal. No this is some kind of emotional war inside me. Since we'll be going home Tuesday, let me call this psychotherapist Dr. Williams tomorrow. I'm feeling this thing subside a bit."

"OK, Darling."

We held each other until we went to sleep for the remainder of the night. It was 2:20 a.m. when Beautiful Dawn turned out the light.

I had no more panic attacks most of the day, Tuesday, March 14th, the actual date of our Anniversary. We were able to enjoy getting back to the beach. I was determined to walk and not faint in the sand. By evening, we had arranged to enjoy a trendy seafood restaurant '*Seacrets*', up on 49th St. and the beach. The evening was going well. I had enjoyed a juicy drink and was sharing it with Beautiful Dawn. I was beginning to believe that maybe these free-floating anxiety attacks were short lived. We shared an entrée Yellow Fin Tuna grilled to perfection. Beautiful Dawn, who loves tuna raved about it and decided that it was the best we had eaten. We concluded with a sumptuous old fashion Ice Cream sundae.

Just as I was ready to the pay the bill, the emotional 'grim reaper' returned.

"Oh, Sweetheart!... Damn!"

My hand with the check in it was trembling, my face grew flush and my heart started pounding. "Aldie, Darling," she grabbed my hand.

"Sit there for a moment and breathe. Look at me and breathe. I love you, Darling. I'm your wife and I'm a nurse. Trust me."

I attempted a long breath, held it for a moment, and then exhaled. I did that repeatedly. I was determined to listen to my wife -the first rule of any marriage- and by the end of the first year with this beautiful woman, I won't fail that test. I breathed in and out, long breaths, holding and releasing slowly.

"This is hard!" I interrupted my breathing to get that out. I must have taken fifty deep breaths. The waitress came by and took my credit card and check and never noticed my deliberate exercise.

"I'll be back in a minute," she said, thanking us and then walking away.

Before long, I noticed that things were slowing down a bit. The crushing wave that had engulfed me with anxiety started to recede. The dread that I was about to die eased up a bit. I stopped the repetitive breathing.

"Thank you, Sweetheart. I'm better."

I was able to walk out of '*Seacrets*' with only the symptoms of sweaty palms and my feet felt as if I was sloshing around in a shallow pool. Beautiful Dawn's arm was around me and she drove the car back to the Hilton. She gave my feet and my back a massage that was heavenly. Her hands have a gentle strength about them, a caring reassurance.

I kissed her and shared: "Sweetheart, it's a strange way to celebrate our one-year anniversary, with this unwieldy anxiety pouncing on me. I must say that I didn't see this coming. One year ago, I rejoiced that you were not only in my life, but were becoming my wife, my truest friend and partner, my lover and soul mate. And now, Darling, I've never regretted one minute of making those promises and I will continue to rejoice that you are my mate. I love you so dearly, Sweetheart!"

She returned.

"Aldie, I wouldn't trade our lives and the experiences of being your wife for a moment. I feel truly blessed to be with you…" – she reached down and kissed… "and in sickness and health!"

I didn't rest well, of course, even though I yawned as if I really needed to. I wondered when my emotional predator might sneak up again. I was learning that part of panic was the dread of a next assault. It was like waiting up in the dark with a shotgun just in case an intruder succeeded with a home invasion. I double-pillowed my side of the bed and just stared at the boardwalk light down below. Beautiful Dawn was off into a deep sleep. If my rude intruder might approach in sleep, I will do everything in my power to suppress my fear – pounding heart, sweaty palms and feet, a feeling that something awful was about to happen. I'd grip the cover, walk around the room and breathe deeply, wash my face in cold water and, perhaps I should have thought of this first… pray! *Oh, God of my fragile being, help me in the helplessness of my fear. Help me to understand your love will never be taken away no matter what my fear. Let me feel your hand. Amen.*

My thinking was doing cartwheels. I was doing a life review –traveling back as far as I could remember to what just makes up this life…Aldron Gerard Seaver. I wondered and marveled at who I might possibly be in the scope of creation: a mere speck of timeless space dust, worthy of nothing, yet begging for everything; virile enough to impregnate the woman of my dreams, scared to death at being a father. I looked at the clock and it was 1 a.m. For what seemed an eternity, my mind just unpacked every rotten thing I had ever done as well as occasional good stuff. Did my life amount to a hill of beans? Who am I to dare to speak as if I understood the mysteries of the Universe? Who am I to declare that wine and bread from my hand meant anything because I'd say, *'This is my Body, broken for you.'* How do I know Jesus really said that? How do I know Jesus even existed? How do I know that this moment in darkness along the sea is real just because I may attach meaning to it? Am I going crazy – is that what this anxiety is about? Is this the ultimate bail out....? Will I live... with this..."

"Aldie?"

I woke with a start. Beautiful Dawn was standing by our bed, kissing my cheek.

"It's nine o'clock, Darling I've been awake for an hour and a half and you were sleeping deeply."

I held her and kissed her lips softly.

"Oh.... I'm not sure what time I got to sleep, Sweetheart. I just kept dreading that the intruder would come again. and... I was doing a life review. I think I remembered everything I had ever done or said in 44 years. I guess I just exhausted the dirty laundry list and drifted off."

Beautiful Dawn put her head on my chest. She knew that I had had an emotional shift in my persona. The unexpected intrusions of anxiety (still to be dealt with medically and psychologically) had come as somewhat of an alarm within my system. 'Something's wrong' was the warning sound, some shifting of the emotional tectonic plates within my psyche. I had experienced an emotional earthquake and the aftershocks were scary.

We put our overnight items together after freshening up and getting dressed. We would check out by 10:30 and find food. The Anniversary Couple would make their way back to Havertown, the two and a half-hour drive. I was aware as we pulled back onto Ocean Highway and headed up coastal Maryland that we had not enjoyed lovemaking the entire several days we were in Ocean City. Strange how anxiety can kill desire! Here we were celebrating our one-year anniversary, remembering one of the most beautiful days of our life, when earth and heaven had kissed each other as we promised a partnership of mutual trust and abiding love...but this intrusion of an anxiety disorder would zap my libido. That was sobering thought!

"Sweetheart, I apologize that this anxiety thing so overcame me that I haven't been much of a lover in these past two days."

"Think nothing of it, Darling. 'caring for you is part of our contract."

Chapter Twenty-Seven

CALMING THE STORMS WITHIN

Matthew 6:34 *"Give your entire attention to what God is doing right now, and don't get worked up about what may or may not happen tomorrow. God will help you deal with whatever hard things come up when the time comes.*

The Message: The Bible in Contemporary Language, Eugene Peterson, NavPress, (2002)

Dr. Jeff Williams had begun his career as a neurosurgeon with a specialty in brain tumors at Thomas Jefferson University Hospital in Philadelphia. He had been one of the pioneers in gamma knife surgery, radiating tumors with potent gamma beams. The science has unfolded into a powerful new cyber knife weapon against all kinds of tumors. As his career unfolded, Dr. Williams became more interested in psychotherapy and especially treating people with bi-polar, anxiety disorders and depression. By the time I had scheduled a consultation, my panic disorder was like a fully involved house fire. Every day attacks were almost certain. I would awake early in the morning with a knot in my stomach and dread at another manifestation of anxiety. On the morning I was scheduled to go over to Dr. Williams' office near the hospital, I had a sharp pain in my chest and thought for sure I was having a heart attack. Beautiful Dawn took all my vitals and assessed no indicators of a heart event. I would spend time in uncontrolled crying as she held me. It felt as if some outside force had chosen me as a land target and was intent on destroying everything in sight. I kept wondering, *'Does this ever end? Will it ever go away?'* A quick visit to the emergency ward that morning showed everything normal.

Beautiful Dawn insisted on going with me to the psychotherapist's consultation. We found parking and walked into an old Georgian-type brick building which houses four medical suites. When I settled into the waiting room and filled out all the necessary

371

paperwork, I found myself in one more manifestation of panic: flushed face and tremors and feeling nauseous. Nausea became a daily symptom, too, and I carried Saltine crackers and packs of Tums and Pepto-Bismol with me all the time just to stem nausea. Strangely, I had never really thrown up with these anxiety symptoms, but just succumbed a few times to dry heaves as soon as I could reach a toilet. I was very much embedded into the anxiety disease– that much I knew.

Dr. Williams was a tall, red-haired man with a pleasant manner about him. He looked to be about my age. He greeted Dawn and congratulated her on the pregnancy. Looking at me with his chart in hand, he said:

"So, you're in full-blown anxiety?"

"Yes, Dr. Williams, it appears it just descended on me within the last week – actually it started when I was on an Anniversary weekend with my wife."

"Uh-oh, that dims the celebration."

He looked at Beautiful Dawn and me with a chuckle and then said with a serious tone:

"Actually, Mr. Seaver, your anxiety probably didn't start during your get-away. Anxiety has antecedents that go back even to childhood. Stress and life changes will trigger them. Were you, for example, nervous as a child or prone to episodes of fear?"

I thought for a moment. "Well, actually I was, Dr. Williams. I was always afraid of letting people down, of not meeting their expectations. My father never wanted me to become an Episcopal priest....

Oh, yes, I see that you are a clergy type! I should have looked closer at your chart. Clergy are some of my 'frequent flyers' around here."

"Really? Clergy?" I was surprised at the comment, since most of the colleagues I know seldom mention anxiety.

"Yes, you folks are die-hard 'people pleasers' and dump unrealistic expectations on yourself. I'm currently working with five male pastors – let's see, two Catholic priests, a Lutheran pastor, an Imam... ecumenical, aren't we? ...and I also have a rabbi I just saw within the last few days. You're number six. Welcome to the FACT club… I call it: 'Frequently Anxious Clergy Types.' He smiled. "I haven't done extensive study, but I'm beginning to believe because of my own practice here that anxiety disease and depression are more prevalent among the ranks of the clergy than probably any other profession."

Then, looking back at my chart, he sighed and looked at me in a moment of silence.

"Okay, the first thing I want to do is to give you a thorough physical. I know you had some of that at O.C., but it's what those of us who work with anxiety disorders study carefully are looking for are the 'panic marker series.' Otherwise known as PMS!' *Beautiful Dawn loved it!* It will include not only checking vitals, but also asking you some pretty pointed questions. Your answers are important, because they will form some of the methodology we use for your psychotherapy. I have to nudge my clergy clients: answer them honestly, because clergy are often reluctant to mention their life warts and bruises."

For the next forty-five minutes, I went through an intensive physical, including monitoring my breathing, an EKG for my heart and taking blood, etc. The interview process included asking me questions to determine every conceivable indicator of anxiety in my life – experiences of childhood, teen years, early adulthood, my sexual growth, the shaping of my own theology, detailed questions of family and how I got along with my colleagues. I could see how this consultation was creating building blocks for the specific approach to psychotherapy for me. Beautiful Dawn was impressed with the thoroughness of my consultation. Dr. Williams used his staff effectively to gather information and document all of it in a way that he could know about 'Aldron Gerard Seaver.' *I was going to become 'a book!'*

Sitting down with me after all the testing - an hour and a half since we entered his office, Dr. Williams said:

"I feel confident that we can not only treat your anxiety, but also keep it safely under wraps for the rest of your natural life. Notice I didn't say 'cure' your anxiety. The cure depends on you, of course, but the psychotherapy and meds, which I'm going to start you on today, will keep it in check and allow you to enjoy the new baby and manage the church and its overwhelming need of you."

I walked out with a prescription for Ativan (Lorazepam) and a notebook written by Dr. Williams and his medical staff entitled *Calming Our Anxious Selves,* which Beautiful Dawn had completely read before we reached home.

With some resolve she turned to me as we pulled into the driveway and said: "We're going to nip this in the bud, Darling. I want you well by April 1ˢᵗ – no fooling!"

I chuckled getting on the expressway. "I will do everything I can, Sweetheart. I've got to be ready for 'B'- Day. It felt good just to get started on dealing with this ruthless interloper. I would meet Dr. Williams for our first psychotherapy session the following Tuesday. I kept reflecting on what he said – *that the antecedents for anxiety often go back into childhood.* The night before last when I had been awake fearful of when the next strike of anxiety would come, my life review did include times when I hid behind dreadful fear. My father's punishment was often physical and severe. He would sometimes take me by the hair of my head and pull me around the kitchen. At the dinner table he had a habit of reaching over and grabbing my ear with his rage in high gear. Once he threw me across the kitchen floor and my head hit the stove. I had a welt the size of a baseball on my forehead.

I learned two things from these unforgettable fits of rage: First, I kept my hair very short as a youth! And secondly, I never sat next to my father at the kitchen table. Allison was my buffer. He never yelled at her or pulled her hair, but, then again, he never said much to her even though she would usually lean toward him at the table with that *'Daddy, please pay attention to me'* look in her eye. It broke my heart. Sometimes I wanted to yell at the old man and say, "For God's sake, Pap, pay attention to your little girl!" Back then I worried about everything: my sister Allison, my mother (who was very passive with my father), my acne, my dry well of girlfriends, my struggle with Math, my rather gangly appearance. I looked like Abe Lincoln with a crew cut! I suffered through a few bullies on the bus who on occasion would punch me and empty my lunch box, throwing my Lebanon Bologna sandwich on the dirty bus floor and then they'd devour my coveted Hostess 'Twinkies.' Then they would hand me back my empty lunch box. Sometimes Mr. Fletcher, our bus

374

driver, would blame me for throwing my sandwich on the bus floor and make me clean it up.

In my childhood, I took everything seriously and responsibly. When I was in groups at school, I always felt I needed to be the one to make things work out- like winning the game of volley ball or making sure a class assignment was finished. It was 'leadership by fear of failure' –feeling responsible for the whole. And with that I was aware of having a nervous stomach. I would report to my Mom frequent stomach pains. My bowels were either loose are dealing with cramping constipation. Our GP, Dr. Henderson called it a 'nervous stomach.' Yes, it was coming back to me.

During the weeks of psychotherapy, with my anxiety disease in full attack mode, I discovered several things to be true: *First,* and most important, I have the most wonderful wife in the world! I already knew that, of course, but even more now. Pregnant and over a month shy of delivering our first child, she proved strong in guiding me through the perils of a generalized anxiety disorder. She cared for me, watched my diet like a hawk, gave me lots of kisses, but didn't coddle me. She kept me focused on the healing, not helplessness. My libido continued to take a nosedive during this period, but it proved to be a welcome time for 'snuggles and cuddles.'

Second, I found that I needed to learn how to embrace my vulnerability. I had assumed at the age of 44, I had the world on a string, the proverbial tiger by the tail, and all those other clichés that I tried to convince others that I was invincible and indestructible. (What a crock!) Looking back, I was glad I got knocked on my ass. It's not something one normally welcomes, but it was necessary. The anxiety was telling me something about myself: *You're a finite human being who needs to care about self as much as you care about others!*

Third, I discovered that the more I learned about the disease - Generalized Anxiety Disorder or GAD, the more I could manage it better. True, *Ativan (Lorazepam)* was helpful and got me through the worst attacks, particularly the ones that came during worship and while I was preaching or while visiting the hospital. But through my visits with Dr. Williams and reading thoroughly his wonderful manual, *Calming Our Anxious Selves,* I learned 'positive self-talk' – *'Aldron, you know what this is, it's anxiety...It's not going to kill you...*

You've had it before... Let it flow through you... don't hold it back. When attacks would come, I'd talk with them. *Oh, you've decided to visit... OK, but I don't need you here... I've got other things to do than worry with you... So please go away.'* I know that sounds weird, but it works for me.

Gradually my anxiety attacks came less frequently and lasted no more than about 5 – 10 minutes –sometimes even less. I did let the anxiety attack flow through me, like a wave that, once ashore, would retreat back to the sea. By two weeks into my psychotherapy, the 'intruder' was subsiding to sometimes as few as 30 seconds per attack. And, of course, the psychotherapy with Dr. Williams was exceptional.

My 'life review' had taken on a decidedly beneficial turn – especially when I could assess what I use to perceive were my failures and lack of approval by my father. And here I was my sister's true sibling! In fact, my life with my Dad had become a centerpiece of the therapy. I hadn't realized how much impact he had on me. Even though he was deceased, my father was still very much 'alive' within me. A number of sessions included several meaningful visits *with* my sister, Allison. It was one of the few times we did anything together since she had married and had kids. Our sharing sessions with Dr. Williams were very beneficial and strategic discussions about our father, 'who art now in heaven' had in this Earth Realm unknowingly created some emotional damage to both of us. Allison and I were able to chat for hours and even cry and hold each other. And trips back and forth in the car were very productive. In fact, I had not realized that she, too, had experienced numerous anxiety attacks, more in her twenties and early thirties.

The News

I was doing fine - even that Saturday morning when Beautiful Dawn got 'the call' from Dr. Greenburg.

"Yes.... Yes, Dr. Greenburg. It was indicated? OK – No, we were anticipating it. No, we'll be fine. Thank you for calling."

Beautiful Dawn hung up the phone. She held me. "We *do* have a child with Downs, Aldie."

We held each other for the longest time, rubbing each other's backs. I could feel my wife crying. I imagined that they weren't tears of 'Why us?'... but tears of acceptance, of reality, of responsibility...of the promise of love we would gladly share with one who will share an abundance of love back. I whispered gently:

"We will be fine, Sweetheart. The Holy One has granted us an opportunity to have a very special child, one who will give far more than we could imagine. I love you! It's all going to work out. There is a gift within you... a beautiful gift we will share."

Gathering composure, Beautiful Dawn looked at me: "I know, Darling. It will be wonderful. Are you going to be OK? Does this trigger anxiety for you at all?"

"I am OK, Sweetheart. Actually, to tell you the truth, it feels like something has been lifted. I don't know."

The pregnancy news of a child with Downs got around our families pretty quickly. Beautiful Dawn's Mom, Lorraine, was the most supportive of all. A coffee meeting at Starbucks brought warmth and love that was unexpected. Lorraine shared that she had worked a short while with a family of a child of Downs - Suzanne. ''

Lorraine smiled from ear to ear. "Suzanne won my heart, Baby. I just loved that little girl. Our days together were sheer delight. She would make me laugh and make me cry. Sometimes I wondered whether I wouldn't just take care of her for free. Of course, I didn't pursue that – I needed the money - but I looked forward to every moment with Suzanne. There was so much love pouring out of that little delight, I had to pinch myself. When I had to give up the job, Suzanne cried all day. She was five then. Her mother told me she went to the window and moved the curtain and cried my name. It just tears my heart out, Baby! Actually, she missed me so much, the family would let me come and visit."

Looking at Beautiful Dawn with a serious eye to eye, Lorraine admitted:

"I'm not saying it will be easy, Baby. Your child may not do some of the 'normal' things a teen likes to do. But she will be able to do many, many things. And most of all, the joys outweigh any of the concerns. Down syndrome kids are just pure joy."

We decided to be candid with the congregation about our news of anticipating a child of Downs. The All Saints folks were wonderfully supportive. A couple of families with children of Downs gathered around us with embraces and pledges of love and support. The only family member we did not tell Beautiful Dawn's father. Dawn was still reeling somewhat about Jack's attempt to keep Dawn separated from Lorraine. She wasn't ready to announce that her pregnancy was with a Downs child. She had shared her news of pregnancy with him, but Jack was strange about things like this. Dawn decided to wait until after her birth to let him know.

Re-Lenting

Time had passed so quickly since our March 14th anniversary and with all the anxiety drama that surrounded it, I had forgotten to mention that Lent had begun in early March. Wouldn't you know it – all of this and Lent, too? I almost forgot how the time of Lent is filled with its own angst (anxiety). Did the makers of the liturgical calendar know me? The Sunday texts were filled with rich symbolism about human angst. Positive events in life, times of great affirmation, moments (such as those fleeting moments when we hear of our 'favored' status from a parent or boss or when praise is heaped upon us.) Such moments led us to places of our greatest testing. Just when I was thinking I was aware of what God wanted me to do or where God might want me to go, surely it would cause me some measure of anxiety.

Interestingly, my Generalized Anxiety Disorder unfolded precisely when I thought I had it all together in my life (now 45.) The unwelcome 'beast within' causing the misfiring of our neurotransmitters must be reckoned with. It is like a demon that knows us and needs acknowledging. I would not have agreed with that at the early onset of my anxiety disorder. The blindsided attacks of anxiety seemed like the enemy, the ruthless marauder. Its massacre of my spirit and body often tested me beyond what I thought were my limits. Those sudden feelings that I was going to die and the dreadful 'portal view' of life (peering outside to what seemed an unreal world from within my aimless vessel) brought emotional war. Some medical writers called it 'de- realization', an awareness that 'normal' was being stripped away and that every anxious moment was *Aldron in Wonderland,* –an unhappy trip with many stones to tumble over.

According to the gospels Jesus was tested in the wilderness after his baptism (a ritual John used with antecedents in the Ancient Near East.) The ritual started as a necessary cleansing for those approaching the Temple in Jerusalem, particularly cleaning oneself with any association with Gentiles and foreigners on the pilgrimage there. Now John the Baptist had transformed baptism into a kind of immersion cleansing in preparation for God's new time approaching. John had become disillusioned with the Temple culture of his priest father, Zechariah. His water baptism gig had opened up to *all people approaching*. They were urged to prepare for the reign of God. Therefore, countless of the curious came out wondering what all the fuss was about.

In his baptism, Jesus heard the divine affirmation as he was raised gasping for his breath in the chilly, dirty waters of the Jordan River. (Matthew 4:1ff). It was such an emotional and mental rush to be singled out, to be chosen. It had the illusion of rank and privilege. We wonder whether Jesus welcomed it or not. Such affirmation could be an overwhelming weight to carry around. What does one do when the Holy One calls one 'beloved,' 'favored, '- worthy to be listened to by many? It must bring scary expectations. *What if I fail? What if I can't do the job? What if I'm a disappointment to my 'Abba- Father?* Whatever his emotions, Jesus must have sensed that the cleansing-though-cloudy-waters of divine affirmation might soon become a torturous mountain of testing and struggle. It's true of the life of many. The CEO with all her perks and power faces an awful executive decision – to lay off hundreds of employees because of an economic crunch facing the company. When faced with such a challenge, the power and the perks seem fleeting, justifying that adage that 'it is *truly* lonely at the top' of that metaphorical mountain.

Jesus *wandered* and *wondered* as the 'tester' (the 'Satan') arrived with a suitcase packed with career options. What does the Chosen One do with being chosen by the Holy One. Using the rhetorical 'you'…

The Tester: *You could be a magical 'human bread king' and turn ordinary rocks into bread, thus feeding a hungry people and reducing regional starvation exponentially. How noble! What would be better than that? Everyone would know you had a special 'in' with the Creator Father that way. That's why you do it, right? To impress the Affirmer.*

Jesus: Well, is daily bread the divine vocation? Is that going to get my Father-Abba's 'Atta boy!'

The Tester: *What about theatrics? You're chosen, so…think how impressed people will be when you can jump off the temple pinnacle and land on your feet with angel wings flapping to land you softly. People would be in wonder of your God-connection. They would applaud you loudly.*

Jesus: Mmph. That sounds like I'm testing my Abba (Father). You're kidding, right?

The Tester: *Or you could be 'Lord of the Lands' for as far as your eyes could see – all of it yours to have and to hold and with kingly power. Think how people would be your subjects and answer to your authority and to no one else! Of course, there would be one slight requirement, Son of God Guy, that you bow down and give me worship.*

Jesus: *Get out of here, you Tester! It's my Abba-Father who gets me on knees for worship. Get out!!! Get out!!!*

The greatest tests always seem to be about *ego*, about *self*-serving, not *God-serving*…or *others*-serving. Wasn't it true of the 'prodigal' boy (i.e. 'wasteful boy'), whose self-serving landed him in pig feces and corn husks. He ended up with a prodigiously generous 'father.' It's as if your earthly father wrote a check of an enormous sum of money and made it out to you and said: *Because you are my beloved child, I give you this to use to serve some humanitarian good in the world.* It seems like the father met the son's wasteful self with his wasteful (prodigal) love. The world is an enormous prodigal (self-serving) mass. How could the Holy One, the Father of the Household, counter it except with gut-wrenching unconditional love.

Jesus, wrenched with thirst and hunger, cold and heat, night and day, had to get out of the 'way,' his own *way*: *to be divinely privileged, to be unmistakably a 'Son' or 'Daughter' of God' – is to be empty of 'self' so the self can serve others.* The Roman Caesar may be considered *'Filius Dei'* (Son of God), but Caesar rules from a different seat of power, one that like today is oppressive and restrictive of freedom. The *filius dei* from Israel is servant of everyone and thus a servant of God.

This road less traveled would take him to serving God's straying people. There would come a day when he would take off his outer garment and submit to washing his students' feet and then give them his own bread (his own life) or surrender his own wine, *his joi d'vive, his very life animation, his blood.* Being 'from God' necessarily means being 'among God's people,' mirroring Godly patience and care. Whatever else one might say about the Holy One, God doesn't seem to sit on a throne barking orders to subjects and demanding worship. God is a deity on the ground in ways we often cannot see.

I had shared in my sermon about my 'testing' - my recent episodes of panic attacks. I confessed my temptation to feel indispensable as a pastor.

"Sometimes pastors believe they are layered with some divine Teflon coating from vulnerability or brokenness. Nothing could be farther from the truth! The pastoral call is a burden - which is what this stole we wear around our necks symbolizes – a yoke on our shoulders that's necessary to My anxiety has been a weird 'friend,' tapping me on my shoulder: *'Pardon me, Seaver, you are not invulnerable.'*

"Pastors get sick, get down, get worn out and sometimes get unexpected attacks of panic - essentially our bodies sounding an alarm that something needs attention – as in my situation, the 'inner me' needed a lot of attention.

"It seems I've been serving an inner illusion about my strength and endurance. At times, I suppose I think it's possible for me to turn stones into bread or imagine I can jump off tall buildings in a single bound. Jesus helps me understand that to know what God wants me to do with my life, I need to remember it's not to become 'Superman,' but rather to become a 'Surrendering Servant.'

I took the point further.

"How else can any of us who carry the label 'Christian' serve our Creator? Doesn't Jesus show the way? It's an invitation (not a coercing) to put aside the egoistic self and see in serving others the greatest possibilities of being a whole person, a healthy person, a 'God person.' It seems true that the greatest 'power' in this world is not dominating others but submitting through servant leadership. Really! I know it's hard to imagine, but Jesus might say to us (having been through his own testing time on the mountain) that *we lead best when we serve the rest.'* Of course, you already know, that won't be the choice most of us make. Our world follows a different rubric. 'Might makes right' wins out over 'servant-hood soars' – or something like that."

"Tricky about anxiety – it rushes me to *self*-focus. Alarm bells begin sounding within me and all my energy is focused on 'me.'

Anxiety really is fear of the unknown. One day in Lent, I was on the couch (a frequent occupation during this disease) and suddenly as if God were calling me, I had to get up off the couch and get moving to help another person – someone I remembered was in rehab. And so off I went, shedding the 'me' focus that drove me to the couch in fear. When I'm absorbed in others' cares and concerns, I'm seldom anxious. Serving others is almost a better prescription than Ativan for healing anxiety." Thus ends the lesson! Mine.

Baby Bound Blues

It was the last week in March that the Baby's Room remodeling was completed by M & K Renovations under Beautiful Dawn's complete supervision. The canary yellow paint was a perfect finish to the room. The baby crib, mobiles, the clothes closet, baby changer and chest of drawers were all in place. The green Berber carpet looked like soft grass on a sunny day and the window trimmings were rainbow colored with images of puppy dogs and cats. The day we signed the final check for completion of work, we stood in it and held each other anticipating the day our little pooper would say 'Hello' to the world.

Beautiful Dawn had me on a learning curve for the day of delivery. Nancy, her mid-wife friend also did some coaching. I had several important jobs, course: First, to be present, of course. Nothing less than the Second Coming of Jesus would be keeping me away. Second, I had to have plenty of coconut oil to massage her breasts and vaginal area. According to Beautiful Dawn and Nancy, sensuality was not to be absent for the occasion. Conception began with pleasure, it was necessary to have it part of the delivery. Third, I was to listen to Nancy's every instruction: bring warm towels, keep warm water available and encourage Beautiful Dawn every minute. ('You're doing a good job delivering our baby, Sweetheart!' 'I love you for all your hard work!' 'You are so beautiful!' etc., etc.) Regardless of the pain or words or expletives ('You did this to me, you bastard!') I was to keep a positive attitude. I was not to say things like: 'Jesus, I can't stand this!' or 'Oh my God, get her to the hospital!' Or 'For God's sake, where is the damned epideral?'

Although my anxiety had subsided substantially since the weekend of our Anniversary Getaway, I was still keeping the Ativan close by for anxious moments -especially on delivery day. Wisely, I had requested a retired Episcopal priest, Russ Grossnickle, from Media, PA, to be on hand to cover Holy Week to Easter. Easter happens to fall on Tax Day, April 15th this year and, since it's possible we may have a little 'deduction' of our own, I certainly want to be prepared. Additionally, a few women in the congregation are on 'baby alert' to provide food and diaper service. The buzz about Beautiful Dawn having the baby at home has generated a lot of conversation. Some women have regarded her as a kind of hero for choosing this path. A few have expressed concern and doubts and are certain at the last minute she will change her mind and go to the birthing center at Mercy. Of course, Beautiful Dawn is under a Taurus sign and she also happens to be of Irish descent – put those two together and you have a Tee shirt reading: *She who must be obeyed!* There are four words my beautiful friend and confidant hates to hear: 'You can't do that.'

On April 1st, Russ Grossnickle, my intended supply for Easter, fell and broke his leg in two places. Russ at 74 is no fragile guy. He was playing on the neighborhood softball league and fell trying to steal home. *Thou shall not steal!* His knee took a direct hit right on the base and they had to carry him out on stretcher and into an awaiting ambulance. He broke his kneecap and his tibia. I visited him at his office and razzed him a little about trying to be a jock at 74. I asked the Diocese to help me with coverage for Easter. Two days later, the diocesan office called me and indicated that suffragan Bishop F. U. Frank was slated to cover for me. I had forgotten that F. U. was now the interim bishop of the Mid-Atlantic Diocese. The bishop had retired, and F. U. had scored enough points in Mid-Atlantic to be the 'head honcho' temporarily. God, I missed Ben Cargill down in the Eastern Virginia Diocese! But with suffragan bishop F. U. holding the fort here in the Mid Atlantic area, I wasn't sure whether this assignment was a terrible omen or an act of grace. Ever since my days at Holyoke Episcopal Parish in Virginia and the searing judgmental tone of F. U.'s letter about my relationship with Dawn, I've had this 'edgy' fantasy going on with F. U., somewhere between wanting a verbal full metal jacket hurled at him to putting him on a large rotisserie spit grill at some public barbecue. Now he was going to cover my baby arrival time at All Saints should it come over Easter? Beautiful Dawn laughed so hard, she almost wet herself. I didn't tell her my edgy fantasy.

"Of all people!" She held her hand over her mouth.

She had met F. U. Frank only once at a diocese gathering on World Hunger. Of course, he was elegantly charming to her, even greeting her with a hug:

"I've heard so much about you. It's nice to meet you in person." That was a little after our wedding celebration, to which he and his wife, Wendy, were invited but were no-shows. Knowledge of the 'letter' - the one in which he demanded the cessation of my relationship with Beautiful Dawn- had reached around the parish and created a few enemies. Word was that F. U. was a bit embarrassed about the letter, especially since All Saints Parish is known to be a generous supporter of the Mid-Atlantic Diocese, especially the work of the Board of Foreign Missions. (A fund in our parish established back in the 1800's had grown from a large sum left by family of a missioner – the Rev. R. Hodges McFinney, missionary to the Mara Region, Tanzania.) One of our former bishops once declared that All Saints Parish in Havertown was the backbone of mission work in all the Mid-Atlantic Diocese.

I found it amusing that I should be sending him my packet of information about worship at All Saints. I also know that F. U. can be a whirling dervish in preaching and worship. He is known for sometimes coming up with the wrong Gospel lesson on a particular Sunday for which he has prepared, obviously, the wrong sermon.

On Palm Sunday, April 8th, the Delaware Valley woke up to a rare April snow, albeit a wet one, that dumped a few inches by the time of our 8AM Mass. Earlier Saturday, a Nor'easter off the Mid-Atlantic had been predicted to move to the East as it approached from the Outer Banks, but the cold front clipper approaching from Canada decided to arrive just as the Nor'easter was approaching and the result was three inches of slushy snow that essentially blanketed the area. The roads were passable by morning, but it sure required a change in our plans for a Palm Processional along the road frontage to the Church Nave. Bob McGyver, my crack Senior Warden stood out at the frontage road and directed everyone to the go to the Church Social room to pick up their palm branches for the processional to the Nave. The 8AM crowd proved thinner than usual, but the indoor processional went off without a hitch. By 11AM, the snow had essentially melted as the sun finally peeked out and the temps moderated.

I had taken an Ativan before the start of the 8AM service, because the beginning of Holy Week was always a stressful time as I anticipated a Maundy Thursday, Good Friday, Easter Vigil and Easter go-for-broke week. Palm Sunday marks the beginning of what Christians call 'Holy Week' – a time of intense preparation for the Vigil of Easter and the crowning liturgical jewel of the lectionary year, the Resurrection of Our Lord/Easter Day.

Beautiful Dawn was becoming more familiar something called 'liturgy' and what a 'lectionary year' was. She grew up Roman Catholic but confessed she had been 'asleep' through most of those years, especially as a teenager. She reminded me that after her date rape and various sexual indiscretions along the way and her disappointment falling in love with Lenny McCracken and then his admission to being gay, she and Christianity parted ways for a time. As it turned out, my openness to her doubts and fears and uncertainties may have paved the way for a new awakening on how important a church community, a gathered body of the resurrected Jesus really was.

She likes to tell people *Aldie sort of 'plugged me in' for the first time. Now, at least, I am learning the language – liturgy, lectionary. Biblical criticism. It's all very fascinating. We have prayer and meditation time together and cogent conversations.*

Chapter Twenty-Eight

NEW BIRTH, A NEW DAWN

Poem for a Daughter
'I think I'm going to have it,' I said, joking between pains. The midwife rolled competent sleeves over corpulent milky arms. 'Dear, you never have it, we deliver it.' A judgment the years proved true. Certainly I've never had you as you still have me, Caroline. Why does a mother need a daughter? Heart's needle, hostage to fortune, freedom's end. Yet nothing's more perfect than that bleating, razor-shaped cry that delivers a mother to her baby. The blood cord snaps that held their sphere together. The child, tiny and alone, creates the mother.

A woman's life is her own until it is taken away by a first particular cry. Then she is not alone but a part of the premises of everything there is: a time, a tribe, a war. When we belong to the world we become what we are.

Poems by Anne Stevenson (From **POEMS 1955-2005** *(2005)*

Wednesday morning, Beautiful Dawn woke with tenderness in her abdomen that set off a little alarm inside me. I wondered if it might be a prelude to labor. But, she assured me that it was probably the Chinese dish we had the evening before at 'Lucky Dragon.' She did promise to stay in bed and rest and I prepared breakfast for her.

I was on schedule to continue my visits to homebound members. At All Saints, we have a bevy of them —some 'homebound', interestingly enough, who are seldom 'home,' when I call them to bring Communion. I've been a priest long enough to know that what homebound people enjoy most with Holy Communion visits is not the communion *per se*, but my undivided attention. Sally Marquette is a case in point. She's 87 years old, a widow for almost thirty of those years and living alone with her Pembrooke Welsh Corgi, 'Mr. McCoombs.' When I visit her, Mr. McCoombs welcomes me with a few yips and then nestles down at Sally's feet. We settle into a long conversation in which I hear every imaginable detail of Sally's week. She has a very small family and a very small world. Her son lives in Ohio with his family and she has a sister in Iowa, who has family there. But that's the extent of it. For Sally Marquette, my visit is the biggest event of her week. Her son usually calls her once a week and her sister occasionally, but few people drop by. She could probably tell you every detail of my life, because she asks a lot of questions and remembers the answers to all. If the truth were known, Sally would want me to visit her every week. In order to set some good boundaries, I always have to tell her when I arrive: 'Sally, will you help me get out the door by 2 p.m., I've got an appointment with Mr. So-and-So.' And she does let me know, because I've given her responsibility. And it works.

"Father Seaver, I see by the clock on the wall that we have ten minutes left."

I set up my floating communion set, prayed and instituted it. Then I was out the door. Otherwise, Sally would enjoy my visiting all afternoon and would invite me for supper. She also reminds me before she leaves, 'I need my kiss!'

On this particular afternoon, I was scheduled to see Ida Mae McCafferty, one of our oldest members at 96. She had never married and had taken care of both her parents until their late ages and buried both of them. Ida was an only child. She has two great nieces who also now live in Shaker Heights outside of Cleveland. Thin, tall and able to get around without a cane, Ida Mae McCafferty is feisty and a staunch Republican. She worshipped Richard Nixon and always believed he got a bad rap over Watergate. I always make it a point never to be sucked into a political discussion with her. Unlike Sally Marquette, Ida Mae loves cats. She has four of them and three of them like me a lot, crawling all over me when I sit in her quaint living room with all the window shades drawn and only one tiny lamp with a 40-watt light bulb turned on. I usually accrue enough cat hair to put a cat together! Thank God I keep a lint remover in my car.

In the middle of our conversation that afternoon I felt a text come to my iPhone – the familiar two buzzes. I excused myself a moment and pulled out my phone. Ida Mae looked away with that 'Oh-these-cell-phones' look. The text from Beautiful Dawn jolted me. *Aldie, come home. My water is breaking.*

I calmly put the iPhone back in its holster and stood up. "Ida Mae, my wife just texted me. She's going into labor!"

"Goodness, Fr. Seaver, by all means, get her to the hospital!" She knew all about my wife's pregnancy and gave a lot of 'home spun' advice, although she had neither been married or pregnant, but had a sister, etc. and etc. I didn't have time to explain to her that we were having the baby at home, but I excused myself and walked hurriedly to the door.

"Be assured, I will bring that communion again soon."

"Don't be silly. You've got fatherhood obligations. Now go!"

I was in my car with a quick text: *'On my way!'* And, while I was doing well with anxiety, I started feeling the flushing in my cheeks and my heart pounding out of my chest. *'Okay, I expected you to come visit,'* I addressed my intruder, *'but I'm busy now and I really need for you to leave. Get out!'* I found myself yelling that at the top of my lungs. And a strange peace blanketed me, a catharsis of sorts. I almost surprised myself that I had managed the outburst. My face still felt flushed and my heart was still pounding, but I was able to re-arrange my demeanor so that practicality, not fear, overtook my thoughts. Now I could run down the list. First, I'm sure Beautiful Dawn had called Nancy. Second, my job was to get out the towels, the basins, the coconut oil, the extra pillows and hospital sheets and the box of instruments that Beautiful Dawn had arranged for. Third, I was going to leave a message for Dr. Greenburg to let her know that my wife's water had broken. I was only two blocks from the apartment, when a second text came in.

'My dilation seems fast, Aldie. Are you soon home?'

'Two blocks,' I returned the text.

Suddenly, I saw emergency lights in the mirror. It was a police officer pulling me over.

"Shit, Shit, Shit!"

He took his time getting out of his cruiser. Finally, he approached me. I almost shouted:

"Officer, my wife is having a baby. I'm only a block away. Can you help me? I need to get there fast. The baby's coming!"

He was a young man, not more than twenty-five or twenty-six. He looked at me with a frozen look, like either I was lying or what the hell was he getting himself into.

"I might need your help delivering it if we don't get there soon. She's dilating fast."

"Are you sure?"

Am I sure? I thought! I shook my head.

"Please, I've got to get there. The number is 510, right side, townhouse."

"Follow me", he said quickly,

"When I see you pull off, I'll turn around and pull in the driveway." He ran back to his cruiser and turned on his light and sped out in front of me. We made it to the house in seconds. He circled and pulled in behind me. I got out and ran quickly into the house. I noticed that I didn't see Nancy's vehicle.

Beautiful Dawn was on the bed holding her abdomen. The officer came in behind me, not realizing that she was there fully naked, her legs spread out.

"Sweetheart, did you call, Nancy?"

"Aldie... oh, oh... I can't get a hold of her!"

"We're having it at home. She has a mid-wife, but I don't see her car."

"This is officer James, Sweetheart." Beautiful Dawn looked up at him

"Hi, Mr. Sweetheart... I'm Dawn... oh! Don't leave, we need your help. We're having the baby at home. A midwife, Nancy, is supposed to be helping us. I'm going to need you..."

I could hear James turn his head and say, 'Jesus Christ!'

"James....uh,' I pointed to the closet. "We don't have much time. Go into that closet and fetch that basin on the upper shelf and fill it with warm water – not hot, but warm water."

"I don't know, sir..."

"Just do it, Jim, or you might be helping me deliver this baby!" I hate ordering cops around, but I was feeling desperate"

He hurried. I could hear him say: *"Shit!"* (Touché!)

Meanwhile, I got the hospital sheets out, the coconut oil and the box of instruments. I placed pillows under her legs.

"Aldie, this is going to happen soon. It's you and me, darling... Oh, oh!"

I started rubbing the coconut oil over her legs and vaginal area and then her breasts. James came in looking a bit pale, holding the basin of warm water.

"Thanks, James. Put them on the table and now I'm going to ask you to pull out four or five folded towels from the linen closet and three folded washcloths. It's over there next to the bathroom entrance."

"Aldie! Oh my goodness. I need you to rub me."

I began massaging her vaginal area and her breasts. James, returning with the folded towels looked as if he couldn't possibly believe what was going on. Nothing in the textbook references in the academy had prepared him for a home natal delivery.

As I massaged my wife to stimulate the contractions, I turned to James with another request:

"James, there's a midwife named Nancy Gresham. She lives in Upper Darby. We need to get in touch with her. She's supposed to be helping deliver our baby. Her number is 610-585-4421. Call her, please."

James was glad to walk out to the kitchen and make the call. Now Beautiful Dawn was feeling enormous pressure. I could tell by caressing her vaginal walls that our little bambino was intent on crawling out of one of the world's smallest spaces in order to make its debut.

"Ooh! Aldie."

"Darling," - remembering I needed to be talking- "I love you, my precious Sweetheart. Thank you for the gift of you and our baby. You are so beautiful through and through."

"Oh, I love you to Aldie. Kiss me."

I came around and reached over and kissed her on the lips and put the cool water on her forehead. Then I kissed her again.

"You are doing a beautiful job, my Love. I cherish you so much."

"Mm... Oh, oh! Nancy... oh, where is she?"

James is calling her. I propped her up and massaged her breasts with my left hand, soaked with coconut oil. I returned to massaging her vaginal walls. "My Beautiful Dawn, you are delivering our baby. How beautiful you are – your spirit, your mind, and your beautiful life-sharing body! I love you so much."

Suddenly, I heard the doorbell. Thank God, it was Nancy. She rushed in.

"Hey, Dawn... you started without me."

"Nancy, I'm so glad to see you. Oh! I tried to call you."

"I was getting my hair done. I saw you had called and decided to forget the styling. Well, what the heck! A bad hair day."

She looked at me.

"Aldie, are you OK?"

I nodded.

"You're doing well so far. Just keep massaging. I'm going to check vitals and dilation. Uh, glad your police officer pal is here, but he looks a little pale."

James came to the doorway. "If you think you're going to be OK now, I'll be on my way."

"Thanks, James. I'd shake your hand, but it's in my wife's vagina right now."

We laughed. James shook his head in disbelief and left. I tried imagining what he'd be telling guys back at the precinct.

Beautiful Dawn was now dilating at such a rapid pace that Nancy could feel the head of the baby. I assumed a position talking to Beautiful Dawn, massaging her breasts, kissing her on the lips, putting my fingers through her hair telling her how absolutely stunning she was, how beautiful her ample breasts were ready to give nourishment to our child.

"Aldie, oh...Ohhh! I love you!"

"I love you, Sweetheart. Keep pushing and keep breathing. You are doing an incredibly beautiful job. You are bringing our baby into the world, Darling. I love you so much!"

She suddenly let out a hauntingly unearthly scream, one I had never heard from this beautiful woman! The sweat rolled down her face and she was squinting; the character of her face was transfigured into a sheer moment of rage. Was this the incomparable cry of birth... pain and pleasure, resolve, a force of life almost unbearable? For a fleeting moment I saw strength in her I've never seen in anyone. She could have lifted an army tank with her bare hands. She squeezed my hand so hard I could almost feel numbness. I quickly applied the cool washcloth.

"Baby is almost here, Dawn. You're doing an amazing job, Honey!" Nancy assured.

A second unearthly scream of birth emitted from Beautiful Dawn, this time louder than the first so that she lifted her head and held her breath, squinting and grabbing both of my wrists and squeezing them as if she wanted to yank them right out of my arms.

"Here comes baby. Her expression reminded me of a scene in Amityville Horrors when the character of Linda Blair became frightening. My Beautiful Dawn looked at me with eyes wide open and a beet-red face. It had the look of: '*You did this to me you son-of-a-bitch... I'm going to rip your testicles off and ram them down your throat!*' I tried not to think of that.

"Keep pushing. Oh my, Dawn... you've done it... it's here." Suddenly Beautiful Dawn caught her breath and looked at me with wide-open eyes. In between intermittent breaths, she said repeatedly,

"I love you, Aldie. I love you... I love you." I began to cry and returned the *'I love you.*' '

And then ... Oh Wonderful Jesus! I heard the most beautiful, welcoming sound I have ever heard in my 45 years of life: *the first cry of our baby.*

"Ohhhh! You've done it, Darling", I said with tears in my eyes. I took a washcloth of warm water and began to wash her brow and her cheeks, her neck and breasts.

"Look Dawn!"

Nancy held up a beautiful baby girl, screeching her little baby screams in rapid successions. I marveled at the sounds of birth - Beautiful Dawn's haunting screams and now the baby's own birthing screams! What an incomparable rush, the sounds and sights of natural birth.

After a few snips of the umbilical and dressing the area, Nancy brought the baby to her mother and laid her on her breast. Beautiful Dawn cried happy tears and I let my own flow freely. I put my head down next to Beautiful Dawn's and looked amazingly at this new life we shared. *Amy Dawn Seaver* had arrived into the world with her loving parents within inches of her tiny screaming mouth. I couldn't resist a quick 'selfie'– Dawn, myself and our screaming baby girl – all of us with tears.

It was 3:45 p.m., Wednesday, April 12th - a beautiful day - a new day in creation with a new life shared with the world. Welcome, *Amy Dawn Seaver.*

Chapter Twenty-Nine

AMY DAWN, OUR PERFECT DOWNS BABY

My Perfect Child

As my children were born, I wanted them to be perfect.

When they were babies, I wanted them to smile and be content playing with their toys.

I wanted them to be happy and to laugh continually instead of crying and being demanding. I wanted them to see the beautiful side of life.

As they grew older, I wanted them to be giving instead of selfish. I wanted them to skip the terrible twos. I wanted them to stay innocent forever. As they became teen-agers, I wanted them to be obedient and not rebellious, mannerly and not mouthy. I wanted them to be full of love, gentle and kind-hearted. "Oh, God, give me a child like this" was often my prayer.

One day He did. Some call (her) handicapped... I call (her) Perfect!!

by Anonymous

The nice thing about having a baby at home is that you don't have to go from the hospital to the house. Our baby 'cave' was ready, of course, but Amy would be in a bassinet in our bedroom for a while. Dr. Greenburg, the OB/GYN physician makes house calls. She was supportive of our having the baby at home. By 6PM that evening, she had stopped by to do a post- delivery check-up. She was very pleased with the job Nancy Gresham had done as a midwife. All of Beautiful Dawn's vitals were normal and little Amy Dawn checked out normal also. Dr. Greenburg gave some suggestions about breastfeeding and post-natal care for Amy Dawn. She also liked our Baby Cave and even took a picture before she left, because, she announced she was also pregnant! Wow! We gave our hearty congratulations.

"I may have to look into this baby delivery at home myself," she said as she left us with a smile.

Beautiful Dawn slept soundly through the late evening until about 1 a.m., Amy Dawn let us know with no uncertainty that she was hungry. Preparations were made for her second breastfeeding and the little pooper took to the nipple so naturally. I lay with Beautiful Dawn while she fed Amy Dawn, kissing my wife on the cheeks and stroking her hair with whispered I love you's as I marveled at the sound of our little chowhound's contented feeding at her mother's nipple.

"Aldie, it's so hard to imagine this little bundle was inside me. I just marvel at the gift of life. Thank you for our love."

"Thank you, Darling, I marvel at the joy of our love-making mingled with the Creator's Big 'L' Love."

I enjoyed listening to Amy Dawn's first burp. Wow! It was a good one and a little later she left us with another little gift. I walked to the Baby Room and initiated the baby-changing table with a little 'scent of Amy Dawn!' as I came to describe it. We did affectionately refer to her as 'our little pooper' and that she was!

I had a tough decision to make. It was Maundy Thursday and the activities for Holy Week and Easter were unfolding quickly. Should I contact F. U. Frank and tell ask him to proceed with coverage for the balance of Holy Week and Easter? I knew that I had to make that call within a few hours. Interim Bishop F. U. Frank was essentially on call for me; it was my decision to make.

"What do you think, Sweetheart? I think you should have the larger part in this decision. And I'll do whatever you want me to do."

She was once again breast-feeding Amy Dawn. She thought for a moment. "I think this is such a magical time to be together, Aldie. I would prefer that you be here."

"That's what I'll do." I was on the phone with Forrest. within minutes.

"Congratulations, Aldie! I wasn't sure when this might be happening, but I'm glad everything is fine. I have this evening, tomorrow evening, Saturday's Easter Vigil and Easter Sunday all open. Thanks for the packet of information details. My wife is looking forward to coming along and meeting the folks of All Saints."

"Thanks, Forrest. Bob McGyver is my Senior Warden and he's ready to help you along the way. He knows the Holy Week routine really well. The Assisting Ministers and altar helpers will guide you through everything. There will be an envelope from me in appreciation for your services."

"You don't' have to do that..."

"I insist, Forest. This is above and beyond the call of duty."

There was a pause. "Well, thanks, Aldie."

I had purchased a Gift Certificate for the Dillworthtown Inn for him and Janice. I recall his saying once that he had never been there. I gave Bob McGyver a call to let him know the news and ask him to have the word passed along through the parish's communication system. And then I let him know that the suffragan Bishop would be handling things through Easter Sunday.

"No, don't be stressed out, Bob. I've left a packet in your mailbox with all the details and Interim Bishop Frank has a copy, too.... Yes, it's pretty detailed, but it will guide you through... Huh? No, he already knows you're there to help tonight, tomorrow at Good Friday Noon and 7:30 p.m. as well as Saturday's Easter Vigil Service at 10 p.m. And Bob, he'll need your help, so please look after him." While I was at my phone, I decided to send out a general Email to the parish contacts I have to attach a picture and let them know the safe arrival of Amy Dawn Seaver, 6 pounds, 10 ounces – mother and daughter doing well, father holding his own.

I announced to Beautiful Dawn that I was 'home for the holidays.' Taking a breakfast order, she responded:

"Mm." I'm starting to get an appetite, Aldie. How would some scrambled eggs, bacon and toast with OJ and coffee be?"

"Coming right up, most beautiful Mommy!'

I was happy that my wife was feeling her appetite return. She admitted to Dr. Greenburg that her vaginal area was pretty sore and, of course, she was feeling fatigue, but having her appetite back was a good sign and I was happily cooking away to accommodate with breakfast. Amy Dawn was asleep in her bassinet next to our bed. The smell of eggs and bacon was welcome. I was able to put a beautiful lavender daisy in a small flower vase and played some relaxing music in the background.

"Aldie, after I eat, I need to call my Mom and Dad. I know they would want to know. I'll write a list of other people you can call for me if you want to."

"Great, I mean, I'm in the business of spreading good news?" I kissed her gently.

As she enjoyed her eggs and bacon, I rubbed her back, which she called 'heaven on earth.'

After breakfast, she called her father, who was fixing a rocking chair in his basement.

"Oh, I've got a granddaughter! Congratulations, Dawn –how's it all goin'? Which hospital are in you in?…You're *not* in the hospital? At home?! Well, I declare -- you did it the old fashion way, huh! … 'Amy Dawn,' well that's a pretty name! Glad you got her mother's name in there. How's that preacher doin'? Uh-huh. Glad he can hang around for few days. It's Easter weekend… oh, got somebody to cover. Good for him. Yes. Okay, Darlin'. Can't wait to see my little grand…. "What?…Huh? She's what?"

Then Beautiful Dawn told him Amy was a Downs Syndrome child. (There was silence on the other end.)

"She's…. retarded? My granddaughter's retarded?"

Beautiful Dawn was expecting that response. She explained that Amy Dawn wasn't retarded. Downs syndrome or a medical condition that affects 1 in 700 babies born in the country. All indications were that Amy Dawn could live a pretty active life. Women who are older seem to be at a higher risk at having a DS baby. She explained it's really caused by the child getting an extra chromosome 21. Scientists don't know why it happens - they just know there's nothing that can be done to prevent the extra chromosome from developing. She told her Dad that she had the required triple screening to determine DS.

There was silence at the other end of the line.

"Daddy, are you there?" Jack said hurriedly: "Well… I hope she does well. Look, Dawn, I've got to get this rocking chair finished and delivered today. I better get back. Take care of yourself."

"Good bye, Daddy."

I looked at Beautiful Dawn. "Sounds like he wasn't taking that well."

"Yea, I sort of expected it. My father's never been one to accept life's differences. When my biological mother, Lorraine, announced to him that she had an extra toe on her right foot, he wouldn't have sex with her for the longest while. Mom told me it felt to him like she was damaged. I don't know, Aldie. I love my Dad, but he's one weird duck at times. I just hope he accepts our daughter." She put her planted a little kiss on Amy's head.

"We'll cross that bridge together," I assured her.

I had called Beautiful Dawn's Mom shortly after Dr. Greenburg left last evening. I could not reach her and we had not heard back from her. I told Beautiful Dawn, so she decided to attempt a call. I handed her the cell phone.

"Mom?"

"Oh my God, Baby. I just got in and listened to Aldie's message! Oh my God. May I come to see you?"

"Of course, you can. I hear her crying right now, so I'm going to feed her. Aldie said he tried to call you."

"Clint and I were down in Atlantic City the last two evenings. I had no idea you'd be going into labor so soon. But I'm home now."

"Okay, Mom, give me about a half hour and I'll be glad to see you."

"Honey..."

"Yes, Mom, she is a child of Downs... but she's a beautiful baby."

"I have no doubt, Baby. Oh my God...We'll love her just the same. I can't wait. Love you, baby."

"Love you, too Mom."

A smile stretched across Beautiful Dawn's face. I brought Amy Dawn over and gently laid her on Dawn's shoulder. Reaching under her nightgown for her nipple, this time her right one, Beautiful Dawn planted a little kiss on Amy Dawn's little head and then placed her nipple to the baby's little mouth.

"Okay, sweet little girl. Mommy's got ample food. Oh, my breasts feel so tender, Aldie. Do you mind gently caressing my left breast? Your hand would feel so good."

I complied and lay my head next to hers with bountiful kisses to share. It was as near to heaven as I could possibly be on earth.

It had been almost a month since we made love. But the feeling of my hand on her left breast and the little lips of Amy Dawn on her right put Beautiful Dawn in a zone of intense pleasure.

"Mm, I'm in a heavenly zone, Aldie!"

She actually drifted off to sleep. Light classical music was still serenading throughout our bedroom. I almost fell asleep with my head on the pillow when I heard the doorbell.

Amy awoke with a start.

I got up and started out the room. "I think it must be your Mom."

Beautiful Dawn realized the baby needed a burp. She was gently patting her back when Lorraine came through the bedroom door.

"Oh my God, Baby!" (She says 'Oh my God, Baby' a lot!) Grinning from ear to ear, Lorraine sat down next to the bed. She looked like a million dollars. She had on a short lavender dress with sparkles. Her hair was peppery and teased back.

"Mom, you look gorgeous."

"Oh, thank you Baby. Oh my God! She's so adorable. Amy Dawn Seaver!"

"Do you like 'Grandma. Granny... Nana... Mom-Mom? What would you like to be called?" Lorraine's eyes widened: "Oh my, I need to think about that. I've never been in this role before. What do you think, Honey?"

"Your choice, Mom. I just finished burping her. Would you like to hold her?"

Lorraine started to cry. She took little Amy Dawn her arms and set down by Beautiful Dawn's bed.

"Sorry, Honey. I've... I haven't had an opportunity to do this for so long..." Tears were streaming down her cheeks.

"Aw Mom, I'm sorry."

"No... it's just that this reminds me of the first time I picked you up in my arms, Honey. You were so adorable too. Oh my God, that I've lived to see this moment! Thank you!" Her eyes cast upward.

She kissed Amy Dawn's head and rocked her in ecstasy. Beautiful Dawn placed her hand on her Mom's arm. As she watched Her, she realized how rare this moment was in her rocky life.

"You'll be a wonderful Grandma."

"Oh, Honey... that's what it will be then - Grandma," she looked at Beautiful Dawn through her tears, "Grandma... Grandma Lorraine. Oh, Amy Dawn, Grandma loves you so much." Suddenly, Amy Dawn burped. "Oh, my goodness, did we have a little burpie in there? Mommy's feeding you well."

"Careful, Mom, she'll leave you another gift," Beautiful Dawn warned. Lorraine laughed. "Oh, I don't mind at all. It's good to know that things are working down there!" It wasn't more than two or three minutes that Amy dawn left her gift, warming Lorraine's hand and providing 'the scent of Amy Dawn.'

"Daddy is proving very proficient in the diaper-changing department."

"Oh yes!" I muttered after the compliment.

Beautiful Dawn chatted with her Mom about the Downs syndrome and her father's response. Lorraine shook her head: "Aw, Honey, he always had a problem with things like this. Don't worry about it."

"Oh, I'm not worried, Mom."

The doorbell rang and I called Lorraine to help finish the diaper changing. She gladly complied. At the door was Ruth McGill, the woman who had served so graciously as our Wedding Coordinator. She had brought five different meals ready-to-heat.

"Oh my gosh, Ruth! What a special treat. Now I won't mess up the cooking after all."

We had a good laugh.

"It comes with a lot of love, Fr. Aldie. We had five different family units preparing five different items for you. I was on my way to the Maundy Thursday service. We're going to miss you this weekend."

"Yea, I know. I'm on Daddy Duty right now. I will miss the services."

"Oh, don't even think about it. Why, when Edward and I had our first son, he was on an oil tanker helping clean up the Valdez mess in Alaska. I would've given anything to have him do what you're doing."

"Well, come on in and see Dawn. Her Mom is visiting, but I'm sure she'd love to see you and hold the baby." Ruth didn't hesitate.

I don't know any woman who doesn't relish moments like this. with a new born baby. She and Lorraine met for the first time and they were off to the races with baby chatter, smiles and laughter. Ruth was overjoyed at seeing Beautiful Dawn and the baby. Ruth relished a few minutes holding our little pooper and then told her that five families had donated meals.

Beautiful Dawn was grateful, of course. She laughed: "I'm sure Aldie's glad to hear that. He's been worried to death his cooking is not going to be adequate. But, he does fine – I told him."

Then Amy Dawn, now asleep, was shuttled off to Lorraine. And they all enjoyed some 'girl-baby time.'

I was wrapping up my Email when the doorbell rang again. When I opened it, I was shocked to see Jack O'Shea!

"Jack!"

"Congratulations, old man". He grinned as he shook my hand. He had a vase of beautiful tulips in his arm and a card. I stood there a bit stunned.

"Well, ain'tcha gonna let Grandpa in?"

"Oh, dumb of me. Come on in, Jack. Let me take your coat."

"Naw, I'm not stayin' long. I just wanted to sneak a peek at my new granddaughter and see how Dawn is holding up."

"Okay. Well, she's got some women up there visiting her, but you're welcome to come in." I chuckled.

"The more the merrier" Jack started up the steps.

I wasn't sure what reaction Beautiful Dawn and her mother would have. Ruth McGill would be a benign presence, of course. But, Lorraine? Oh well, let it be what it might be.

"Well, I don't need to stay long, if they don't mind." I led Jack upstairs.

"Uh, who is it, Aldie?.... Daddy?"

Jack's eyes fell on Beautiful Dawn and then on Lorraine... then back to Beautiful Dawn... then to Lorraine.

"Lorraine," Jack nodded.

"Jack."

Then he turned to Ruth. "Howdy, Ma'am. I'm Jack O'Shea... I guess you might say, I'm the Grandpa too." Then his eyes fell on little Amy Dawn fast asleep on Beautiful Dawn's bosom.

"Oh, my... what a beautiful little girl."

He set the vase of tulips down on the table next to the bed and pulled out his handkerchief. His eyes had begun watering.

"Thanks, Daddy. The flowers are beautiful."

Lorraine's eyes never looked up. It couldn't have been more awkward for her —especially mindful how Jack had prevented her from having a relationship with Beautiful Dawn. But that was ancient history now. Lorraine and Jack were no longer an 'item' and nothing could possibly keep Beautiful Dawn from having a relationship with her mother. In fact, Beautiful Dawn now wondered why she hadn't pressed her father more about her mother's identity.

"Uh, I don't want to interrupt you woman talking and such, but I wonder if I might be able to have a few moments with my daughter and granddaughter. I promise you, it won't take long. "

Something in Jack's tone worried me a bit, but I knew that Beautiful Dawn would handle whatever her father wanted to say. So, I escorted the girls back downstairs and offered more coffee.

"What is it, Daddy?"

Jack looked down and then looked at Beautiful Dawn.

"I've been a damn fool, Dawn" He pulled out his handkerchief and blow his nose. "I didn't mean to react the way I did about my granddaughter being a Downs baby. I just want to apologize. She's a beautiful little girl and I'll treasure her as my granddaughter And"... looking out the window... "I've been aware that I wasn't honest with you about the early days of your life. You always thought Lydia was your mother. And now you know that Lorraine is your birth Mom."

"Daddy, how did you know that I found that out?"

"Oh, things get around... you know. But Dawn, I kept it from you, because I didn't want you think that you were a mistake." The truth is that after I left Lydia and Lillian, I fell deeply in love with Lorraine. Oh my, did I fall! I would have married her in a moment. Well, when I found out she was pregnant...."

Jack looked down and shook his head... "I was embarrassed. I thought we were using the right protection and all. But I was a fool. After the pregnancy, Lorraine and I had an on again, off again relationship. I think she was in love with me, but having a child... well, it wasn't in the cards. I let my dumb pride get in the way. When she gave birth to you, I supported her financially, I set her up in an apartment, but I didn't want to have anything to do with her."

"Well, Christ, she pleaded for me to marry her! But I kept putting her off. Then, by the time you were three years old, I filed custody to get you, because I found out that Lorraine was with another man. It was my own damn fault. I should never have left her go. Nevertheless, I filed custody and won. Well, it broke Lorraine's heart and she had none of the resources to fight the custody. But... just as I thought I had rid myself of Lorraine, I met her one night and, well, I fell back in love with her. In order to see her, I had to promise to bring you with me. So practically every night of the week, I'd put you in the truck and take you along to Lorraine's apartment and she'd spend the first hour loving you and holding you. And then, we'd...well, you know... "

Dawn nodded with a smile.

"...I know I'm rambling on here," Jack rubbed his stubble, "but the truth is that I refused to marry her and learned later that she was again with someone else. And again, I got angry and forbid her from having contact with you. And it's been that way until...."

Beautiful Dawn looked at him, tears streaming down her cheek and said:

"...until I tried to find out myself, Daddy." Dawn sat up a little. "I had to search for my biological mother on my own. I've been a puppet on string, haven't I, Daddy? I've been leverage between you and Lorraine. She wanted so desperately to see me! Don't you know what it did to me?

There was a long pause and some sighs from Jack. He shook his head a couple of times.

"Darlin', I've been so bad. When I found out you had a baby, I knew that I had to come clean on this. I'm tired of lyin' and hidin'. He wiped tears from eyes. "I just came by to say I'm sorry... to see if it might be possible to make amends. I think I've said enough."

"Let's try, Daddy. Let's really try."

Beautiful Dawn thanked him for coming forward with the truth. She told him that, although it hurts deeply, she loved him and hoped that he would accept Amy Dawn as his granddaughter.

"I will. I know that with a sincere mother like you and a good person like Aldie, she will get through this condition." (Condition?)

He kissed Beautiful Dawn on the forehead and touched the shoulder of Amy Dawn and took his hat and left the room.

I wished Jack good-bye as he proceeded toward the door. He turned and acknowledged Ruth McGill, what a pleasure it was to meet her. Then he looked at Lorraine.

"Lorraine, good to see you."

She smiled at Jack in a detached sort of way —as if perhaps years had melted away a distant memory.

Jack said, 'So long' to Aldie and left. Aldie told the girls he'd see how Beautiful Dawn was and they were welcome to return. "She'd want to say, 'Good bye' at least." I ran up the steps and knocked lightly.

"Are you OK, Darling? "

"Oh, Aldie... I am. My father is a mess. I love him, but he's a train wreck. I'll tell you more about it later. Did Ruth and my Mom leave?"

"No, I invited them to come back up if you're OK."

"Please, Aldie, have them back up. The baby is fast asleep if you could put her in the bassinet." Ruth and my Mom hit it off well. It turns out that Ruth and Mom knew each other from a shoe store they frequented in Haverford called 'Wallach's.' "Most comfortable shoes I've ever had on my feet," my Mom said. Also, coincidentally Ruth used to work there as a young woman while she was attending Haverford Community College. They talked continuously while Jack was upstairs with Beautiful Dawn I placed Amy Dawn in her bassinet and left them to their girl talk and straightened up in the kitchen. Eventually, Ruth came downstairs and told me that she had to help out with the Mass at the 7:30 p.m. Maundy Thursday service.

"I'm glad you're taking some time off, Aldie. I'll miss your sermon tonight..." Ruth patted him on the shoulder.

"Thanks, I almost had it written, Ruth.... but I can't think of a better place for you to be right now than here. The interim bishop seemsready to jump in to cover this weekend, too. I'll miss you all. I hope it goes well... especially the Oratorio 'The Weeping Tree' the Senior Choir will be presenting on Good Friday. I've listened in on a couple of rehearsals the choirs had on it. I'm looking forward to hearing it on line."

Ruth gave Aldie a hug and thanked him for letting her visit. "I even got to hold her!" I thanked Ruth for the abundance of food and goodies she brought, how generous and kind it was. "Everything is just to heat up, Aldie. Pretty simple, huh?"

"It's so wonderful, Ruth." I gave her a big hug of appreciation and asked her to thank folks from Beautiful Dawn and myself.

Chapter Thirty

NEW LIFE IN A GOOD FRIDAY WORLD

Luke 24:1-8
At the crack of dawn on Sunday, the women came to the tomb carrying the burial spices they had prepared. They found the entrance stone rolled back from the tomb, so they walked in. But once inside, they couldn't find the body of the Master Jesus. 4-8 They were puzzled, wondering what to make of this. Then, out of nowhere it seemed, two men, light cascading over them, stood there. The women were awestruck and bowed down in worship. The men said, "Why are you looking for the Living One in a cemetery? He is not here but raised up. Remember how he told you when you were still back in Galilee that he had to be handed over to sinners, be killed on a cross, and in three days rise up?" Then they remembered Jesus' words.
The Message (MSG) Copyright © 1993, 1994, 1995, 1996, 2000, 2001, 2002 by Eugene H. Peterson

Good Friday morning brought sunshine and warmer temperatures. The cold snap that had moved quickly through the Delaware Valley earlier in the week had given way to a welcome springtime feel. I walked out to get the *Inquirer* and stretched. The temperatures were in the fifties, but I could feel a decidedly warmer breeze on my face.

I thought to myself, '*Good Friday.' How strange that I would normally be putting the finishing touches on the Noontime meditation for the Passion According to St. John or, as I had originally planned, a meditation on the Last Words of Jesus.*

I remember once meditating on the word 'Good' for Good Friday and my struggle to see in this world the 'good' that God intended through the death of Jesus. I struggled to embrace the notion that a 'Good' God would allow an instrument of death like the Roman cross to be the final narrative of Jesus' life among his people. Words like 'atonement' and 'sacrifice' and 'scapegoat' may have had cultural significance in ancient Judaism, but I was hard pressed to correlate Jesus with the ancient system of sacrifice in order to appease God for human wrongs. I know it's doctrinally foundational to Christianity and at the heart of what 'gospel' (good news) means, but at 45 I was finding it tougher than ever to believe atonement theology. On one hand, it seemed logical that early theologians would borrow from the imagery of the Jewish sacrificial system and ascribe to Jesus a 'lamb to be slaughtered' parallel or that the ancients would see human behavior as sinful and needing divine atonement for its wrongs. But that ancient worldview shifted dramatically to a world of iPads and GPS's, enormous terabytes of information and incalculable scientific and medical advances, penetrations into outer space and inner space and understanding of the working of the human brain. How is it possible to attribute 'atonement' theology and 'retributive justice' to this world? Some faith groups thrive on the imagery of retributive justice... i.e., the more threats and punishment for human wrongs the better. I'm more inclined now in my life to believe this faith tradition is more powerful than atonement theology and retributive justice. I'm gradually awakening to trust in Jesus' self-giving, tortured and surrendered life as his own choice and not of his Holy Abba-Creator's doing. I've imagined at times Jesus' Abba Father trying to talk him out of his collision course with Rome. It's so lopsided – Rome's enormous weapon of public humiliation for a sentence like sedition. Jesus could hardly be a threat to Roman government. He may have stirred up the moneychangers before animal sacrifice at the Temple, but he was hardly a threat to the *Pax Romana*. Or was he? His plea for non-violence and distributive justice as germane to his mission might have been the greatest threat to worldly power by domination systems. His strong passivity (evidenced in the passion narratives of the gospels.) was even a threat to his own faith leaders.)

Passivity likely was not an early messianic trait. And despite the 'servant leadership' passages in Isaiah, public opinion among Jewish kings and leaders anticipated their Messiah as a warrior-king.

Jesus was hardly a warrior-king. He would teach: *As I surrender and serve, so I invite you?* That's certainly a different way from 'might makes right.' Did Jesus want to reform and transform the human spirit by his servitude model to others? Might it not be that the real *revolution* that his life was unveiling was a *spiritual* revolution through which the world could be spared of its downward spiral ethically and spiritually? I'm wondering this on a Good Friday morning as I scan the *Inquirer*.

The feedback from Bob McGyver, my Senior Warden, was that the suffragan bishop, F. U. Frank was a 'control freak.' Bob called me early.

"Aldie, Maundy Thursday was a nightmare," he lamented. "The suffragan wanted to control every aspect of the service. The Choral Director was angry, the acolyte was crying, and the organist almost walked out. I've got to get this guy calmed down!"

This was the last thing I needed to hear on 'Daddy duty' at home. I recalled that F. U. had a way of bringing disarray to parishes he served, which is why they made him a suffragan bishop back when. I decided I needed to call him. The Good Friday Noon service was a spoken service and he needed to follow the script, the plan.

I called him. "Forrest, how's it going at All Saints?"

"Well.....Aldie, your people are a little disorganized. I had to bring them up to date on a few things."

I was trying to curtail my indignation: "Forrest, you don't need to do that or change anything. I have it all organized – you know, the stuff I E-mailed to you. Just follow the game plan."

"Well..."

"Today's Noon time is spoken with two hymns. My Music Team has the same script you do. Just follow that or they will be out of sync. Now you've got to promise me you'll do that."

"OK, Aldie, but the mass is a mess!"

"Forrest, listen. I intended variations on that. These folks are used to the way we do it. Don't rearrange it. Come on, Forest. 'Blended' liturgies are part of the emergent church. You know that."

"Well... OK."

"Thanks, I appreciate your help. Now...you'll find that the Easter Vigil really does follow the book."

"Yeah, I saw that... that'll be good. Okay. We'll take care of it, Aldie."

"Please. Thank you, Forrest," I sighed. I hung up and lamented to Beautiful Dawn: "Why did I think that having the suffragan fill in at worship for the Three Days would be easy?"

Beautiful Dawn was nursing Amy Dawn and listening to me gripe about my favorite nemesis. "There are always going to be people like F. U. Frank to mess up the game plan, Aldie, aren't there? I'm sorry it's such a worry to you." She tried to comfort me.

I returned, "Well, when you're a priest, the parish is somewhat like your child... you feel responsibility for everything and you always have to keep after those who have anything to do with your child – the teachers, the coaches, other parents... I suppose it will be that way with our little Amy Dawn when she gets to be a certain age."

Beautiful Dawn looked down at Amy Dawn, getting nourishment from her breast. Beautiful Dawn smiled: "It's true. We have an enormous responsibility for guiding her through this jungle called 'the world.'"

"What may I get you, Darling?"

Oh, Sweetheart..... Mmm, I think today I need to come downstairs and have breakfast with you there. Dr. Greenburg wanted me to get out of bed as soon as I felt comfortable. I just burped Amy Dawn and I think she's ready for a nap."

"Sure thing, Darling."

Gently, I took Amy Dawn in my arms and kissed her head and placed her in the bassinet. Then I helped Beautiful Dawn out of bed. We stopped at the bassinet. The morning light was coming through the window and glowing on her face. I twisted the blinds a little so there was subdued sunlight. Then Beautiful Dawn held onto my arm as we went downstairs. This was her first venture downstairs since Amy Dawn's birth on Wednesday.

"It feels good to get out of bed and move around. There's not as much vaginal soreness, Aldie."

I sat her down at the kitchen table and went about making breakfast. "What'll it be, my lady?"

"Uh...I sort of feel like pancakes, Aldie."

"My specialty, of course."

As I prepared the pancakes mix, we talked about Good Friday. Beautiful Dawn was still trying to embrace this Church Year stuff.

"I know that you've told me how the worship sort of follows the life of Christ, Aldie. I just don't understand this Holy Week stuff. That hasn't been on my learning curve."

"Oh... well, first I should say that one of the reasons the Gospels were written was to record that part of Jesus' life having to do with his surrender and death for the sake of his mission... uh, well to point to the bringing on God's kingdom. Jesus had a message and a mission and they were sort of one and the same... point to God's presence (or the Day of the Lord) in the world and prepare people for how that presence was going to come about in their lifetime. In fact, Jesus was certain it would happen in their lifetime. The prophet Jeremiah had predicted that one day God would be 'known' by everyone and they wouldn't have to learn about God, because God was going to carve God's love on their hearts."

"Okay, I think I'm with you. It's all about God and people getting closer," Beautiful Dawn observed.

I raised my eyebrows in appreciation: "Precisely."

"That hadn't happened with Laws, it needed to be more personalized."

"Yes, it's like going to visit rather than just sending a letter!" she mused.

Beautiful Dawn had a way of capturing the essence in ways that I do not. "Yes, you're getting it, Love! I should put you in the pulpit."

She chuckled: "When the pope takes a wife!"

I placed the orange juice and coffee and table plate for the pancakes before her. The pancakes were ready to be flipped over. The maple syrup was fetched and I continued: "So, Jesus arrived in Jerusalem, he taught in the temple and made a final full court press with his message- i.e. God's time has arrived, Jesus was eventually seized for creating a stir among the folks. And for the first time, his public message and popularity were observed as a threat to organized religion in Jerusalem itself - the Sadducees, the Pharisees, the Jewish legal system, the Temple guards. It was a kind of perfect storm. Roman domination of Jerusalem was already problematic for Jews. And here comes a country preacher with a zealous message about spiritual reform and challenging their fragile religious infrastructure and the Temple system."

"He might have just been 'run out of town' if it had been up to the Jewish authorities. They really did not intend that he should be crucified on a Roman cross. A big 'no-no!' Even though the text has the crowds shouting, 'Crucify him!' when given the choice between Jesus and a rabble-rouser named Barabbas," they would rather have Barabbas (whose name interestingly means 'Son of the Father') released from jail. And Barrabas had been an insurrectionist and a murderer!"

"My opinion is that the Roman authorities were getting antsy about Jesus' popularity and his stirring up what was heretofore a tolerable situation. He was becoming a threat to the *Pax Romana* – the 'peace of Rome'. So, they accused him of sedition and chose to publicly crucify him just to show others the consequences of civil disobedience."

Beautiful Dawn was now enjoying her pancakes as I made one for myself. I continued:

"So, this local historical event – what was essentially a police action leading to a quick trial and public execution – prompted a tsunami of what Jesus had been talking about in his ministry – the ushering of a new time of God in the world among many. Jesus' death by crucifixion triggered a wave of 'Spirit' -(some would say '*Holy* Spirit) -that eventually forged a new community around God's presence in the world of believers. Now all kinds of people would learn to live together in harmony and care for one another and, in Jeremiah's vision, each would know God without someone having to teach them. That's what Spirit makes possible."

I realized that I had shared a 'bootleg narrative' of the sweep of the Gospel's Passion message. Every other parish priest, bishop, etc., would likely have said it differently and perhaps better. Seeing Beautiful Dawn looking quizzically at me, I continued:

"So, okay, Darling... to sum it up: Holy Week is the Church's way of remembering the story Jesus' message and mission and how it links us to God's purpose of loving the world. How God loves the world is to share someone like Jesus so that we might know for ourselves 'God loves the world.' through him."

Beautiful Dawn smiled. "Thank you, Aldie. And, by the way, these pancakes are delicious!"

Thankfully F. U had heeded my request to 'follow the script,' so I heard from Bob McGyver, who texted me that Forrest seemed somewhat subdued at Good Friday noon. He had been moved by our organist Helen's adaption of Samuel Barber's *Adagio*. It always had a somber effect on me when she'd play it. Nevertheless, there were over hundred people who attended the Noontime gathering, some coming from neighboring workplaces and most from our senior communities around Havertown. A special quartet from the choir offered a Joseph Martin version of the old hymn *'Were You There?'* Beautiful Dawn and I watched the simulcast showing of the service. Bob McIver had arranged for the simulcast through WPHI-TV Community Access. Forrest's sermon was surprisingly good. He focused on the Last Seven Words —especially the last word Jesus supposedly uttered from the cross *"It is accomplished!"* It's actually the 6th Word, but according to John's Gospel this was Jesus' *fait accompli,* when Jesus 'hands over his spirit.' Forest spoke of the believer's surrender to God is always surrendering of everything she or he is to the One who breathed into them in the first place. I reflected: *In the end, to whom do we belong? For Jesus, there wasn't any doubt. Ultimately we are the Creator-Father's scattered children held within divine love and care. With that conviction and in his own physical agony, Jesus uttered his last breath -'It is finished!' It is accomplished! His purpose was fulfilled and now he could return to his Ground of Being, the Author of Creation.*

I was relieved to hear that F. U. had followed the script. I hoped that the evening service would be the same. There wasn't any preaching at the Tenebrae service. The Choral Offering was the centerpiece of proclamation: Joseph Martin's beautiful oratorio *The Weeping Tree.* The Tenebrae Service, from the Latin 'shadows' or 'darkness' comes from the tradition of the special services on the eve of and morning of Holy Saturday. Our modification of the worship included gradually extinguishing candles until the Nave is completely dark. In the quietness of the dark, the worshipers are suddenly aware of a great noise (usually by slamming a book shut or, as I did in Holyoke, slamming a door, which had a greater effect, symbolizing the earthquake at Jesus's death.) After a moment, a lighted candle is returned to the altar, signifying the return of Christ to the world. As the lighted candle remains the only light, people leave the Nave mindful that, as dark as the world can be, the light of Christ cannot be extinguished. It's a very beautiful service – and all Forrest needed to do was follow the script!

To my relief that service went well also. All Saints' Tenebrae setting must have moved Forrest. Bob McGyver told me his voice was deep and resonant. He may have been short of stature, but he was capable of that deep resonant voice. Our choir outdid itself with the Joseph Martin's *The Weeping Tree*. Our music team had gathered a small orchestra of strings and reeds to help with the accompaniment. The soloists added so much – Mike McGyver, Bob's son, is a Bass soloist in the Westminster Choir College. Jocelyn Brady sings with the Temple University choir. She was the Soprano soloist. Carol Churchill works for the City of Philadelphia and at one time was a member of the Philadelphia Orchestra Choral Group – an excellent Alto or Mezzo Soprano. And Edward Green, a high school music teacher, was masterful as the Tenor soloist. I had heard the Oratorio on line when the choral director selected the music, so I was excited that our Tenebrae service included it in lieu of preaching.

I regretted not being there. Beautiful Dawn had encouraged me to go, but I knew that it would only be a distraction for me to slip into the Nave. So, having the service simulcast on WPHI was a great alternative. Amy Dawn slept right through it!

Since Beautiful Dawn had been breastfeeding, the nights have been interesting. I find that I cannot sleep when she's up feeding our little pooper. Perhaps its guilt, I don't know. Those are meaningful times, lying beside her as she sits up in bed. I stroke her back and caress the unused breast with coconut oil. I miss making love and she does too. We know it's been three weeks and three days since I last lay behind her, gently servicing her. Sometimes we look at each other longingly. But my wife knows as a nurse that at least a month after delivery is needed to allow for the healing of the vaginal area. Beautiful Dawn did not have excessive bleeding, but Dr. Greenburg did have to provide for some healing salve.

Beautiful Dawn shared: "Sweetheart, a woman's libido is min-imal after delivery. Perhaps its Nature's way of allowing her energies to shift to care for the baby, like breastfeeding. It's not that I'm not thinking about you and us and our beautiful lovemaking. It will happen.

We were enjoying the tasty dinners Ruth McGill had dropped by on Maundy Thursday. The women of All Saints were exceptional cooks. In fact, when I first arrived there, a Cook Book of recipes (with many of their pictures) had been published to help pay for the Lounge renovation. Some of the women had published their own special recipes of dishes that I would love to have tried (if I had been passionate about cooking). So, we were enjoying some of them – and gaining pounds from them. I still needed to get out and get some grocery shopping done. It was Holy Saturday (by the church calendar) and there were countless people out, enjoying yet another beautiful and even warmer day in the Delaware Valley. At Giant Eagle I wondered where everyone had come from. The parking was limited, and the aisles were full. I was fortunate to find a grocery cart. One thing I knew I would likely find as I made my way up and down the crowded aisles – I would bump into parishioners who might protract my shopping venture. And I did. Another 'Ruth' in the congregation, Ruth Wharton, our Altar Guild chair and E-Newsletter Editor, spotted me and hugged me.

Surprisingly I didn't see anyone else from the parish, but Ruth's lament reminded me to never ask Forest to do another coverage for me. He can do his interim bishop thing but stay away from worship leadership unless he's just invited to preach. Even at that, I'm glad he was at least available for my Holy Week coverage, because there weren't many clergy available for that duty. I needed to get him through the Easter Vigil, which thankfully followed the 'Book' closely and was pretty well orchestrated by the choir, organist and altar guild, congregational readers, etc. Even an anally frustrated liturgist like F. U. Frank would be proud of how the Vigil was arranged.

When I got back home from groceries, I noticed Lorraine's car parked in front of the house. She and Beautiful Dawn were in the den and Lorraine was holding the baby.

We greeted her and offered to make some tea. Lorraine didn't give me much eye contact, I assumed because her focus was on the baby. But Beautiful Dawn sort of rolled her eyes. Okay, so there was something other than tea brewing here... some Mother issue. Lorraine had her emotional baggage, I'm sure. First, it was Jack and his dirty laundry. (ZIPS!) Now I wondered what else gave with Mom.

I decided to be 'out of the way' so they could talk, so I went to my study (the third bedroom of the townhouse) and, as I often do, opened Safari to see what was happening in the world. Up popped a picture of a cute little cottage. I had bookmarked a Realtor page offered by Wagner, Inc. of Havertown. Ty Wagner was a friend of a pastor friend of mine. I told him once that I often imagined a cottage for Beautiful Dawn and me – to get out of the townhouse setting.

I looked at the specs of this attractive house. Large kitchen and dining room, comfortable Living Room with fireplace... Mm... Large Master Bedroom with walk-in closet and half bath, stand up shower and tub, two guest bedrooms with adjoining bath, downstairs family room with half bath and enclosed in back porch... one-quarter acre wooded lot located next to Rolling Green Golf Club on Northcroft Rd.

This seems too good to be true. I bookmarked it and sent an Email to Tyler Wagner just to get an inquiry response. Interestingly, he E-mailed me back immediately. The house had a contract on it, but the time was running out. He would keep me informed. I tend to feel pessimistic about real estate that has contracts on it, because it tends to work out. But I thanked Ty and just put it aside.

I had lots of E-mails from parishioners, some still belatedly sending congratulations and others lamenting about various and sundry things happening in the parish. I realize that my absence (especially on the premises) is going to draw complaints. People know I'm around and won't hesitate to vent – either in person (like Ruth Wharton and Ruth McGill) or on-line. Some of the laments were not about the interim bishop's behavior, but also about people not following through with assignments – supplies that weren't ordered or staff not following up, people not being visited. The list goes on, of course.

As a rector, I preside over a kind of 'household' where, among other things, I'm sort of the head householder. I know that's not true in principle, but often I find I have to make sure the house is running And, of course, most often it isn't. As a householder, I sometimes keep the kids from fighting. Often, they fight over my attention or inattention. They look to me to wonder where the money is going to come from. Or sometimes they expect me to be an advocate for their individual programs to be funded over someone else's program. When I preach (even the householder has to do that now and again), they're certain my sermon is not directed toward them, but to the people across the aisle. I remember even my Senior Warden, Bob McGyver, once teasing me.

"Aldie, as far as I'm concerned a good sermon is one that's over my head.... and directed at the guy sitting behind me!" Bob McGyver is a tease. So, the Email laments are directed to the householder who is away for a few days on Daddy Duty.

The new Email coming in as I was reflecting on this, caught me by surprise:

Fr. Seaver. Jeff Boone here. I liked Bishop Frank's sermon from Good Friday Noon. Can we have him back some time?

Mm. Not on my watch, Jeff.

Maureen McCarty, home from college for Spring Break wrote. "*I'm missing not seeing you Fr. Seaver. I need to talk with you in confidence before I return to Radford University, Virginia. I have the whole week off.*"

Wonder what's on Maureen's mind? I enjoy guessing... and I've been wondering whether she's pregnant. Her sister, Jan, came home with that announcement. You know sisters! Of course, it's not funny. But there's a permissive side to Emily and Jan I've wondered about since their confirmation instruction.

There were three wedding requests – two for the same day next year. Grace McKenna e-mailed and requested baptism for her granddaughter, Adrianne McKenna. Baptism? Mmm, I need to think about Amy Dawn's baptism. I scanned the calendar, which although full, does have some Saturday and Sunday spaces for this. Here's the most interesting one – a gay guy writes to ask if I would officiate he and his partner's wedding on Thanksgiving Day 2013.

Unfortunately, I cannot. But it may be coming sooner rather than later. (Pennsylvania has putting off on marriage equality.) *Thanks for your inquiry.* (Thanksgiving Day?!)

Lorraine left and didn't say 'Good bye' as she passed. A lot of silent time had passed. Something a little bizarre is going on here. She looked a little forlorn. After she left, Beautiful Dawn appeared with little Amy Dawn in tow.

"Oh, brother! My mother! Clint wants to move to Costa Rica and wants Lorraine to join him. He has property there and he's tired of what's going on in our country – the economy, the Democrats, the liberal press. He claims life would be better there. What's worse, he wants to do this by the end of April!"

Beautiful Dawn shook her head. "She told me. 'Baby, I've never been out of the country and the thought of living there is just downright scary!' Aldie, in the last three weeks I've found my Mom, uncovered my Dad's sordid past and had a baby – that being the most enjoyable of all. She chuckled, kissing Amy Dawn on the forehead.

"Mmm. I take it your Mom was looking for advice."

Beautiful Dawn nodded.

"She doesn't know what to do. She feels that her reconnection with me and her love for this little pooper is a bright spot in her life. But now her life is suddenly being detoured. I told her, 'Mom, you have to go where your heart leads and where your head can go with you.' I told her to sleep on it, because Clint is almost demanding an answer. Since he's kind of bankrolling her life right now, she knows that she'd be lost without his support. After all, she's moved in with him, you know?"

"I think I know where this is heading."

"Me too." I told my Beautiful Dawn that, unfortunately, her mother was too weak to say 'No', as scary as a transition like that would be.

"Yeah, I know. She's moving to Costa Rica." She chuckled, "Amazing, Aldie. First I find my mother, we reconnect and then I lose my mother to a Central American nation!"

Easter Vigil and Easter thankfully were glorious at All Saints. I was so relieved. F. U. Frank was superb in leading the Vigil, following the script, engineering the high mass at Midnight. I think he enjoys high liturgy. I know there are always little foul up's in any worship, but it's hard to screw up Easter. You smile a lot and tell everyone 'He is risen! He is risen indeed!' –the early Church's paschal incantation. No sermon should be, of course, sour or sobering. And no hymn should be ponderous and slow. Yes, there should be brass. We were fortunate enough to have the Fairmont Brass Quartet from Philadelphia. I watched the simulcast and it brought chills up and down my spine to the opening hymn 'Jesus Christ is Risen Today!' preceded by the liturgical dancers silently processing to this makeshift tomb and finding it empty with dramatic surprise. Our dancers do this so beautifully while the organ plays a subtly counter melody to the hymn tune. Our Worship Team wonderfully crafted what appears to be a tomb and garden (essentially an Easter garden that has been ever so slowly growing since Lent began back in February). Now among the flowers the liturgical dancers (which includes Reed O'Connor, one of our young men from Haverford Community College) look into the open tomb. A light within brightens as does their faces. The dancers pull a sheer white veil from the tomb, connected to a thin wire, which is hoisted up almost to the organ pipes and connected there by another liturgical dancer standing near an alcove. The sheer veil almost glitters as it moves, animated by a few fans blowing into it. It almost seems like Jesus' very spirit is springing out the tomb. The organist begins to rumble a low crescendo that gets louder, and the Brass begin a stirring fanfare, staring with the horns and baritone and the trumpets chattering in almost counter rhythm against the faint under tone of the approaching hymn – all crescendos to a feverish pitch of harmonic eighth notes and sixteenth notes. Suddenly the Nave lights come on and the first of several banners announcing resurrection appears as the procession begins. Led by the choral director, the congregation breaks into *Jesus Christ is Risen Today.'*

The choir processes two by two behind the torchbearers and the cross-bearer. Their stoles are glittering gold. Then I see Bishop F. U. Frank wearing his cape and carrying his miter following the Word-bearer, holding the large Missal with the Gospel Words printed and open, the two Assisting Ministers follow him, the elements bearers and last but not least the acolytes process for lighting the altar candles –fourteen on each side. Finally, the Paschal Candle bearer follows at the end of the procession and the sacristan, Bob McGyver, receives it from the bearer, turns and places it on a stand next to the pulpit. One of the acolytes moves to the side and lights it just as the hymn finishes with trumpet flourishes, their dancing eighth and sixteenth notes gradually concluding in notes of perfect harmony.

The simulcast did the processional justice by filming from the balcony, perfectly centered behind the brass. It was for us the 'next best thing to being there.' It was past 12 Noon when the celebration concluded with the chatter of church members and the announcer saying '*You have been listening to a live broadcast from All Saints Episcopal Church, West Chester Pike in Havertown, Pennsylvania. Rector, The Reverend Aldron G. Seaver, with guest preacher, The Rev. Forrest Ulysses Frank, Interim Bishop of Episcopal the Diocese of Pennsylvania. This is WPHI Community Access TV...*'

Beautiful Dawn had been nursing Amy Dawn and finally got the all-important burp before taking her upstairs and placing her in her bassinet. She seemed content and more than ready for her nap. She didn't even wake up with the burp. I began preparing one of those delicious ready-made meals the Parish had provided.

"Hey there, Aldie Seaver, I know you miss being there," Beautiful Dawn said to me as she returned to the kitchen.

"I do, Sweetheart, but it isn't anything compared to the 'new life' thing going on right here with our beautiful bambino."

I kissed her gently on her lips and gave her a gentle hug. She sat down and scanned the Sunday *Inquirer* while I warmed up the meal.

"Aldie, I haven't heard anything from the girls at Children's. I thought sure someone would call." Now, I know things like this don't happen often – especially on Easter Sunday, but the phone did ring almost as soon as Beautiful Dawn said that. It turned out to be Tabitha Hunter, the head nurse on her unit!

"Girl, I'm so sorry to be getting to you so late. I could give the excuse that we can't get anything done here without you, but you'd think I was pulling your leg."

"God, Tab (her nickname), it's good to hear your voice!"

"I know you said you were going to have your baby at home. Did you...did you give up that silliness and find a hospital."

"No, Tab, I did the 'silly thing' and had her at home." Dawn went on to give her the 'full girl talk' details, including the reluctant police officer who saw her bulging vagina and the drama with her father and mother and, most importantly, that Amy Dawn arrived safe and sound and weighing in at 6 lbs. and 11 oz. Looking at me and winking, she said:

"And Aldie was so helpful, but I won't bore you with the details."

Tab had not supported Dawn having our baby at home. She was kind of an 'old school' nurse who believed that only a sanitary medical facility was the right place to deliver babies. She would argue, "Honey, don't be silly you have mega germs all around that house."

"Tab, we have mega germs there in the hospital, probably more than we'd find at our house!" Dawn countered.

"Yeah, but what if something goes wrong and your midwife panics? That's what hospitals are for." But Dawn couldn't be persuaded. "Anyway, Dawn, I was told on behalf of the staff to give you a call and find out the news."

"Thank you, Tab. We're very happy. Dr. Greenburg gave us all an A+ for the job well done and really, it all turned out well. I'd say I miss you guys, but I'm getting so pampered here between my husband and the folks at All Saints, I'd be lying."

"We miss you too, girl. The staff is sending you over a little 'Welcome, Baby, gift.' Jenny McPherson, your teammate on PICU, told me to send a hug and tell you 'Get your ass back here soon!'"

Chapter Thirty-One

Sonnet 7 - The face of all the world is changed, I think

The face of all the world is changed, I think, since first I heard the footsteps of thy soul Move still, oh, still, beside me, as they stole Betwixt me and the dreadful outer brink

Of obvious death, where I, who thought to sink, was caught up into love, and taught the whole of life in a new rhythm. The cup of dole God gave for baptism, I am fain to drink,

And praise its sweetness, Sweet, with thee anear. The names of country, heaven, are changed away. For where thou art or shalt be, there or here; And this . . . this lute and song . . . loved yesterday, (The singing angels know) are only dear

Because thy name moves right in what they say.
by Elizabeth Barrett Browning

Amy Dawn's baptismal date stirred up more schedule conflicts than if we were planning for the Second Coming of Christ. Lorraine and Clint (now world travelers) were planning a trip to Paris during one weekend in early May. My Mom had a weekend with her Red Hat Society up at Longwood Gardens. Allison's 'Soccer Mom' mania was showing most weekends in April because of an insane soccer schedule. We never did hear back from her father, Jack, who always said *'the only way he would darken the door of a church again is in pinewood box –and then it wouldn't matter.'* (Of course, he did come to Grace's Service of Remembrance at All Saints).

After much agonizing over calendars, we decided that we would have the baptism the third Sunday in May (the day before Lorraine and Clint would be off to Paris). My Mom said the Red Hat ladies would be home from their weekend Saturday night before the Sunday baptism. Things were finally going to come together for that elusive date – May 16th. Amy Dawn would be baptized at the 11 o'clock liturgy. We would invite people to a reception after

Church at the Courtyard Marriott Philadelphia Devon up in Wayne. Bob McGyver has a brother who caters there and we worked out a menu and invited family and some close friends to join us after the baptism.

I had asked my good friend, Lutheran Pastor, Mark Crenshaw, who is in his fifth year at his Elkton, Maryland parish, to come to Havertown and lead the worship and preach that day. My joy would be to baptize our daughter with Beautiful Dawn holding her in a beautiful little baptismal gown that her Great Grandmother, Mary Shannon O'Shea (her father's grandmother) had worn. Somehow it got handed down to someone who could care for it. In a little 'dress' rehearsal for her baptism, Amy Dawn fit perfectly into this knitted treasure that Dawn counted as one of her greatest heirlooms. Our plan was that she would hold our daughter as I baptized her, with my arm around Dawn and my other hand sharing in pouring water from a baptismal shell over her head with the words, *Amy Dawn Seaver, I baptize you in the Name of the Father (+) and of the Son, and of the Holy Spirit. Amen.* It required a little bit of choreography to do this, but we actually practiced and got it worked out.

We invited Mark over for dinner the evening before the Sunday baptism and got into a big discussion about the 'why' of baptism. Mark and I are close friends from many years when we were classmates at Temple. Discussions over coffee about religion had brought us together in the coffee shop of the Student Union building. But soon we became avid pool players, slipping over to Broad Street Billiards for an afternoon of beer and camaraderie (meeting up between 3 – 5pm). It's been a great friendship ever since and we still meet for lunch somewhere between Havertown and Elkton and occasionally we find billiards at the McLaren's Irish Pub on Concord Pike north of Wilmington.

In a little bit a 'devil's advocate' role, Dawn asked:

"Let's just say, guys, for the sake of discussion, that our little Amy Dawn would not be baptized. Would it make a difference?"

I looked at Mark, raising my eyebrows. "What's your answer, my friend?"

He shared that he couldn't imagine an omnipotent, omnipresent, omniscient God holding any judgment on an unbaptized child. He considers baptism an outward celebration of a spirituality reality – that our daughter is a child of God regardless of whether we had her publicly baptized or not.

I added:

"So, honey, we're inviting our families and our friends to listen in on our promise to raise Amy Dawn up in the faith we both share. We get a chance to do that out in the open, so others perhaps can be reminded of their own baptismal promises. "

Mark shared that public celebrations of spiritual realities are really the mark of Christian community – we do that with marriages. We do that with the Sacrament of Holy Communion, where we share openly what we believe inwardly through this contrived meal of bread and wine – that Christ is within and all around us as we share it. Everything about our faith can be expressed outwardly. of a deeply meaningful spiritual connection (although I know that means different things for different people) – not for showiness, but to recall God's infinite promise to be with us through this earthly trek.

"I agree," Mark continued "that life has the duality of outer actions drawing upon inner realities or inner realities creating outward expressions. Belief is an inner reality that needs expression symbolically and communally. John the Baptist believed that a river cleansing symbolically bathed a person inwardly to prepare them for God's new presence on the horizon. After more than two thousand years, ours is a baptism of initiation. We are children of our Father-Creator. And water and Word (the Bible) merge to give expression to that reality that we do belong to the Creator."

Dawn shook her head. "Well, my eyes are a bit glazed over "... then she laughed...."but you two sound convincing.'

The baptism went off without a hitch – save for Amy Dawn's decision that her hunger for Mommy was more important than her initiation into some spiritual journey she couldn't begin to comprehend. Her whimper during the baptism brought smiles. Beautiful Dawn rocked her gently as Daddy spread water upon her head' The sprinkling actually changed her demeanor... she quieted down and smiled one of those 'I've-got-gas, Daddy' smiles. Although I like to think she was just giving Daddy a happy smile.

More than fifty people attended the luncheon at the Courtyard in Wayne. Amy Dawn, well fed after her baptism, slept through the entire luncheon. And we have tons of pictures if you ever want to see them!

As a postscript, Dawn's Dad never did show for the baptism, but did come to the Marriott for the luncheon. I actually saw Jack O'Shea smile once or three times and, at some particular point after the reception, hold Amy Dawn. (Yes, it's true!) Even Lorraine marveled to see the elusive Jack O'Shea being a bit of a bowl of jelly with a beautiful little girl in his arms. It was good therapy – for him and for Dawn as well. It's too bad he missed the baptism (albeit keeping to his promise that he wouldn't darken the door of a church except in a pinewood box). He might have learned that the Creator never stops desiring us and sustaining us through the thickets we encounter all our earthly days. It takes the powerful symbol of water (washing, nurturing, cleansing) plus the untamed energy of Spirit (which blows where it wills) and Word (God's teaching impulses) to navigate us through a world of lies and delusions. Martin Luther had many difficult days being who had to be – reformer, evangelist, teacher, preacher, pastor, etc. When things got bad, Luther would look in the mirror and shout *Ich bin Getauft! (I am baptized!)* Sometimes we have to remind ourselves that we *do* belong to a cosmic-yet-incarnating God, who gets a kick out of us.

My friend Mark gave an excellent sermon on precisely the above point – how our wilderness wandering in faith can make us forget our baptismal initiation into God's mindfulness. He echoed the biblical narrative of Jesus' own baptism where God's claim on him ('You are my beloved son') was not a promise that the journey of his life would be easy, but that regardless where the road would lead, he would have an Abba-Father companion alongside.

'*Life's greatest tests,*' Mark reminded us, '*come when we are certain that Abba-Father delights in us and we feel confident of his claim on us. Doubt and disbelief are pretty easy. The world helps with that. But saying 'I believe' is one tough road to travel and yet, possibly the most meaningful travel we will make.*"

Jack O'Shea didn't hear that message, but he should have. I recall him saying that he didn't know whether he was baptized or not, but it didn't matter to him. He would laugh and say: *If there is a hell, I am heading in that direction with a one-way ticket!* But the Spirit blows regardless and maybe it will blow something of God's unconditional grace through his already rough journey of hard work and fleeting relationships.

Chapter Thirty-Two

'THE COTTAGE'

Dream House

It is the dream house for her built with love and charm the coolest clouds ever there where the hot sunny rays are the light! taking bath in the showering rain and the mist is the mirror for her wearing the blue sky where the rainbow decoring her flowing hair twinkling star in her studded nose brighten her face in shy and warm!

dew as ear ring and the shine reflect the moon rays.... the house in vermillon colour built in the sky with love and charm flying around with her green carpet plains pouring silver falls golden desert dunes shining flowers in the sky roaring sea in the night it is the dream house me flying with her built in the sky with love and charm.........

lily peace lago every by to ph

Beautiful Dawn's townhouse was a lovely setting for the start for our marriage and the arrival of Amy Dawn. But I hadn't forgotten about Ty Wagner's listing of a house on Northcroft Rd., backing up the Rolling Green Golf Club. We affectionately called it "The Cottage." About the second week in May, I decided to look at it. I was shocked to find out it was still on the market!

"Why didn't you let me know, Ty? I'm still interested. "

"Believe it or not, Aldie, it just went off contract. The couple couldn't find the money and turned it down. It's now on the market again."

"All right Ty, please let me talk to Dawn and have an opportunity to come and see it." We agreed and I told him that I would call him back.

On her return from her walk, I reminded Dawn of the cottage I had mentioned in April, the day her mother had visited to talk about Costa Rica, etc. At the time I was enthusiastic, but not particularly optimistic about having a chance at a contract on the cottage. I showed it to her on line and she loved it.

"Oh my goodness, Aldie. I remember that. It seemed too good to be true."

When I didn't hear back from Ty Wagner, I just assumed that the contract on the cottage had gone forward. We had gotten so busy with the demands of watching over Amy Dawn and her mother's reluctant move to Costa Rica with Clint that we had forgotten about 'The Cottage.' Now we were excited to hear it was still on the market.

Well, it turns out Lorraine and Clint never did move to Costa Rica. The real estate deal he was trying to finalize, to buy property there, fell through and he lost about five thousand dollars on his investment. The broker involved had not checked out the deal thoroughly enough to discover it was a fraudulent tax dodge from a third-party rogue investment group from Indiana trying to get rich quick. Clint had been ready to put down another fifteen thousand dollars when his broker called him and waved the red flag on the whole deal. Clint was furious, of course, and totally lost interest in moving to Costa Rica. Lorraine was elated and this peppy 62-year-old brunette returned to being' Grandma' to Amy Dawn and my Beautiful Dawn was relieved. Clint decided to invest in a time-share with Wyndham Resorts that would allow them to travel four weeks out of the year. And that was just fine with Lorraine.

I had a wedding at All Saints that Saturday afternoon in May, but afterward, we bundled up Amy Dawn and drove over to 'The Cottage.' It turned out to be three minutes from Jackie Riordon's house and a closer route for Beautiful Dawn to take to Children's. For me it would be a shorter commute to All Saints Church.

'The Cottage' took our breath away. Picture an L-shaped struc-ture on one floor, built with real stone facing, a large center fireplace, three bedrooms, one a Master Bedroom larger than our townhouse bedroom, with walk-in closet, a large bathroom with walk-in shower as well as a tub. The Living Room and Dining Room with the large center fireplace adjoined the rooms. an eat-in kitchen and a family room where there had been a garage. In the back, off the Family Room was a screened-in porch that faced a gradually sloping backyard. The house included Central Air and Heating and modern eat in kitchen. The house is actually on Northcroft Rd., backing up to a wooded area and the number 5 hole at Rolling Green Golf course.

Aldie. This doesn't seem real! There must be something wrong with it that someone hasn't snatched it up."

I looked at Ty Wagner, wondering the same. He scratched his head. "Well, to be honest possibly one thing. "

We gasped.

"It does need a new roof. That's been one of the holdbacks for at least two families. However, the owners have come down in price by $20,000. The last couple was eager to buy it, but their financial package fell through. So here we are."

Beautiful Dawn and I looked at each other. We knew the asking price originally was $420,000. Now the price reduction to $400,000 made it seem more possible. I currently had over $100,000 left from my Aunt Char's inheritance. My mother had promised me $100,000 of her sister's generous inheritance toward our future home. Beautiful Dawn had received some monies from her Grandma Wilma's estate. We had already discussed the possibility of pooling our resources together and making a home purchase. Not the least, her townhouse in Havertown was worth about $275,000 on the current market.

"Ty, I'd like to put a contract down on this house today."

I took his hand and shook it and Ty promised to have something by Email to print out, signed and returned to him before the afternoon was out. We walked around 'The Cottage' for about another hour. Ty told us how to secure the door on the way out. There was an unfinished basement, but not a full basement that I already could imagine fixing up. The washer- dryer room was right off from the kitchen in a pantry area. It was clear the property had been well cared for. The lawn was well manicured and Beautiful Dawn could already see great possibilities for flowerbeds. It really felt like home. But I knew we had to get from point A to point C. If we purchased it, I would immediately have the roof replaced and a few little modifications that would turn one of the bedrooms into a nursery for Amy Dawn. Wow! Our heads were spinning. By late afternoon we had the contract signed and faxed back to Ty and now the real challenge would begin: mortgaging.

We knew that Wells Fargo Bank would be our choice. Jaime Franchot of All Saints was a Wells Fargo Bank Mortgage lender. I knew that she would do everything possible to get us in 'The Cottage.' And, as if coincidences weren't already evident, Jaime lived four doors down the street from 'The Cottage.'

All dreams have their drawbacks, of course. We hit a few snags getting from point A to point C (if C is the signing of a mortgage).

The first drawback was my Mom. I should never have taken her word for the availability of the $100,000 from her sister's will. She said with verbal passivity, "Well to be honest, Aldie, my investment counselor believes I should leave that money in long-term securities, you know, like a 'rainy day' fund just in case something catastrophic happens. I'm sorry."

I didn't even allow myself a look of disappointment. I was my Mom's Executor and I knew that Allison and I would eventually share whatever came out of her estate. I had to look at the long term and let Mom enjoy the balance of her life feeling secure. We would make this hurdle somehow.

The second drawback was that Ty discovered a lien on the property from a previous contractor who had done some work on the house and the previous owners had defaulted on paying the balance on the work. That had to be settled before the house could be sold. Why the contractor had not pursued this sooner, the attorney could not understand. Of course, the owners had moved out of the state – maybe to Costa Rica! But they were going to try to locate them before any sale. If not, the price would increase to cover the defaulted payment.

Everything comes in three's. Ty called me on a week later and indicated that PEPCO was planning to update their lighting system along Northcroft Rd. in the near future and there would be significant amount of street work there. (This was more of an inconvenience than a drawback.)

The brighter side of things was that Jaime Franchot was wonderful in working out the best possible deal for us to buy the house. She knew the drawbacks and wasn't going to see them as obstacles to overcome. Beautiful Dawn and I had excellent credit ratings. Our vehicles were paid for and, apart from some student loans and the mortgage on her townhouse, we had a green light for some kind of mortgage loan. With the lien on the property because of the unpaid work and the absence of the money I thought my Mom was happily making available, Beautiful Dawn and I were still looking at coming up with almost $250,000 down and mortgaging the new balance (with the lien adjustment) of $200,000. We knew it was still possible for the delinquent payment on the construction bill to be retrieved if they should find the previous owners. If that happened, it would be a reimbursement.

On Monday afternoon at Wells Fargo, Jaime Franchot looked over the paperwork. "Fr. Aldie, this is exceptional, believe me! If I had more customers coming in here ready to put more than fifty percent of the money down on a 30-year fixed, I'd be jumping for joy. So, I'm saying if you have that kind of money or even less, to bring to the table, Wells Fargo will guarantee a mortgage. Just to let you know, Wells Fargo normally requires at least 10% down on a 30-year fixed. We could probably approve your loan based on significantly less than the $250,000 you're bringing. So, I have to offer to you upfront-you technically would only need $42,000 to buy this house. You have an excellent credit rating – both of you. Your debt-to-income ratio is significantly low, and this is a first- time mortgage for you as a family. Do you want to think about it?"

Beautiful Dawn and I thought it over in less than a minute and decided that the accelerated equity upfront money would bring would be beneficial in the long run. We were already being guaranteed a Home Equity Line of Credit through Wells Fargo at 3%. Since I needed to repair the roof immediately, I would use the HELOC to get that work done. My end-game plan was to someday purchase a second home somewhere for getaways. Right now, it just seemed right to have a manageable monthly mortgage payment. With the eventual sale of Beautiful Dawn's townhouse (which would begin as soon as the new mortgage was issued), we knew that we could apply that to some investment plan that included Amy Dawn's future and the unforeseen expenses down the road.

On May 2nd, following Beautiful Dawn's workday, we met Jaime at Wells Fargo with the Title Rep and with Ty Wagner and the Attorney and signed an endless assortment of papers for a mortgage on the property along Northcroft and were presented the keys with a bottle of Champaign and a free weekend in the Pocono's to boot. I presented a cashier's check to Wells Fargo for $250,000. Amy Dawn was with us and seemed to giggle and coo her approval at the new residence as we were presented the keys. Handshakes and hugs were shared. Jaime Franchot said: "Well, Fr. Aldie and Dawn, welcome to my neighborhood!"

We arrived at 'The Cottage'. Ty joined us to do a walk-through. Interestingly, PP&L had already started doing some landscaping on Northcroft Lane with their trucks parked near the house. We knew things would be messy with their work in the next couple of weeks. But it didn't dampen our joy at our acquisition.

After Ty left, we just stood in the center of the Living Room and held each other. Amy Dawn was hungry. It was dinnertime. Even my own stomach was growling. As she sat on the only chair in the living room, she gave Amy Dawn nourishment and we kissed.

"Aldie, Darling, thank you for making this possible. This is so incredible!"

"Sweetheart, you made it possible too," I said as I held her in a threesome embrace with Amy Dawn between us.

She smiled:

"I know I helped financially, but it was your tenacity and not giving up and keeping after it all that did the lion's share of the work. Thank you. I love you."

I kissed her and then we walked around a bit to take it all in.

We had already contracted Havertown Movers to schedule a Friday, June 1st as our moving date. With our new baby and everyone's busy schedule, I wanted the movers to do everything - door to door - including unpacking and box removals at 'The Cottage.' It was worth it.

Moving Day

Nothing like moving day to ratchet up your anxiety! My mother, who, I had failed to mention, had also made visits to enjoy her new granddaughter, but was subdued about Amy Dawn being a child with Downs. And Lorraine came to provide childcare as we watched the townhouse being boxed up. Some folks at All Saints joined in the festivities, bringing a few pick-up trucks for transporting personal items and, of course, plenty of food to share. The folks at All Saints are just no-holds-barred excellent gourmet-quality cooks! Jerry and Bob of Havertown Movers were super friendly guys, making a lot of fuss over Amy Dawn.

Even Jaime Franchot stopped by on her way to work to bring a bunt cake and a carafe of coffee. She got a chance to hold Amy Dawn and to tell me that there was a gift on my desk at the office.

"And, just to let you two know, Bob and I would love to offer dinner this evening. We know you likely won't have things ready to have a meal. So, come on over around 6 pm – if that time is suitable"

"Hey, that's very kind of you, Jaime." Beautiful Dawn agreed and thanked her. Her husband, Bob Franchot, was City Solicitor for Havertown. Bob wasn't much of a church-attender, but we shared rounds of golf together. Like a lot of other guys, his handicap was significantly lower than mine, but we had a lot of fun on the course. Beautiful Dawn enjoyed Jaime, too, because Jaime and Bob had a teenage son who was also a Downs Syndrome person. Jeremy Franchot, now a teen. I had baptized Jeremy soon after I arrived at All Saints. I remember having met with Jaime and Bob about the baptism. Jeremy was already ten years old, but Jaime and Bob had questioned whether a baptism for a Downs child was OK nor. I shared that Jeremy was as welcome into the faith and a spiritual journey in his life as any other child. God invites everyone into a knowing relationship with the divine and why not make the opportunity possible for Jeremy.

Jeremy turned out to be loved by all the kids in his Sunday School class. Even the 'macho' guys turned to Jell-O around Jeremy and would love playing games with him. So, when I baptized Jeremy, I almost lost it when he looked up at me and said, *Thank you, Fr. Seaver. Now am I a Jesus boy?* I remember choking back tears and saying, *Jeremy, you'll always be a Jesus boy!* Then I kissed him on his head.

Of course, I believe the same about our beautiful daughter, Amy Dawn, now a 'Jesus girl.' God has blessed us with a very special little child who will plow through this world with as much love and strength as she can possibly share. She has already been a gift to us, but she will be even more as she grows. I had looked forward to her baptism as a celebration of this huge expanse of God's love in this crazy world!

Moving day was Friday, June 1ˢᵗ and was hampered a bit by a rain that had decided to blanket the Delaware Valley. But by afternoon, things had cleared out and the moving truck was well on its way - a total distance of 3.1 miles from the Town House to Northcroft Rd. The Havertown Mover's van was actually waiting on us while we gathered up last-minute personals and closed up the townhouse (now empty, vacuumed and clean). In fact, they had already begun to unload a few larger items by the time we pulled into the driveway.

"Don't you guys ever eat lunch?" I asked Jeremy?

"Oh, we ate in the truck on the way," Jeremy smiled.

"Well, there's plenty of food we'll put out as soon as the dining room table gets brought in."

Lorraine held Amy Dawn (still napping) while Beautiful Dawn directed Jeremy and Bob where to place furniture. We had purchased a number of items that we agreed would enhance our new beginning at 'The Cottage,' items replacing some hand-me-down and 'Early Goodwill' furniture that Beautiful Dawn had gathered along the way and pieces that I also had brought from my old house. Our purchases included a new bedroom set for the Master Bedroom, a new Dining Room Set as well as kitchen table and chairs. Not the least, we enjoyed a fabulous new Living Room arrangement with coffee table and lamps and stands that Beautiful Dawn had fallen in love with from Grossman's Furniture Store in Philadelphia, where we bought most of the new items. She liked Jeremy and Bob, but she was pretty attentive to how they carried the new furniture into the house. Even with that, she noticed a small scratch on one of the end tables for the Living Room. It was likely something that happened in transport, but it was hardly noticeable to the human eye. Nothing's perfect.

By late afternoon everything was unloaded, furniture in its proper place and the boxes folded and Jeremy and Bob were on their way. Amy Dawn was fed and already asleep in her bassinet in what would become the new baby room. Lorraine had left. My Mom, lingering awhile to admire the house and take a few pictures, finally left too. It was Beautiful Dawn and I holding each other, looking around at our new digs, smelling the new furniture, admiring it in its new setting and looking at each other as if a dream had come true (which, of course, it had).

There were smiles of satisfaction being able to make this milestone in our lives – not that we owned the house outright, but that we had a piece of real estate unattached from another structure. We walked into the screened-in porch. Although we could hear the sounds of the Expressway in the distant, it wasn't a dominating sound. *Be it ever so humble, there is no place like home. (John Howard Payne)*

"You know what today is, Aldie?" Beautiful Dawn said as she kissed my lips

"You mean other than 'Moving Day? 'Mm....'"

"How old is Amy Dawn, Darling?" She was testing me.

I thought for a moment... "She's three and a half months old?"

"That's right. I talked to Dr. Greenburg this morning and she gave us the green light to..."

"Oh my gosh!" I put my hands on my head.

My eyes opened widely with discovery.

Beautiful Dawn was already holding me and pressing against me... to which I responded with 'ardor.' 'Woodie' was attentive. Dawn was wearing a flowery print skirt and white blouse. My hands could not stop as I went on my knees and found my way to her softness and we melted.

"Hurry, Woodie!.... I mean, Hurry, Aldie!" she demanded.

We both laughed and fell onto the soft carpeting near the new couch. My hands quickly slipped off her white cotton panties as she unbuckled the belt on my blue jeans. She stood up and pulled at them until I was on my back in my whitie-tightie's. She got on top of me and practically ripped off my shirt.

"Damn it, Aldie, help me take off these pants!" She laughed at her moment of frustration.) There's only one word that can describe six weeks without intimacy with the one you love – E-C-S-T-A-S-Y! Enough said!

Our ecstasy must have awakened Amy Dawn; she began some 'where are you' whimpers. We could have easily fallen asleep after the strenuous day. Moving, I was reminded, is high on the stress scale along with divorce and death and jobs, etc. My cell phone was buzzing as Beautiful Dawn went quickly into the Nursery Room.

A call was coming from Mercy Hospital. The news shared by the ER nurse was bad. Jake Glyndon had been rushed to the ER and died of a massive heart attack. June was there with her sister. I explained to Beautiful Dawn, kissed her and the baby, and was out the door. (My first pastoral call from 'The Cottage.')

Many things run through a pastor's mind on his or her way to bad news. I thought, of course, about how tragic it had been a year ago when Bryce Glyndon was murdered at our church. I remember how devastated June and Jake were. I remember that I had had a bad cold when I was visiting them. I recall the expressions on their faces when I entered their home. Then there was the difficult Service of Remembrance where I stood at the very place Bryce had been shot and attempted a sermon of sustaining comfort to everyone. And not the least, I remember their generosity for my services – their gift of our getaway to the Victorian Inn in Cape May, New Jersey. Now a new chapter is added – the unwelcome intruder has struck again. Jake was probably 67 or 68; June was near that age, perhaps younger.

Mercy Community Hospital is part of the Kindred Hospital of Greater Philadelphia. The ER room number was 15, the curtain closed. The ER nurse took me to the room and pulled back the curtain. June and her sister were standing by Jake's body. She came over and held onto me and sobbed.

"June! I'm so sorry!" I just can't fathom this!"

"Aldie, I can't believe it. Forty-four years of marriage and suddenly this! He seemed Okay, except he was awfully tired. He went out and play golf today. He told me he wanted to get 18 holes in…" She stopped and sobbed more. Her sister gave her a tissue and I took her hand in a gesture of comfort as if to say, 'Sorry we have to meet this way.'

June continued. "He was just finishing up and putting his clubs away and his good friend Joe, saw him slump over at the locker bench. He was… he was dead on arrival. I can't believe it." She seemed inconsolable until she wiped her tears.

We proceeded over to the gurney, Bob still had his intubation tube in, but they quickly removed it and I got out of my anointing oil and prayed for a Gracious God to welcome home a son of His own making, a sheep of His own fold, a sinner of His own redeeming.

I asked June to hold his hand and her sister's and I held Jakes right hand as we prayed and concluded with the doxology. *The Lord bless him and keep him. The Lord's face shine on him with grace and mercy. The Lord look upon him and give him peace* I placed the sign of the cross on his forehead in oil... *In the name of the Father, and of the Son and of the Holy Spirit. Amen.*

I spent another 30 minutes with June and her sister, whose name was Barbara (from Conshohocken, PA). I had not met her at Bryce's funeral. June and Barbara shared memories – not the least of which was Bryce and the tragedy that had befallen him.

"You know, Aldie, Jake never got over Bryce's tragedy. He'd go through periods where he didn't want to talk about him. Then there were times he'd sit in his chair and cry and cry.... Now I suppose they're back together again... father and son... I hope so."

"June, I trust beyond my own reason that it is true. I would hope for it myself."

After the men from Stretch's Funeral Home arrived, I suggested that we go into the waiting room while they prepared his removal. I never liked it when the body bag is visible to the survivors. I did want to talk with Hank, the owner about considering possible dates. June was in no position to look at calendars. June and Barbara were chatting a little, so I excused myself and went out with Hank to give him a heads up:

I arrived back at The Cottage around dinner. I had called Beautiful Dawn to see if I could bring something home to share. She reminded me that Jaime and Bob were having us over at 6 p.m. She had been resting on our new couch as Amy Dawn returned to her infant rest, contented so at her mother's breast.

"Oh yes, I completely forgot with this hospital emergency. I'll put on another shirt."

We went over to Jaime's and Bob's for a delightful dinner on their screened-in porch. and chatted about the neighborhood, moving day, the death of Jake Glyndon and, of course, Amy Dawn right in the center of all our admiration. We said 'good bye' not long after dessert. Jaime and Bob certainly understood the physical and emotional demands of the day. We were spent. I felt my tired eyes and sore muscles.

After changing Amy Dawn's poopy drawers, I placed her in bassinet and sat with Beautiful Dawn on the comfy chaise lounge that the owners had left at The Cottage in the screened porch. The good folks at Wagner Realty were kind enough to do a thorough cleaning of the house and spruced up the chaise lounge and several individual chairs.

"What a difference, Aldie! I know I'll miss certain nuances of the townhouse, but I'm sitting here with you and gazing out over a back yard and trees, a peek of the golf course and the sound of birds! I can't believe this is really ours."

I chuckled a little.

"Well, partly ours, Sweetheart. Wells Fargo's still has a chunk of it."

The evening was quiet with only muted sounds of sirens and traffic on the Veterans Memorial Highway (I-476) and train horns in the distance. We were used to the sounds of the city and didn't mind that at all. The important thing, we could hear nature and feel breezes and share a little bit of heaven on earth in this moment. Regardless of what tomorrow might bring – like helping June prepare for the funeral of her husband... and whatever came by way of phone or E-mail or letter... right now it was heavenly to be alive and here on Northcroft Rd. in our brand new (to us) 'Cottage.'

The next morning, Dawn's cell phone was buzzing and buzzing. I looked at my clock and realized it was 6:45 a.m. Beautiful Dawn looked at me with that questioning hunch.

"Hello, Daddy. No, I was up."

"Well...yes, we moved in yesterday. Yes. Well, I meant to call you, I'm sorry (she looked at me and rolled her eyes). Well, yes, there are other people we haven't told yet. It's all happened so quickly... Well, of course you're part of my life. Daddy, calm down! She put her hand over her forehead like she was getting a headache. I'm not going to carry on conversation with you when you're yelling at me. Now, can we have a civil...?"

"He hung up on me! Aldie! My father hung up on me! He's spitting mad that he wasn't in on our buying the house. Good Lord, I've had a baby in the last month and a half! And he accused me of deliberately withholding the information about Amy Dawn having Downs..."

"Geez, I'm sorry, Darling," I placed my hand over her shoulder.

She looked at me with that 'What a way to start a day?' look. I kissed her on the forehead.

"Well, it's his problem. He's the one who's stayed away from me for so many years and then he waltzes back into my life thinking that I've got to divulge everything as if we never missed a beat."

"Let me bring our precious Amy Dawn in, Sweetheart." I knew she needed some Amy Dawn therapy. It was the only smile I could eek out of her this beautiful first dawn at 'The Cottage.'

It was the only smile I could eek out of her this beautiful first dawn at 'The Cottage.' She kissed Amy Dawn and began preparation for breastfeeding. As she settled in, she looked at me and smiled.

"I'm sorry. My father is being unreasonable right now, Aldie. It's not going to upset the goodness of our first day in our new house."

"OK, now... I believe that our first morning in 'The Cottage' is occasion for some breakfast in bed for the most beautiful mother and daughter one could lay eyes on. What'll it be, Madam? Pancakes... French toast... Scrambled Eggs... Poached Eggs. I believe that Aldie's Kitchen is about to open.

"You silly goose! I think I'll have a piece of French toast with a lightly-poached egg on the side."

"Merci, mon cheri, Magnifique! "

Then I realized I was staring at the oven in this house that was very sophisticated. This new oven had knobs and parts that I wasn't all together familiar with. There was a learning curve that was going to be necessary here. I went into our bedroom:

"Madame, there has been a little change of plans. Pardon... I'm needing to learn how to use our new oven. So, I'm only a few blocks from West Chester Pike where there is a McDon-*oud's* French Café. I shall return with French toast and an Egg McMuf*fan*, OJ and Café for Madam!"

Shaking her head, she laughed "You are a silly goose, Aldie! "

McDonald's on West Chester Pike was, unfortunately under reconstruction. Hanne's was not far away, so I decided to order a take-out of French toast and some scrambled egg sandwiches there.

With OJ and Coffee. It took longer than I cared to. I made a mental note that one of the first two things on our 'to do' list this Saturday morning was to go grocery shopping and learn how to use the oven. When I returned, Beautiful Dawn was crying, the baby asleep in her arms.

"Sweetheart?"

"I'm sorry, Aldie... my father's harshness just seems cruel. He didn't even ask what kind of house we moved into, how the baby was, how I was... he was so sweet when he came to our townhouse when Amy was born... and now this. Just when I thought we had bridged the gap in our relationship with Amy Dawn's arrival... and his apology... it's as if he's back to his old ways."

I handed her a tissue and put my arm around her.

"Your Dad's just a loner of sorts, Sweetheart. I'm just not sure what he's trying to work out in his life. I mean... I'd say he's definitely unhappy. I think he wants a relationship with you, but he doesn't know how to go about it."

"I don't want to dwell on it, Aldie, but I feel like I've always been this' little mistake' of his. It's so screwy. He had an affair with my mother while he was married to Millie, having had a tryst with her while he was still married to Lydia....I really did grow up in a dysfunctional family, didn't I?

I dried her tears, then told her that McDonald's was under renovation over on MacDade in Darby and that I had gone to Hanne's Breakfast Nook, where I knew I could order take-out. I put the bed-top table on her lap and presented the *Feaste d'Hanne's*. The morning offered an uncharacteristically brilliant blue sky for summer and the sun was coming across our bedroom window.

Chapter Thirty-Three

TOWARD A BEAUTIFUL DAWN

My Beautiful Sunrise

As dawn greets the day. And sunlight sparkles Rays pouring down Senses come alive Moments to enjoy

Life to be lived When the sun rises up The sky suffusing with light A calming ensues

I think of you And all of the moments That you have brought me light As my heart feels your love I know that you are My beautiful sunrise.

-Lillian Jamison (From Poem Hunter.com, submitted 2008)

August in the Delaware Valley had been brutally humid and hot. There hadn't been any rain in a month and a half. AC's were whirring on steroids and water restrictions were being issued for lawns and washing cars - $200 penalty if caught! Still, I saw cars being washed all over Havertown. It's tough to enforce restrictions. We enjoyed some shade on Northcroft. (Technically we were in Springfield, PA, but it sure felt like Havertown.) The three of us were enjoying our digs in the flower bed. Our little Amy Dawn was having a ball getting acquainted with the outdoor flora and fauna, with butterflies and bugs and touching trees and leaves and listening to the sounds of the truck traffic over on I-476. Almost four months old now, her little personality was beginning to blossom, including her curiosity and laughter at the silly little games we played with her. As Beautiful Dawn replanted flowers, our little pooper sat in her wee swing set and watched everything Mommy were doing. Dawn talked to her with a smile, which always received smiles back. Now and again she'd bring potting soil over and let Amy Dawn smell it. Or she'd let her touch a flower bulb or smell one of the summer roses that she had planted. I was raking grass clipping and let her put her hands in the clippings. Of course, her first instinct was to put them in her mouth! For a recently born child, there are two significant orifices –the intake and outtake!

On this particular Saturday, I was on 'Daddy Diaper Duty.' So, when I heard her little whimper, I suspected and confirmed our familiar 'scent of Amy Dawn' and into the house we went for a change. Her little B.M.'s were, to say the least, pungent. Beautiful Dawn always reminds me (being the Nurse): *'Poop is good, Aldie. It means things are working!'*

I agreed, of course, I just wasn't sure why God made poop so pungent! Anyway, with diapers changed, all fresh and baby deodorized, she was back into her little summer attire and out to the swing once again. Of course, this happened again not more than 10 minutes later. So, Amy Dawn's pooping is working just fine, thank you!

I caught a glimpse of my Beautiful Dawn squatting and planting flowers, wearing her Phillies baseball cap in the sun. She is so in her 'zone' when working her flower garden. I whispered a *'Thank you, God!'* as I watched her adoringly.

Mountain Springs Lake Resort

We decided to make our first trip outside of Havertown with Amy Dawn the second week of August. The heat that dominated most of June and July and, in early August, had subsided somewhat after a super thunder storm. In fact, late August was proving to be a cooler month than any since May. We decided to take a Tuesday and Wednesday and drive up to the Pocono Mountains to 'Mountain Springs Lake Resort,' (part of the weekend-getaway gift from Jaime Franchot and the staff at Wells Fargo.) We reserved a log cabin on the lakefront. Located just south of Big Pocono State Park, 'MSL' Resort is situated east of I-476 and west of I-80 off of Route 715 and Mountain Springs Drive. We arrived as the evening shadows were stretching out over the lake. Once inside the cabin, Amy Dawn safely in her bassinet for the evening, we sat on the porch and listened to the 'music of the night'- especially the robust songs of cicadas. There is such peacefulness in the repetitive sound of these nighttime serenades.

Holding Beautiful Dawn on the chaise lounge, I offered:

"Sweetheart, I'm told the sunrises can be spectacular here. What if we were to rise before the sun and greet the dawn?"

"Oh, I'd rise for that, Aldie," she nodded.

We used the occasion, snuggling amid sounds of this nocturnal symphony of the woods, to reflect on this narrative of our love I've been writing about and how it grew and became what it is now. All through this narrative, we've been adding to what I call the 'Love Memory' that narrates our journey as it has unfolded. We are living that story even to this final chapter. How is it possible that we found each other? Why did it unfold the way it did? We marveled at that as we continued listing to the enchantment around us. Does a love like this just happen accidentally? Or does it have some cosmic 'mindfulness' behind it? (I've always wondered whether there is 'mindfulness' within the universe – a 'God-mindfulness.' I can't imagine there isn't divine thought so vastly different from human thought) We have wondered about the cosmic source of this particular love we share. We're not sure we can answer 'how' or 'why,' but it has been a wonderful journey. The chaise lounge was so comfortable as we chatted away, but the silences became greater, the distances between our soft words wider and pretty soon, without our willing it, we were asleep in each other's arms, a restful sleep and a light blanket around us to take the edge off of a night chill. I awoke to the sound of a night owl close by and looked at my watch. We had been asleep two hours. I kissed Beautiful Dawn on the forehead and wrapped the blanket around her and walked her gently to our bed.

A Beautiful Dawn

It was 4:50 A.M. In the predawn light, so I nudged my Beautiful Dawn.

"Sweetheart, I can see those ribbon-like hues of dawn. 'This is the Day the Lord has made... let us rejoice and be glad in it."

Amy Dawn was already making noises of being hungry for Mommy's natural food supply. It was 'table for one on the left' this time for our Little Pooper. We sat on the chairs of the deck as we waited this momentous dawn. It was August 22nd. The sun began to edge its way up over the mountain behind the lake. As it appeared, its spray of light flashed an irresistible splash on our faces.. It was an astoundingly beautiful dawn like the name I have used throughout this novel to address my dearest companion in the world. We turned Amy Dawn toward the warm, splash of the dawn. It was like every day - a 'day the Lord had made.' All of them have been all the more from the moment I realized that this journey of my life was truly heaven-sent.

We have few dawns like this one, the one the brochure talks about 'where the sun first bursts across the mountain and skips a bright sheen across the lake'. It's such an occasion for unspoken praise.

"Oh my goodness, Aldie, I don't want this moment to end!"

"I know," I returned, "life has too few moments like this." I kissed her on her forehead.

"Aldie, it's taken me a long while, but now I'm certain that the Creator God brought us together. Even with numerous doubts about faith and religion looming over my life, the mess I found myself in during my teen years and, of course, my dysfunctional family, I've grown in my soul and my love for God and now feel I want to believe. In the complexity of 'what if's' and 'what may come's,' I've just felt we were meant for each other.

"Me too, Darling," I said as I wrapped my arms around her. "I've always rejoiced in seeing your smile and the kindness and care that just radiate from you. You are truly *my* new Dawn. I wasn't drawn to you out of lust, although I sensed within that you were a beautiful creature. I was drawn to your beautiful personality And now with Amy Dawn so much a part of our lives, I can honestly say that God is Love. I've felt that deep within... and touched it like a sacred vessel."

"Would you give me one moment, Sweetheart", I said as I gently tapped my finger on her nose (one of my frequent affectations for Beautiful Dawn). I went into the bedroom and pulled out of my overnight bag a rather voluminous printout of papers. I brought it to her and said,

"Here it is, Darling" I said showing her the novel 'The Rector's New Dawn' (working title.) "Our love story," she said with excitement! "Yes, all these past several years, I've been writing this narrative and you have added so much to it with your additional thoughts. I brought it along thinking we could complete it right here, this Saturday, August 22ⁿᵈ. "

I had carried my laptop with me every day and when moments could be spared, I wrote our love story. Before we had come up to the lake, I went to Staples and printed out over almost four hundred pages all that I had written and all that we recalled as this beautiful experience of 'us' happened.

"Do you think people would be interested in reading this, Aldie?" She thumbed through it.

"Perhaps... perhaps not, I responded. I suppose to some people our romance would seem so ordinary. We dine, we travel a lot and make passionate love. And yet when you think about it, these past several years haven't been all that ordinary. We've just filled in the spaces between events like the murder in our church, a gun pointed at me by one of my homeless men, forgeries of my name in Florida and children catching fire on Christmas Eve... all of this mingled with church and intimacy,"

Beautiful Dawn laughed. "I guess church and sex do seem like strange bedfellows, Aldie! "

I wondered out loud whether I had overdone the intimacy narratives of our love story. I realized that we had been very transparent about our lovemaking. Folks who are church types might be shocked how graphic they are. Our culture generally isn't inclined to mix those two together.

"Come on, Aldie, I think our intimacy has been a beautiful part of this romance. I don't think it goes overboard at all, even if some may think so." She chuckled: "Although I still don't think I'm ravenous as you've made me out to be!"

"Sweetheart Dawn, you are so uninhibited in matters of sensuality. I love that we're free to be ourselves...playful, teasing, rich in fantasy," I offered.

She teased me with: "Yes, but you did exaggerate my ravenousness a wee bit - you nasty boy! Didn't you?"

I looked down,

"A wee bit, I think, Sweetheart."

Amy Dawn had fallen asleep at her mother's breast and now she was stirring again. Beautiful Dawn's breasts were still tender and waiting. We smelled pee and poop, so, first things first, things first, we changed her together. Fussy as she was, it was a beautiful sound – a mother and father welcoming the beautiful dawn with their infant child getting ready for breakfast. Beautiful Dawn sat down on the big wicker chair facing the sunrise – now gloriously risen. I went to the kitchen to begin making coffee, scrambling eggs and putting some sausage links in the pan. I caught a glimpse of her awash in the light of morning. I've called her what she most has been since I've known her – my 'Beautiful Dawn.'

I paused from making our breakfast and wondered how I might conclude this intimate love story of the rector and his wife his exceptional daughter, Amy Dawn. I wrote what a powerful memory I had of the first time we met at Eve and Dewey's, where she was providing care as a Certified Nursing Assistant to Dewey. When her work was finished, I invited her to stay and take communion with us. Reluctantly and appreciatively, she did stay. I remember placing the wafer in her hand and she looked into my eyes, smiled and told me her name…'*Dawn. My name is Dawn*'

Beautiful Dawn looked at me suggesting: "Aldie, could we end this intimate love story with simply….. 'I love you?'" I responded, "I can't think of a better way, Sweetheart." And, with a sustained kiss... we did. It was 9:10 a.m. I closed my lap top.

Chapter Thirty-Four

AN EPILOGUE

'I can't help loving you more than is good for me; I shall feel all the happier when I see you again. I am always conscious of my nearness to you - your presence never leaves me. Adieu, you whom I love a thousand times.'

- Johann Wolfgang von Goethe

Dawn and Amy Dawn drifted off to sleep following breakfast. The sun was now reaching higher with its shadow-draped brilliance and the warmth and light bathing them on the porch chaise. I could hear the echoes of the morning hawk perched along lakeside pines. Boaters whose crafts were moored at the cabin docks across the way were now revving up their outboards for morning fishing ventures or just trolling about the lake. The skies were a deep blue in low morning humidity and not a cloud could be seen on the horizon. Fish were splashing about the glistening sunlight. It's hard to imagine a morning so perfect as this one had begun. Maybe this is a glimpse, as fleeting as it seems, of what we know as an earthly 'heaven.' Surely all mornings are not like this. It could have been a rain-soaking morning with fog hanging low over the lake. It still would have been beautiful, of course, to be alive and feeling life brimming all about us. But it was a day full of boundless beauty serenaded by nature's own symphony. It was a day that could not be ordered up, but only hoped for or imagined. I thought it might have been 'accidental perfection' and I just sat for a while and watched it being 'perfect.' Or maybe it wasn't accidental at all. I am a grateful observer. I gazed at Beautiful Dawn cradling our love child, our perfect Downs infant, our perky almost-five-month old Amy Dawn Seaver, and I thanked the Creator for Life and Love and for every moment my human clock has ticked through this time we both have shared…every moment…

I finished typing the above paragraph on my laptop, still savoring the memory of telling my wife I loved her and feeling her sweet lips on mine. Even as I closed out the story of our romance, I continued reflecting on what might become my Epilogue for this story.

Beyond the Perimeter

'The Last Word' takes me beyond the perimeter of all my theological musings, all the stuff I've said throughout this love story related to my priestly work. It takes me into the unfamiliar but imagined realm of 'The Other Side,' about which many have written, some claiming they've actually traveled there. Some in Eastern thought have referred to it as the Akashic Field[1] - a term coined in the 1800's as an ethereal space where all human thoughts and events are kept.[1] It's a subject we seldom if ever talk about as clergy. What I imagine is that when I die, my kaki coil is turned in for 'new duds' – like going to the cleaners! What's that world like? The dream sequence of my father that night at 'The Fairbanks Inn' on Amelia Island, FL - that cosmic re-connection I made with him after his death - got me *real* curious about life after this life.

------

[1]*Mystics and sages have long maintained that there exists an interconnecting cosmic field at the roots of reality that conserves and conveys information, a field known as the Akashic record. Recent discoveries in the new field of vacuum physics now show that this Akashic field is real and has its equivalent in the zero-point field that underlies space itself. This field consists of a subtle sea of fluctuating energies from which all things arise: atoms and galaxies, stars and planets, living beings, and even consciousness. This zero-point Akashic-field—or "A-field"– is not only the original source of all things that arise in time and space; it is also the constant and enduring memory of the universe. It holds the record of all that ever happened in life, on Earth, and in the cosmos and relates it to all that is yet to happen. (note: There's no scientific proof that the Akashic Field exists, but it's sure intriguing.)*

I've heard from accounts of people who tootled off and come back that we are invited by whatever spiritual entity meets us to 'review' our lives as they completed them. It's curious that we would 'review' life because it seems like we don't often do that while we live here in Earth Realm –unless we are perhaps in some therapeutic process or are just reflective people. I do imagine the 'review' is not for the purpose of judgment nor the beginning of some retributive process, but it is like a self-review in 'raw' mode - the camera setting that allows the eye not to miss anything. I get a chance to see 'me' re-wound and observed as I really went about it day by day in Earth Realm. If this is true (and I don't have a stitch of proof), it's enough to scare the bejesus out of me! Who in their right mind wants to 'review' his life? If there is 'judgment,' maybe that's what 'judgment' *really* is – not some deity mitigating punishment on us, but more allowing us to review the tape rolling every minute I lived: Aldron Gerard Seaver, in raw mode. Time might be totally different so that I see it all in a short span of earthly *chronos*. And I might be thinking: *'Dear God! That really sucked of me'*...or *'Oh, God, I remember that day'*... or maybe, *'Wow, I lived that time authentically'*... or *'Crap, I'm embarrassed to see that!'*... or *'Well, that shouldn't have happened!'*... or *'What was I thinking?'* (Likely the more frequent responses!) I might also think *'That was good of me,* OK *of me, brave, kind and compassionate of me, maybe even 'brilliant of me!'* We can be sometimes so clueless in real time. So, I imagine that in real life I did 'swim in denial' and let things slip past me. Maybe 'judgment' on The Other Side is our consciousness of who we really were along that dusty road or all the winding roads of daily life. It's the final review, the summing up – and we get to see it.

This is your life, Aldron!' I shudder! What will I see? Will I cringe at the review?

Let me guess. My 'life review' would be a myriad of images of me –first as a toddler with all the little selfish things I only knew how to do. It would include all the little lies I told and all the big ones, the 'bail out' lies, the messes I made and the all the times I wasted. There were so many of those! It would have accounted for my struggling teen years, my preoccupation with my genitals! I didn't know what the word 'testosterone' meant back then. And there was the worry over my sister Allison's endless pursuit of being loved and accepted by my father. Add to that my obsession over my acne. It would include my hopeless, obsessive attraction to Susie Frost between the years 1960 -1964. It was one of those dramas with her I endured. I was so invisible, so *not* what she was looking for. All the while I carried this burning torch! 'Why,' I wondered, 'had I put so much energy into that?'

My life review might include episodes of anxiety when I lost so much weight that my mother took me to the doctor swearing I was anorexic. It would also include those anxious days in the 12th Grade when I lacked the confidence to fill out a college application for fear that I wouldn't be chosen for anything. (I lived with a chronic fear of rejection.) It might also show how my Aunt Charlotte's persistence and motivation gave me courage to apply to college and how I became provisionally accepted at Temple University (with a B+ average and adequate SAT scores)

Added, my life review might take a glimpse of my anguish over my father's and grandfather's disdain for my becoming an Episcopal priest and my lack of courage to confront them about it or to believe I could have convinced them otherwise, that it was a legitimate way to spend my professional life. It would show how little my parents could afford to support me in an academic education and my many part time jobs through college –from being a waiter in Philadelphia area restaurants, to that of being a nighttime school custodian, various security jobs and microfilming in the Temple University Library.

On the brighter side, it would have included the unsolicited but accidental gift of meeting and falling in love with Dawn Briana O'Shea, such a God-*sent* to me. She beautifully rounded out my life. She was the 'yin' of my 'yang.' She was the that part of me that I once craved years earlier in Susie Frost (so appropriately named, creating a chill that had frozen my immature 'high school butt.')

The review seems fast and yet endless. It's incredible, seeing my life flowing like an endless panel of animation before my eyes and capturing every detail and yet, in reviewing, I'm observing me in living color! Who was rolling this camera of brutally real scenarios… does the Holy One film us, all of us…every breath, every action, thought? I become exhausted to the point of wanting to push away

448

from where I am perched. I plead for mercy. *I can't...I can't view this. I'm sorry.* And suddenly, I'm aware that I had fallen into some kind of sleep.

I hear my name and I look up and see some angelic attendant touching my chest gently.' I sand and gaze around into an unearthly panoramas I could never have imagined.

"Dear Aldron, you have drawn new breath. Your last breath left you in earth time and your new life is born."

Now... between my last earthly breath and this astral life in this Akashic field, my angelic attendant might ask me: *'Are you ready to pass through this corridor of life review to the God Realm? Are you convinced you have accomplished what you sought to accomplish in the Earth Realm?'*

I respond: 'I've got a choice? You mean I could go back and work this all out again?' My host responds: *It is your choice.* I finally surrender that if meeting Dawn helped me to know what it was to love another person so authentically, then I suppose I have accomplished all that was important to accomplish. If this encounter was the highpoint, I might even say the 'Godpoint' - then I am certainly ready to step through the abyss.

It's difficult to imagine the countless people we connect with in the course of our days in 'Earth Realm' – it would be in the many thousands, of course. The enormous span of connections would likely include the day to day, up and down encounters with our families; it would include those few whom we might call our truest friends. Added to the list are colleagues, workmates, helpers, caregivers, countless, nameless people who served us, provided for us, talked with us, directed us from one place to another, cared for our things, taught us, kept us safe, protected us, challenged us, and sometimes competed with us. There is a matrix of human caring around us every day that is like a durable and sustaining web, holding us in its firm but gentle grasp.

We're not always aware of it and sometimes those grasps may seem impersonal, even controlling or condescending, but as I review my life, when it comes to the times of human care, the Eternal Holy One might say: *'I've been watching over you and caring for you more than you have realized.'* God, I believe, has been there in the shadows of 'Aldie-time' with pure, embracing Love. I was cradled in it more than I knew. In all of my life, had I made promises to God? Yes, but forgotten all too quickly! Did I bail out on my life story? More than once or three times – too many to name! Did I fail to remember who I really was? Countless times. And yet this awesome, unconditionally loving Deity graced me all through my hubris and forged me with a spirit life anyway! How could I not be deeply aware of it? Because daily life's preoccupations can cause us to be numb to the gifts that come from outside and inside us.

I recall that in Earth Realm I seemed free to do my own will much like the wind blows where it wills. And yes, things went awry now and again. Earth Realm has its own will and I matched it with my own minutes and hours and days. On earth, my willfulness produced accidents and miscalculations. I was whirling willfulness.

Nature unleashes its fury without regard for the just or the unjust. Medical procedures are not perfect and sometimes people die. Personalities take on dark forms and do terrible things to innocent people (as in war and human violence). We are cared for, but we're not always defended. The nature of the Divine is not as the proverbial intervening 'Superman' acting in the nick of time to save individuals or whole peoples from ruthlessness and injustice. Yet the Psalmist captures an ancient image of the Divine Shepherd nurturing, tending, feeding and leading so that God's people are cared for along the uncertain path they are led (Psalm 23).

Across the beautiful field, I am aware of people coming and going – some floating, most just walking. Transport in the God Realm varies. There is public conveyance that appears to be like rapid transit. People get on and off. Some air transport seems to hover about the ground. Everything seems to move in sync and at safe proximity between conveyances. Many people are walking or floating as if on an imaginary conveyer (like those long airport conveyor people movers.) Most people walk. Many bike (as they probably did in Earth Realm.)

"Aldron!"

I hear my name called and I am looking at – dear God, it's Kathy Jones Kramer, my talented cellist ex-wife in Earth Realm"

"Kathy!" We embrace…"You look incredible!"

Her smile radiates. She glowed with a peace all around her.

"And you look radiant, Aldron."

"Aldron, how beautiful it is here! And there's so much to tell you. My partner, Anita, is here, but after you and I parted, Anita and I both struggled with periodic illnesses. Life became a challenge beyond measure for her. She passed from earth before me, but we are reunited! After she passed, I stayed with the Philadelphia Orchestra. How I love you in the Holy One, Aldron, for your earthly patience. You allowed me a life I was so fearful to embrace. I have so much peace I never thought possible. And I gave you very little"

"It was the Universe finding a way of love for both of us. I'm glad you found peace and happiness. And I see your cello is with you. I hope you are sharing your gift here in the Astral Realm."

"I am Aldron. I am heading to experience new scores that have been written here on this side, never experienced by earthly ears!" She hugged me once more. "It's incredible to be playing this music on the Astral Plane. I hope you will enjoy hearing us. Peace be with you, Aldron!" And she left. Her cello was already making music – I could hear it.

For a moment, I was confused. Why was I here? What was the event of my death? Where is my earthly Dad, who met me in a dream at the Fairbanks Inn in Florida?

While on our uncertain paths in the cosmos, it always seems there is one person, one very special person the Creator sends us who completes our very selves. For some it could be a spouse. Others would consider perhaps an unconditionally loving friend. And, too, others might consider a parent or grandparent or teacher. A Godsent reality, Beautiful Dawn came to me from some benevolent energy in the cosmos.

If my spirit guide in that heavenly abyss helped me to finally reach *'there'* (wherever 'there' is), I imagine it somewhat like a Maxfield Parrish painting. I am standing on the portico of an enormous monolith of a building with large columns on a bright, late afternoon, the brilliant sunlight casting long shadows. Standing there is the most satisfying feeling I could imagine, an incomparable ecstasy of oneness with everything around me. I look out over a sweeping panorama of beautiful gardens and dwellings, animals and rivers and people moving about. Still, as indescribably beautiful as this moment is,

I am aware of a deeper sense of aloneness, as if something is missing in me – some heart connection. Even at that, how could I know what I was 'missing' when all about me seems so serene and satisfying? It is a bit like the biblical Adam ('Earth Human' *adamah*) aware of his created-ness and oneness with animals and vegetation and his Creator, but not finding one like himself. The Creator looks at all that is created and sees that the Human is alone. So, it seems that the divine crafting is not complete until there is *companionship*. Companionship is what the Earth Realm dwellers long for –those with whom one can feel a completion of self. We were meant to be in relationships, (imperfect or dysfunctional as they may be). Sadly, many Earth Realm humans prefer isolation – to be the unshared self. They have imagined instead a bottomless trove of hoarded treasures from which, once gathered, they might find ease and completeness and wholeness. But, of course, that is the lie and illusion. Life is always meant to be whole – and wholeness happens when the community is knit together as a beautiful tapestry. 'Sharing and caring' are God-like virtues. The Biblical 'Good News' is always *Immanuel (God with us)* and it is transfixed in all Eternity as **We Are One.** How wonderfully that Wisdom (Spirit) chose to penetrate Earth Realm in God's self-revealing connection with humans. In God Realm that Earth Realm spell of isolation is broken, otherwise cobwebs of self-delusion would follow us around as we move through the inestimable beauty on The Other Side. (Perhaps that was my father's plight in my eerie dream in Florida.)

A New Dawn

And now in the distant reach of my eyes, far down from that enormous alabaster porch on which I am standing, I see a figure approaching me, silhouetted against the late afternoon sun. And as the image gets closer, I begin to stir within. It is someone who seems familiar ...and soon I recognize that it is...*Oh Eternal Love!* ...my Beautiful Dawn! She is wearing a beige robe draping her beautiful presence. She is even more beautiful - if I could even imagine- than I experienced her in Earth Realm. She doesn't speak, yet I hear my name coming from her: *Aldron... my love for all time! We're together again!* Her eyes are fixed on me, her warmth radiating toward me and she holds out her hand and we embrace each other in that familiar incomparable *'one-anotherness.'* *(Ubuntu)*. I am happy... no, I am ecstatic, at reuniting with my friend, my lover, my soul mate - the completion of my very self. Our connection makes me aware of 'Love Memory.' It is as if the memory of love has been carried from a distant place and now settles within us. Earth Realm was a precursor to such perfect, cosmic *Ubuntu*.

I could almost burst! It seems like a fountain springing up and flowing out of me. We hold each other tenderly. We feel our lips merge with distinctive mindfulness of earthly kisses. At once we are transported to rest upon a soft bed surrounded by beautiful sheer drapes that flap gently in astral breezes – not cold, but comfortably soothing. Our bodies merge with incomparable *Eros*-Love – far exceeding our sweaty, entangled bodies in Earth Realm and far more arousing than we could ever have imagined back there.

It is almost impossible to describe in earthly terms what 'merging' (love-making) is like on the Astral Plane. The worrisome limits of physical intimacy on earth are not worrisome on The Other Side. We are at once sans robes and enveloped in such a purely erotic way that we are vibrating wildly with our astral bodies. It is love memory that heightens the merging. Our intimacy on this side is infinitely more satisfying and more complete than in Earth Realm. Our bodies seem ageless, lean and sensual, yet we still have the personas we had in Earth Realm, continuing to grow with body-mind-spirit synchronicity toward a *'divine persona.'*[1]

[1] *This is one of the most complex concepts in the Astral Word. The expression 'divine persona' hardly captures it. We are aware in the astral realm that we are not perfect yet have within us the impulse to grow toward a completeness that allows us to be at one with the Creator and yet still carry within us a unique 'us' that can live both outside of the Whole and yet within the Divine. Perhaps it is as if the soul recognizes its divinity even as it is a God-astral being. It's what we might imagine the soul to be if it didn't have an earthly body.*

Further, we are truly *Aldron and Dawn*, but we are new versions of 'us' with bodies fitted for a new life beyond the limits of Earth Realm. She is radiantly beautiful as on earth, but more so in this new realm in both body, mind and spirit. Now my physique is male, but not muscle-powered. It is a comfort to Dawn as it was in

453

earth realm. We can rest and snuggle in each other's arms as we did on earth. Even at that, our spiritual selves are equally attractive and able to experience a never-before expanded reality and beauty and being creative and imaginative – all of this serving the infinitely Holy One.

We are not 'married' as we were on earth. Rather, we are connected to the whole of Eternal Love like two drops of water in the magnificent sea: two drops, yet no less the Sea itself. Our love vibrations are so genuine, like a symphony -all its parts are in beautiful synchronicity.

In the astral world and greater God Realm, our awareness of the Whole allows us to enjoy the *Eternal Now* of every experience. We simply experience a greater sense of our love on earth – an unparalleled mutual attraction to which our hearts had been drawn.

The Eternal Now

There is, I believe, an *Eternal Now* that shapes this world and the next. From that Akashic plane our understanding of the Eternal Now dismisses Earth Realm time, when we gazed at our watches endlessly. Nothing of measured time *(chronos)* exists beyond the perimeter of Earth Realm. The Astral side can easily replicate the familiar, but without earthly limits. In fact, measured time itself does not exist in the Astral Plane. Life is about meaning. It is measured as Kairos – the meaningful flowing of experiences that reflect the divine in all things. Thus, lies and deceit and fear and hiddenness (even if attempted) cannot survive in the Astral. They are like a sticky web that weighs down the attempter and requires aid from caring souls whose love energy removes the web.

There are places here much like our earthly hospitals that provide intervention for all those who drag their weighty earthly attitudes to the Other Side. They are so comingled with Eternal Love as to provide cosmic healing and release. Often the healed ones are seen leaving these healing places like doves flapping their wings joyfully. I wondered whether my father, Ken Seaver, might be there.

On the Other Side we comprehend thoughts with greater clarity and vividness than all earthly words could ever communicate.

Our conversations are not spoken words. Language is not necessary. Everything is *'thought-ness'* – unutterable and yet understood. The astral heart is connected to thought expressions with compassion and a willingness to understand. Our ears are the familiar decorum on our astral bodies, but we do not hear. We listen with our hearts and hear with our hearts.

In this realm, we are One –even as we are myriads and myriads of entities radiating God-being-God – timeless, indivisible, uniquely expressive, yet always understood and valued. Thoughts and deeds and actions are part of the Whole. We are rays of light and yet still One Light. We are personas -*Aldron and Beautiful Dawn* - and yet we are inseparable from the 'Universe.' We can be away from one another, enjoying flowers or music or art or we can at the same time enjoy mutual 'thought-*ness*.' We see with our hearts even though our eyes are astral body decorum. The heart is everything and that which is most closely connected to the Eternal Being, the Holy One.

We are *Everyone-in-One* within the God Realm, always finding each other, always within reach, sharing in some library or viewing a film or watching a competition, tending flowers or reviewing Earth Realm history or worshipping the Creator with others or enjoying a symphony of great Earth Realm masters like Beethoven or Brahms or Bach or maybe Heavy Metal or Broadway musicals, whatever our Earth Realm interests. Too, we can be in solitude watching a beautiful sunrise lifting high in the astral realm.

I can only describe it as *timeless fluidity* of the self and togeth-erness flowing together –ever energetic and in places we choose. We can rest, even sleep. We can actually be at several places at one time without being distracted or disconnected by our fluidity. Comparable to more advanced computer technology, the Astral Field allows for multi-tasking without straining consciousness We are like multiple open apps. All of this happens in *multilarity (new word!)* vs in *singularity)* because we are part of a 'one-in-many' universe.

We never grow weary of these rhythms of living on the Other Side, because there is such enormous opportunity to live One's Self into the Whole that we can only be mindful of eternal quality. Again, there is no *chronos (time)*.

Most staggering of all is the notion that even as our Love Memory has a particularity about it – as *Dawn and Aldron* - our 'togetherness' is a cosmic plurality – a cosmic journey of togetherness as everyone's journey of togetherness and everyone's cosmic journey part of ours. *There is 'oneness' as in Ubuntu (one-anotherness).*

There is no need to assert orthodoxy on the Other Side. In fact, there is no 'orthodoxy,' only praise of the divine impulse everywhere we go. 'Knowing' and 'Ideas and 'Imagination' blend together to bring continuing awareness of the Divine Energy and Eternal Presence. (DEEP). All expressions articulate or affirm the Whole, the One in All. Prayer on the Other Side is exclusively channeled to Earth Realm's kindred souls. Here people see prayer as an urgent mindfulness, with light and love released like rays from the Eternal Now to quicken human response in compassion toward others. Where that Eternal Now's rays reach on earth allow us to see bright places of compassion: hospitals and worship groups, hospice communities, counseling centers, support groups, care facilities, etc. Even though prayers reach us, they can seem impenetrable at times. Still, it's amazing to think that those beyond are praying for us.

Suddenly, I feel the rush of wind all about me. I feel an unsteadiness beneath my feet as if an earthquake is shifting my footing. I begin wondering where I truly am or how I got here.

I'm not sure what's happening! Am I imagining all of this - I feel suddenly like a painter seeking to create a seascape. I'm aware I am experiencing it and yet it seems so unreal…. My brush strokes are so fast, the colors are almost jumping off the canvas. I may be on the Other Side, but I'm confused about what I'm really doing… where I really am. I see it. I feel it. I wonder if I am dreaming it, but it is so vivid. I hear the wind blowing, the trees swaying, and I seem to be swaying with them. Now I am running with the wind, a kite is flying and picking me up. Then I am back to earth, feeling warm…I am in front of my laptop and it's overheating, my hand upon it is hot. I worry that it might explode, and all the pictures might explode like volcanic ash out of my laptop. I hear the rush… my head is spinning. I've got to finish this… love…. story…

Suddenly I am startled by the whirring sound of a… boat motor! Where am I? The throttle jolts me awake. The boat makes Amy Dawn cry and Dawn is awakened with an 'Oh!' As I rub my eyes, I'm aware that I had fallen asleep and my images of life beyond this world were a dream. I had not written one word of my epilogue! My heart was racing. "I was dreaming, my Darling!" I touched her hand.

"That boat motor scared us all, Aldie. I think the boat was just below us. There... there, sweet Amy."

As things settled down and Beautiful Dawn walked to our room to change a diaper, I began to write:

'This epilogue was a dream imagining what heaven (the astral world) is like. It was so vivid... and yet, the Other Side was deep in my dream state. I did not see my father there. It was a busy dream....'

As I conclude this love story, I will say there is more to be written, more to be lived, more to be shared, more to be revealed and certainly more loving to be savored. This is my testimony of the journey we've made up to and including this day. I thank you, dear reader, for traveling with me along these pages, for permitting me to let this litany of accidental romance unfold, for letting me wander through my own world of theological speculation and thank you for letting me open the windows of love's fragrance. I had questioned, as I began this love story, whether such love was possible. I now know that it is, although it's certainly not an easy traverse. Dawn and my opposites on matters of religious faith and beliefs and Dawn's torturous family life and sexual abuse were part of our hubris with the ordinary and extraordinary experiences we lived. From our differences we cultivated a love that has carried us along the cosmos, perhaps many times before. *We rejoice that we have tasted its eternal delicacies.*

I believe, against all odds, that Love (capital 'L') must ultimately prevail to become the signature of all life. That seems to be the divine impulse. Divine Love is life's true beginning and, tested along the uncertain paths of each person, waits for us with welcome embrace at life's end. Even with the horrific human conditions that are part of this earth's density, we will be welcomed into Divine Love mightily. We are all One.

I decided to end my epilogue with a piece of love poetry - a Rumi Love poem, which seems to be a fitting way to express the sentiments of two thankful hearts, sitting on the porch of a lake cottage on a beautiful dawn:

'A moment of happiness, you and I sitting on the veranda, apparently two, but one in soul, you and I. We feel the downflowing water of life here, you and I, with the garden's beauty and the birds singing. The stars will be watching us, and we will show them what it is to be a thin crescent moon. You and I unselfed, will be together, indifferent to idle speculation, you and I. The parrots of heaven will be cracking sugar as we laugh together, you and I. In one form upon this earth, and in another form in a timeless sweet land.'

Kulliyat-e Shams, 2114 Jalal ad-Din Muhammad Rumi (1207-1273)

About the Author

Ron Reaves was born in 1946 and grew up near Gettysburg, PA. He is a graduate of York Junior College (now York College of Pennsylvania), Gettysburg College and the Lutheran Theological Seminary Gettysburg. During his studies he was a part-time Park Ranger and Interpretive Ranger with the National Park Service. Professionally, he has served as a pastor of churches throughout Maryland and Delaware. During those years he attended  a Pastor's School at Stetson University in DeLand, FL. He is a wedding officiant, a liturgical artist, musician, photographer and has hosted group travel throughout Europe and the Middle East. He has written faith formation curricula and meditation works. This is his first novel. He has two adult children, Pam, an elementary school teacher, and Brad, a pastor. He has three grandchildren, Delaney, Jordyn and Noah. He is married to Lucretia (Leather) Reaves and lives in Frederick, MD. Email: ronrv@comcast.net

www.ingramcontent.com/pod-product-compliance
Lightning Source LLC
Chambersburg PA
CBHW051508250626
47156CB00001B/7